THE STRUGGLE

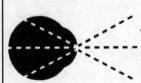

This Large Print Book carries the
Seal of Approval of N.A.V.H.

THE STRUGGLE

WANDA E. BRUNSTETTER

THORNDIKE PRESS

A part of Gale, Cengage Learning

GALE
CENGAGE Learning

Detroit • New York • San Francisco • New Haven, Conn • Waterville, Maine • London

GALE
CENGAGE Learning®

Copyright © 2012 by Wanda E. Brunstetter.
Kentucky Brothers Series #3.
All scripture quotations are taken from the King James Version of the Bible.
All German-Dutch words are taken from the Revised Pennsylvania German Dictionary found in Lancaster County, Pennsylvania.
Thorndike Press, a part of Gale, Cengage Learning.

LIBRARY OF CONGRESS CATALOGING-IN-PUBLICATION DATA

Brunstetter, Wanda E.
   The struggle / by Wanda E. Brunstetter. — Large print ed.
    p. cm. — (Kentucky brothers series; #3) (Thorndike Press
large print Christian fiction)
  ISBN-13: 978-1-4104-4181-2 (hardcover)
  ISBN-10: 1-4104-4181-4 (hardcover)
  1. Married people—Fiction. 2. Accidents—Fiction. 3. Amish—Fiction.
4. Kentucky—Fiction. 5. Large type books. I. Title.
PS3602.R864S77 2012
813'.67mdash;dc23   2012022956

Published in 2012 by arrangement with Barbour Publishing, Inc.

Printed in the United States of America
1 2 3 4 5 6 7 16 15 14 13 12

DEDICATION/ ACKNOWLEDGMENT

To Richard and Betty Miller, our dear Amish friends who know what it's like to deal with the adjustment of having family members move away.

If ye forgive men their trespasses, your heavenly Father will also forgive you.

MATTHEW 6:14

Fisher Family Tree

Abraham and Sarah (deceased) Fisher's Children

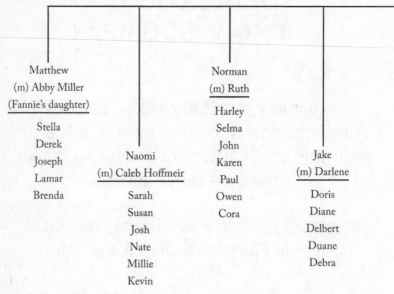

Matthew
(m) Abby Miller
(Fannie's daughter)

Stella
Derek
Joseph
Lamar
Brenda

Naomi
(m) Caleb Hoffmeir

Sarah
Susan
Josh
Nate
Millie
Kevin

Norman
(m) Ruth

Harley
Selma
John
Karen
Paul
Owen
Cora

Jake
(m) Darlene

Doris
Diane
Delbert
Duane
Debra

Abraham and Fannie Fisher's Children

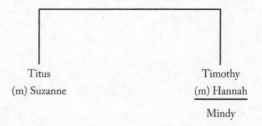

Titus
(m) Suzanne

Timothy
(m) Hannah

Mindy

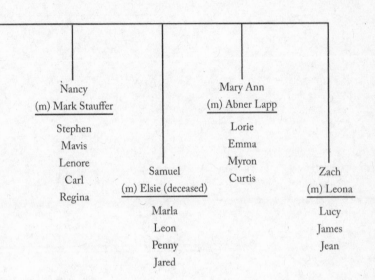

Nancy
(m) Mark Stauffer

Stephen
Mavis
Lenore
Carl
Regina

Samuel
(m) Elsie (deceased)

Marla
Leon
Penny
Jared

Mary Ann
(m) Abner Lapp

Lorie
Emma
Myron
Curtis

Zach
(m) Leona

Lucy
James
Jean

Fannie's Children from Her First Marriage

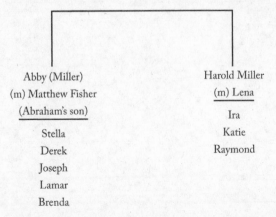

Abby (Miller)
(m) Matthew Fisher
(Abraham's son)

Stella
Derek
Joseph
Lamar
Brenda

Harold Miller
(m) Lena

Ira
Katie
Raymond

CHAPTER 1

Paradise, Pennsylvania

Timothy Fisher approached his parents' home with a feeling of dread. Good-byes never came easy, and knowing Mom disapproved of his decision to move to Kentucky made this good-bye even harder.

He stepped onto his parents' porch and turned, trying to memorize the scene before him. He liked the rolling hills and rich, fertile land here in Pennsylvania. As much as he hated to admit it, he did have a few misgivings about this move. He would miss working with Dad in the fields. And just thinking about the aroma of Mom's sticky buns made his mouth water. But it was time for a change, and Christian County, Kentucky, seemed like the place to go. After all, his twin brother, Titus, and half brother Samuel were doing quite well in Kentucky. He just hoped things would work out for him, too.

Shrugging his thoughts aside, Timothy opened the back door and stepped inside. Mom and Dad were sitting at the kitchen table, drinking coffee and eating sticky buns.

"*Guder Mariye,*" he said with a smile, trying to ignore his throbbing headache.

"Mornin'." Dad motioned to the coffeepot on the stove. "Help yourself to a cup of coffee. Oh, and don't forget some of these," he added, pushing the plate of sticky buns to the end of the table.

"I'll get the coffee for you." Mom started to rise from her seat, but Timothy shook his head.

"I can get the coffee, Mom, but I can't stay long because I have some last-minute packing to do. Just wanted to see if there's anything either of you needs me to do before I leave."

Tears welled in Mom's brown eyes. "Oh Timothy, I really wish you weren't going. Isn't there anything we can do to make you stay?"

Timothy poured himself a cup of coffee and took a seat at the table. "I've made up my mind about this, Mom. Samuel's gotten really busy working for Allen Walters, and he's finding a lot of paint jobs on his own, so he has enough work to hire me."

"But you had work right here, helping

your *daed* and painting for Zach."

"I realize that, but Dad's already hired someone else to work the fields, and Zach has other people working for him." Timothy blew on his coffee and took a sip. "Besides, I'm not moving to Kentucky because I need a job. I'm moving to save my marriage."

"Save your marriage?" Mom's eyebrows furrowed. "If you ask me, taking Hannah away from her *mamm* is more likely to ruin your marriage than save it! Hannah and Sally are very close, and Hannah's bound to resent you for separating them."

"Calm down, Fannie." Dad's thick gray eyebrows pulled together as he placed his hand on Mom's arm. "You're gettin' yourself all worked up, and it's not good for your health."

Her face flamed. "There's nothing wrong with my health, Abraham."

"*Jah,* well, you may be healthy right now, but with you gettin' so riled about Timothy moving, your blood pressure's likely to go up." He gave her arm a little pat. "Besides, if he thinks it's best for them to move to Kentucky, then we should accept that and give him our blessing."

Mom's chin quivered. "B–but we've already lost two sons to Kentucky, and if Timothy goes, too, you never can tell who might

11

be next. At the rate things are going, our whole family will be living in Kentucky, and we'll be here all alone."

Timothy's gaze went to the ceiling. "You're exaggerating, Mom. No one else has even mentioned moving to Kentucky."

"That's right," Dad agreed. "They're all involved in their businesses, most have their own homes, and everyone seems pretty well settled right here."

"I thought Titus and Samuel were settled, too, but they ran off to Kentucky, and now they've talked Timothy into moving." Mom sniffed, and Timothy knew she was struggling not to cry.

"They didn't talk me into moving," Timothy said, rubbing his forehead. "I made the decision myself because I'm sick of Hannah clinging to her mamm and ignoring me." He huffed. "I'm hoping things will be better between us once we get moved and settled into a place of our own. Hannah will need a bit of time to adjust, of course, but once she does, I'm sure she'll see that the move was a good thing." He smiled at Mom, hoping to reassure her. "After we get a place of our own, you and Dad can come visit us. Please, Mom, it would mean a lot to know you understand my need to do this."

Mom sighed. "If you're determined to go, I guess I can't stop you, but I don't have to like it."

Timothy smiled when Dad gave him a wink. Mom would eventually come to grips with the move — especially when she saw how much happier he and Hannah would be. He just hoped Hannah would see that, too.

Hannah stood at the kitchen sink, hands shaking and eyes brimming with tears. She could hardly believe her husband was making them move to Kentucky. She couldn't stand the thought of leaving her family — especially Mom. Hannah and her mother had always been close, but Timothy was jealous of the time they spent together. He wanted her all to himself — that's why he'd decided they should move to Kentucky. She wished she could convince Timothy to change his mind, but he wouldn't budge.

She sniffed and swiped at the tears running down her cheeks. "It's not fair! I shouldn't be forced to move from my home that I love to a place I'm sure I will hate! I can't believe my own husband is putting me through this!"

Hannah jumped when the back door banged shut. She grabbed a dish towel and quickly dried her tears. If it was Timothy, she couldn't let him know she'd been crying. It would only cause another disagreement like the one they'd had earlier this morning, and they sure didn't need any more of those. Timothy didn't like it when she cried and had often accused her of using her tears to get what she wanted.

When Hannah was sure all traces of tears were gone, she turned and was surprised to see her mother standing near the kitchen table. Hannah breathed a sigh of relief. "Oh Mom, it's you. I'm so glad it's not Timothy."

"Are you okay? Your eyes look red and puffy." Mom's pale blue eyes revealed the depth of her concern.

Hannah swallowed a couple of times, unsure of her voice. "I . . . I don't want to move. Just the thought of it makes me feel ill. I want to stay right here in Lancaster County."

Mom stepped up to Hannah and gathered her into her arms. "I wish you didn't have to move, either, but Timothy's your husband, which means your place is with him." She gently patted Hannah's back. "Your daed and I will miss you, but we'll come to visit as soon as you get settled in."

"But that probably won't be for some

time." Hannah nearly choked on the sob rising in her throat. "We'll be staying with Timothy's brother Samuel until we get a place of our own, and I–I'm not sure how that's going to work out."

"I understand your concerns. From what you've told me, Samuel has a lot on his hands, having four *kinner* to raise and all. He'll no doubt appreciate your help."

Hannah stiffened. "Do you think Samuel will expect me to watch the children while he's at work?"

"Maybe. It would mean he wouldn't have to pay anyone else to watch them — unless, of course, he decides to pay you."

"It's my understanding that Esther Beiler's been watching them, but I suppose that could change with me living there."

Mom pulled out a chair at the table and took a seat. "You'll just have to wait and see, but hopefully it'll all work out."

Hannah wasn't sure about that. She hadn't planned on taking care of four more children. "Moving to a strange place and being around people she isn't used to seeing will be difficult for Mindy. My little girl is going to need my attention more than ever."

"That's true. It will be an adjustment. But Mindy's young, and I'm sure she'll quickly adapt to her new surroundings," Mom said.

Hannah sighed. She didn't think anything about their move to Kentucky would work, and to be honest, she hoped it wouldn't, because if things went badly, Timothy might see the light and move back to Pennsylvania where they belonged.

CHAPTER 2

Lexington, Kentucky

Hannah shifted on the seat, trying to find a comfortable position. After tearful good-byes to their families last night, she, Timothy, and Mindy had left home at four this morning and spent the last ten hours on the road. The few hours of sleep Hannah had managed to get while riding in Charles Thomas's van had done little to relieve her fatigue and nothing to soften the pain of leaving Pennsylvania.

Why couldn't Timothy understand the closeness she and Mom felt? Didn't he care about anyone's needs but his own? When they'd first gotten married, he'd said he loved her and wanted to spend the rest of his life making her happy. Apparently he'd lied about that. Maybe he'd told her what she wanted to hear so she would agree to marry him. He probably only wanted a wife to cook, clean, and give him children, because he sure didn't seem to care about her wants or needs — or for that matter, what was important to her. Hannah's inner voice told her this wasn't true, but somehow it just felt better to think so.

She glanced at her precious daughter sleeping peacefully in the car seat beside her. Mindy resembled Hannah's mother in some ways. She had the same blond hair and pale blue eyes, but she had her daddy's nose and her mama's mouth. If they had more children, Hannah wondered what they would look like. Oh, how she wished for another baby. A little brother or sister for Mindy would be so nice. She thought about the miscarriage she'd had last year and wished once more that the baby had lived.

Seems like I never get what I want, Hannah thought bitterly. *Makes me wonder why I even bother to pray.*

Hannah's inner voice told her again that she shouldn't feel this way. Looking at Mindy, she knew how blessed she was to have such a special little girl.

She glanced toward the front of the van where Timothy sat talking to their driver. It made her feel sick to hear the excitement in Timothy's voice as he told Charles about the phone call he'd had with his twin brother, Titus, last night. Titus was married to Suzanne now, and Samuel and Esther would probably be married soon, as well. Both Samuel and Titus were happy living in Kentucky, but Hannah was certain she would never be happy there.

Hannah leaned her head against the window and closed her eyes as the need for sleep overtook her. She wished she could wake up and discover that this was all just a bad dream and find herself home in her own bed. But of course, that was just wishful thinking. At least for now, sleep was her only means to escape the dread that kept mounting the closer they got to their destination.

Timothy glanced at the backseat and was pleased to see that his wife and daughter were both sound asleep. They'd pushed hard all day, only stopping to get gas, eat, and take bathroom breaks. If all went well, they should be in Pembroke by this evening.

A sense of excitement welled in Timothy's soul. It would be good to see his brothers again, and he could hardly wait to start a new life in Kentucky, where he'd been told that land was cheaper and more abundant. Since their house in Pennsylvania had already sold, he had the money to begin building a home. The problem would be finding the time to build it, since he'd only be able to work on it when he wasn't painting with Samuel. Of course, it might be better if he could find a home that had already been built — maybe a place that needed some work and he could fix up in his spare time. Well, he'd decide about that once he'd had a chance to look around.

"How are you holding up?" Charles asked, running his fingers through his slightly thinning gray hair, while glancing over at Timothy. "Do you need to take a break?"

"Naw, I'm fine. Just anxious to get there is all."

Charles nodded. "I'm sure. It's been a long day, but we're making good time. According to my GPS, we should be in Pembroke by six-thirty or so, barring anything unforeseen."

"That sounds good. If I can borrow your cell phone, I'll call and leave a message for Samuel so he knows what time to expect us."

"Sure, no problem." Charles handed Timothy his phone.

Timothy dialed Samuel's number and was surprised when a young boy answered the phone. He hadn't expected anyone to be in the phone shanty.

"Hello. Who's this?" he asked.

"It's Leon. Who's this, and who are ya

callin' for?"

"It's your uncle Timothy, and I'm calling to let your daed know that we're in Kentucky and should be at your place around six thirty."

"Oh, good. Should I tell Esther to have supper ready then?"

"Is Esther there now?"

"Jah. *Daadi's* still at work, and Esther's here with me, Marla, Penny, and Jared."

"Okay, will you let your daed know when he gets home from work what time to expect us? Oh, and if Esther doesn't mind holding supper till we get there, we'd surely appreciate it. It'll save us some time if we don't have to stop and eat somewhere."

"Sure, no problem. I'll tell 'em both what you said."

"*Danki,* Leon. See you soon." Timothy hung up and put the phone back in the tray. "I think Esther will have supper waiting for us when we get there," he said to Charles. "So we shouldn't have to stop again except if you need gas or someone needs a bathroom break."

"Sounds good. Nothing like a good home-cooked meal to look forward to. Would you mind letting the other drivers know?"

"Don't mind a'tall." Timothy called each of their drivers, who were transporting his

21

family's belongings, then settled back and closed his eyes. If he slept awhile, the time would pass more quickly.

Just think, he told himself, *in a few more hours, I'll be sitting in my brother's kitchen, sharing a meal and catching up on all his news. Sure hope I get to see Titus and Suzanne this evening, too. I can't wait to find out how they're doing.*

CHAPTER 3

Pembroke, Kentucky

"We're here, Hannah! Better wake Mindy up so we can greet Samuel and his family."

Hannah's eyes snapped open, and she bolted upright in her seat. The moment she'd been dreading was finally here. She could see by his expression that Timothy was excited. Too bad she didn't share his enthusiasm.

Hannah fiddled with her head covering to be sure it was on straight then gently nudged her rosy-cheeked daughter's arm. "Wake up, Mindy," she said softly, so as not to frighten the child. Ever since Mindy had been a baby, she'd been a hard sleeper, and if she was awakened too abruptly, she either cried or became grumpy. It was better if she was allowed the freedom to wake up on her own, but right now that wasn't possible.

"Let's get out and stretch our legs before we go inside." Timothy had the van door open before Hannah could even unbuckle the seat belt holding Mindy in her car seat. They'd no more than stepped out of the van when Samuel rushed out the door to greet them. "It's mighty good to see you, brother!" he said, giving Timothy a big bear hug.

"It's good to see you, too." Timothy's smile stretched ear to ear as he pounded Samuel's back.

"It's nice to see you, as well," Samuel said, turning to Hannah and giving her a quick hug. "How was your trip?"

"It was long, and I'm stiff and tired." Hannah knew her voice sounded strained, and probably a bit testy, but she couldn't help it. She didn't want to be here, and there was no point in pretending she did. Life was perfect back home in Pennsylvania — at least, she thought so.

Samuel nodded with a look of understanding. "I remember how tired the Kinner and I felt when we got here last year." He smiled at Mindy and reached his hand out to her, but she quickly hid behind Hannah.

"She's a little shy — especially since she hasn't seen you in a while," Timothy said. "I think she just needs some time to get reacquainted."

Woof! Woof! A black lab bounded out of

the barn and headed straight for Mindy. When Mindy screamed, Timothy quickly scooped her into his arms.

"Sorry about that." Samuel grabbed the dog's collar. "Lucky gets excited when he sees someone new to play with," he said.

Hannah frowned. "Mindy's too little to play with a dog that big. She's obviously afraid of it."

"I'll put the dog away. Come on, boy." Samuel led the dog back to the barn.

I don't think our daughter wants to be here any more than I do, Hannah thought. *Why can't you see that, Timothy? Why couldn't we have stayed in Pennsylvania? How can you expect Mindy or me to like it here? I'll never consider Kentucky my home.*

Samuel had just returned from the barn when his four children rushed out of the house, followed by a pretty, young Amish woman with dark hair and milk-chocolate-brown eyes.

"Esther, you remember Timothy when he came for Titus and Suzanne's wedding, and I'd like you to meet his wife, Hannah, and their daughter, Mindy," Samuel said. It was obvious from his smiling face that he loved her deeply.

Esther smiled warmly and gave Hannah a hug.

25

"It's nice to meet you," Hannah said, forcing a smile.

"It's real good to see you again," Timothy said, shaking Esther's hand.

Samuel smiled down at his children. "So what do you think, Timothy? Have the kinner grown much since you last saw 'em?"

Timothy nodded. "They sure have. I hardly recognize Leon, he's gotten so tall, and when I called earlier, I didn't realize at first it was him on the phone. And would you look at Marla, Penny, and Jared? They've all grown a lot, too!"

Charles stepped out of the van, and Timothy introduced him to Samuel and Esther.

"The trucks with all of Timothy and Hannah's things aren't far behind," Charles said. "Should we start unloading as soon as they get here?"

"Maybe we could eat supper first," Esther said. "It's almost ready, and it won't be good if it gets cold. Believe me, there's plenty of food for everyone, even the drivers, so make sure you tell them to stay and eat with us."

"That sounds good to me." Timothy patted his stomach. "With all the work we have ahead of us yet tonight, I'll need some nourishment to give me the strength to do it."

"I'd suggest that we wait till tomorrow, but since it'll be Sunday, that won't work," Samuel said.

Sunday. Hannah groaned inwardly. If this was the week Samuel's church district had church, she'd be forced to go and try to put on a happy face when she met a bunch of people she didn't want to know.

"Where are we going to put everything?" Timothy asked his brother. "Will there be room enough in your barn?"

"I think so," Samuel said with a nod. "And if there isn't, we can always put some of your things in Titus's barn."

"Speaking of my twin, where is he?" Timothy questioned, looking back toward the house. "I figured he might be here waiting for us."

"He and Suzanne are coming, and I'm sure they'll be here soon. Titus probably had to work a little later than usual this evening."

Esther touched Hannah's arm. "You look tired. Why don't you come inside and rest while I get supper on the table?"

Resting sounded good, but Hannah didn't want to appear impolite, so she forced another smile and said, "I appreciate the offer, but I should help you with supper."

"There really isn't that much left to do.

27

Marla set the table awhile ago, and the chicken's staying warm in the oven. But if you really want to help, you can cut up the veggies for a tossed salad while I mash the potatoes."

"Sure, I can do that."

Hannah reached for Mindy, and when Timothy handed the child over, Hannah followed Esther into the house.

While Mindy played with her cousins in the living room, Hannah helped Esther in the kitchen.

"How long have you and Samuel been courting?" Hannah asked, feeling the need to find something to talk about.

"We started courting this past summer, but then Samuel broke things off for a while because he was afraid of being untrue to his wife's memory. Since he'd promised Elsie before she died that he'd always love her, he felt as if he was betraying her memory when he fell in love with me. But something miraculously changed his mind, and Samuel renewed his relationship with me." Esther smiled brightly. "We hope to be married sometime next year."

I wonder if Timothy would find someone else if something happened to me, Hannah mused as she washed and patted the lettuce dry. *With the way things have been between us lately, he might be glad if I was gone. He might find another wife right away.*

Hannah knew she couldn't continue with these negative thoughts, so she watched out the window as the two big trucks pulled into the yard. Timothy greeted the drivers and unloaded their two horses, Dusty and Lilly, from the trailer that had been pulled behind one of the trucks. All their furniture and household items were in those trucks, along with the buggy they used for transportation and all of Timothy's tools and farming equipment. Nothing had been left in Pennsylvania except their empty house, which would soon have new owners living in it. Everything seemed so final, and it was hard to even think about someone else living in their house.

"It's so nice that you and Timothy are here," Esther said. "I know Samuel's pleased that Timothy has made the move. And of course, Titus will be happy to have his twin brother living nearby. He's often mentioned all the fun times he and Timothy had growing up together."

Hannah was about to comment when she spotted a horse and buggy pull into the yard. A few minutes later, Titus and Suzanne climbed down, and Timothy and his twin brother embraced. When they pulled apart, Titus snatched Timothy's straw hat and tossed it into the air. When the two brothers started whooping and hollering, Hannah wondered if they would ever settle down. They acted like a couple of kids — the way they had during their running-around years. Timothy and Titus looked so much alike, and they'd always been very close. They had the same thick, dark brown hair and brown eyes; although Titus's left eye was slightly larger than his right eye. That was the only way some folks were able to tell them apart. They were obviously happy to be together again.

But I'm not happy, and nobody seems to care. Hannah fought the urge to give in to the tears stinging the backs of her eyes. They'd been in Pembroke less than an hour, and already she hated it. Pennsylvania was where her heart remained, and Kentucky would never replace it. No matter how long they lived here, Pennsylvania was the only place she'd ever call home.

Titus asked, bumping Timothy's arm as he joined him at the fence.

"Oh, nothing much."

"Come on now." Titus nudged Timothy's arm a second time. "This is your twin *bruder* you're talkin' to, so you may as well say what's on your mind."

Timothy smiled, knowing how it had always been between him and his twin. They could sense things about each other, good or bad. It was as if they knew what the other one was thinking. "I'm worried about Hannah," he admitted. "I'm afraid she may never adjust to living so far away from her mamm."

"I wouldn't worry too much. I'm sure she'll get used to it. But if you're really concerned, I'll speak to Suzanne and ask her to make sure Hannah feels welcome. Maybe they can hire a driver and go shopping in Hopkinsville soon or just get together for lunch or something."

"Danki. I'd appreciate that. At this point, anything's worth a try."

"You know, Timothy, you might be rushing things a bit. Maybe you just need to relax and let Hannah work through it all," Titus added. "You've only been here for one day."

"I was just thinking the same thing. You

CHAPTER 4

As Timothy sat in church on Sunday morning, he looked across the room and noticed that Hannah wasn't paying attention to the message being preached by one of the ministers. Ever since they'd taken their seats on the backless wooden benches inside Suzanne's mother's home almost three hours ago, she'd either stared out the window or fussed with Mindy, whom she held on her lap. Fortunately, Mindy had recently fallen asleep, so Hannah should have been paying attention, but she seemed completely bored, as though her mind was elsewhere. When they lived in Pennsylvania, Hannah had always appeared interested during church. Was her disinterest now because she hadn't enjoyed any of the messages, or was it simply because she didn't want to be here at all? Timothy guessed the latter, because so far, Hannah had made it clear that she didn't like anything about moving to Kentucky. He'd hoped that once she accepted the idea that this was their new home, she would learn to fit in and end up actually liking the area.

When Timothy realized that he, too, wasn't paying attention to the message, he pulled his thoughts aside and, for the rest of the service, concentrated on what was being said.

When church was over, the men and women ate the noon meal in shifts, so Timothy wasn't sure how Hannah was doing or if she'd met any of the women. Once everyone had eaten, a few people went home, but most gathered in groups to visit.

Timothy meandered around the yard for a bit then stopped for a spell to lean against the fence. Behind him he could hear cows mooing in the distance, but he preferred to watch the activities around him. He glanced at the big maple tree nearby, now barren with the approach of winter, and noticed his wife sitting on a chair with Mindy in her lap, looking more forlorn than ever. He'd seen some of the women try to talk to Hannah, but then a short time later, they would leave and join the others who were visiting on the opposite side of the yard. This caused him even more concern, wondering if his wife may have given these women the cold shoulder.

Hannah had been quiet and moody ever since they'd left Pennsylvania, and even during the time they'd spent with family last night, she'd remained aloof — as if her thoughts were someplace else. *Probably back in Pennsylvania with her mamm,* Timothy thought with regret. Keeping to herself so much was not a good thing. Worse yet, she was hovering over Mindy again, not letting her play with the other children. Timothy had hoped that by coming to Kentucky, Hannah would want to make some friends. But if she continued to remain aloof, making new friends probably wouldn't happen. He worried that people might get the impression that his wife was standoffish. But then how could they think otherwise with the way she'd acted so far?

Maybe she just needs a bit more time, Timothy told himself. *Once Hannah gets better acquainted with Suzanne and Esther, she'll fit right in. At least, I hope that's the case, because I sure wouldn't want her to mope around all the time. It could have a negative effect on Mindy, and it won't do any good for our marriage either. I'm probably rushing things and need to be more patient.*

"You look like you're somewhere far-off What are you thinkin' about, brother?

and I always did think alike."

"Jah. So changing the subject," Titus said, "have you had a chance to talk to Samuel about working with him?"

Timothy nodded. "He said he's been really busy lately, doing a lot of jobs for Allen, plus some he's lined up on his own. Starting tomorrow, I'll be working with both Allen and Samuel on a job in Crittenden County." He shifted, feeling uncomfortable all of a sudden. "You know, with this being the Lord's Day and all, guess we really shouldn't be talkin' about work."

Titus gave a nod. "You're right, so why don't we go find Samuel and some of the other men here and see if we can get a game of horseshoes started?"

Timothy smiled. "Sounds good to me. Let's go!"

"Everything looks so different here," Hannah said after they left the Yoders' place and were heading down the tree-lined road in their horse and buggy toward Samuel's house. "The grass in the fields is an ugly brown, and from what I can tell, there aren't many houses or places of business nearby. Christian County is nothing like Lancaster County at all."

"That's true," Timothy agreed, "but it's

peaceful and much quieter here, and there aren't nearly so many cars or tourists."

"I've gotten used to the tourists. In fact, if it weren't for the tourists, my daed's bulk food store wouldn't do nearly as well as it does."

"Guess you're right about that, but I still think it's nice to be here where the pace is slower."

Hannah grimaced when Mindy, who was asleep in her lap, stirred restlessly as their buggy bounced over the numerous ruts in the road. She turned in her seat a bit to look at Timothy and frowned. "The pace may be slower here, but the roads in Christian County need some work, don't you think?"

"I suppose, but there are some rough roads around Lancaster, too."

Hannah knew her husband was trying to look on the positive side of things, but so far she didn't like one thing about being here. In fact, Timothy's bright outlook actually irritated her. Every time she complained, he had some way of twisting things around to make it all sound good.

"See that driveway over there?" Timothy pointed to the right. "It leads to the bed-and-breakfast I told you about. It's run by a young English woman, Bonnie Taylor." He gave Hannah a dimpled smile. "I met Bon-

36

nie when I came here for Titus and Suzanne's wedding, and she seemed very nice. Samuel and Allen did some work on her house before she opened the B&B, and Esther's been working for her part-time ever since. She helps Bonnie in the mornings before heading to Samuel's to keep house and watch the kinner. Then she goes back to help at the B&B again in the evenings after Samuel gets home from work."

Hannah grunted in response. She wasn't interested in hearing about the B&B or the woman who owned it. She wished Timothy hadn't gone to his brother's wedding, because it wasn't long after that he'd come up with the crazy notion to move here.

Maybe I should have gone with him to the wedding, she thought. *Then I could have discouraged him from the very beginning.*

"So what did you think of the church service today?" he asked, moving their conversation in a different direction.

She sighed. "It was okay, I guess."

"Did you hear what the bishop said in his message about remembering to count our blessings and learning to be content?"

"I . . . I don't really remember."

"Well, he said contentment helps to keep one's heart free from worry. It also teaches us to live simply and think of others more than ourselves. I think his message was a good reminder for us, don't you?"

Hannah stiffened. "What are you trying to say, Timothy? Do you think I'm supposed to be thankful and content that you forced me to leave the home I loved and come here to a place I already hate? How can you even accept that someone else will be living in our house in Pennsylvania?"

Timothy gripped the reins a bit tighter. "You only think you hate it here because you didn't want to move, but if you'll give it half a chance, I think you might change your mind. Besides, the house in Pennsylvania is not ours anymore, remember?"

"Jah, you made sure of that, didn't you? And I doubt I'll ever like it here. I mean, what's to like? We're stuck living with Samuel and his kinner, and —"

"We won't be living with him forever," Timothy interrupted. "As soon as we find some suitable property, I can start building a house."

"But it's the middle of November, Timothy. Even if we could find the perfect property right away, you'd never get a house built for us before winter sets in."

"You're right, but spring will come sooner than we think."

"I can't imagine us being cooped up with

Samuel and his rowdy kinner throughout the winter months." Hannah frowned. "If we have to live here, I'd really like to have a place of our own."

"And we will — just as soon as I can get one built."

"Can't we see about buying a house that's already built? We could move in quicker, and our stay with Samuel would be brief."

He shrugged. "Samuel said there's not much for sale in this area right now. He feels fortunate to be renting the house owned by Esther's folks."

"What's going to happen after he and Esther are married?" Hannah asked. "Will they continue renting the place from her folks, or will they end up buying it?'

"I'm not sure. Samuel hasn't said anything about that. And as far as I know, he and Esther aren't officially engaged yet."

"I'll bet they will be soon. Samuel needs a *mudder* for his kinner, and it's pretty obvious that he's smitten with Esther."

"I don't think *smitten* is the right word for what my bruder feels for Esther," Timothy said. "All ya have to do is watch how they interact to see that they're obviously in love with each other."

Hannah looked down at Mindy and stroked her soft cheek. *Well, at least I have you,* she thought. *That's something to be thankful for. Mindy, you are my one constant blessing.*

CHAPTER 5

"Wake up, sleepyhead." Timothy shook his wife's shoulder.

"I'm tired. It can't be time to get up already." Hannah moaned and pulled the quilt over her head.

Timothy nudged her arm through the covers. "It's Monday morning, and Samuel and I need to get an early start because we'll be working out of the area today. Allen will be coming by to pick us up soon."

Hannah just lay there, unmoving.

"Hannah, please get up. I was hoping you'd fix us some breakfast and pack lunches for us to take to the job."

She pulled the covers aside and yawned noisily as she sat up. "Oh, all right." Her long, tawny-brown hair hung around her shoulders in an array of tangled curls. Hannah's thick hair had always been naturally curly — which meant she had to work hard at getting it parted down the middle, twisted on the sides, and pulled back into a bun. When she took it down at night, she spent several minutes brushing it out. During the first year of their marriage Timothy had often brushed Hannah's hair. That had been a special time for him, when he felt really close to her. He hoped they could bring those days back again now that they were making a new start.

Timothy leaned down and kissed Hannah's cheek. It was warm and soft, and he was tempted to forget about going to work with Samuel and stay here with Hannah. But he knew he couldn't do that. He had to earn a living and provide for them.

"I'll see you downstairs in the kitchen," he said, before giving her another quick kiss. Then he moved away from the bed and stopped for a minute to gaze at Mindy, sleeping peacefully on a cot across the room, her golden curls fanned out across the pillow. She looked like an angel, lying there so sweet. Mindy could have shared a room with Penny, of course, but Hannah had insisted that their daughter needed to be close to them — at least until she felt more familiar with this new place. Timothy figured it was just an excuse. Hannah, following in her mother's footsteps, was too clingy and overprotective where their little girl was concerned.

Mindy's so sweet and innocent, he thought. *She's always smiling and full of curiosity.* Timothy hoped in the years ahead that he and Hannah would have a few more children, whom he was sure would be equally special. His stomach clenched as he thought about the baby Hannah had lost last year and how hard she'd grieved after the miscarriage. It had taken some time for her to pull out of her depression, but with the help and encouragement of several family members, she'd finally come to accept the baby's death, although he didn't think she had ever fully understood why God had allowed it.

Of course, God's ways aren't our ways. Sometimes it's better if we don't try and figure things out — just accept life's disappointments and trust God to help us through them, because He's in control of every situation anyhow, Timothy reminded himself as he slipped quietly out of the room.

After fixing breakfast for Timothy and Samuel and packing them both a lunch, Hannah, still feeling tired, was tempted to go back to bed. But she knew she couldn't do that because Samuel's children would be up soon, and then she'd have to fix them breakfast and see that the two oldest were

43

off to school. Esther had been caring for Samuel's children, but since Samuel hadn't mentioned Esther coming over, Hannah assumed she'd be watching them. She'd been worried that it might be expected of her, but now that she was here, she'd changed her mind. Truth was, she thought she could do a better job with the kids than Esther, not to mention with keeping the house running smoother. Good habits began at an early age, and as far as Hannah was concerned, Samuel's children needed more structure.

After Leon and Marla left for school, she would find something for the little ones to do while she unpacked some of her and Timothy's clothes and got things organized in the bedroom they shared with Mindy. Hannah had suggested that Mindy sleep in the bed with her and Timothy for a few nights, but he'd put his foot down and insisted that she sleep on the cot. Didn't he care that Mindy was being forced to adjust to new surroundings and needed the comfort of her mother?

With determination, Hannah forced her thoughts aside, knowing if she didn't keep busy she would feel even more depressed. "Maybe I should organize around here today," she muttered as she put away the bread. The whole house, while clean enough, seemed quite cluttered — not nearly as tidy as she'd kept their home in Pennsylvania.

"Who ya talkin' to?" a small voice asked.

Startled, Hannah whirled around. Seven-year-old Leon, still in his pajamas and barefoot, stared up at her, blinking his brown eyes rapidly.

"No one. I mean, I was talking to myself." She suppressed a yawn.

"Are ya bored? Is that why you were talkin' to yourself?"

"No, I'm not bored, I was just. . . . Oh, never mind." Hannah motioned to the table, where the box of cold cereal she'd served the men for breakfast still sat. "Would you like some cereal?"

He shook his head.

"Would you rather have eggs?"

"Don't want no *oier.* I was hopin' for some *pannekuche.*"

"I don't have time to make pancakes this morning."

"Esther fixes us pannekuche whenever we want 'em." Leon, who had his father's light brown hair, made a sweeping glance of the entire room. "Where is Esther, anyways? She's usually here before we get up."

"I don't think she'll be here today."

45

He tipped his head and looked at her curiously. "How come?"

"Because I'm here, and I'll be fixing your breakfast this morning."

Leon studied her a few more seconds then shrugged. "So can we have pannekuche?"

Hannah shook her head. "I said no. I don't have time for that this morning." *This child is certainly persistent,* she thought.

He pointed to the battery-operated clock on the far wall. "It's still early. Marla, Penny, and Jared ain't even outa bed yet."

"The correct word is *aren't,* and I'm not going to fix pancakes this morning, so you may as well go back upstairs and get dressed. By the time you come down, I'll have a bowl of cereal and a hard-boiled egg ready for you to eat."

"Don't want an *oi,*" Leon mumbled, shuffling toward the door leading to the stairs.

"Make sure you wake Marla," Hannah called after him. "I don't want either of you to be late for school."

Leon tromped up the stairs.

Hannah cringed. She hoped he didn't wake Mindy. Like Hannah, Mindy wasn't a morning person, and if she got woken out of a sound sleep, she was bound to be cranky.

She listened for a few minutes, and when

46

she didn't hear her daughter, she went to the refrigerator and took out a carton of eggs. She'd just gotten them boiling on the stove when both Leon and Marla showed up.

"Leon said Esther's not comin' today. Is that true?" Blond-haired, nine-year-old Marla, asked, casting curious brown eyes on Hannah.

Hannah nodded. "I'm sure that's the case, because if she was coming, she would have been here by now." She motioned to the table. "Have a seat. You can eat your cereal while the eggs are boiling."

"I told ya before — I don't want no boiled oi," Leon said. "It'll get stuck in my throat."

Hannah grimaced. Was there no pleasing this child?

"Just eat your cereal, then," she said, placing two bowls on the table.

The kids took a seat and bowed their heads for silent prayer. Hannah waited quietly until they were finished; then she poured cereal into the bowls and gave them each a glass of milk. She'd just turned off the stove when she heard Mindy crying upstairs. "I'll be right back," she said to Marla before hurrying up the stairs.

Hannah was about to enter the bedroom she and Timothy shared with Mindy when three-year-old Jared and Penny, who was five, padded down the hall.

"*Wu is* Daadi?" Penny asked. Her long, sandy-brown hair hung down her back in gentle waves, and she blinked her brown eyes as she looked up at Hannah curiously.

"Your daddy went to work," Hannah said. "Now go downstairs to the kitchen. I'll be there as soon as I get Mindy."

"*Kumme,* Jared," Penny said, taking her blond-haired little brother's hand.

As the children plodded down the stairs, Hannah went to see about Mindy. She found the child curled up on the cot sobbing. No doubt she was confused by her surroundings. After all, they'd only been here two nights, and waking up and finding herself alone in the room probably frightened her.

"It's okay, my precious little girl. Mama's here." Hannah bent down and gathered Mindy into her arms. Truth was, she felt like crying, too. Only there was no time to give in to her tears right now. She had to feed the little ones and get Marla and Leon off to school.

When Esther stepped into Samuel's kitchen, she was surprised to see Marla and Leon at the table eating cereal.

"Where's your daed?" she asked, looking at Marla.

"He and Uncle Timothy went to work."

Esther glanced at the clock. She knew she was running a little behind but didn't think she was that late.

"Daadi left early this mornin'," Leon explained. "Had a paint job to do up in Marion."

"Oh, I see." Esther smiled. "So did you two fix your own breakfast?"

Marla shook her head. "Aunt Hannah fixed it for us."

"I guess that makes sense. Where is Hannah?"

"Went upstairs 'cause Mindy was cryin'," Leon answered around a mouthful of cereal.

Just then, Jared and Penny entered the kitchen, both wearing their nightclothes. As soon as Penny caught sight of Esther, she grinned and held up her arms.

Esther bent down and scooped the little girl up, giving her a kiss on the cheek. Penny was such a sweet child — easygoing and so compliant. Her little brother, on the other hand, could be a handful at times, but he was still a dear. Esther loved him, as well as all of Samuel's children, as if they were her own. After she and Samuel got married, these little ones would be hers to help raise, and she could hardly wait. It would be wonderful to leave the guesthouse where she'd been staying on Bonnie's property and move back here to the home where she used to live with her parents. The best part of moving back would be that she would finally be Samuel's wife.

Esther had missed her folks dearly after they'd moved to Pennsylvania to help care for her brother, Dan, who had multiple sclerosis. Her family was never far from her thoughts.

Esther removed her shawl and black outer bonnet, placing them on a wall peg near the back door. Then she returned to the kitchen to fix Jared and Penny's breakfast. She'd just gotten them situated at the table when Hannah, carrying Mindy, stepped into the room.

Hannah blinked her eyes rapidly. "*Ach,* you scared me, Esther! I didn't expect to see you here."

"I come over every morning to watch the kinner while Samuel's at work. I assumed you knew."

"I did hear that, but since we'll be living here until we have a home of our own, I figured I would be watching the children." Hannah shifted Mindy to the other hip. "It only makes sense, don't you think?"

Esther couldn't think clearly enough to say anything. It probably didn't make sense for them both to care for the children, but Samuel had been paying her to watch them, and she enjoyed being here. Besides, some of the money Esther earned went toward her brother's medical expenses, so it was important that she keep working right now. Should she speak up and say so, or let Hannah take over? Maybe it would be best to wait until Samuel got home and let him decide who would watch the children. In the meantime, she was here now, and she planned to stay.

CHAPTER 6

Marion, Kentucky

"This is my first time in Marion," Samuel said as he, Allen, and Timothy worked on a storefront Allen had been contracted to remodel. "It's really a nice little town."

"Yep, and there's a lot of interesting history here," Allen said while sanding around one of the large window casings.

Timothy listened with interest as Allen talked about the Crittenden County Historical Museum, which had been built in 1881 and was originally a church. "It's the oldest church building in Marion, and the interior includes original wood floors, pulpit, balcony, and stained-glass windows," Allen said, pushing his dark brown hair under his baseball cap. "The church held on for over 120 years, until it was finally forced to close its doors due to a lack of membership. Soon after that, the building was donated to the historical society. Now it houses a really nice collection of memorabilia, pictures, and many other things related to the history of Marion and the surrounding communities that make up Crittenden County." Allen looked over at Timothy and grinned. "Guess that's probably a bit more than you wanted to know, huh?"

Timothy smiled as he opened a fresh bucket of paint. "Actually, I thought it was quite interesting. Anything that has to do with history captures my attention."

"My brother's not kidding about that," Samuel chimed in. "I'm anxious to show him the Jefferson Davis Monument, because I'm sure he'll be interested in that."

"Titus told me all about it," Timothy said. "He said the view from inside the monument is really something to see."

"He's right about that," Samuel said with a nod. "Maybe in the spring, we can go there and take our kids. I think they'd get a kick out of riding the elevator and being up so high."

"I'd sure like to go," Timothy said, "but I don't know about Mindy. She's pretty young to enjoy something like that, and Hannah might not go for the idea either." He paused long enough to grab a paint stick and stir the paint in the can. "As you probably know, my *fraa* tends to be pretty

53

protective of our daughter."

"*Fraa* means *wife,* right?" Allen questioned.

Timothy nodded. "How'd you know that?"

Allen motioned to Samuel. "Between him and Esther, they've taught me several Pennsylvania-Dutch words." His face sobered. "There was a time when Samuel thought I was interested in Esther because I talked to her so much."

"But you set me straight on that real quick," Samuel said, winking at Allen. "And now everyone knows Bonnie's the love of your life."

Allen's face reddened. "I hope it's not that obvious, because I haven't actually told Bonnie the way I feel about her yet."

Samuel snickered. "Well, you'd better do it quick, 'cause if you don't, someone else is likely to snatch her away."

Allen's dark eyebrows furrowed. "You really think so?"

Samuel shrugged. "You never can tell, but I sure wouldn't chance it if I were you."

Timothy grinned as he continued to paint while listening to Samuel and Allen kibitzing back and forth. The two men had obviously become really good friends.

I like working with both of them, he decided.

In fact, so far, Timothy liked everything about being in Kentucky. The countryside where Samuel lived, as well as here in Crittenden County, was nice, and the land was fertile — just right for farming. *Now if Hannah will just catch on to the idea, we might make a good life for ourselves here,* he thought.

"How does Zach feel about you moving to the Bluegrass State?" Allen asked, looking at Timothy. "I know you used to work for him."

"Zach's fine with it. Since I only painted part-time and mostly farmed with my dad, I don't think Zach will miss having me work for him that much. Besides, he's employed several Amish men."

Allen smiled. "Zach's been my good friend since we were kids. I was hoping he might move his family here, too, but I guess that's not likely to happen."

"I'd be surprised if he ever did move," Samuel said. "After being taken from our family when he was a baby and then spending the next twenty years living in Washington State without even knowing his real name or who his Amish family was, once Zach got back to Pennsylvania, he vowed he'd never leave."

"I can't blame him for that," Allen agreed.

"I know our folks are glad Zach's staying put," Timothy said, "because Mom hasn't taken it well that three of their other sons have moved out of state."

Paradise, Pennsylvania

Fannie had just entered Naomi and Caleb's general store when she spotted Hannah's mother, Sally, looking at some new rubber stamps.

"Wie geht's?" Fannie asked, noticing the dark circles under Sally's pale blue eyes.

Sally sighed and pushed a wisp of her graying blond hair back under her white head covering. "I wish I could say that I'm doing well, but to tell you the truth, I'm really tired."

"That's too bad. Haven't you been sleeping well?"

Sally shook her head. "Not since Hannah and Timothy left. I'm concerned about how my daughter is doing."

"How come? Is Hannah *grank?*"

"She's not physically sick, but when I spoke to her on the phone Saturday evening, she said she already doesn't like Kentucky and wishes she could come home. I'm not sure that's ever going to change."

Fannie wasn't sure what to say. She wasn't any happier about Timothy leaving Pennsyl-

56

vania, but it was what her son wanted, and if getting Hannah away from her mother strengthened their marriage, then it probably was for the best. Hannah and her mother were too close, and Fannie knew from some of the things Timothy had shared with her that Hannah's unhealthy relationship with her mother had put a wedge between the young couple. It was a shame, too, because Timothy really loved his wife and wanted her to put him first, the way a loving wife should.

"Don't you miss your son?" Sally asked. "Don't you wish he would have stayed in Pennsylvania?"

Fannie glanced at her stepdaughter, Naomi, who stood behind the counter, and wondered if she was listening to this conversation. She had to be careful what she said, because if Naomi repeated it to her father, he'd probably lecture Fannie about letting their children live their own lives and tell her not to discuss Timothy and Hannah with Sally.

Sally touched Fannie's arm. "Is everything okay? You look *umgerrent.*"

"I'm not upset." Fannie lowered her voice to a near whisper. "You know, Sally, I haven't lost just one son to Kentucky; I've lost three. And if I can deal with it, then I think you can, too."

Sally's forehead wrinkled. "Are you saying you're okay with the fact that three of your boys live two states away?"

"I'm not saying that at all. I've just learned to accept it because it's a fact, and short of a miracle, none of my sons will ever move back to Pennsylvania."

Sally tapped her chin, looking deep in thought. "Then I guess we ought to pray for a miracle, because I really want Hannah to come home."

CHAPTER 7

Pembroke, Kentucky

"How would you like to go over to the B&B and meet Bonnie?" Esther asked Hannah after Leon and Marla had left for school.

Hannah shrugged. "I suppose that would be okay." Truth be told, she didn't really care about meeting Bonnie but guessed it would be better than sitting around Samuel's house all day, trying to keep Mindy occupied and making idle conversation with Esther, whom she barely knew. *Of course, I don't know Bonnie either,* she reasoned. *But it'll be good to get out of the house and go for a buggy ride.*

"We can take my horse and buggy," Hannah said. "After being confined in the trailer with Timothy's horse on the trip here, Lilly's probably ready for a good ride."

Esther hesitated a minute then finally nodded. "I'll get the kinner ready to go while you hitch your horse to the buggy."

Hannah wasn't sure she wanted Esther to do anything with Mindy, so she quickly said, "On second thought, maybe we should take your horse and buggy, because I'm not used to the roads here yet, and neither is Lilly."

"If that's what you'd prefer." Esther went over to Jared and Penny, who sat beside Mindy playing with some pots and pans, and explained that Hannah would help them wash up and get their jackets on because they were all going to Bonnie's.

Samuel's children leaped to their feet and started jumping up and down. Following suit, Mindy did the same.

"*Ruhich,* Mindy," Hannah said, putting her fingers to her lips. "You need to calm down." She looked sternly at Penny and Jared. "You need to be quiet, too."

The children looked at Hannah and blinked several times as tears welled in their eyes.

"Now don't start crying," Hannah said.

"They're just excited." Esther spoke in a defensive tone. "They love going over to Bonnie's and playing with her dog, Cody."

"Well, they're getting Mindy all worked up, and it's hard for me to get her settled down once that happens."

"Be still now," Esther said, placing her hands on Penny and Jared's heads. "Listen

60

to Hannah and do what she says while I go out and hitch Ginger to my buggy."

The children calmed down right away, and so did Mindy. Then as Esther went out the door, Hannah led the three of them down the hallway to the bathroom to wash up. When that was done, she took their jackets down from the wall pegs in the utility room and helped the children put them on.

By the time they stepped onto the back porch, Esther had her horse hitched to the buggy. When she motioned for them to come, Hannah ushered the children across the yard. Once they were seated in the back of the buggy, she took her seat up front on the passenger's side.

"Everyone, stay in your seats now," Hannah called over her shoulder as Esther directed the horse and buggy down the driveway. "This road is bumpy."

"You're right, the driveway is full of ruts right now," Esther said, looking over at Hannah. "That's because we've had so much rain this fall."

Hannah grimaced. She knew the damage too much rain could cause. A few years ago, they'd had so much rain in Lancaster County that many of the roads had flooded. She wondered if that ever happened here.

After they turned onto the main road and

had traveled a ways, Esther pointed out various church members' homes. "Oh, and there's the store my folks used to own before they moved to Strasburg to help care for my brother, Dan."

"Who owns the store now?" Hannah asked.

"Aaron and Nettie Martin. They're a Mennonite couple, and they're fairly new to the area."

"I see. Is that where you do most of your shopping?"

"Jah, but when we're able to go into Hopkinsville, I shop at Walmart."

They rode silently for a while; then Hannah turned to Esther and said, "I understand that your brother has MS."

Esther nodded. "The disease has progressed to the point that he has to use a wheelchair most of the time."

"That's too bad. I can't imagine how I would feel if something like that happened to Timothy."

"It's been hard on his wife, Sarah, because she has a lot more responsibility now, but with my mamm and daed there to help, it makes things a bit easier."

"Easier? How could anything be easy if you have someone in your family in a wheelchair or with a severe disability?"

"Mom and Dad don't see it as a burden, and neither does Sarah. They love Dan very much, and there isn't anything they wouldn't do for him."

Hannah nodded. Some people might be able to sacrifice that much, but she wasn't sure she could. And she hoped she'd never have to find out.

Someone tapped Hannah's shoulder, and she turned around to see Penny. "What is it?" she asked, trying to keep the edge out of her voice.

Penny pointed at Mindy and said, *"Schuck."*

Hannah looked at Mindy and noticed that she'd taken one of her shoes off. "It's fine. Don't be a *retschbeddi*," she said, frowning at Penny.

"I don't think she means to be a tattle-tale," Esther said, jumping to Penny's defense. "She was probably concerned that Mindy might lose her shoe."

"Well, it's not her place to worry about Mindy — especially when she wasn't doing anything wrong."

Hannah couldn't help but notice Esther's icy stare. *She obviously doesn't like me, but I don't care. I don't care if anyone here in Christian County likes me.* She swallowed around the lump in her throat. *But if nobody likes me, I'll never fit in. Maybe I should try a little harder to be nice.*

"Just look at those maple trees," Esther said, bringing Hannah's thoughts to a halt. "It's hard to believe that just a few short weeks ago they were a brilliant reddish gold, and now they've lost most of their leaves." She sniffed the air. "That pungent odor tells me that someone in the area is burning leaves."

"It sure is chilly today," Hannah said. "I wonder if we'll have a cold winter."

"I wouldn't be surprised. A few years ago we had a terrible ice storm that left many Englishers without power. A lot of us Amish pitched in to help out wherever we could."

"I'm sure everyone needed help during that time," Hannah said.

Esther nodded. "They sure did."

They rode a little farther, and then Esther guided the horse and buggy up a long, graveled driveway. "See that big house at the end of the drive?" she said, pointing out the front buggy window. "That's Bonnie's bed-and-breakfast."

Hannah studied the stately old home. On one end of the long front porch was a swing, and two wicker chairs sat on the other end. A small table was positioned between them, holding a pot of yellow mums. The place looked warm and inviting. Even the yard was neat, with bushes well trimmed and weed-free flower beds in front of the house. "The outside of the home looks quite nice," Hannah said. "Where's the guesthouse you stay in?"

"Over there." Esther pointed to a smaller building that was set back from the house. It didn't look like it had more than a couple of rooms, but Hannah figured it was probably big enough for Esther's needs. Since she spent most of her time helping out at the B&B or watching Samuel's kids, she really only needed a place to sleep.

Just then a little brown-and-white mixed terrier bounded up to the buggy, barking and leaping into the air like it had springs on its legs.

"That's Bonnie's dog, Cody," Esther said. "He gets excited as soon as he sees my horse and buggy."

"*Hundli!* Hundli!" Mindy shouted from the backseat.

"No, Mindy," Esther said. "Cody's a full-grown dog, not a puppy."

"All dogs are puppies to her," Hannah said in Mindy's defense.

Esther silently guided her horse up to the hitching rail and climbed down from the buggy. After securing the horse, she came

65

around to help Penny and Jared down, while Hannah put Mindy's shoe back on and lifted her out of the buggy.

Then, with the dog barking and running beside them, they made their way up to the house.

When they stepped inside, Hannah sniffed at the scent of apples and cinnamon. She figured Bonnie must have been baking. A few seconds later, a young woman with dark, curly hair and brown eyes stepped into the hallway. "Oh Esther, it's you," she said with a look of surprise. "I didn't expect to see you again until this evening."

"I came by because I wanted you to meet Samuel's sister-in-law, Hannah. They've moved here from Pennsylvania." Esther motioned to Mindy, who clung to Hannah's hand. "This is their daughter, Mindy; she's three."

"It's nice to meet you, Hannah. I'm Bonnie Taylor." Bonnie shook Hannah's hand; then she bent down so she was eye level with Mindy and said, *"Brauchscht kichlin?"*

"Why would you ask if my daughter needed cookies?" Hannah questioned.

"Oh my!" Bonnie's cheeks flamed as she straightened to her full height. "I've learned a few Pennsylvania-Dutch words from Esther and Samuel and thought I knew what I was saying. What I meant to ask was if Mindy would *like* some cookies." She looked down at Jared and Penny, who were smiling up at her with eager expressions, then motioned for them to follow her into the kitchen.

"What's that delicious smell?" Hannah asked, sniffing the air.

"Oh, you must smell my new apple-pie fragrance candle." Bonnie pointed to the candle on the table. "I bought it the other day at Walmart in Hopkinsville."

"I hope I'll get to go there soon," Hannah said. "I could use a few things that I probably can't find at the Mennonite store in this area."

"I'd be happy to drive you to Hopkinsville whenever you want to go." Bonnie motioned to the table. "If you'd all like to take a seat, I'll give the children a glass of milk and some of the peanut butter cookies I made yesterday, and we ladies can enjoy a cup of tea."

"Can we have a few cookies, too?" Esther asked, wiggling her eyebrows playfully while smiling at Bonnie. It was obvious that the two women were good friends, and Hannah felt a bit envious.

After the children finished their cookies and milk, Penny asked if she and Jared could take Mindy outside to play with the dog and see Bonnie's chickens.

"I don't think so," Hannah was quick to say. "Mindy's never been here before, and she might wander off. I'd feel better if she stayed inside with me."

Esther instructed Penny to keep an eye on her little brother and told Jared to stay close to his sister and remain in the yard. The children nodded, and after being helped into their jackets, they skipped happily out the back door.

Hannah gathered Mindy into her arms. She couldn't believe Esther would send two small children into the yard to play by themselves. She wondered what Samuel would think if he knew how careless Esther was with his children.

Bonnie took a seat at the table, and as she visited with Hannah and Esther, she couldn't help but notice the look of sadness on Hannah's face. The young woman was polite enough and appeared to be interested in hearing how Bonnie had acquired the bed-and-breakfast, but her voice seemed flat, almost forced, like she was making herself join in the conversation. Bonnie remembered when Timothy had come for Titus and Suzanne's wedding, she'd been surprised that his wife hadn't been with him. He'd said Hannah stayed home to take care of her mother, who'd sprained her ankle, but Bonnie had a feeling it was more than that. She was pretty intuitive and had a hunch that Hannah didn't like it here. Probably hadn't wanted to leave Pennsylvania at all.

"It's so nice to just sit and visit like this, with a warm cup of tea and some delicious cookies," Esther said. "I enjoy such simple pleasures."

Bonnie nodded. "I remember when I was a girl visiting my grandparents here, Grandma once said to me, 'Whatever your simple pleasures may be, enjoy them and share them with someone else.' She also said that we sometimes take for granted the everyday things that give us a sense of joy and well-being. These simple things are often forgotten when problems occur in our lives." She lifted her cup of tea and smiled. "Since I've moved here I've been trying to savor all the down-to-earth pleasures I possibly can."

Hannah smiled and nodded. At least she was responding a bit more.

Bonnie was about to ask if either Esther or Hannah would like another cookie when the back door bounced open and Penny and

Jared rushed in.

Penny dashed across the room and clutched Bonnie's hand. "Eloise is *dot!*"

"Eloise is dead?" Bonnie looked over at Esther for confirmation. "Is that what she said?"

"I'm afraid so," Esther said with a nod.

"Oh my! I'd better go see about this!" Bonnie jumped up and hurried out the door.

CHAPTER 8

Hannah shuddered at the thought of someone lying dead in Bonnie's yard. "Wh–who is Eloise?" she asked in a shaky voice.

"She's one of Bonnie's laying hens," Esther replied. "If you don't mind keeping the kinner in here with you, I think I'll go outside and have a look myself."

"No, I don't mind." Hannah said with a shake of her head. Truth was, she had no desire to see a dead chicken, and she didn't think the children needed to be staring at it either.

Esther leaned down and gave Jared a kiss on the cheek. "Be a good boy now."

After Esther went out the door, Hannah seated the children at the table and gave them each a piece of paper and some crayons she had brought along in her oversized purse.

While they colored, she studied her surroundings some more. The kitchen was

71

cozy, with pretty yellow curtains at the window. There was a mix of modern appliances — a microwave, portable dishwasher, and electric coffeemaker, along with an older-looking stove and refrigerator on one side of the room. Several older items — a butter churn, a metal bread box, some antique canning jars, and an old pie cupboard that looked like it had been restored — added character to the room. Everything in the kitchen looked neat and orderly, much the way Hannah had kept her kitchen back home. It was nice that Bonnie had been able to use her grandparents' place as a bed-and-breakfast so others could enjoy it. Hannah hoped when Bonnie came in that she might show her the rest of the house.

Being here, in this place so warm and inviting, made Hannah miss her home all the more. She felt like a bird without a tree to land in, and it just wasn't right. She knew, according to the Bible, that she needed to be in subjection to her husband, but it was hard when she felt he'd been wrong in insisting they move to Kentucky.

I mustn't dwell on this, Hannah told herself. *It's not going to change the fact that I'm stuck in a place I don't want to be, so I need to try and make the best of my situation — at least until Timothy wakes up and realizes we were better off in Pennsylvania.*

"What do you think killed Eloise?" Bonnie asked after she and Esther had dug a hole and buried the chicken.

"I'm pretty sure she died from old age, because her neck wasn't broken and there were no tears in her skin or any feathers missing. You can be glad it wasn't a fox, because they can really wreak havoc in a chicken coop. In fact, a fox probably would have killed every one of your chickens," Esther said.

Bonnie breathed a sigh of relief. Taking care of chickens kept her busy enough; she sure didn't need the worry of keeping some predator away.

"Shall we go back inside and give Hannah a tour of the B&B?" Esther asked once they were done.

Bonnie shrugged as she jammed the shovel into the ground and leaned on it. "Do you think she'd be interested? She seems kind of distant."

"I believe so. She did comment on the outside of your house when we first pulled into your yard. In fact, she seemed impressed by what she saw."

"Well, she wouldn't have been if she'd

seen the way it looked before Samuel and Allen did all the repairs on this place."

"It just goes to show that there's hope for almost any home, even those that are really run down," Esther said with a chuckle.

Bonnie laughed, too. "This old house was definitely rundown. I think if my grandparents were still alive, they'd be pleased with the way it looks now. And I know they'd appreciate their home being put to good use."

"I believe you're right, and I'm glad your business is doing well."

"You get the credit for some of that, because if you hadn't taught me how to cook, I couldn't offer my patrons a decent breakfast as part of their stay."

Esther smiled. "I'm glad I was able to help, and I'm appreciative for the job you've given me."

"You'll have it for as long as you like, because I have no plans to go anywhere." Bonnie gave Esther's arm a gentle squeeze. "You, on the other hand, might have other plans that don't include the B&B."

Esther tipped her head. "What other plans?"

"Marrying Samuel, of course. Once you two are married, I'm sure you'll want to be a full-time mother to his children and any other children you may have in the future."

Esther's cheeks flushed to a deep pink. "Samuel and I haven't set a date to be married yet, but I hope it'll be soon."

"Well, whenever it happens, once you're married, your first obligation will be to him and his children."

Esther smiled. "What about you and Allen?"

"What about us?"

"Has he hinted at marriage yet?"

"No, but if he had, I would have avoided the subject."

"How come?"

"You know why, Esther."

"So you haven't told him yet about the baby you had when you were sixteen?"

Bonnie shook her head. "No, and I'm not sure I ever will. I'm afraid it might ruin our relationship."

"You can't have an honest relationship if you're not truthful with him about your past." Esther's sincere expression was enough to make Bonnie tear up.

"I know I should tell him, but I need to be sure our bond is strong enough before I do."

"How long do you think that will be?"

Bonnie shrugged. "I don't know. I'll have to play it by ear." She started walking toward the house. "Now changing the subject, after I give Hannah a tour of my house, would you all like to stay for lunch?"

"That'd be nice, but we wouldn't want to impose."

"It wouldn't be any trouble, and I'd enjoy not having to eat alone."

"If it's okay with Hannah, then it's fine with me," Esther said.

When they stepped back into the house, they found Hannah watching as the children colored pictures while seated at the table.

"I was wondering if you'd like to stay for lunch," Bonnie said.

Hannah looked at Esther, as though seeking her approval. When Esther nodded, Hannah smiled and said, "That'd be nice."

"Before we eat, though, would you like a tour of my bed-and-breakfast?"

"Yes, I would," Hannah replied. "I've been admiring some of the things you have here in the kitchen, and I'd enjoy seeing what the rest of the house looks like."

Bonnie found a game for the kids to play and situated them on the living-room floor; then she motioned for Esther and Hannah to follow her upstairs.

"I've seen all the rooms many times, so I think I'll stay down here with the children," Esther said.

"That's fine. Since you're up there cleaning every morning, you probably get tired of looking at the rooms."

Esther shook her head. "Not really. I enjoy my work, but I think it's best if I stay with the children."

"I agree," Hannah spoke up. "They might end up coloring everything in Bonnie's kitchen." A hint of a smile crossed her face, and Bonnie was pleased. It was the first time Hannah had seemed this relaxed. Maybe as Bonnie got to know Hannah better, they might even become friends.

CHAPTER 9

When Hannah and Esther returned from Bonnie's that afternoon, the first thing they did was put the kids down for their naps. All three of them were tired and cranky. Jared and Mindy had screamed and fussed so much on the way home that Hannah thought she would go insane. She'd figured the ride home would lull them to sleep, but it apparently had the opposite effect. They were probably full of sugar from the cookies they'd eaten. Hannah would have to watch Mindy a little closer from now on and make sure she ate properly. She didn't like it when her daughter became hyper.

"I'm going out to the phone shanty to make a call," Hannah told Esther after she'd put Mindy down and made sure she was asleep.

"That's fine." Esther smiled. "While you're doing that, I'll start cutting up the vegetables for the stew I'm going to make for supper this evening."

Hannah frowned. "Actually, I was planning to fix a meat loaf for supper. I saw some ground beef in the refrigerator and thought I'd use it for that."

"Oh, well, Samuel really likes stew, and that's what I told him I'd make for supper tonight."

Hannah's jaw clenched. Esther and Samuel weren't even married, but she acted like she was in charge of his kitchen. For that matter, she acted like she was in charge of everything in this house, including Samuel's children.

"Will you be staying here to eat supper with us?" Hannah asked.

Esther nodded. "I usually eat supper and then do the dishes before I head back to Bonnie's."

"Now that I'm living here, you won't need to stay."

"Oh, but I want to. I enjoy eating supper with Samuel and the kinner." Esther's cheeks colored. "Unless you'd rather that I didn't join you for supper. If that's the case, I can just fix the meal and be on my way."

Hannah folded her arms. "It's not that I don't want you to stay. I just don't see the need for you to fix supper when I'm perfectly capable of doing it."

"I'm sure you are, but . . ." Esther's voice trailed off. "If you'd prefer to fix meat loaf, that's fine with me."

Hannah nodded in reply then scooted out the back door. She was anxious to call Mom and tell her about Bonnie's B&B. Seeing the antiques there had given her an idea about how she might earn some money. She was eager to tell Timothy about it as well.

When Hannah stepped into the phone shanty, she was pleased to discover a message from her mother. But as Hannah listened to Mom talk about going shopping at Naomi and Caleb's store in Paradise and then eating at Bird-in-Hand Family Restaurant, a wave of homesickness rolled over her. She sat for several minutes, fighting the urge to cry, then finally laid her head on the table and gave in to her tears.

When the tears finally subsided, Hannah dried her face on her apron and headed back to the house, not bothering to return Mom's call. When she stepped inside, she was surprised to see Esther standing in front of the kitchen sink. "Oh, you're still here?"

Esther nodded. "I'll leave as soon as Marla and Leon get home from school."

"Since I'm here to greet them, there's really no need for you to wait."

Esther, looking more than a bit hurt, nodded. "I'll see you tomorrow then."

Not if Samuel agrees to let me watch the kinner, Hannah thought.

Bonnie had just taken a pan of cinnamon rolls from the oven, when she heard the distinctive *clip-clop* of horse's hooves. She set the pan on the cooling rack and looked out the kitchen window, surprised to see Esther's horse and buggy coming up the driveway.

"I wonder what she's doing here at this time of the day. I hope nothing's wrong."

Bonnie slipped into a sweater and hurried outside, just as Esther was tying her horse to the hitching rail. "I didn't expect to see you until later this evening. Is something wrong?" she asked.

"Yes, I'm afraid so."

Bonnie felt immediate concern. "What is it?"

Esther's chin trembled as tears welled in her brown eyes. "Hannah doesn't like me, Bonnie. I'm sure of it."

"Did you two have a disagreement?"

"Not exactly. She pretty much told me how it's going to be."

"What do you mean?"

"Hannah let it be known that she'd rather I not stay for supper, and she didn't want

81

me to fix the stew I'd promised Samuel I would make." Esther stroked Ginger's velvety nose, as though needing the horse's comfort. "She thinks my services aren't needed now that she and Timothy are living in Samuel's house."

"That's ridiculous! Samuel hired you to watch the kids, cook meals, clean the house, and do the laundry."

"I know, but now that Hannah's there, I feel like I'm in the way. I'm sure she's quite capable of doing everything I've been doing, and it would save Samuel some money if he didn't have to pay me."

"Have you talked to him about this?" Bonnie questioned.

"Not yet. I was hoping to speak with him this evening, but that was before Hannah practically pushed me out the door."

Bonnie put her arm around Esther and gave her a hug. "Now, don't you give in so easily. You need to talk to him soon, because Hannah has no right to just come in and take over like that."

Esther sniffed and slowly nodded. "I'll go over there a little early tomorrow morning. Hopefully, I can discuss things with him before he leaves for work."

"That's a good idea. In the meantime, you can come up to the house and have supper with me."

Esther smiled. "Thank you, Bonnie. I don't know what I'd do without your friendship."

"You've been a good friend to me, as well." Bonnie shivered, feeling a sudden chill. She hoped Hannah wouldn't do anything to mess things up between Esther and Samuel. They'd already had their share of struggles, and if anyone deserved some peace and happiness, it was them.

CHAPTER 10

"Where's Esther?" Marla asked when she and Leon arrived home from school.

"She went home." Hannah motioned to the stairs. "You'd better go up to your rooms and change out of your school clothes so you can get your chores done before it's time to eat supper. Oh, and go quietly, please, because the little ones are napping."

Leon looked up at Hannah with a wide-eyed expression. "Esther went home?"

"That's what I said." Didn't the child believe her, or was he hard of hearing?

"But Esther never goes home till after supper." Leon's brows furrowed; he looked downright perplexed.

"That's right," Marla put in. "And after supper, Esther and I always do the dishes together before she goes back to Bonnie's."

Hannah looked directly at Marla. "From now on, I'll be fixing supper, and you can help *me* do the dishes."

Marla opened her mouth as if to say something more, but Leon spoke first. "But what about Esther?"

Hannah sighed. "I just told you. Esther won't be here for supper."

Leon's forehead wrinkled. "But she'll still be comin' in the morning to fix our breakfast and take care of Penny and Jared while we're in school, right?"

"That hasn't been decided yet. I'll be talking to your daed about it when he gets home from work," Hannah said, her irritation mounting. "Since your uncle Timothy and I will be living here until we get our own home, there's no reason I can't watch your brother and sister during the day while you're at school and your daed's at work."

"But Jared and Penny like Esther, and so do we." Marla looked over at Leon, who agreeably bobbed his head.

"I'm sure you do, and you'll have plenty of time to spend with her once she and your daed get married."

Leon's mouth opened wide. "Daadi and Esther are gettin' married? How come nobody told us about it?"

Hannah flinched. *Oh great. Now I've said something I shouldn't have said.* "What I meant to say was that if your daed keeps courting Esther, then I'm sure in time he'll

85

ask her to marry him."

A smile stretched across Leon's face as he hopped up and down and clapped his hands. "That's really good news! I'm gonna ask Daadi to marry Esther right away!"

"That's not a good idea," Hannah was quick to say. "I'm sure your daed will let everyone know once he and Esther have set a date."

"But he might do it quicker if we ask him to." Marla grabbed Leon's hand and gave it a squeeze. "Won't it be *wunderbaar* when Esther's our mamm?"

He nodded vigorously.

"Well, it hasn't happened yet, so you need to keep quiet about it." Hannah wished she'd never brought the subject up. And she certainly hoped that by the time Samuel married Esther, she and Timothy would be living in their own place, because two women in the same house, each trying to do things her own way, would never work.

Hannah had just finished making a tossed green salad when she heard the rumble of a truck coming up the driveway. Looking out the window and seeing Timothy and Samuel climb out of Allen's truck, she hurried to set the table.

A few minutes later, Samuel and Timothy

entered the kitchen.

"Mmm . . . it smells good in here, but it doesn't smell like stew," Samuel said, sniffing in the air. "Esther said she'd fix my favorite stew for supper this evening." He glanced around. "Where is Esther anyway? Is she in the living room?"

"No, uh . . . Esther went home, and we're having meat loaf."

Samuel's eyebrows furrowed, and even Timothy shot Hannah a questioning look. "Why'd she go home? Was she feeling grank?" Samuel asked.

"No, she's not sick. I just told her that since I was here she wouldn't need to help with supper and could go home."

"You sent Esther home?" Samuel's eyebrows lifted high, and his voice raised nearly an octave.

Hannah looked at Timothy, hoping he would come to her rescue, but he just stared at her as though in disbelief.

"Well . . . uh, I didn't send her home exactly. I just told her that I could fix supper and that her help wasn't needed."

"What gives you the right to be tellin' Esther that?" A vein on the side of Samuel's neck bulged just a bit.

"That ain't all, Daadi," Leon said, rushing into the room. "Aunt Hannah said she didn't think Esther would be comin' here in the mornings no more. Least not till the two of you get married."

"Is that so?" Samuel's sharp intake of breath and his pinched expression let Hannah know he was quite upset.

"I . . . I didn't actually say Esther wouldn't be coming over. I just said I'd need to talk to you about it, because I really don't see a need for her to be here when I'm perfectly capable of taking care of your kinner, cleaning the house, and cooking the meals." Hannah's cheeks warmed. "And I mistakenly mentioned that you might marry Esther."

"I do plan to marry her," Samuel said. "But it's not official yet, and I haven't talked to her about a wedding date." He leveled Hannah with a look that could have stopped a runaway horse. "I'd appreciate it if from now on you don't tell my kinner anything they should be hearin' directly from me." Samuel turned and started for the door.

"Where are you going?" Timothy called to him.

"Over to the B&B to speak with Esther!" Samuel let the door slam behind him.

"We need to talk about this," Timothy said, taking hold of Hannah's arm and leading her toward the door.

"What about supper?" She motioned to

the stove. "The meat loaf's ready, and I really think we should eat."

"The meal can wait awhile. Let's go out on the porch where we can speak in private."

Before Hannah could offer a word of protest, he grabbed her jacket from the wall peg, slung it across her shoulders, and ushered her out the door.

"Now what gives you the right to send Esther away when you know she's been watching Samuel's kinner?" Timothy asked, guiding her to one end of the porch. "Do I need to remind you that this is Samuel's home, and he's been kind enough to let us live here?"

"You don't need to talk to me so harshly." Hannah's voice whined with the threat of tears.

"I'm sorry, but surely you could see how upset Samuel was. He loves Esther very much and wants her to care for his kinner when he's not at home." Timothy's voice softened some but remained unyielding. "Things shouldn't have to change just because we're living here right now."

Hannah stiffened and started to snivel. "Well, they've changed for me! But I guess you don't care about that."

"I do care, and I hope we can either build or find a place of our own really soon so we can feel settled here in Kentucky," Timothy said. "And Hannah, please turn off the waterworks. There's no reason for you to be whimpering about this. There's no question that what you said to Esther was wrong — especially when those arrangements had been worked out between Samuel and Esther long before we moved here."

"I didn't suggest that Esther leave because I was trying to change anything. I just thought it wasn't necessary for both of us to take care of the house and kinner, and I figured Samuel would appreciate me helping out." Hannah folded her arms and glared at him, wiping tears of frustration away. "And I doubt that I'll ever feel settled living here, because my home is in Pennsylvania, not Kentucky!"

"You've said that before, Hannah, and it's gettin' kind of old." He placed his hand on her shoulder. "Life is what we make it, and unless you're willing to at least try to accept this change and make the best of it, you'll never be happy. I'm tired of our constant bickering, and I'm worn-out from trying to keep the peace between us. You need to focus on something positive for a change."

Hannah stared at the wooden floorboards on the porch; then she lifted her gaze to meet his. "I think I know something that might make me happy — or at least, it would give me something meaningful to do."

"What's that?"

"Esther and I took the little ones over to see Bonnie Taylor this morning, and while we were there, I was impressed with all the antiques Bonnie has."

His forehead wrinkled. "I'm confused. What's that got to do with anything?"

"I was thinking maybe I could start my own business, buying and selling antiques. It would help our finances, and —"

He held up his hand. "You can stop right there, Hannah, because your idea won't work."

"Why not?"

"For one thing, Samuel's barn is full of our furniture, so you wouldn't even have a place to store any antiques. Second, most antiques can be quite expensive, and we don't have any extra money to spend on something that might not sell. Third, I seriously doubt that antiques would sell very well around here."

"What makes you say that?"

"There are no tourists here — at least not like we had in Lancaster County, and there aren't nearly as many people living in this area." Timothy slowly shook his head. "You need to find something else to keep yourself busy, because selling antiques is definitely out — at least for right now. It would be too big of a risk. Now let's get inside and eat supper."

Resentment welled in Hannah's soul. She was getting tired of Timothy telling her what to do all the time, and it didn't surprise her that he'd been against her idea right from the start. He didn't even want to consider it. Was there anything they could agree on, or was this a warning of how things were going to be from now on?

Samuel fumed all the way to Bonnie's. *Just who does Hannah think she is, sending Esther home when she should have been taking care of the kinner and sharing supper with us? Hannah has a lot of nerve coming into my house and trying to take things over!* Samuel wondered how his brother put up with a wife like that. Of course, Hannah, being the youngest child and only girl in her family, had always been a bit spoiled. Even back when she was a girl growing up in their community, he'd noticed it. And it didn't help that she was under her mother's thumb, which he knew was why she'd been opposed to the idea of moving to Kentucky in the first place.

I wonder what made Timothy decide to marry Hannah, Samuel thought as he gripped the horse's reins a bit tighter. *It must have been her pretty face and the fact that she could cook fairly well, because Timothy was sure blinded to the reality that Hannah's tied to her mamm's apron strings.*

Samuel drew in a couple of deep breaths, knowing he needed to calm down before he spoke to Esther. He sent up a quick prayer, asking God for wisdom.

By the time he pulled up to the hitching rail in Bonnie's yard, he felt a bit more relaxed. He climbed down from the buggy, secured his horse, and sprinted across the lawn to the guesthouse, where he rapped on the door and called, "Esther, are you there?"

No response.

He knocked again, but when Esther didn't answer, he figured she might be up at the main house with Bonnie.

Hurrying across the lawn, he took the steps two at a time and knocked on Bonnie's door. Several seconds went by before Bonnie answered the door. "I came to see Esther. Is she here?" Samuel asked.

Bonnie nodded. "We were about to have supper."

"I'm sorry to interrupt, but I need to talk

to Esther for a few minutes, if you don't mind."

Bonnie smiled. "Come in. I'll wait in the living room while you two visit."

"Thanks, I appreciate that."

Bonnie turned toward the living room, and Samuel headed for the kitchen.

"Samuel, I'm surprised to see you here. I figured you'd be at home having supper with your family," Esther said when Samuel stepped into the room.

He frowned. "I figured that's where you'd be, too, but when Timothy and I got home, Hannah said you'd come here."

Esther nodded. "I think my being there made her feel uncomfortable. I sensed a bit of tension between us all day."

Samuel pulled out a chair and joined her at the table. "When I go back home, I plan to tell Hannah in no uncertain terms that I want you to keep watching the kinner, and that includes bein' there for supper."

"But Samuel, if it's going to cause trouble with Hannah, maybe it might be best if —"

Samuel shook his head. "It won't be best for the kinner, and it sure won't be best for me." He reached for Esther's hand. "I know it won't be easy for you to deal with Hannah, but I'm asking you to keep working for me and to try and get along with Hannah."

He smiled and gently squeezed her fingers. "I'd set a date to marry you right now so you could be with us all the time, but I think we'd better wait till Timothy and Hannah find a place of their own. We have to keep reminding ourselves that these arrangements are only temporary."

Esther's eyes sparkled with unshed tears. "Oh Samuel, let's pray it won't be too long."

Timothy stepped outside after the evening meal was finished, while Hannah cleaned up and occupied the children. It felt good to breathe in the fresh air, especially when things had gone downhill after arriving home. He didn't blame Samuel for being upset with Hannah, and he hoped it didn't put a further strain on their living arrangements until they had a place of their own.

Timothy thought about Hannah's desire to sell antiques. He had to admit her eyes had been shining when she'd shared her thoughts with him about it. It was the first time since they'd arrived in Kentucky that Hannah had showed any kind of enthusiasm.

Was I wrong to discourage her? he wondered. *Maybe something like that would help Hannah adjust to her new surroundings. Guess I was wrong for not listening more to what she had to say. I'll think about it more once we're able to get a place of our own. By then, I'll have a better idea of what our expenses will be like.*

For now, though, he should go out to the barn to make sure everything was secured for the evening. He'd wait for his brother and hope he could smooth things over with him, because the last thing he needed was for Samuel to ask them to leave. If he did, where would they go? They sure couldn't move in with Titus and Suzanne in their small place.

Now, don't borrow any trouble, he told himself. *Things will work out. They have to.*

Chapter 11

Leaves swirled around the yard, and the wind howled eerily under the eaves of the porch as Hannah stood waiting for Bonnie to pick her and Mindy up. She gazed at the gray-blue sky and the empty fields next to Samuel's place and wished it was spring instead of fall. They were going into Hopkinsville today to do some shopping, so maybe that would lift her spirits. Hannah looked forward to the outing because it had rained every day last week and she was tired of being cooped up in the house with Esther and the children. She'd had to learn how to deal with Esther coming over every day to watch Samuel's children, but it wasn't easy. Esther did things a lot differently than Hannah, but she found if she kept busy writing letters to Mom and cleaning house, the days were bearable. It wasn't that Esther didn't keep the house clean — she just wasn't as structured and organize

as Hannah had always been. Many tim
Esther had tried to engage Hannah i
conversation, but since they really didn'
have much in common, there wasn't a lot
to talk about. They'd worked out an agreement to take turns fixing supper, so at least
that gave Hannah a chance to do some
cooking, which she enjoyed.

Hannah watched as Esther hung some
clothes on the line, using the pulley that ran
from the porch to the barn. Mindy must
have seen her, too, because she left Hannah's side, darted across the porch, and
tugged on Esther's skirt. Esther stopped
what she was doing, bent down, picked
Mindy up, and swung her around. Hannah
cringed as Mindy squealed with delight. It
really bothered Hannah to see how Mindy
had warmed up to Esther. It seemed like
she was always hanging on Esther, wanting
to crawl up into her lap to listen to a story,
or just sitting beside Esther at the table.
This was one more reason Hannah hoped
she and Timothy could find a place of their
own soon, where she and Mindy could
spend more quality time together without
Esther's influence. Everyone seemed to love
Esther.

Hannah looked away, her thoughts going
to Timothy. He'd been keeping very busy

helping Samuel. They'd had several indoor paint jobs, which was a good thing on account of the rain. The downside was that most of the jobs were out of town, and by the time the men came home each evening, Timothy was tired and didn't want to talk with Hannah or even spend a few minutes playing with Mindy before she was put to bed. He often went to bed early and was asleep by the time Hannah got Mindy down and crawled into bed herself. Where had the closeness they'd once felt for each other gone? What had happened to Timothy's promise that everything would be better once they had moved? So many things had gotten in the way of what had brought them together in the first place.

When Esther went back inside, Hannah glanced at Mindy, now frolicking back and forth across the porch, amusing herself as she pretended to be a horse. *Your daadi hardly spends any time with you anymore, either. Will we ever be like a real family again?*

Hannah's musings were halted when Bonnie's car pulled into the yard and she tooted her horn. Grabbing Mindy's car seat from the porch, Hannah took Mindy's hand and hurried out to the car.

"Where's Esther?" Bonnie asked when Hannah opened the car door. "Aren't she and Samuel's little ones coming with us today?"

Hannah shook her head. "Jared and Penny have the beginning of a cold, and she thought it'd be best if she kept them in today."

"I guess that makes sense. Is everyone else well?"

"So far, and I hope it stays that way, because I sure don't want Mindy coming down with a cold." Hannah put Mindy's car seat in the back and lifted Mindy into it, making sure her seat belt was securely buckled. Then she stepped into the front seat and buckled her own seat belt.

Bonnie smiled. "I appreciate the fact that you use the seat belts without me having to ask. I know that the Amish don't have seat belts in their buggies, so I sometimes have to remind my passengers to use them when they're riding in my car."

"I've sometimes wished we did have seat belts," Hannah said, "because when someone's in a buggy accident, they're often seriously injured."

Bonnie nodded with a look of understanding. "Getting to know my Amish neighbors has been one of the biggest blessings in my life, and I don't like hearing about accidents of any kind. I pray often for my Amish and

English friends, asking God to keep everyone safe."

"Esther mentioned that you're a Christian and that you go to a small church in Fairview," Hannah said.

"Yes, that's right." Bonnie pulled out of Samuel's yard and headed down the road in the direction of Hopkinsville. "It's a very nice church, and I enjoy attending the services. When my grandma was alive, she and Grandpa used to go to that church."

"Have you ever attended an Amish church service?" Hannah asked.

"Not a Sunday service, but I did go to Titus and Suzanne's wedding, which I understand was similar to one of your regular preaching services."

Hannah nodded. "So what did you think of the wedding?"

"It was nice. Quite a bit different from the weddings we Englishers have, though."

"When you and Allen get married, will it be at the church in Fairview?"

Bonnie's mouth dropped open. "Where did you get the idea that Allen and I will be getting married?"

"Samuel said so. I heard him talking to Timothy about it during supper a few nights ago."

"What did he say?"

"Just that he knew Allen was planning to marry you, and he hoped it'd be soon."

Bonnie gave the steering wheel a sharp rap. "That's interesting — especially since Allen hasn't even asked me to marry him."

"He hasn't?"

"No, but he has dropped a couple of hints along the way."

"Maybe he's waiting for just the right time."

Bonnie kept her focus on the road.

Did I do it again and say something I shouldn't have? Hannah wondered. *Maybe Bonnie doesn't love Allen enough to marry him.*

Oak Grove, Kentucky

"Samuel, I wanted to tell you again how much I appreciate your understanding after we had our little talk concerning Hannah and Esther," Timothy said before hauling one of their paint cans across the living room of the older home they were painting.

"Hey, it's okay. I'm glad we had the chance to talk things out." Samuel smiled. "We're family, and it's important that we all get along, for our sake, as well as the kinners'. It's not good having unspoken tension between us."

"I don't want that either," Timothy said.

"Hannah has seemed a little more content this past week, now that she and Esther are taking turns with the cooking. I'm hoping maybe with Hannah getting into some sort of a routine while getting better acquainted with life in Kentucky she'll learn to like it here as much as I do."

"I hope so, too," Samuel said, "because I'm really glad you're here."

"How are things going for you two?" Allen asked Samuel when he entered the house, interrupting their conversation.

"Real well," Samuel replied. "We should have it done before the week is out." He motioned to Timothy, who was kneeling on the floor, painting the baseboard an oyster shell white. "With all the work we've had lately, it's sure good to have my brother's help. Even though Timothy only worked part-time for Zach, he learned some pretty good painting skills."

"I can see that he's doing a fine job." Allen moved closer to where Samuel stood on a ladder. "I'm sure the folks who live here will be glad to hear that all the painting will be finished before Thanksgiving."

"Speaking of Thanksgiving, what are you doing for the holiday?" Samuel asked.

"I'm going over to Bonnie's."

"That's good to hear. I was going to invite

you to join us at Titus's house if you didn't have plans."

"I appreciate the offer," Allen said, "but I'm really looking forward to spending the day with Bonnie. We've both been keeping so busy and haven't seen much of each other lately."

Samuel chuckled. "You'll never get her to agree to marry you if you don't spend some time with her."

"I know. That's why I accepted her invitation for Thanksgiving dinner. And if everything goes well, I'll ask her to marry me before the day is out."

Samuel grinned. "Well now, isn't that something? Be sure and let me know how it goes."

"I'd like to hear that news myself," Timothy called from across the room.

Allen nodded. "You two will be the first ones I tell — after my folks, of course. Oh, and I'll also tell your brother Zach, because I'm sure he'll be happy to hear I'm finally willing to give up the single life and have found a woman I want to marry."

Paradise, Pennsylvania

"Johnny, are you sure you don't need my help at the store today?" Sally asked her husband as they sat at the kitchen table eating breakfast. "Since Hannah's been gone, I've been bored and really need something to occupy my time and thoughts."

"Our niece, Anna, and her friend, Phoebe Stoltzfus, are working out really well. I'm not needed there all the time, so you wouldn't find much to do either." Johnny pulled his fingers through the ends of his nearly gray beard. "Makes me wonder if I ought to retire and buy a little place for us in Sarasota. We could live in the community of Pinecraft, where so many Plain folks retire or vacation."

Sally frowned as she shook her head. "Then we'd be living even farther from Hannah. Unless Timothy brought his family down to Florida for a vacation, which I doubt, we'd rarely see them."

He patted her arm. "Now don't look so worried. It was only wishful thinking on my part. I'm not really ready to retire just yet, but when the time comes for me to sell the store, I'd like to move to a place where it's warm and sunny all year."

Sally felt a huge sense of relief. At least she didn't have to worry about that for a while. She picked up her cup of tea and took a drink. "I've been wondering about something."

"What's that?"

"Thanksgiving's just a week away, and I was hoping we could go to Kentucky for the holiday. It would be nice to see Hannah and find out for ourselves how she, Timothy, and Mindy are doing."

Johnny shook his head. "I don't think so."

"Why not?"

"It's too soon for us to pay them a visit. Hannah needs to adjust to living in Kentucky, and seeing us right now might make it harder on her."

"But Johnny, our daughter's miserable. Every time she calls, I can hear by the tone of her voice how distressed she is. And the letter I got from her the other day made me feel so sad, reading how much she misses us and wishes she could come home."

"Just give her more time. She'll get over her homesickness after a while." Johnny gulped down the rest of his coffee, scooted his chair away from the table, and stood.

"I'm not so sure about that. Hannah liked it here in Pennsylvania, and she doesn't like much of anything about living in Kentucky."

"I don't have time to debate this with you right now. I need to get my horse and buggy ready so I can get to the store."

"But you said you weren't needed there."

"I said I wasn't needed as much as before, but there are still some things I need to do.

I may have some boxes to unpack and move if the newest shipment came in yesterday afternoon when I left Anna in charge." Johnny grabbed his straw hat, slipped into his jacket, and hurried out the door like he couldn't get out of there soon enough.

Tears welled in Sally's eyes. *I don't think he cares how miserable our daughter is or even how much I miss her. If I thought for one minute that Johnny wouldn't get angry with me, I'd catch a bus to Kentucky and go there for Thanksgiving myself!*

CHAPTER 12

Fresno, California

Trisha Chandler sat at the head of her small dining-room table, hands folded in her lap, and lips pursed with determination. She'd just shared a delicious noon Thanksgiving meal with her two closest friends, Shirley and Margo, whom she'd met at a widow's support group after her husband died of a heart attack two years ago. As soon as they'd finished eating, she'd given them some news that hadn't been well received. But she wasn't going to let them talk her into changing her mind. No, she'd waited a long time to do something fun and adventurous, and their negative comments were not going to stop her from fulfilling a dream she'd had for several years.

"I've always wanted to travel, and now that the restaurant where I've worked since Dave passed away has closed its doors, I think it's time for me and my trusty little car to go out on the road," Trisha said.

"But it's not safe for a woman your age to be out on her own," Margo argued. "What if something happened to you?"

Trisha grunted. "Nothing's going to happen, and I'm not that old. I just turned fifty-eight last month, remember? Besides, it doesn't matter how old I am. In this crazy world, there's no guarantee that any of us are ever really safe."

Tears welled in Shirley's blue eyes. Always tenderhearted, Shirley had joined their widow's group six months ago when her husband lost his battle with colon cancer. "After thinking it through a bit more, maybe it's not such a bad idea after all. Truthfully, I wish I could be brave enough to venture out on my own," she said. "We're going to miss you, Trisha, that's for sure."

Trisha gave Shirley's hand a gentle squeeze. "Why don't you come with me? Just think of all the wonderful things we can see."

Shirley shook her head. "I can't be gone for six months, the way you plan to do; my children would never allow it. Besides, I really don't like being too far from home."

Trisha nodded in understanding. "Since I don't have any children, there's really nothing to keep me here."

"Does that mean you plan to sell your condo and be gone for good?" Margo asked, her dark eyes widening.

"Oh no. I'm sure I'll be back."

"You know this really isn't a good time of the year to be driving across the United States," Margo pointed out. "You could run into all kinds of foul weather."

"I've thought about that, but I'll start out in the southern states, and then as the weather warms up in the spring, I'll head up the East Coast and see some of the historical sights."

Shirley took a drink of water. "What about the expense? A trip like that could cost plenty. I don't mean to pry, but can you afford the gas and hotels you'll need along the way?"

"Dave had a pretty good-sized life insurance policy, and I'm sure it'll be more than enough to provide for my needs on this trip I've always dreamed about taking."

Margo leaned forward and leveled Trisha with one of her most serious looks. "And there's nothing we can do to talk you out of it?"

Trisha shook her head determinedly. "I've made up my mind, and I'm confident that God will be with me as I venture out to see some of the beautiful country He created."

"Let's see now. . . . The turkey is in the oven, green beans and potatoes are staying warm on the stove, a pumpkin and an apple pie are in the refrigerator, and the table is set." Bonnie smiled as she surveyed her dining-room table. She'd used a lace tablecloth her grandmother had made many years ago, set the table with Grandma's best china, and placed a pot of yellow mums from Suzanne's garden in the center of the table with pale orange taper candles on either side. Everything was perfect and looked very festive. Now all she had to do was wait patiently for Allen to arrive.

Bonnie moved over to the window and pulled the lace curtains aside. The morning had started out with some fog, but then the fog had lifted and revealed a beautiful day with blue skies and white, puffy clouds, with no rain in sight. It was quite a contrast from the last few weeks when they'd had nothing but gray skies and too many rainy days.

She stepped into the hall to look in the mirror and check her appearance. She'd chosen a pretty green dress to wear today, and her dark, naturally curly hair framed her oval face. Bonnie also wore a cameo pin, one of the few pieces of jewelry that had belonged to her grandmother. She kept the brooch safely tucked away in her jewelry box except for special occasions such as this. A touch of lipstick, a little blush, and some pale green eye shadow completed her look. She'd always been told that she was attractive and didn't need makeup, so she'd never worn much. But it wasn't her natural beauty she hoped Allen was attracted to. She wanted him to see and appreciate her inner beauty as well.

Should I share my past with him today? Bonnie wondered. *Or would it be best to wait for another time? I wish I could just tell him right out, but I'm so afraid of his reaction.* Since she didn't know how he would deal with hearing she'd once had a child, she didn't want to chance spoiling the day — or worse, their relationship.

The closer Bonnie and Allen had become, the more she struggled with her insecurities and fears. Her thoughts and reality seemed to be at odds with each other these days. It was unnerving at times. She would talk herself into telling him, but then her fears got in the way and she'd chicken out.

The sound of a vehicle rumbling up the driveway put an end to Bonnie's musings. She looked through the peephole in the front door and saw Allen's truck pull up to her garage. With a sense of excitement, she waited until Allen stepped onto the porch before she opened the door.

"Happy Thanksgiving!" they said at the same time.

He grinned. "Wow, you look absolutely beautiful!"

"Thanks. You look pretty good yourself," Bonnie said, admiring his neatly pressed gray slacks, light blue shirt, and black leather jacket.

Allen followed her into the house and paused in the hall to sniff the air. "Mmm . . . Something sure smells good."

She smiled. "Everything's ready, so it's just a matter of putting the turkey on the platter, carving it, and serving things up. Then we can eat."

He handed her his jacket. "I'm starving! If you'll hang this up for me, I'd be happy to cut the bird for you."

"That would be great. I don't know about you, but I've always loved seeing the Thanksgiving turkey sitting in the center of the table. You know, like one of those Norman Rockwell paintings." Bonnie hung Allen's jacket on the coat tree in the hall and followed him to the kitchen. While he carved the turkey, she put the potatoes and green beans into bowls and took them out to the dining-room table, along with some olives, pickles, and the whole-wheat rolls Esther had made for her the day before. She laid a serving spoon next to the spot for the turkey platter. That way they could scoop the hot stuffing right out of the bird and onto their plates.

Oops! Guess I'd better make more room for the turkey, Bonnie thought, as she moved the yellow mums to the far end of the table. Then she returned to the kitchen to make the gravy while Allen finished up with the turkey.

"I think we're all set," Allen said, rubbing his hands briskly together. "For now, I think I've carved off enough meat for the both of us."

"Yes, it looks wonderful, and I'm right behind you with the gravy," Bonnie replied as they started for the dining room.

Once they were seated, Allen took hold of her hand. Bowing his head, he prayed, "Heavenly Father, I thank You for this wonderful meal that's set before us. Bless it to the needs of our bodies, and bless the hands that prepared it. Be with our family and friends on this special Thanksgiving Day, and keep them all safe. Thank You for the many blessings You've given to us. Amen."

Allen opened his eyes, looked at Bonnie,

and winked. "As our Amish friends often say, 'Now, let's eat ourselves full!' "

"You carved the turkey, and you're my guest, so you go first," she said, pointing to the golden brown bird. "If you want some stuffing, you can use the large spoon to scoop some onto your plate."

Allen forked a few pieces of turkey onto his plate and got some stuffing as well. Then they served themselves the side dishes. As they ate, they visited about various things that had happened in the area lately. Bonnie noticed that one minute Allen seemed very relaxed and the next minute he seemed kind of nervous and fidgety and would lose his train of thought. She knew he'd been working long hours lately and figured he might be tired or uptight. Hopefully, after he finished eating, he'd feel more relaxed.

"I'm surprised you didn't go to Washington to spend Thanksgiving with your folks," Bonnie said when the conversation began to lag.

"I'd thought about it, but Mom and Dad aren't home right now. Their thirty-fifth wedding anniversary is tomorrow, so they're on a two-week vacation in Kauai."

"I'm sure they must be having a good time." Bonnie sighed. "I've always wanted to visit one of the Hawaiian islands, but I guess it's not likely to happen. At least not anytime soon."

"How do you know?"

"I'm too busy running the B&B. Besides, I'm sure a trip like that would be expensive."

"You never know. You might make it there someday. Maybe sooner than you think." Allen fiddled with his spoon. "What about you? How come you didn't go to Oregon to spend the holiday with your dad?"

"For one thing, I have some guests checking into the B&B on Saturday. Besides, my dad is coming to Kentucky for Christmas, so it's only a month before I get to see him."

Allen smiled, seeming to relax a bit. "That's good to hear. I'm anxious to meet your dad."

"I'm eager for you to meet him, and I'm sure he'll enjoy getting to know you as well."

They sat in companionable silence awhile, finishing the last of their meal. Then Bonnie pushed back her chair and stood. "As much as I hate to say it, I think it's time to clear the table and do the dishes." She motioned to the adjoining room. "If you'd like to make yourself comfortable in the living room, I'll join you for pie and coffee as soon as my kitchen chores are done."

Allen shook his head. "I wouldn't think of letting you do all the work while I kick back and let my dinner settle." He stood. "If we both clear the table and do the dishes together, we'll be done in half the time. Then we can spend the rest of the day relaxing."

"That sounds nice, and I'll appreciate your help in the kitchen."

An hour later, when the food had all been put away and the dishes were done, Bonnie gave Allen a cup of coffee and told him to go relax in the living room while she got out the pies.

"This time I won't argue," he said, offering her a tender smile. He really was a very nice man, and as hard as Bonnie had fought it, she'd fallen hopelessly in love with him.

Allen took the cup of coffee, gave her a kiss on the cheek, and headed for the living room.

Bonnie went to the refrigerator and took out the pumpkin pie and whipped cream. She was on her way to the dining room when she heard Cody barking outside.

"Would you mind checking to see what Cody's yapping about?" she called to Allen. "Sounds like he's in the backyard."

"Sure, no problem." Allen went through the kitchen and opened the back door.

Woof! Woof! Cody rushed in and darted right in front of Bonnie, causing her to stumble. The pie slipped out of her hands and landed on the floor with a *splat,* and the can of whipped cream went rolling across the room, stopping at Allen's feet.

Cody didn't hesitate to lick up the pie, and Bonnie didn't know whether to laugh or cry.

When Allen started laughing, she gave in to the urge, too. "I hope you like apple pie," she said, "because that's the only kind I have left."

"Apple's my favorite anyway, and since the whipped cream came right to me, I can just spray some on," he added, leaning over to pick up the can.

Bonnie didn't know if apple really was Allen's favorite or if he was just trying to make her feel better, but the easygoing way he'd handled the situation helped a lot. Gazing at the pie splattered all over the floor, they both gave in to hysterical giggles.

At last, Bonnie put the dog outside and, with Allen's help, cleaned up the mess on the floor.

"This might not be the most romantic place to say it," Allen said, taking Bonnie into his arms, "but I'd like to spend the rest of my life with you — cooking, cleaning, and getting after the dog."

Bonnie tipped her head and looked up

him. "Wh–what exactly do you mean?"

"I mean that I love you very much, and if you'll have me, I want to make you my wife."

Bonnie felt like all the air had been squeezed out of her lungs, and she leaned against Allen for support.

"Can I take that as a yes?" he asked, kissing the top of her head.

"No. Yes. I mean, maybe." She pulled away. "What I really mean is I'd like to think about it a few weeks, if you don't mind."

Allen's forehead wrinkled. "In all honesty, I was hoping you'd say you love me, too, and that you'd be happy to be my wife."

"I . . . I do love you, Allen, but marriage is a lifelong commitment, and I — well, I don't want to make a hasty decision. I'd really like a little time to think and pray about it before I give you my answer."

He nodded slowly. "I guess that makes sense. When do you think you'll have an answer?"

Noticing his disappointment, she searched for the right words as she moistened her lips with the tip of her tongue. "Umm . . . How about Christmas Eve? Would that be soon enough?"

"That's only a month away, so I guess I can hold out that long." Allen lowered his head and kissed her gently.

Dear Lord, Bonnie prayed when the kiss ended. *Help me to have the courage to tell Allen about my past. I'm just not ready to do it today.*

CHAPTER 13

Paradise, Pennsylvania

"What can I do to help?" Fannie asked when she entered her daughter-in-law Leona's kitchen on Thanksgiving Day.

Leona, red-faced and looking a bit anxious, smiled and said, "I appreciate the offer, because you and Abraham are the first ones here, and I really could use some help." Her metal-framed glasses had slipped to the middle of her nose, and she quickly pushed them back in place. "Would you mind basting the turkey while I peel and cut the potatoes?"

"I don't mind at all." Fannie grabbed a pot holder and opened the oven door of the propane stove, releasing the delicious aroma of the Thanksgiving turkey that was nicely browning. "Mmm . . . Just the smell of this big bird makes me *hungerich*," she said, while reaching for the basting brush lying on the counter to her right.

Leona nodded. "I know what you mean. The smell of turkey has been driving me crazy ever since it started roasting."

"Where are the kinner?" Fannie asked after she'd covered the turkey again and shut the oven door.

"James is out in the barn helping Zach clean out a few of the stalls so the rest of our guests will have a place to put their horses if they'd rather not use the corral."

"That's where Abraham went, too, so he'll probably end up helping them," Fannie said. "Now, where are the girls hiding themselves? I didn't see any sign of them when I came into the house."

Leona pointed to the door leading upstairs. "They're tidying up their rooms so their cousins won't see how messy they can be."

Fannie chuckled. "I guess that's what you can expect with most kinner. Of course, my Abby wasn't like that at all. Even when she was little, she kept her room neat."

"Maybe I should ask her to have a little talk with Lucy and Jean. They might be more inclined to listen to their aunt than they are to me."

"I know what you mean. Someone else usually has a better chance of getting through to our kinner than we do ourselves.

And that doesn't change, even when they're grown with families of their own." Fannie motioned to the variety of vegetables on the table. "Would you like me to make a salad from those?"

"I'd appreciate that." Leona placed the cut-up potatoes in a kettle of water and set it on the stove. "Now that I've finished that chore, I can help you cut up the vegetables. Have you heard anything from Timothy lately? I was wondering what he and Hannah will be doing for Thanksgiving."

"I talked to him a few days ago," Fannie replied, reaching for a head of lettuce. "He said they'd be having dinner at Titus and Suzanne's place today."

"Who else will be there?"

"Samuel and his kinner and Esther, as well as Suzanne's mother, grandfather, brothers, and sisters."

"None of Suzanne's siblings are married yet, right?"

Fannie shook her head. "Nelson's the oldest, and from what Titus has said, Nelson used to court a young woman from their community, but they broke up some time ago because they weren't compatible."

Leona reached for a tomato and cubed it into several small pieces. "If he was thinking about marriage at all, then it's good that he realized before it was too late that she wasn't the right girl for him."

Fannie sighed deeply. "I worry about Timothy, because I don't think he and Hannah are compatible. They've struggled in their marriage almost from the beginning."

"A lot of that has to do with Hannah's mamm, don't you think?"

"I'm afraid so. Sally King is a very possessive woman, and she's clung to Hannah ever since she was born. Hannah's always turned to her mamm when she should've been turning to her husband."

"Moving to Kentucky has put some distance between mother and daughter, so maybe things will improve for Hannah and Timothy with Sally out of the picture."

"I certainly hope so." Fannie stopped talking long enough to shred some purple cabbage. "I saw Sally at the health food store the other day, and she was really depressed because Johnny said they couldn't go to Kentucky for Thanksgiving."

"Did he give a reason?"

"Said he thought it was too soon — that they needed to give Hannah and Timothy some time to adjust to their new surroundings before making a trip there."

"Did Sally accept his decision?" Leona asked.

"I guess so. She said they'd be having Thanksgiving at one of their son's homes, but I could see that she was pining for Hannah."

Leona reached for a stalk of celery. "I hope I never interfere in my girls' lives once they get married. I wouldn't want my future son-in-law to move away because he felt that I was coming between him and his wife."

Fannie shook her head. "I doubt that would ever happen, Leona. You and Zach are raising your kinner well, and you're not clingy with them the way Sally is to Hannah."

Leona smiled. "Danki. I appreciate hearing that."

The sounds of horses' hooves and buggy wheels crunching on the gravel interrupted their conversation.

"Looks like more of the family has arrived," Leona said, looking out the window. "I see Naomi and Caleb's buggy pulling in, and behind them is Nancy and Mark's rig."

Fannie smiled. It would be good to spend the holiday with some of their family. The only thing that would make it any better would be if Samuel, Titus, Timothy, and their families could join them.

Maybe next year we can all be together, she thought. *And when Esther and Samuel get married, I'm sure most of us will go for the wedding, so that's something to look forward to.*

Pembroke, Kentucky

"If everything tastes as good as it smells, I think we're in for a real treat," Timothy said as he and the rest of the family gathered around the two tables that had been set up in Suzanne and Titus's living room. Even though their double-wide manufactured home was short on space, Suzanne had wanted to host the meal, and it was kind of cozy being together in such a crowded room. Fortunately, it was a crisp but sunny fall day, and the kids could go outside to play after the meal. That would leave enough room for the adults to sit around visiting or playing board games.

"You're right about everything smelling good," Titus said. "I think the women who prepared all this food should be thanked in advance."

All the men bobbed their heads in agreement.

"And now, let us thank the Lord for this food so we can eat," Suzanne's grandfather said.

The room became quiet as everyone bowed their heads for silent prayer. Timothy recited the Lord's Prayer; then he thanked God for the meal they were about to eat and for all his family in Kentucky, as well as in Pennsylvania.

When the prayers were finished and all of the food had been passed, everyone dug in.

"Yum. This turkey is so moist and flavorful," Suzanne's mother, Verna, said. She smiled at Esther. "You did a good job teaching my daughter to cook, and we all thank you for it."

Suzanne's cheeks colored, and Titus chuckled as he nudged her arm. "That's right, and my fraa feeds me so well I have to work twice as hard in the woodshop to keep from getting fat."

Everyone laughed — everyone but Hannah. She sat staring at the food on her plate with a placid look on her face. Timothy was tempted to say something to her but decided it would be best not to draw attention to his wife's sullen mood. No doubt she was upset that her folks didn't come for Thanksgiving, but she should have put on a happy face today, if only for the sake of appearances. It embarrassed Timothy to have Hannah pouting so much of the time. Just when he thought she might begin to adjust, something would happen, and she'd be fretful again. He worried that some people might think he wasn't a good husband because he couldn't make his wife happy. Well, it wasn't because he hadn't tried, but nothing he did ever seemed to be good enough for Hannah. He worried that it never would. What if he'd made a mistake forcing her to move? What if she never adjusted to living in Kentucky and remained angry and out of sorts? Was moving back to Pennsylvania the only way to make his wife happy?

But if we did that, we'd be right back where we were before we left. Hannah would be over at her mamm's all the time, and I'd be fending for myself. If we could just find a place of our own, maybe that would make a difference. Hannah might be happier if we weren't living at Samuel's, and if we weren't taking up space in Samuel's house, he and Esther could get married and start a life of their own.

"Hey, brother, did ya hear what I said?"

Timothy jumped at the sound of Titus's voice. "Huh? What was that?"

"I asked you to pass me the gravy."

"Oh, sure." Timothy took a little gravy for himself and then handed it over to Titus.

"I thought about inviting Bonnie to join us for dinner," Suzanne spoke up, "but Esther said Bonnie had invited Allen to eat at her place today."

"Allen could have joined us here, too,"

Titus said. "He knows he's always welcome in our home."

Samuel cleared his throat. "Well, I probably shouldn't be broadcasting this, but I happen to know that Allen had plans to propose to Bonnie today."

"Oh, that's wunderbaar," Esther said. "I can hardly wait until I see Bonnie tomorrow morning and find out what she said."

"She'll say yes, of course." Titus grinned. "I mean, why wouldn't she want to marry a nice guy like Allen?"

"Speaking of Allen," Samuel said, looking at Timothy, "did he say anything to you about the house that's for sale over in Trigg County, near Cadiz?"

Timothy shook his head. "What house is that?"

"It's a small one, but I think it could be added on to. Allen went over to look at it the other day because the owners were thinking of remodeling the kitchen before they put it up for sale, and they wanted him to give them a bid."

Timothy looked at Hannah. "What do you think? Should we talk to Allen about this and see if he can arrange for us to look at the place?"

Hannah shrugged, although he did notice a glimmer of interest in her eyes. Maybe this was God's answer to his prayers. While he wasn't particularly fond of the idea of living thirty-seven miles from his brothers, he was anxious for them to find a place they could call home.

"All right, then," Timothy said. "Tomorrow morning I'll talk to Allen about showing us the house."

Hannah said nothing, but she did pick up her fork and eat a piece of meat, and that made Timothy feel much better about the day.

CHAPTER 14

Esther woke up early on Friday morning and hurried to get dressed so she could get up to the main house and speak to Bonnie. She found her friend sitting at the kitchen table with a cup of tea.

"I wasn't sure if I'd see you this morning," Bonnie said, looking up at Esther. "Since I don't have any guests checking into the B&B until tomorrow, I figured I wouldn't see you until this evening."

"I wanted to find out how your Thanksgiving dinner with Allen went."

Bonnie smiled. "It was nice. At least I didn't burn anything."

"I didn't think you would. You've gotten pretty efficient in the kitchen."

"Yes, but I'll probably never be as good a cook as you." Bonnie's face sobered. "The pumpkin pie I made got ruined."

"Oh no! What happened?"

"Cody was outside barking, and when

Allen opened the door to see what the dog was yapping about, Cody came running in." Bonnie chuckled. "After that, it was like watching a comedy act. I tripped, the pie went flying, and the can of whipped cream rolled across the room and landed at Allen's feet. Afterward, we just stood there, laughing like fools. Fortunately, I'd also made an apple pie, or we wouldn't have had any dessert at all."

"Oh my. I can almost picture it." Esther laughed. "That sounds terrible and funny at the same time."

Bonnie nodded. "But the day ended on a good note, because Allen asked me to marry him."

Esther clapped her hands. "Oh, that's such good news. I hope you said yes."

Bonnie shook her head. "I told him I needed to think about it for a few weeks."

"What's there to think about? You love Allen, and he loves you. I think you'll be very happy together."

"I still haven't told him about my past, and I'm not sure I can do it."

"Of course you can. Allen's a good man; he'll understand."

"Maybe, but I'm afraid to take the chance."

"What are you going to do?"

"I'm not sure. I told Allen I'd have an answer for him by Christmas Eve, so if I'm going to tell him about the baby I adopted out when I was a teenager, I'll need to do it before I agree to marry him." She groaned. "It wouldn't be right to wait until after we're married and then spring the truth on him."

"No, and it wouldn't be right to keep the truth from him indefinitely either."

"Guess I need to pray a little more about this and ask the Lord to give me the courage to tell Allen the truth," Bonnie said, while warming her hands on the teacup.

Esther smiled. "I'll be praying for you, too."

"Thanks, I appreciate that." Bonnie motioned to the teapot. "I don't know where my manners are. Would you like to have a cup of tea?"

"That sounds nice. Since we don't have to do any baking this morning, there's plenty of time for me to sit and visit awhile."

"How was your Thanksgiving?" Bonnie asked after Esther had poured herself a cup of tea and taken a seat.

"The food was delicious." Esther frowned. "But Hannah was in a sullen mood most of the day, and that made us all a bit uncomfortable."

"I'm not surprised," Bonnie said. "With this being the first holiday she's spent away from her family, she probably felt sad."

"I suppose so, but I dread going over to Samuel's today, because Hannah might still be in a bad mood. I realize that she misses her family in Pennsylvania, but I wonder if the family she has right here will ever be good enough for her."

"I'm sure she'll adjust eventually," Bonnie said. "Time heals all wounds, and it will help if we all try to make her feel welcome. Right now I think what Hannah needs most is friends."

Esther nodded. "That's what I think, too, and I've been trying, but I don't think Hannah likes me. Even though she seems to have accepted the idea of me coming over every day to watch Samuel's children and cook supper every other evening, I think she still resents me. It's like she's turned this into some sort of competition or something."

"Just give her a bit more time, Esther. Once Hannah gets to know you better, she'll come to love you and treasure your friendship as much as I do."

Esther forced a smile. "I hope you're right, because if we're going to be sisters-in-law, I wouldn't want any hard feelings between us."

■ ■ ■ ■

Hannah glanced at the battery-operated clock on the far kitchen wall and frowned. The men had left early this morning for a job in Elkton, which meant she'd had to get up early in order to fix breakfast and pack their lunches. In a few minutes, the children would be getting up, and then she'd have to fix their breakfast as well. Why was it that Esther always seemed to be late on the days she was needed the most?

Not that I really want her to be here, Hannah thought as she reached for her cup of coffee and took a sip. *It's just not fair that I should have to be responsible for two men and five children — four who aren't even my own.*

She tapped her fingers along the edge of the table. *If I wasn't here right now, and Esther was late, I wonder what Samuel would think about that. Was she ever late before we came to live here? Should he really be thinking of making her his wife?*

"For goodness' sake," she said aloud. "I don't even know what I think anymore. It wasn't long ago that I didn't want Esther here at all. Now I'm complaining that she's not here to help me."

Hannah got up from the table and moved over to the window, letting her thoughts focus on yesterday and the close friendship she'd noticed between Suzanne and Esther. It seemed like they had their heads together, laughing and talking, most of the day. Again, she found herself wishing for a friend — someone with whom she could share her deepest feelings and who wouldn't criticize her for the things she said or did — someone she could be close to the way she had been with Mom.

Oh, how she wished her folks could have joined them for Thanksgiving, but maybe they could come for Christmas. She hoped she, Timothy, and Mindy would be living in their own place by then. The house Allen had mentioned to Timothy might be the one. Hannah hoped they could look at it soon, because she really wanted to be moved out of Samuel's house before Christmas.

CHAPTER 15

"What time will Allen be here?" Hannah asked as she, Timothy, and Samuel sat at the kitchen table drinking coffee on Saturday morning.

"Said he'd be here by nine o'clock." Timothy glanced at the clock. "So we have about ten more minutes to wait."

Hannah rose from her chair. "I'd better get Mindy's coat on so we can be ready to go as soon as he arrives."

Timothy shook his head. "I don't think taking Mindy with us to look at the house is a good idea."

Hannah quirked an eyebrow. "Why not?"

"We need to concentrate on checking out the house that Allen's found, and having Mindy along would be a distraction. You know how active she can be sometimes."

Hannah pursed her lips. "We can't expect Samuel to watch her. He'll have enough on his hands watching his own kinner today."

"I don't mind," Samuel spoke up. "Penny and Marla will keep Mindy entertained, and she shouldn't be a problem at all. The kids are all playing upstairs right now, so they'll probably keep right on playing till they're called down for lunch."

Hannah tapped her foot as she contemplated what Samuel had said. He was pretty good with his children, so maybe Mindy would be okay left in his care. "Well, if you're sure you don't mind . . ."

Samuel shook his head. "Don't mind a bit."

"Okay, we'll leave Mindy here." Hannah glanced at the clock again. It was almost nine, and still no Allen. She really wished he'd show up so they could be on their way. And oh how she hoped the house he'd be taking them to see was the right one for them.

"Take a seat and have some more coffee," Timothy said, motioning to her empty chair. "Allen's probably running a little late this morning. I'm sure he'll be here soon."

With a sigh, Hannah reluctantly sat down. She'd only taken a few sips of coffee when she heard Allen's truck pull in. "Oh good, he's here," she said, jumping up and peeking out the kitchen window. "I'll get my shawl."

"Guess I'd better wear a jacket," Timothy said, rising from his seat. "When I went out before breakfast to help Samuel and Leon with the chores, I realized just how cold it is out there."

"Jah," Samuel said with a nod. "Wouldn't surprise me if we got some snow pretty soon."

Hannah wrinkled her nose. "I hope not. I'm not ready for snow."

"Well, the kinner might not agree with you on that." Samuel chuckled. "I think they'd be happy if we had snow on the ground all year long."

Hannah wrapped her shawl around her shoulders, set her black outer bonnet on her head, and hurried outside without saying another word. She had thought about going upstairs to tell Mindy good-bye but decided it would be best if she snuck out the back door. If she'd gone upstairs and Mindy started crying, she would have felt compelled to take her with them, which, of course, might have caused dissension between her and Timothy.

"Are you sure you don't mind driving us all the way to Cadiz?" Timothy asked Allen after they'd gotten into his truck.

Allen shook his head. "I don't mind a bit, and it's really not that far. Maybe when

139

we're done looking at the house we can stop in Hopkinsville for some lunch."

"That sounds nice," Hannah was quick to say, "but Samuel might need some help fixing lunch for the kinner, and since today is Esther's day off, he'd probably appreciate me being there to help." Truth was, Hannah doubted Samuel's ability to fix a nutritious lunch for the children. He'd probably give them whatever they asked for instead of what they needed.

"Eating lunch at a restaurant sounds good to me," Timothy spoke up, looking straight at Hannah. "And I'm sure Samuel can manage to fix something for the kinner just fine."

Hannah was tempted to argue the point but didn't want to make a scene in front of Allen. "Okay, whatever," she said with a nod. She supposed it wouldn't hurt Mindy to have an unhealthy lunch once in a while. Forcing herself to relax, Hannah focused on the passing scenery as they headed for Trigg County.

Sometime later, Allen turned off the main road and onto a dirt road — more of a path, really. "The house is just up ahead," he said, pointing in that direction.

A few minutes later, a small house came into view. *It's too small for our needs,* Hannah thought at first glance, *but I suppose it could be added on to. Well, I'll give it the benefit of the doubt — at least until we've seen the inside of the place.*

As Tom Donnelson, the real estate agent, showed them through each room of the house, all Timothy could think was, *This place is way too small.* The kitchen, while it had been recently remodeled, didn't have a lot of cupboard space. He didn't see any sign of a pantry, either, which would have helped, since the cabinet area was so sparse. The living room and dining room were both small, too, and there were only three bedrooms. If he and Hannah had more children, which he hoped they would someday, a three-bedroom house wouldn't be large enough — especially if any overnight guests came to visit. They would definitely have to add more bedrooms to the house, as well as enlarge the living room and kitchen. And of course, since this was an Englisher's home, they would have to take out all the electrical connections.

The other thing that bothered Timothy was the distance between Trigg and Christian Counties. If they moved here, they'd have to hire a driver every time they wanted to see Samuel, Titus, and their families. And how would that work with him working with

Samuel? It would be inconvenient and costly to hire a driver every day for such a distance, not to mention the miles his brothers would have to travel if they helped him with renovations on the small house. It would be expensive for Titus and Samuel to get someone to bring them here whenever they came to visit, too, and he wouldn't feel right about putting that burden on his brothers.

Timothy glanced at Hannah, hoping to gauge her reaction to the place. She'd commented on how nice it was to see new cupboards in the kitchen and bathroom and even said how convenient it would be to have everything on one floor. If she liked it here, it would be hard to say no to buying it, because keeping Hannah happy in Kentucky would mean she'd be less likely to hound him about moving back to Pennsylvania. *Is this a sacrifice I'd be willing to make?* he asked himself.

"The owners are motivated to sell," Tom said. "So I'm sure they'd be willing to consider any reasonable offer."

Timothy looked at Hannah, but she said nothing. It wasn't like her not to give her opinion — especially on something as important as buying a house.

Timothy cleared his throat, searching for

the right words. "I . . . uh . . . think my wife and I need to talk about this, but we appreciate you taking the time to show us the place."

Tom rubbed the top of his bald head. "Sure, no problem. Just don't take too much time making a decision, because as nice as this place is, I don't think it'll be on the market very long."

"We'll get back to you as soon as we can." Timothy ushered Hannah out the door and into Allen's truck, where he'd been waiting for them.

"That didn't take too long," Allen said. "So, what'd you think of the house?"

Timothy glanced at Hannah, but she didn't say a word — just sat with her hands folded in her lap, looking straight ahead.

"Well, uh . . . It's a nice little house, but I'm not sure it's the right one for us," Timothy said. "I can see we'd be sinking a lot of money into the place just to enlarge it for our needs."

Hannah released a lingering sigh. "Oh, Timothy, I totally agree."

"You do?"

She nodded vigorously. "The place is way too small, and it's so isolated out here. I wouldn't think you'd want to be this far from your brothers either."

A sense of relief flooded over Timothy. She was as disappointed in the place as he was. Even so, she was probably unhappy that they would have to continue living with Samuel for who knew how much longer.

"It's okay," he said, whispering in Hannah's ear. "I'm sure some other place will come up for sale, and hopefully it'll be closer to home."

"Home?" She tipped her head and looked at him curiously.

"What I meant to say was, closer to Samuel and Titus's homes."

"It'll need to be a much larger house and not so isolated." Her lips compressed, and tiny wrinkles formed across her forehead. "I think I'd go crazy if we moved way out here."

"Not to worry," he said, resting his hand on her arm. "We'll wait till we find just the right place. Anyway, we can consider this as a practice run in knowing what we need to look for. Live and learn, right?"

Hannah gave a quick nod; then she leaned her head against the seat and closed her eyes. Was she still hoping he'd give up on the idea of living in Kentucky and move back to Pennsylvania? Well, if she was, she could forget that notion.

CHAPTER 16

Hannah glanced out the kitchen window and grimaced. It had started snowing last night and hadn't let up at all. Christmas was just two weeks away, and if the weather turned bad, it could affect her folks' plan to come for the holiday. Timothy's parents were planning to come, too. In fact, their folks planned to hire a driver and travel together. Andy Paulsen, the driver they'd asked, was single, owned a nice-sized van, and had some friends who lived in Hopkinsville, so it was the perfect arrangement.

Hannah wondered if Timothy was as anxious to see his folks as she was hers. It was different for Timothy; he had family here. She didn't. He never talked about home the way she did either, so maybe he was happy just being here, where he could see his twin brother and Samuel whenever he wanted. Despite a bit of competition between Timothy and Titus, they'd always been very close. Hannah remembered one evening when she and Timothy were courting that Titus, who liked to play pranks, had taken her home from a singing, pretending to be Timothy. Since it was dark and she couldn't see his face well, he'd managed to fool her until they got to her house and one of the barn cats had rubbed against his leg when he was helping Hannah out of the buggy. He'd hollered at the cat and called it a stupid *katz*, something Timothy would never have done. Hannah knew right away that she'd ridden home with the wrong brother.

She chuckled as she thought about how she'd decided to play along with the joke awhile and had picked up the cat and thrust it into Titus's arms. When the cat stuck its claws into Titus's chest, the joke ended.

"What's so funny?"

Hannah whirled around. "Ach, Esther, you shouldn't sneak up on me like that."

"I didn't mean to frighten you," Esther said apologetically. "I just came into the kitchen to check on the soup I've got cooking and saw you standing in front of the window laughing. I thought something amusing must be going on outside."

Hannah shook her head. "The only thing

146

going on out there is a lot of snow coming down."

Esther stepped up to the window. "It doesn't seem to be letting up, does it?"

"Do you get much snow in this part of Kentucky?" Hannah asked.

"Some years we do. Other times we hardly get any at all." Esther motioned to the window. "If this is an indication of what's to come, we might be in for a bad winter this year."

Hannah frowned. "I hope not. The weather needs to be nice so Timothy's folks and mine can get here for Christmas."

Esther smiled. "From what Samuel's told me, his folks are really excited about coming, so it would probably have to be something bad like a blizzard to keep them at home. Maybe the snow will stick around, if it stays cold enough, and give us a white Christmas."

"My parents are looking forward to coming here, too, and I guess if this is the only snow we get until they arrive, it would be nice to have it around for Christmas."

"Can we go outside and play in the *schnee*?" Penny asked as she, Jared, and Mindy raced into the kitchen.

"That sounds like fun," Esther said. "And when you're done playing in the snow, you can come inside for a warm bowl of chicken noodle soup."

Jared and Penny squealed, jumping eagerly up and down.

"Schnee! Schnee!" Mindy hollered, joining her cousins in their eagerness to play in the snow.

Hannah put her finger to her lips. "Calm down." She looked at Esther. "I'm sure it's frigid out there, and I don't think any of them should go outside to play."

"They'll come in if they get too cold," Esther said.

Hannah shook her head. "I don't want my daughter getting cold and wet."

"I understand that, but I don't think a few minutes in the snow will hurt her any. I'm sure when you were little you loved the snow. Didn't you?"

"Jah, but I was never allowed to play in it very long because my mamm always worried about me getting chilled."

"Please . . . please . . . can Mindy go outside with us to play?" Penny pleaded.

All three children continued to jump up and down, hollering so loudly that Hannah had to cover her ears. "Oh, all right," she finally agreed. "But I'm going outside with you, because I want to make sure Mindy doesn't wander off or slip in the wet snow and get hurt."

"I think I'll turn down the stove and join you," Esther said. "It's been awhile since I frolicked in the snow."

After all the fuss, Esther was surprised to actually see Hannah laughing and romping around in the snow like a schoolgirl. She even showed the children how she liked to open her mouth and catch snowflakes on the end of her tongue.

"This is *schpass!*" Penny shouted as she raced past Esther, slipping and sliding in the snow.

"Jah, it's a lot of fun!" Esther tweaked the end of Penny's cold nose. "Should we see if there's enough snow on the ground to make a snowman?"

All three children nodded enthusiastically, and even Hannah said it sounded like fun.

Hannah helped Mindy form a snowball, and they began rolling it across the lawn while Esther helped Jared roll another snowball. Since Penny was a bit older, she was able to get a snowball started on her own.

As the children worked, they giggled, caught more snowflakes on their tongues, and huffed and puffed as their snowballs grew bigger. Esther was pleased to see Hannah actually enjoying herself. It was the first time she'd seen this side of Hannah. Maybe she was warming up to the idea of living here. There might even be a possibility that the two of them could become friends. It wasn't that Esther needed more friends; she had Suzanne and Bonnie. But Hannah needed a friend, and if she could act happy and carefree like she was doing now, she'd probably make a lot of friends in this community. Unfortunately, though, since Hannah had arrived in Kentucky, her actions had made her appear standoffish.

After they finished building the snowman, Esther suggested they look for some small rocks to use for the snowman's eyes and buttons for his chest.

The children squatted down in an area where some dirt was showing and started looking for rocks, and Esther joined them.

"Maybe I should run inside and check on the soup," Hannah said. "Just to be sure it's not boiling over."

"I turned the stove down, so I'm sure it's fine." Esther reached for a small stone she thought would be perfect for one of the snowman's eyes. "And Hannah, I just thought of something."

"What's that?"

"I was wondering what your thoughts are

on the two desserts I'm hoping to make for Christmas."

"What did you have in mind?" Hannah asked.

"One of the things I wanted to make is pumpkin cookies, because I know Samuel and the kinner like them. I also found a recipe for Kentucky chocolate chip pie, and I was thinking of trying that, too. I've never made it before, but it sounds really good."

"I could make the pie if you like," Hannah said. "I'm always looking for new recipes to try."

"That'd be great." Esther was glad Hannah had made the offer. It was what she'd been hoping for. Maybe baking together would bridge the gap that still seemed to be between them.

Hannah smiled. "Timothy loves anything with chocolate chips in it, so I know at least one person who'll be eager to try out the pie. That is, if it turns out okay."

"You're a good cook, so I'm sure it'll turn out fine." Esther felt hopeful. She was glad today had been going so well.

"I can only hope so. Now, I think somebody ought to check on that soup," Hannah said. "So, if you'll keep a close eye on Mindy, I'll go do that."

"Sure, no problem." Esther glanced up at

Hannah to make sure she'd heard her, and when Hannah turned and headed into the house, she continued to look for more rocks.

Esther was only vaguely aware that Jared and Mindy had begun chasing each other around the yard, until she heard a bloodcurdling scream.

Dropping the rock she'd just found, she hurried across the yard, where Mindy stood holding her nose. Blood oozed between Mindy's gloved fingers and trickled down the sleeve of her jacket. The children had obviously collided. So much for fun in the snow!

Just then, Hannah rushed out of the house. Seeing Mindy's bloody nose, she glared at Esther. "What happened?"

"The children were running, and I think Jared and Mindy collided with each other," Esther said.

Hannah knelt down to take a look at her daughter's nose. "I thought you promised to keep an eye on Mindy for me," she said, taking a tissue from her jacket pocket and holding it against Mindy's nose. "If you'd been watching her, Esther, this wouldn't have happened!"

"I'm sorry," Esther said above Mindy's sobbing.

Hannah grabbed Mindy's hand and ushered her into the house.

That's just great, Esther thought. *Things were going so well between Hannah and me. Now this is one more thing for Hannah to complain to Samuel about when he gets home from work tonight. If Hannah and Timothy don't move into a place of their own soon, Hannah will probably have Samuel convinced that I'm not fit to be his wife or the kinner's stepmother.*

CHAPTER 17

Branson, Missouri

"Is this your first time here?" an elderly woman with silver-gray hair asked Trisha as she took her seat in one of the most elaborate theaters in Branson. She'd gone to the women's restroom before entering the theater and was surprised to see that even it was ornately decorated.

Trisha nodded, feeling rather self-conscious. "Does it show?"

The woman chuckled. "Just a little. I couldn't help but notice the look of awe on your face as you surveyed your surroundings. It is quite beautiful, isn't it?"

"It is a magnificent theater," Trisha said. "I've never seen anything quite like this before."

"You know the old saying, 'You ain't seen nothin' yet'? Well, you just wait until you see this show. The star attraction is a violinist, and his Christmas show is absolutely incredible. I've seen him perform before, and I guarantee you won't be disappointed."

Trisha smiled in anticipation. "I'm looking forward to it."

"So, are you here alone?"

Trisha nodded. "I'm from California, and I'm making a trip across the country to take in some sights I've always wanted to see. After I spend a few days here, I'll be heading to Nashville. From there, I'm going to Bowling Green, Kentucky, to see an old friend."

Just then the show started, ending their conversation. As the curtain went up, Trisha turned her attention to the stage, listening with rapt attention to the beautiful violin music that began the show. So far this trip was turning out well, and she looked forward to spending Christmas with her friend Carla.

Hopkinsville, Kentucky

"I'm so glad the weather's improved and there's no snow on the ground," Hannah said as she and Suzanne pushed their carts into Walmart's produce section. Since it was Saturday, and Samuel and Timothy had volunteered to watch the children, Hannah and Suzanne had hired a driver to take them to town so they could do some grocery shopping and buy a few Christmas gifts.

"It would be nice to have a white Christmas," Suzanne said wistfully, "like the ones I remember from my childhood."

"Esther said the same thing about having a white Christmas. Maybe so, but snowy weather makes it harder to travel, and I don't want anything to stand in the way of my folks coming for Christmas."

"I'm sure their driver will have either snow tires or chains for his van, so driving in the snow shouldn't be a problem. Unless, of course, it became a blizzard."

Hannah nodded. "That's what worries me. I'd be so disappointed if my folks couldn't come, and I'm sure Timothy and his brothers would feel bad if their folks couldn't make it either."

Suzanne patted Hannah's arm. "Not to worry. I'm sure everything will be fine and we'll all have a really nice Christmas, with or without the snow."

Pembroke, Kentucky

"I've got some good news and some bad news," Timothy said when he returned to the house after checking the messages in Samuel's phone shanty.

"Let's have the good news first," Samuel

said, placing his coffee cup on the kitchen table.

"Mom and Dad's message said they're still planning to come for Christmas and they can stay until New Year's."

Samuel grinned. "That is good news. It'll be great to see our folks again, and we'll have plenty of time to visit and catch up on things." He picked up his cup and took a drink. "So, what's the bad news?"

"Hannah's mother left a message saying she and Johnny won't be coming after all." Timothy groaned. "I sure dread telling Hannah about it, because I know she's gonna be very upset. She's been looking forward to her parents' visit for weeks now."

"Why can't Sally and Johnny come?" Samuel asked.

"Johnny injured his back picking up a heavy box at the store. He's flat in bed, taking pain pills and muscle relaxers. Sally has to wait on him hand and foot because he can't do much of anything right now and was advised by his doctor to stay in bed for the time being."

"That's too bad. I remember last year when Allen hurt his back after falling down some stairs. He was cranky as a bear with sore paws and none too happy about his mom coming to take care of him."

"Doesn't he get along well with her?" Timothy asked, taking a seat beside Samuel.

"They get along okay, but from what I could tell, his mom tried to baby him, and Allen didn't go for that at all."

"I guess most men don't like to be babied. We want to know that our women love us, but we don't want 'em treatin' us like we're little boys."

"That's for sure." Samuel reached for one of the cinnamon rolls Esther had baked the day before and took a bite. "So how are you gonna break the news to Hannah?"

"Guess I'll just have to tell her the facts, but I'm sure not looking forward to it." Timothy grimaced. "Hannah's been in a better mood here of late, but I'm afraid that'll change once she hears about her folks."

Later that night after Hannah had put Mindy to bed, she and Timothy retired to their room, and she told him what a good time she'd had shopping. "Suzanne and I found all of the Christmas gifts we had on our lists." Hannah smiled, realizing how good it felt to tell Timothy the events of her day. The outing with Suzanne had been just what she needed to vanish some of the tension she'd felt since arriving in Kentucky.

"Oh Timothy, I'm so excited about my

folks coming for Christmas. It will be wunderbaar to have all of our parents here for the holidays. I think I actually feel some of that special holiday spirit." Hannah plumped up their pillows, feeling a sense of lightheartedness she hadn't experienced in some time. But then she noticed a strange look on her husband's face.

"Hannah, I'm really glad you had such a nice day with Suzanne," Timothy said, "but there's something I need to tell you."

"What is it?"

"I wanted us to be alone when I told you this, and there's no easy way to soften the blow, so I may as well just come right out and say it. Your parents won't be able to make it for Christmas."

She hoped she'd heard him wrong. "What do you mean? Why aren't they coming?"

"Your daed hurt his back and won't be able to travel for a while."

"Oh no." She groaned, plopping down on the bed. "I just can't believe it."

"I'm sorry," Timothy said. "I know how disappointed you must be."

Hannah sniffed, trying to hold back the tears that threatened to spill over. "Jah." Her hands shook as she stood and pulled the covers back on the bed. Changing into her nightgown and climbing under the covers, she could almost feel Timothy watching her. Yet he remained quiet as he slid into bed next to her. After a few minutes, she heard his steady, even breathing and figured he must have fallen asleep.

Hannah knew it had probably been hard for Timothy to break the news about her folks not coming, and she was grateful he'd waited until they were alone to do it. But couldn't he have at least given her a hug instead of turning his back on her and falling asleep? Staring at the ceiling and feeling worse by the minute, Hannah realized there was nothing she could do but accept the fact that her folks weren't coming, but that didn't make it any easier.

Poor Dad, she thought as tears slipped from her eyes. *He must be in terrible pain, and both he and Mom are probably just as disappointed as I am that they can't come here for Christmas.*

Hannah rolled over and punched her pillow. *I'll accept it, but I don't have to like it! If I wasn't so far from home, I'd be able to help Mom and Dad right now. If . . . If . . . If . . .* She buried her face in the pillow, trying to muffle her sobs. *Why do things like this always happen to me?*

CHAPTER 18

"Just look at all that snow coming down. I think it's safe to say that we're gonna have a white Christmas," Timothy said as he and Samuel headed out to the barn to do their morning chores on Christmas Eve. "Sure hope Mom and Dad make it before this weather gets any worse."

"I hope so, too." Samuel's boots crunched through the snow. "This could mean we're in for a bad winter."

"If the snow and wind keep up like this, it could also mean Mom and Dad might have to stay longer than they planned." Timothy glanced toward the road. "I wonder if the snowplows will come out our way today."

"It's hard to say. Guess it all depends on how busy they are in other places."

When Samuel opened the barn door, the pungent aroma of horse manure hit Timothy full in the face. "Phew! There's no denying that the horses' stalls need a good cleaning."

"You're right about that. Guess we should have done them last night, but since we got home so late from that paint job in Hopkinsville, I was too tired to tackle it."

"Same here."

As they stepped into the first stall, Samuel asked, "Do you think Hannah and Esther are getting along any better these days?"

Timothy shrugged. "I don't know. Why do you ask?"

"I was thinking if they were, maybe Esther and I could get married sometime after the first of the year, even if you and Hannah haven't found a house by then."

"I have no objections to that, but I think it's something you and Esther will need to decide." Timothy reached for a shovel. "I know I've said this before, but I really do appreciate you letting us stay with you and giving me a job. You've helped to make things a lot easier for us, which has given me a few less things to worry about."

Samuel thumped Timothy's back. "That's what families are for. I'm sure if the tables were turned, you'd do the same for me."

Timothy gave a nod, although he wasn't sure his wife would be so agreeable about Samuel and his kids staying with them. Hannah was more desperate to find a place of their own than he was, and he figured it was because she wanted to have the run of the house and didn't want to answer to Esther. Of course, if they'd been living with Hannah's folks all this time, Hannah wouldn't have a problem with her mother telling her what to do. And if Sally and Johnny needed a place to live, Hannah would welcome them with open arms.

Ever since he'd given her the news that her folks wouldn't be coming for Christmas, she'd gone around looking depressed and had even refused to do any baking with Esther, saying she wasn't in the mood. Timothy was fairly certain that Hannah didn't know that he'd lain awake for at least an hour after she'd cried herself to sleep that night, not knowing what to say that would make her feel better. He felt even worse because, before he'd given her the news about her folks, she'd seemed upbeat about her day with Suzanne. Had it not been for the bad news, Hannah's day of Christmas shopping might have been a turning point in helping her to be more comfortable with living in Kentucky. Instead, her Christmas spirit had disappeared.

Sure hope Hannah's able to put on a happy face while my folks are here, Timothy thought, gripping the shovel a little tighter. *I don't need to hear any disapproving comments about my wife from Mom. And Hannah's negative attitude won't help Mom any, since she is already none too thrilled about any of her sons living here.*

The whole idea of moving had been to improve their marriage, and if Timothy's mother didn't see any sign of that, he'd probably have more explaining to do. Instead of getting easier, things seemed to be getting harder.

Timothy directed his thoughts back to the job at hand, and after he and Samuel finished cleaning the stalls, they left the barn.

"We must have gotten at least another two inches of snow since we started shoveling the manure," Samuel mentioned as they tromped back to the house.

"I'll say!" Timothy jumped back when a snowball hit him square on the forehead. "Hey! Who did that?" he asked, looking around as he wiped the snow off his head.

"There's your culprit!" Samuel pointed to Leon, sprinting for the back porch. "Come on. Let's get him!"

Leon squealed as Timothy and Samuel pelted him with snowballs.

"That ain't fair! It's two against one!" Leon jumped off the porch, scooped some snow into a ball, and slung it hard. This one landed on Samuel's back.

In response, Samuel turned and pitched a snowball at Timothy. Pretty soon snowballs were flying every which way, and no one seemed to care who they were throwing them at.

"This has been a lot of fun," Samuel finally said, "but we'd better go into the house and get warmed up."

Timothy, gasping for breath, nodded, but he was grinning as he headed for the house. He felt like a kid again and was sure from the look on his brother's face that Samuel did, too. It had been good to set his worries aside for a few minutes and do something fun. He'd forgotten that playing in the snow could be such a good stress reliever. He'd also forgotten the enjoyment he and Hannah had in the earlier years of their marriage when the first big snowstorm hit Lancaster County. It had only been a few years, yet it seemed so long ago.

Peeking into the oven at the pumpkin cookies, Esther was pleased to see that they were almost done. She planned to serve them this evening, along with hot apple cider. Since Hannah hadn't made the Kentucky chocolate chip pie like she'd planned, Esther had also baked an apple and a pumpkin pie to serve for dessert on Christmas Day.

Esther looked forward to spending Christmas Eve with Samuel and his family, and was glad she could be here at Samuel's all day to help with the cooking and cleaning. She felt sorry for Hannah, though, knowing how disappointed she was over her folks not being able to come. Yet despite Hannah's sullen mood, she was upstairs right now, putting clean sheets on the bed in the guest room. Fannie and Abraham would stay here for a few nights, and since they didn't plan to return home until New Year's Day, they would spend a few nights with Titus and Suzanne. Esther knew Titus, Timothy, and Samuel were looking forward to seeing their folks. She'd hoped her own folks might be able to come for Christmas, but they'd decided it was best to stay in Pennsylvania to be with Sarah and Dan. Esther hoped they'd be able to come for her wedding — whenever that would take place. At the rate things were going, she was beginning to wonder if she'd ever become Samuel's wife.

Esther had been relieved that Hannah hadn't said anything to Samuel about Jared causing Mindy's nose to bleed the other day. If Hannah had mentioned it, then Samuel hadn't brought it up to Esther, which probably meant he either didn't know or didn't blame her. She hoped that was the case, because she didn't want anything to come between her and Samuel.

Esther had just taken the last batch of pumpkin cookies from the oven when Samuel, Timothy, and Leon entered the kitchen laughing and kidding each other.

"Brr . . . It's mighty cold out there," Samuel said, rubbing his hands briskly together.

"And it's snowing even harder now." Timothy rubbed a wet spot on the bridge of his nose. "Sure hope our folks make it here soon, 'cause I can't help but be concerned about them."

"Worrying won't change a thing," Samuel said.

"Your brother's right," Esther agreed. "Whenever I find myself worrying, I just get busy doing something, and that seems to help. It makes the time go by faster, too."

"Guess you're right. While we were out in the snow chasing each other with snowballs, I didn't even think about my worries. But now that I'm back inside, I have a nagging feeling that the weather is going to cause some problems on the roads."

"Well, I don't think it'll bother Mom and Dad," Samuel said with an air of confidence. "They've hired an experienced driver with a reliable van, and I'm trusting God to keep them all safe."

"I need to trust Him, too." Timothy moved across the room toward Esther. "Any chance I might have one of those Kichlin?"

"The cookies are really for this evening, but since I baked plenty, it's fine if you have a few. I'm sure you guys must have worked up an appetite playing out there in the snow. You can let me know if they're any good."

"If they taste as good as they smell, you don't need to worry." Timothy grabbed two cookies. "So, where's my Fraa and *dochder?*"

"Hannah's upstairs making the bed in the guest room," Esther replied. "And Mindy's playing with Samuel's kinner up in Penny's room. I think I heard Leon running up the stairs to join them. No doubt he wants to tell them about that snowball fight you all had."

"Think I'll go up and see how Hannah's doing," Timothy said, holding up one of the cookies. "I know she's feeling pretty down today, so maybe I can cheer her up with one of these." He ate the other cookie he'd taken. "Mmm . . . This is really good, Esther. Think I may need to have a couple more when I come back downstairs."

Esther chuckled. "Just don't eat too many

or you'll spoil your appetite for supper."

He wiggled his eyebrows playfully. "After that snowball battle, not a chance."

When Timothy left the room, Esther turned to Samuel and said, "I doubt that one of my cookies will help Hannah. I think she'll be down in the dumps tonight and tomorrow as well."

"You're probably right." Samuel, his hair still wet from the snow, moved to stand beside Esther. "I've been thinking about something," he said, slipping his arm around her waist.

"What's that?" Esther asked as Samuel wiped a drip of water that had splashed from his hair onto her cheek.

"I was wondering how you'd feel about us getting married right after the first of the year."

Esther drew in a sharp breath. The thought of marrying Samuel so soon made her feel giddy. "Oh Samuel, I'd love to marry you as soon as possible, but Timothy and Hannah haven't found a home of their own yet."

"I realize that, but I was hoping we could get married anyway."

"You mean two families living under the same roof?"

He nodded.

"I don't think it would work, Samuel. Hannah and I do things so differently — especially concerning the kinner. It's been hard enough for us to get along with me here just a few hours each day. If I was here all the time, I'm afraid Hannah would resent me even more than she does already. Sometimes things are fine, and other times I can feel the tension between us. It's uncomfortable being constantly on edge."

Samuel nuzzled her cheek with his nose, where the drip of snow had just been. "So would you prefer to wait to get married till after Timothy and Hannah find a place of their own?"

Esther's heart fluttered at his touch. "Jah. As difficult as it will be to wait even longer, I think that would be best."

Hannah had just finished putting the quilt back on the guest bed when Timothy entered the room. "What's that you have behind your back?" she asked, blowing a strand of hair out of her eyes.

Timothy held up the cookie. "Thought you'd like to try one of Esther's pumpkin kichlin. They're sure good." He smacked his lips and handed her the treat.

As much as Hannah disliked hearing her husband rave about Esther's cookies, her stomach growled at the prospect of eating one. The whole house smelled like pumpkin, and she had to admit when she bit into the cookie that it was really good.

"You should have seen the snowball battle Samuel and I just had with Leon. Foolin' around in the snow like that made me feel like a kid again." Timothy grinned and kicked off his boots. "Remember when we first got married, how we enjoyed doing things like that?"

"I did see you three down there in the yard," she said, ignoring his comment. "I was watching out the window and thinking how nice it would be if you spent more time with Mindy and played games with her like you did with Leon." Hannah tromped across the room and picked up Timothy's boots. "You should have taken these off downstairs. I hope you didn't track water all the way up the stairs," she grumbled. "Now please take them over to our room and put them on the throw rug. I just got this room all nice and clean for your parents, and now you're dripping water all over the floor."

Hannah watched as Timothy picked up his boots and did as she asked, not saying a word as he walked across the hall to their room. She knew his good mood had evaporated once she'd started lecturing him. But it irritated her to see Timothy have fun with Samuel's son instead of their own daughter. And couldn't he see that the room for his parents was all nice and clean?

"I guess not," Hannah muttered. "Timothy and I just don't see things the same way anymore. Maybe we never did, but it seems like it's gotten worse since we moved to Kentucky."

Nashville, Tennessee

"It sure is good to see you," Bonnie said as she and her dad left the airport terminal and headed for her car.

He grinned and squeezed her hand. "It's good to see you, too, and I appreciate you coming all this way to pick me up."

"It's not that far, Dad. Besides, this is the closest airport to where I live. I just wish you could stay longer than a few days," she said, opening her trunk so he could put his suitcase inside.

"I do, too, but I need to be back at work by next Monday."

"I'd hoped you might have put in for a few more days' vacation than that."

"Maybe I can come and stay longer sometime this spring or summer." He climbed into the passenger's side and buckled his

172

seat belt.

As they drove toward Kentucky, they got caught up with one another's lives. "I'm really anxious to show you all the changes that have been made to your folks' old house," Bonnie said. "I think Grandma and Grandpa's place makes the perfect bed-and-breakfast."

He smiled. "I'm looking forward to seeing it, too."

As they neared Clarksville, it began to snow, so Bonnie turned on the windshield wipers and slowed down a bit. "It started snowing in Pembroke last night," she said. "And when I left to come to the airport, it was still snowing, but as I got closer to Nashville, it quit."

"I sure didn't expect to see snow on this trip," Dad said. "We haven't had any in Oregon yet."

Bonnie frowned as she stared out the front window. If the snow kept coming down like it was right now, by this evening it could be a lot worse. She hoped Samuel's folks would make it safely and said a mental prayer for everyone who might be driving in the snow throughout the day.

CHAPTER 19

Out of politeness, Hannah stood on the front porch, watching as Timothy and Samuel greeted their parents. From the joyous expressions on the brothers' faces, she knew they were happy to see their folks. Fannie and Abraham were equally delighted to be here.

Hannah couldn't deny them that pleasure, but it was hard to be joyful when she missed her own parents so much. Her chin quivered just thinking that at this very moment she could have been greeting her parents as well. She looked away, trying to regain her composure and knowing she'd have to put on a happy face. She'd make every attempt to do it, if for no other reason than for Mindy's sake, because she wanted her daughter to have a nice Christmas with at least one set of grandparents. But she'd only be going through the motions, because inside she was absolutely miserable.

When Fannie finished greeting her sons, she turned to Hannah and gave her a hug. "Wie geht's?" she asked.

"I'm doing okay. How about you?"

Fannie smiled. "I'm real good now that we're here safe and sound."

"That's right," Abraham said, nodding. "The roads on this side of Kentucky are terrible, and we saw several accidents. Fortunately, none of 'em appeared to be serious."

"Let's go inside where it's warmer." Samuel opened the door for his parents. Everyone followed, including Fannie and Abraham's driver, who said he could really use a cup of coffee before heading to his friend's house on the other side of Hopkinsville.

Esther greeted Fannie and Abraham as soon as they entered the kitchen; then she and Hannah served everyone steaming cups of coffee.

"I made plenty of cookies for our dessert tonight, so we may as well have some of them now." Esther smiled as she placed a plate of pumpkin cookies on the table.

"Those look *appenditlich*," Fannie said, reaching for one.

"You're gonna enjoy 'em." Timothy grinned at his mother. "I already sampled a few, and they are delicious."

"I can vouch for that," Samuel agreed. " 'Course, everything Esther bakes is really good." He smiled at Esther, and the look of adoration on his face put a lump in Hannah's throat. It had been such a long time since Timothy had looked at her that way or complimented her on her baking.

Maybe he doesn't love me anymore, she thought. *If he did, then why'd he force me to move here?* Hannah's mood couldn't get much lower. *Just listen to them. Everybody loves Esther's cookies.* It made her want to escape upstairs to her room. They'd probably be enjoying that Kentucky chocolate chip pie she'd volunteered to make if she hadn't changed her mind about it. But her heart just wasn't in it. Without her parents coming to celebrate Christmas with them, Hannah wasn't in the mood for much of anything. She might try making the pie some other time. Maybe after she and Timothy had a place of their own. If she baked something Timothy really liked, he might compliment her for a change.

Hannah's thoughts were quickly pushed aside when five young children darted into the room. With smiling faces, Fannie and Abraham set their coffee cups down and gathered the children into their arms.

"Ach, my!" said Fannie, eyes glistening.

"We've missed you all so much."

"We've missed you, too," Marla said, hugging her grandma around the neck. The other children nodded in agreement.

After all the hugs and kisses had been given out, the children found seats at the table, and Esther gave them each a glass of milk and two cookies.

"That's plenty for Mindy," Hannah said. "If she eats too many kichlin, it'll spoil her supper."

"We won't be eating the evening meal for a few hours yet," Timothy said. "So I don't think a couple more cookies will hurt her any."

Hannah, though irritated, said nothing, preferring not to argue with her husband in front of his parents.

"I'm sorry your folks weren't able to make it." Fannie offered Hannah a sympathetic smile. "We stopped by their place before we left town to pick up the gifts they asked us to bring, and your daed seemed to be in a lot of pain."

"That's what Mom said when I spoke with her on the phone this morning." Hannah blinked against the tears pricking the back of her eyes. Not only was she sad about her folks being unable to come, but she still felt bad that Dad had injured his back, and she wished she could be there to help Mom take care of him.

"I know your mamm was really looking forward to coming here," Fannie said, "but I'm sure they'll make the trip as soon as your daed is feeling better."

"It probably won't be until spring," Hannah said, her mood plummeting even lower. "I'm sure they won't travel when the roads are bad, and I wouldn't want them to."

"Speaking of the roads," their driver, Andy, spoke up, "I'd better head to my friend's house now, before this weather gets any worse."

Timothy and Samuel both jumped up from the table. "We'll get Mom and Dad's stuff out of your van so you can be on your way," Timothy said.

"I'll come with you." Abraham pushed his chair aside and stood.

After the men went outside, the children headed back upstairs to play. "I think I'll go out to the phone shanty and call Bonnie," Esther said. "Her dad is supposed to arrive today, so I want to see if he made it okay." She slipped on her jacket and hurried out the door.

Thinking this might be the only time she'd have to speak with Fannie alone, as soon as everyone else had left, Hannah moved over to sit next to her mother-in-law.

"I know how close you've always been to your twins," she said, carefully choosing her words, "and I'm sure having them both move to Kentucky has been really hard for you."

Fannie nodded slowly. "I never thought any of our kinner would leave Pennsylvania."

"I didn't think they would either — especially not Timothy. I thought he enjoyed painting for Zach and farming with his daed."

"I believe he did," Fannie said, "but Timothy wanted a new start, as did Samuel and Titus."

"I don't like it here," Hannah blurted out, wanting to get her point across. "I want to go back to Pennsylvania, and I was hoping you might talk Timothy into moving back home."

Fannie sat quietly, staring at her cup of coffee. With tears shimmering in her eyes, she said, "I can't do that, Hannah. I've already expressed the way I feel to Timothy, and if I say anything more, it would probably make him even more determined to stay in Kentucky. It could drive a wedge between us that might never be repaired."

Hannah lowered her gaze, struggling not

to cry. "Then I guess I'll have to spend the rest of my life being miserable."

Fannie placed her hand on Hannah's arm. "Happiness is not about the place you live. It's about being with your family — the people you love."

"That's right, and my family lives in Pennsylvania."

Fannie shook her head. "When you married my son, you agreed to leave your mother and father and cleave to your husband. You must let go of your life in Pennsylvania and make a new life here with your husband and daughter."

Hannah knew Fannie was right. When she'd said her vows to Timothy on their wedding day, she'd agreed to cleave only unto him. But she'd never expected that would mean moving away from her mother and father and coming to a place where she didn't even have her own home. Maybe if they could find a house to buy soon, she would feel differently, but that remained to be seen.

"It's nice to meet you, Ken," Allen said when Bonnie introduced him to her father.

"Nice to meet you, too. Bonnie's told me a lot about you." Ken grinned at Bonnie and gave her a wink.

"I hope it was all good," Allen said, taking a seat in the living room next to the Christmas tree.

"Of course it was all good," Bonnie said before her father could reply. She looked over at Ken and added, "Allen's never been anything but kind to me."

Allen smiled. Hearing her say that made him think she might be ready to accept his marriage proposal. The only problem was, he couldn't bring it up in front of her dad. He'd have to wait and hope he had the chance to speak with Bonnie alone at some point this evening. He had even gone over in his mind what he wanted to say when he finally did pop the question.

His gaze went to the stately tree he'd helped her pick out a week ago. It looked so beautiful with all the old-fashioned decorations and even a few bubble lights mixed in with the other colored lights. He wished he'd brought the subject of marriage up to her that day when they'd been alone and in festive moods. But since he'd promised to wait until Christmas Eve, he hadn't said anything.

Tonight Bonnie seemed a bit tense. Maybe she was nervous about her dad being here. It was the first time he'd come to visit since Bonnie had left Oregon and turned her grandparents' home into a bed-and-breakfast. Allen knew from what Bonnie had told him that her dad had lived here with his folks during his teenage years but had hated it. It wasn't the house or even the area he hated, though; it was the fact that he'd been forced to leave his girlfriend in Oregon. When she'd broken up with Ken, he'd blamed his folks for forcing him to move, and once he graduated from high school, he'd joined the army and never returned to Kentucky.

"I have some open-faced sandwiches and tomato soup heating on the stove, so if you're ready to eat, why don't we go into the dining room?" Bonnie suggested.

"Sounds good to me." Allen rose from his chair, and her dad did the same.

After they were seated at the dining-room table, Bonnie led in prayer and then dished them each a bowl of soup, while Allen helped himself to an open-faced egg-salad sandwich. "These really look good," he said, passing the platter to Ken.

"They sure do. When Bonnie's mother was alive, she used to make sandwiches like these every Christmas Eve. It was part of her Norwegian heritage to make the sandwiches open-faced and garnish them with tomatoes, pickles, and olives."

Bonnie smiled. "And don't forget the fancy squiggles of mustard and mayonnaise Mom always put on the sandwiches."

Allen took a bite. "Boy, this tastes as good as it looks."

"The soup's good, too," Ken said, after he'd eaten his first spoonful. "Bonnie, you've turned into a real good cook."

"I owe it all to Esther," she said. "She's an excellent cook and taught me well. Without her help, I'd never have been able to come up with decent breakfast foods to serve my B&B guests."

"Esther's your Amish friend, right?" Ken asked.

Bonnie nodded. "I'm anxious for you to meet her, but she's with Samuel's family this evening, so you won't get the chance until tomorrow morning."

"Will she join us for breakfast?" Ken asked.

"I think so. Then she'll be going back to Samuel's to spend Christmas Day."

"I hope you intend to join us tomorrow for Christmas dinner," Ken said, looking at Allen.

"Most definitely." Allen grinned at Bonnie. "I wouldn't miss the chance to eat some of that delicious turkey you're planning to roast. The meal you fixed on Thanksgiving was great, so I'm sure Christmas dinner will be as well."

Bonnie smiled. "Thank you, Allen."

As they continued their meal, Allen got better acquainted with Ken. When he wasn't talking, he was thinking about whether he'd get the chance to speak with Bonnie alone. It made him a little nervous, hoping he'd remember what he'd practiced saying all week. Allen thought he was about to get that chance when Bonnie excused herself to get their dessert.

"Would you like some help?" he offered.

"That's okay. Just sit and relax while you visit with Dad." Bonnie disappeared into the kitchen. Allen hoped he'd get a chance to speak to her before the evening was out.

"I hear you're in the construction business," Ken said after he'd taken a drink of coffee.

"Yes, that's right." Allen glanced at the kitchen door, wishing he could be in there with Bonnie. Not that he didn't enjoy her dad's company; he just really wanted to know if she'd made a decision about marrying him.

"How do you like what Bonnie's done with the house?" Allen asked, looking back at Ken. "She's really turned this place into a nice bed-and-breakfast, don't you think?"

"Yes, it's amazing the transformation that's taken place," Ken agreed. "Not that I didn't have faith in my daughter's abilities, but to tell you the truth, this house was pretty rundown, even when I lived here, so I really didn't know what to expect."

Allen smiled. "Your daughter's pretty re-markable."

"Bonnie says you want to marry her," Ken blurted out.

Allen nearly choked. "Well, uh . . . yes, but I didn't realize she'd mentioned it to you."

Ken gave a nod. "Yep. Said she's supposed to have an answer for you soon."

"That's right. Tonight, to be exact."

"Are you planning to start a family right away?"

"I don't know. That's something Bonnie and I will have to discuss — if she agrees to marry me, that is."

"She'll make a good mother, I think. She's older and ready for that now. Not like when she was an immature sixteen-year-old and had to give her baby up."

"Wh–what was that?" Allen thought he must have misunderstood what Ken just said. *Baby? What baby?*

"She was too young to raise a child back then, and with my job at the bank and trying to raise Bonnie alone, I sure couldn't help take care of a baby. So I insisted that she give the child up for adoption."

Allen's spine went rigid. Bonnie had given birth to a baby when she was sixteen, and she hadn't said a word to him about it? What other secrets did she have?

He leaned forward and rubbed his head, trying to come to grips with this news.

"Are you okay?" Ken asked.

"Uh — no. I have a sudden headache." Allen pushed his chair aside. "And I think I'd better go before the weather gets any worse." He rushed into the hall, grabbed his jacket from the coat tree, and hurried out the door. He couldn't get out of there fast enough.

CHAPTER 20

Bonnie had just placed some slices of chocolate cheesecake on a platter, when she heard the rumble of a vehicle starting up. She went to the window and peered out. It was snowing pretty hard, but under the light on the end of her garage she could see Allen's truck pulling out of the yard.

Now where in the world is he going?

Bonnie hurried into the dining room. Dad sat at the table, head down and shoulders slumped. "I just saw Allen's truck pull out of the yard. Did he say where he was going?"

Dad looked up at her and gave a slow nod. "He's going home."

Bonnie frowned. "Why? What happened?"

"Said he had a headache, but I think it had more to do with me and my big mouth."

"What are you talking about, Dad? Did you say something to upset Allen?"

Dad rubbed the bridge of his nose. "I'm

afraid so."

"What'd you say?"

"We were talking about his desire to marry you, and I asked if he wanted children." Dad paused and took a sip of water. "Then I . . . uh . . . mentioned the child you'd given up for adoption."

Bonnie gasped and sank into a chair with a moan. "Oh Dad, you didn't! How could you have told Allen that? It was my place to tell him about my past, not yours."

"I know that, but I figured it was something you had already told him. I mean, if you're thinking of marrying the guy, then you should have told him about the baby."

"I was planning to, but I couldn't work up the nerve, and there just never seemed to be the right time. I would have told him before I'd given an answer to his proposal though."

"Good grief, Bonnie, you can't wait to spring something like that on a man right before you agree to become his wife. What in the world were you thinking?"

Bonnie stiffened. She didn't like the way Dad was talking to her right now — as though she was still a little girl in need of a lecture.

"I'm sorry, honey," Dad said before she could offer a retort. "I wasn't thinking when

I blabbed to Allen. I was wrong in assuming you had already told him. I'm sure when he comes here for dinner tomorrow you'll be able to talk things out."

Tears welled in Bonnie's eyes, and she blinked to keep them from spilling over. "I hope so, Dad, because I really want things to work out for us. I love Allen so much."

"Does that mean you're going to accept his proposal?"

She gave a slow nod. "If he'll have me now that he knows the truth about my past."

"I'm sure he just needs some time to process all of this. He loves you, Bonnie. I'm certain of it." Dad pushed his chair aside and stood. "You know, I'm really bushed, so if you don't mind, I think I'll head upstairs to bed."

"That's fine. I'll just clear things up in here, and then I'll probably go to bed, too."

"Things will work out for you and Allen. Just pray about it, honey." Dad gave her a hug. Before he headed up the stairs, he turned and looked back at her. "As I said before, I'm really sorry I blurted all that out to Allen."

Noticing her dad's remorseful expression, Bonnie said, "What's done is done, Dad. I should have told Allen sooner, and it's too late now for regrets."

"It'll work out, honey. You'll see. Allen probably just needs some time to think about it."

"I hope so. Good night, Dad. Sleep well."

"You, too."

After Dad went upstairs, Bonnie remained in her chair, staring at the lights on the Christmas tree. It had helped to hear Dad's reassuring words. Now if she could only believe them. *Does Allen really have a headache, and if so, why didn't he come to the kitchen and tell me himself? Did he leave because he couldn't deal with the truth about my past? Will he be back for Christmas dinner tomorrow? Should I give him a call or just wait and find out?*

Trisha squinted as she tried to keep her focus on the road. With the snow coming down so hard, it was difficult to see where she was. This was so nerve-wracking, especially since she didn't have a lot of experience driving in the snow. She figured she should be getting close to Hopkinsville though, where she could get a hotel room and call her friend in Bowling Green to let her know she wouldn't arrive tonight after all but would try to get there tomorrow. At the rate the wind was blowing the snow all around, she began to question where she was. She'd lost service on her GPS and wasn't sure if she was supposed to go straight ahead or turn at the next crossroad.

Maybe Margo was right, she thought. *It might have been a mistake to venture out on my own.*

When a truck swooshed past Trisha's car, throwing snow all over the windshield, she swerved to the right and nearly hit a telephone pole. Heart pounding and hands so sweaty she could barely hold on to the steering wheel, Trisha sent up a prayer as she made a right turn. *Please, Lord, let this be the way to Hopkinsville.*

Driving slowly, with her windshield wipers going at full speed, she proceeded up the road. There were no streetlights on this stretch of road, and she had a sinking feeling she'd taken a wrong turn.

Should I turn around and head back to the road I was on or keep going? she asked herself. *Maybe I'll go just a little farther.*

Trisha saw a pair of red blinking lights up ahead. She slowed her car even more as she strained to see out the window. Then, as she approached the blinking lights, she realized the vehicle in front of her was an Amish buggy. While doing some online research of the area before making this trip, Trisha had learned that there were Amish and Mennonite families living in Christian County, Kentucky. Apparently the Amish in this buggy had been out somewhere on Christmas Eve and were probably on their way home.

Afraid to pass for fear of frightening the horse, Trisha followed the buggy until it turned onto a graveled driveway. It was then that she noticed a sign that read: BONNIE'S BED-AND-BREAKFAST.

Maybe there's a vacancy and I can spend the night, she thought, hope welling in her soul. *Then in the morning, I'll ask for directions to Bowling Green and be on my way.*

Trisha turned in the driveway and stopped her car several feet from where the horse and buggy had pulled up to a hitching rail. When a young Amish woman climbed down from the buggy, Trisha got out of her car.

"Excuse me," she hollered against the howling wind, "but are you the owner of this bed-and-breakfast?"

The woman shook her head. "I just work here part-time, and I live over there in the guesthouse." She pointed across the yard, but due to the swirling snow, Trisha could barely make out the small building. She could, however, see the large house in front of her, which was well lit and looked very inviting right now. It was obviously the B&B.

"Is the owner of the bed-and-breakfast here right now?" Trisha asked, pulling her scarf tighter around her neck to block out the cold wet flakes that were now blowing sideways from the storm.

"I'm sure she is, but —"

"Thanks." Being careful with each step she took, Trisha made her way across the slippery, snowy yard and up the stairs leading to a massive front porch. As she lifted her hand to knock on the door, a sense of peace settled over her. She had a feeling God had directed her to this place tonight, and for that she was grateful. She just hoped she wouldn't be turned away.

Bonnie had just put away the last of the dishes she'd washed when she heard a knock on the front door. Hoping Allen might have come back or that maybe it was Esther returning from Samuel's, she hurried to the foyer. When she opened the door, she was surprised to see a middle-aged English woman with snow-covered, faded blond hair on the porch.

"May I help you?" Bonnie asked.

"My name is Mrs. Chandler, and I was wondering if you might have a room available for the night." The woman pushed a lock of damp hair away from her face. The poor thing looked exhausted.

"The B&B isn't open during Christmas," Bonnie said.

"Oh, I see." The woman's pale blue eyes revealed her obvious disappointment, and she turned to go.

Bonnie's conscience pricked her. Like the innkeeper on the first Christmas Eve, could she really fail to offer this person a room? Thankfully, she could provide something much better than a lowly stable.

"Don't go; I've changed my mind," Bonnie called as the woman walked toward the stairs. "I have a room you can rent. This weather isn't fit for anyone to be out there — especially if you aren't familiar with the area. Come on in and warm up."

The woman turned back, and a look of relief spread across her face as she shook the snow out of her hair and entered the house. "Oh, thank you. I appreciate it so much. You're right. The roads are horrible, and I didn't want to get stuck. I could hardly see where I was going with all the snow coming down. I hate to keep rambling on about this, but this storm is a bit scary, and I had no idea where I was."

"It's not a problem." *After all,* Bonnie thought, *it's Christmas Eve, and I can't send a stranger out into the cold.*

CHAPTER 21

Bonnie awoke early on Christmas morning and, seeing that Mrs. Chandler was still in her room, made her way quietly into the kitchen. Once she had a pot of coffee going, she slipped into her coat and went out the back door. She was glad it wasn't snowing at the moment, even though there was more than a foot of the powdery stuff on the ground. From the way the sky looked, Bonnie figured more snow was probably on the way.

She paused on the porch to breathe in the wintry fresh air. The sight before her looked like a beautiful Christmas card, and she couldn't take her eyes off the wintry scene. Except for a few bird tracks under the feeders, the snow was untouched. Nothing had escaped the blanket of snow. In every direction was a sea of white. The mums that had long lost their autumn color were covered with snow, forming a pretty design. The pine branches were decorated with fluffs of powder, and the pinecones were like nature's ornaments.

Bonnie stepped off the porch, turned, and looked up. The rooftop on the house was covered with heavy snow, giving it an almost whimsical look. Bonnie was glad for a white Christmas. It was what all kids, young and old, dreamed of having.

Glancing at the place where Allen's truck had been parked the night before, she noticed that the snow was so deep that it had erased all signs his vehicle had ever been there. Her heart was heavy after what had happened last night, but the beautiful white snow helped to lighten her spirits a bit. Besides, it was Christmas — a time for joy, hope, love, and a miracle. Bonnie felt it would take a miracle for Allen to understand why she hadn't told him about her past and to forgive her for holding out on that important part of her life.

Forcing her thoughts aside, she carefully made her way out to the guesthouse, knowing Esther was usually up by now. She rapped on the door, and a few seconds later, Esther, bundled in her shawl and black outer bonnet, opened the door.

"I was just on my way up to the house to see you," Esther said. "I wanted to wish you a merry Christmas and let you know that I'm heading over to Samuel's to watch the children open their gifts."

"So you won't be joining us for breakfast?" Bonnie asked, feeling a bit disappointed. "I was hoping you could meet my dad."

"How about if I stop by this evening after I get back from Samuel's?"

"That's fine. Your place is with Samuel and his children this morning." She nodded toward the road, which hadn't been plowed. "I'm a little concerned about the weather and the road conditions, though. Do you think you can make it to Samuel's okay?"

Esther nodded. "Ginger's always been good in the snow, and it's much easier for our buggies to get around in this kind of weather than it is for a car. Since I'm leaving early, there shouldn't be many vehicles on the road yet."

"You're probably right." Bonnie hesitated a moment, wondering if she should tell Esther what had happened last night between her dad and Allen.

"You look as if you might be troubled about something," Esther said, as though reading Bonnie's mind. "Is everything all right?"

"I don't know."

Esther opened the door wider. "Come

inside where it's warm, and tell me what's wrong."

"Are you sure you have the time? I don't want you to be late getting to Samuel's."

"It's okay. I'm sure they won't start opening presents until I get there."

"All right, thanks. I really do need to talk."

Esther removed her shawl and outer bonnet as she led the way to her small kitchen. "Let's take a seat at the table and have a cup of tea," she said, placing her garments over the back of a chair.

"I really don't need any tea, but if we could just spend a few minutes talking, it might help me sort out my feelings."

Bonnie told Esther all that had transpired between her dad and Allen, and how Allen had told Dad he had a headache and gone home without even saying good-bye.

"But I thought you were planning to tell Allen about your past," Esther said.

"I was, and I would have done it before I gave him an answer to his proposal, but I had no idea Dad would blurt it out like that before I had a chance to explain things to Allen." Tears welled in Bonnie's eyes. "I'm afraid the reason Allen left is because he's upset with me for not telling him the truth before this. He probably thinks I'm a terrible person for what I did when I was sixteen. I doubt that he'd want to marry me now."

"Even if Allen was upset about it, I'm sure that after you talk to him, he'll understand why it was hard for you to share this part of your past with him. You can explain things when he comes over for dinner this afternoon," Esther said, placing her hand gently on Bonnie's arm.

"*If* he comes for dinner." Bonnie fought back tears of frustration. "I'm afraid the special relationship Allen and I had might be spoiled now."

"I'm sure it's not, Bonnie, and I'm almost positive he'll come for dinner. Allen's too polite not to show up when he's been invited to someone's house for a meal. I'm equally sure he'll want to talk with you about all of this."

"I hope you're right, because we really do need to talk, although if he does come for dinner, we won't be able to say much in front of my dad or Mrs. Chandler."

"Mrs. Chandler?"

"My B&B guest."

"Oh, that must be the woman I met last night when I got back from Samuel's."

"You did?"

"Yes, and she asked if I was the owner of the bed-and-breakfast. When I told her I work for you part-time and that you were probably at home, she took off for the house before I could explain that you weren't open for business on Christmas. The poor woman looked pretty desperate."

"It's okay," Bonnie said. "After Mrs. Chandler explained her need for a room, I didn't have the heart to say no. There was no way I could have made her go back out in that blizzard last night."

Esther smiled. "I figured that might be the case." She got up and gave Bonnie a hug. "You're always so kind to others. No wonder you've become such a good friend."

Bonnie smiled. "You've been a good friend to me, as well."

"I do hope everything will work out for you and Allen."

"Me, too," Bonnie murmured. "I've waited a long time for love to come my way, and if things don't work out, I'll never allow myself to fall in love again."

"Guder mariye. En hallicher Grischtdaag," Timothy said, joining Hannah at the bedroom window, where she stared out at the snow.

"Good morning, and Merry Christmas to you, too," she said, in a less than enthusiastic tone.

Timothy's heart went out to her. This was the first Christmas she'd spent away from her parents, and he knew she was hurting. *I hope the gift I made for Hannah will make her feel a little happier.*

"I have something for you," he said, reaching under the bed and pulling out a cardboard box.

She tipped her head and stared at it curiously. "What's in there?"

"Open it and see."

Hannah set the box on the bed and opened the flaps. As she withdrew the bird feeder he'd made, tears welled in her eyes. "Oh Timothy, you made it to look like the covered bridge not far from our home in Pennsylvania."

"That's right. Do you like it, Hannah?" he asked.

"Jah, very much."

"I know how much you enjoy feeding the birds, so I decided to make you a different kind of feeder. See here," he said, lifting the roof on the bridge. "The food goes in there, and then it falls out the ends and underneath the bridge, where the birds sit and eat."

Hannah smiled. "Danki, Timothy. As soon as we find a house of our own, I'll put the feeder to good use."

"You don't have to wait till then," he said. "I can put the feeder up for you in Samuel's backyard. With all this snow, I'm sure the birds, and even the squirrels, will appreciate the unexpected treat."

She shook her head. "I don't want to put it here at Samuel's place."

"Why not?"

"I just don't, that's all." Hannah hurried across the room and opened the bottom dresser drawer. "I have a Christmas present for you, too," she said, handing him a box wrapped in white tissue paper.

Timothy took a seat on the bed and opened the gift. He was a little hurt that Hannah didn't want to use the bird feeder right away, but he hid his feelings, not wanting anything to ruin the day. Inside the package he found a pale blue shirt and a pair of black suspenders.

"Danki," he said. "These are both items I can surely use."

Excited voices coming from outside drew Timothy back over to the window. "Looks like Esther just arrived, so Samuel will soon present his kinner with the new pony he bought them for Christmas," he said. "Let's get Mindy up and go outside and join them."

"You go ahead," Hannah said. "Mindy

needs her sleep. Besides, I don't want her getting all excited over the pony. She might think she should have one, too."

"In a few years, maybe we ought to get her one," Timothy said.

Hannah shook her head vigorously. "Ponies are a lot of work, and I don't want our daughter thinking she can take a pony cart out on the road. That would be too dangerous." She frowned. "If you want my opinion, Samuel shouldn't be giving his kinner a pony, either. They're all too young and irresponsible."

"What Samuel does for his kinner is none of our business, and since Mindy's too young for a pony right now, there's no point in talking about this anymore." Timothy turned toward the bedroom door. "You can stay here if you want to, but I'm going outside to see the look of joy on my nieces' and nephews' faces when they see that new pony for the first time." Timothy hurried out the door.

Arguing with Hannah was not a good way to begin the day — especially when it was Christmas. But he wasn't going to let her ruin his good mood. Why couldn't things stay positive between them, the way they had been when he'd given her the bird feeder? Would they ever see eye to eye on anything that concerned raising Mindy? Was he foolish to hope that at least Christmas would be a tension-free day?

Allen sat at his kitchen table drinking coffee and stewing over what Bonnie's dad had told him last night. Now he wasn't sure what to do. Should he go over to Bonnie's for dinner this afternoon or call her and say he'd decided to stay home? He could probably use the weather as an excuse. The roads had been terrible last night, and from the looks of the weather outside, they most likely weren't any better today. Besides, with it being Christmas, the state and county road workers were probably stretched pretty thin, with only a skeleton crew filling in on the holiday. But blaming the weather for his absence would be the coward's way out, and running from a problem wasn't how he handled things. Of course, he'd never asked a woman to marry him, only to find out from her father that she'd given birth to a baby and given it up for adoption. It might not have been such a shock if Bonnie had told him herself. But the fact that she'd kept it from him made Allen feel as if she didn't love or trust him enough to share her past. Was she afraid he would judge her? Did she think he would condemn her for something that had taken place when she was young and impressionable?

How do I really feel about the fact that the woman I love had a baby out of wedlock? Allen set his cup down and made little circles across his forehead with his fingers, hoping to stave off another headache. *Is that what really bothers me, or is it the fact that she didn't tell me about the baby? If we'd gotten married, would she ever have told me the truth? Do I really want to marry her now?* There were so many questions, yet no answers would come.

Allen sat for several minutes thinking, praying, and meditating on things. The words of Matthew 6:14 popped into his head: *"If ye forgive men their trespasses, your heavenly Father will also forgive you."*

He groaned. *I know I'm not perfect, and I've done things I shouldn't have in the past. It's not my place to judge Bonnie or anyone else. The least I can do is give her a call and talk about this — let her explain why she didn't tell me about the baby.*

Allen was about to reach for the phone, when the lights flickered and then went out. "Oh great, now the power's down. Someone must have hit a pole, or it's due to the weather. Guess I'll have to use my cell phone."

Allen went to the counter where he usually placed the cell phone to be charged and discovered that it wasn't there. "Now what'd I do with the stupid thing?" he mumbled.

He checked each room, looking in all the usual places. He also searched the jacket he'd worn last night, but there was no sign of his cell phone.

Maybe I left it at Bonnie's, he thought. *If I could use the phone and call her, I could find out. Guess I'd better drive over there now and hope she has power at her place, because if I stay here with no heat and no way to cook anything, I'll not only be cold, but hungry besides.*

Allen grabbed his jacket and headed out the door. When he stepped into his truck and tried to start it, he got no response. Either he'd left the lights on last night, or the cold weather had zapped the battery, because it was dead.

"This day just keeps getting better and better. That settles that," he muttered as he tromped through the snow and back to the house. "Looks like I'll be spending my Christmas alone in a cold, dark house and nothing will be resolved with Bonnie today."

CHAPTER 22

"That's a mighty cute pony Samuel bought for the kinner, isn't it?" Fannie said as she, Hannah, and Esther worked in the kitchen to get dinner ready.

"Jah, it certainly is." Esther smiled. "And I think the name Shadow is perfect for the pony, because it sure likes to follow the kinner around."

"Looks like they all took to the pony rather quickly, too," Fannie added.

Hannah rolled her eyes. "If you ask me, Samuel's kinner are too young for a pony. They can barely take care of their dog."

"They're not too young," Fannie said with a shake of her head. "Marla and Leon are plenty old enough to take care of the pony."

"I agree with Fannie," Esther said, reaching for a bowl to put the potatoes in. "Having a pony to care for will teach the children responsibility."

Hannah made no comment. Obviously

her opinion didn't matter to either of these women. She picked up a stack of plates and was about to take them to the dining room when Esther said to Fannie, "When Suzanne and Titus were here last night, she mentioned that she's been feeling sick to her stomach for the last several weeks. I was wondering if she said anything to you about that."

"No, but it sounds like she might be expecting my next *kinskind*." Fannie grinned. "And if that's the case, I think it would be wunderbaar, because Abraham and I would surely welcome a new grandchild."

Hannah swallowed hard. She couldn't help but feel a bit envious — not only because she wanted to have another baby and hadn't been able to get pregnant again, but because she saw a closeness developing between Esther and Fannie.

It's not right that Fannie's nicer to Esther than she is to me. I'm her daughter-in-law, after all. Esther isn't even part of this family yet. Hannah wished, yet again, that her parents could have been here for Christmas. It would help so much if she and Mom could sit down and have a good long talk. Hannah's mother had always been there for her and would surely understand how she felt about things.

■ ■ ■ ■

Trisha yawned, stretched, and pulled the covers aside. She couldn't remember when she'd slept so well. "Oh my, it's so late," she murmured after looking at her watch and realizing it was almost noon.

She sat up and swung her legs over the edge of the bed, just as her cell phone rang. "Hello," she said, suppressing a yawn.

"Trisha, this is Carla."

"It's good to hear from you! Merry Christmas."

"I wish it was a merry Christmas. Jason and I just received some bad news."

"I'm sorry to hear that. What's wrong?"

"Jason's mother was taken to the hospital this morning, so we'll be heading to Ohio right away."

"That's too bad. I hope it's nothing serious."

"They think she had a stroke."

"I'll be praying for her, and for you and Jason as you travel."

"Thanks, we appreciate that." There was a pause. "I'm sorry we won't be here to have Christmas dinner with you."

"That's okay. I understand. Now be safe, and I'll talk to you again soon."

When Trisha hung up, she hurried to take a shower and get dressed. She probably should have checked out by now and might even be holding things up for the owner of the bed-and-breakfast if she had Christmas plans, which she probably did. Most everyone had plans for Christmas — everyone but her, that is.

Maybe I should have stayed in Fresno instead of taking off on this trip, she thought. *At least there I could have spent Christmas with Margo and Shirley. Well, it's too late to cry about that now. I'm not in Fresno, and I need to get back on the road. With any luck, I may be able to find a restaurant in Hopkinsville that's open on Christmas Day. That is, if I can even find Hopkinsville.*

Trisha picked up her suitcase and went downstairs, where a tantalizing aroma drew her into the kitchen.

"I apologize for sleeping so late," she said to Bonnie, who stood in front of the oven, checking on a luscious-looking turkey. "I was snuggled down under that quilt, feeling so toasty and warm, and I didn't want to wake up."

Bonnie closed the oven door, turned to Trisha, and smiled. "That's okay. I'm glad you slept well. I figured you must be tired after your drive here last night. I know from experience that driving in such bad conditions can really exhaust a person, especially when they are unfamiliar with the roads." She motioned to a tray of cinnamon rolls on the counter. "Would you like a cup of coffee and some of those?"

Trisha's mouth watered. "That sounds so good. I'll just eat one and be on my way."

"Do you have any plans for today?" Bonnie asked.

"Not anymore." Trisha told Bonnie about the call she'd had from Carla. "So, if you'll be kind enough to tell me how to get to Hopkinsville, I'll see if any restaurants are open there. After I eat, I'll probably head on down the road."

"I doubt that any restaurants will be open today. And if you did find a restaurant, what fun would it be to eat alone?"

"It's never fun to eat alone," Trisha admitted, "but I've gotten used to it since my husband passed away."

"Why don't you stay here and join me and my dad for Christmas dinner?" Bonnie offered.

"It's kind of you to offer, but I wouldn't want to impose."

"It's not an imposition. There's plenty of food, and if you'd like to spend another night here, that's fine, too."

211

"Really? You wouldn't mind?"

"Not at all."

"Thanks, I think I'll take you up on that." Truth was, this charming B&B had captivated Trisha — not to mention that it would be much nicer to have a home-cooked meal in the company of Bonnie and her dad than to sit alone in some restaurant to eat.

Trisha glanced around the room. "Is there anything I can do to help you with dinner?"

"I appreciate the offer, but there's nothing that needs to be done until closer to dinnertime. So why don't you just relax for now?"

"Maybe I'll take my coffee and cinnamon roll upstairs. I really should call a few of my friends from California and wish them a merry Christmas."

A few minutes after Trisha left the kitchen, Bonnie's dad came in.

"Did you meet my B&B guest out in the hall?" Bonnie asked. During breakfast she'd told him about Mrs. Chandler.

"Nope. I came from the living room, but I did hear footsteps on the stairs, so I guess that must have been her."

"I hope you don't mind, but I invited Mrs. Chandler to join us for dinner today. Oh, and she'll be staying one more night, too."

Dad smiled. "You're sure accommodating, Bonnie. Most people running a business that is supposed to be closed for the holiday wouldn't have welcomed a guest at the last minute the way you did."

"I couldn't very well send her out into the cold. Besides, the poor woman looked tired and lonely. And she's not from around here."

"How do you know?"

"When she was filling out the paperwork to check into the B&B last night she said she was from California."

"She's a long ways from home then."

"Yes, and she could have easily gotten lost in that blinding snow."

"Have you heard anything from Allen today?" Dad asked.

Bonnie shook her head. "I tried calling him at home awhile ago, but the phone just rang and rang."

"Maybe he's on his way here. Did you try his cell phone?"

"No, I didn't. Even if he was coming for dinner, I didn't think he would have left already, so I only called his home phone."

"Why don't you give his cell phone a try?" Dad suggested.

"Good idea." Bonnie picked up the phone and dialed Allen's cell number. She was surprised when she heard a phone ringing somewhere else in the house. It sounded like it was coming from the dining room.

"What in the world?" Moving quickly into the dining room, she discovered Allen's cell phone lying in the chair where he'd been sitting last evening.

"It must have fallen out of his pocket," Bonnie told Dad when he followed her into the dining room. "I guess now all we can do is wait and see if Allen shows up for dinner."

"I hope he does," Dad said with a nod. "I owe him an apology for what I blurted out last night, and I know you're anxious to talk to him, too."

"Yes, I am, although I'm feeling nervous about it." Hearing the wind howling outside, Bonnie glanced out the window and saw that it was snowing again. "I hope if Allen is on his way over that he'll be safe. Whatever roads have been plowed will probably drift shut again since the wind has picked up."

"Try not to worry; I'm sure he'll be fine," Dad said.

"You're right. Worry won't change a thing, so I'll pray and trust God to bring Allen here safely today."

"Good idea." Dad moved toward the living room. "If you don't need me for anything, I think I'll go relax in front of the fire for a while. Since I don't have a fireplace in my house, I'd forgotten how nice one can be."

Bonnie noticed a faraway look in his eyes. He'd obviously had some good memories from living in this place.

"I remember how my mom used to sit in front of the fireplace humming while she knitted," Dad continued. "I can still almost hear the click of her knitting needles, as though keeping time to her music."

"Yes, I recall her doing that when I came here to visit sometimes." Bonnie patted Dad's arm. "You go ahead and relax. I'll call you when dinner's ready."

"Thanks, honey."

When Dad left the room, Bonnie said a prayer for Allen; then she picked up his cell phone and returned to the kitchen to check on the meal. By the time she had everything on the dining-room table, it was two o'clock, and still no Allen. She was sure he wasn't coming.

Bonnie was about to call Mrs. Chandler for dinner when the lights went out. Fortunately, she was done cooking, so at least they wouldn't have to worry about eating cold food.

While Dad added more wood to the fireplace, Bonnie lit some candles, grabbed a flashlight, and headed upstairs to the room she had rented to Mrs. Chandler.

She knocked on the door, and a few seconds later, Mrs. Chandler, looking half-asleep, answered. "Oh, I'm so sorry. After I made my phone calls, I laid down on the bed to rest and must have fallen asleep." She yawned and stretched her arms over her head. "I can't believe with all the sleep I had last night that I could still be so tired. I slept like a baby, though. It's so peaceful and quiet here, and as soon as I reclined on the bed and pulled that beautiful quilt over me, I was out like a light."

"That's okay. You must have needed the extra rest, and you know, I think there's something about being wrapped up in a quilt that makes a person feel safe and comforted."

"You're so right. I was asleep almost before my head hit the pillow. If you'll give me a minute to freshen up, I'll be right down."

Bonnie explained that the power was out and gave Mrs. Chandler the flashlight, because there were no windows in the hall. Then she carefully made her way down the stairs, where she opened all the curtains to let what little outside light there was into the house.

A short time later, Bonnie's guest came down and joined them in the dining room. Bonnie introduced Dad to Mrs. Chandler, and they all took their seats. Even though she'd opened the curtains, the room was quite dark, but the flickering candles helped. Bonnie thought the candlelight made it seem more relaxing and festive — sort of like back in the days of old.

After Bonnie prayed, giving thanks for the meal, she passed the food around.

Dad looked over at her and said, "It doesn't look like Allen's coming, does it?"

"No, I'm afraid not. Once the lights come back on, I'll try calling him again. He needs to know that his cell phone is here, because I'm sure he's going to need it when he goes to work tomorrow morning."

"You mean, *if* he goes to work," Dad said. "With the way the snow's been coming down, the roads might not be passable by morning."

The conversation changed as Bonnie asked Mrs. Chandler a few questions about herself, including her first name.

"Oh, it's Trisha. My husband and I used to live in Portland, Oregon, but we moved to Fresno, California, shortly after we got married."

"What was your maiden name?" Dad

asked with a peculiar expression.

"It was Hammond."

Bonnie heard Dad's sharp intake of breath and wondered if he'd choked on something. Just then, the lights came back on, and Bonnie worried more, because Dad's face looked as white as Grandma's tablecloth.

"Dad, are you all right?"

He just sat staring at Trisha as if he'd seen a ghost.

Trisha studied him for several seconds, and then she gasped. "Kenny Taylor? Is that you?"

Dad nodded. "What are you doing here in Kentucky? Did you know I'd be here at my folks' old house?" His eyes narrowed and deep wrinkles formed across his forehead.

Trisha shook her head vigorously. "Of course not. I had no way of knowing you were here, or that this was where you used to live. How would I have known that?"

"You sent me a letter after I moved here, remember? Or did you forget about that?"

Trisha's brows furrowed as she slowly nodded. "I'd almost forgotten about that, and I sure didn't remember your address after all these years. When I pulled in here last night, I had no idea this used to be where you lived."

"So what are you saying — that it was just

a twist of fate that brought you here?"

"Maybe; I don't know. The snow was really bad, and I had to get off the road. I didn't even know where I was. Thankfully, I saw the blinking lights on a horse-drawn buggy and followed it here." Trisha paused, and her voice lowered as she looked at him and said, "Maybe it was God, and not the weather, who led me here."

Dad grunted. "Yeah, right."

Bonnie, feeling as shocked as Dad obviously was, could almost feel the tension between him and Trisha. She wished there was something she could do. What a stressful Christmas this had turned out to be. It was bad enough that the man she loved was so upset with her that he didn't want to join them for Christmas dinner. Now, as fate would have it, Dad's old girlfriend had shown up out of the blue, and Dad's Christmas had been ruined, too. How much worse could it get?

Chapter 23

"I'm sorry about what happened between me and your dad yesterday. I'm sure it ruined your Christmas," Trisha said the following morning when she entered the kitchen and found Bonnie sitting at the table reading her Bible.

Bonnie looked up and smiled. "It's not your fault. Dad should be the one apologizing — and mostly to you, because you had no way of knowing he was here."

Trisha sank into a chair with a sigh. "I'm glad you realize that, but even after all these years, I believe he's still angry with me for breaking up with him. I don't understand it, though. It's not like we were engaged to be married or anything. We were just teenagers back then and thought we were in love."

"I think the reason Dad was so upset is because when you broke up with him, he believed it was due to the fact that he was moving to Kentucky. So he was upset with his parents and blamed them for the breakup."

"But I sent him a letter telling him I'd fallen in love with Dave, and that was the only reason I broke up with him shortly before he moved. After reading my letter, Kenny should have realized that our breakup had nothing to do with him moving, and most of all, that it wasn't his parents' fault."

Bonnie shook her head. "Dad never got your letter."

"How do you know that?"

"Soon after I moved here, I found the letter stuck between some papers in an old pie cupboard in the basement. The letter was unopened," Bonnie explained. "Then later, when I went to Portland to take care of Dad after he'd been in a car accident, I showed him the letter."

"What'd he say about that?"

"He was stunned and said he'd never seen the letter before. After he read it, he regretted having blamed his parents for making him move to Kentucky and wished he could tell them how sorry he was. But since they'd both passed away, it was too late for that," Bonnie added.

"So Ken's more upset about how our

breakup affected his relationship with his folks than he is with me for choosing Dave over him?"

"I think so. Although I know from the few things Dad's told me that he really did care about you. I believe it was a long time before he got over you breaking up with him." Bonnie motioned to her Bible. "Dad's a Christian now, and he needs to remember what God says about forgiveness."

"I'm a Christian, too," Trisha said. "I found the Lord soon after Dave and I moved to Fresno and started going to a neighborhood church."

"Since you and Dad are both Christians, you ought to be able to work this out." Bonnie rose from her seat and pointed out the window, where huge snowflakes swirled around the yard. "And from the looks of this weather that's set in, I'd say you're both going to be stuck here for a few more days, which should give you enough time to make peace with each other."

Paradise, Pennsylvania

"How's Johnny doing?" Naomi asked when Sally entered her store shortly after it had opened.

"He's still in quite a bit of pain." Sally frowned. "He's also cranky and impatient."

"A back injury can cause a person to be out of sorts. I hope it didn't ruin your Christmas."

Sally shrugged and picked up a shopping basket. "Our sons and their families came over for a while on Christmas Day, so that helped, but I wish we could have gone to Kentucky like we'd planned."

"I talked to my daed earlier this morning, and he said they're having blizzard-like conditions in Christian County right now, so maybe it's a good thing you had to stay home."

"Is everyone okay there?" Sally questioned, feeling concern.

"Dad said everyone's fine, but if the weather doesn't improve, they may end up having to stay a few days longer than they'd planned. He also mentioned that many people have been without power in the area, which is affecting quite a few of their English neighbors."

"If there's no power, how'd Abraham manage to call you this morning?"

"The power was on in Samuel's phone shanty, but Dad said with the wind blowing like crazy, there was a good chance they might lose power there, too."

"I'd better do my shopping in a hurry so I can get home and call Samuel's number. I want to check on Hannah and be sure she and the others are okay." Sally started down the notions aisle and nearly bumped into Phoebe Stoltzfus. "What are you doing here?" she asked.

"I came in to get some sewing supplies for my mamm," Phoebe replied with a smile.

"Shouldn't you be at the bulk food store right now? You can't expect Anna to handle things by herself, you know." Sally hoped Phoebe wasn't the kind of person who shirked her duties.

"I don't expect that at all." Phoebe's face turned red. "Since the store doesn't open for another half hour, I figured I'd have time to make a quick stop here before going to work."

"Oh, I see." Sally didn't know why, but she didn't quite trust Phoebe. She remembered how a few years ago the rebellious young woman had been going out with Titus Fisher but broke things off and headed for California with a friend. If Phoebe hadn't done that, Titus would still be living in Pennsylvania because the only reason he'd moved to Kentucky was to start a new life and try to forget about Phoebe.

Maybe that's why I don't care much for Phoebe, Sally thought. *Her foolish actions set the wheels in motion for three of the Fisher men to move to Kentucky. If Phoebe had stayed put in Lancaster County, she'd probably be married to Titus by now, and none of the brothers would have moved away, so Hannah would still be here, too.*

Turning her attention back to the issue at hand, Sally said to Phoebe, "Well, just see that you're not late for work today. Johnny and I don't want any of our employees sloughing off on the job."

"No, I won't be late," Phoebe mumbled before hurrying down the aisle.

Pembroke, Kentucky

Hannah glanced out the living-room window at the swirling snow and frowned. She hated being cooped up in the house — especially with so many people. Why couldn't Fannie and Abraham have stayed with Titus and Suzanne the whole time? Having them here was just a reminder that her folks were at home and Dad was down with a sore back. With the exception of the bird feeder Timothy had given Hannah, it had not been a very good Christmas. And now this horrible weather only made her feel worse. She knew it had upset Timothy that the bird feeder he'd given her would remain in the box until they got a place of their own. But she didn't want the feeder put up in Samuel's yard, even if temporarily. Hannah wanted the feeder in her own yard, not someone else's.

Then, to give her one more thing to fret about, this morning after breakfast, Samuel and Timothy had taken off with Samuel's horse and buggy for Hopkinsville, because they hadn't been able to get ahold of Allen and were worried about him. Hannah had tried talking Timothy out of going, reminding him that the roads were bad and it was hard to see. But he'd been determined to go, and nothing she'd said made any difference. It seemed as though whatever Hannah wanted, Timothy was determined to do just the opposite. Or at least that's how it had been since they'd moved to Kentucky.

"I think I'll go out to the phone shanty and see if there are any messages from my mamm," Hannah said to Fannie, who sat in the rocking chair by the fire with Jared and Mindy in her lap.

"It's awfully cold out there," Fannie said. "Abraham said so when he went out to help Samuel clean the barn this morning."

"I'll be fine." Hannah stepped into the hall and removed her heavy woolen shawl from a wall peg. After wrapping it snugly around her shoulders, she put on her outer bonnet, slipped into a pair of boots, and went out the door.

The snow was deeper than she'd thought it would be, and she winced when she took her first step and ended up with icy cold snow down her boots. By the time she reached the phone shanty, her teeth had begun to chatter, and goose bumps covered her arms and legs. To make matters worse, Hannah's feet were soaking wet and fast getting numb from the snow that kept falling inside her boots.

I should have thought to put on some gloves, she told herself as she stepped inside the shanty and turned on the battery-operated light sitting on the small wooden table beside the phone. She blew on her fingers to get the feeling back in them, took a seat in the folding chair, and wiggled her toes, hoping to get some warmth in her boots before punching the button to listen to their voice-mail messages. There was one from Mom, saying she'd heard about the bad weather they were having and asking if everyone was all right. Hannah picked up the phone and dialed her folks' number, but since no one was in the phone shack, she had to leave a message. "Hi, Mom, it's Hannah. I wanted to let you know that we're all fine here, but the weather's awful, and I really miss you. I wish we could have been in Pennsylvania for Christmas instead of here."

Hannah hung up the phone, and with a feeling of hopelessness, she trudged back to the house, trying not to get more snow in her already-soaked boots.

Hopkinsville, Kentucky

Allen shivered as he pulled a blanket around his shoulders and made his way to the kitchen. He couldn't believe he'd been without power for twenty-four hours, and with no phone or battery for his truck, it looked like he would be stuck here until the power came on and he could call someone for help.

"Man, it's sure cold in here! Guess this is what I get for building my home where there are no neighbors close by," he grumbled. If he had, he could have asked one of them to give him a ride into town where he could buy a new battery for his truck.

"Let's see now, what do I want to eat?" he asked himself, peeking into the refrigerator, which had stayed plenty cold despite the loss of power. A peanut butter and jelly sandwich would be real good about now, but he knew there was no peanut butter. It was on his grocery list. There was no jelly either, but he did find a package of cheddar cheese, a bottle of orange juice, two sticks of butter, and a carton of eggs. He wasn't in the mood for raw eggs, so he took out the cheese and orange juice, got down a box of crackers from the cupboard, and took a seat at the table. "Dear Lord," he prayed, bowing his head, "bless this pitiful breakfast I'm about to eat, restore power to the area soon, and be with my family and friends everywhere. Amen."

Allen's thoughts went to Bonnie. Did she have power at her place? Was she doing okay? He wished he could just jump in the truck and head over there now — or at least call to check up on her. "I'm such a fool," he muttered. He regretted the way he'd left on Christmas Eve and knew he needed to apologize for not showing up yesterday, too, although that was completely out of his control. Things had sure changed from when he had fretted over not flubbing up his proposal to Bonnie. He wished now her answer was all he had to worry about. One thing for sure: he needed to talk to Bonnie soon.

Allen had just eaten his second cracker when a knock sounded on the front door. He jumped up and raced over to the door to see who it was. Timothy and Samuel stood on his porch dressed in heavy jackets and straw hats.

"We've been trying to call and became worried when we didn't get an answer," Samuel said, his brows furrowed. "When Esther mentioned that Bonnie said you never showed up for Christmas, we decided we'd better come and check on you."

"How'd you get here?" Allen asked, looking past their shoulders.

"Came with Samuel's horse and buggy." Timothy motioned to where they'd tied the horse to a tree near Allen's garage.

"Wow, it must have taken you awhile to get here," Allen said. "Especially in this horrible weather."

Samuel nodded. "Took us over an hour, but there weren't any cars on the road, so we moved along at a pretty good clip."

"I'm glad you're here," Allen said, "because the power's out, and to top it off, the battery in my truck is dead. Since yesterday morning, I've been stranded with no heat, and I can't find my cell phone, so I haven't been able to call anyone for help."

"You left your cell phone at Bonnie's on Christmas Eve," Samuel said. "She told Esther that, too."

"Oh, I see. I kind of figured that might be the case." Allen opened the door wider.

"You two had better come inside. It's not much warmer in the house than it is outside, but at least it's not snowing in here," he added with a chuckle.

"Why don't you gather up some clothes and come home with us?" Samuel suggested after they'd entered the house.

"I appreciate the offer, but I wouldn't want to impose."

"It's not an imposition," Samuel said. "Besides, if you stay here and the power doesn't come on soon, you'll either freeze to death or die of hunger."

"You've got that right. Although, I guess I could have tromped through the snow and pulled my barbecue grill out of the garage." Allen's nose crinkled. "But I don't have much food in the house, and even if I did, I don't relish the thought of bein' out in the cold trying to cook it."

"I can't blame you there," Timothy said.

"Give me a minute to throw a few things together, and then we can head out." Allen started for his room but turned back around. "Say, I have an idea."

"What's that?" Samuel asked.

"Instead of taking me to your place, how about dropping me off at Bonnie's? That way I can get my cell phone, and if she's still speaking to me, maybe I can talk her into letting me have one of her rooms at the B&B for the night."

"Why wouldn't she be speaking to you?" Timothy questioned.

"It's a long story. I'll tell you both about it on the way."

Samuel nodded. "If it doesn't work out and you still need a place to stay, you're more than welcome to come home with us."

"Thanks. Depending on how things go with Bonnie, I may need to take you up on that offer."

CHAPTER 24

Pembroke, Kentucky

"It looks like Bonnie must have a guest," Allen said when Samuel pulled his horse and buggy up to the hitching rail. A small blue car, mostly covered in snow, was parked near the garage.

"That's right, she does," Samuel said. "Esther mentioned that the woman is from California and she arrived here late on Christmas Eve."

"I thought the B&B was closed for the holidays," Allen said, climbing down from the buggy.

"It was, but Bonnie made an exception because the woman couldn't find her way to Hopkinsville in the snow and needed a place to stay."

Allen smiled. That sounded like Bonnie. She was a good person, and they really did need to talk.

"Maybe you'd better come inside where

it's warmer and wait until I see if Bonnie will rent me a room," Allen said, looking first at Timothy and then Samuel.

"Sure, we can do that," Samuel said, "but I doubt that Bonnie would turn you out in the cold."

Allen wasn't so sure about that. He'd walked out Christmas Eve without a word of explanation or even telling her good-bye. No doubt, Bonnie's dad had told her about the conversation they'd had regarding Bonnie's past, so by him not showing up for dinner yesterday, she probably thought he was angry with her.

Well, I was at first, he admitted to himself as he tromped through the drifts of snow in the yard. *I was angry and hurt, but I'm going to fix things now if I can.*

After the three men stepped onto the porch, Samuel knocked on the door. A few seconds later, Bonnie opened it, and she looked at them in disbelief. Then her gaze went to the yard, where the horse and buggy stood. "I'm surprised to see you out in this horrible weather." She glanced over at Allen. "Did you come here in Samuel's buggy?"

He nodded.

"Where's your truck?"

"At home with a dead battery. I've been

stranded there since Christmas morning, with no electricity, no vehicle, and no cell phone."

"Your cell phone is here. We found it on the chair you sat in on Christmas Eve." Bonnie opened the door farther and moved aside. "Come in, everyone, where it's warmer."

As they stepped into the entryway, Allen caught a glimpse of a middle-aged woman sitting in front of the fireplace in the living room to his right. He figured she must be Bonnie's unexpected guest.

"Let's go into the kitchen," Bonnie suggested. "I'll pour you some coffee, and how about a piece of pumpkin pie or some chocolate cheesecake to go with it?"

Allen's mouth watered. "Mmm . . . that sounds really good."

"Same here," Samuel and Timothy said in unison.

"Which one do you want — the cheesecake or the pie?" Bonnie asked.

"Both," Allen replied with a grin. "I've had very little to eat in the last twenty-four hours, and I'm just about starved to death."

"No problem. I have pie and plenty of leftovers from yesterday's Christmas dinner."

Allen grimaced. If he'd been there yesterday to eat with them, there wouldn't be so many leftovers, and he wouldn't feel as though he was close to starvation right now.

"Is your dad still here?" Samuel asked as he removed his jacket and took a seat at the table, along with the others. "I was hoping I'd get the opportunity to meet him."

"Yes, he's in his room right now, but I'll call him down before you leave." Bonnie poured them all coffee, and then she took a delicious-looking pumpkin pie from the refrigerator, cut three slices, and gave them each a piece. Following that, she placed a dish of chocolate cheesecake on the table and said they could help themselves.

"Dad was planning to leave today, but with the weather turning bad, he called the airlines and canceled his flight," Bonnie said. "He doesn't want to go until the weather improves, because he's concerned about me driving him to the airport on snowy roads."

"My truck has four-wheel drive, so I'd be happy to take him," Allen offered as he helped himself to a generous slice of pumpkin pie. "As soon as I get a battery for it, that is."

"I appreciate the offer, but I'm sure I can manage to get him there." Bonnie smiled, but it appeared to be forced.

She is upset with me, and I need to talk to her about my actions on Christmas Eve, but I can't very well say anything with Timothy and Samuel sitting here. Allen blew on his coffee and took a drink. "Uh . . . the reason we came over is, I was wondering if I could rent a room from you for the night."

She shook her head.

"You won't rent me a room?" He couldn't believe she would turn him out in the cold.

"No, but I will let you stay in a room free of charge." Her smile softened, reaching all the way to her eyes this time.

Allen relaxed and released a deep breath. "Thanks. I appreciate that very much."

They sat quietly for a while as the men drank their coffee and ate the pie. Then, when they were just finishing up, Bonnie excused herself and left the room. When she returned several minutes later, she had Allen's cell phone, and her father was with her.

"Dad, I'd like you to meet Samuel Fisher," she said, motioning to Samuel. "And this is his brother Timothy."

"It's nice to meet you both," Ken said, shaking their hands. "You did some real nice work on this old house," he added, looking at Samuel.

Samuel motioned to Allen. "I can't take

237

all the credit. My good friend here did some of the work."

Ken looked at Allen and smiled. "It's good to see you again. We missed you on Christmas Day."

Allen explained his situation and why he was here right now. What he didn't admit was that even if he hadn't been stranded, he might not have come for Christmas dinner. He'd really needed the time alone to spend in thought and prayer. So at least something good had come from him being alone on Christmas Day, sad as it was.

"I'm sorry you were stranded but glad you're here now," Ken said, clasping Allen's shoulder. "I think you and my daughter need to talk."

Before Allen could respond, Samuel pushed his chair aside and stood. "Since Allen has a place to spend the night, I guess Timothy and I will be on our way. We've been gone quite awhile, and we don't want Esther, Hannah, or our mom to start worrying about us."

"Knowing Hannah, she's probably been worried since the moment we left," Timothy said.

"I'll walk you to the door," Ken offered.

Timothy and Samuel said their good-byes and started out of the kitchen.

"We'll be back to check on you tomorrow, Allen," Samuel called over his shoulder.

"Okay, thanks."

"Would you like another cup of coffee?" Bonnie asked Allen as the other men left.

He nodded. "That'd be nice. I hadn't had anything hot to drink since I lost power at my place."

"Oh, and would you like something more than just the pie to eat? I can fix you some eggs and toast."

"That does sound good, but if you don't mind, I'd like to talk to you first." He glanced toward the door to see if Ken might come back to the kitchen and was relieved when he heard footsteps clomping up the stairs.

"What did you want to talk about?" Bonnie asked, taking a seat across from him.

Allen cleared his throat a few times. "First, I need to apologize for rushing out of here on Christmas Eve without saying goodbye."

Bonnie sat staring at him.

"And second, I want you to know the reason I left."

"I think I already know," she said. "Dad told you about the baby I had when I was a teenager, and you were upset by it, so you went home." Tears welled in her eyes. "You probably think I'm a terrible person now, don't you?"

He shook his head. "We all make mistakes, Bonnie. You were just a confused teenager with no mother to guide you and a father who was struggling to raise you on his own."

She nodded slowly. "But that's still no excuse for what I did. I'd been brought up with good morals, and —" She stopped talking and reached for a napkin to wipe the tears that had dribbled onto her cheeks.

"Beating yourself up about the past won't change anything," Allen said. "And just so you know — the fact that you had a baby out of wedlock wasn't really why I left."

"It . . . it wasn't?"

"No. The main reason I left was because I couldn't deal with you having kept it from me — especially when I'd thought we'd been drawing so close."

"I was planning to tell you, Allen. I just couldn't seem to find the nerve or the right time to say it."

"How come? Did you think I wouldn't want to marry you if I knew about your past?"

"That's exactly what I thought." Bonnie blew her nose on the napkin. "I was afraid you might not want me if you knew what I'd done."

Allen left his chair and skirted around the table. Gently pulling Bonnie to her feet, he whispered, "I love you, Bonnie Taylor, and if you'll have me, I want to be your husband."

"Oh yes, Allen. I'd be honored to marry you," she said tearfully.

A wide smile spread across his face. "I was hoping you'd say that, and I'm also hoping you'll accept this." Allen reached into his jacket pocket and pulled out a small velvet box. When he opened it, Bonnie saw the beautiful diamond ring inside and gasped.

"Oh Allen, it's perfect!"

He removed it from the box and slipped it on her finger then pulled her into his arms.

They stood together for several minutes, holding each other and whispering words of endearment. Then, when Allen's stomach gurgled noisily, Bonnie laughed and pulled away. "I think I'd better give you something more to eat before you starve to death."

Allen chuckled and patted his stomach. "That might be a good idea, because I feel kind of faint. Of course," he quickly added, "it probably has more to do with the excitement I feel about you accepting my proposal than it does with my need for food. It isn't exactly how I wanted to propose; I had this big long speech I'd practiced for days that I was gonna give on Christmas Eve."

She gave him a quick kiss on the cheek. "Your proposal was perfect — simple and sweet. Now, take a seat and relax while I get some bacon and eggs cooking, and then I'll tell you about the woman who showed up here after you left on Christmas Eve."

"The one good thing about being snowed in like this is that it's given us more time to spend with the *kinskinner,*" Abraham said to Fannie as they stood in front of the window in Samuel's guest room, looking out at Marla and Leon, who were in the yard tossing snowballs at each other and giggling.

"You're right about that," she said with a nod. "And even though I miss our grandchildren at home, I've enjoyed being here with Samuel's four kinner and Timothy's little Mindy." She sighed deeply. "It's just too bad they have to live so far away, which means we can't see them very often."

Abraham grunted. "Now, don't waste time on trivial matters."

"It's not a trivial matter to me. I miss my boys and their families."

"I understand that, because so do I, but it won't do any good for you to start feeling sorry for yourself. We'll come here to visit whenever we can, and I'm sure that our boys will bring their families to Pennsylvania as often as they can, too."

"Humph!" Fannie frowned. "I doubt that'll happen too often. With Suzanne most likely expecting a *boppli,* she and Titus will probably stick close to home. And as busy as Samuel seems to be, I'll bet we won't see him before he and Esther are married — whenever that's going to be." She folded her arms. "Then there's Timothy, who might never come back to Pennsylvania to see us."

"What makes you say that?"

"Think about it, Abraham. He moved here to get his wife away from her interfering mamm. If he takes his family home for a visit, Hannah will want to stay, and then Timothy will have an even bigger problem on his hands."

Abraham quirked an eyebrow. "Bigger problem?"

She nudged his arm. "He already has a problem with a wife who does nothing but complain and doesn't want to be here. To tell you the truth, I don't think she wants us here either."

"Now, Fannie, you shouldn't be saying things like that."

"Why not? It's the truth. Hannah's just not accepting of me the way our other daughters-in-law are. She rarely makes conversation, and when she does say something to me, it's usually a negative comment or she's expressing her displeasure with something I've done."

"Now what could you possibly have done to upset Hannah?" he asked.

"For one thing, just a little while ago she became upset when I was about to give Mindy some Christmas candy." Fannie sighed deeply. "It's not like I was going to give her the whole box or anything; it was just one piece."

"Well, Hannah is the child's Mudder, and it's her right to decide when and if Mindy should have candy."

"But it's not fair that Mindy's cousins got to have a piece of candy and she didn't." Fannie moved away from the window. "I wish Timothy had never married Hannah. She's selfish, envious, and too overprotective where Mindy's concerned. She even wanted me to convince Timothy to move back to Pennsylvania."

Abraham's brows shot up. "Really? What'd you say?"

"Told her I couldn't — that Timothy wouldn't appreciate it." Fannie sighed. "You know, Abraham, Timothy and Hannah's marriage is already strained, and it makes me wonder if things will get worse in the days ahead." She clasped Abraham's arm. "I just have this strange feeling about Timothy and Hannah. Of all our Kinner, he's the one I'm the most worried about. Timothy and Hannah certainly need a lot of prayer."

CHAPTER 25

For the next several days, the bad weather prevailed. But by Monday, the snow had finally stopped and the roads were clear enough to drive on, so Abraham, Fannie, and their driver left for home. Hannah felt relieved, because Fannie was beginning to get on her nerves. Not only that, but Samuel's kids had been noisier than usual with their grandparents here, always vying for their attention and begging Abraham for candy, gum, and horsey rides. Mindy had also been whiny and often begged for candy and other things Hannah didn't want her to have. If that wasn't bad enough, it had sickened Hannah to see the way Esther acted around Fannie — so sweet and catering to her every whim. Was she trying to make an impression, or did she really enjoy visiting with Fannie that much?

Maybe it's because Esther's folks live in Pennsylvania, Hannah thought as she stared out the living-room window. *Is it possible that Esther misses her Mamm as much as I do mine?*

"As much as I hate to say this," Timothy said, slipping his arm around Hannah's waist, "Samuel and I have a paint job in Oak Grove this morning, and our driver just pulled in, so I need to get going."

Hannah squinted at the black van. "That doesn't look like Allen's rig."

"You're right; it's not. We won't be working for Allen today. This house is one Samuel lined up on his own, so he called Bob Hastings for a ride because his vehicle is big enough to haul all our painting equipment."

"Oh, I see." Hannah turned to look at Timothy. "Do you have any idea how long you'll be working today?"

He shrugged. "It'll probably be seven or eight before we get back home. Since we've been hired to paint the whole interior of the house and the owners would like it done by the end of the week, we'll need to put in a long day."

Hannah sighed. "It's my turn to cook supper this evening, so would you like me to fix it a little later than usual?"

He shook his head. "You and the kids should go ahead and eat. Maybe you can keep something warm in the oven for Samuel and me, though."

"Sure, I can do that."

When Timothy went out the door, Hannah headed for the kitchen, where Esther was doing the breakfast dishes.

"Would you like me to dry?" Hannah asked.

Esther turned from the sink and smiled. "That'd be nice."

Hannah grabbed a clean dish towel and picked up one of the plates in the dish drainer. "It seems quiet in here with Fannie and Abraham gone, Samuel and Timothy off to work, and Samuel's two oldest kinner at school," she said.

"Jah, but I kind of miss all the excitement."

Hannah couldn't imagine that. She preferred peace and quiet over noise and chaos. She was actually glad Christmas was over.

They worked quietly for a while; then Hannah broke the silence with a question that had been on her mind. "Do you miss not living close to your mamm?"

"Of course I do." Esther placed another clean plate in the drainer. "But I know Mom and Dad are needed in Pennsylvania so they can help my brother and his family. I also know that my place is here."

"How can you be sure of that?"

"Because this is where Samuel lives, and I love him very much."

"So love is what's keeping you here?"

"Jah. That, and the fact that this is my home. I mean, I like it here in Kentucky, but if Samuel wanted to move back to Pennsylvania after we got married, I'd be willing to move there, too."

"So I guess that means I should have been willing to move here because it's what Timothy wanted?" Hannah couldn't keep the sarcasm out of her voice.

"A wife's place is with her husband," Esther said. "It's as simple as that."

Hannah cringed. Maybe a wife's place was with her husband, but wasn't the husband supposed to care about his wife's needs and wishes, too?

"Are you sure you don't mind taking me to the airport this afternoon? I feel bad asking you to drive after the snowy weather we've had these last few days," Bonnie's dad said as the two of them sat in the living room enjoying the warmth of the fireplace.

"Of course I don't mind, and since the roads are pretty well cleared, I'm sure we'll be fine."

"Excuse me," Trisha said, entering the room with her suitcase in hand. "I wanted

249

to let you know that I'm ready to head out, so if you'll print out my bill, I'll settle up with you now."

"Where will you be going from here?" Bonnie asked, leading the way to her desk in the foyer.

"Since my friend and her husband from Bowling Green are still away, I won't be stopping there. So I'll probably head for Virginia and check out some of the sights that I've read about."

"This sure isn't a good time of year to be traveling anywhere by car," Dad called from the other room. "Maybe you should head back to California."

Trisha looked at Bonnie and rolled her eyes. "He always did like to tell me what to do," she whispered.

Bonnie smiled. That didn't surprise her one bit, because Dad was a take-charge kind of guy.

Once Trisha's bill had been taken care of, she stepped into the living room and said good-bye to Dad.

"Have a safe trip," he mumbled.

Trisha hesitated a minute. Then she moved closer to him and said, "It was nice seeing you again, Kenny, and I'm truly sorry for whatever hurt I may have caused you in the past."

"It's Ken, not Kenny," Dad mumbled.

Trisha stood a few seconds, as if waiting for some other response, but when Dad said nothing more, she picked up her suitcase and opened the front door.

"It's been nice meeting you. Feel free to stop by if you're ever in this area again," Bonnie said, stepping onto the porch with Trisha.

Trisha turned and smiled. "I appreciate the offer, but if I do come back this way, I'll be sure and call first. I wouldn't want to be here if your dad's visiting, because it's obvious that I make him feel uncomfortable."

"Well, he needs to get over it and leave the past in the past — forgive and forget. Life's too short to carry grudges, and I plan to talk to him more about that. You just call, no matter what, if you should ever come by this way again."

Trisha gave Bonnie a quick hug then started down the stairs. She was almost to the bottom when her foot slipped on a still-frozen step and down she went.

"What did I go and do now?" Trisha wailed. She tried to get up but was unsuccessful. "Oh, my ankle . . . It hurts so much!"

Bonnie, being careful not to slip herself, made her way down the porch stairs and knelt beside Trisha. After a quick look at Trisha's already swollen ankle, she determined that it could very well be broken. "Stay right where you are," Bonnie said when Trisha once more tried to stand. "I'll get Dad's help, and we'll carry you into the house."

CHAPTER 26

"I can't begin to tell you how much I appreciate you letting me stay here while my ankle heals," Trisha said to Bonnie as she hobbled into the kitchen with the aid of her crutches.

"It's not a problem," Bonnie said. "Since you broke it after falling on my slippery steps, the least I can do is offer you a room free of charge." She motioned to the table. "Now if you'll take a seat, I'll fix you some breakfast."

Trisha still felt bad about imposing on Bonnie like this, but she really did appreciate all she had done for her since she'd fallen two days ago. Bonnie had even gone so far as to call her fiancé, Allen, and ask that he take her dad to the airport so she'd be free to take Trisha to the hospital to have her ankle x-rayed. And when they'd learned that it was broken, Bonnie had stayed with Trisha at the hospital and brought her back here to care for her. It was definitely more than she had expected.

Being with Bonnie was a taste of what it might have been like if Trisha had been able to have children. She'd always longed to be a mother and had wanted to adopt, but Dave wouldn't even discuss that option. He'd said on more than one occasion that if they couldn't have children of their own, then he didn't want any at all. Trisha thought it was selfish of him to feel that way — especially when there were children out there who needed a home. But out of respect for her husband, she'd never pushed the issue. Besides, she'd always felt that a child needed love from both parents.

"Would you like a bowl of oatmeal and some toast this morning?" Bonnie asked, breaking into Trisha's thoughts.

"Yes, thank you; that would be fine." Trisha seated herself at the table and watched helplessly as Bonnie made her breakfast. "I feel like I ought to be doing something to earn my keep," she said.

Bonnie shook her head. "It's no bother, really. I have to fix breakfast for myself, anyway."

"But you've done so much for me already — even giving up your room downstairs and moving into one of your upstairs guest rooms.

"I'm happy to do that. After all, you can't be expected to navigate the stairs with your leg in a cast and having to use crutches."

"I'm just not used to being waited on or pampered," Trisha said. "I've always been pretty independent, and after Dave died, I really had to learn how to fend for myself."

"I understand. Dad was the same way after Mom passed away from a brain tumor."

"How old were you when she died?"

"Thirteen."

"That must have been hard for both you and your dad."

"It was." Bonnie went to the cupboard and took out a box of brown sugar, which she placed on the table. "Mom was a very good cook, and she didn't like anyone in her kitchen, so I never learned to cook well. After she died, Dad and I just kind of muddled by."

"But you obviously learned how to cook somewhere along the line, because that Christmas dinner you fixed was delicious."

Bonnie smiled. "I had a good teacher."

"Who was that?"

"Esther Beiler. When I moved into Grandma and Grandpa's house and decided to open the B&B, Esther came to work for me. At first she did most of the cooking, but then she took the time to teach me." Bonnie moved back to the stove to check on the oatmeal. "Of course, I'll probably never be as good a cook as Esther, because she just has a talent for it."

"Guess everyone has something they're really good at," Trisha said, reaching for two napkins from the basket on the table. She folded them and set them out for the meal.

"That's true. Where do you feel your talents lie?" Bonnie questioned.

"I don't know if I'm as good a cook as Esther, but I used to be the head chef for a restaurant in Fresno, and the customers often raved about some of the dishes I created. So I guess if I have a talent, it's cooking."

"Oh my!" Bonnie's cheeks turned pink. "I had no idea there was a chef who could no doubt cook circles around me sitting at my table on Christmas Day. If I'd known that, I probably would have been a complete wreck."

Trisha laughed. "I've never considered myself anything more than someone who likes to cook, so you really don't need to worry about whether anything you fix measures up."

"That's good to know, because the oatmeal's a little too dry. I probably didn't put enough water in the kettle."

Trisha waved her hand. "Don't worry about that. It's funny, but whenever someone else does the cooking, no matter what it is, the food always tastes so much better. I used to tell my husband that his toast was the best-tasting toast I'd ever eaten. Anyway, a pat of butter and some milk poured over the top, and I'm sure the oatmeal will be plenty moist."

"I know exactly what you mean about someone else's cooking. It's kind of like eating outdoors. When does the food taste any better than that?" Bonnie set two bowls on the table and took a seat. "No wonder my dad fell so hard for you when you were teenagers. You're a very nice woman, Trisha Chandler."

Trisha smiled. "Thanks. I think you're pretty nice, too."

When breakfast was over and Trisha was resting comfortably on the living-room sofa, Bonnie did the dishes. She'd just finished and was about to mop the kitchen floor when Esther showed up.

"I'm surprised to see you," Bonnie said.

"I figured you'd be over at Samuel's by now."

"I told Hannah last night that I'd be coming over late because I had some errands to run," Esther said. "To tell you the truth, I think she was glad."

"Are things still strained between you two?"

"A bit, although I believe they are somewhat better. We've been talking more lately, and I think that's helped."

Bonnie smiled. "I'm glad. You should bring Hannah and the little ones over to see me again. Maybe Suzanne would like to come, too."

"That sounds like fun. And speaking of Suzanne, I found out yesterday that she and Titus are expecting a baby. She's due sometime in August."

Bonnie squealed. "Now that is good news! I'm sure everyone in Suzanne's family must be very excited."

"They are, and so are Titus's parents. We suspected it when they were here for Christmas, and when Titus called his folks and told them the official news, they were delighted."

"I'm sorry I didn't get to see Abraham and Fannie while they were here this time," Bonnie said. "I enjoyed meeting them when they came for Titus and Suzanne's wedding. They seem like a very nice couple."

"They are, and I look forward to having them as in-laws."

"How soon will that be?" Bonnie asked, taking a seat at the table and motioning for Esther to do the same.

Esther lowered herself into a chair. "I don't know. Samuel would get married tomorrow if it was possible, but I really think we should wait until Hannah and Timothy have found a place of their own."

"I understand, but what if it's a long time before they find a place? Will you change your mind and marry Samuel anyway?"

Esther shrugged. "I don't know. Guess I'll have to wait and see how it all goes." She reached over and touched Bonnie's arm. "Speaking of weddings, have you and Allen set a date for your wedding yet?"

"Not a definite one, but we're hoping sometime in the spring."

"I've never been to an English wedding before, so I hope I'll get an invitation."

"Would you be allowed to go? I mean, it's not against your church rules or anything, is it?"

Esther emitted a small laugh. "No, it's not."

"Then you'll definitely get an invitation.

In fact, I'm sure Allen will want to invite all our Amish friends."

"Will Allen sell his house and move here to the bed-and-breakfast, or will you sell this place and move into his house with him?"

"We haven't actually discussed that. And you know, until this minute, I hadn't even given it a thought." Bonnie's forehead wrinkled as she mulled things over. "I sure would hate to give up this place, and I do hope Allen doesn't ask me to."

"I don't think he will. He knows how much you enjoy running the B&B."

"That may be so, but some men expect their wives to do things they don't really want to do. Take Hannah, for instance. She didn't want to move to Kentucky, but Timothy insisted."

"And with good reason," Esther said. "He had to get Hannah away from her mother in order to make her see that her first priority was to him."

Bonnie's lips compressed. "Hmm . . . I wonder if Allen will make me choose between him and the bed-and-breakfast."

Hannah had just sent Marla and Leon off to school when she looked out the kitchen window and spotted Suzanne's horse and buggy pull into the yard. A few minutes later, there was a knock on the door.

"Brr . . . It's cold out there," Suzanne said after Hannah opened the door and let her in.

"Do you think it's going to snow again?" Hannah asked.

"I don't believe so. The sky's clear with no clouds in sight, so that's a good thing."

"After that blizzard we had, I don't care if I ever see another snowflake," Hannah said.

Suzanne laughed. "I'm with you, but I think the kinner might not agree."

"So what brings you by here this morning?"

"I need to go to the store to pick up a few things, and since Samuel's place is right on the way, I decided to stop by and see how you're doing."

Hannah could hardly believe Suzanne would ask how she was doing. No one else seemed to care — least of all Timothy. "I'm okay," she murmured. "How about you? I heard you've been having some morning sickness."

"That's true, and I felt nauseous when I first got up today, but after I ate something and had a cup of mint tea, it got better." Suzanne removed her shawl and black outer bonnet then placed them on an empty chair before taking a seat.

"Would you like something to drink?" Hannah asked. "There's some coffee on the stove, or I could brew a pot of tea."

"No thanks. I'm fine."

Hannah was tempted to start washing the dishes but figured that could wait. The idea of visiting with Suzanne a few minutes seemed appealing, so she also took a seat. "I remember when I was expecting Mindy, for the first three months I felt nauseous most of the day. After a while, it got better though."

"Speaking of Mindy, where is she right now? She's so sweet. I was hoping I'd get to see her today."

"She's still sleeping, and so are Jared and Penny."

"Now, that's a surprise. I figured they'd all be up, running all over the house by now."

Hannah frowned. "Those kids of Samuel's are just too active."

"They do have a lot of energy," Suzanne agreed. "But then I guess most kinner do." She placed her hand against her stomach. "I know I have seven more months until the boppli is born, but Titus and I can hardly wait for our little one to get here."

"Are you hoping for a *bu* or a *maedel?*"

"I think Titus would like a boy, but I don't really care what we have; I just want the baby to be healthy."

Hannah cringed, remembering the miscarriage she'd had last year. *I wish the baby we lost would have gone to full-term and been healthy. I wish I was pregnant right now.*

CHAPTER 27

"Get your coat; there's something I want to show you," Timothy said to Hannah one Saturday morning toward the end of January, when he entered the kitchen and found her doing the dishes.

"What is it?" she asked, turning to look at him.

"It's a house I want you to look at."

"Is it for sale?"

He nodded. "Samuel and I spotted the FOR SALE sign yesterday on our way home from work."

"How come you didn't mention it last night?"

"Because I knew we couldn't look at it until this morning, and I didn't want you bombarding me with a bunch of questions I couldn't answer till I knew more about the house."

She flicked some water at him. "I wouldn't have bombarded you with questions."

"Jah, you would." He dipped his fingers into the soapy water and flicked some water back in her direction, enjoying the playful moment — especially since things were so up and down between him and Hannah.

She moved quickly aside. "Hey! Stop that!"

He chuckled. "I figured if you wanted me to have a second shower of the day, then you'd probably want one, too."

"I don't think either of us needs another shower, but I do want to see that house. So let me finish up here, and we can be on our way." She paused, and tiny wrinkles formed across her forehead. "Will Samuel be able to watch Mindy, or do we need to take her along?"

"I've already talked to him about it, and he said he's fine with watching her, since he'll be here with his kinner anyway."

"Okay, great. I'll just be a few more minutes."

Timothy leaned over and kissed Hannah's cheek. She'd been so sullen since their move. It was good to see her get excited about something. He just hoped she wouldn't lose her enthusiasm once she saw the house he was interested in buying.

Bonnie had just finished feeding the chickens when she spotted Allen's truck coming up the driveway. She'd spoken to him on the phone several times but hadn't seen him for a while because he'd been so busy with work and bidding new jobs. It was amazing that he'd have so much work to do at this time of the year, but she was glad for him, as she knew many others were out of work.

"It's good to see you," she said when he stepped out of the truck and joined her near the chicken coop.

He leaned down and gave her a kiss. "It's good to see you, too. Are you busy right now? I'd like to talk to you about something."

"I've got the time, but let's go inside where it's warmer."

He smiled and took her hand. "That sounds like a plan, but I'd like to talk to you in private, and I know Trisha's still with you right now, so I thought maybe we could go for a ride."

"Trisha came down with a cold and is in her room resting."

"Sorry to hear she's not feeling well." Allen flashed Bonnie a look of concern. "I hope you don't get sick, too. You've been doing extra duty taking care of her since she broke her ankle, so your resistance might be low right now."

"I'm fine," she said as they strode hand in hand toward the house. "I take vitamins, eat healthy foods, and try to get at least eight hours of sleep every night."

He squeezed her fingers gently. "That's good to hear."

When they entered the house, the smell of something burning greeted them.

"Oh, no . . . my cookies!" Bonnie raced into the kitchen and opened the oven door. The entire batch of oatmeal cookies looked like lumps of charcoal. "That's what I get for thinking I could multitask," she muttered. "I figured I'd be finished feeding the chickens in plenty of time before the cookies were done."

Allen stepped up behind Bonnie and put his arms around her waist. "It's my fault for keeping you out there so long."

"It's okay. I have more cookie dough in the refrigerator, but I'll wait until after our talk before I make any more." Bonnie turned off the oven and took the burned cookies out. "I think I'll set these on the back porch so they don't smell up the house more than they already have. I can crumble them up later for the birds. I'm sure they'll eat them."

"Here, let me do that." Allen picked up another pot holder, took the cookie sheet from her, and went out the back door. When he returned, Bonnie had a cup of coffee waiting for him, and they both took seats at the table.

"So what'd you want to talk to me about?" she asked.

He reached for her hand. "Now that we're officially engaged, I think it's time we decide on a wedding date, don't you?"

She smiled. "Yes, I do."

"So how about Valentine's Day?"

Her eyebrows shot up. "Oh Allen, I could never prepare for a wedding that soon. Valentine's Day is just a couple of weeks away."

His shoulders drooped. "I figured you'd say that, but I'm anxious to marry you, and you can't blame a guy for trying."

She giggled. "I'd really like to have a church wedding and invite all our friends — Amish and English alike. Of course, my dad and your folks will also be invited, and we'll need to give them enough time to plan for the trip."

"That's true. So how long do you think it'll take for us to plan this wedding?"

"How about if we get married in the middle of May? The weather should be pretty nice by then, and we could have the reception here — maybe outside in the yard."

"That would mean a lot of work for you, making sure everything looks just the way you want it."

"I'm sure some of our Amish friends will help me spruce up the yard, and I'll ask Esther to make the cake and help with all the other food we decide to have."

He leaned closer and kissed the end of her nose. "Sounds like you've got it all figured out."

"Not really, but I'm sure it'll all come together as the planning begins." She paused and moistened her lips, searching for the right words to ask him a question. "There's something else we haven't talked about, Allen."

"What's that?"

"Where we're going to live once we're married."

"Oh, that." He raked his fingers through the ends of his thick, dark hair. "I'm guessing you don't want to give up the B&B?"

She shook her head. "This place has come to mean a lot to me. But I suppose if you don't want to live here —"

He put his finger against her lips. "I have no objections to living in this wonderful old house with you. After all, I did have a little something to do with making it as nice as it is." He winked at her.

"Yes, you sure did." Bonnie tapped her fingers along the edge of the table. "But what about your house? I know you built it to your own specifications, and —"

"It's just a house, Bonnie. I can be happy living anywhere as long as I'm with you."

She gently stroked his cheek, not even caring that it felt a bit stubbly. "I'm a lucky woman to be engaged to such a wonderful man."

"No, I'm the lucky one," he said before giving her a heart-melting kiss.

"How far away is this place?" Hannah asked when she stepped outside and found Timothy standing beside their horse and buggy. "I figured we'd have to hire a driver to take us there."

"Nope. It's just a few miles from here."

"That's good to hear." Hannah wasn't thrilled with the idea of living too far from Timothy's brothers and their families. She figured Timothy would be excited to hear that from her, but for some reason she wasn't ready to share those new feelings just yet. She had to admit, if only to herself, that since she'd gotten to know Esther and Suzanne better, she wanted to be close enough so they could visit whenever they wanted to.

"We'd better get going," Timothy said, helping her into the buggy. "I told the real estate agent we'd meet him there at nine o'clock."

With a renewed sense of excitement, Hannah leaned back in her seat and tried to relax. If they could get this house, they might be able to move out of Samuel's place within the next few weeks.

As they traveled down the road, Timothy talked about how much he was enjoying painting with his brother, and then he told Hannah that the place they'd be looking at had fifty acres, which meant he could do some farming if he had a mind to.

Hannah knew he'd enjoyed farming with his dad in Pennsylvania, but if he was going to keep working full-time for Samuel, she didn't see how he'd have time to do any farming. Maybe they could lease some of the land and only farm a few acres for themselves. She kept her thoughts to herself though. No point in bringing that up when they didn't even know if they'd be buying the house.

A short time later, Timothy guided the horse and buggy down a long dirt driveway with a wooden fence on either side. A rambling old house came into view. It looked like it hadn't been painted in a good many years, but Hannah knew Timothy could take care of that. What concerned her was that the shutters hung loose, the front porch sagged, the roof had missing shingles, and several of the windows were broken. If that wasn't bad enough, the whole yard was overgrown with weeds.

"Ach, my!" she gasped. "This place is an absolute dump! Surely you don't expect us to live here!"

CHAPTER 28

Timothy's mind whirled as he groped for something positive to say about the house before Hannah insisted that they turn around and head back to Samuel's place.

"Listen, Hannah," he said, clasping her arm, "I think we need to wait till we've seen the inside of the house before drawing any conclusions. Let's try to keep an open mind — at least for now."

She wrinkled her nose. "If the inside looks even half as bad as the outside does, then I'm not moving here."

"Well, let's go inside and take a look. I see the agent's car over there, so he's probably in the house waiting for us."

Hannah sighed. "Okay, but where are you going to tie the horse? I don't see a hitching rail, which probably means this house belongs to an Englisher."

"That may be, but if we buy the place, we can put up a hitching post, and of course we'll have to remove the electrical connections." He directed Dusty over to a tree. "I'll tie my horse here, and he should be fine for the short time we'll be inside the house."

When they stepped onto the porch a few minutes later, Timothy cringed and took hold of Hannah's hand. There were several loose boards — the kind that looked like if you stepped on them the wrong way, they'd fly up and hit you on the back of the head. The porch railing was broken in a couple of places, too.

"I know this porch looks really bad right now, but imagine if the boards and railing were replaced and it was freshly painted," Timothy said with as much enthusiasm as he could muster. "And look, the front of the house faces east. Think of all the beautiful sunrises we can watch from here on warm summer mornings."

"I guess that's one way of looking at it," Hannah said in a guarded tone.

Timothy was about to knock on the door when it swung open. Tom Donnelson greeted them with a smile. "It's good to see you both again. Come on in; I'm anxious to show you around."

As they entered the living room, where faded blue curtains hung at the window,

Tom explained that the elderly man who'd owned the house had recently passed away, and his children, who lived in another state, had just put the place on the market. He then took them upstairs, through all five bedrooms, each needing a coat of fresh paint, and pointed out that there was an attic above the second story that would give them plenty of storage. The wide woodwork around the floor base, as well as the frames around the doors, were impressive, but they were badly scratched and needed to be sanded and restained.

When they got to the kitchen, Hannah's mouth dropped open. Timothy was sure she was going to flee from the house in horror. Not only did it need to be painted, but the sink was rusty from where the faucet had been leaking, the linoleum was torn in several places, the counter had multiple dings, and some of the hinges on the cabinet doors were broken. An old electric stove and refrigerator sat side-by-side and would need to be replaced. Most of the rooms had been wallpapered with several layers that had been put on over the years. So before any painting could be done, the walls would have to be stripped clean.

"I think this old house has some potential," Tom said. "It just needs a bit of a face-lift."

"A bit of a face-lift?" Hannah exclaimed with raised brows. "If you want my opinion, I'd say it needs to be condemned." She turned to Timothy and frowned. "Don't you agree?"

He shrugged his shoulders. "I know it's hard to see, but if you could just look past the way the house looks right now and imagine how it could look with some re-modeling —"

"But that would take a lot of time, and probably a lot of money, too," she argued.

"I'll bet with the help of Samuel and Titus we could have this place fixed up and ready to move into by spring."

"The beginning of spring or the end of spring?" she questioned.

He turned his hands palms up. "I don't know. Guess we'd have to wait and see how it all goes."

Hannah's dubious expression made Timothy think she was going to refuse to even consider buying the house, but to his surprise, she turned to him and said, "If you really think you can make this place livable, then let's put an offer on it."

"Are you sure?"

She nodded.

"All right then." Timothy looked at Tom. "Can we do that right now?"

Tom gave a nod. "There's no time like the present. Let's head over to Samuel's house, and we can discuss a fair offer, and then you can sign the papers."

That afternoon after Timothy and Hannah got back to Samuel's house and shared the news that they hoped to buy the house they'd looked at, Samuel decided to head over to the B&B and tell Esther. This was not only good news for Timothy and Hannah, but for him and Esther, as well, because it meant they could be married soon.

"Can we go with you, Daadi?" Leon asked as Samuel took his horse out of the barn. "We haven't gone over to play with Cody in a long time."

"And since Esther didn't come over here today, she's probably busy bakin' cookies," Marla added as she joined her younger brother. She licked her lips. "Sure would like some of those."

"I suppose you can go along, but Jared and Penny will probably want to go, too, and if they both go, then Mindy will want to be included, and I'm not sure Hannah will go for that."

"Can we at least ask?" Leon looked up at Samuel with pleading eyes. "If Aunt Hannah says Mindy can't go, then just the four of us will go with ya, okay?"

"Jah, and then Mindy will cry. You know she will." Marla frowned. "She's a whiny baby, and besides that she's spoiled."

Samuel reached under the brim of his hat and scratched his head. "You think so?"

"Sure do," Marla said with a nod.

"Hmm . . . Seems to me that Hannah's always telling Mindy no about something or other," Samuel said. "So I wouldn't call that spoiled."

"Mindy may not get everything she wants, but she's a big mama's baby, and Aunt Hannah's always fussin' over her," Leon interjected.

For fear that whatever he said might get repeated, Samuel didn't agree with the children, but he didn't disagree either. Truth was, he got tired of watching the way Hannah doted on Mindy, but if Timothy didn't say anything to his wife about it, then it wasn't Samuel's place to comment. He'd watched Esther with his children many times and was glad she didn't smother them with too much attention. He knew she loved them very much and felt sure that she'd make a good wife and mother.

"I'll tell you what," Samuel said, looking at Leon. "You run into the house and tell Aunt Hannah that you, Marla, Penny, and

Jared are going over to see Esther with me, and if she doesn't mind, Mindy is welcome to come along."

"Okay. I'll be back soon!" Leon raced across the yard and into the house.

Samuel bent and gave Marla a hug. "You can get in the buggy if you want to."

"Okay, Daadi." Without waiting for Samuel's assistance, Marla climbed into the buggy and took a seat in the back.

He smiled. His oldest daughter was such a sweet little girl. In many ways she reminded him of Elsie. How glad he was that Marla and Leon had both been old enough when their mother died so they would have some memories of her as they grew up. Penny might remember some, too, but little Jared would only know whatever he was told about his mother. At least the children had Esther, and in fact, Jared and Penny often called her "Mama." Samuel had no problem with that.

Hearing the sound of laughter, Samuel glanced toward the house. Leon, Penny, and Jared, wearing straw hats, jackets, and scarves, pranced like three little ponies across the lawn. When they reached the buggy, they grabbed hold of Samuel's legs and squeezed.

"We can head out now, Daadi," Leon said.

"Hannah said Mindy can't go."

"I figured as much," Samuel mumbled before lifting Penny and Jared into the buggy. *It's a shame Mindy couldn't join us,* he fumed. *Hannah is way too protective of that child.*

Leon climbed in last and took a seat up front on the passenger's side. "Hold the reins steady now while I untie my horse from the hitching rail," Samuel told the boy.

When Samuel took his seat on the driver's side, Leon handed him the reins and smiled. "Sure can't wait to play with Cody!"

Paradise, Pennsylvania

As Sally meandered up their driveway after getting the mail, she decided to stop at the phone shack and see if there were any new messages. She'd just stepped inside when she heard the phone ring, so she quickly grabbed the receiver. "Hello."

"Hi, Mom. This is a pleasant surprise. I wasn't expecting anyone to pick up the phone."

"Hannah, it's so good to hear your voice! How are you? How are Mindy and Timothy doing?"

"We're all fine. Mindy's taking a nap, and Timothy's in the house with our real estate agent, going over the paperwork we need to sign."

"Paperwork?"

"Jah. We found a house today, and we're going to put an offer on it."

"Wow, that was quick."

"Jah, quick as dew."

"I guess that means you'll be staying in Kentucky?" Sally couldn't keep the disappointment she felt out of her voice.

"That's what Timothy wants, so I suppose we are."

Sally had expected Hannah to say she didn't want to stay in Kentucky, like she had so many other times when they'd talked. Maybe she'd resigned herself to the idea, knowing it was the only way to keep her husband happy.

"So tell me about the house. Is it close to where Timothy's brothers live?" Sally asked.

"It's just a few miles down the road from Samuel's place and not far from Titus's home either."

"Is it nice and big?"

"It's big, but . . . well, not so nice. In fact, it needs a whole lot of work."

Sally grimaced. "If it needs a lot of work, then why are you buying the place?"

"Because it's reasonably priced, and Timothy thinks he can have it fixed up enough so we can move in sometime this spring. With him and his brothers doing most of the work, it will save us a lot of money, too."

"I see."

"You and Dad will have to visit us after we get moved in. There are five bedrooms, so there's plenty of room for us to have company."

"Jah, we'll have to do that."

"How's Dad's back? Is he doing a lot better now?"

"He's working a few days a week at the store again but still has to be careful not to overdo. He had quite a siege with his back this time."

"I'm glad he's doing better." Hannah paused. "It's been good talking to you, Mom, but I'd better hang up now. I need to check on Mindy and see if the paperwork is ready to sign."

"Okay. Take care, Hannah, and please keep in touch."

"I will. Bye, Mom."

When Sally hung up the phone, a sick feeling came over her. Now that Timothy and Hannah were buying a house, she was almost certain they would never move back to Pennsylvania. If only there was something she could do to bring her daughter back home where she belonged. But what would it be?

With the mail in her hand and a heavy heart weighing her down, Sally trudged wearily toward the house. When she stepped inside, she found Johnny sitting in the recliner with a fat gray cat in his lap.

"You know I don't like that critter in the house," Sally snapped. "She gets hair everywhere!"

"I'm not letting her run all over the place, Sally. As you can see, I'm holding Fluffy in my lap."

Sally ground her teeth together, not even bothering to mention that there was cat hair clinging to her husband's pants, and tossed the mail onto the coffee table in front of the sofa. "I just spoke with Hannah on the phone, and guess what?"

"I have no idea." Johnny stroked the cat behind its ears and stared up at Sally with a smug expression. It only fueled her anger, watching more cat hair fly each time Johnny petted the feline.

"Hannah and Timothy are buying a house."

"That's good to hear. Samuel's been nice in letting them stay with him, but they really do need a place of their own."

Sally stepped directly in front of Johnny,

her hands on her hips. "Don't you realize what this means?"

"Jah. It means they'll have a place of their own where we can stay when we go to visit."

She clenched her teeth so hard her jaw started to ache. "It means they aren't moving back to Pennsylvania. They wouldn't be buying a house unless they planned to put down roots and stay in Kentucky."

"I think you're right about that, and it's probably for the best."

"What's that supposed to mean?"

"It means Timothy moving his family to Kentucky was the best thing he could have done for his marriage." Johnny stared at Sally over the top of his glasses, as if daring her to argue with him. "We've been through all this before, but I'm going to remind you once more that the Good Book says when a couple gets married, they are to leave their parents." Johnny let go of the cat and spread his arms wide. "And they are to cleave to each other. Leave and cleave!" He brought his hands together quickly and made a tight fist. "And that's the end of that, no matter what you may think."

CHAPTER 29

Pembroke, Kentucky

As soon as Samuel pulled his horse and buggy into Bonnie's yard, Cody leaped off the porch and darted into the yard to greet them. The children were barely out of the buggy when the dog was upon them, yapping excitedly and leaping into the air.

"Calm down, Cody," Samuel scolded, snapping his fingers at the dog. He remembered how once last year Cody had gotten his horse riled up and the critter ended up getting kicked pretty bad. The end result was a broken leg for the dog. Samuel sure didn't want anything like that to happen again.

"Take the dog over there to play," Samuel told Marla as he pointed to the other side of the yard. "That way he won't get kicked by the horse like he did last year."

She bent down and grabbed Cody's collar then led him across the yard. The other children quickly followed.

Samuel secured his horse to the hitching rail and hurried up to the house. He was about to knock when the door opened and Bonnie stepped out.

"Oh, it's you and the children. I heard Cody barking and wondered what all the commotion was about."

Samuel chuckled. "Yeah, that critter can get pretty worked up sometimes — especially when my kids come around."

Bonnie smiled. "Maybe the kids would like to come in for some cookies and hot chocolate."

"I don't know about the kids, but I'd like some." Samuel jiggled his eyebrows playfully, which was easy to do because of his good mood. "I'd like to talk to Esther first, though. Is she here or at the guesthouse?"

"She's upstairs right now, cleaning one of the rooms. I have some guests checking in later today." Bonnie motioned to the stairs. "Feel free to go on up if you'd like to talk to her, and then when you're done, you can join me and the kids in the kitchen for a snack."

"Sounds good to me." Samuel hung his jacket and hat on the coat tree in the entryway and sprinted up the stairs, hearing his kids squealing with delight as Bonnie called them in for a snack. He found Esther in one of the guest rooms sweeping the floor.

"Guder mariye," he said, stepping into the room.

Esther jumped. "Ach, Samuel, you startled me! I didn't realize you were here."

"Sorry about that. I'm surprised you didn't hear my noisy boots clomping up the stairs," he said.

"Well, I did, but I thought it was Bonnie."

"Bonnie has loud-clomping boots?"

Esther giggled, and her cheeks turned a pretty pink. "Her snow boots are a bit loud, but since we don't have any snow right now, I guess she wouldn't have been wearing any boots."

Samuel grinned. Esther looked so sweet when she looked up at him, almost like an innocent little schoolgirl. His heart ached to marry her, but he was trying to be patient.

"So what are you doing here?" she asked, setting her broom aside.

"Came to see you, of course." He took a few steps toward Esther. "I wanted to share some *gut noochricht.*"

"What's the good news?"

"Timothy and Hannah are buying a house. Their real estate agent's at my place right now, and they're signing papers to make an offer on the place. If their offer's accepted, they hope to be moved in by spring." He moved closer and took Esther's hand. "So you know what that means?"

"I guess it means Hannah will be happy to be living in a place of her own, where she won't have to share a kitchen or worry about anyone giving Mindy too much candy."

"That's probably true, but what it means for us is that once they're moved into their own home, we can get married."

"But what if their offer's not accepted?"

"I think it will be. It's a fair offer, and Tom Donnelson told Timothy that the owner of the house has passed on, and his adult children are anxious to sell the place."

"If they're so anxious to sell, then why would it take until spring before Timothy and Hannah can move in?" Esther questioned.

"The place is pretty run-down, and it's going to take a few months to get it fixed up so it's livable." Samuel gave Esther's fingers a gentle squeeze. "But if Titus and I help with the renovations, I think we can have it done in record time."

"I believe you could. It didn't take long for you and Allen to fix this old place up, so I'm sure with three very capable brothers working on Timothy's place, it could be done in no time at all." Esther's eyes sparkled as she smiled widely. "Oh Samuel, after all these months of waiting to become your wife, I can hardly believe we could actually be married in just a few months." Her face sobered. "I think it's best if we don't set a definite date yet, though — just in case the owners of the house don't accept Timothy and Hannah's offer."

Samuel pulled Esther into his arms and gave her a hug. "I'm sure it'll all work out, but we can wait to set a date until we know something definite. Now, why don't you take a break from working and come downstairs with me? Bonnie's promised to serve hot chocolate and cookies to me and the kids, and I'd like you to join us."

"I'm almost done here. Just let me finish sweeping the floor, and I'll come right down."

"Okay, but you might want to hurry. The kinner are in the kitchen with Bonnie, already enjoying those kichlin, and I'm going down now and make sure there are some left for us." Smiling, and feeling like a kid himself, Samuel gave her a quick kiss and hurried from the room.

Esther smiled as she finished sweeping the floor. Did she dare hope that she and Samuel could be married in a few months — or at least by early summer? Of course, she'd need a few months to make her wedding dress and plan for the wedding. Since Samuel was a widower, they wouldn't have nearly as large a wedding as younger couples who'd never been married. But there would still be some planning to do.

Oh, I wish Mom could be here to help me prepare for the wedding, Esther thought wistfully. *But it wouldn't be fair to ask her to come when she's needed to help Sarah care for Dan.*

Esther knew she could probably count on Suzanne to help with wedding details, but with Suzanne being pregnant and possibly not feeling well by then, she might not be able to help that much.

I could ask Bonnie, but then she has her own wedding to plan for, and I'm sure that's going to take up a lot of her time. Then there's Hannah, but I'm not sure she'd even want to help — especially now that they may be buying a house that needs a lot of work.

Even though Hannah had been a bit friendlier to Esther lately, she still kept a little wall around her — like she didn't want anyone to get really close. Esther hoped that wall would come down someday, because she still wanted to be Hannah's friend.

I'd better wait and see first if Hannah and Timothy get that house. Then I can begin planning my wedding and decide who to ask for help.

Once Esther finished sweeping, she emptied the dustpan into the garbage can she'd placed in the hall and went downstairs to join everyone for a snack. She didn't realize how hungry she'd gotten.

She'd just stepped into the kitchen, where Samuel and his children sat at the table, when the telephone rang.

"Hello. Bonnie's Bed-and-Breakfast," Bonnie said after she'd picked up the receiver. There was a pause; then she said, "As a matter of fact, Esther is right here. Would you like to speak with her?" She handed Esther the phone. "It's your mother."

With a sense of excitement, Esther took the phone. "Mom, I was just thinking about you. I wanted to tell you that —"

"Esther, your daed's in the hospital." Mom's voice quavered. "They've been treating him for a ruptured appendix, and now he's in surgery."

Esther gasped. "Ach, Mom, that's *baremlich!* I'll either hire a driver or catch the bus, but I'll be there as soon as I can."

"What's terrible?" Samuel asked when Esther hung up the phone.

She relayed all that her mother had said and then asked Bonnie if she could have some time off.

"Of course you can," Bonnie was quick to say. "Other than the guests coming in later today, I have no one else booked until Valentine's Day."

Esther looked at Samuel. "Do you think Hannah would be willing to take over full responsibility of your kinner and all the household chores until I get back from Pennsylvania?"

"I'm sure she will," Samuel said. "And if she's not, then I'll find someone else to help out. Your place is with your family right now."

Esther smiled, appreciating the understanding of both Samuel and Bonnie. She felt sick hearing about Dad's ruptured appendix, knowing how serious something like that could be. She closed her eyes and sent up a quick prayer. *Lord, please help my daed to be okay.*

CHAPTER 30

A ray of sunlight beckoned Hannah to the window in Marla's bedroom, where she'd been cleaning. Esther had only been gone a week, and already Hannah was exhausted. Samuel's children were a handful — especially Jared, who was a lot more active than Mindy. Hannah never knew what the little stinker might get into, and she had to stay on her toes to keep up with him. Jared was also a picky eater, often refusing to eat whatever she'd fixed for meals. Esther had usually made him something he liked, but Hannah felt that Jared could either eat what was on his plate or do without. She figured in time he'd learn to eat what the others ate, even if he didn't particularly like it.

Then there was all the extra cleaning she had to do. It seemed that no matter how many times she got after the children to pick up in their rooms, they just ignored her. Penny and Jared were the worst, often scattering toys all over the place. It was either nag them to clean up or do it herself, which was what she was doing today. She was glad Marla and Leon were both in school, and she'd put the three younger ones down for a nap. It was easier to get things done when they weren't underfoot. Hannah often found herself wishing Esther hadn't gone to Pennsylvania, because she now realized that it had been much easier to share the work.

Hannah sighed and bent to pick up one of Marla's soiled dresses that should have been put in the laundry basket. The only good thing that had happened this week was that the offer she and Timothy had made on the old house had been accepted. So she could now look forward to the day when they'd be able to move in. As soon as the deal closed, which should happen in a few weeks, Timothy would begin working on the interior. He and his brothers would take care of exterior work as well, but most of those renovations could be done once they were moved in.

Samuel had heard from Esther a few days ago, giving him an update on her dad's condition. Even though he'd made it through surgery okay, there'd been a lot of infection in his body, and he was still in the hospital being carefully watched and getting heavy doses of antibiotics. The family had been told that he'd probably be there at least another week. After that, he would need a good four to eight weeks for a full recovery. So Esther had decided that she would stay and take over the stands her dad had been managing at two of the farmers' markets in the area. The stands really belonged to Esther's brother, but with Dan's MS symptoms getting worse, he certainly couldn't manage them anymore. Esther's mother probably could have taken over the stands, but she felt Dan's wife needed her help to care for their home and two children, as well as Dan.

As Hannah moved across the room to make Marla's bed, her thoughts went to Bonnie. *I wonder how she's managing without Esther's help.*

Hannah knew the woman from California was still at the B&B because her ankle wasn't completely healed. No doubt, having her there created more work for Bonnie. She probably felt as overwhelmed as Hannah did right now.

"I was wondering if you've heard anything from Esther," Trisha said when Bonnie joined her in the living room in front of the fireplace.

"Her father is still quite sick, and Esther plans to stay in Pennsylvania and take care of the stands he's been running. It could be up to eight weeks before she returns to Kentucky," Bonnie said.

"So who will take her place helping you here at the bed-and-breakfast?"

Bonnie shrugged. "I don't know. If things get too busy, I'll probably have to place a help-wanted ad in the local newspaper."

"I could help. I'm getting tired of sitting around so much, so it would give me something meaningful to do."

Bonnie's eyes widened. "But your leg's still in the cast, and once you get it off, you'll need physical therapy. I sure can't expect you to climb the stairs and service the guest rooms."

"I could do some of the cooking. I'm pretty good at that, even if I do say so myself."

Bonnie folded her arms and leaned against the bookcase behind her. "That's right. Since you used to work as a chef, I'll bet you could create some pretty tasty dishes for my B&B guests."

Trisha nodded. "I could make them as fancy or simple as you like. I'd even be happy to work for my room and board."

Bonnie shook her head. "If you're going

to work for me, then I insist on paying you a fair wage, as well as giving you room and board. I was doing that for Esther, you know."

Trisha smiled as a sense of excitement welled in her chest. Maybe God had sent her here on Christmas Eve for a reason. She might even end up staying in Kentucky permanently. Of course if she did, she'd no doubt be seeing Bonnie's dad again.

Would I mind that? she asked herself. *Maybe not.*

CHAPTER 31

By the middle of February, Timothy and his
brothers had done a lot of work on the
house. If things went well, they hoped to
have it fixed up enough so that Timothy,
Hannah, and Mindy could move in by the
middle of March, even if some things still
needed to be done. Hannah thought she
could live with that — as long as it didn't
take too much time to finish the house after
the move. She was so anxious to have her
own place.

On this Saturday, Timothy and Titus were
working at the house while Samuel went to
Hopkinsville to run some errands. Hannah,
tired of being cooped up in Samuel's house
with five active children, decided to bundle
the kids up and go over to her house to see
how things were progressing. She'd also
made the men some sandwiches because
they'd left early this morning before she'd
had a chance to fix them anything for lunch.

"You're the oldest, so I want you to keep an eye on the other children and wait here in the house while I get the horse and buggy ready," Hannah told Marla.

Marla looked up at her with a dimpled grin. "Okay, Aunt Hannah. I'll watch 'em real good."

Hannah patted Marla's shoulder. Of all Samuel's children, Marla was the easiest to deal with. She was usually quite agreeable and seemed eager to please. She was also the calmest child, which Hannah appreciated, because Samuel's other three could think of more things to get into than a batch of curious kittens. She did notice, though, that Marla had a funny habit. Every so often, the child put her hand inside the opposite sleeve of her dress, as if hiding it or maybe trying to warm it up. No one else mentioned this or seemed to take notice, and Hannah didn't spend much time wondering about it herself. *After all, I used to chew my fingernails when I was a girl.* Fortunately, she gave up the habit before she reached her teen years, so she figured Marla would probably do the same.

"I shouldn't be too long, but give me a holler if you need anything," Hannah said before going out the back door.

Since the buggy was already parked in the

yard, all she had to do was get her horse. When Hannah entered Lilly's stall, the horse flicked her ears and swished her tail.

"Would you like to go for a ride, girl?" Hannah patted the horse's flanks. "You need the exercise, or you'll get fat and end up in lazy land." She smiled to herself, remembering how Mom had often used that term to describe someone who didn't want to work.

Lilly whinnied in response and nuzzled Hannah's hand. She was glad they had been able to bring both of their horses when they'd moved. Having them here was a like a touch from home. Hannah glanced at the other side of the barn where all their furniture had been stacked under some canvas tarps. Once they could bring their belongings to the new house, she hoped it would help her feel closer to the home she used to know and love in Pennsylvania. Starting over was difficult, but it would be a bit easier when they could use their own things again. While Samuel's house was comfortable enough, nothing in it belonged to Hannah, and she still felt out of place — like a stranger at times.

Hannah was about to put the harness on Lilly when a little gray mouse darted out of the hay and zipped across her foot. Startled, she screamed and jumped back. There were a few critters she really didn't like, and mice were near the top of her list.

Hearing Hannah's scream must have frightened Lilly, for she reared up and then bolted out of the stall. Hannah chased after the horse, and realized too late that she'd left the barn door open.

"Come back here, Lilly!" Hannah shouted as she raced into the yard after the horse.

Around and around the yard they went, until Hannah was panting for breath. She knew she had to get Lilly back in the barn or she'd never get her harnessed and ready to go. And if the crazy horse kept running like that, she might end up out on the road, where she'd be in jeopardy of getting hit by a car.

"Whoa! Whoa, now!" Hannah waved her hands frantically, but it did no good. Lilly was in a frenzy and wouldn't pay any attention to her at all.

Hannah heard someone shout, and when she turned her head, she was surprised to see Leon running out of the house, waving his arms and hollering at Lilly. While the boy might be young, he must have known exactly what he was doing, because it wasn't long before he had Hannah's horse under control and running straight for the barn.

Hannah hurried in behind them and quickly shut the door. "Whew! Lilly gave me quite a workout! Danki for coming to my rescue, Leon."

The boy looked up at her and grinned. "I've helped Daadi chase after his horse before, so I knew just what to do. And if our pony ever gets outa the barn, bet I can get him back in, too." Leon's face sobered. "Marla said I wasn't supposed to go outside, but when I saw your horse runnin' all over the place, I had to come out and help. Sure hope that's okay."

She smiled and gave his shoulder a gentle squeeze. "I'm glad you did. Would you like to help me put the harness on Lilly?"

"Jah, sure."

A short time later, Hannah's horse was hitched and ready to go. Now all she needed to do was load the children into the buggy, and they could be on their way.

"Could you give me a hand with this drop cloth?" Timothy called to Titus, who was on the other side of the living room, removing some old baseboard that needed to be replaced.

"Sure thing." Titus stopped what he was doing and picked up one of the drop cloths. "Do you want to cover the whole floor or just this section for now?"

"If you're about ready to paint your side of the room, we may as well cover the entire floor," Timothy said.

"I will be as soon as I put the new baseboard up."

"Okay then, let's just cover the floor on my side for now. Sure am glad we both know how to paint," Timothy said as they spread out the drop cloth.

"Jah, but you've done more painting than I ever have, so your side of the room will probably look better than mine. Think I'm better at carpentry than painting."

"You are good with wood," Timothy agreed, "but your painting skills are just fine. I think you sell yourself short sometimes."

Titus shrugged. "That's what Suzanne says, too."

"Speaking of Suzanne, how's she feeling these days?"

"She's still havin' some morning sickness, but at least it doesn't last all day like it did at first." Titus's forehead wrinkled. "Since we've only been married a few months, we weren't expecting a boppli this soon. But then God knows what we need and when we need it, so we've come to think of it as a blessing."

Timothy thought about his brother's remark. He'd always felt that God knew what he needed and when he needed it, but he wasn't so sure Hannah shared that belief. Sometimes her faith in God seemed weak, and she usually had little to say about the sermons they heard at church. He felt that this move to Kentucky had been God's will, but he didn't think Hannah had come to accept it just yet. They still quarreled a lot, and Hannah often nagged him about little things. But since they'd bought this house, her outlook seemed a bit more positive. He hoped after they moved in and she arranged things to her liking she'd feel more like Kentucky was her home.

The brothers worked quietly for a while, until Timothy heard a horse and buggy pull in. Thinking it was probably Samuel coming to help, he didn't bother to look out the window.

A few minutes later, the front door opened, and Hannah stepped into the room carrying a wicker basket. Marla, Leon, Penny, Jared, and Mindy traipsed in behind her.

That's just great, Timothy thought. *The last thing we need is the kinner here getting in the way.* He was about to ask Hannah what they were doing when Mindy rushed over to

Titus, who was crouched down with his back to them, and threw her little arms around his neck. "Daadi!"

With a look of surprise, Titus whirled around, nearly knocking the child off her feet. Mindy took one look at Titus's face and started howling. She'd obviously mistaken him for her daddy, but after seeing his beard, which was much shorter than Timothy's because he hadn't been married as long, she'd realized her mistake.

Hannah placed the basket on the floor, hurried across the room, and swooped Mindy into her arms. "It's all right, little one. That's your uncle Titus. Don't cry. Look, daadi's right over there." She pointed to Timothy.

Hannah set Mindy down, and the child, still crying, darted across the room toward Timothy. In the process, she hit the bucket of paint with her foot and knocked it over. Some of the white paint spilled out, but at least the drop cloth was there to protect the floor. When Mindy saw what she'd done, she started to howl even louder — like a wounded heifer.

Timothy, grabbing for the paint can and more than a bit annoyed, glared at Hannah and said, "What are you doing here, and why'd you bring the kinner? This is not a place for them to be when we're tryin' to get some work done!"

Hannah pointed to the basket she'd set on the floor. "You left so early this morning that I didn't get a chance to make your lunch, so I decided to bring it over to you." She motioned to the children, who stood wide-eyed and huddled together near the door. "I could hardly leave them at home by themselves, now, could I?"

"Of course not, but —"

"And I wanted to see how you're doing and ask if there's anything I can do to help," she quickly added.

"Jah, there is," Timothy shouted. "You can just leave the lunch basket and head back home with the kinner while I clean up the paint that got spilled!"

Hannah's chin quivered, and even from across the room he could see her tears. "Fine then," she said, bending to pick up Mindy. "I guess that's what I get for trying to be nice!" She ushered the kids quickly out the door, slamming it behind her.

"Hey, Timothy, you need to calm down. You caught the paint before too much damage was done, so did you have to yell at Hannah like that?" Titus asked, moving over to the basket. "I'm hungerich, and I'm glad she brought us some lunch."

"It was a nice gesture," Timothy agreed, "but she should have left the kinner in the buggy while she brought the lunch basket in here. She ought to know better than to turn five little ones loose in a room that's being painted." He shrugged his shoulders. "But what can I say? Sometimes my fraa just doesn't think."

"No one is perfect, Timothy. Maybe you're just too hard on Hannah. It might help if you appreciated the good things she does, rather than scolding her for all the things she does that irritate you."

A feeling of remorse came over Timothy. He didn't know why he'd been short on patience lately. Maybe it was because he wanted so badly to get this house presentable enough so they could move in. Even so, that was no excuse for him losing his temper — especially in front of the children.

"You're right, and I appreciate the reminder. I should have handled it better," Timothy said, watching out the window as the buggy headed down the road. "Guess it's too late now, but as soon as I get home, I'll apologize to Hannah and try to make things right." He dropped his gaze to the floor. "Guess I'd better say I'm sorry to the kinner, too — especially my sweet little girl, who probably thinks her daadi's angry with her."

CHAPTER 32

Trisha had just taken a loaf of banana bread from the oven when the telephone rang. Knowing Bonnie was outside emptying the garbage, Trisha picked up the receiver. "Hello. Bonnie's Bed-and-Breakfast."

"Bonnie, is that you?"

"No, this is Trisha." Then, recognizing the voice on the other end, she said, "How are you, Kenny?"

"I'm okay, and if you don't mind, it's Ken, not Kenny." There was a pause. "How's your ankle doing?"

"It's better. I got the cast off a week ago, but now I'm doing physical therapy."

"How much longer will you be staying at Bonnie's?" he asked.

"I don't know. I guess that all depends on when Esther returns from Pennsylvania."

"What's she doing in Pennsylvania, and what's that got to do with you?"

Trisha explained about Esther's dad and

then told Ken that she'd been doing the cooking for Bonnie and that Bonnie was taking care of servicing the rooms. "I thought Bonnie would have told you that," she added.

"Nope. She never said a word."

Hmm . . . that's strange, Trisha thought. *I know Bonnie's talked to her dad since Esther left. I wonder why she didn't mention any of this to him.*

"She probably didn't mention it because she thought I wouldn't approve," Ken said, as though anticipating the question on the tip of her tongue.

"And would you?" she dared to ask.

"The B&B is Bonnie's to do with as she likes, so whomever she hires to work there is her business, not mine."

"So you're okay with me working here?"

"I didn't say that. Just said —"

The back door opened suddenly, and Bonnie stepped in. "It's your dad." Trisha held the receiver out to Bonnie. "I'm sure he'd rather talk to you than me."

After Bonnie took the phone, Trisha left the room, wondering once again if things would ever be better between her and Ken. She hoped they would, because over these last several weeks, she and Bonnie had become good friends. She'd gotten to know

310

Allen, too, and appreciated the way he always included her in the conversation whenever he came to see Bonnie, although Trisha usually tried to make herself scarce so he and Bonnie could have some time alone.

I wish I could be here for Bonnie and Allen's wedding, Trisha thought as she entered the living room and took a seat in the rocker. *Maybe when Esther comes back I can find another job somewhere in the area and rent an apartment in Hopkinsville — at least until after Bonnie and Allen are married.*

If she and Ken hadn't broken up when they were teenagers, would she have visited him at this house? What if she had married Ken instead of Dave? Would they have ended up living in Kentucky instead of Oregon?

"Shoulda, woulda, coulda," she murmured, leaning her head back and closing her eyes. "There's always more than one direction a person can take. I guess there's no point in pondering the 'what if 's.' "

It had taken Hannah awhile to get the children settled down after they'd gone back to Samuel's. They'd clearly been upset by Timothy's outburst. After they'd had silent prayer before lunch, Leon looked up at

Hannah and said, "How come Uncle Timothy's mad at us?"

"I don't think he's mad at you," Hannah assured him. "He was just upset because we went over to the house when he was really busy, and when the can of paint got spilled, he was left with a mess to clean up. I think he was more upset with me than anyone," she added.

"When we first moved to Kentucky, Daadi used to yell at us like that," Marla spoke up, putting her hand inside the sleeve of her dress.

"He did?"

"Jah. Esther said it was because he missed our mamm so much, but we thought he didn't love us."

"But you know now that he loves you, right?" Hannah questioned.

Leon bobbed his head. "Daadi got better after I ran away from home. Maybe you oughta run away, too, Aunt Hannah. Then when ya come back, Uncle Timothy might be nicer to ya."

Hannah smiled despite her sour mood. "Sometimes I do feel like running away, but it probably wouldn't be the answer to our problems."

"What is the answer?" Marla asked.

Hannah shrugged. "I'm not sure. I guess I

just need to let your uncle Timothy work on the house and not bother him when he's there." She reached over and wiped away a blob of peanut butter Mindy had managed to get on her chin.

Truth was, when Timothy snapped at her like he had today, it made her long to be back in Pennsylvania, where she'd have Mom's love and support. That wasn't likely to happen, though — especially now that they'd bought a house. Hannah figured she'd better make the best of things and try to stay out of Timothy's way when he was busy working on the house. That would be easier than quarreling all the time or being hurt when he said something harsh to her, which seemed to be happening a lot lately. She knew Timothy didn't like to argue either, but they seemed to do it frequently.

Maybe he thinks I'm hard to live with, Hannah thought.

The children had just finished their lunch, when Hannah heard the sound of horse's hooves coming up the driveway. When she went to the window, she was surprised to see Timothy's horse and buggy pull up to the hitching rail. *I wonder what he's doing back so early. Maybe he forgot a tool. Or maybe he came to lecture me some more.*

Fearful that Timothy might say something

313

to upset the children, Hannah told them to go upstairs to their rooms.

"What about our *schissel?*" Marla asked. "Don't you want us to clear them first?"

Hannah shook her head. "That's okay. I'll take care of the dishes." She lifted Mindy from her stool and told her to go upstairs to play with Marla and the others.

When the children left the room, Hannah started clearing the table. She'd just put the last dish in the sink when Timothy entered the kitchen.

"What are you doing here?" she asked over her shoulder. "I thought you planned to work at the house all day."

"I do, but I had to come home for a few minutes." He stepped up to Hannah and placed his hands on her shoulders. *"Es dutt mir leed."*

"You're sorry?"

"That's right. I shouldn't have gotten so angry about the spilled paint and spouted off like I did. Will you forgive me, Hannah?"

She nodded, feeling her throat tighten. "I'm sorry, too," she murmured. Hannah couldn't believe he'd come all the way home just to say he was sorry, but it softened her heart. She felt more love for her husband than she had in a long time. Did she dare hope that things would be better between them from now on?

CHAPTER 33

By the middle of March, Timothy and Hannah were able to move into their home. Not everything had been fixed, but at least it was livable. Since Esther was still in Pennsylvania, Hannah had agreed to watch Samuel's children at her house, which meant he had to bring them over every morning, but he seemed to be okay with that.

One sunny Monday, Hannah decided to take advantage of the unusually warm weather and hang her laundry outdoors, rather than in the basement. As she carried a basket of freshly washed clothes out to the clothesline, she wondered if they'd made a mistake in buying this old house. So much remained to be done. Several upstairs windows needed new screens. Some screens were broken, and some were missing altogether. The barn needed work, too, which was important because it not only housed their horses, but also Timothy's farming tools, painting supplies, and many other things, including hay and food for the animals. Then there was the yard. Hannah didn't know if she'd ever get the weeds cleared out in time to plant a garden this spring. The fields behind the house looked like they hadn't been cultivated in a good many years, and they'd need to be plowed and tilled before Timothy could plant corn. It was all a bit overwhelming, and having to take care of Samuel's children during Esther's absence only made it worse for Hannah. However, she'd agreed to do it, and the money Samuel insisted on paying her was nice for extra expenses.

Hannah shifted the laundry basket in her arms. On a brighter note, soon after they'd moved in, Timothy had mounted the covered-bridge bird feeder he'd given her for Christmas on a post in their backyard. Hannah glanced at the feeder and smiled when she saw several redheaded house finches eating some of the thistle seed she'd put out. She found herself humming and enjoying the joy spring fever always brought.

Redirecting her thoughts, she set the laundry basket on the ground and turned to check on the children. Penny, Jared, and Mindy sat on the porch steps, petting the pathetic little gray-and-white cat that had wandered onto their place the day they'd moved in. The kids had named the cat Bobbin because he bobbed his head whenever he walked. The poor critter had trouble with his balance and sometimes fell over when he tried to run. Hannah figured he'd either been injured or been born with some kind of a palsy disorder. One thing for sure, the cat had been neglected and was looking for a new home. While Hannah wasn't particularly fond of cats, she couldn't help feeling sorry for Bobbin, so she'd begun feeding him, which of course meant the cat had claimed this as his new home. For the sake of Mindy, who'd latched on to the cat right away, Hannah had allowed Bobbin to stay. But she'd made it clear that he was not to be in the house. She didn't want to deal with cat hair everywhere, not to mention the possibility of fleas.

As Hannah hung a pair of Timothy's trousers on the line, she thought about how hard he and his brothers had worked on the house. Looking around, she had to admit they really had accomplished a lot in a short amount of time.

She giggled to herself, thinking back to the day when their new propane stove had been delivered. When they were moving the appliance into place, part of the floor gave way, and the stove became wedged halfway between the kitchen floor and the basement ceiling. Everyone stood with looks of shock until someone had the good sense to suggest that they secure the stove before it fell any farther through the floor. Then they worked together to get the stove hoisted back up in place. Apparently, the wood floor had weakened in that area from a leaky pipe, because originally the sink was located there. It wasn't funny at the time, and it set them back a few days, but Timothy, Samuel, and Titus managed to get the floorboards replaced and a nice square area inlayed with brick for the stove to set on. Except for a few scratches on her new stove, which Hannah wasn't happy about, it had all worked out.

"Frosch schpringe net."

Hannah looked down, surprised to see Jared standing beside her, and wondered what he meant about a frog not jumping. She was about to ask when he pointed to her laundry basket. A fat little frog sat looking up at her.

Hannah screamed. She hated frogs. Even the sight of one sent chills up her spine. "Get that frosch out of there!"

Jared looked up at her like she was a horse with two heads as he picked up the frog.

"Put it over there," she said, pointing to a clump of weeds near the barn. She would have told him to take it all the way out to the field, but she didn't want him going that far from the house.

As Jared walked off, Hannah shook her head and continued to hang up the laundry. *That boy is really something,* she thought with a click of her tongue. *I hope Esther knows what she's getting herself into by marrying Samuel.*

She'd just finished hanging the last of the towels when she spotted a car coming up the driveway. When it pulled up next to the barn, she realized it belonged to Bonnie.

"Guder mariye," Bonnie said as she joined Hannah by the clothesline. "That is how you say *good morning,* isn't it?"

Hannah nodded, surprised that Bonnie knew some Pennsylvania-Dutch words.

"It's so nice out today, and I decided to take a ride and come by to see your new house. Oh, and I brought you a few house-warming gifts." Bonnie motioned to her car. "They're in there."

"I'd be happy to show you the house, but you didn't have to bring me anything," Hannah said.

Bonnie smiled. "I wanted to welcome you to the neighborhood. You know, my B&B

isn't too far from here, so feel free to drop by any time you like."

"Thanks." Hannah bent to pick up the empty laundry basket. "Let's go inside, and I'll show you around."

"Sounds good. I'll get your gifts from the car and follow you up to the house."

Hannah skirted around the weeds and stepped onto the porch. "You all need to come inside now," she said to the children.

"Can't we stay out here?" Penny asked in a whiny voice. "We want to pet the katz."

"You can pet the cat later. I need you inside where I can keep an eye on you."

Penny's lower lip jutted out, and when Mindy started to howl, Jared did, too. Their screams were so loud Hannah feared their nearest neighbor might call the police, thinking something horrible had happened. She held the laundry basket under one arm and against her hip then put her finger to her lips. "Hush now, and come inside, *schnell*."

But the children didn't come quickly, as she'd asked them to do. Instead, they sat on the porch step, with Mindy still holding the cat, and all three of them crying.

Just then, Bonnie showed up carrying a wicker basket. She placed it on the little wooden table on the porch, reached inside, and handed each of the children a chocolate bar. Even though Hannah didn't normally allow Mindy to have candy — especially so close to lunchtime — she offered no objections, because Bonnie's gift to the children was all it took to stop their crying.

"You can eat the candy, but only if you come inside," Hannah said, opening the door. The children put the cat down, and as he bobbled off to chase after a bug, they followed Bonnie and Hannah inside.

Once inside, Hannah instructed them to go to the kitchen to eat their candy bars, while she gave Bonnie a tour of the house.

"This is a nice-sized home," Bonnie said when they stepped into one of the bedrooms upstairs. "Plenty of room for a growing family and extra room for any company you may have."

"Our family's not growing at the moment," Hannah said. "Unless you count Bobbin, the cat."

"I assume you and Timothy will want other children?" Bonnie asked.

Hannah nodded. "I had a miscarriage last year, but I haven't been able to conceive since then. Timothy says it's because I'm always stressed out, but I think my womb might be closed up."

Bonnie gave Hannah's arm a gentle

squeeze. "I'll pray for you."

"Thanks, I appreciate that." Hannah was surprised to see such compassion on Bonnie's face. It made her think maybe Bonnie might want children, too.

"The men did a good job painting all the rooms," Bonnie said, as they moved on to another bedroom.

"Yes, they did. It took them awhile to strip off the wallpaper, but it turned out nice. There's still some work that needs to be done up here, though." Hannah motioned to the windows. "Some of the screens are missing, and some are old and loose, so they'll all need to be replaced. But considering the repairs that have been done since we bought this place, we're fortunate that we could move in so quickly."

"There were a few missing screens at the B&B when I first moved in," Bonnie said. "But between Samuel and Allen, those were taken care of before the warm weather arrived last year."

"Hopefully, Timothy will get all the screens replaced here soon. With nicer weather on the way, it will be good to have fresh air circulating through the house."

Hannah left the room and stepped into the hall. "I think we should go downstairs now and see what the kids are up to in the kitchen."

"Oh yes, and I want to give you my housewarming gifts, too."

When they entered the kitchen, the children were gone. Hannah checked the living room and found them sitting on the floor with a stack of books. "Go to the bathroom and wash up," she instructed. "You probably have chocolate on your hands, and I don't want that getting on any of Mindy's books."

The children did as she asked, but they didn't look happy about it.

Hannah turned to Bonnie and said, "Those kids of Samuel's can sure be stubborn."

Bonnie chuckled. "I guess all kids can be that way at times."

The two women continued on into the kitchen, and Bonnie removed a carton of eggs, a cookbook, several dish towels, and a loaf of homemade bread from the wicker basket she'd set on the table. "The eggs are from my layers," she said. "Oh, and Trisha made the bread, I made the dish towels, and the cookbook was put together by some of the women at my church. I have one, too, and all the recipes I've tried so far have been very good."

"Thank you for everything," Hannah said

as they both took a seat at the table.

Hannah thumbed through the cookbook and stopped when she came to a recipe for Kentucky chocolate chip pie. "You know, I was planning to make this pie for Christmas, but I didn't feel like doing any baking. I really do need to try it sometime though. Timothy likes anything with chocolate chips in it, and I bet he'd enjoy the pie."

"It does sound tasty," Bonnie agreed. "If you try it, let me know how it turns out. I could even be your guinea pig," she added with a gleam in her eyes.

"I might just do that." Hannah laughed. "Would you like a cup of tea?" She offered, feeling cheerful. "It won't take long to get the water heated."

"That sounds nice, but I really should get going. I need to drive Trisha to her physical therapy appointment this afternoon, and if we get an early start, I may try to get some shopping done while we're in Hopkinsville."

Bonnie was just starting for the door when a fat, little frog hopped out of the sink onto the counter, then leaped onto the floor by Hannah's feet. She screamed and jumped up. "Jared Fisher, did you bring that frosch into the house?"

Wearing a sheepish expression, Jared shuffled into the kitchen. Hannah pointed at the frog. "Take it outside, right now!"

Hannah was relieved when the child did as she asked but embarrassed that she'd made a fool of herself in front of Bonnie. "I've had a fear of frogs ever since my oldest brother put one in my bed when I was a little girl," she explained. "And I sure never expected to see a frog this early in the year."

"It must be the warm weather that brought it out." Bonnie smiled. "And believe me, I understand about your fear. I think we all have a fear of something."

"Not Timothy. I don't think he's afraid of anything."

"Most men won't admit to being afraid because they want us to think they're fearless." Bonnie chuckled and moved toward the door. "It was nice seeing you, Hannah, and thanks for giving me a tour of your new home."

"Thank you for stopping by and for all these nice things."

Hannah stood at the door and watched as Bonnie walked out to her car. It had been nice to have an adult to visit with for a while. Even though Hannah kept busy watching the children, she often felt lonely and isolated. Oh, what she wouldn't give for a good visit with Mom.

CHAPTER 34

As Esther's driver, Pat Summers, turned onto the road leading to Pembroke, Esther's excitement mounted. Here it was the first Saturday in April, and she could hardly believe she'd been gone two months. But her help had been needed in Pennsylvania, and she'd stayed until Dad was well enough to take over working the stands at both farmers' markets. It had been good to spend time with her family, but as hard as it was to leave, she knew her place was here in Kentucky with Samuel and his children. She would stop by the B&B first to drop off her luggage and let Bonnie know she was back, and then she would head over to see Samuel and the children.

"I hope the woman you work for at the bed-and-breakfast will have a room available for me to spend the night," Pat said as they neared Bonnie's place. "If there are no vacancies, I'll have to look for a hotel in

Hopkinsville. I've done enough traveling for one day and need to rest up."

Esther smiled at her. "When I spoke to Bonnie on the phone a few days ago, she said she didn't have any guests coming until next weekend. So unless things have changed, I'm sure she'll have a room for you."

"I'm anxious to see the B&B," Pat said. "From what you've told me, it sounds like a real nice place."

Esther nodded. "It is now, but you should have seen the house before Samuel and Allen fixed it up. Both men are good carpenters, and Samuel's an expert painter, so Bonnie was very pleased with how it turned out." Esther motioned to the B&B sign on her right. "Here we are. Turn right there."

Pat drove up the driveway and parked her van on the side of Bonnie's garage. When they got out of the van, Cody leaped off the porch and ran out to greet them.

"Oh, I hope he doesn't bite," Pat said when the dog jumped up on Esther.

"No, he's just excited to see me." Esther told Cody to get down; then she bent over and stroked his head. "Good boy, Cody. Have you missed me?"

Woof! Woof! Cody wagged his tail.

"I've missed you, too," Esther said with a

chuckle. "Now be a good dog and go lie down."

Cody darted over to Pat and sniffed her shoes before making a beeline for the porch, where he flopped down near the door.

Esther found the front door open, so she didn't bother to knock. They'd just entered the foyer when Bonnie stepped out of the kitchen. "Oh, it's so good to see you!" she said, giving Esther a hug. "I knew you were coming back today, but I wasn't sure what time you'd get here."

"We spent last night in a hotel in Louisville and got an early start this morning," Esther explained. She turned to Pat and introduced her to Bonnie.

"I was wondering if I might be able to rent a room for the night," Pat said after shaking Bonnie's hand.

Bonnie nodded. "I have no other guests right now, so you can take your pick from any of the rooms. Shall we go upstairs and take a look right now?"

"Sure, that'd be great."

While Bonnie took Pat upstairs, Esther meandered into the kitchen. She found Trisha baking cookies. "Ah, so that's the source of the wonderful aroma," she said, motioning to the cookies cooling on racks.

"It's nice to see you, Esther," Trisha said.

"I'm sure you're glad to be back."

Esther nodded. "Yes, I am. I've missed seeing all of my friends here."

"How soon will you want to start working at the B&B again?" Trisha asked.

"I'm not sure. I'll need to talk to Bonnie about that." Esther motioned to the cookies. "If those taste as good as they smell, I'd say any B&B guests who might get to eat them are in for a real treat."

"I hope so."

"I hope you'll stay here for a while," Esther said. "At least until I know what my plans are going to be."

Trisha quirked an eyebrow. "What do you mean? Are you saying you might not continue to work for Bonnie?"

"I'm not sure. It'll depend on how soon Samuel and I get married, and whether he wants me to keep working or not." Esther leaned on the edge of the counter. "I probably shouldn't have said anything until I've talked to Samuel, so I'd appreciate it if you didn't mention this to Bonnie."

"I won't say anything."

"If I should decide to quit, would you stay to help Bonnie?" Esther asked.

Trisha shrugged. "Maybe. I do like it here, and Bonnie and I have become quite close. In fact, I've begun to feel like she's the daughter I never had."

Esther smiled. "I'm glad."

Just then Bonnie and Pat entered the kitchen. "You were right. This place is wonderful," Pat said, looking at Esther.

"Which room did you choose?" Esther asked.

"The one with the Amish theme. I love that Log Cabin quilt on the bed."

"It is nice," Esther agreed. "But then I like most Amish quilt patterns."

"Why don't we all take a seat?" Bonnie motioned to the table. "We can have some of Trisha's delicious cookies and a cup of hot tea."

A crisp afternoon breeze brushed Hannah's face, and she shivered. It might be officially spring, but the chilly weather said otherwise.

I wish Timothy didn't have to spend the day plowing the fields, Hannah thought as she hitched Timothy's horse to the buggy. She'd wanted to spend the day as a family — maybe hire a driver and do some shopping in Hopkinsville — but Timothy said he didn't have time. It seemed like whenever he wasn't painting with Samuel, he had work to do here. Hannah kept busy during the week, taking care of Samuel's kids and keeping up with things around the house, but when the weekend came, she was ready to do something besides work. Since Timothy wasn't available today, she'd decided to take Mindy and go over to see Bonnie for a while. Hannah's horse, Lilly, had thrown a shoe, so Hannah knew if she wanted to go anywhere, she'd have to take Dusty. She hoped he would cooperate with her and take it nice and easy, because there had been times when she'd ridden with Timothy that he'd had to work hard to keep the horse under control. Since Dusty had been let loose in the pasture this morning and had a good run, Hannah figured he might be ready for a slower pace.

As she guided the horse and buggy down the lane, Hannah saw Timothy out in the field. He must have seen her, too, for he lifted his hand in a wave. Hannah waved back and stopped the horse at the end of the lane to check for traffic. Seeing no cars coming, she directed the horse onto the road. They'd only gone a short ways when Dusty started to trot, but it quickly turned into a gallop. Hannah tightened her grip on the reins and pulled hard, but that didn't hold the horse back. "Whoa!" she hollered, using her legs to brace the reins. "Whoa, Dusty! Whoa!"

Dusty kept running, and the foam from

his sweat flew back on Hannah, but she was concentrating so hard, she barely took notice. As the horse continued to gallop, the buggy rocked from side to side. If she didn't get Dusty under control soon, the buggy might tip over.

The sound of the horse's hooves moving so fast against the pavement was almost deafening as Hannah struggled to gain control. Dusty clearly had a mind of his own.

This is what I get for taking a horse I really don't know how to handle, Hannah fumed. *Guess I should have stayed home today and found something else to do.*

The buggy swayed, taking them frighteningly close to a telephone pole, and Mindy, sitting in the seat behind Hannah, began to cry.

"It's gonna be okay, Mindy," Hannah called over her shoulder. "Hang on tight to your seat, and don't let go!"

Chapter 35

Hannah's fingers ached as she gripped Dusty's reins and pulled with all her strength. Why wouldn't the crazy horse listen to her and slow down? If she wasn't able to get control of him soon, she didn't know what would happen.

Another buggy was coming from the opposite direction. As it drew closer, she realized it belonged to Titus and Suzanne. They must have known she was in trouble, for as soon as they passed, Titus whipped his rig around and came up behind Hannah's buggy. A few minutes later, his horse came alongside hers. Grateful for the help, but fearful a car might come and hit Titus's buggy, all Hannah could do was cling to the reins and pray.

Titus's horse was moving fast, and he managed to pass and move directly in front of Hannah's horse and buggy. Hannah knew if Dusty kept running he'd smack into the back of Titus's rig, but thankfully, the horse slowed down. When Titus pulled over to the side of the road, she was able to pull in behind him. Titus then handed Suzanne the reins, hopped out of his rig, and came around to Hannah's buggy. "Are you okay?" he asked with a worried expression.

Out of breath and barely able to speak, she nodded and said, "Dusty got away from me, and I couldn't slow him down."

"Well, slide on over and let me take the reins," Titus said. "I'll drive your horse and buggy, and Suzanne can follow us in my rig."

"Danki. I appreciate your help so much," Hannah said, blinking back tears and grateful that nothing serious had happened — especially since she had Mindy with her.

"Where were you heading?"

"I was going to visit Bonnie, but I've changed my mind. I just want to go home."

Titus climbed into the buggy and took a seat beside Hannah. Then glancing into the backseat, where Mindy was still crying, he said, "It's okay, Mindy. Everything's gonna be fine."

Hannah was so relieved that Titus had come along and taken control of Timothy's horse. One thing she knew for sure: she'd never take Dusty out again by herself!

Esther's heart raced as she neared Samuel's house. Rather than taking the time to hitch her horse to the buggy, she'd ridden over on her scooter. Since Samuel's place wasn't far from Bonnie's, it hadn't taken her long to get there.

Esther parked the scooter near the porch and hurried up the steps. Just then the door opened and Samuel, as well as all four of his children, rushed out to greet her.

Samuel gave Esther a hug. "It sure is good to see you!"

She smiled. "It's good to see all of you, too."

The children began talking at once, asking Esther questions and vying for her attention.

"All right now," Samuel finally said, "you can visit more with Esther later on. Right now I'd like some time to visit with her alone. Why don't you all go to the kitchen and eat a snack? There's some cheese and apple slices in the refrigerator."

"I'm not hungerich." Penny pointed to her stomach. "My silo's still full from lunch."

"So your silo's still full, is it? Didn't know my little maedel had a silo right there."

Samuel gave Penny's stomach a couple of pats; then he leaned his head back, and the sound of his laughter seemed to bounce off the porch ceiling.

Esther and the children laughed, too. It was good to be back with Samuel and his family. She'd missed them all so much. These children had become like her own, and she couldn't wait to become their stepmother.

When the laughter subsided, the children gave Esther another hug and bounded into the house.

As Esther and Samuel sat on the porch visiting, she studied the man with whom she'd fallen so hopelessly in love. Samuel's light brown hair, streaked with gold from the sun, was thick and healthy-looking. His dark brown eyes, so sincere, spoke of his love for her.

"Now that you're back," Samuel said, reaching for Esther's hand, "can we set a date for our wedding?"

She smiled. "I'd like that."

"How about next month?"

Esther shook her head. "Oh Samuel, as much as I would like that, it's just a bit too soon. I'll need some time to make my wedding dress, and with Bonnie and Allen getting married soon, and then going on a two-week honeymoon, I'll also need to help at the B&B. Could we get married the last Tuesday in June?"

"I'd sure like it to be sooner, but I guess June isn't that far off," he said.

"No, it's not, and we do need to give our folks some advance notice so they can plan for the trip." Esther's face sobered. "I hope Mom and Dad will be able to come. With my brother not doing well, they may feel that they can't leave Sarah to care for him on her own."

"I'm sure they can get someone else to help with Dan's care for a few days," Samuel said. "I don't think your parents would miss your wedding."

"I hope not. I'd really like to have them here."

"Speaking of your parents, maybe when they come for the wedding I can ask about buying this house. I've appreciated being able to rent the place from them, but I'd really like to have a house I can call my own."

Esther nodded. "It's good that you mentioned it, because that topic came up while I was in Pennsylvania. Mom and Dad said they'd be willing to sell the house to us for a reasonable price, and I'm sure Dad will discuss the details with you soon."

Samuel grinned. "Now, that's good news!"

"There's something else we need to discuss," Esther said.

"What's that?"

"I was wondering if you'd like me to quit my job at the B&B after we're married."

Samuel pulled his fingers through the ends of his beard and sat quietly as he contemplated her question. Finally, he smiled and said, "It's really your decision, but if it were left up to me, you'd quit working for Bonnie and be a full-time wife and mother."

"I feel that way, too," Esther said. "And I think Trisha might be willing to stay on and keep working for Bonnie. She seems really happy there. In fact, if she agrees, then I can quit even before we get married."

"That's good to hear. Sounds like it will all work out."

"As I said, I'll need to help out at the B&B while Bonnie and Allen are on their honeymoon. If things get busy, Trisha will need some help."

"That's fine with me." Samuel smiled widely. "I can't wait to share the news with my family that you and I will be getting married in June."

CHAPTER 36

"Are you getting nervous yet?" Trisha asked when Bonnie came down to breakfast two days before her wedding.

Bonnie nodded. "I'd be lying if I said I wasn't."

"I understand. My stomach was tied in knots for two full weeks before my wedding."

"I think I'll feel better once I get busy around here. Since Allen and I will be going to Nashville tomorrow to pick up my dad and his folks at the airport, I need to get as much done today as I can in preparation for the reception."

"I'll do everything I can to help, and don't forget, Esther will be coming over."

"I'm sure Dad and Allen's folks will help when they get here, too." Bonnie opened the refrigerator and took out a boiled egg. "Guess I'd better hurry and eat so I can get going."

"You'd better have something more than an egg to eat, or you'll run out of steam before you even get started." Trisha placed a plate of toast on the table and poured Bonnie a glass of orange juice and a cup of coffee.

"Thanks." Bonnie smiled. "You certainly do take good care of me."

A lump formed in Trisha's throat. "You've become very special to me, and it gives me pleasure to do things for you."

"You're special to me, too," Bonnie said as she took a seat at the table. "Are you going to join me for breakfast?"

"I already ate, but I'll have a second cup of coffee and visit while you eat."

After Trisha joined her at the table, Bonnie said a prayer, thanking God for the food and for her and Trisha's friendship. When the prayer ended, she reached for a piece of toast and spread some strawberry jam on top. "Are you sure you can manage on your own for the two weeks Allen and I will be in Hawaii?" she asked Trisha.

"Esther will be helping as much as she can, so between the two of us, we'll manage just fine."

Bonnie placed her hand on Trisha's arm. "I'm so glad you've decided to stay here permanently."

"I'm happy about it, too; although some of my friends in California weren't too thrilled when I called and gave them the news."

"I'm sure that's only because they're going to miss you and had hoped you might be returning to California soon."

"I suppose." Trisha pursed her lips. "I just hope your dad won't mind when he hears the news."

"Why would he mind?"

Trisha shrugged. "He might not like the idea of his ex-girlfriend working for his daughter."

"Dad already knows you're working for me, and he hasn't said anything negative about it."

"He may not have said anything to you, but when I spoke to him on the phone the last time, he made it pretty clear that he wasn't thrilled about me being here." Trisha's forehead wrinkled. "He probably didn't say anything to you because he assumed my working at the B&B was temporary. He may have figured by the time he came here for your wedding, I'd be long gone."

"I think you're worried for nothing. I'll bet when Dad gets here he won't say a negative thing about you working for me." Bonnie gave Trisha's arm a little pat. "Now, I'd better finish my breakfast, because this is going to be a very long day."

The slanting afternoon sun glared in Hannah's face as she gripped the hoe and chopped at the weeds threatening to overtake her garden. Weeding was no fun, but it needed to be done. She'd planted several things a few weeks ago, and already the weeds looked healthier than the plants coming up. Maybe what they needed was more water. They'd had a dry spring so far, and Hannah had to water her vegetable garden, as well as the flowers she'd planted close to the house, by hand. Oh how she wished they would get some much-needed rain.

Mo-o-o! Mo-o-o! A brown-and-white cow in their neighbor's pasture peered across the fence at Hannah with gentle-looking eyes but a forlorn expression that matched Hannah's mood. She would much rather be doing something else, but if she didn't stay on top of the weeds, she wouldn't have any homegrown food to can in the fall.

Of course, she thought ruefully, *all the homegrown food in the world won't stave off the loneliness I've often felt since we moved to Kentucky.* In Pennsylvania she'd had some friends, and Hannah's mother had always been available whenever she'd needed help. *If Mom were here right now, she'd be helping me with the weeding.*

Hannah knew she should quit dwelling on the same old thing. After all, she was making some new friends here in Kentucky, and things had been a little better between her and Timothy since they'd moved into their new home.

Hannah's thoughts were halted when she heard buzzing to her left. Three hummingbirds fluttered around the glass feeder she'd hung on a shepherd's hook in one of her flower beds. It was always fun to watch the tiny birds skitter back and forth between the trees and the feeder. If more hummingbirds came, she'd need to put up a second feeder.

Just then the van belonging to Timothy's driver came up the lane. Hannah smiled. Timothy was home early today. Maybe he'd get those screens put in the window like he kept promising to do. Or maybe they could spend some time together this afternoon and do something fun with Mindy.

After Timothy told his driver good-bye, he joined Hannah by the garden. "Looks like you've been busy," he said.

She nodded. "It's a lot of work to keep up a garden."

"Jah, but it'll be worth it when we have fresh produce to put on the table, not to mention whatever you're able to can for our use during the winter months."

"I'm surprised to see you back so early," she said, changing the subject.

"Samuel and I finished our job in Clarksville sooner than we thought, and he figured it was too late in the day to start something else, so he said I should go home."

"I hope you won't have to work this coming Saturday," Hannah said. "It's Bonnie and Allen's wedding day, remember?"

"Don't worry. Neither Samuel nor I will be working that day, and Titus won't be working at the woodshop either, so we'll all be free to go to the wedding."

"I've never been to an English wedding," Hannah said. "I wonder what it'll be like."

"We'll find out soon enough, but right now I'm going to get some work done around here."

"Are you going to be able to replace those screens for the windows today?" she asked.

He shook his head. "I need to get some more planting done in the fields, but I'll get to the screens as soon as I can."

"But it's hot and stuffy upstairs, and it's only going to get worse as the weather gets warmer."

"So open the windows awhile."

"Flies and other nasty insects will get in."

"If you can't stand the flies, just keep the doors and windows downstairs open during the day, and that should help."

"It seems like you never finish anything when I ask," Hannah mumbled. "At least not since we moved here."

"I'll get the screens done as soon as I can. Right now, though, I'm going into the house to get something to eat before I head out to the field."

"Don't eat too much," she admonished, "or you'll spoil your supper."

"Well what can I say?" he said with a sheepish grin. "I'm a hardworking man, and I need to eat a lot in order to keep up my strength. You wouldn't want me to waste away to nothing, would you?"

"No, of course not."

He started to walk away, but she called out to him, "Don't make a bunch of noise when you go inside. Mindy's taking a nap. Oh, and please don't make a mess in the kitchen. I just cleaned the floor this morning."

He grunted and strode quickly up to the house.

Hannah sighed. Since Timothy seemed in a hurry to get out to the fields, she hadn't even bothered to mention them doing anything fun together this afternoon. What was the point? She was sure he would have said no. Between Timothy's paint jobs and his work in the fields, they rarely spent any quality time together anymore. And what time they did spend, Timothy either had work on his mind or ended up talking about Samuel and Titus. With the exception of church every other Sunday, they hardly went anywhere as a family. They'd talked about going to see the Jefferson Davis Monument, which wasn't far from where they lived, but they hadn't even done that. Hannah was beginning to wonder if all Timothy wanted to do was work. Maybe he thought she would be happy working all the time, too. As it was, she kept busy doing things she didn't really enjoy in order to keep from being bored. She'd all but given up on the idea of buying and selling antiques. The last time she'd mentioned it to Timothy, he'd repeated his objections.

Timothy has his brothers and Allen for companionship, Hannah thought. *But who do I have? Just Mindy most of the time, and of course that dopey little cat who likes to lie on the porch with his floppy paws in the air. Bonnie and Esther are busy planning their weddings, and Suzanne only comes around once in a while.*

Hannah knew she was giving in to self-pity, but she couldn't seem to help herself. Her resolve to make the best of things was crumbling. *Maybe I should join Timothy for a snack. I could really use something cold to drink, and at least it would give us a few minutes to visit before he heads out to the fields.*

She set the hoe aside, stretched her aching limbs, and hurried toward the house. When she stepped into the kitchen, she halted, shocked to see Timothy sitting on a chair with Mindy over his knees, giving her a spanking.

"What do you think you're doing?" Hannah shouted over Mindy's cries.

Timothy looked at Hannah, but he didn't speak to her until he'd finished spanking Mindy. Then he set the child on the floor and told her to go upstairs to her room.

Mindy looked at Hannah with sorrowful eyes, tears dribbling down her cheeks. Hannah reached out her arms, but Timothy shook his head. "She's a *nixnutzich* little girl and deserved that *bletsching.*" He pointed to the door leading to the stairs. "Go on now, Mindy, schnell!"

Alternating between sniffling and hiccupping, Mindy ran out of the room.

Hannah placed her hands on her hips and glared at Timothy. "Now what's this all about, and why do you think Mindy is naughty and deserved to be spanked?"

"When I came in to get a snack, I figured Mindy was still taking a nap," Timothy said. "But what I found instead was our daughter with a jar of petroleum jelly, and she was spreadin' it all over the sofa. When I told her to come with me to the kitchen, she wouldn't budge — she just looked up at me defiantly. So I picked her up and carried her to the kitchen. After she started kicking and screaming, I'd had enough, so I put her across my knees and gave her a well-deserved spanking."

"She shouldn't have been playing with the petroleum jelly," Hannah said, "but she's only a little girl, and I think you were too harsh with her." Irritation put an edge to Hannah's voice, but she didn't care. As far as she was concerned, Timothy had punished their daughter in anger, and that was wrong.

"I may have been angry, but I didn't spank her that hard. I just wanted Mindy to learn that it's wrong to get into things and make a mess, and that her disobedience will result in some kind of punishment."

"It doesn't have to be a bletsching." Hannah's tone was crisp and to the point. "There are other forms of punishment, you know."

"Sometimes a spanking's the best way to teach a child as young as Mindy that there are consequences for disobedience."

Hannah's mouth quivered as she struggled not to give in to the tears pricking the back of her eyes. *I won't let him see me cry. Not this time.*

Timothy stood and pulled her gently into his arms. "Let's not argue, Hannah. I love you, and I love Mindy, too."

"You have a funny way of showing it sometimes."

He brushed a kiss across her forehead. "I'm doing the best I can."

Hannah shrugged and turned away.

"Where are you going?" he called as she headed for the stairs.

"Upstairs to comfort Mindy!" Hannah raced from the room before he could say anything else. Timothy might think he was doing his best, but at the moment, she wasn't the least bit convinced.

CHAPTER 37

Hopkinsville, Kentucky

When Allen stepped out of his bedroom, he heard his parents' voices coming from the kitchen. Hearing his name mentioned, he paused and listened, even though he knew it was wrong to eavesdrop.

"I can't believe our son is finally getting married," Mom said. "I was about to give up."

Allen rolled his eyes. Mom could be so dramatic about things.

"I know," Dad agreed. "This is a very special day for him, and for us, too."

"Maybe there's some hope of us becoming grandparents."

"That would be nice. Think I'd enjoy having little ones to buy Christmas gifts and birthday presents for."

"I wonder if Allen and Bonnie are planning to start a family right away."

"Are you two talking about me behind my

back and planning my future to boot?" Allen asked, stepping into the kitchen. He wasn't really irritated — just surprised by their conversation.

Mom smoothed the lapel on Allen's white tuxedo. "You and Bonnie do want children, don't you?"

Allen nodded. "Yes, Mom, we do."

She smiled. "You know, when I came here last year to help out after you'd injured your back, I had a hunch you and Bonnie would get together."

He tipped his head. "Oh, really? What made you think that?"

"I could see the gleam in your eyes whenever you spoke of her. After spending time with Bonnie yesterday when you two picked us up at the airport, I could see how well you complement each other."

"I agree with your mother," Dad said. "Bonnie's a great gal, and I do believe she was worth waiting for, son."

Allen smiled. "You're right about that. Bonnie is all I could ever ask for in a wife, and I hope we have as good a marriage as you two have had."

Fairview, Kentucky

"Dad, there's something I've been wanting to talk to you about," Bonnie said after she'd pulled into the church parking lot and turned off the car.

"What's that?" he asked, turning in the passenger's seat to face her.

"Trisha plans to make Kentucky her permanent home. She'll be working for me at the B&B full-time."

His mouth dropped open. "How come?"

"Because Esther will be getting married toward the end of June, and she won't be working for me any longer."

He folded his arms and stared straight ahead. "I see."

"I have a complaint." Bonnie readily listened to the complaints of others, but rarely spoke of her own. Today she would make an exception.

"What's the gripe?" he asked.

"I'm not happy about the way you give Trisha the cold shoulder."

"I don't do that."

"Yes you do. I have a hunch you're still angry with her for breaking up with you when you were teenagers. You know, you shouldn't think negative thoughts about someone until you have all the facts."

Dad frowned deeply. "Facts about what? Trisha broke up with me; I blamed my parents; and I can't go back and change any of it — end of story."

"But you're still angry about it."

"So?"

"So, you need to forgive Trisha as well as yourself. And remember, what lies behind us and what lies before us are small matters compared to what lies within us."

Dad rubbed his forehead, as though mulling things over.

"Remember when you asked what I'd like for a wedding present?"

He nodded.

"Well, the one thing that would give me the greatest pleasure would be for you to make peace with Trisha. Is that too much to ask?" She sat quietly, hoping he'd take her words to heart.

He turned his head and gave her a faint smile. "I'll give it some thought."

Pembroke, Kentucky

As Samuel stood in front of the bathroom mirror combing his hair, he smiled. Two of his good friends were getting married today, and he couldn't be happier for them. He was glad Allen and Bonnie had invited him and the kids to attend the wedding, but he was a bit nervous about going. He'd never been to an English wedding before and wasn't sure what to expect. The ceremony would be quite different from Amish wed-

354

dings, and he hoped the kids wouldn't say or do anything to embarrass him.

They usually behave themselves during our church services, he reminded himself. *So, hopefully they'll be on their best behavior today.*

Setting his comb aside, Samuel opened the bathroom door and was surprised to see Penny standing in the hallway.

"I smell peppermint candy," she said when Samuel stepped out of the bathroom. "Were you eatin' candy in there, Daadi?"

Samuel chuckled and patted the top of her head. "No, silly girl. Daadi washed his hair with some new shampoo that smells like peppermint."

Penny stuck her head in the bathroom and sniffed the air. "Are ya sure 'bout that?"

"Of course I'm sure. Now go tell your brothers and sister that it's time for us to pick Esther up. We don't want to be late for Allen and Bonnie's wedding."

Penny looked up at him with a serious expression. "I wish it was you and Esther gettin' married today."

"I wish that, too, but just think . . . by the end of June, Esther will be my fraa, and your new mamm."

Penny offered him a wide grin. "I can hardly wait for that!"

Samuel smiled and nodded. "No more than I can, little one."

CHAPTER 38

Fairview, Kentucky

"You make a beautiful bride," Trisha said as she helped Bonnie set her veil in place. "And your dress is absolutely gorgeous!" She gestured to the hand-beaded detail on the bodice and hem of the long, full-gathered skirt made of an off-white satin material.

"You don't think it's too much, do you?"

Trisha shook her head. "Absolutely not. Your wedding gown is as lovely as the woman wearing it, and you deserve to look like a princess today."

Bonnie smiled. "You're a pretty matron of honor, too."

Tears pooled in Trisha's eyes. "I'm honored that you would ask me to stand up with you."

Bonnie gave Trisha a hug. "You've become a good friend."

"But Esther's your friend, too, and I

figured you'd want her to stand up with you."

"You're right, Esther's a very special friend, but I'm fairly sure that her church wouldn't allow her to be part of my bridal party, so I only asked you." Bonnie re-adjusted her lacy veil just a bit. "I'm glad most of my Amish friends will be able to attend the wedding, however."

"Will you be invited to Esther and Samuel's wedding?" Trisha questioned.

"Oh yes. I went when Titus and Suzanne got married, so I'm sure I'll get an invitation to Esther and Samuel's wedding, too."

"Are Amish weddings much different than ours?"

"They definitely are." Bonnie smiled at Trisha. "Since you and Esther have gotten to know each other quite well, I'm almost sure you'll get an invitation to her wedding."

"I hope so. That would truly be an honor for me."

A knock sounded on the door of the little room in the church where Bonnie and Trisha had gone to get ready.

"Would you like me to see who that is?" Trisha asked.

Bonnie nodded. "If it's Allen, I don't want him to see me until I walk down the aisle, so please don't let him in."

"Don't worry. I won't." When Trisha opened the door, Bonnie's dad walked in. He stepped up to Bonnie and stared at her as though in disbelief.

"Doesn't your daughter look beautiful in that dress?" Trisha asked.

"Yes, she's stunning." Dad smiled and gave Bonnie a hug. Then he turned to Trisha and said, "You look very nice, too."

Trisha's cheeks flushed. "Why, thank you, Kenny — I mean, Ken. You look pretty spiffy yourself."

Bonnie smiled. For the first time, she felt the barrier between Dad and Trisha come down a wee bit. *Thank You, God, for this answered prayer.*

"I believe it's time for me to walk you down the aisle," Dad said, extending his arm to Bonnie. "Your groom is waiting for you and probably growing anxious."

"No more than I am," Bonnie said, blinking back tears.

They followed Trisha from the room, and when they reached the back of the sanctuary, Trisha turned and gave Bonnie's dress and veil a quick once-over. After offering Bonnie a reassuring smile, she made her way slowly down the aisle in time to the soft organ music.

Bonnie clung to Dad's arm as they followed Trisha down the aisle. Just as all the wedding guests stood, an explosion of sunlight spilled through the stained-glass windows. The light seemed to guide Bonnie down the aisle, where her groom waited beside his cousin, Bill, whom he'd chosen to be his best man. Every fiber of Bonnie's being wanted to be Allen's wife. He was like a magnet drawing her to him.

Bonnie glanced to her left and spotted Esther sitting with Samuel and his children. In the pew next to them sat Titus and Suzanne, along with Timothy, Hannah, and little Mindy. To the right, she saw Allen's parents, and behind them Allen's friend, Zach, with his wife, Leona. They'd come from Pennsylvania for this special occasion and would be staying at Titus's place. Others from Bonnie's church and some from the community had also come to witness the wedding. It was wonderful to know she and Allen had so many good friends.

When Bonnie and Dad joined the wedding party at the altar, Pastor Cunningham smiled and said, "Who gives this woman to be wed?"

"I do," Dad answered in a clear but steady voice. When he kissed Bonnie's cheek and hugged her before taking a seat in the first pew, Bonnie noticed tears in his eyes.

■ ■ ■ ■

Hannah sat straight as a board as she watched this very different wedding ceremony and recalled her own wedding day. She wondered what it would have been like to wear a long white gown with a veil and walk down an aisle in a church with people sitting on both sides of the sanctuary watching her every move. At least in an Amish wedding, the bride and groom were able to sit throughout most of the service. They didn't stand before the minister until it was time to say their vows.

"Dearly beloved," the pastor said, capturing Hannah's attention, "we are gathered together in the sight of God and the presence of these witnesses to join this man and this woman in holy matrimony, which is an honorable estate instituted by God in the time of man's innocence, signifying unto us the mystical union that exists between Christ and His Church. It is, therefore, not to be entered into unadvisedly, but reverently, discreetly, and in the fear of God. Into this holy estate these persons present now come to be joined."

The pastor's expression was solemn as he continued: "Allen and Bonnie, I require and charge you both as you stand in the presence of God, to remember that the commitment to marriage means putting the needs of your mate ahead of your own. The act of giving is a vivid reminder that it's all about God and not you. Be an encourager to your mate. The more you bless each other, the more God will bless you."

Hannah cringed. She had fallen short when it came to encouraging Timothy — especially when he'd decided to move to Kentucky. She rarely put his needs ahead of her own.

"Remember, too, that it's a privilege to pray," the pastor continued. "Turn your thoughts toward God in the morning, and you'll feel His presence all day. Make each day count as if it were your last, and forget about the *if only*s, for they can only lead to self-pity. Tell yourself each morning that this day is what counts, so you may as well make the most of it. Finally, don't harbor bitterness toward God or your marriage partner."

Hannah shifted uneasily in her seat. She'd been harboring bitterness toward Timothy ever since they moved to Kentucky, and when he'd spanked Mindy the other day, it had fueled her anger.

She turned her head and smiled at Timothy and was glad when he smiled in response. Maybe they could start over. Maybe if she tried harder to be a good wife, things would go better between them.

CHAPTER 39

Paradise, Pennsylvania

Sally had just finished washing the supper dishes when she looked out the kitchen window and spotted a horse and buggy coming up the driveway. When the driver stopped near the barn, she recognized who it was.

"Abraham Fisher is here," she called to Johnny, who sat at the table reading the newspaper.

"He must have come to look at the hog I have for sale." Johnny left his seat and hurried out the back door.

A few minutes later, Sally saw Fannie standing near the buggy, so she opened the back door and hollered, "You're welcome to come inside if you like!"

Fannie waved and started walking toward the house.

"Let's go into the kitchen and have a glass of iced tea while the men take care of business," Sally suggested when Fannie entered the house.

Fannie smiled. "That sounds nice. It's been hot today — too hot for the first day of June, if you ask me."

"I agree. Makes me wonder what our summer's going to be like."

Sally poured them both a glass of iced tea, and they took seats at the table.

"I haven't heard from Timothy in a while," Fannie said. "Have you heard anything from Hannah?"

"No, not for a week or so."

"The last I heard from Timothy, he mentioned that he and Hannah were going to Allen Walters's wedding."

"Hannah mentioned that, too, but I haven't heard anything from her since," Sally said. "To tell you the truth, I haven't been phoning Hannah as often as before."

"How come?" Fannie took a sip of iced tea.

"Johnny pointed out that I need to give our daughter some space." Sally sighed. "I still miss Hannah something awful, and it's hard having her living so far away."

"I understand," Fannie said. "Try as I may, it's still hard to accept the fact that three of my sons have moved to Kentucky. I'd always hoped and believed that when

Abraham and I reached old age we'd have all our kinner and kinskinner living close to us. But I've learned to accept that it's not meant to be."

"The problem for me," Sally said, "is that I'm not as emotionally close to our sons and their wives as I am to Hannah. That's made it doubly hard for me since she moved away."

"I understand, but you can still be close to your daughter without her living nearby." Fannie smiled. "Just be there for her, if and when she needs you. That'll count for a lot."

Pembroke, Kentucky

Trisha couldn't believe how lonely she'd felt since Bonnie and Allen had left on their honeymoon. She'd become used to fixing supper and sharing it with Bonnie and didn't enjoy eating all her meals alone. She didn't have any guests at the B&B right now, either, so things had been unusually quiet.

"Now quit feeling sorry for yourself," Trisha mumbled as she entered the kitchen. "You've been living alone since Dave died and managed okay, so why's this any different? Besides, you should be enjoying this little rest before things start to pick up again."

Resolved to make the best of the situation, Trisha took a container of leftover soup from the refrigerator and poured the contents into a kettle. She was about to turn on the stove when the telephone rang. She quickly picked up the receiver. "Hello. Bonnie's Bed-and-Breakfast."

"Trisha, this is Ken."

"Oh, hi. How are you?"

"I'm doing okay, but I was wondering if you've heard anything from Bonnie lately. I'm worried about her and Allen."

"How come?"

"I just heard on the news that one of those tour helicopters from Kauai went down, and I know they were planning to go up in one, so I'm wondering if —"

"Did you try calling them, Ken?"

"Yes, I did, and I had to leave a message on both of their cell phones. I'm telling you, Trisha, this has me really worried."

"I'm sure they're fine. If Bonnie and Allen were involved in that crash, I'm certain you would have heard about it by now." Trisha cringed. *Oh, I hope they weren't in that helicopter. What a tragedy that would be.*

"You know, I never used to worry so much, but the older I get, the more I fret about things."

Trisha gave a small laugh, hoping to reassure him. "I know what you mean. I'm the same way."

"How are things going there?" he asked. "Have you been really busy since Bonnie and Allen left?"

"No, not really. Actually, business has been kind of slow, but I'm sure it'll pick up now that summer's almost here. I guess I should enjoy this little break before it gets busy again."

Trisha jumped as a gust of wind blew against the house, causing the windows to rattle. Rain pelted down on the roof. When the lights flickered, she said, "I hate to cut this short, Ken, but I'd better hang up. It's raining really hard, and the wind's howling so much that I'm afraid the power might go out. I need to get out some candles and battery-operated lights, just in case."

"Okay, I'll let you go. Oh, and Trisha, if you hear anything from Bonnie, would you please ask her to give me a call?"

"Yes, of course I will." The lights flickered again then went off, leaving Trisha in total darkness.

Exhausted after a hard day's work, Timothy flopped onto the sofa with a groan. He'd put in a full eight hours painting in Clarksville then come home and worked in the fields until it had started raining real hard. Every muscle in his body ached.

He leaned his head against the back of the sofa and closed his eyes, allowing his mind to wander. Things had been better between him and Hannah lately — ever since Allen and Bonnie's wedding, really. They hadn't argued even once, and Hannah seemed much sweeter and more patient with him. She hadn't nagged when he'd left his shoes in the living room the other day or complained because he'd tracked dirt into the house. Timothy didn't know the reason, but Hannah had definitely changed her attitude and actually seemed more content.

He smiled. Hannah was in the bathroom right now giving Mindy a bath. He'd promised when she was done and had put Mindy to bed that the two of them would share a bowl of popcorn while they relaxed. He looked forward to spending time alone with his wife but wasn't sure he had the strength to stand in front of the stove and crank the lever on the corn popper. He figured Hannah would probably be awhile, so if he rested a few minutes, he might feel more like popping the corn by the time she was done bathing Mindy.

Timothy was at the point of nodding off when Mindy bounded into the room wearing her long white nightgown and fuzzy slippers. She climbed onto the sofa and put her little hands on both sides of his face. "*Gut nacht,* Daadi."

"Good night, little one." Timothy's heart swelled with love as he kissed her forehead. "Sleep tight."

Hannah smiled. "I'm taking her up to bed now, and I shouldn't be too long, so if you want to start the popcorn, I'll pour the lemonade as soon as I come down."

"Okay." How could he say no when Hannah was being so sweet?

As Hannah and Mindy headed up the stairs, Timothy pulled himself off the sofa and ambled into the kitchen. He glanced out the window. It was pitch dark, and the rain pelted the house so viciously it was almost deafening. It was hard to believe a day that had begun so sunny and warm could turn into such a stormy night.

Sure hope it'll be better by morning, he thought. *Samuel and I won't be able to finish the outside of that house we started on today if it's still raining tomorrow.*

By the time Hannah came downstairs, Timothy had made the popcorn and drizzled it with melted butter.

"That smells wunderbaar," she said, sniffing the air. "If you'll take it into the living room, I'll join you there in a few minutes with some lemonade."

"Sounds good."

A short time later, Timothy and Hannah were on the sofa with a large bowl of popcorn between them and glasses of cold lemonade.

"It sure is a stormy night," Hannah said. "A lot different than today was, that's for sure."

"You're right about that." Timothy frowned. "I'm afraid if the rain doesn't quit, I might lose my corn. It's coming down pretty fierce out there."

"I know how hard you worked planting that corn," she said. "I hope you don't lose it."

He nodded. "Working with the land reminds me that it's the Lord's creation, and it makes me feel at one with nature. We need that corn for our own use, and it would also be nice to have some to sell."

She gave him an encouraging smile. "My daed once said that disasters often bring a person back to what really matters. And if you have to replant, then there's no shame in asking your friends and family to help."

"Your daed's a wise man." Timothy's gaze came to rest on the faint smattering of freckles on Hannah's nose that had been brought out by the sun. He leaned over and nuzzled her cheek. "And as my daed always says, 'If we let God guide, He will provide.' "

The house was quiet, and the kids had gone to bed some time ago. Samuel removed his reading glasses and rubbed his eyes then put his Bible on the table. He was wide awake and had the house all to himself — a rare opportunity for him these days.

"Guess if I'm gonna be any good tomorrow, I better get some sleep." he murmured, slowly rising from the chair in the corner of the living room. Quietly, he walked down the hall to his room, so as not to waken anyone. His body was weary from putting in long days, but he was thankful Allen had several jobs lined up for him and Timothy. It was a blessing to have steady work, especially in these hard economic times.

When Samuel entered his bedroom, he didn't bother to turn on the battery-operated light; he just got undressed and crawled into bed. Outside the wind was blowing so strong it made the window sing. The heavy rain sounded like pebbles being thrown against the side of the house. In an effort to drown out the noise, he grabbed his pillow and put it over head. But it was no use.

Samuel groaned and stretched, trying to get the kinks out of his muscles. It was going to be one of those nights where sleep would not come quickly. True, he was bone tired, but maybe he was just too tired to sleep. Normally the rain would have lulled him to sleep, but for some reason, it had the opposite effect on him tonight. Maybe he ought to go back to the living room and read more from the Bible. Or a glass of warm milk might help him become drowsy enough to fall sleep.

Stepping into the kitchen a short time later, Samuel was surprised to find Marla sitting at the table in the dark.

"What are you doin' in here, sweet girl?" he asked, turning on the gas lantern overhead.

Marla sighed. "Oh, just thinking is all. I woke up and couldn't get back to sleep."

"I couldn't sleep either. That's some storm out there, isn't it?"

She nodded.

"The wind's blowing so hard it made my windows sound like they were singing." Samuel smiled, thinking Marla might get a chuckle out of that, but then he noticed tears glistening on her cheeks. "What's wrong? Are you afraid of the storm?" he asked.

She shook her head. "Daadi, do you think Mama would mind that you're gonna marry Esther, and that Penny and Jared have already started callin' her 'Mamm'?"

Samuel studied Marla's face and was reminded again how much she was like her mother. The child was kind and always concerned about others — just the way her mother had been. His little girl seemed to have grown up right before his eyes. She seemed more like a young lady than the nine-year-old that she was.

"Is there a reason you're thinking about this, Marla?" Samuel asked. "I thought you liked Esther."

"Oh I do, Daadi. In fact, I like Esther a lot. I just hope if Mama's lookin' down from heaven that she's not upset."

Before Samuel could respond, Marla continued. "I had a dream tonight before I came down, and it got me to thinkin'."

"Was it a bad dream?" he asked.

She shook her head. "It was kind of a nice dream, but somethin' strange happened."

"What was that?"

"I was dreamin' that we were all back in Pennsylvania, like it used to be before . . ." Marla looked down as if struggling for the word.

"Before what, Marla?'

"Before Mama died. We were sittin' by this pond, havin' a picnic. All of us were eatin' and laughin' and havin' a good time. Then, just like that, we were back in Kentucky, still sittin' by a pond havin' a picnic — only Mama's face disappeared, and it was Esther's instead." Marla sniffed. "Then the dream ended, and when I woke up, it made me wonder if Mama would be sad about Esther comin' into our lives."

Samuel's heart almost broke for his daughter's concern. She was such an innocent child with grown-up feelings. He decided right then and there to be honest with her.

"You know, Marla, I used to ask myself that same question. And before I go on, let me say that it's important for you to know that Esther is in no way replacing your mamm. No one could ever do that. You also need to know that I was torn about letting Esther into my heart when we started to have feelings for each other. I prayed about it and almost moved us back to Pennsylvania because I thought it was wrong." Samuel noticed that Marla seemed to be hanging on his every word.

"Then, while I was struggling with what to do, your mamm spoke to me in a very special way," he continued.

"She did? How'd she do that, Daadi?" Marla questioned.

Samuel didn't want to reveal just yet about Elsie's journal, because one day when Marla was an adult, he planned to give her the diary on a special occasion. He would know when the time was right.

"Well, it's kind of personal to me right now, and one day I'll share with you how I know." Samuel smiled and tousled his daughter's hair. "Believe me when I tell you that your mamm did let me know that it was okay for me to love Esther."

Marla grinned, and Samuel was glad to see her relax. They sat together in silence awhile, until he noticed that Marla was holding something and kept wrapping it through her fingers.

"What have you got there?" he asked.

"It's one of Mama's hankies." Marla's voice grew shaky. "I . . . I hope you don't mind, Daadi, but last year on my birthday when you gave me Mama's teacup and it broke, I knew you went out to the barn. So I left my room and was gonna ask Esther if you were okay, but when I walked past your room, I saw a box sittin' on the floor. I knew it was wrong, but I went into your room to see what was in the box. When I saw Mama's hankie with the butterfly on it all folded up nice and neat with all the other things, I took it." Tears gathered in the corners of Marla's eyes. "I'm real sorry, Daadi. I shouldn't have done that, but I've taken good care of the hankie. Ever since that night, I keep it with me under the sleeve of my dress. Then at night, I put it under my pillow to keep it close. It makes me feel like Mama's right here with me. When I'm hurtin', I can just reach my hand into my sleeve and hold the hankie, and it's like Mama's holdin' my hand and makin' me feel better."

Samuel was so choked up it took a moment before he could speak. "Ach, Marla," he whispered, taking her into the comfort of his arms and rocking her as he'd done when she was a baby. "It's okay; don't you worry now. Keep your mamm's hankie close and never let it go, and do whatever you have to so that you won't forget her."

Samuel paused a minute, trying to keep his emotions under control. "Your mamm left wonderful memories behind for me, you, and your brothers and sister. They were so young at the time, but someday when Penny and Jared are older, they'll be coming to you and Leon and wanting to hear all that you remember about their mamm. Never be afraid to talk about her, even to

Esther. That's what keeps her memory alive — remembering our time with her."

Samuel sat with his arm around Marla a few more minutes, enjoying this tender moment. Then, when she said good night and headed to her room, he remained at the table and bowed his head. *Thank You, Lord, for special moments like this and a memory that will be with me forever.*

Chapter 40

When Timothy came in from doing his chores the following morning, he wore a sorrowful look. "Sometimes I just want to give up." He flopped into a chair at the table with a groan. "Why is it that a person can feel so good about things one day, and a day later everything just comes tumbling down?"

"What's wrong?" Hannah asked, feeling concern as she handed him a cup of coffee.

"It's the corn crop," he said with a slow shake of his head. "Almost all of it's ruined, and of course after all that rain we had, it's hot and muggy now."

"I'm sorry," she said. "Did the rain cause the damage, or was it the high winds that came up last night?"

"I think it was mostly the wind, because much of the corn is lying flat. I'll either have to forget about having a corn crop this year or replant and hope the warm weather stays long enough for all the corn to grow and mature." Timothy groaned. "It's a shame, too. The corn was looking so good before the storm blew in and ruined it."

"What are you going to do now?" Hannah asked, joining him at the table.

"I don't know. What do you think about all of this?"

Hannah blew on her coffee as she contemplated the situation. She was tempted to tell Timothy that this might be a sign that they shouldn't have moved to Kentucky but knew that would probably make him all the more determined to stay. Besides, after hearing what the pastor had said during Bonnie and Allen's wedding, Hannah had resolved to be a more supportive wife. And lately she'd been thinking that living here might not be so bad after all.

"Well," she said, "since you're so busy painting right now and really don't have the time to replant, maybe you ought to forget about trying to grow corn this year. We could plant some in the garden for our own personal use and see how that does. We could always lease some of the land and keep a few acres for our own use. That way it won't be so much for you to handle."

He offered her a weak smile and reached for her hand. "I think you might be right about that."

Hannah smiled, too. It felt good to be making a decision together.

The phone rang, and Trisha hurried into the foyer to answer it. "Hello. Bonnie's Bed-and-Breakfast."

"Hi, Trisha, it's Ken."

"Oh, I'm surprised you're calling so early." She glanced at the clock on the mantel in the living room. "It's eight o'clock here, so it must only be six in Oregon."

"Yeah, it's early yet, but I had a hard time sleeping last night and got up at the crack of dawn."

"How come? Are you still worried about Bonnie and Allen?"

"Yes, I am, but I'm also worried about you."

Now that's a surprise. "Why are you worried about me?" she asked.

"When we talked last night, you said the weather was bad and you might lose power."

"The electricity was out for several hours, and we had pounding rain with harsh winds most of the night. But the weather looks much better this morning. The sun's out now, and it's warming up fast, so I think things will dry fairly quickly this morning."

"That's good to hear. I'm glad you're

okay. But I don't think it's good for you to be in that big house all alone."

Trisha smiled. She could hear the concern in Ken's voice, and it made her feel good that he might care more for her than he was willing to admit. Or maybe it was just wishful thinking. Even if he did feel something for her, with him living in Oregon and her in Kentucky, it wasn't likely that they'd ever begin a relationship.

They talked awhile longer, until Ken said, "I'd better let you go. I'm going to keep trying to get ahold of Bonnie, and I'd appreciate it if you'd let me know if you hear anything from her or Allen."

"I certainly will. You take care and try not to worry. Goodbye, Ken." Trisha hung up the phone and leaned against the doorjamb with a sigh. She knew it was silly, but talking to Ken on the phone reminded her of when they were teenagers and used to spend hours talking to each other. Part of her missed those carefree days, yet she really wouldn't want to go back to being a teenager again.

"It's time to get some breakfast and begin my day," she told herself as she headed for the kitchen.

"You look kind of down in the dumps this

morning," Samuel said when Timothy showed up at his house. "Did you and Hannah have a disagreement?"

"Nope. We've been gettin' along much better lately," Timothy said. "But that nasty weather we had last night completely ruined my corn crop."

"I'm sorry to hear that. It's supposed to be dry the rest of this week, and there's even going to be a full moon. Would you like me to help you plant more corn?"

Timothy shook his head. "You're busy enough, and so am I. After talking things over with Hannah, I've decided to forget about trying to grow more corn this year. Might even consider leasing some of the land next year so I don't have so much to take care of. For now, though, I think I'll just concentrate on our jobs and on getting the rest of the things done at my house that still need to be taken care of."

"Are you sure? I'd be happy to help if you want me to."

"No, that's all right. You and Esther will be getting married in a few weeks, and you're gonna be busy preparing for that."

"I can't believe it's finally going to happen." Samuel grinned and thumped Timothy's back. "Won't it be great to have most of our family here for the wedding?"

Timothy nodded. "It'll be good to see everyone again."

"Esther talked with her folks the other day, and they're planning to be here, too. It's going to be a great time."

Hannah swatted at a pesky fly. She'd been working in the garden all morning while keeping an eye on Mindy, who was squatted in the grass nearby, picking dandelions. It was hot and humid, but the rustle of grass gave Hannah some hope that the wind might bring relief from the muggy weather. She guessed this kind of weather was better than the awful storm they'd had last night. As much as they'd needed some rain, they hadn't wanted that much. Hannah knew how hard Timothy had worked planting the corn, and she felt bad when he'd told her that it had been ruined. Well, some things couldn't be helped. They'd just have to try again next year or think about leasing some of the acreage out like they'd discussed.

Maybe this afternoon I'll bake that Kentucky chocolate chip pie I've been wanting to try, she decided. *It might cheer Timothy up when he comes home to a dessert that I'm almost sure he'll enjoy.*

Hannah glanced at Mindy, who had moved closer to the house. *My little girl is growing so much, and she's so full of curiosity. I hope Mom and Dad can come for a visit soon. They're missing so much by not being able to see all the little things Mindy does.*

Hannah leaned her hoe against the fence and headed for the house. Like it or not, it was time to start lunch. Her bare feet burned as she hobbled across the gravel but found relief as soon as she stepped onto the cool grass.

"It's time to go in for lunch," Hannah said to Mindy. "After that, Mama's going to bake a pie."

Mindy looked up with a sweet expression and extended her hand, revealing one of the dandelions she'd picked earlier. *"Der bliehe."* Apparently she didn't care about pie today.

"Jah, I see the flower. Leave it on the porch and come into the house with me now." Hannah opened the door and held it for Mindy. The child, still clutching the dandelion, trotted into the house.

Hannah washed her hands at the kitchen sink and took out a loaf of bread for sandwiches. While she was spreading peanut butter, a fly buzzed noisily overhead. It was hot in the kitchen, and Hannah fanned her face with one hand while swatting at the bothersome insect with the other. Would she spend the whole summer killing bugs and trying to find a way to stay cool? Of course, the reason there were flies in the house was because she'd opened the upstairs windows this morning, trying to get some ventilation.

Mindy tromped into the kitchen and tugged on Hannah's apron. "Der bliehe," she said, showing Hannah the dandelion she still held in her hand.

Hannah, feeling a bit annoyed, said, "Mindy, I want you to go to the living room and play until I call you for lunch."

Mindy gave Hannah's apron another tug. "Der bliehe."

"Not now, Mindy! Just do as I say and go to the living room."

Mindy's lower lip protruded as she turned and left the room.

Bzz . . . bzz . . . Hannah gritted her teeth as the irksome fly kept buzzing around her head. Finally, in exasperation, she grabbed the newspaper Timothy had left on the counter last night, waited until the fly landed on the table, and gave it a good whack.

"That's one less thing I have to deal with right now," she said, scooping the fly up with the paper and tossing it in the garbage can.

Hannah went to the sink and wet a sponge. Then she quickly wiped the table where the fly had landed and went back to finishing the sandwiches she'd started.

When their lunch was ready, Hannah went to the living room to get Mindy. The child wasn't there. She opened the front door and looked into the yard but saw no sign of Mindy there either.

I wonder if she went upstairs to her room.

Hannah hurried up the stairs, and when she entered Mindy's bedroom, she spotted the child's favorite doll lying on the floor under the window. Then her gaze went to the open window. Now, the once-broken screen was no longer there.

With her heart pounding, Hannah moved slowly forward, while her brain told her to stop. She felt cold as ice as she approached the window. She held her breath as her gaze moved from the horizon, down to the yard below. She already knew what she would see but prayed it wouldn't be so. Mindy lay on the ground in a contorted position. She wasn't moving.

Hannah dashed down the stairs and out the front door, her fear mounting and making it hard to breathe. When she reached Mindy, she noticed that her daughter still held the shriveled-up dandelion she'd tried to give Hannah only a short time ago.

Hannah dropped onto the grass and

checked for a pulse, but there was none. Stricken with fear such as she'd never known, Hannah raced for the phone shanty to call for help, while whispering a desperate prayer, *"Please, God, don't let our precious Mindy be dead."*

CHAPTER 41

Trisha had just started baking some bread when the telephone rang. She wiped her floury hands on a clean towel and picked up the receiver. "Hello. Bonnie's Bed-and-Breakfast."

"Hey, Trisha. It's Bonnie."

"Oh, it's so good to hear from you!" Trisha sighed with relief. "Your dad and I have both tried calling you and Allen, but all we ever got was your voice mail. We've been worried about you two ever since we heard about a helicopter crash on Kauai. Your dad was afraid you might have been on that 'copter, but thank goodness, you obviously weren't, and I'm so relieved."

"Yes, it's been all over the news, and it was a terrible tragedy. Allen and I might have been on the helicopter had we not decided to go on a boat cruise instead. I'm so sorry we made you worry. I lost my cell phone on the beach, and the battery in

Allen's phone was dead and wouldn't recharge. So he got a new battery this morning. And I never did find my cell phone but decided to wait until we get home to buy a new one."

"Oh, that's too bad. Have you called your dad yet to let him know you're all right?"

"Yes, I did, and he was thankful to hear from me."

"The last time Ken and I talked, I told him that I was sure we'd have heard if something tragic had happened to you and Allen." Trisha took a seat at the desk that held the phone. "Speaking of tragedies, we had one in this community three days ago."

"What happened?" Bonnie asked.

Even though she'd only known the people in this community for a short time, Trisha struggled to convey the news and explain about Mindy's death without breaking down.

"Oh no, that's terrible! I can't imagine how Timothy and Hannah must feel." Bonnie paused before continuing. "Have they had the funeral yet? I wish we could be there for it."

"Her funeral is today, but I'm not going because I don't know the family that well and wasn't sure if I'd be welcome."

Trisha could hear Bonnie sniffling.

"I hope this hasn't ruined your honey-moon," Trisha said. "I thought you should know so you can be praying for Mindy's family."

"Yes, we'll definitely do that."

"Oh, and some of Timothy's relatives are staying here at the B&B since there wasn't enough room at all the brothers' homes for everyone who came."

"I'm glad you had the rooms available. Oh, and Trisha, please let them know that there will be no charge for the rooms. It's the least I can do to help out during this difficult time."

"That's very generous of you. I'll let them know." Trisha paused then quickly added, "Try to relax and have a good time during the rest of your honeymoon, okay?"

"Yes, we will, though it won't be easy. It's so hard to believe Mindy is dead, but thank you so much for letting us know."

Hannah, dressed in black mourning clothes, stood in front of a small wooden coffin in shock and disbelief. The body of the little girl inside that box just couldn't be her precious daughter. It wasn't possible that they were saying their final good-byes. Hannah's eyes burned like hot coals. She wished this was just a horrible nightmare. But as hard as she tried to deny it, she knew Mindy was gone.

Over and over, Hannah had replayed the horrible event that had taken place three days ago. Looking out Mindy's bedroom window and seeing her daughter's body on the ground below had nearly been Hannah's undoing. After she'd gone to the phone shanty to call for help, she'd returned to Mindy and stayed there until the paramedics came. Hannah, though clinging to the hope that it might not be true, had known even before help arrived that Mindy was gone. Yet in her desperation, she'd continued to pray for a miracle — asking the Lord to bring Mindy back to life the way He had the little girl whose death was recorded in Matthew 9.

If God could do miracles back then, why not now? Hannah asked herself as she gazed at Mindy's lifeless body. But Hannah's pleas were for nothing. Mindy was dead, and God could have prevented it from happening — and so could Timothy. *If only he had put in those screens when I asked him to.* A deep sense of bitterness welled in Hannah's soul. *If Mindy hadn't fallen through that broken screen, she would still be alive — running, laughing, playing, picking dandelions.*

Her stomach tightened as she thought

about the comment their bishop's wife had made when she and the bishop had come to their house for the viewing. "I guess our dear Lord must have needed another angel."

He shouldn't have taken my angel! I needed Mindy more than He did. Hannah lowered her head into the palms of her hands and wept.

"It's time for us to go the cemetery now," Timothy said, touching Hannah's arm.

Hannah didn't budge. *I don't want to go. I don't want to watch as my only child is put in the cold, hard ground.*

Hannah's mother stepped between them and slipped her arm around Hannah's waist. "Everyone's waiting outside for us, Hannah. We need to go now."

Hannah, not trusting her voice, could only nod and be led away on shaky legs. How thankful she was for Mom's support. Without it, she would have collapsed.

Outside, a sea of faces swam before Hannah's blurry eyes — her brothers and their families, Timothy's parents and most of his family, as well as many from their community. Most were already seated in their horse-drawn buggies, preparing to follow the hearse that would take Mindy's body to the cemetery. A few people remained outside their buggies waiting to go.

Hannah shuddered. She'd attended several funerals, but none had been for a close family member. To lose anyone was horrible, but to lose her own child was unbearable — the worst possible pain. Hannah feared she might die from a broken heart and actually wished that she could. It would be better than going through the rest of her life without Mindy. Yes, Hannah would welcome the Angel of Death right now if he came knocking at her door.

Once Hannah's parents had taken seats in the back of the buggy, Hannah numbly took her place up front beside Timothy. She blinked, trying to clear the film of tears clouding her vision, and leaned heavily against the seat. Oh, how her arms ached to hold her beloved daughter and make everything right. If only there was some way she could undo the past.

As the buggy headed down the road toward the cemetery, the hooves of the horse were little more than a plodding walk. Even Dusty, who was usually quite spirited, must have sensed this was a solemn occasion.

When they arrived at the cemetery, Hannah sat in the buggy until the pallbearers removed Mindy's casket from the hearse and carried it to the grave site. Then she and all the others followed.

After everyone had gathered around the grave, the bishop read a hymn while the coffin was lowered and the grave filled in by the pallbearers. With each shovelful of dirt, Hannah sank deeper into despair, until her heart felt as if it were frozen.

Even though Hannah hadn't actually spoken the words, Timothy knew she blamed him for Mindy's death. Truth was, he blamed himself, too. If only he'd taken the time to replace the screens, the horrible accident that had taken their child's life would not have happened. If he could just go back and change the past, they wouldn't be standing in the cemetery right now saying their final good-byes.

A lump formed in Timothy's throat as he tried to focus on the words of the hymn their bishop was reading: *" 'Ah, good night to those I love so; Good night to my heart's desire; Good night to those hearts full of woe; Out of love they weep distressed. Tho' I from you pass away; In the grave you lay my clay; I will rise again securely, Greet you in eternity.' "*

Timothy glanced at his parents and saw Mom's shoulders shake as she struggled with her emotions. Dad looked pale as he put his arm around her.

Timothy looked at Hannah's parents and saw Sally sniffing as she swiped at the tears running down her cheeks. Johnny stood beside her with a pained expression.

Nearly everyone from Timothy and Hannah's families had come for the funeral, and each of their somber faces revealed the depth of their compassion and regret over the loss of Mindy. *Do they all think I'm responsible for Mindy's death?* he wondered. *I wouldn't blame them if they did.*

Timothy's gaze came to rest on Hannah. Her face looked drawn, with dark circles beneath her eyes. She hadn't slept much in the last three days, and when she had gone to bed, she had slept in Mindy's room — probably out of a need to somehow feel closer to her. Timothy missed having Hannah beside him at night, for he desperately needed her comfort. If she could just find it in her heart to forgive him, perhaps he might be able to forgive himself.

The bishop's reading finally ended, and everyone bowed their heads to silently pray the Lord's Prayer. Timothy noticed how the veins on Hannah's hands protruded as she clasped her hands tightly together and bowed her head. He suspected she was only going through the motions of praying, because that's what he was doing. What he really wanted to do was look up at the sky and shout, "Dear God: How could You have taken our only child? Don't You care how much we miss her?"

When the prayer ended, most of the mourners moved away from the grave site, but Hannah remained, hands clasped, rocking back and forth on her heels.

"Hannah, it's time for us to go now. We must return to the house and spend time with our guests," Timothy said, gently touching her shoulder.

Hannah wouldn't even look at him. Finally, Hannah's mother and father led her slowly away.

Timothy stayed at the grave site a few more minutes, fighting to gain control of his emotions. He knew he had to find a way through the difficult days ahead, but he didn't know how. Worse yet, he feared that his wife, who'd been so close to their daughter, might never be the same.

CHAPTER 42

Paradise, Pennsylvania

"I'm worried about Timothy and Hannah," Fannie told Abraham as they ate breakfast a week after they'd returned from Kentucky.

"I know you are, Fannie, but worrying won't change a thing." Abraham rested his hand on her arm. "We're told in 1 Peter 5:7 to cast all our cares on Him."

"I realize that, but it's hard when you see a loved one hurting and know there's nothing you can do to ease their pain."

"There most certainly is. We can pray for them, offer encouraging words, and listen and be there when they want to talk."

"You're right." Fannie sighed. "I just wish we could have stayed in Kentucky longer. I really think Timothy and Hannah need us right now."

"But remember, Fannie, Hannah's folks are still there, and I think it might have been too much if we'd stayed, too."

"But we could have stayed with Samuel," she argued. "There's plenty of room in that big house of his, and we would have been able to go over often and check on Timothy and Hannah."

Abraham stroked Fannie's hand. "We'll be going back in a few weeks for Samuel and Esther's wedding. I'm sure Hannah's folks will be gone by then, and it'll give us a chance to spend more time with Hannah and Timothy."

"That's true, but how can we celebrate what should be a joyous occasion when our son and his wife are in such deep grief?"

"While there will be some sadness, it'll be good for everyone to focus on something positive," he said. "Samuel went through a lot when he lost Elsie, and he deserves to be happy with Esther."

Fannie nodded. "You're right. And since I've come to know Esther fairly well, I believe she's the right woman for Samuel and his kinner."

"I agree, and I hope Timothy and Hannah are able to be at the wedding, too, because I'm sure Samuel would be disappointed if they didn't come."

"Do you really think Hannah will be up to going? You know how upset she's been since Mindy died." Fannie paused, feeling the pain of it all herself. "Abraham, it about broke my heart to see the way she shut Timothy out. She barely looked at him the day of Mindy's funeral."

"I know."

"Timothy thinks she blames him for Mindy's death." Fannie's forehead wrinkled. "Do you think our son is responsible for the tragedy?"

Abraham shrugged. "Guess there's a little blame on everyone's shoulders. Timothy for not putting in new screens; Hannah for not keeping a closer watch on Mindy; and even little Mindy, who shouldn't have been playing near the window." He sighed. "But as I told Timothy when I spoke to him on the phone last night, blaming himself or anyone else will not bring Mindy back."

Fannie nodded slowly. "You're right, of course, but it's a hard fact to swallow."

"I also reminded our son that in order to find the strength to press on, he needs to spend time alone with God."

"That was very good advice," Fannie said. "I just hope Timothy will heed what you said."

Pembroke, Kentucky
"You really need to eat something," Sally said, offering Hannah a piece of toast.

Hannah shook her head. "I'm not hungry."

Sally frowned. She was worried sick about her daughter. Over the last week, a number of women from the community had brought food, but Hannah wouldn't eat anything unless she was forced to. She simply sat quietly in the rocking chair, holding Mindy's doll.

If all I can do is offer comfort and sit beside Hannah, then that's what I'll do, Sally thought, taking a seat beside Hannah. "You can take comfort in knowing that Mindy is in a better place," she said, placing her hand on Hannah's arm.

"Better place? What could be better for my little girl than to be right here with me?" Hannah's eyes narrowed into tiny slits. "It's Timothy's fault Mindy is dead! If he'd just put new screens in the windows like I asked —"

"Kannscht ihn verge ware?" Johnny asked as he entered the room.

Hannah slowly shook her head. "No, I don't think I can ever forgive him."

Johnny stood beside Hannah and placed his hand on her shoulder. "If there's one thing I've learned over the years, it's that we don't get to choose our fate. We can only learn how to live through it."

Hannah just continued to rock, staring

401

straight ahead.

"God doesn't spare us trials," Sally said. "But He does help us overcome them."

Hannah made no reply.

"Maybe we should leave her alone for a while." Johnny nudged Sally's arm and motioned to the kitchen. "Let's go eat breakfast. Timothy's finishing his chores in the barn, and I'm sure he'll be hungry when he comes in."

Sally hesitated. She really wished Hannah would join them for breakfast but didn't want to force the issue. Maybe Johnny was right about Hannah needing some time alone; she had been hovering over her quite a bit this week. With a heavy sigh, Sally stood and followed Johnny to the kitchen.

When Timothy joined them a few minutes later, Sally couldn't help but notice the tears in his eyes. He was obviously as distressed about Mindy's death as Hannah was, but at least he continued to eat and do his chores. Yet Timothy spoke very little about his feelings. Maybe he thought not talking about it would lessen the pain. Sally knew otherwise.

The three of them took seats at the table, and after their silent prayer, Sally passed a platter of scrambled eggs and ham to Timothy. He took a piece of the ham and a spoonful of eggs; then after handing the platter to Johnny, he said, "I appreciate all that you both have done, but you've been here almost two weeks now, and I think it's time for you to go home."

"But Hannah's not doing well, and she needs me," Sally argued. She couldn't believe Timothy would suggest that they return to Pennsylvania right now.

With a look of determination, Timothy shook his head. "Hannah and I need each other in order to deal with our grief. As long as you're here, she'll never respond to me."

Sally winced, feeling as if he'd slapped her face. Did Timothy honestly believe that Hannah, who hadn't said more than a few words to him since Mindy's death, needed him more than she did her own mother? She was about to tell him what she thought about that when Johnny spoke up.

"I believe you're right, Timothy. Sally and I will leave in the morning."

CHAPTER 43

Timothy leaned against Dusty's stall and groaned. It had been three weeks since Mindy's death, and things seemed to be getting worse between him and Hannah. He'd figured once Hannah's parents went home, Hannah would return to their own room at night, but she'd continued to sleep in Mindy's bedroom. To make matters worse, whenever Timothy spoke to Hannah, she barely acknowledged his presence. Didn't she realize how horrible he felt about Mindy's death? Didn't she know that he missed their daughter, too?

Despite his grief, Timothy knew he needed to get back to work or they wouldn't have money to pay their bills and buy groceries. Yet he couldn't leave Hannah by herself all day — not in the state she was in. So he'd called and left a message for Suzanne last night, asking if she'd be willing to come and sit with Hannah. He hoped that either she or Titus had checked their voice mail, because Samuel and his driver would be coming by in an hour to pick him up. If Suzanne didn't come over by then, there was no way Timothy could go off to work. He couldn't ask Esther to stay with Hannah. Between taking care of Samuel's kids and doing last-minute things for her upcoming wedding, she had her hands full. Thankfully, Bonnie and Allen had returned from their honeymoon a few days ago, so Esther's help wasn't needed at the B&B anymore.

Forcing his thoughts aside, Timothy finished feeding Dusty and Lilly then went back to the house. Hannah was sitting in the rocking chair with Mindy's doll in her lap.

"We need to talk," he said, kneeling on the floor in front of her.

Hannah kept rocking, staring straight ahead, with no acknowledgment of his presence. If her pale face and sunken eyes were any indication of how tired she felt, she hadn't slept much since the accident, but then, neither had he. How could he get any quality sleep when his wife stayed two rooms away and wouldn't even speak to him? He longed to offer Hannah comfort and reassurance, but it wouldn't be appreciated. Hannah had shut him out, and he wasn't sure she would ever let him into her world again. Her brown eyes looked so sorrowful behind her tears, yet she wouldn't express her feelings.

Timothy was even more worried because he'd noticed that Hannah had lost a lot of weight since the accident. She ate so little, and then only when someone practically forced her to do so. Did she think that not eating would dull her pain, or was she trying to starve herself to death? He hoped she wasn't so depressed that she wanted to end her own life. He couldn't deal with another tragedy — especially one of that magnitude. He'd just have to try harder to get through to her.

"I love you, Hannah. Please talk to me." Timothy's fingers curved under her trembling chin.

She winced and pulled away as if she couldn't stand the sight of him. Her reluctance to look at him or even speak his name was so strong he could feel it to the core of his being. Even his gentle touch seemed to make her cringe. If only there was something he could do to bridge the awful gap between them.

"Why are you shutting me out?" he asked, trying once again. "Don't you think I miss Mindy, too?"

Hannah turned in her chair, refusing to make eye contact with him.

Timothy swallowed around the lump in his throat. It hurt to know she didn't love him anymore.

A knock sounded on the back door, and he went to answer it.

"I got your message," Suzanne said when he found her standing on the porch. "I'd be happy to stay with Hannah while you go to work today."

Timothy breathed a sigh of relief, trying to stay composed. "Let's go into the kitchen so we can talk," he said.

When they entered the kitchen, Timothy shared his concerns about Hannah. "I know it's only been a few weeks since Mindy died, but Hannah's still grieving so hard it scares me. What if she doesn't snap out of it? What if —"

"I'll try talking to her," Suzanne said. "Maybe she'll open up to me."

"You might be right. Since she doesn't blame you for our daughter's death, she probably won't give you the cold shoulder the way she does me. I can't get her to respond to me at all."

Suzanne offered Timothy a sympathetic smile and patted his arm. "Things will get better in time; you'll see."

Timothy sighed. "I hope so, because the guilt I feel for not putting in new window screens is bad enough, but having my wife shut me out the way she has is the worst kind of pain."

"I can only imagine."

A horn honked, and Timothy looked out the window. "Samuel and his driver are here, so I'd better go. Thanks again for coming, Suzanne."

"You're welcome."

As Hannah continued to rock, her shoulders sagged with the weight of her depression. She almost felt paralyzed with grief and was sure that her life would never be normal again.

When she'd refused to talk to Timothy, she'd seen the pained expression on his face, but she didn't care. Because of him, she was miserable. Because of him, she'd never see her precious little girl again.

Hannah stopped rocking, lifted Mindy's doll, and studied its face. *If Mindy had lived and been crippled, that would have been better than her dying,* she thought. Then she remembered a conversation she'd had with Esther some time ago about her brother, Dan, who was struggling with MS. Hannah had mentioned that she didn't think she could take care of someone like that. If she could have Mindy back, she'd gladly make the sacrifice of caring for her, even if she was disabled.

Suzanne stepped into the living room, disrupting Hannah's thoughts. "I'm here to spend the day with you," she said, handing Hannah a cup of hot tea.

Hannah shook her head. "I don't want anything to drink, and I don't need you to babysit me."

Suzanne set the teacup on the small table near the rocking chair and took a seat on the sofa across from Hannah. "Timothy is really worried about you."

Hannah said nothing.

"We're all worried, Hannah."

Hannah started the rocker moving again. *Creak . . . Creak . . . Creak . . .* It moved in rhythmic motion.

"I know you're going through a hard time, but if you ask God for strength, He will give it to you. When you're hurting, He will give you comfort in ways that no one else can."

Hannah's throat constricted, and a tight sob threatened to escape. "God doesn't care about me."

"He most certainly does. God loves and cares about all His people."

"Then why'd He take Mindy?"

"I don't know the answer to that, but I do know that accidents happen, and —"

Hannah's face contorted. "It was an accident that shouldn't have happened! God could have prevented it, and so could Timothy. He should have put new screens on the windows when I asked him to. Now our daughter is gone, and she's never coming back!"

Hopkinsville, Kentucky

"Are you sure you're ready to begin working again?" Samuel asked Timothy as he set a ladder in place inside the doctor's office they'd been hired to paint.

"Whether I'm ready or not is beside the point. I have to work. We need the money, and I need to keep busy so I don't think too much," Timothy said after he'd opened a bucket of paint.

"It's good to be busy, but I'm concerned that you might not have given yourself enough time to heal before returning to work," Samuel said. "You look like you haven't been sleeping well."

"I haven't. It's kind of hard to sleep when I know it's my fault that my daughter is dead. And knowing Hannah blames me for the accident makes it even worse." Timothy clenched his fingers tightly together. "When

I look in the mirror these days, I don't like what I see."

"That's *narrish*. Blaming yourself will only wear you down."

"It might seem foolish to you, but that's the way I feel." Timothy dropped his gaze as he continued. "I keep hearing Hannah that day, asking me to fix the window screens upstairs. But I was too worried about planting the field. I kept putting it off and finding other things to do. Now in hindsight, I keep asking myself, *What was I thinking?* Replacing those screens, especially in my daughter's room, was far more important than the corn crop that ended up getting destroyed. Same goes for the rest of the projects I did instead of taking care of the screens. Mindy's life was at stake, and now I'm paying the price for being so stupid."

Samuel moved across the room and clasped Timothy's shoulder. "It takes a strong person to deal with hard times, and you're a strong person. So with God's help, you can choose to forgive yourself and go on with your life. And never forget that you have a family who loves and cares about you. We're all here to support you through this difficult time. Remember, Timothy, I was in a similar situation over a year ago when I lost Elsie. I know it's not exactly the

411

same, but the pain is just as strong. In time, good things will happen again in your lives. I never would have believed it myself, but good things have happened for me."

"I appreciate hearing that, and I know as time passes it might get easier. I couldn't get through this without my family's support, but I sure wish I had Hannah's. She won't even speak to me. In fact, she avoids looking at me." Timothy groaned. "I really don't know what to do about it."

"Would you like me to talk to her? With all I went through after Elsie died, I might be able to help Hannah through her grief."

"You can try if you like. Suzanne said she'll attempt to get through to Hannah, too, but I doubt it'll do any good." Timothy picked up his paintbrush. "Guess we'd better get to work, or this job will never get done."

Samuel nodded. "Just remember one thing: I'm here for you, day or night."

CHAPTER 44

Pembroke, Kentucky

"Mom, Dad, it's so good you could be here for my wedding today," Esther said as she sat with her folks eating breakfast at Bonnie's dining-room table. Mom and Dad had arrived yesterday afternoon and would be staying for a few days after the wedding. Esther's brother James and his family, who lived in Lykens, Pennsylvania, had also come. But due to Dan's failing health, he and his family had remained in Pennsylvania.

"We're glad we could be here, too," Mom said, smiling at Esther. "There's no way we could miss our only daughter's wedding."

Dad bobbed his head. "Your mamm's right about that."

Esther glanced across the table at Samuel's sister Naomi. She and her husband, Caleb, as well as some other members of Samuel's family, were also staying at the bed-

and-breakfast. Esther appreciated the fact that Bonnie had graciously agreed to let them all have their rooms at no cost. They'd set up a cot for Trisha in the guesthouse, and she'd slept there last night, since they needed all the extra rooms for their guests. Trisha would be living in the guesthouse full-time after Esther was married.

"I can't believe this day is finally here," Esther murmured. "I just feel a bit guilty getting married when Timothy and Hannah are still grieving for Mindy. Samuel and I had thought about postponing the wedding for another month or two, but Timothy wouldn't hear of it."

"One thing I've always thought was special about you is that you can't look the other way when someone you know is hurting," Mom said, smiling at Esther. "But postponing your wedding won't bring Timothy and Hannah's little girl back, and I'm sure they would want you to go ahead with your plans."

Esther nodded. "That's exactly what Timothy told Samuel."

"Life goes on even when people are hurting. Maybe going to the wedding will help them focus on something else, if only for a little while," Naomi spoke up. "I remember when my little brother Zach was kidnapped.

Nothing seemed right. But we forced ourselves to keep on with the business of living despite the pain we felt over losing him."

"That's right," Naomi's sister Nancy said. "It was hard going on without our little brother all those years, but God helped us get through it."

"And He will help Timothy and Hannah, too," Allen said. "They just need to stay close to Him and rely on others for comfort and support."

"Do you think they'll attend the wedding?" Bonnie asked, turning to look at him.

"Well, Timothy's back working with Samuel again, and when I spoke to him yesterday, he said he was planning to go and that he hoped Hannah would feel up to it."

When Timothy entered the kitchen, Hannah was standing in front of the stove making a pot of coffee. That was a good sign, because ever since Mindy died he'd had to make his own coffee in the mornings.

"I'm just going to have a bowl of cereal, and then I'll need to get ready for the wedding," he said, stepping up beside her.

No reply. Not even a nod.

"Hannah, are you planning to go Esther and Samuel's wedding with me?"

She slowly shook her head.

"Maybe I shouldn't go either, because I don't want to leave you here alone."

"Just go on without me; I'll be fine," she mumbled. Well, at least she was talking to him again.

"Are you sure you won't go? It might do you some good to get out of the house for a few hours."

She whirled around and glared at him. "You can't expect me to put on a happy face and go to the wedding when I feel so dead inside!"

Normally, Timothy preferred to listen rather than talk, but something needed to be said, and he planned to say it. "You know, when we first made plans to move to Kentucky —"

Her eyes narrowed. "Your plans, don't you mean? You never considered whether I wanted to move. All you thought about was yourself!"

"I wasn't just thinking of me. I was thinking of us and our marriage."

She folded her arms. "Humph!"

"We can make this work, Hannah, but it's going to take both of us to do it."

"It's never going to work, and I don't see how you can expect it to," she said. "If we were still in Pennsylvania, none of this would have happened. Don't you realize that the day our daughter died, a part of me died, too? You took her from me, Timothy. You took our precious little girl, and she's never coming back!" Hannah turned and rushed out of the room, leaving him staring after her, eyes wet with tears.

It had been hard for Timothy to hitch his horse to the buggy and go over to Samuel's for the wedding, but out of love and respect for his brother, he'd made himself do it. Now, after turning his horse loose in the corral and starting in the direction of the house, he was having second thoughts. Maybe he should have stayed home with Hannah. She was terribly upset when he left. But if he couldn't get through to her in the kitchen this morning, it probably wouldn't have mattered if he'd stayed there all day and talked to Hannah. Suzanne had tried, Samuel had tried, and Esther had tried, but no one could get through to her. Hannah blamed Timothy for Mindy's death, and she obviously wasn't going to forgive him. Short of a miracle, nothing he could say or do would change the fact that she no longer loved him. He feared that for the rest of their married life they'd be living in the same house, sleeping in separate bedrooms, with Hannah barely acknowledging his presence. That wasn't the way God intended marriage to be, but Timothy didn't know what he could do about it.

As he neared the house, he spotted Bonnie and Allen on the front porch talking to Trisha. He wasn't surprised that they'd been invited, since Allen and Samuel were good friends and so were Bonnie and Esther. And since Trisha and Esther had been working at the B&B together for the last several weeks, it was understandable that she'd received an invitation to the wedding as well.

"It's good to see you," Allen said, clasping Timothy's shoulder as soon as he stepped onto the porch.

"Thanks. It's good to see you, too."

"How's Hannah doing?" Bonnie asked. "I was hoping she might be here today."

Timothy shook his head. "Hannah's still not doing well. She didn't feel up to coming."

"That's too bad. I've been meaning to drop by your place and see her," Bonnie said. "I was busy getting ready for the out-of-town wedding guests, and I'm sorry I didn't take the time to check on her. I'll try to do that within the next day or so."

Timothy forced a smile. "I appreciate that, and hopefully Hannah will, too." He motioned to the house. "Guess the service will be starting soon, so I'd better get inside."

When Timothy took a seat beside his dad, he noticed that Samuel and Esther had already taken their seats, facing each other. They fidgeted a bit, an indication that they were nervous, but their eager smiles let him know how happy they were. They'd both been through a lot, so they deserved all the happiness of this special day.

Timothy glanced to his right and saw his other five brothers sitting beyond his dad. On the benches behind them were his three brothers-in-law. His sisters sat together on the women's side of the room with his sisters-in-law. Many of his nieces and nephews had also come to the wedding, making quite a large group from Pennsylvania. They'd hired several drivers with vans to make the trip.

As the first song began, Timothy thought about how this was the second of his brothers' weddings he'd attended alone. Last October, Timothy had left Hannah and Mindy in Pennsylvania when he'd come to Kentucky to attend Titus and Suzanne's wedding. Hannah had used the excuse that her mother needed help because she'd sprained her ankle, so she'd insisted on staying home. Now Timothy was at Samuel and

419

Esther's wedding, and he was alone once again. This time he understood why Hannah hadn't wanted to come. It had been difficult for him to come, but he was happy Samuel had found love again, and Timothy wanted to witness his brother's marriage.

As the service continued, Timothy thought about his own wedding. He'd loved Hannah so much back then — and still did, for that matter. But things had changed for Hannah. Even before Mindy's death, she'd often been cool toward him. He'd shrugged it off, figuring she was still upset with him for making them move to Kentucky. But there had been times, like the week before Mindy died, when he thought Hannah was beginning to adjust to the move and had actually warmed up to him. Just when he'd felt there was some hope for their marriage, Mindy's tragic death had shattered their world. Timothy was convinced that Hannah's love for him was dead. Their tragedy was so huge, nothing short of a miracle could mend their relationship.

Timothy's thoughts were halted when Bishop King called Esther and Samuel to stand before him. Their faces fairly glowed as they each answered affirmatively to the bishop's questions. When the vows had been spoken, the bishop took Esther and Samuel's hands and said, "So go forth in the name of the Lord. You are now husband and wife."

I hope they will always be as happy as they are right now, Timothy thought. *And may nothing ever drive them apart.*

As Hannah entered the cemetery to visit Mindy's grave, she spotted a lone sheep rubbing its nose on one of the headstones. At least she thought it was a sheep. Due to the tears clouding her vision, she wondered if she might be seeing something that wasn't actually there.

Hannah moved forward and stopped when she heard a loud *baa.* There really was a sheep by that headstone. But why would the creature be in the cemetery, and who did it belong to?

Hannah heard another *baa* and glanced to her left. Several sheep grazed in the field on the other side of the cemetery. Apparently one had found a way out and ended up over here. Well, the sheep could stay right where it was, for all she cared.

Hannah ambled slowly through the cemetery until she came to the place where Mindy's body had been buried. The simple granite headstone inscribed with Mindy's name, date of birth, and date of death had been set in place, making the tragedy even more final. Tears welled in Hannah's eyes, and she swayed unsteadily. The anguish that engulfed her was so great she felt overcome by it. She dropped to the ground and sobbed. "Oh Mindy, my precious little girl . . . How can I go on without you?"

CHAPTER 45

After Hannah returned home from the cemetery, she sat on the porch awhile, holding Bobbin and hoping the cat would offer her some comfort. He didn't. She just felt worse because she was reminded of how Mindy had enjoyed playing with the animal. One time Bobbin had lost his balance and rolled down the stairs like a sack of potatoes. Mindy had been so concerned and looked so relieved when she'd seen that the cat wasn't hurt.

Even with the memories she had left of Mindy, Hannah didn't think anything would ever bring her the comfort she so badly needed. She barely noticed the birds singing in the trees and refused to look at the flowers she'd planted in the spring. She thought about the dandelions Mindy had picked on the morning of her death and winced. It was such a bittersweet memory.

Bobbin rubbed his nose against Hannah's

hand and purred, as though sensing her mood; yet Hannah felt no comfort.

When the sun became unbearably hot, Hannah set the cat on the porch and went inside for a glass of water. She took a seat at the table and sat staring at the stool Mindy used to perch on during their meals. This house was way too quiet without the patter of Mindy's little feet and the sound of her childish laughter bouncing off the walls. She'd been such a happy girl — curious, full of energy, so cute and cuddly. Hannah's arms ached to hold her and stroke her soft, pink skin.

Giving in to her tears, Hannah leaned forward and rested her head on the table. She'd been on the brink of tears every day since Mindy died, and often let herself weep, as she was doing now.

"Oh how I wish I'd had the chance to say good-bye, kiss my precious girl, and tell her how much I love her," Hannah sobbed. Overcome with fatigue and grief, she closed her eyes and drifted off.

Sometime later, Hannah was awakened when Timothy entered the kitchen, touched her shoulder, and said, "How come you're sitting here in the dark?"

Hannah sat up straight and rubbed her eyes. "I must have dozed off."

Timothy lit the gas lamp above the kitchen table. "Sorry I'm so late. There were lots of people from my family at the wedding, and I wanted to visit with them."

Hannah glanced at the clock on the far wall. It was almost seven o'clock. Had she really been asleep nearly two hours?

"Mom and Dad said to tell you hello. They'll be over to visit in the next day or so. I think tomorrow they're going to help Esther and Samuel with the cleanup from the wedding."

Hannah shrugged. She didn't care whether Fannie and Abraham came over to see her. She wasn't good company and really had nothing to say to either of them.

"Have you eaten supper yet?" Timothy asked.

She shook her head. "I'm not hungry."

"Hannah, you need to eat. I'm worried because you've lost so much weight, and it's not good for your health to skip meals like you do."

"Why'd the Lord bring us here, only to forsake us?" she wailed.

"God hasn't forsaken us, Hannah. He knows the pain we both feel." Timothy rested his hands on her trembling shoulders, and for just a minute, Hannah's pain lessened a bit.

"Why don't the two of us go for a ride?" he suggested. "It'll give us a chance to enjoy the cool evening breeze that's come up, and I think it would be good for you to get out of the house for a while."

She shrugged his hands away. "I don't want to go for a ride. I just want to be left alone."

"Not this time, Hannah. You need me right now, and I . . . I need you, too."

Hannah just stared at the table, fighting back tears of frustration.

"Don't you love me anymore?" he asked, taking a seat beside her.

His question burned deep in her heart, and she shifted in her seat, unsure of how to respond.

He leaned close and moaned as he brushed his lips across her forehead. "I love you, Hannah, and I always will."

Overcome with emotion, she took a deep breath and forced herself to look at him. His eyes held no sparkle, revealing the depth of his sadness. When he pulled her into his arms, she felt weak, unable to resist.

As Timothy's lips touched Hannah's, a niggling little voice in her head said she shouldn't let this happen, yet her heart said otherwise, and she seemed powerless to stop it.

Finding comfort in her husband's embrace, Hannah closed her eyes and allowed his kisses to drive all negative, hurtful thoughts from her mind.

When Timothy awoke the following morning, he glanced over at his sleeping wife and smiled. She looked so peaceful with her long hair fanned out on the pillow and her cheeks rosy from a good night's sleep. He decided not to wake her. After all, he'd been fixing his own breakfast for the last few weeks, so he could do it again this morning.

He grabbed his work clothes, bent to kiss Hannah's forehead, and slipped quietly out of the room. There was extra pep to his step because, for the first time in weeks, he actually felt hopeful.

As Timothy fixed a pot of coffee in the kitchen, he thought about last night and thanked God that he and Hannah had found comfort in each other's arms. Timothy was certain her response to him had been the first step in helping them deal with the pain of losing Mindy. He felt hopeful that they could now face the loss of their daughter together and find the strength they both needed to go on.

When Timothy walked out the door to wait for his driver, he leaned against the porch railing. Watching the sunrise, he thought it had never looked more beautiful.

Hannah yawned and stretched her arms over her head. Her brain felt fuzzy — like it was full of thick cobwebs. She must have slept long and hard.

When Hannah sat up in bed and looked around, she felt as if a jolt of electricity had been shot through her. She was in her own bedroom, not Mindy's! *How in the world did I end up here?*

Hannah rubbed her forehead. Then she remembered Timothy's kisses and words of love. She'd needed his comfort and let her emotions carry her away.

"What was I thinking?" Hannah moaned. She hadn't forgiven Timothy for causing Mindy's death and didn't think she ever could. One night of being held in his arms wouldn't bring Mindy back to them, and it may have given Timothy false hope.

Hannah pushed the covers aside and crawled out of bed. With tears blinding her vision, she stumbled across the room. She couldn't stay here anymore. She had to get away.

As Hannah packed her bags in readiness to leave, pain clutched her heart. If they hadn't moved to Kentucky, none of this would have happened. Mindy would still be with them, and they'd be living happily in Pennsylvania.

After Hannah got dressed, she opened the bedroom door, set her suitcase in the hallway, and headed for Mindy's room. When she stepped inside, she stared at her daughter's empty bed. She hadn't even changed Mindy's sheets since the tragic day of her death. A deep sense of sadness washed over Hannah as she sat on the bed and buried her face in Mindy's pillow. She took a deep breath, trying to keep her daughter's essence within her. But sadly, she was reminded once again that Mindy was never coming back. Hannah wouldn't see her little girl's sweet face again — not in this life, anyhow. The only way she could deal with this unrelenting pain was to leave this place, where painful memories plagued her night and day, and return to Pennsylvania. At least there she would have Mom and Dad's love and support. Yes, that's what she needed right now.

With one last glance, Hannah spotted Mindy's favorite doll. She picked it up and carried it, along with her suitcase, down the stairs. Upon entering the kitchen, she found a notepad and pen and quickly scrawled a note for Timothy, which she left on the table.

Hannah pushed the screen door open and stepped onto the porch. A blast of warm, humid air hit her full in the face, yet she still felt chilled. She heard a pathetic *meow*. Looking down, she saw Bobbin lying on his back on the porch, paws in the air. Did the poor cat know she was leaving? Did he even care?

Shoulders slumped and head down, Hannah stepped off the porch and made her way down the lane, where she would stop at the phone shanty to call her driver for a ride to the bus station in Clarksville.

As she ambled slowly past the fence dividing the lane from the pasture, Mindy's doll slipped from her hand, unnoticed. Squinting against the morning sun, blazing like a fiery furnace, Hannah kept walking and didn't look back. It was best to leave all the painful memories behind.

When Timothy's driver dropped him at the end of their lane that evening, Timothy winced with each step he took. He hurt all over — even the soles of his feet. He and Samuel had worked on a three-story house in Hopkinsville today, and he'd been up and down the ladder so many times he'd lost count. It had been easier to work, however, knowing things were better between him and Hannah and that she'd be waiting for him when he got home. He hoped she'd have supper ready and that they could sit outside on the back porch after they ate and visit while they watched the sun go down and listened to the crickets sing their nightly chorus.

As Timothy continued his walk up the lane, he kicked something with the toe of his boot. He looked and was surprised to see Mindy's doll lying facedown in the dirt.

"Now what's that doing here?" he murmured. Could Hannah have gone out to get the mail today and taken the doll along? She'd had it with her almost constantly since Mindy died and often rocked the doll as though it were a baby. Hannah had probably dropped it on the way back from the mailbox and just hadn't noticed.

Timothy picked up the doll and carried it under one arm. When he entered the house, all was quiet, and he didn't smell any food. It was a disappointment, but he was used to it because Hannah hadn't done any of the cooking since Mindy died. Timothy stepped into the utility room and put the doll on a shelf then went to the kitchen. Hannah wasn't there, and he was about to call for her when he spotted a note on the table. He picked it up and read it silently.

Timothy,

I'm sure you'll be disappointed when I tell you this, but I can't stay here any longer. Every time I look at you, I remember that you could have prevented our daughter's death, and it's too painful for me to deal with. I'm returning to Pennsylvania to be with Mom and Dad. Please don't come after me, because I won't come back to Kentucky, and I can no longer live with you. It's better this way, for both of us.

— Hannah

Timothy sank into a chair and groaned. He couldn't believe it. After last night, he was sure things were better between them. Why had she let him kiss her and then slept in their room if she hadn't forgiven him for being the cause of Mindy's death?

He shuddered and swallowed against the sob rising in his throat. He'd not only lost his daughter, but now his wife was gone, too. He didn't know if he'd ever see Hannah again. She hadn't even signed the note with love. Should he go after her — insist that she come home? Or would it be better

432

to give her some time and hope she'd come back on her own? After so many weeks of trying to remain strong, Timothy could no longer hold in his grief. He leaned forward and sobbed so hard it almost made him ill. He didn't care anymore. He was exhausted from trying to be strong for Hannah, and now he had nothing left. How much more could a man take?

CHAPTER 46

Paradise, Pennsylvania

Sally had just entered the phone shack to make a call when the telephone rang. She quickly picked up the receiver. "Hello."

"Sally, is that you?" a male voice asked.

"Yes, it's me. Who's this?"

"It . . . it's Timothy."

"Is everything all right? You sound *umgerennt.*"

"I am upset. I came home from work today and found a note from Hannah." There was a pause. "She said she was leaving me and returning to Pennsylvania."

Sally drew in a sharp breath. "Hannah's on her way here?"

"Jah. I'm not sure if she hired a driver or caught a bus." Another pause. "I thought maybe you would have heard from her."

"No, but then maybe she didn't call because she was afraid we would have told her she shouldn't come."

"Would you have?"

Sally sank into the folding chair, unsure how to respond. If Hannah had told her that she was coming, it would have been hard to dissuade her. But she was fairly sure if Hannah had talked to Johnny about this, he would have told her to stay put — that her place was in Kentucky with her husband.

"Sally, are you still there?"

"Jah, I'm here."

"What are you gonna do when Hannah gets there?" Timothy asked.

Sally was glad he hadn't forced her to answer his previous question. She shifted the phone to her other ear.

"We'll make her feel welcome, of course."

Timothy grunted. "Figured as much."

"Hannah's obviously in great distress or she wouldn't have felt the need to leave Kentucky. Seriously, we can hardly ask her to go as soon as she gets here."

"No, I suppose not, but Hannah's place is with me."

"Maybe she needs some time away — time to think and allow her broken heart to heal."

"You might be right, but I'm hurting, too, and I think I should be the one to help Hannah through her grief."

"You may not realize this now, but a time

435

of separation might be what you both need."

"It's not what I need, Sally. When Hannah gets there, will you please ask her to come home?"

"Pennsylvania has been Hannah's home since she was a baby."

"Not anymore," Timothy said forcefully. "Her home's here with me!"

"I can't talk anymore," Sally said. "I need to fix supper for Johnny. One of us will call and let you know when Hannah arrives so you won't worry about her. Good-bye, Timothy. Take care." Sally hung up the phone quickly, before he could respond.

She sat for several minutes, mulling things over. *So Hannah's coming home. I wonder what Johnny will have to say about this?*

Pembroke, Kentucky

When Timothy hung up the phone, he sat in disbelief. After his conversation with Sally, he was convinced that she had no intention of trying to persuade Hannah to return to Kentucky.

Needing some fresh air, he stepped out of the hot, stuffy phone shanty. He needed to talk to his brothers about this, and he'd start with Titus, since he lived the closest.

Timothy sprinted up to the barn to get his horse and buggy, and a short time later he was on the road. He let Dusty run, and as the horse trotted down the road, Timothy's thoughts ran wild. He remembered the day he'd told Hannah he wanted to move to Kentucky. She'd argued with him and begged him to change his mind. When she'd asked if he would be sad to leave Pennsylvania, he'd replied, "As long as I have you and Mindy, I'll never be sad." Little did he know then that less than a year later, he'd be sadder than he ever thought possible.

"Maybe Hannah was right about my decision to move here," he mumbled. "But if we'd stayed in Pennsylvania, Hannah would have continued to put her mamm's needs ahead of mine, and she'd have spent more time with her than she did me."

Who am I kidding? My marriage to Hannah is in more trouble now than it's ever been. I'd thought things were better last night, but I was wrong. Hannah obviously doesn't love me. She probably had a moment of weakness and, when she woke up this morning, realized her mistake and wanted to get as far away from me as possible. No doubt she'd rather be with her Mamm right now.

By the time Timothy pulled into Titus's place, he felt even more confused and stressed out. He really did need to talk to someone who'd understand the way he felt about things.

"What brings you by here this evening?" Titus asked, stepping out of the barn. "Is everything okay?"

"No, it's not," Timothy said, climbing out of the buggy. "Hannah's gone!"

"What do you mean?"

Timothy explained about the note he'd found and told Titus about the conversation he'd had with Hannah's mother.

"Would you like my opinion?" Titus asked.

"Jah, that's why I came over here. I'd also like Suzanne's opinion. Is she in the house?"

"No, she's feeding the cats in the barn. You want me to call her, or should we go in there?"

"Let me secure my horse, and then we can go in the barn."

When they entered the barn a few minutes later, Timothy spotted Suzanne sitting on a bale of hay with Titus's cat, Callie, in her lap. Seeing Suzanne so large in her pregnancy reminded him of Hannah when she was carrying Mindy. How long ago that now seemed.

"Oh hi, Timothy," she said, smiling up at him. "Is Hannah with you?"

He shook his head then quickly explained the situation. "I can't believe she would just

438

up and leave me like that," he said.

"She's been an emotional wreck ever since Mindy died, and people like that don't think things through before they act," Suzanne said. "If you want my opinion, I think you should give her some time."

"So you don't think I should go after her?"

Suzanne shook her head. "That might make matters even worse."

Timothy looked at Titus. "What are your thoughts?"

"I agree with my wife. If you try to force Hannah to come back to Kentucky, she might resent you more than she already does. It could drive a wedge between you that will never break down."

"What if Hannah never gets over Mindy's death? She blames me for the accident, and I'm afraid —" Timothy stopped talking and drew in a shaky breath. "You don't think Hannah will divorce me, do you?"

Suzanne gasped. "That would be baremlich, and it goes against our beliefs."

"Jah, it would be terrible," Titus said, "but I really don't think Hannah would do such a thing."

"How do you know?" Timothy questioned.

"If she got a divorce, she'd have to leave the Amish faith. Can you really see Hannah doing something that would take her away from her family — especially her mamm — and in such a tragic way?"

"I hope not, but in Hannah's current state of mind, she might do anything." Timothy sank to a bale of hay and let his head fall forward into his hands. All he could do was wait and pray for a miracle.

CHAPTER 47

Paradise, Pennsylvania

Hannah sat in a wicker rocking chair on her parents' front porch, watching two of Dad's cats leaping through the grass, chasing grasshoppers. It made her think of Mindy and how she'd loved playing with Bobbin. Mindy had also liked playing with her doll, but a few days after she'd arrived at her folks', Hannah had realized that Mindy's doll must still be in Kentucky. She'd had it with her when she was walking down the lane to call for a driver, so she assumed in her grief, she must have dropped it along the way. It was probably just as well. Seeing it all the time would be a constant reminder of what Hannah had lost.

Tears sprang to her eyes. She remembered the time she'd entered the living room and spotted Mindy leaning against the wall, wearing Timothy's sunglasses and a grin that stretched from ear to ear. She'd been such a happy child — so spontaneous and curious about things.

"Mind if I join you?" Mom asked, joining Hannah on the porch.

"No." Hannah motioned to the chair beside her.

"Are you doing okay?" Mom asked, taking a seat. "You look like you're deep in thought."

"I was thinking about Mindy and how much fun she used to have playing with the cat." Hannah sniffed. "Thanks to us moving to Kentucky, you and Dad missed so many of the cute little things Mindy said and did. I wish. . . ." Her voice trailed off, and she stared down at her hands, clasped firmly in her lap.

Mom reached over and took Hannah's hand. "It's all right, Hannah."

"Would you like to hear about some of the things Mindy did?"

"Of course."

"One day Mindy and I were walking on the path leading from our house to the mailbox. She stopped all of a sudden and looked up at me with a huge smile. Then she said, 'I love you Mama.' "

Hannah stopped talking and drew in a shaky breath, hoping to gain control of her swirling emotions. "Another time, Mindy was picking dandelions and kept calling them 'pretty flowers.' She had a dandelion in her hand when she died, Mom." Hannah paused again, barely able to get the words out. "I . . . I will never forget the shock of seeing my precious little girl lying there so still, with a withered dandelion in her hand." Hannah nearly choked on the sob rising in her throat. "I don't think I can ever forgive Timothy for causing Mindy's death."

Pembroke, Kentucky

"Not long ago, Trisha and I were talking about how food always tastes so much better when it's eaten outside," Bonnie said as she and Allen sat on the front porch of the B&B eating supper. They'd invited Trisha to join them, but she'd declined, saying she wanted to give the newlyweds some time alone and would fix something for herself in the guesthouse.

"You're right about the food tasting good," Allen agreed, after taking a bite of fried chicken. "The only problem with eating outside is this hot July weather. Whew! It makes me glad for air-conditioning! I don't know how our Amish friends manage without it."

Bonnie smiled. "I guess one never misses what one's never had."

"That's true."

"By the way," she asked, "have you seen Timothy since he ate supper with us last week? I've been wondering how he's doing."

"Not very well. I saw him yesterday, and he's so despondent. It's a miracle he's been able to keep going at all."

"I wish Hannah hadn't walked out on him. She may not realize it, but she needs her husband as much as he needs her."

"I agree." Allen reached for Bonnie's hand. "If we ever had to go through anything like that, I'd want you right by my side."

She nodded. "I'd want you near me as well, but I hope we're never faced with anything like what Hannah and Timothy are going through right now."

In the two weeks Hannah had been gone, it had been all Timothy could do to cope. He missed his wife so much and longed to speak with her. He'd called her folks several times and left voice messages for Hannah, but she never responded. He'd gotten one message from Sally the day Hannah got there, but it was brief and to the point. She didn't think Timothy should try to contact Hannah and said Hannah would contact him, if and when she felt ready.

"What a slap in the face," Timothy mumbled as he made himself a sandwich for supper. Since he wasn't much of a cook, he'd been eating sandwiches for supper every evening unless he ate at one of his brothers' homes. Both Esther and Suzanne were good cooks, so he appreciated getting a home-cooked meal. He'd eaten supper at Bonnie and Allen's one night last week, and that meal had been good, too.

If I could just talk to Hannah, he thought, *I might be able to convince her to come home.*

Timothy wanted to go to Pennsylvania and speak to her face-to-face, but Samuel and Titus had both advised him to stay put and give Hannah all the time she needed. Trisha, who had lost her husband a few years ago, had reminded Timothy that everyone was different and that it took some people longer than others to deal with their grief. Timothy understood that because he was still grieving for Mindy. He really believed he and Hannah needed each other during this time of mourning. He also feared that the longer they were apart, the harder it would be to bridge the gap between them.

Through prayer and Bible reading, Timothy had been trying to forgive himself, but it was difficult knowing Hannah might never forgive him or come back to Kentucky. How could he go on without her? Nothing would ever be the same if they weren't together as husband and wife.

Timothy set his knife down and made a decision. He would call his mother and ask her to speak to Hannah on his behalf. He just hoped Hannah would listen.

Chapter 48

On Monday morning, during the second week of August, Titus showed up at Samuel and Esther's house with a big grin. "Suzanne had the baby last night, and it's a boy!" he announced, after he'd entered the kitchen, where they sat with the children having breakfast.

Samuel jumped up and hugged Titus. "That's really good news! Congratulations!"

"How are Suzanne and the baby doing?" Esther asked.

"Real well, all things considered. Her labor was hard, but then I guess that's often the case with first babies. The boppli is healthy and has a good set of lungs. Oh, and he weighs nine and a half pounds, and he's almost twenty-two inches long."

"That's a pretty good-sized baby," Samuel said with a low whistle. "Much bigger than any of my kinner when they were born. I think Leon was the biggest; he weighed seven pounds, eleven ounces. The other three were all six and seven pounds."

"What'd ya name the boppli?" Marla asked.

Titus's grin, which had never left his face, widened. "Named him Abraham, after my daed. 'Course we'll probably call him Abe for short."

"I like that name," Leon spoke up. "It'll be nice to have another boy cousin."

"I'm sure Dad will be happy to hear you named the baby after him." Samuel motioned to the table. "If you haven't had breakfast yet, you're welcome to join us."

"I appreciate the offer, but I'm too excited to eat anything right now. I've gotta call the folks and leave 'em a message. And I want to stop and tell Timothy the news. Then I'll be heading back to the hospital to see how my fraa and boppli are doing."

"What about Suzanne's family?" Esther questioned. "Do they know about the baby?"

Titus bobbed his head. "Suzanne's mamm went with us to the hospital last night, so she was there when the boppli came."

"I'll bet she was excited," Esther said. "Especially since this is her first grand-child."

"Jah. Since Nelson seems to be in no

hurry to find himself a wife, our little Abe will probably be the only grandchild for Suzanne's mamm to dote on for some time." Titus rolled his eyes. "Which means he'll probably end up bein' spoiled."

"We're really happy for you," Samuel said. "There's nothing quite like becoming a parent." He patted the top of Jared's head.

Esther smiled. She knew how much Samuel loved his children and hoped it wouldn't be long before they could have a child of their own to add to this happy family.

Paradise, Pennsylvania

Fannie had just finished making french toast for breakfast when Abraham ambled into the kitchen with a smug-looking smile. "I've got some good news," he said, clasping Fannie's arm.

"Glad to hear it, because it'll be nice to get some good news for a change. Seems like there's too much bad going on in our world these days."

"I just came from the phone shack, and there was a message from Titus."

"Oh? What'd it say?"

"Suzanne had her boppli last night, and they named him after me."

Fannie smiled widely. "They had a boy?"

"Jah. A big, healthy boy, at that."

449

"That's wunderbaar! Just think, Abraham, this gives us forty-eight kinskinner, not counting dear little, departed Mindy. Oh, I wish we could go to Kentucky right now so we could see the new boppli."

"We'll go soon, Fannie — unless Titus and Suzanne decide to come here first."

She shook her head. "That's not likely to happen. From what Titus said the last time we talked, things are really busy in the woodshop right now, so I doubt he'll be taking time off for a trip anytime soon. Besides, it's a whole lot easier for us to travel than it would be for a young couple with a new baby."

"You're probably right, so we'll go there soon. But I think we should give 'em some time to adjust to being parents before we barge in, don't you?"

She nodded slowly. "I suppose you're right, and when we do go, it'll be nice to see Samuel and his family, as well as Timothy."

Abraham took a seat. "Speaking of Timothy, have you been able to talk to Hannah yet? You did promise him you'd try to talk her into going back to Kentucky, right?"

"Jah, I did, but every time I've gone over to the Kings' place, I've only seen Sally." Fannie sighed deeply. "She always gives me the excuse that Hannah's resting or isn't feeling up to company. Makes me wonder if I'll ever get the chance to speak to Hannah face-to-face."

"Well, don't give up. One of these days when you stop over there, Sally's bound to be gone, and then she won't be able to run interference for Hannah." Abraham grunted. "Wouldn't surprise me one bit if she doesn't do it just so she can keep Hannah all to herself. You and I both know that Hannah's mamm had such a tight hold on Hannah before Timothy moved them to Kentucky that it was choking the life out of their marriage. Now that Hannah's back home and livin' under her folks' roof again, Sally will probably do most anything to keep Hannah there."

"Oh, I hope that's not the case." Fannie set the platter of french toast on the table and took a seat beside Abraham. "As soon as we're done with breakfast, I'm going over to see Hannah again. Since I promised Timothy I would talk to her, I need to keep trying."

Hannah had just entered the kitchen when a wave of nausea ran through her. She clutched her stomach and groaned. This was the third day in a row that she'd felt sick to her stomach soon after she'd gotten out of bed. *Could I be pregnant?* she wondered. *Oh, surely not. I don't see how. . . .*

Hannah's thoughts took her to the last night she'd spent in Kentucky. She remembered how she'd allowed herself to find comfort in Timothy's arms and had awakened the next morning fearful that because of her willingness to be with him, he'd gotten the wrong idea. Had Timothy believed she'd forgiven him and that things were better between them? Well, he ought to know that just wasn't possible! Even if Hannah was carrying Timothy's child, she could never return to Kentucky and be the wife Timothy wanted and expected her to be. The only way Hannah could cope with Mindy's death was to stay right here in the safety of her parents' home.

Hannah had just put the teakettle on the stove when her mother entered the kitchen. "I'm going shopping as soon as we're done with breakfast, and I was hoping you'd come with me," Mom said.

Hannah shook her head. "I don't feel like it, Mom. I just want to stay here."

"Oh, but Hannah, you've been cooped up in this house ever since you came home, and I think it would be good for you to get out for a few hours."

"I can't. I might see someone from Timothy's family, and then they'd probably tell me I was wrong to leave Timothy and that my place is in Kentucky with him." Hannah leaned against the counter as another wave of nausea rolled through her stomach.

"Are you feeling all right? You look pale," Mom said with a worried frown. "Are you grank?"

"I'm fine. Just tired, is all."

"That's because you're not sleeping well. I think you should let me take you to the doctor and see if he'll prescribe some sleeping pills."

Hannah shook her head vigorously. "I don't want any sleeping pills. I sleep when I need to — sometimes during the day. I'm sure I'll feel better once I've had some breakfast."

Mom pulled Hannah into her arms for a hug. "I can't help but worry about you. Maybe I should wait until tomorrow to do my shopping."

"I'll be fine. Go ahead with your plans."

"All right, then. Is there anything you'd like me to pick up for you while I'm out and about?"

Hannah shook her head. "There's nothing I need." *Except a sense of peace I may never feel,* she added to herself.

■ ■ ■ ■

Soon after Mom left, Hannah decided to sit on the porch for a while because it was so hot and stuffy in the house. With a cup of peppermint tea in one hand, she took a seat on the porch swing and tried to relax. Besides the nausea that still plagued her, the muscles in her back and neck were tense. She leaned heavily against the back of the swing and concentrated on the noisy buzz of the cicadas coming from the many trees in her parents' yard.

Hannah had only been sitting a few minutes when a horse and buggy pulled into the yard. Her first impulse was to dash into the house, but curious to see who it was, she stayed. When she saw Fannie Fisher climb down from the buggy, Hannah felt her heart pound. *Oh no! Not her! I can't deal with the questions I'm sure she's likely to ask.*

Hannah jumped up and was about to run into the house when Fannie called, "Stay right there, Hannah! I need to speak to you!"

Feeling like a defenseless fly trapped in the web of a spider, Hannah collapsed onto the swing. She supposed she couldn't avoid Timothy's mother forever, so she might as well get it over with. Maybe after she explained how she felt about things, Hannah wouldn't be bothered by Fannie again.

"Wie geht's?" Fannie asked as she joined Hannah on the porch.

"I'm surprised to see you," Hannah mumbled, avoiding Fannie's question about how she was doing.

"I've come by several times to see you, but your mamm's always said you weren't up to company."

Hannah didn't say anything — just waited for the barrage of questions she figured was forthcoming.

Fannie shifted from one foot to the other; then without invitation, she took a seat in one of the wicker chairs. "I understand that you're hurting, Hannah. Losing Mindy was a horrible tragedy, and we all miss her."

Just hearing Mindy's name and seeing the look of compassion on Fannie's face made Hannah feel like crying.

"I also understand why you may have felt that you needed to get away from Kentucky for a while," Fannie continued. "But have you considered how much this is hurting Timothy? He's grieving for Mindy, too, you know."

Hannah's jaw clenched. "I'm sure he is, but it doesn't change the fact that it's his fault our little girl is dead."

A pained expression crossed Fannie's face. "Timothy blames himself, too, but all the blame in the world won't bring Mindy back."

"Don't you think I know that? When I discovered Mindy lying on the ground so still, I begged God for a miracle, but He chose not to give me one. Instead, He snatched my only child away when He could have stopped it from happening in the first place." Hannah couldn't keep the bitterness out of her voice, and it was a struggle not to give in to the tears pricking the back of her eyes.

"You know, even with a brand-new screen on a window, someone could still fall through if they ran into it too hard or leaned heavily against it. Screens are only meant to keep bugs out, not prevent people from falling out of windows."

Hannah offered no response. She was sure Mindy had fallen out the window because the screen was broken, and nothing Fannie could say would change her mind.

"You're right that God could have prevented Mindy's death," Fannie said with tears in her eyes. "He could let us go through life protected from every horrible thing that could hurt us."

"Then why doesn't He?"

"I don't know all of God's ways, but I do know that whenever He allows bad things to happen to His people, He can take those things and use them for good." Fannie slipped her arm around Hannah's shoulder. "But we have to decide to let it work for our good and not allow bitterness and resentment to take over. We can choose to let God help us with the hurts and disappointments we must face."

Hannah's throat felt so clogged, she couldn't speak. What Fannie said, she'd heard before from one of the ministers in their church. But letting go of her hurt wouldn't bring Mindy back, and besides, she didn't think she could do it. Hannah felt the need to hold on to something — even if it was the hurt and bitterness she harbored against Timothy.

As though sensing Hannah's confusion and inability to let go of her pain, Fannie said, "The only way you'll ever rise above your grief is to forgive my son. Bitterness and resentment will hurt you more in the long run, and when you do the right thing, Hannah, God will give you His peace. Won't you please return to Kentucky and try to work things out with Timothy?"

Hannah looked away, tears clouding her

vision. "I just can't."

Fannie sat for several minutes; then she finally rose to her feet. "I pray that you'll change your mind about that, for your sake, as well as my son's." She moved toward the porch steps but halted and turned to look at Hannah. "Oh, before I go, I thought you might like to know that Suzanne had a baby boy last night. They named him Abraham, and I guess they're planning to call him Abe for short."

It took all that Hannah had within her, but she forced herself to say she was glad for Suzanne and Titus. Inside, however, just hearing about Suzanne's baby made her hurt even more. It was one more painful reminder that Hannah no longer had any children to hold and to love.

"We'll be going to Kentucky to see the boppli in a month or so. Maybe you'd like to go along," Fannie said.

Hannah shook her head. A wave of nausea came over her, and she thought she might lose her breakfast. "I don't mean to be rude, but I'm not feeling so well, and I need to lie down." Before Fannie could respond, Hannah jumped up and rushed into the house.

Pembroke, Kentucky
When Timothy arrived home from work

that day, the first thing he did was head to the phone shanty to check for messages. He found only one — it was from Mom, and it wasn't good news. She'd spoken to Hannah but couldn't get her to change her mind about coming back to Kentucky.

With a heavy heart, Timothy dialed his folks' number to leave a message in return. He was surprised when Mom answered the phone.

"It's Timothy, Mom. I just listened to your message about seeing Hannah today. Is there anything else you can tell me about your visit with her?" he asked.

"Hannah isn't the same woman you married, Timothy," Mom said. "Losing Mindy has changed her. She's bitter and almost like an empty vessel inside. I fear she may never be the same."

"Does she still blame me for Mindy's death?"

"Jah, and she's not willing to return to Kentucky."

Sweat beaded on Timothy's forehead, and he reached up to wipe it away. "She didn't mention divorce, did she?"

"No."

"Well, that's a relief. Maybe it's for the best that she's not with me right now. Seeing her every day and knowing how she feels about me would only add to the guilt I already feel for causing Mindy's death."

"I think maybe Hannah needs more time, Timothy. We're all praying for her, and for you as well. You've got to stop blaming yourself, son, because all the blame in the world won't bring Mindy back, and it's not helping your emotional state, either."

"I know, Mom, but if I could, I'd give my life in exchange for my daughter's."

"That's not an option, and you need to find a way to work through all of this. You need to get on with the business of living."

"How can I do that when my wife hates me and won't come back to our home?"

"I don't think Hannah hates you, Timothy. I just think she's so caught up in her grief that she needs someone to blame. I also believe in the power of prayer, so let's keep praying and believing that someone or something will help Hannah see that her place is with you. I don't think you should try to force her to come back."

"I would never do that, Mom. If Hannah decides to return to Kentucky, it has to be her decision of her own free will." Timothy blinked as a trickle of sweat rolled into his eyes. "And I . . . I want more than anything for Hannah to say that she's forgiven me and can love me again."

CHAPTER 49

"There's something I need to tell you," Bonnie said to Allen as they shared breakfast together one Saturday morning in mid-September.

Allen set his cup of coffee down. "You look so somber. I hope it's not bad news."

She shook her head. "It's good news. At least it is to me. I'm hoping you'll think it's good news, too."

He wiggled his eyebrows. "Then tell me now, because I can't stand the suspense."

Smiling and taking in a deep breath, Bonnie said, "I'm pregnant."

Allen stared at her like he couldn't believe what she'd just said. "Are . . . are you sure?" he asked in a near whisper.

"I took a pregnancy test earlier this week, and I saw the doctor yesterday afternoon. It's official, Allen. The baby's due the first week of April."

"How come you waited till now to tell

me?" Allen's furrowed brows let Bonnie know he was a bit disappointed. Was it because she hadn't told him sooner, or was he upset about her being pregnant?

"I know we've only been married four months, and I'm sorry if you're disappointed because we didn't expect to start a family so soon, but —"

Allen placed his finger against her lips. "I'm not the least bit disappointed. I'm thrilled to hear such good news. You just took me by surprise, that's all." He smiled widely then leaned over and gave her a kiss. "Wow, I can't wait to tell my folks this news. Mom will be so excited when she hears that she's gonna be a grandma. Have you told your dad yet?"

"No, you're the first one I've told, and I would have given you the news last night, but you fell asleep soon after we ate supper."

"I don't usually conk out like that," Allen said, "but I've been working such long hours lately, and I can't seem to get enough sleep."

She smiled. "I understand. Things have been busier around the B&B recently, too, and it's keeping me and Trisha hopping."

"You should probably slow down now that you're expecting a baby. Maybe you ought to consider hiring someone else to help Trisha so you can take it easy and get plenty of rest."

"I promise I won't overdo it, but I can't sit around doing nothing. It's not in my nature."

He nodded. "Okay. I guess you know what you're capable of doing."

Bonnie finished eating her scrambled eggs then pushed away from the table. "I think I'll call my dad right now. After that, I'm going to share our good news with Trisha."

"Sounds like a plan. While you're calling your dad, I'll use my cell phone and give my folks a call." Allen grinned. "Something tells me that once the baby comes, they'll be making a lot more trips to Kentucky."

Bonnie nodded. "I'll bet Dad comes to visit us more often, too."

"You look like you're in a good mood this morning," Trisha said when she found Bonnie humming as she did the breakfast dishes.

Bonnie turned from the sink and smiled. "I sure am. In fact, I'm feeling very blessed and happy."

"Would you like to share some of that happiness with me?"

"That's exactly what I was planning to do." Bonnie motioned to the table. "Let's have a seat, and I'll tell you about it."

Leaning her elbows on the table, Bonnie smiled and said, "Allen and I are going to have a baby. I'm due the first part of April."

Trisha grinned and reached for Bonnie's hand. "Oh, that is good news! I'm so happy for you, Bonnie."

"I appreciate God giving me a second chance at motherhood since I was forced to give up my baby when I was sixteen."

"I know you'll make a good mom. I've seen how patient and kind you are with Samuel's kids. And Allen will make a good daddy, too."

"Yes, I believe he will." Bonnie tapped her fingers along the edge of the table.

"Is there a problem?" Trisha asked.

"Well, no, not for me, but you might not see it that way."

"What is it?"

"When I called Dad to give him the good news, he was very pleased."

"I imagine he would be."

"Well, the thing is . . ." Bonnie paused and moistened her lips. "He said something about quitting his job at the bank and moving here so he can be closer to me and the baby."

"I can understand him wanting to do that."

"How would you feel about it if Dad decides to move?"

Trisha shrugged. "Whatever Ken does is his business."

"I know there has been some tension between you two, and if he moves here, you'll be seeing him fairly often, so I thought —"

"It's not a problem, Bonnie. When your dad came to your wedding in May, things were better between us, so I don't anticipate any issues if he should decide to move here."

"That's a relief. I want having this baby to be a positive experience, and I was a little concerned that you might decide to leave if Dad moves to Kentucky."

Trisha shook her head. "As long as you want me to help at the B&B, I'm here for you."

"I'm glad to hear that, because my business has picked up since you came to work for me. Besides, you and I have become good friends, and I'd miss not having you around."

Trisha smiled. "I'll stay as long as you want me to."

Paradise, Pennsylvania

Hannah sat in the rocking chair inside her parents' living room and placed both hands

465

against her stomach. It hadn't taken very long for her to realize that she was definitely pregnant. Due to the morning sickness, Mom had figured it out, too. Hannah was okay with her folks knowing, but she didn't want anyone else to know — especially not anyone from Timothy's family. If they knew she was expecting a baby, they'd tell Timothy. And if he knew, Hannah was sure he would come to Pennsylvania and insist she go back to Kentucky with him. So Hannah had asked her folks not to tell anyone, and they'd agreed to keep her secret. But Dad had made it clear that he wasn't happy about it. He'd said several times that he thought Hannah's place was with her husband, no matter how she felt about him. "Marriage is for keeps, and divorce is not an option," Dad had said the other night.

Hannah grimaced. She'd never said she was going to get a divorce, but one thing she did know: she couldn't be with Timothy right now.

A tear trickled down her cheek as she thought about the baby she carried. She wasn't ready to be a mother again — wasn't ready to have another baby. She wasn't even sure she could provide for this child and wondered whether Mom and Dad would be willing to help her raise it.

"As time goes on, I become more worried about Timothy," Samuel said as he dried the breakfast dishes while Esther washed. "When Hannah left three months ago, Timothy hoped she would change her mind and come back to him, but the longer she's gone, the more depressed he's become. I really don't know how much longer he can go on like this."

Esther nodded. "It's sad to think of him living all alone in that big old house, feeling guilty for causing Mindy's death and longing for Hannah to come home."

"I've tried everything I know to encourage him, but nothing I've said has made any difference." Samuel reached for another plate. "My mamm tried talking to Hannah several weeks ago, but it was all for nothing. Mom told Timothy that Hannah wasn't very cordial and she isn't willing to forgive him or come back to Kentucky."

Esther slowly shook her head. "I've said this before, Samuel, and I'll say it again. All we can do for Timothy is pray for him and offer our love and support. What Hannah decides to do is in God's hands, and we must continue to pray for her, too."

Chapter 50

Paradise, Pennsylvania

Fannie had just entered her daughter's quilt shop when she spotted Phoebe Stoltzfus's mother, Arie, on the other side of the room by the thread and other notions. Fannie and Arie had been close friends when Titus and Phoebe had been courting, but after the couple broke up, the two women saw less of each other. Of late, Fannie hadn't seen much of Arie at all. She figured that was probably because Arie had been busy helping Phoebe plan her wedding, which would take place in a few weeks.

"It's good to see you," Fannie said when Arie joined her at the fabric table. "It's been awhile."

Arie nodded. "I've been really busy helping Phoebe get ready for her wedding, this is the first opportunity I've had to do some shopping that doesn't have anything to do with the wedding."

Fannie smiled. "I know how that can be. When Abby was planning her wedding, I helped as much as I could. Of course, the twins were still little then, so I couldn't do as much as I would have liked. But then, Naomi and Nancy helped Abby a lot, so that took some of the pressure off me."

"Speaking of your twins, I saw Timothy's wife the other day," Arie said.

"Oh, really? Did you pay her a visit?" Fannie was anxious to hear about it, because she wondered if Hannah had been more receptive to Arie than she had to her.

"I saw Hannah coming out of the doctor's office in Lancaster," Arie said.

"Has she been grank?"

"I don't know if she's sick or not. I didn't say anything to Hannah, because as soon as I approached her, she hurried away." Arie's forehead wrinkled. "That young woman, whom I remember as always being so slender, has either put on a lot of weight or else she's pregnant."

Fannie's mouth dropped open. "Are you sure it was Hannah?"

"Of course I'm sure. Her belly was way out here." Arie held her hands several inches away from her stomach.

Fannie frowned. "Hmm . . ."

"Have you seen Hannah lately?" Arie

questioned. "Do you know if she's pregnant?"

"I saw her some time ago but not recently. She's been staying with her folks for nearly five months, so I don't see how she could be pregnant. Unless maybe . . ." Fannie set her material aside. "I've got to go. It was nice seeing you, Arie."

"Where are you off to?"

"I'm going to pay a call on Hannah," Fannie said before hurrying toward the door.

When Fannie arrived at the Kings' place a short time later, she found Sally on the porch hanging laundry on the line that had been connected by a pulley up to the barn.

"Is Hannah here?" Fannie asked, joining her.

"Jah, but she's not up to visiting with anyone right now," Sally said, barely looking at Fannie.

"She never is. At least not when I or anyone from my family has come by. What's going on, Sally?"

"Nothing. Hannah's just not accepting visitors right now."

"Why not?" Fannie's patience was waning.

"Well, you know how sad Hannah feels

470

about losing Mindy, and she doesn't want anyone bombarding her with a bunch of questions. I thought you understood that she needs to be alone."

"Wanting to be left alone for a few weeks or even a month after losing a loved one might be normal, but this has gone on far too long, and it doesn't make sense."

Sally's eyes narrowed. "What are you saying, Fannie?"

"I'm saying that it isn't normal for a wife to leave her husband the way Hannah did and then stay cooped up in her parents' house and refuse to see anyone but them."

"Everyone grieves differently."

"That may be so, but most people know when they're going through a rough time that they need the love and support of their family and friends. That should include Hannah's husband's family, too, don't you think?"

Sally said nothing. She picked up a wet towel and hung it on the line. Then she bent down to pick up another one.

"Is Hannah expecting a boppli?" Fannie blurted out.

Sally dropped the towel and whirled around to face her. "What made you ask such a question?"

"Someone saw Hannah coming out of the

doctor's office in Lancaster the other day, and they said she looked like she was pregnant." Fannie took a step closer to Sally. "Is it true? Is Hannah pregnant?"

Sally lowered her gaze. "Hannah's asked me not to discuss anything about her with anyone."

Fannie tapped her foot impatiently. "I'm not just anyone, Sally. I'm Hannah's mother-in-law, and if she's carrying my grandchild, I have the right to know."

Sally lifted her gaze, and tears filled her eyes. "I really can't talk about this right now."

Fannie stood several more seconds then hurried away. Even without Sally admitting it, she was quite sure Hannah was expecting a baby. It wasn't right that she was keeping it a secret. Timothy deserved to know, and Fannie planned to call him as soon as she got home.

CHAPTER 51

"If Fannie suspects I'm pregnant and tells Timothy, I don't know what I'll do if he shows up here," Hannah said after her mother told her about Fannie's most recent visit.

"Now, you need to calm down and relax," Mom said, handing Hannah a cup of herbal tea. "Since I didn't admit anything to Fannie, she would only be guessing if she told Timothy you were expecting a boppli."

Hannah got the rocking chair she was sitting in moving harder and grimaced when the baby kicked inside her womb. This baby was a lot more active than Mindy had been when she was carrying her. It seemed like the little one was always kicking. Sometimes it felt as if the baby was kicking with both feet and both hands at the same time. When that happened at bedtime, it was hard for Hannah to find a comfortable position so she could sleep.

"Was that Fannie Fisher's rig I saw pulling out when I came in?" Dad asked, stepping into the living room.

Mom nodded. "She wanted to speak to Hannah, but I wouldn't let her."

"Any idea what she wanted to talk to her about?" he asked.

"Fannie suspects that I'm pregnant," Hannah said. "I . . . I'm afraid she may tell Timothy."

Dad crossed his arms. "That might be the best thing for everyone concerned. I never did think Timothy should be kept in the dark. I've been tempted to tell him myself, but I knew if I did, I'd have you and your mamm to answer to."

"You've got that right," Mom said with a huff. "If Hannah doesn't want Timothy to know, we need to respect her wishes."

"That's kind of hard to do when I think she's wrong." Dad's forehead wrinkled as he narrowed his eyes and looked right at Hannah. "I think you should forgive that husband of yours and go on back to Kentucky."

"I just can't." Hannah placed her hands on her swollen stomach, and even though she knew the next words were ridiculous, she couldn't seem to stop them. "Even if I could forgive him for causing Mindy's

474

death, how could I trust him not to do something that could hurt this boppli, too?"

Pembroke, Kentucky

"How'd things go for you today?" Esther asked when Samuel came in the door around six o'clock.

"Okay. Timothy and I are almost done with the house we've been painting in Herndon. If all goes well, we should be able to start on another house in Trenton by the end of this week." Samuel slipped his arm around Esther's waist. "How was your day?"

"Good. Trisha and Bonnie picked me up, and the three of us went to see Suzanne and the boppli." Esther smiled. "Little Abe is so cute, and I really enjoyed holding him. Even Jared and Penny were taken with the little guy."

Samuel chuckled. "I'll bet those two would like to have a baby brother or sister of their own to play with."

Esther sighed. "Are you disappointed that I haven't gotten pregnant yet?"

" 'Course not," Samuel said with a shake of his head. "We haven't been married half a year yet, so there's plenty of time for you to get pregnant."

"But what if I don't? Maybe I won't be able to have any children."

475

Samuel gave Esther's arm a tender squeeze. "Try not to worry. It'll happen in God's time, and if it doesn't, then we'll accept it as God's will."

Esther smiled. She appreciated her husband's encouraging words. She was about to tell him that supper was almost ready when she heard several bumps followed by a piercing scream.

Esther and Samuel raced into the hall, where they found Penny lying at the foot of the stairs, red-faced and sobbing. Leon, Marla, and Jared stood nearby, eyes wide and mouths hanging open; they looked scared to death.

Samuel dropped to his knees. "Are you hurt, Penny?" he asked, checking her over real good.

"I . . . I'm okay, Daadi." Penny sniffed and sat up.

"What happened?" Esther asked. "Did you trip on the stairs?"

Penny turned and pointed to a small wooden horse.

Samuel's face flushed. "How many times have I told you kids not to leave your toys on the stairs? Now I hope you see how dangerous that can be!"

The children nodded soberly.

Esther knew Samuel's first wife had died

476

after falling down the stairs, so she could understand why he would be upset, but she thought he was being a little too hard on the children.

"I'm sorry, Samuel," she said. "I should have kept a closer watch to make sure that nothing was left on the stairs."

"It's not about things getting left on the stairs," Samuel said, shaking his head. "The toy horse shouldn't have been there in the first place."

"You're right." Tears welled in Esther's eyes. "I guess I'm not doing a very good job with the kinner these days."

"That's not true," Marla spoke up. "You take real good care of us."

All heads bobbed in agreement, including Samuel's. "Marla's right, Esther. You've done well with the kinner ever since you started taking care of them, but you can't be expected to watch their every move." He gave each of the children a stern look while shaking his finger. "It's your job to watch out for each other, too, and that includes keeping the stairs and other places free of clutter so you'll all be safe." He smiled at Esther. "And I want you to be safe, as well."

"I talked to my dad today," Bonnie told Allen as they sat at the dining-room table, eating supper that evening.

"What's new with him?"

"He'll be moving here next week."

Allen's eyebrows shot up. "Here, at the B&B?"

"Only for a little while — until he finds a place of his own. If it's okay with you, that is."

"Sure, I have no problem with that."

"He got word that he'll be managing one of the banks in Hopkinsville."

"That's all good news." Allen grinned. "Does Trisha know about this?"

Bonnie nodded. "To tell you the truth, I think she was rather pleased."

"Well, who knows? There might be a budding romance ahead for those two."

Her eyebrows arched. "You really think so?"

"Would you be okay with it?"

Bonnie smiled. "Most definitely. I think Dad and Trisha would be perfect for each other."

"Hmm . . . you might be right about that." Allen reached for his glass of water and took a sip. "So tell me about your day. Did you get some rest?"

"I didn't work, if that's what you mean. Trisha and I took Esther over to see Suzanne's baby, and holding little Abe made me even more excited about having our own baby."

Allen grinned. "I'm looking forward to that, too."

Bonnie handed him the bowl of tossed salad. "And how was your day?"

"Busy. I bid two jobs in Hopkinsville and then stopped at the house Samuel and Timothy have been working on this week."

"How's Timothy doing?" she asked, reaching for her glass of water.

"Not very well, I'm afraid. He doesn't look good at all, and he's pushing himself way too hard. He probably believes working long hours will help him not think about Hannah so much." Deep wrinkles formed across Allen's forehead. "If Timothy's not careful, though, he'll work himself to death."

CHAPTER 52

On Friday afternoon after Timothy got home from work, he fixed himself a sandwich. Then he headed for the barn to feed the horses, muck out their stalls, and replace a broken hinge on one of the stall doors.

Ever since Hannah had left, he'd worked on some unfinished projects — including new screens for all of the windows in the house. His most recent project was the barn. So far, he'd reinforced the hayloft, replaced a couple of beams, and fixed a broken door. Tomorrow, with the help of Samuel, Titus, and Allen, he planned to re-roof the barn. It felt good to keep busy and get some of the projects done that he'd previously kept saying he would do later. It was the only way he could keep from thinking too much about Hannah and the guilt he felt for causing Mindy's death.

It was dark by the time Timothy finished up in the barn, and he was so tired he could barely stay on his feet. He shook the grit and dust from his hair and headed for the house, not caring that he hadn't gone to the phone shanty to check for messages. Stepping onto the porch, he barely noticed the hoot of an owl calling from one of the trees.

When Timothy entered the house, he trudged wearily up the stairs, holding on to the banister with each step he took. After a quick shower, he headed down the hall toward his room. But as he neared Mindy's bedroom, he halted. Other than the day he'd replaced the screen in her window, he hadn't stepped foot in this room. For some reason, he felt compelled to go in there now.

Timothy opened the door, and a soft light from the moon cast shadows on the wall.

"Oh Mindy girl, I sure do miss you," he murmured. "Wish now I'd spent more time with you when you were still with us. If I could start over again, I'd do things differently." Tears coursed down Timothy's cheeks as a deep sense of regret washed over him. "If I'd just put a screen on your window when your mamm asked me to, you'd be here right now, sleeping peacefully in your bed, and your mamm would not have left me."

Timothy moaned as he flopped onto Mindy's bed and curled up on his side. With his head resting on her pillow, he could smell the lingering sweetness of his precious little girl. After Hannah had left, he'd thought about changing Mindy's sheets but hadn't gotten around to it. Right now he was glad.

Mindy . . . Mindy . . . Mindy . . . Timothy closed his eyes and succumbed to much-needed sleep.

"Daadi . . . Daadi . . . I love you, Daadi."

Timothy sat up and looked around. Had someone called his name? The voice he'd heard sounded like Mindy's, but that was impossible — she was dead.

"Daad–i."

Timothy blinked, shocked to see Mindy standing on the other side of her bedroom. Her clothes glowed — illuminating the entire room.

"I . . . I must be seeing things!" Timothy rubbed his eyes and blinked again. Mindy was still there, moving closer to him. Her golden hair hung loosely across her shoulders, and her cherubic face glowed radiantly.

"I'm sorry, Daadi," she whispered, extending her hand to him.

"Sorry for what, Mindy?"

"I shouldn't have been playin' near the window that day. Don't be sad, Daadi. It's not your fault. You work so hard and just got busy and forgot about the screens."

Timothy drew in a shaky breath, struggling to hold back the tears stinging his eyes. He reached out his hand until his fingers were almost touching hers. Mindy looked like a child, but she sounded so grown-up. "Mindy, my precious little girl. Oh, I've missed you so much."

"Don't cry, Daadi. I'm happy with Jesus, and someday you and Mama will be with us in heaven."

Timothy nearly choked on a sob as he lifted his hand to stroke her soft cheek. Then she was gone, and the room lost its glow.

"Mindy, don't go! Come back! Come back!"

Feeling as though he were in a haze, Timothy pried his eyes open and sat up. Sunlight streamed in through the bare window, and he knew it was morning.

Timothy glanced down at himself and realized he must have fallen asleep on Mindy's bed. He sat for several minutes, rubbing his temples and trying to clear the cobwebs from his brain. He'd seen a vision last night. Or was it a dream? Mindy had spoken to him and said he shouldn't blame himself for the accident. She was happy in heaven, as he knew she must be, and that gave him a sense of peace.

Timothy rose to his feet and ambled over to the window. "Thank You, God," he murmured with a feeling of new hope. "I believe You gave me that dream last night so I would stop blaming myself. Now if Hannah would only forgive me, too."

Paradise, Pennsylvania
"Mama. I love you, Mama."

"Mindy, is that you?" Hannah sat up in bed with a start, rubbing her eyes in disbelief.

"I'm over here, Mama."

A bright light illuminated the room, and Hannah gasped. Mindy stood by the window, dressed all in white with golden flecks of sunlight glistening in her long hair.

"Mindy! Oh, my precious little girl!" Hannah gulped on a sob, grasping the quilt that still covered her.

"Don't cry, Mama. Don't be sad. I'm happy livin' in heaven with Jesus. Someday you and Daadi will be with us, too."

Hannah couldn't speak around the lump in her throat. All she could do was hold out her hands.

"Don't blame Daadi anymore, Mama. He just got busy and forgot about the screens.

484

Daadi needs you, Mama. Go back to him, please."

Hannah sniffed deeply as tears trickled down her cheeks. She was unable to take her eyes off her precious angel.

"Go soon, Mama. Tell Daadi you love him."

Hannah blinked. Then Mindy was gone.

Hannah's eyes snapped open when she heard the clock ticking beside her bed. It was early — not quite five o'clock. She'd had a restless night, trying to turn off her thoughts and find a comfortable position for her sore back. "I had a dream about Mindy," she murmured. The dream had been so real, Hannah wondered if it hadn't been a dream at all. If it was a dream, could it have been God's way of getting her attention — making her realize that she needed to forgive Timothy and return to Kentucky?

Hannah swung her legs over the side of the bed and ambled across the room. Then she lowered herself into the rocking chair near the window. *You must forgive Timothy,* a voice in her head seemed to say. *Mindy wants you to.*

Hannah thought about a Bible verse she'd learned as a child and quoted it out loud: " 'If ye forgive men their trespasses, your heavenly Father will also forgive you,' Matthew 6:14."

A sob tore from Hannah's throat, and in the dimness of the room, she bowed her head and closed her eyes. "I forgive him, Father," she prayed. "Forgive me for feeling such resentment and anger toward my husband all these months."

Hannah opened her eyes and gently touched her stomach. "Timothy and I can be one again. Together we can welcome this miracle into the world," she whispered.

Bracing her hands on the arms of the chair, Hannah stood and gazed out the window, watching the light of dawn as it slowly appeared in the horizon. It was almost December, and mornings were chilly in Pennsylvania this time of the year, but feeling the need for a breath of fresh air, she opened the window. Taking in a few deep breaths, Hannah felt as if a heavy weight had been lifted from her shoulders. "I need to return to Kentucky. I need to go now."

CHAPTER 53

Sally had just starting making breakfast when Hannah came into the room, looking bright-eyed and almost bubbly. It was the first time since her daughter had been home that Sally had seen a genuine smile on her face.

"You look like you're in a good mood this morning," Sally said. "Did you sleep well last night?"

Hannah nodded. "I had a dream, Mom. It was a dream about Mindy."

"Oh? Was it a good dream?"

"Jah, it was a very good dream. Mindy said I shouldn't blame her daed for the accident. She also said she was happy in heaven." Hannah took a seat at the table. "Mindy was right, Mom. My unwillingness to forgive Timothy was wrong."

Mom touched Hannah's shoulder. "Perhaps God gave you that dream so you would realize the importance of forgiveness."

"I need to return to Kentucky," Hannah said. "Timothy needs to know that I've forgiven him. I also want to tell him about the boppli I'm carrying."

Sally was quiet for a few minutes as she processed all of this. She knew Hannah's place was with her husband, but she would miss her daughter. *I can't say or do anything to prevent her from going,* she told herself. *Timothy wishes to make his home in Kentucky, and even though I'm going to miss her, I know that's where my daughter belongs.*

Sally was about to voice her thoughts when Johnny entered the room. "Is breakfast ready yet?" he asked. "I need to get to the store and open it, 'cause neither of my helpers can come in till ten this morning."

"I think I ought to start working in the store again, and then we can let those two young women go," Sally said. "Once Phoebe gets married, she'll probably want to stay home and start raising a family, anyway."

"You're welcome to work in the store if you want to," Johnny said, "but I thought you liked staying at home."

"I do, but now that Hannah's going back to Kentucky, I'll be alone and will need something meaningful to do."

Johnny's eyebrows shot up. "Hannah's returning to Kentucky?"

"That's right, Dad." Hannah repeated the dream she'd had and told him about the decision she'd made to be reunited with her husband.

"Well all I've got to say is it's about time you saw the light." Johnny shook his head. "I never did think you should have left Timothy, and not telling him about the boppli wasn't right, either."

"Hannah doesn't need any lectures this morning," Sally was quick to say. "What she needs is our love and support."

Johnny bobbed his head and smiled at Sally, obviously happy to hear her say that. "She definitely has my support, and I think I know a way she can head for Kentucky today."

"How's that, Dad?" Hannah asked.

"Abraham Fisher came by my store yesterday, right before closing time. He mentioned that he'd hired a driver to take him and Fannie to Kentucky to see Titus and Suzanne's baby. He said he'd arranged it without Fannie knowing, and that he was going to surprise her with the news this morning. Guess the plan is for them to leave sometime this afternoon, and they'll get to Titus's place tomorrow." He grinned at Hannah. "I'm sure their driver would have room for one more if you'd like to go along."

Hannah's eyes brightened. "I definitely would! It's like this was meant to be."

"Great! I'll stop by Abraham's place on my way to work and set it all up." Johnny clapped his hands together. "Now I think we'd better have some breakfast so I can get going and you can pack."

Pembroke, Kentucky

"This roof is even worse than I thought," Timothy called to Samuel, who stood on the ground below picking up the shingles his brother had already thrown down to him.

Samuel cupped his hands around his mouth and shouted, "When Titus and Allen get here, one of 'em can go up there and help you!"

"Okay, whatever!" Timothy gave a quick wave and continued to almost frantically tear off more of the shingles.

Samuel was still worried about his brother. Timothy had been driving himself too hard. Truth was, he probably shouldn't be working on the barn roof at all today. But the weather had been nicer than usual for this time of year, and Timothy had insisted on getting the roof done before bad weather set in. Samuel had suggested that Timothy rest awhile and let him take over the job of removing shingles, but Timothy wouldn't hear of it. Samuel was afraid if Timothy didn't slow down soon, he'd keel over from exhaustion. Maybe when Allen and Titus showed up, one of them could talk some sense into him.

As Hannah rode in Herb Nelson's van, along with Fannie and Abraham, all she could think about was her dream. She'd shared the details of the dream with Fannie and Abraham and thanked them for allowing her to travel to Kentucky with them. Now, as they neared Pembroke, Hannah felt compelled to tell Fannie something she hadn't shared with anyone yet.

"All this time, I've been blaming Timothy for Mindy's accident, but I really think I'm the one to blame," Hannah said.

Fannie's eyes widened. "Wh–what do you mean?"

"When Mindy came into the kitchen that day, she held a dandelion in her little hand that she wanted to give me. But I sent her away — told her to go out of the room and play." Hannah swallowed hard. Just thinking about it made her feel sad. "If I hadn't done that, she wouldn't have gone upstairs to her room, and if I'd kept her in the kitchen with me, she'd still be alive."

491

Fannie reached across the seat and took Hannah's hand. "It was an accident — perhaps one that could have been avoided — but if it was Mindy's time to go, then she could have died some other way."

Hannah nodded slowly. "One thing I do know is that Mindy's happier in heaven than she ever could be here on earth, and the dream I had gave me a sense of peace about things."

Fannie smiled. "I'm glad, and I'm also pleased that you're going back to Timothy. I know he will be so happy to see you."

"He'll also be glad about the boppli you're expecting, just as we are," Abraham said from the front passenger's seat.

Hannah looked down at her growing stomach. "I'm grateful God's given us another chance to be happy, and I pray that we'll do a good job raising this baby."

"You'll do fine, Hannah," Fannie said. "I just wish we'd known about the boppli sooner."

"I didn't feel like I could tell anyone. I was afraid if Timothy found out, he'd insist that I go back to Kentucky. Until I had that dream about Mindy, I just wasn't ready to go back. Now this van we're riding in can't seem to get me there fast enough."

As they turned onto the road near her

house, Hannah leaned toward their driver and said, "Would you mind dropping me off by the mailbox? Then I can walk up to the house and surprise Timothy. I'd like a few minutes alone with him before you all join us," she added, looking at Fannie.

"I have a better idea," Abraham said. "How about if after we drop you off, we head over to Suzanne and Titus's place to see their new boppli? Then in a few hours, we'll go over to your house and surprise Timothy, because he has no idea we're coming."

"That'll be fine," Hannah said with a nod. "After I've greeted Timothy and we spend some time together catching up, I plan to make him something special. It seems like ages ago now, but I've been wanting to bake Timothy a Kentucky chocolate chip pie. We can all have some when you come over later on."

Abraham grinned. "Sounds good to me. Never have been known to turn down a piece of pie. Isn't that right, Fannie?"

"Absolutely!" Fannie reached over the seat and gave his shoulder a pat.

When their driver pulled over by the mailbox a few minutes later, Hannah got out of the van, took her suitcase, and said, "I'll see you in a few hours." Then she turned and headed down the lane with a sense of confidence, letting her hand bounce between the boards on the fence. Her heart picked up speed as the path curved, taking her closer to the house. She could hardly wait to see Timothy.

Just as Hannah stepped into a clearing, she spotted a red-and-blue ambulance with its lights flashing. She tensed. Something terrible must have happened. Clutching her stomach, she let the suitcase drop to the ground. Her breath came hard as she ran the rest of the way. *Please, God, I pray that nothing's happened to Timothy.*

When Hannah got closer to the house, she spotted Samuel, Titus, and Allen near the ambulance. "Wh–what happened?" she panted. "Where's Timothy?"

"Hannah?" Titus looked stunned. "What are you doing here?"

"I'll explain later. Please tell me what's going on. Has someone been hurt? Is . . . is it Timothy?"

Samuel clasped Hannah's shoulders. "Jah. Timothy was working on the barn roof, and he slipped and fell."

Hannah swayed unsteadily, and Titus reached out to give her support. "Oh, dear Lord, no!" she cried, looking toward the sky. "Please, don't take my husband from me now, too!"

CHAPTER 54

"Would you mind if I skip out on you for an hour or so while I run a few errands?" Bonnie asked Trisha as she finished putting some bread dough into two pans.

"Of course not. I've never minded when you run errands without me," Trisha said.

"Well, since my dad will be arriving sometime later today, I don't want you to worry that I might not make it back before he gets here. He's driving instead of flying this time, so there's no way I can be sure what time he'll arrive. When I spoke to Dad on the phone last night, he said he thought it would probably be later this afternoon, so I'm sure I have plenty of time."

Trisha put the loaves of bread in the oven and closed the door. "If for some reason you're not, I'll show him which of the guest rooms you have reserved for him."

Bonnie smiled. "What would I ever do without you, Trisha?"

"You'd be fine. Just like you were before I showed up at your door last Christmas."

"I was managing okay," Bonnie said, "but things have gone even smoother since you started working here. I never thought anyone could cook better than Esther, but I think you're a pro."

Trisha's face heated with embarrassment. "I appreciate the compliment, but the only reason I cook as well as I do is because I've had a few more years' experience than Esther. For a young woman in her twenties, she's not only a good cook, but a very capable wife and mother to Samuel's four lively children."

"That's true, and I don't know how she does it all." Bonnie patted her protruding stomach. "When this little one makes his or her appearance, I hope I can be even half as good a mother as Esther is to those kids."

"I'm sure you will be."

Bonnie slipped into her jacket and grabbed her purse. "I'd better get going, or Dad will definitely be here before I get home." She hugged Trisha and hurried out the door.

For the next two hours, Trisha kept busy cleaning the kitchen, mixing cookie dough, and answering the phone. She'd just taken a reservation from a couple who would be staying at the B&B in a few weeks when she heard a car pull into the yard. She figured it must be Bonnie but was surprised when she glanced out the kitchen window and saw Ken getting out of a black SUV. Her heart skipped a beat. Even in his late fifties, he was as handsome as he had been in his teens.

Now stop these silly schoolgirl thoughts, she reprimanded herself. *I'm sure Ken doesn't feel all giddy inside every time he sees me.*

Drawing in a deep breath to compose herself, Trisha wiped her hands on a paper towel and went to answer the door.

"It's good to see you," she said cheerfully when Ken entered the house. "How was your trip?"

"Long and tiring, but at least there were no problems along the way."

"That's good to hear. Bonnie's out running errands at the moment, but I can show you to your room if you'd like to rest awhile," Trisha offered.

He shook his head. "If I lie down, I'll probably conk out and won't wake up till tomorrow morning. Think I'll just sit in the living room and wait for Bonnie to get home. I'm anxious to find out how she's feeling."

"She's doing real well," Trisha said. "Not

much morning sickness and not as tired as I figured she'd be."

"That's because she comes from hardy stock," he said with a chuckle.

Trisha laughed, too, and felt herself begin to relax. "Would you like a cup of coffee, Ken?"

"Sure, that'd be great."

"I was just making some cookies when you pulled in," she said. "If I put a batch in the oven now, you can have some of those to go with the coffee."

He smacked his lips. "Sounds good. I'm always up for cookies."

Ken followed Trisha into the kitchen, and after he'd taken a seat at the table, she handed him a cup of coffee.

"Why don't you join me?" he asked. "The cookies can wait a few minutes, can't they?"

"Sure." Trisha was pleased that he wanted her to sit with him. "So when will you be starting your new job?" she asked after she'd poured herself some coffee.

"Monday morning. I'll need to start looking for a house pretty soon, too, because I don't want to take up a room here that Bonnie could be renting to a paying customer."

"I'm sure Bonnie won't mind you staying here for however long it takes to find a place."

"That may be so, but I'm not going to take advantage of my daughter's good nature."

Trisha smiled. "Oh, I have something I'd like to show you."

"What is it?"

Trisha went to the desk and removed a manila envelope from the bottom drawer. "Bonnie found this in the attic a few days ago. It's full of pictures — some of you and me when we were teenagers." She handed Ken the envelope and sat down across from him.

Ken pulled out the pictures and smiled. "We made a pretty cute couple, didn't we?"

Trisha nodded, looking at the photos again. "We had a lot of fun together back then."

"Have you ever wondered how things would have turned out if you'd married me instead of Dave?" he asked, surprising her.

"Yes, I have," she answered truthfully. "But if you'd married me, you wouldn't have Bonnie for a daughter."

"You're right. We would have had some other child, or maybe we'd have several."

Trisha slowly shook her head. "No, Ken. We wouldn't have any children."

"How do you know?"

"Because I'm not able to have children of

my own." Tears welled in Trisha's eyes, blurring her vision. "I wanted to adopt, but Dave wouldn't hear of it. Since I'm an only child, and so was Dave, I don't even have any nieces or nephews to nurture and enjoy. So to help fill the void in my life and because I love kids, I taught the preschool Sunday school class at our church for several years, and I volunteered once a month for nursery duty during worship services."

"Trisha, I'm so sorry," he said sincerely. "I know not having children or being able to adopt must have been hard for you."

She nodded, swallowing around the lump in her throat.

Ken left his chair, and taking the seat beside Trisha, he pulled her into his arms.

His kindness was her undoing, and she dissolved into a puddle of tears.

When Bonnie drove into her yard, she was surprised to see Dad's SUV parked alongside the garage. She really hadn't expected him this soon.

After she turned off the engine and gathered up her packages, she quickly headed for the house, anxious to greet him. When she stepped into the kitchen, she halted, surprised to see Dad sitting at the table hugging Trisha. She stood in disbelief, and when she cleared her throat, they both quickly pulled away.

"Sorry," Bonnie apologized. "I didn't mean to startle you." Seeing the tears in Trisha's eyes, she said, "Is everything all right? You look upset, Trisha."

Trisha reached for a napkin and dried her eyes. "It's nothing to worry about. I was just telling your dad about my inability to have children, and I got kind of emotional."

"I . . . I was comforting her." Dad's cheeks were bright red, and Bonnie was sure he was more than a little embarrassed. Could something be happening between Dad and Trisha? Maybe some sparks from their teen-age years had been reignited. She hoped it was true, because they both deserved a second chance at happiness.

"Come here and give your old man a hug." Dad stood and held his arms out to Bonnie.

"It's so good to see you," she said after she'd set down her packages and given him a hug. "I didn't expect you so soon, though. How was your trip?"

"I made good time, so I can't complain, and the trip was fine." He gave her stomach a gentle pat. "How's that little grandson of mine doing?"

Bonnie shook her head. "Dad, that's wishful thinking on your part. We don't know if it's a boy or a girl."

"Well you ought to find out. I thought most pregnant women were doing that these days."

"Not me. Allen and I want to be surprised when the baby comes."

Dad grunted. "But if I knew for sure it was a boy, I could start buying things for the little fellow."

"You can decide what to buy after the baby gets here, and it might end up being girl toys and pretty pink dresses."

He nodded. "Guess you're right about that. I'll try to be patient, and I want you to know, I'll be just as happy if the baby's a girl."

Bonnie smiled. Like Dad had ever been patient about anything.

"Why don't you sit down and visit with your dad while I bake some cookies?" Trisha suggested. "I was getting ready to do that when he arrived."

"Thanks. I'm kind of tired, so I think I will take a seat."

Bonnie talked with Dad about his trip until he changed the subject. "So where's that son-in-law of mine?" he asked. "Is Allen working today?"

"Not his usual job, but he is helping Timothy re-roof his barn. Samuel and Titus are supposed to be there helping, too."

Dad smiled. "I've said this before, and I'll say it again: that man of yours is a keeper."

Bonnie nodded vigorously. "You're right about that, and I love him very much."

Just as Trisha took the first batch of cookies from the oven, Allen showed up.

"Look who's here," Bonnie said, motioning to Dad. "He arrived earlier than expected."

Allen smiled and shook Dad's hand. "I'm glad you made it safely." Then he turned to Bonnie and said, "I have some bad news."

"Oh dear. What is it?"

"Timothy fell off the roof of his barn, and he's in the hospital."

Bonnie gasped. "Oh no. Was he hurt badly? Is he going to be okay?"

"I don't know yet. After the ambulance came, I drove Hannah, Titus, and Samuel to the hospital, and then —"

"Hannah was there?"

Allen nodded. "She showed up unexpectedly, and you know what else?"

"What?"

"She's pregnant."

"Wow! Now that is a surprise!" Bonnie hardly knew what to say. She'd never expected Hannah to return to Kentucky, although she had been praying for that. And the fact that Hannah was expecting a baby was an even bigger surprise.

"I can't stay long," Allen said. "Timothy's folks are over at Titus and Suzanne's place, and I need to let them know what's happened. They'll no doubt want a ride to the hospital." He touched Bonnie's arm. "Do you want to go along?"

"Definitely," she said with a nod.

Hannah felt as if everyone in the waiting room was staring at her as she paced back and forth in front of the windows. She was just too nervous and worried to sit still. Before Allen, Bonnie, Fannie, and Abraham got there, she'd explained to Titus and Samuel what made her decide to return to Kentucky. Then when the others arrived, she'd told Bonnie and Allen.

After that, Hannah hadn't said much because all she could think about was Timothy. What could be causing them to take so long in finding out the extent of his injuries? What would she do if Timothy didn't make it? How would she find the strength to go on? She'd exhausted her storehouse of endurance.

"Lord, we need Your help," Hannah whispered tearfully. "Please be with Timothy, and let us hear something soon."

"Why don't you come and sit with us?" Bonnie said, gently touching Hannah's shoulder. "You look worn-out, and you're not doing yourself any good by pacing."

Hannah couldn't deny her fatigue, but just sitting and doing nothing made her feel so helpless. "I wish we'd hear something," she said, fighting tears of frustration. "It's so hard to wait and not know how Timothy is doing. I . . . I'm so afraid he won't make it."

"I understand, but I'm sure you'll hear something soon." Bonnie took hold of Hannah's arm. "You must never give up hope. Just put your trust in the Lord, Hannah."

Trust. It was hard to trust when her future was so uncertain, but Hannah knew that she must. Reluctantly, she allowed Bonnie to lead her to a chair.

"Is it all right if I say a prayer out loud for you and Timothy right now?" Allen asked.

Hannah nodded and bowed her head. She knew they needed all the prayers they could get.

"Heavenly Father," Allen prayed, "we come to You now, asking that You'll be with the doctors and nurses as they examine and care for Timothy. Give them wisdom in knowing what to do for him, and if it be Your will, we ask that Timothy's injuries are not serious. Be with Hannah, and give her a sense of peace as she waits to hear how her husband is doing. We thank You in advance for hearing our prayers. In Jesus' name we ask it, amen."

Hannah had just opened her eyes when a middle-aged man entered the room and walked over to her. "Mrs. Fisher?"

Hannah nodded and swallowed hard. She didn't know if she could stand hearing bad news. *Help me, Lord. Please help me to trust You.*

"I'm Dr. Higgins," he said, offering Hannah a reassuring smile. "I wanted you to know that your husband has suffered a mild concussion. He also has several nasty bruises, a few broken ribs, and a broken arm. But as bad as that might sound, he's not in serious condition and should be able to go home in a day or so."

Hannah breathed a sigh, almost fainting with relief. "Oh, I'm so thankful. Can I please see him now?"

The doctor nodded. "Certainly. Follow me."

Hannah looked at Timothy's family members. "Would you mind if I go in alone and speak to him first?"

"Of course not," Fannie spoke up. "You're his wife, after all."

Hannah smiled and gave Fannie a hug. Then, sending up a prayer of thanks, she followed the doctor down the hall.

When she entered Timothy's room, she found him lying in the hospital bed with his eyes closed. Quietly, she took a seat in the chair beside his bed. It scared Hannah to see her husband all bandaged up and his arm in a cast, but she knew it could have been so much worse. She'd only been sitting there a few seconds when Timothy opened his eyes and turned his head toward her.

"Am I seeing things, or am I dreaming? Is that really you, Hannah?" he asked, blinking as he gazed at her with disbelief.

Hannah's eyes burned as she thought of how close she'd come to losing him. Jumping up and reaching for his hand, she blinked against the tears that sprang to her eyes. "Yes, Timothy, it's really me — you're not dreaming. The doctor said you're going to be all right, and it's the answer to my prayers."

"But how'd you get here? When did you arrive? Wh–what made you come?"

Hannah explained everything to Timothy,

including the dream of Mindy that she'd had.

"That's really strange," he said, "because I had a dream about Mindy, too." Hannah placed her hand gently on Timothy's arm. "I want you to know that I've forgiven you, and I . . . I need to ask your forgiveness, too. It was wrong of me to leave the way I did, and I'm sorry for putting all the blame on you for Mindy's death. I've had a long time to think about things, and I know now that I'm also at fault for what happened to our daughter."

"Wh–what do you mean?"

"I should have been watching her closer that day, and I never should have sent her out of the kitchen because I thought I was too busy and couldn't be bothered."

Tears pooled in Timothy's eyes. "It's okay, Hannah. I forgive you, and I'm grateful that you've found it in your heart to forgive me. Now we both need to forgive ourselves."

She nodded solemnly. "There's . . . uh . . . something else you should know."

"What's that?"

Hannah pulled her coat aside.

Timothy's eyes widened as he stared at her stomach. "You . . . you're expecting a boppli?"

"Jah." She seated herself in the chair

again, feeling suddenly quite weary. "It'll be born next spring."

"Oh Hannah, what an unexpected blessing! Even in our grief, God has been so good to us."

"And He was watching out for you today," she said. "Falling off the barn roof could have ended in tragedy. How grateful I am that your injuries aren't life-threatening."

"I'm thankful for that, too, and from now on, whenever I'm working up high, I'll be a lot more careful than I was today."

"I don't know what I would have done if something had happened to you." Hannah leaned close to him, and despite her best efforts, she couldn't hold back the tears.

"I love you, Hannah," Timothy said as he reached out his hand and wiped away the tears trickling down her cheeks. "Oh, how I've prayed for this moment!"

"And I love you," she murmured. "Forever and always."

EPILOGUE

Six months later

Hannah hummed as she placed one hand on each of her twins' cradles in order to rock the babies to sleep. Little Priscilla Joy was the first to doze off, but Peter John wasn't far behind.

Hannah sighed. God had surely blessed them with these two precious bundles, and she was ever so grateful — not just for the privilege of raising these special babies, but for the opportunity to be Timothy's wife. She loved him so much and knew with assurance that he loved her, too.

Once Hannah was sure the babies were asleep, she stopped rocking their cradles and moved to the living-room window to look out at the beautiful spring day. The birds were singing so loud she could hear them from inside the house. To her, they'd never sounded more beautiful. A multitude of flowers had popped up in the garden, and the grass, which had recently been mowed, was lush and green. Their home looked beautiful. *Yes, our home,* she thought. It had been a long time in coming, but Hannah knew without a doubt that this was where she belonged.

Hannah's gaze went to the field where Timothy had been working all morning. She didn't see any sign of the horses or plow, so she figured he must have stopped to take a break. She glanced toward the kitchen and chuckled. Even the scratches on her new stove made her smile, remembering how it had happened all those months ago. She'd been upset about it at the time. Now Hannah couldn't believe she had let something so trivial bother her. She saw the mishap with the stove as a reminder of how hard her husband and his brothers had worked to turn this house into a real home. It had also become a good conversation topic when friends or family came to visit. The story of how the stove fell halfway through the floor always gave everyone a good laugh.

Hannah's thoughts took her back to the day they'd brought Timothy home from the hospital, two days after he'd fallen from the roof of their barn. Hannah had seen that he was settled comfortably on the sofa and then gone to the kitchen to prepare something for supper. Going into the utility room to get a clean apron, she'd been surprised to discover Mindy's doll on a shelf. When she'd asked Timothy about it, he'd explained that he had found the doll lying on the path leading to the mailbox. Hannah couldn't have been more relieved. After that, she'd taken the doll and tucked it safely away. One day she would give it to Priscilla Joy and let her, as well as Peter John, know all about their sister, Mindy.

Hannah had struggled with discontentment and bitterness when they'd first moved to Kentucky, but now she saw the Bluegrass State for its beauty and peacefulness and was happy to call it her home. She was thankful for English friends like Bonnie, whose baby girl, Cheryl, had been born two weeks before the twins. Things were going well for Trisha, too. She'd sold her condo in California and was planning to marry Bonnie's dad in June. Hannah had also established a closer bond with Suzanne and Esther. Suzanne's baby, Abe, was growing like a weed, and Esther had told her the other day that she and Samuel were expecting a baby in October. The Fisher family in Christian County, Kentucky, was definitely growing, and Hannah was happy to be part of their clan.

Hannah sighed contently. Everything seemed right with the world.

"Are you wishin' you were outside working in the garden on this nice spring day?" Hannah smiled at the sound of her husband's deep voice as he came up behind her. "I guess you are taking a break. I didn't think I'd see you until suppertime."

"The horses needed a break more than I did, but I used it as an excuse to come up to the house."

Hannah heard the laughter in Timothy's voice and knew even before she turned around that there must be a smile tugging on his lips. "I'm glad you came in."

"Me, too. I decided while the team rested I'd spend a few minutes with my fraa and bopplin, which is where I'd rather be, anyway."

Hannah gently squeezed his arm. "The babies are sleeping right now, but you're just in time to have a piece of the Kentucky chocolate chip pie I baked this morning."

"Mmm . . . that sounds good." He wiggled his eyebrows playfully. "But aren't you worried that it'll spoil my appetite for supper?"

She shook her head. "Supper won't be ready for a few hours yet. By then, I'm sure you will have worked off that piece of pie and will be good and hungry."

He grinned and nuzzled her cheek with his nose. "You know me so well, Hannah."

"That's right, I do. I know and love you, Timothy Fisher. And you know what else?" she asked, tipping her head to look up at him.

"What's that?"

"Despite any struggles we may encounter, I know in my heart that we can make it through them because we'll have each other." She stepped into her husband's embrace. "And most importantly, we'll have the Lord."

"That's right," he agreed, brushing his lips across her forehead. "For as we are reminded in Psalm 71, He is our rock and our fortress."

HANNAH'S KENTUCKY CHOCOLATE CHIP PIE

Ingredients:
1 stick butter or margarine, melted
2 eggs, beaten
1 cup sugar
1 teaspoon vanilla
1 cup chocolate chips
1 cup nuts, chopped
1 (9 inch) unbaked pie shell

Preheat oven to 325 degrees. In small kettle, melt the margarine and set aside. In bowl, beat eggs, sugar, and vanilla. Add chocolate chips and nuts and stir. Add margarine and beat well. Put in unbaked pie shell. Bake for 50 minutes or until done.

DISCUSSION QUESTIONS

1. Hannah had a hard time accepting her husband's decision to move from Pennsylvania to Kentucky because she knew she would miss her family, especially her mother. What are some things people can do to accept a move and adjust to their new surroundings?

2. Was there anything, other than moving, that Timothy could have done to improve his marriage and help Hannah realize that she was too close to her mother?

3. What are some things that parents can do to help their grown children who are married not to be so dependent on them and to cleave to their mates?

4. When Timothy and Hannah were forced to live with Timothy's brother Samuel for a time, it put further strain on their mar-

riage, and it became difficult for Samuel and his future wife, Esther, to continue with their plans to be married. What are some ways a family can deal with having other people living with them for a time?

5. When a tragedy occurred in this story, Hannah blamed her husband and pulled away from him emotionally as well as physically. What are some ways we can work through a tragedy without blaming someone else?

6. Bonnie felt guilty for something she'd done when she was a teenager and was afraid to tell Allen about it. Is there ever a time when we should keep information about our past from a loved one?

7. Allen had a hard time forgiving Bonnie for not telling him about her past. He not only felt betrayed but wasn't sure he could trust her anymore. How can being unwilling to forgive others affect our relationship not only with that person, but also with God? What does the Bible say about forgiveness?

8. The Amish believe strongly that once they are married, God wants them to stay

together until death separates them. What impact do you think it would have on an Amish community if one of their members left their spouse and perhaps even got a divorce?

9. What differences did you see in this story between the Amish in Lancaster County, Pennsylvania, and the Amish who live in Christian County, Kentucky?

10. What verses of scripture did you find the most helpful in this story? In what ways might you apply them to your own life?

ABOUT THE AUTHOR

Wanda E. Brunstetter is a *New York Times* bestselling author who enjoys writing Amish-themed, as well as historical, novels. Descended from Anabaptists herself, Wanda became deeply interested in the Plain People when she married her husband, Richard, who grew up in a Mennonite church in Pennsylvania.

Wanda and her husband now live in Washington State but take every opportunity to visit their Amish friends in various communities across the country, gathering further information about the Amish way of life. Wanda and her husband have two grown children and six grandchildren. In her spare time, Wanda enjoys photography, ventriloquism, gardening, beach-combing, stamping, and having fun with her family.

In addition to her novels, Wanda has written two Amish cookbooks, two Amish devotionals, several Amish children's books, as well as numerous novellas, stories, articles, poems, and puppet scripts.

Visit Wanda's website at www.wandabrun stetter.com, and feel free to e-mail her at wanda@wandabrunstetter.com.

The employees of Thorndike Press hope you have enjoyed this Large Print book. All our Thorndike, Wheeler, and Kennebec Large Print titles are designed for easy reading, and all our books are made to last. Other Thorndike Press Large Print books are available at your library, through selected bookstores, or directly from us.

For information about titles, please call:
(800) 223-1244

or visit our Web site at:
http://gale.cengage.com/thorndike

To share your comments, please write:
Publisher
Thorndike Press
10 Water St., Suite 310
Waterville, ME 04901

THE SCENT OF SAKE

JOYCE LEBRA

KENNEBEC LARGE PRINT
A part of Gale, Cengage Learning

GALE
CENGAGE Learning·

Detroit • New York • San Francisco • New Haven, Conn • Waterville, Maine • London

GALE
CENGAGE Learning™

Copyright © 2009 by Joyce Lebra.
Kennebec Large Print, a part of Gale, Cengage Learning.

Kennebec Large Print® Large Print Superior Collection.
The text of this Large Print edition is unabridged.
Other aspects of the book may vary from the original edition.
Set in 16 pt. Plantin.
Printed on permanent paper.

LIBRARY OF CONGRESS CATALOGING-IN-PUBLICATION DATA

Lebra-Chapman, Joyce, 1925–
  The scent of sake / by Joyce Lebra.
    p. cm. — (Kennebec large print superior collection)
  ISBN-13: 978-1-59722-943-2 (pbk. : alk. paper)
  ISBN-10: 1-59722-943-1 (pbk. : alk. paper)
  1. Rice wines—Japan—History—Fiction. 2. Rice wines industry—Japan—History—Fiction. 3. Japan—History—19th century—Fiction. 4. Large type books. I. Title.
PR9499.3.L43S34 2009b
823—dc22
                                  2009006238

Published in 2009 by arrangement with Avon, an imprint of HarperCollins Publishers.

Printed in the United States of America
1 2 3 4 5 6 7 13 12 11 10 09

To those who preserve the tradition.

When Amaterasu came forth [from the dark cave]
the Plain of High Heaven in the Central Land of the Reed Plains
. . . became light.

the *Kojiki*

THE CHARACTERS

Kinzaemon IX
Hana, his wife
Rie, their daughter
Jihei, Rie's mukoyoshi
Fumi, Rie's daughter by Saburo Kato
Seisaburo, Rie and Jihei's son
O-Toki, Jihei's favorite geisha, mother of Yo-shitaro
Yoshitaro, Jihei's son of O-Toki
Tama, Yoshitaro's wife
Teru, Jihei's daughter of O-Toki
Kazu, Jihei's daughter of O-Yumi
Eitaro, Fumi's mukoyoshi
O-Sada, Yoshitaro's geisha
Ume, daughter of Yoshitaro and O-Sada
Hirokichi, son of Fumi and Eitaro
Mie, daughter of Fumi and Eitaro
Mari, Seisaburo's wife
O-Haru, Sawaraya proprietress
Masami, O-Toki's lover
Goro, son of O-Toki and Masami

Nobuo, son of Seisaburo and Mari
Masako, daughter of Seisaburo and Mari
Naoko, Hirokichi's wife
Hana, daughter of Hirokichi and Naoko
Toji, brewmaster
Kin, banto, chief clerk
Shin'ichi, Kinnosuke, his successor
Nobu, wife of Kinnosuke
O-Natsu, faithful family servant
O-Yuki, maid
Mrs. Nakano, marriage go-between
Hirano, Seisaburo's banto
Buntaro, Hirano's son, Kinnosuke's successor
Yamaguchi, competing brewer
Yusuke, his banto

CHAPTER 1

It was a day Rie would never forget, the day her mother told her who her husband would be. That day she had knelt in the frigid courtyard scrubbing the wooden sake barrels, barrels so large they had to be lifted by ropes and pulleys. She gripped the big brush in both hands and scrubbed back and forth, back and forth until her muscles ached. She rubbed her blue-cold hands together and held them over her nose and mouth. Then she scratched under the cotton scarf that held back her long thick hair and shifted on the rush mat on which she was kneeling. As she did so, she glanced through the misty screen of her breath at the door of the brewery and inhaled the pungent, mildewy smell of yeast, the smell that permeated every corner of the drafty old wooden house and brewery buildings. Women were never to enter the forbidden door that gaped darkly before her.

"Let a woman enter the brewery and the sake will sour," the old ones always said. Her mother had warned her of this since childhood. But Rie relished the yeasty smell of brewing sake that hung in the air. She had always played near the door and the barrels as a child. As a little girl, she had waited, terrified, for the news that the sake had soured. It never had. Now that she was grown, now that she had her own secret opinions of what women could accomplish, she made it her duty to wash the barrels, a task she took on when she knew her father was not looking. As atonement.

This time he caught her. "Rie! Haven't I warned you to stay away from the brewery door? It's too dangerous to be so close to the *kura,* brewing building, and washing barrels is not your responsibility."

Rie looked up to see her father looming over her, frowning, hands thrust into the sleeves of the indigo work kimono he always wore. His white chicken-feather eyebrows were dusted with frost and seemed to stand erect in anger.

Understand me, she longed to say. *See me as doing my best for you and the house.* But she couldn't say it.

Rie stood and bowed, looking down at her feet. Her father, Kinzaemon IX, head of the

House of Omura, was the one person in the world she most wanted to please. He represented all nine generations of the ancestors, a long line to which both he and now Rie owed *on,* the obligation that could never be repaid but toward which one must strive throughout one's life.

At first when her brother had died, so had all her father's hopes and dreams. But after weeks of grieving, he had uttered the portentous words that would change her life: "So now, Rie, the future of the Omura House rests with you. You alone are the one who will maintain the honor and prosperity of the house. Remember, this is a heavy responsibility."

Everyone knew that sake brewing was a man's world, and Kinzaemon could have brought a geisha's son into the house. But with the Kansai *chonin,* the merchants, they often preferred to adopt a husband for a daughter, an adult clerk who had proven his mettle and would be an asset to the family business. It was common practice among brewers, a good business strategy.

And she had felt it, felt the weight of the generations fall upon her, the hope her father had bestowed upon her. She could not bear his sad eyes or the way her mother got busy every time she neared so as not to let on that she had been crying. Rie had promised herself then that she would take this loss from their shoulders, this burden, and carry it as her own.

Now, as she washed the barrels, she pictured her little brother Toichi's large brown eyes, his sweet face. She should have been watching him closer, her father's only son. He had been her responsibility, and now he was gone. Her guilt was a burden she would bear the rest of her life, the result of her own carelessness and disregard of her responsibility to the house. As she finished scrubbing the last of the barrels all she got was blue-cold hands and a scolding from her father. "Yes, Father. But I do not want to leave this job to others. It's too important. And I'm not so near the door." She glanced up briefly, and looked down again.

"Get back to the kitchen!" Kinzaemon bellowed.

Rie was careful not to let her anger and disappointment show. She bowed, dropped the brush, and ran toward the door leading through the earthen corridor to the rooms of the house. The kitchen. That was the place of women. How unreasonable of her father to expect her to be only a confined "girl in a box."

Now she was the first and only child. The

samurai knew what to do about barren wives who had only daughters. A mistress could always be found to provide an heir for the house. Still, the Kansai merchant houses found daughters useful. The midwives liked to announce with the birth of a daughter: "It's a girl, so the house will prosper." With a son you really had a gamble, true enough. You had to take what you got, and that could be a bright boy or a dull one. Her baby brother Toichi had been bright. Still, with a daughter, intelligent or not, you had a range of choices for an adopted husband for her. And for an important house like the Omuras, there were plenty of prospects, excellent ones.

With Toichi gone, it was imperative that Rie take an interest in the business, this she knew, to learn as much as she could from her imperious father and chief clerk, Kin. "Knowing about the brewery will help your husband in the future, the house. I want our brewery to be number one," her father had always said.

And so, as Rie glided rapidly along the pounded earthen corridor to the polished platform hallway and rooms of the house, she determined to fulfill her father's wish. As penance. But how, she wondered as she ran her hand along the dark brown woodwork that gleamed in the faint, frozen morning light? She turned and ran her hand along the sturdy aged cypress pillar that supported the house, the House of Omura, the house whose head she had so far disappointed. At nineteen, her arms could barely reach to embrace this post that had supported the house for nine generations. She walked more slowly to the kitchen door.

"Oh, there you are," said a smiling plump maid whose apple cheeks bespoke her country origins. O-Natsu held out a cup of tea to warm Rie's hands. "O-Josama," O-Natsu said, using the title reserved for the younger woman of the house, "your mother wants to see you. She is in her room waiting." She bowed again.

"Thank you, O-Natsu." Rie sipped tea and held the cup in both hands for a moment to warm them. She handed the cup back to O-Natsu, adjusted her scarf and apron, and walked along the chilly corridor and up the steep slippery wooden stairs to her mother's second-floor room.

"I have returned," she announced, kneeling outside the door.

"Come in," her mother's soft voice greeted her.

The strength concealed beneath Hana's voice was a source of wonder to Rie. She opened the sliding screen with both hands, bowed, and glanced at her mother's refined face, a face that did not reveal the manifold concerns behind it. A brewer's wife was responsible for the food, housing, clothing, health, and well-being of all the brewery workers. Rie entered the room on her knees and moved toward the hibachi to warm her hands. She looked down at her chapped red fingers and held them over the glowing coals, rubbing gently.

Her mother was sitting opposite Rie, her back to the paulownia dressing cabinet, sewing together sections of a kimono that had been taken apart for laundering. Her mother's room was a large eight-tatami room with a two-tatami dressing room adjacent. It was sparsely furnished according to Japanese sensibility: a low lacquerware table, the hibachi, the paulownia dressing cabinet, and *zabuton* completed the appointments. "Where have you been, Rie? Out in front of the kura again?"

Rie hesitated, bowing slightly. "Yes, Mother. I was washing barrels." She moved her back and wet feet closer to the warm coals and reached to pour tea for her mother and herself.

"You know, Rie, your father doesn't like you there. And so close to the kura. I've

17

always felt we shouldn't be anywhere near the kura door. You know how great the danger of pollution is."

Hana snipped a thread and looked at her work critically. She had tried to show Rie the lock stitch, but Rie could not sew stitches as fine as her mother's and always felt awkward and inadequate when faced with a sewing task.

Rie put down her cup and poked at the hibachi coals with long metal chopsticks. "I know, Mother. But I'm not really so near the door. I must work there in order to wash the barrels. That's where the *kurabito* leave them when they're finished. And that's where the well is." She cringed, remembering the well. If she'd been closer that day, little Toichi wouldn't have fallen in. Rie was eight at the time, and Toichi had only been walking a few months. How was she to guess that he could have pulled himself up, fallen in. Gooseflesh crawled up her arms as she remembered. "I can't move the barrels, you know. And Toji-san has never complained."

"No, I don't suppose he would. He has always been so fond of you. He even let you play in the barrels as a little girl. He knows he can count on you to continue the traditions of our house. But you know the Ikedas lost their whole cellar last year when the sake went sour. And you must listen to Father. You must obey him."

Warmth crept up Rie's cheeks as she pressed her lips together and reached for a cup of tea, warming both hands and inhaling the comforting green tea fragrance.

"I know." She put down the cup and moved her hands back to the hibachi without speaking further. She knew better.

"Have another cup of tea, Rie." Her mother smiled ever so slightly.

Rie glanced again at her mother's face with its patrician Kyoto nose, the distinctive downward curve that marked aristocratic women from the old capital. It was known that someone in Hana's family had had a liaison with a Kyoto woman. Rie's mother had inherited the woman's best feature.

"Another thing, Rie. . . ."

Rie glanced again at her mother, and lowered her eyes. This must be why her mother had called her.

"You are close to twenty now, and it's high time we were serious about your marriage. And we have several good candidates. Your father and I are especially interested in the Okamoto son, Jihei. He has been apprenticed to the Ohara house, so we know he has had excellent training, and the reports we hear are good."

Jihei?

Rie looked up in alarm. She tried to remember what Jihei looked like. She knew he was one of the clerks who came on errands to the office.

"*Ah,* I remember now," she murmured, her heart sinking. She recalled a boy with a large nose and eyebrows that stood up straight like her father's. Not the handsomest of clerks by any means. Not as handsome as the Kato's third son, the son whose elegant bearing, fine chiseled features, and long fingers bespoke a certain sensitivity. On the day of Toichi's funeral, Saburo Kato had stood before her, murmured his apologies, then had looked up at her with such intense brown eyes that she knew then he shared her wound in some way. Understood it. Since then, she had noticed him more than once. *He* would be her husband, given a choice. But no choice would be given, of course.

"We have arranged the *o-miai* meeting for early next month. The Okamotos have been approaching us, and they are serious." Hana paused to turn a teacup around in her hand. "We don't want to delay too long or they will get discouraged and look elsewhere. We can have the wedding before summer."

"I see." Rie slowly put her cup down, her hand trembling.

"You know Father and I have your best interests at heart."

Rie sighed and tried to put Jihei's face out of her mind. Luckily, his face was very forgettable. Unluckily, she knew it was the interests of the house that mattered, not her own preferences.

Hana glanced at Rie's face before continuing. "Personal feelings have so little to do with marriage. Your father and I were fortunate. We grew fond of each other after we married. That is what you must hope for." She paused. "We know you understand. So we'll ask Mrs. Nakano to go ahead with the *o-miai* arrangements. We'll choose a good fortune day in May. I've always liked spring weddings. Summer is too hot."

Hana leaned forward slightly. "And you must try to be a good wife, Rie. Be compliant. Your feelings must not intrude." Hana put down her sewing and looked at Rie's face. "Women often find it necessary to 'kill the self.' Otherwise life becomes too difficult."

Kill the self. Isn't that what she'd done when her brother died? A sliver of guilt wedged inside her heart.

Her mother picked up her sewing again

21

and bent over it. "And remember how fortunate you are. You won't have to live with a mother-in-law. Your husband is the one who will. He will have the bigger adjustment to make." She glanced again at Rie.

Rie put her hand over her mouth. She wondered how her mother had had to "kill the self." Was it the suffering at the loss of little Toichi? Remorse made her cheeks glow hot like the coals from the hibachi. "Yes, Mother." She bowed to her mother, excusing herself before leaving the room.

She walked slowly down the stairs and along the wooden walkway above the earthen floor, deliberately putting one slipper just in front of the other. She glided into the wooden *geta* and walked out to the gated garden. She opened the creaking weathered gate and stepped onto the large round stones toward a huge boulder. She leaned against it and gazed toward the koi pond.

Of course this was bound to happen. Once parents neared fifty, they were anxious to get the succession settled. Her marriage could not be postponed. Besides, her mother said she and Rie's father cared for each other, and she knew this to be true. Maybe the same would be true for Rie and her husband. At any rate, there was no choice. She would have to marry Jihei. She would have to forget Saburo Kato. Not that she could.

That night Rie sat musing in front of her dressing cabinet. "Kill the self," her mother had said. *How would it ever be possible to kill the self and still continue to live, to survive,* she wondered? She recalled the death a few years ago of one of the kurabito, something her mother had grieved long, almost as long as with Toichi, as it was her responsibility to ensure the health of all the workers in the brewery.

Rie gazed at her reflection, at the face she overheard someone in the office say belonged to a farm woman, something he had dared to say only when her father was not in the room. She sighed. Although her eyes were large and arresting, her teeth protruded slightly, there was no denying. She knew she was not a beauty, in the classical sense. She thought suddenly of the way her father banished her to the kitchen, wanted to keep her away from the business side of the brewery, especially transactions involving cash, something to which women of Kansai merchant houses had no access. How was she to fulfill her responsibility to the house if she wasn't allowed to be involved in the business of brewing? She sighed deeply and sat several minutes at the mirror before laying out the futon.

Arranged marriage was the way. She would not *kill the self.* She would find a way to survive.

The most elegant tearoom in Kobe was reserved for the formal meeting of the two families, with Mr. and Mrs. Nakano presiding as go-betweens. Rie bit her lip and held her breath as, attired in an elegant pale blue kimono of the finest silk, she entered the gold screened room behind her parents. She was able to see, even with her head properly bowed throughout the meeting, that she was right about Jihei. He did have a large nose and startling eyebrows. She continued to gaze at the lacquer plate before her as her parents and the Okamotos exchanged the perfunctory courtesies that sealed her fate. She sat perfectly still, her emotions tightly in check as she listened with a sinking feeling in the pit of her stomach.

A few days after the meeting the Omuras offered their formal proposal. The Okamotos accepted, and the last good fortune day in the May calendar was selected.

Rie spent the next days and weeks trying on the kimono she would own for the rest of her life. As she fingered the *kasuri,* silk and brocade fabrics, and counted the days, she wondered about the stranger her parents had selected as her husband. Would he be as boring as his face? Or would he surprise her? The wedding day approached, the day every woman knew was the most important day in her life. Then why did she have such a feeling of foreboding?

CHAPTER 2

Rie's wedding, her father told her, would be remembered in Kobe as a major event of the year 1825. He often talked to Rie about major events, unwittingly piquing her interest in matters supposedly of no concern to women. The shogunate and its neo-Confucian maxims was one of his favorite topics. The shogunate was in deep financial crisis, something her father discussed with fervor.

"What do we care for the Neo-Confucianism of the shoguns, this so-called philosophy that puts us at the bottom of society, below the samurai, the farmers, even the craftsmen? Empty words! Everyone knows we merchants hold the real wealth, that we are the arbiters of culture, not only in Kobe but everywhere."

Whatever the officials of the shogunate did, including the measures of Chief Councilor Mizuno, all had failed. He had tried to solve the financial crisis through a series of reforms: sumptuary edicts to curtail extravagance, restrictions on festivals and Noh and Kabuki performances, and limits on the activities of pawnbrokers. Nothing worked. As Kinzaemon said, it was the merchants, chonin, who held the real wealth. And of the merchants it was the sake brewers and pawnbrokers who were wealthiest. Most brewers of substance were pawnbrokers and moneylenders as well. If the country were to be saved, it would be houses like the Omuras that would save it.

It was natural, then, for the marriage of two major brewing houses to be viewed as an event of great importance. The engagement followed the o-miai, the formal meeting, and the wedding date was fixed. Mrs. Nakano, the most respected go-between in Kobe, was in her element. The plump, energetic brewer's wife boasted the news of the impending wedding to everyone she encountered, and she had without doubt the widest acquaintance in town. Soon the marriage was eagerly anticipated throughout the whole brewing community.

With the exception of Rie herself, of course.

The match was the talk of the May Brewers Association meeting. The meeting was attended, as usual, by a representative of each brewing house, generally the house head. The chief rival of the Omura House was there, Kikuji Yamaguchi, a bombastic man nearly as large as a sumo wrestler. His *obi* strained over his barrel stomach, and he surveyed the assembled brewers arrogantly. He swaggered and belched as he walked, and boasted loudly that Ogre-Killer would soon be the number one brand of sake in Japan. Kinzaemon overheard him say *"Huh! She's marrying Jihei Okamoto. Some choice! What can he do for White Tiger? Well, so much the better for us!"* Yamaguchi gloated. During the previous year he had succeeded in capturing ten percent of White Tiger's market, a serious blow in the competitive world of the brewers.

Kinzaemon, who had sunk into depression following Toichi's death, seemed discouraged by Yamaguchi's words. Rie knew this from a conversation she overheard while standing outside the office. He was speaking to Kin, she was sure. "This is a bad blow to us, to our position and honor. And he was insulting as well, talking about Rie's marriage to the Okamoto son." Listening, Rie felt her anger rising. *How dare Yamaguchi!* "We have lost part of our market to Yamaguchi too." She had to do something,

28

somehow, to redeem the status of the house and to prove that the Omura House was superior to the Yamaguchi House.

Now, more than ever, marriage to Jihei would be crucial for the continuity and prosperity of the house, Rie knew. Kinzaemon had carefully chosen Jihei after a thorough investigation by Mrs. Nakano. The family of the groom, its reputation and standing, the training of the groom, the absence of contagious disease in the family — all these things had been weighed by Kinzaemon and his wife so that Yamaguchi could have nothing bad to say about the marriage. But everyone knew Yamaguchi was always bragging.

"Most unseemly for a man in his position. The other brewers should have enough sense not to take Yamaguchi's remarks seriously," Hana said one evening, seeking to comfort her husband.

Preparations for the wedding prompted a steady stream of vendors in the office and house of the Omuras: caterers for the reception, weavers and dyers from Nishijin in Kyoto, and seamstresses coming and going in a seemingly unending procession each day.

"Must we invite three hundred guests?" Rie asked. "All those return gifts will be such an expense."

Hana looked at Rie and smiled thought-fully. "This is a modest list, Rie. You know it would be a bad oversight if we omitted even one of the major brewing houses. The list is critical. Besides, you are our only child and this is one of the most important events for our house."

But even Rie's mother had to admit the trousseau was impressive: three four-drawer aromatic cedar *tansu* chests with copper fittings, several sets of cotton and silk linens, and two dozen silk kimonos and brocade obis of every color, including formal black, sewn by the best Nishijin seamstresses.

Dressing the bride took all morning. Rie had to rise at dawn for a bath. Her mother and O-Natsu watched as two women unfolded the silk under-kimonos. They adjusted the sleeves and collars as Rie held out her arms for the many layered undergarments. She tried to stand patiently as the women worked, but her growing anxiety made it hard to stand still. Finally she lifted her arms so the outer kimono could be adjusted in place. The kimono was white silk with an exquisite design of pine, plum, and bamboo below knee level, signifying strength, courage, and harmony. The obi was adorned with a complimentary pattern outlined in gold thread. To Rie, tying the wide obi seemed to take forever. At the neck the collar was arranged so that the proper amount of under-kimono revealed the subtlest variations of white.

Rie's hair was piled into three sections over which was laid the wide white silk band to hide the bride's "devils' horns," symbolizing that a wife was never to display jealousy, whatever her husband chose to do. She doubted Jihei *could* make her jealous! Her face and neck were painted chalk white. Fitting for how she felt.

"But Mother, I feel twice as large as normal. I won't be able to move," Rie complained. She looked in the mirror that O-Natsu held for her and gasped. "I don't even look like myself," she mumbled.

"Don't worry, dear, you need only walk slowly, with very small steps. Remember to keep your knees together and bent and your toes pointed inward, won't you?" Her mother smiled and appraised Rie from every angle. "Very fine," she pronounced.

"You look beautiful," O-Natsu breathed.

The brief ceremony was presided over by a white-robed priest at the city's principal Shinto shrine. At the entrance of the shrine the bride and groom and family guests each took a sip of purifying water with a bamboo

31

dipper from a tank engraved with the characters "cleanse the spirit." The ceremonial room was spare, the floorboards polished to a gleaming gloss, the only furnishing being the zabuton on which guests sat facing the priest and the bridal couple, whose parents sat closest to the bride and groom. The priest waved his paper wand over the bride and groom to invoke the blessing of the gods. Rie and Jihei exchanged the traditional three sips of sake from a black lacquer cup. Her head modestly bowed, Rie was nevertheless able to steal a nervous glance at Jihei. He was standing stiffly in his black wedding kimono, looking straight ahead. She wondered what he was thinking. Was he pleased with his bride? Or did he feel as she did? Rie had no clue to Jihei's feelings, other than his stiff, formal bearing, which was really fitting for the occasion. She would have to wait, she knew, for what lay ahead at night. She wanted to glance at his face, but forced herself to keep looking demurely down, as her mother had instructed.

The teahouse with the largest garden in the city was reserved for the reception. All the city's luminaries were present: shogunal commissioners, town officials, and representatives of each of the major brewing houses with their wives. Women paraded in their elegant kimonos and admired the azaleas while husbands gathered in clusters and discussed the significance of the adoption of the Okamoto second son as successor to the House of Omura. The bride and groom were toasted in the top grade of White Tiger and their virtues extolled by Mr. Nakano and the head of the Kobe Sake Brewers Association.

And so she was married. Jihei, this stranger, was her *husband*.

Standing in the reception line Rie caught her breath when she happened to glance up just as Saburo, the Kato third son, was passing. She looked directly into his arresting eyes, and smiled slightly before looking down. She thought she caught an answering smile as she murmured a greeting and bowed. He was so handsome! And she felt drawn to him, there was no question. Her emotions were in turmoil as she recalled his sympathetic reassurance at little Toichi's funeral, the way he had caught her elbow when she felt faint. The strength he'd somehow transferred to her in that small gesture. She would never forget it, or him. She wondered if negotiations were under way for the marriage of this man she found so appealing. Her shoulders tensed and she pressed her hands more tightly together.

Her thoughts lingered on Saburo Kato during the rest of the reception as she stood beside her new husband.

Rie tensed as Kinzaemon turned to look at her. She made sure her head was modestly bowed, her hands folded in front of her as guests congratulated Jihei at her side. Rie knew that for Kinzaemon the marriage was the culmination of a successful negotiation to ensure the future of the house. But for Rie it felt like a death sentence.

When they returned to the Omura House following the reception it was late evening. Rie's mother helped her out of her obi. "O-Natsu will help you with your kimono, Rie."

Rie's parents vacated the second floor room for the newlyweds and moved downstairs to Rie's former room. Hana said, "The stairs are becoming too much for us, dear. We'd rather you had the room."

"Only if it's really difficult for you, Mother," Rie had demurred.

Rie put on the kimono especially selected for the wedding night, trembling as she did, beads of sweat forming on her brow. Jihei had already been shown to their quarters, but had drunk so much that he stumbled on the stairs. Rie heard him grumbling, his speech slurred, as he staggered around the room bumping into the *shoji. Please be so drunk that you fall asleep the moment you lie down,* she prayed.

As Rie walked up the stairs, she hesitated. The stairway and her mother's room above were so familiar, but tonight they seemed strange, almost forbidding. She put her hands on the yellow plaster walls on either side of the stairway for reassurance, for support on this portentous night.

When she entered the anteroom she saw that Jihei was already recumbent on the futon, eyes closed, his breath smelling of sake even from where she stood. Had her prayers been answered? She entered the room slowly, sat at the dressing table and took down her hair, glancing at Jihei's reflection in the mirror as she combed the glossy locks. When she could delay no longer she went to the futon that had been laid out beside Jihei's and quietly slipped under the covers. She breathed as lightly as possible, hoping that Jihei was already asleep. It seemed an eternity that she lay there wakeful, apprehensive. This man beside her on the futon was a complete stranger.

Some time during the night, she could not say just when, Jihei came to her abruptly, grunting and sweating, without saying anything, without a word that might have shown consideration for her. The shock of his sharp, piercing thrusts caused her to gasp and struggle to stifle a cry of pain. When he stopped, she tried to move but was pinned by Jihei's moist, slack body. *Disgusting!* She lay wakeful, barely able to breathe, the pain between her thighs acute as she listened to Jihei's heavy breathing. A single tear fell. Was this what their life together would be like? If she'd had a dagger, she would have cut her throat now rather than face this nightly humiliation. She thought of Kato, of the tenderness he'd shown her at her brother's funeral. Now she would forever be locked away with a man who would control her destiny. No, she could not think about it. Her mother was right. To survive, one must kill the self.

She closed her eyes, then opened them, determined to get as far away from this man as possible. Finally she was able to edge out from under him. Despite the ache in her heart and the sense of violation, she knew she would have to be with her husband in this way to bear an heir for the house. She bit her lip and tried to sleep, but the pain and sense of outrage made it impossible.

She rolled gingerly out of the futon, drew her kimono around her, and, picking up her padded wrapper, glanced at her still-sleeping husband. She slid open the shoji, then crept quietly down the stairs and along the drafty dark corridor past the kitchen to the bathroom. As she dropped her kimono into the wicker basket in the dressing room, she wrinkled her nose in distaste when she noticed bloodstains. Shivering, she entered the room where the wooden tub stood. Scooping up the tepid water still standing from the evening's baths, she sloshed bucket after bucket over her body until every trace of blood, dried perspiration, and sticky fluids was washed away. Then she wrapped both kimonos around herself and walked softly toward the inner office. She entered and sat in the silent darkness at the main working table. She breathed in slowly. The comforting aroma of musty ledgers mingled with the hint of yeast that never left the house. For the next several minutes, the tears fell in earnest. She listened to her muffled sobs, saw her breath in the dim, wintry light.

As she was busy feeling sorry for herself, a barrel on the floor bearing the White Tiger logo caught her eye, the brand name under which the Omura sake had been sold for nine generations. She gazed at the leaping white beast, talisman of all those ancestors before her father. Of Toichi, had he lived.

Something swept over her, stronger than feeling.

Whatever was necessary to ensure the birth of an heir she would do, *must* do, for the house. That was not only her obligation, but her atonement for the lapse that had ended her brother's life. Yes, she would fulfill her obligation, but the inner office here, the core of the brewery, this she would make her own sphere, a place to forget that other life with Jihei. Here she would work for the house, do her best for White Tiger and for her father. Just how she would accomplish this she was not sure. But she would do it. She would work to redeem herself to her father and position herself to defeat the braggart Yamaguchi, the White Tiger enemy. Kinzaemon would come to know that she was indispensable to the business, far more than "a girl in a box." She would find a way into the business, maybe through Kin, the chief clerk. She knew he was fond of her and had been since she was a small child. He had given her clues about the business from time to time. Sniffling, she rested her arms on the table, then glanced at the White Tiger logo again.

"I will do this, and Father will know," she murmured.

CHAPTER 3

As soon as her eyes opened, Rie extricated herself from her futon, rose, and folded it away in the wall cupboard. She turned to glance at her husband. He showed no sign of waking. Relieved, Rie opened the shoji and quickly changed in the dressing room. She knew her mother would be expecting her to prepare her husband's first breakfast in his new home, and she padded rapidly down the slippery stairway.

Jihei appeared in the breakfast room several minutes later, and as soon as he had eaten the rice, miso soup, and pickles Rie placed before him, he rose abruptly and followed Kinzaemon into the office. Wasn't he able to speak, to acknowledge her at all?

Rie wanted to erase her memories of the night before, of Jihei's body on hers, his breath smelling of sake. She shuddered at the memory, and forced her attention to brewery concerns. Even as a child she had taken an interest in her father's business, and now she felt a greater urgency. He would be retiring soon, and with him Kin. They had been looking for a successor. But before a decision was made about who would succeed Kin, she needed to find out what they were planning, especially in regard to Jihei. Curious to see Kin's reaction to Jihei, but also mindful of Yamaguchi's evaluation of her new husband, she slid quietly along the corridor toward the inner office and peered cautiously around the shoji that stood open. Her father's back was to her, she was relieved to see.

Kinzaemon had taken Jihei into the office to introduce him to Kin, chief clerk and manager of the entire White Tiger operation. A spare spidery figure of a man, prominent front teeth barely covered by his lips, Kin had been with the family business almost as long as Kinzaemon. He was consulted in any major decision. Close in age to Kinzaemon and equally dedicated to family traditions, Kin nevertheless also had more of an eye to the future. Each autumn he insisted on projecting White Tiger's markets three years in advance.

Rie had been watching her father and had noticed how tired he seemed lately, how depressed he'd become as he neared retirement. Always he'd dreamed of a son to carry on the family business, to help him create the dynasty that he'd envisioned long ago. Her shoulders slumped as a familiar weight rested on them. She was more determined than ever to make her father's dream a reality.

"This is Jihei Okamoto, Rie's new husband and my successor," Kinzaemon said. "Now we have a man to succeed me." Rie bit her lip as she heard this.

Kin bowed lower than Jihei, as was appropriate. "Good." He nodded to Kinzaemon and Jihei.

Rie backed quickly out of sight but lingered to hear more. A man to succeed made her father happy, of course. She expected it of her father and was glad that it pleased him, but for her the union had been an outrage that even now left her feeling unclean. Her throat tightened at the memory as she ducked farther out of sight. She did not wish to be seen by her husband, or by Kin either. She would have to catch Kin sometime alone and talk to both him and Jihei about increasing market share. There was nothing to prevent her from going to the office in the evening after her father had left.

She heard Kin open the ledgers and begin

to relate a summary of White Tiger's main suppliers, customers, and sales routes to Jihei. She tried to remember everything Kin said. "In this ledger here you see all our suppliers of Yamada Nishiki rice, *koji* mold, and yeast. And in this one here are all our major customers." As Kin talked, Rie heard the shoji to the outer office open and the men's voices grow fainter. She moved along the corridor toward the outer office so as not to miss any of the valuable summaries of White Tiger's operations.

Rie brought a flask of heated sake to the bridal room that evening and turned to Jihei, her hands shaking as she handed him his drink. She needed to prepare for the future growth of the business, but she could only do so if her husband was in concurrence with her wishes. She took a steadying breath before launching in.

"You know you will be house head as soon as Father retires," she said hesitantly. "And it isn't far off now. He is fifty. So is Kin, therefore we may have a double retirement."

"That would be a problem if they both retired at the same time, wouldn't it?" Jihei asked. He pulled at his bristling eyebrows.

"Oh, we're sure to find someone to apprentice with Kin before that happens, maybe one of the boys from Tamba. Anyway, Father and Kin will soon be on the lookout among the brewing houses."

Jihei picked up a small cup, and Rie leaned over to pour for him.

"Maybe we should be looking now," Jihei offered.

"Yes, I've started looking myself."

Jihei worked at his eyebrows again and shifted uneasily. "I wonder if the daughters of other houses are as active as you."

"Well, I'm an only child and have always loved brewing, even when I was little." She smiled, tentatively.

Jihei leaned back and drained a second cup. "I was trained as a child too, but then it was always my elder brother who would succeed, so there wasn't the same pressure on me. Still, my father always said there was sake running in our veins, not blood," Jihei said, smiling at his joke.

"Yes, we all felt that way," Rie responded, beginning to relax in his presence. Maybe last night was an aberration, and tonight would go better. She hoped so. And yet she couldn't bring herself to think of it.

When Rie drew their futon from the cupboard for the night she deliberately placed hers as far from Jihei's as possible. After they had lain on their separate futon for a few minutes Jihei slid out of his and moved over to Rie. He lifted her quilt and began to move closer.

"*Uh!*" She grabbed the futon tightly around herself. "Let's wait until we both feel ready," she said more gently. She knew she couldn't continue this way, that she would have to relent, and soon, but the thought of his breath, his clumsy moves, put an ache in her chest. Rie guessed that the reason he didn't insist was that he felt a stranger in the house, his position as a *mukoyoshi* without much power as he saw it.

To his credit, Jihei moved back to his futon, picked up a flask of sake from his tray, and drained it without a cup. With a sigh of relief, she heard Jihei slump back onto his futon. *Saved. For tonight at least.*

A few days later Rie overheard her father and Jihei talking at the dinner table. She paused beyond the shoji to listen, a sake flask in her hand. As Kinzaemon aged, his quick timing and nose for business had gradually diminished. Although her father loved her, she knew he didn't put the same faith in her as he would have in a son, but she had promised herself that one day she would make her father proud. Be the son he couldn't have. She knew that if they

44

didn't act quickly, Yamaguchi would soon own a much larger share of the market and she could not allow that, she decided, as she held her breath so as not to be heard. She couldn't wait for Jihei to learn the business. For years she'd been watching and listening in silence, learning so that one day she could act. Now was the time.

"Yes," Kinzaemon was saying in his heavy, husky voice. "Our shipments to Edo are doing well, very well."

Rie entered the room and poured sake for her father and husband.

Jihei made no response to Kinzaemon other than to pick up his sake cup and drain it. Well, *she* would have a lot to say were she in Jihei's position! She put down the flask and glided back through the corridor to the inner office, where Kin still sat bent over a ponderous ledger. He worked later than anyone else, even her father.

"*Ah,* excuse me, Kin-san. May I disturb you for a moment?" Rie bowed and sat down on the tatami opposite Kin.

He looked up. "Good evening, O-Josama." He smiled, his teeth protruding over his lower lip. "Yes, what is it?"

"You know it's difficult for me to speak with Father of any business matter," she began.

"Yes, it seems so, doesn't it? Well, you know, most men in Nada don't want women entering the business side or handling cash."

"But I have an idea, Kin-san." Rie picked up a writing brush and twirled it between her fingers before continuing. It was important to appear nonchalant. "Our shipping to the Edo market has been going well, hasn't it?"

Kin nodded. "Yes, perhaps better than we anticipated."

"Wouldn't this be a good time, then, to expand our shipments to Edo, to try to sell, say another twenty percent in that growing market? Can't we take advantage of it and recover the ten percent of our market we lost to Yamaguchi?" Rie stopped to look intently at Kin.

He sucked in his breath, folded his arms, leaned back against the wall, and closed his eyes. For several minutes he said nothing.

Rie inhaled her favorite yeasty aroma and waited. Would he listen to the merits of her idea or dismiss what she said just because she was a woman, or because he knew her father didn't want her intruding in business decisions? She kept her eyes on Kin's face. *Come on, come on. Agree!*

At length he opened his eyes and looked at Rie. He nodded. "Yes, maybe so. Yamaguchi has caused us a loss. But twenty percent . . . I wonder if your father would agree?"

"Oh, if you agree, then I know you could persuade him. He always follows your opinion, values your judgment so highly."

Kin sucked in his breath again. "Well, now, it isn't only your father. I'd also have to convince your husband, Rie. It might be difficult."

Rie tapped the handle of the brush on the table. "I don't think my husband will object to something you suggest, Kin-san, with your experience, especially if you convince Father." She leaned forward. "You will talk to Father, won't you?"

"It may be difficult, Rie." He glanced at her eager face.

She bowed. "Please, Kin-san."

"Well, then, all right. I'll try." He rubbed his face.

"Thank you so much. I'll come again tomorrow evening after Father has left the office." Rie smiled as she bowed out of the room. Kin could be her ally.

The following evening Rie again took a sake flask to the dining room where her father sat with Jihei. She paused beyond the shoji to listen to their conversation, hoping to glean something that would help her learn more about the business, as well as about Jihei.

"You know both Kato and Yamaguchi have increased their Edo shipments in the past two months," Kinzaemon said. "It might be a good time to raise our shipments twenty percent."

Good work, Kin. Rie smiled, peered cautiously into the room, and glanced at Jihei.

He pulled at his collar uncomfortably. "But twenty percent? Isn't that quite risky? Shouldn't we start more gradually, say five percent?"

Kinzaemon paused. "Well, as Kin says, we have to watch Kato and especially Yamaguchi. Perhaps Kin is right. The market in Edo looks very good. You know the samurai there love their sake as much as anyone. And they have more leisure time than we do."

Jihei shifted on his zabuton. He snorted. "*Leisure!* We don't know the meaning of the word." He reached for his cup. "And we don't want to do anything to jeopardize our local sales, do we? They're secure." He pulled at his eyebrows.

Fool! Rie thought, trying to contain her anger.

"Kin assures me they will remain secure."

Her father folded his arms and leaned back, his eyes closed.

Rie kicked at the wall. So Jihei would resist any forward move by White Tiger. How could he be a worthy successor to the house with so little business acumen? What would become of her father's dream? The dream she'd vowed to uphold. She closed her eyes and forced herself to think. She would somehow have to intervene, so that her father wouldn't realize he had made a poor choice in Jihei. That Jihei could not be worthy of the house Rie had no doubt now. And that he had been a poor choice for a husband, she was certain. No love was growing between them as her mother had hoped, only an uneasy alliance. She thought of Saburo and felt an unnamed yearning so strong it almost made her stagger. No. She could not give in to weakness right now. She straightened her obi before entering the room to pour sake for the men. And to listen, closely.

In the ensuing months White Tiger did begin to increase its sales to Edo, reaching a total rise of twenty percent.

"You were right, Kin-san," Rie overheard her father say in the inner office one day. "The risk was well worth it."

She peered in around the shoji, equal bursts of pride and relief inside her.

Kin bowed. "Now we are moving up to Yamaguchi in our Edo shipping."

Rie smiled to herself and walked back to the kitchen. *She'd been right! Now she knew she had what it took to make her father's dream a reality.* Later in the evening she found a chance to slip into the inner office when she knew her father and Jihei were dining.

"Good evening, Kin-san." Rie bowed as she entered the room.

"*Ah,* O-Josama." Kin beamed. "The increase in our shipping to Edo has succeeded."

"You didn't tell Father that I spoke with you, did you?"

"No. I believe he thought it was my idea."

"Thank you, Kin-san. I knew I could count on you." Rie nodded slightly, but inside she was dancing. "This is a big step for White Tiger." Rie was so pleased that even the thought of her inept husband couldn't subdue her good mood.

After her experience of the wedding night, Rie had shuddered at the thought of a repetition, but knew there was no choice if she were to fulfill her major obligation and produce an heir for the house. For many nights over the next weeks and months she forced herself to succumb to Jihei's drunken groping and thrusting, wishing it were Saburo instead of this horrid man who disgusted her. She imagined Saburo soft, tender, those intense brown eyes watching hers . . . unlike Jihei, who didn't seem to notice whether or not she responded, caring only for himself. Rie wondered how other women felt, endured, to produce an heir, but she had no sisters to enlighten her. Each time Jihei touched her, she closed her eyes and forced back tears as she imagined herself in a faraway place. When she extricated herself, she slipped down the stairs, along the dark corridor and into the o-furo room, where she washed herself vigorously, then stopped in the outer office to sit and breathe deeply, glancing at the White Tiger logo on a barrel. This became her regular ablution ritual. Thus she kept her spirit intact and enabled herself to survive the distasteful nighttime ventures.

One night as Rie was dressing and washing herself she heard slippers slapping toward the *o-furo* room. The shoji opened and her mother stood there.

"Ri-chan, are you all right?" her mother asked, frowning.

"Yes, Mother, I'm just washing."

Her mother stepped into the dressing room and looked at her hesitantly before speaking. "We know you are trying to do your duty, dear. And, well . . . your father and I appreciate it. It will be so important for the house."

"I know," Rie murmured softly, yet feeling a tightness in her chest as she thought of what it was costing her.

"Sleep well, dear," her mother said, bowing slightly as she left.

So long as her parents understood, Rie would continue, would endure, until she became pregnant. She prayed it would happen soon, that she would be relieved of the unpleasant but pressing duty. In the meantime, she would continue to think of Saburo. No one could control her feeling for him.

One morning a few months following the wedding Rie did not feel her normal self. She lingered in her room later than usual. Jihei had already gone downstairs. She heard O-Natsu's voice outside the shoji.

"Good morning. May I come in?"

"Yes, O-Natsu."

O-Natsu stepped in with a tea tray, which she set down on the tatami in front of Rie. "You did not come to breakfast, so I wondered, are you all right?"

"There may be something wrong. I don't feel like eating."

O-Natsu paused and glanced at Rie's eyes, a sign of pregnancy, so the midwives had told her. "I wonder, could you be pregnant?"

"Oh, I thought of that, O-Natsu. I skipped the last two months." She had kept that to herself, until she was sure. Today she *knew.* She smiled for O-Natsu's benefit.

"Shall I call your mother?"

"I guess so, thank you."

"Meanwhile, try to sip some tea. I'll bring up some rice gruel."

Rie nodded, unenthusiastically. She picked up a teacup, then set it down. If she really were pregnant, she would have succeeded in her duty to the house. Her parents would be delighted. She would be relieved of further responsibility toward Jihei at night. Why did she not feel happy, then? She heard steps on the stairs, and her mother and O-Natsu entered. O-Natsu set a tray with a bowl of rice gruel and chopsticks in front of Rie.

Hana sat on the zabuton next to the hibachi and looked intently into Rie's face. "How do you feel, dear? I know you have missed a month, or is it two? And O-Natsu tells me your eyes indicate pregnancy. Let me see." Her mother gazed at her intently. "Can you eat some rice gruel?"

Rie looked down at the food and put a hand on her stomach. "I don't really feel like eating, Mother."

"I know, dear, but you must eat. I'll send O-Natsu to the old herbalist to get something for you."

There was no doubt that Rie was pregnant. That evening Rie and her mother joined Kinzaemon and Jihei around the table. It was Hana's prerogative to make the announcement to her husband and Jihei.

Hana put down her chopsticks and straightened. "We have an important announcement for the future of the house." She paused and looked from Kinzaemon to Jihei, then she continued. "Rie is going to have a child, an heir for the house."

Rie excitedly awaited her father's reaction.

Kinzaemon smiled broadly. "That's wonderful, Rie. A most important child. And you must be especially careful of your health now."

She smiled back.

"Yes, Father. I have always been quite healthy." Rie knew her father would hope for a boy, but she herself would welcome a girl.

"I have sent O-Natsu for some powders

from the herbalist, the same ones I used," Hana said.

Jihei nodded but said nothing, Rie noted. He pulled at his eyebrows and reached for a sake flask. Jihei rarely had anything to say or reacted to what she did or said.

In succeeding days Rie noticed that her father spoke less about Yamaguchi, and the depression that had lowered his spirit seemed to have lifted. His step became sprightlier, and there was a general air of well-being in the household. O-Natsu and Rie's mother were continuously solicitous of Rie, and her mother cautioned her to slow down, to leave more responsibilities to others.

Hana purchased several sets of clothing and wrappers for the baby. She insisted on sewing tiny kimonos of her favorite cotton patterns. One afternoon she took out some baby clothes she had saved from her own son who had died. She fingered them lovingly as she showed them to Rie. Rie smiled and nodded, touching the clothes. Her beloved Toichi. How she missed him still. And now the clothes reminded her of her duty — her duty that she was fulfilling.

Late one afternoon three months later, Rie felt a gripping pain in her abdomen. She hurried to the lavatory, feeling weak and perspiring heavily. O-Natsu saw her hurrying to the lavatory and followed her. Rie opened the shoji quickly and stepped inside, squatting over the hole in the floor. A sharp pain stabbed at her. She huddled over and felt something slipping out and heard a splash below. *No,* she screamed silently. *No! No!* She looked down and saw that her legs were covered with blood. She could not stifle an anguished wail. She stood weakly, her hand clutching the wall for support. The shoji opened, and O-Natsu stepped in with towels and rags, which she handed to Rie.

"I've lost the heir," she moaned. "I've failed the house."

CHAPTER 4

Gloom pervaded the house following the loss of Rie's baby. Her father and mother tried to be sympathetic toward Rie, but they were also depressed. O-Natsu tried to cheer Rie, but she could not be consoled. Jihei, as usual, had nothing to say about the loss of the heir.

One night as Rie was preparing for bed she wondered where Jihei was, hoping to avoid him somehow. He was nowhere to be found, nor did he return that night until long after Rie was asleep. She was relieved, but still wondered. Where was he? Two nights later the same thing happened.

Rie tried to broach the subject indirectly one day when they were alone upstairs. Jihei shifted uneasily and tugged at his ear as she spoke.

"You remember I mentioned when you came into the house that Father has not been as active as he was, because of his health. Perhaps you should spend more time here in the evening, get a firmer grasp of the financial side." She tapped her fan against her shoulder and glanced at Jihei, who was turning his teacup around in his hands, admiring it closely.

"This is a fine cup. Is it old Shino?" he asked.

Rie frowned, ignoring his question. "I think Kin would like to see you in the office more, in the evening. You know he spends long hours here."

Jihei sighed. "Yes, he never seems to stop. Well, you know, between you and Father and Kin, it seems everything gets decided. I sometimes wonder where I fit in, where I should focus my attention." He twirled his eyebrows. "Of course I work here every day with Father and Kin."

How lazy he was! She wouldn't mind twirling *him* by those eyebrows. "A brewer's work is never done, day or night. That's what Mother always says. Father hasn't said anything to Mother or me about retiring, but I can see him slowing down. We don't know when he'll decide the time has come to step down. It's a big decision. But when he does you'll have final authority in everything. You want to be prepared to take charge. Father felt you had the experience for it, coming from the Okamoto House."

Jihei put down his cup. "Of course we were never this big. But I feel I'm as much a brewer as anyone, after so many generations." He smiled tentatively at Rie.

Rie put a hand over her mouth to stop herself from cackling. Did he really believe that? "Yes, of course we all do. I can't remember a time when I wasn't surrounded by barrels or inhaling anything but the smell of yeast. And the sound of the kurabito singing in the kura has always given me a sense of well-being. So then you understand, don't you?"

Jihei bowed slightly and murmured in response to Rie's spoken and unspoken questions.

Late that night Rie lay alone on her futon. She had left the shutters open because she enjoyed watching the moonlight filter into the room, casting mysterious shadows from carvings on the lintel above onto the sliding screens. She listened to the haunting flute of the blind masseuse who walked by each night at the hour of the boar. The fire watcher went by too, clacking his wooden sticks together to warn residents to be careful to put out their stoves and lamps before they went to sleep.

It was, she supposed, too much to expect

that she would have strong feelings for Jihei, or he for her. Rie turned and moved out of her futon. She realized she felt no fondness for her husband, none at all. She went to the open window and looked out into the stone and gravel garden, gray stones on gray pebbles, gleaming in the moonlight. She gazed at the full moon, and looked at the shadows that ghosted through the garden. No sound broke the stillness. She moved her hand over her face.

Her mother's response to most problems was, "Can't you try to endure, Rie?" Her mother was an authority on endurance.

Rie closed the wooden outer shutters and lay down on her futon. Where Jihei was at this hour of night she could only imagine. It dawned on her that she could not count on her husband for anything, that the future of the house rested with her alone.

She turned and closed her eyes.

One blustery evening Jihei managed to once again elude Rie and other family members on the pretext of an errand. He hailed a ricksha at the corner bridge. As he stepped up into the seat he said, "The Sawaraya," and the ricksha puller made off down the road at a run. The Sawaraya was one of the more elegant teahouses where patrons could ask that their favorite geisha be called for an evening's entertainment. Jihei had sent a clerk ahead to make sure that O-Toki would be called from her *okiya* this evening. A cold drizzle began and Jihei drew the collar of his gray cloak closer around his ears. He peered into the darkness as the ricksha drew into the brighter entertainment quarter of the city. The rain could not dampen his spirits as he took in the lively activity of the district, listened to the voices of gesticulating, shouting hawkers, and watched brilliantly kimonoed geisha fluttering through narrow lanes to their evening's assignations. He alighted quickly at the carved wooden gate, handed coins to the puller, and announced himself at the entrance hidden from the street behind a high wooden wall.

He heard footsteps scurrying toward the front entrance.

"Yes! Yes! Please come in!" O-Haru, the ample, faultlessly groomed owner, greeted Jihei effusively and bowed again and again. "Ah, Master! Welcome! How pleased O-Toki will be to see you this evening!"

Jihei felt a sense of relief as he appraised the most fashionable house in the whole district. Raku ware stood on the cabinet that held guests' getas. Above the shoji, beyond the entrance, was a cryptomeria carving that extended the length of the shoji leading to the reception room. An *ikebana* arrangement of three white lilies in a flat obsidian vase was visible on a corner cabinet. The aroma of freshly polished wood assailed him.

Jihei slipped out of his geta and stepped from the stone entryway up to the highly polished cedar floor. O-Haru leaned over to place slippers in front of his feet, then swished down the long corridor, motioning Jihei to follow. Up the slippery wooden stairway she led him along the plaster-walled corridor, down another hall and around a corner to the most exclusive private tatami room at the rear of the house. She opened the sliding screen and ushered him to the low table at the center of the room, indicating the seat of honor that backed to the tokonoma alcove, adorned with another ikebana arrangement of the season's yellow chrysanthemums in an oblong white vase. She opened the shutters that looked out on the koi pond and garden, lit so it glittered like a flight of fireflies.

"Won't you have a bath while you wait?" she invited. "O-Toki will be here shortly."

Jihei acknowledged her invitation, and O-Haru hurried out. He inhaled the distinctive mown-grass aroma of fresh tatami and turned to admire the white crackleware vase holding the chrysanthemums, above which hung a kakemono of a misty Chinese landscape. If there was one thing Jihei appreciated, besides O-Toki, it was fine pottery. He sighed, felt his senses quicken. Again he heard the sound of slippers rapidly slapping toward the room. A maid entered with towels and a house yukata and bowed as she held the robe for Jihei to change.

"Please come to the private bath downstairs. This way, you know." She bowed gracefully and swayed as she guided Jihei down the back stairway, polished until it was slippery, opened the door to the steamy outer room and placed towels in a straw basket, then slipped out. Jihei shrugged off his yukata and dropped it carelessly over a basket, opened the sliding door to the bath and entered. Immediately he was enveloped in a warm earthy mist so damp that everything in the room dripped. He sat on the small wooden stool to wash and rinse at the tap, then put his toes gingerly into the bath. The water was close to boiling, and his foot soon resembled a lobster. He inched himself slowly into the steaming water, slapped a hot towel on top of his head, closed his eyes and sighed.

A bath at the Sawaraya was so much more

relaxing than one at home, with Kinzaemon preceding him, maids hovering about, and Rie following him, dropping hints about this business deal or that one. He felt eternally on inspection, judged. He had to be cautious at home, always on guard. The house was growing more and more oppressive. It was like a cage, a trap that brooked no escape. They had no appreciation for his talents. He felt overshadowed by Kinzaemon and Kin, with Rie ever ready to catch him in an error of some kind. What a woman to have as a wife! But what could he do about her? The Sawaraya was his refuge. Here they treated him with the respect befitting the heir to the Omura House, one of the largest and most prestigious in the city.

"Excuse me!" The mellifluous voice of O-Toki wafted into the room. Jihei opened his eyes and saw her emerge like a vision through the vapor, a young woman whose impeccable grooming and stark white face and neck only enhanced the sinuous eroticism that she exuded. He smiled.

O-Toki knelt at the edge of the tub, tied up the sleeves of her kimono, and began to massage Jihei's shoulders. He moved them in appreciation.

"*Ah!* Your wonderful touch!"

"You have a lot of tension in your neck

and shoulders. You must have had a difficult day." She continued kneading his shoulders and arms.

"What day isn't difficult at White Tiger? But I can forget it here, can't I?"

O-Toki moved her hands down Jihei's back and around to his stomach, just below the navel. *Ah.* And Rie was so unresponsive, even resistant. Hardly what a man needed.

"Of course you know you can."

She stopped with a final thrust toward his groin, then rose and handed Jihei a dry towel.

"Excuse me. I'm going to bring sake to your room. I'll be right there."

As O-Toki left, Jihei emerged from the tub, dried himself in the outer room, and put on the geometrically patterned blue-and-white cotton yukata. He swaggered back to the room and stood a few moments gazing down at the stone garden. He enjoyed the hollow sound of the bamboo dipper as it emptied of water, filled, then emptied again in endless motion. O-Toki's returning footsteps prompted him to take his seat at the table.

She entered bearing a black lacquer tray with a heated sake bottle and two small cups. She knelt and placed the tray on the table, every gesture part of the well-rehearsed tableau Jihei knew so well. Then, hands before her on the tatami, she bowed her head to her hands. Raising her head, she greeted Jihei formally.

"Welcome, Master! How good to see you!" Again she bowed. With both hands she handed Jihei a small cup, then filled it with White Tiger as she smiled and bowed again.

"I have a special treat for you tonight."

Jihei downed the sake in a single gulp. "A special treat? A surprise? Something to eat? Some delectable concoction?"

O-Toki laughed. "Yes, all of those."

"Well, then?"

O-Toki smiled enchantingly. "A surprise can't be rushed if you really want to relish it."

"Oh, I see you mean to keep me in suspense, right?"

O-Toki's smile became more coquettish. "Of course. That's the only way to really enjoy a surprise. But I guarantee you will be very pleased, maybe even happy."

She filled his cup again. After emptying it he handed a cup in return to O-Toki and filled it. She sipped delicately, glancing at Jihei between sips.

He leaned forward. "*Ah,* you said happy. Now that sounds most promising!"

Jihei admired the way O-Toki's peach-flowered kimono and collar revealed an enticing amount of flesh at the nape of her neck, the most erotic part of a woman's anatomy.

"You must be hungry after your bath. Please excuse me while I bring your food."

"Your sense of timing, O-Toki! I'm more interested in happiness. That is much rarer than food, in my experience."

"Well, there is no reason you can't have both, is there? I'll be right back." She smiled as she glided from the room.

Jihei continued to sip slowly, his face reddening as he anticipated O-Toki's touch again. Then he rose and went back to the window overlooking the garden. He hummed a drinking song off-key, then turned back and sat down heavily at the table.

O-Toki returned with a large tray on which were numerous small dishes, followed by a maid with more items. O-Toki set these out on the table one by one, each arranged like an ikebana exhibit with a tidbit of fish or vegetable on it. She bowed and looked at Jihei expectantly.

"You really know how to tantalize a man, don't you?"

O-Toki's hand did not muffle her throaty

laugh. She focused her attention on serving food and sake rather than responding. She picked up a delicate mountain mushroom and held it out toward Jihei on a pair of lacquer chopsticks.

"Here, try this." She popped the choice morsel into his mouth.

"You're right. Delicious!" He grinned, food and juice dripping down his chin.

When Jihei finished eating he sighed, belched, and picked his teeth with a toothpick from a small red lacquer box O-Toki opened and offered him. He leaned back as O-Toki continued to pour sake for him. His face was by now bright red from the hot bath, hot sake, and hot food. He loosened his yukata. O-Toki reached over to fan him with a gold-leaf fan.

"*Ah!* This is always the best time of day, or night. I feel so good!"

"Are you happy?"

"As nearly as is possible in this life."

"You sound philosophical. And speaking of night, I was hoping you would stay tonight. It has been a while." She smiled and bowed.

Bemused, Jihei asked, "Is this a bribe? No surprise unless I agree?"

O-Toki tittered. "Well, I do have a surprise, as I said."

Jihei always enjoyed the repartee, something O-Toki, like all geishas, was skilled at as a qualification. "And will it take all night?" he asked.

"Well, part of it anyway." O-Toki relaxed, leaning on one hand.

"You are always so persuasive." Jihei smiled.

O-Toki straightened, as though sensing she had won. "Your wife won't expect you?" It was a question she did not ordinarily ask of customers, but with Jihei, who was, after all, her patron . . .

"I doubt she'll even notice my absence. Her mind is always on sake, producing, not drinking." Jihei's speech was becoming slurred and his yukata fell open further. They both laughed. "She's always trying to stick her nose into the business, to influence decisions, increase our production. I'll stop her the next time she tries to influence a business decision. You know women can't manage a business."

O-Toki glanced at Jihei and opened her mouth but said nothing. She rose, went to the storage cupboard, and brought out the futon. She cleared the table rapidly, moved it to the side of the room, set the tray out in the hall, and closed the wooden shutters for the night. Jihei fell back on the tatami, his head resting on the futon. When O-Toki tried to arrange the futon, Jihei grabbed her.

"Oh! How can I manage the futon?" she cried in mock distress.

"I think we'll manage together very well. We always seem to."

O-Toki fell into Jihei's embrace. He moved her onto the futon and fumbled with her kimono. She undid her obi and kimono and Jihei moved over her, grunting.

"Is this the surprise?" Jihei whispered in her ear.

"Who is surprised?" she laughed.

Jihei thrust her thighs apart and moved abruptly, then moments later rolled off, turned over, his back toward O-Toki. Soon he was snoring.

Toward morning Jihei stirred, sat up and looked at O-Toki, who awoke slowly and yawned.

"Actually, the surprise is something I must tell you," she said, rubbing her eyes and sitting up.

"*Ah,* at last."

She looked at Jihei and hesitated. "I'm pregnant with your child."

Fear mingled with excitement at the prospect as Jihei leaned toward O-Toki, looking at her intently. "Really?" he cried. "My first child! A son for the Omura

House!" He caressed her abdomen. "When is it due? My wife shows no sign, after she lost our child. I was beginning to wonder if I would ever have one."

"In six months' time. And what makes you think it's a son?" she asked. "What if it's a daughter?"

"Then there will be rejoicing in the Omura House, an adopted husband for another generation. Merchant houses always welcome a daughter, you know."

"But if you acknowledge the baby, I'll lose him. I can't give up my own baby!"

"You won't, I promise," Jihei said, putting a hand on her arm. "You'll be able to see his wedding. I'll tell you whatever you want to know about him. And you know, as first son he will succeed me and have a great future in our house." He did not need to add, far better than he would have here in the water world of geisha houses.

When Jihei returned home in the early morning hours he was relieved to find that Rie had already left their room. He lay down on the futon and closed his eyes. He knew he would have to tell her soon. It was a conversation he dreaded.

CHAPTER 5

Several seasons had passed, and Rie had yet to become pregnant. Instead, she poured herself into her work. Early one evening, Hana sat in her room sewing while Rie hunched over an account book on the other side of the hibachi.

"You know that's not really your responsibility, Rie. Father and Kin may be annoyed if they discover the ledger missing from the office."

"Mother, I always keep track of accounts now. Kin realizes that I need to know where we stand. And he says our finances have improved since I have been following them and making suggestions. Father doesn't need to know." She smiled proudly.

"Well, it isn't expected of a woman, you know, even here in Nada. Women don't handle the cash. It's always been that way. And Father and Jihei could do it, with Kin." She paused and held up her work to examine the fine embroidery with a crane pattern, symbol of longevity.

Rie rested her hands on the ledger and looked at her mother. "You didn't have an adopted husband, Mother. And I'm not actually handling cash. Kin does that. And Father. So no need to object if I'm helping the house."

Hana said nothing further, no doubt glad that Rie had begun to take an interest in the house, after her tragic miscarriage.

They were interrupted by a high-pitched voice beyond the shoji.

"Excuse me!"

The shoji opened and O-Natsu entered, bowing. For a moment she said nothing as she glanced at Rie and her mother. Then she acknowledged Hana's gesture and sat on her haunches, smoothing her kimono under her.

"Yes, O-Natsu, what is it?" Hana asked.

"I have some news, Oku-san," she said, using the title befitting the female head of the household.

"So you've been gossiping again?"

O-Natsu's apple cheeks grew redder. "Well, I thought you should know. . . ." She glanced at Rie, then back at Hana and looked down.

"I was talking with a maid in the market

today, who knows one of the Sawaraya maids."

"Tell us!" Hana said, speaking sharply.

O-Natsu looked at the floor and took a deep breath. "They say Rie's husband is friendly with a geisha, O-Toki, and that she is going to have a child." On the verge of tears, O-Natsu put her hands to her face.

Rie and Hana both looked at O-Natsu. Rie's mouth opened and she frowned.

Hana gasped. "Are you certain, O-Natsu?"

"I'm told there is no doubt. She is due in a few weeks." O-Natsu looked down again and bowed apologetically.

"Thank you, O-Natsu," Hana said, more gently. "You may be excused now."

O-Natsu bowed and left the room, glancing at Rie as she left.

With a sharp intake of breath, Rie looked down at her clenched fists and avoided her mother's gaze for several minutes. Shame burned her cheeks as she thought of her husband with the geisha and a child together, so soon after her own miscarriage! Anger quickly suffused shame.

"Well, Rie, I'm afraid this may be the result of your constant involvement in the affairs of the house. Maybe you are intimidating Jihei. As I've said, a mukoyoshi often feels a stranger in his new home. You know, his position is not so different from a bride's."

The rebuke sent a flush of warmth through Rie, but she was silent, stealing a glance at her mother to try to detect any sign of emotion. She pressed her clenched fists against the edge of the table and rocked back and forth.

"Yes, Mother . . . but he is from a brewing house too. What we do is no mystery to him." Her voice rose slightly. "And I know our family traditions better than he does, so I've tried to help him ever since we were married. This is what you and Father trained me to do, isn't it?"

Her mother's tone softened. "Maybe you should leave any advice to Father and Kin. It may be difficult for Jihei to accept suggestions from a woman."

Rie was silent. Her mother was often right when it came to understanding human beings and why they behave as they do. But Rie had a sense of foreboding, and the gloom that had blanketed her since first hearing about Jihei's indiscretion returned. If she couldn't bear a child, it meant the geisha's son or daughter might be the successor to the house. The thought sent a chill racing through her.

"Try to be more gentle, Rie."

Rie leaned back from the table and frowned. "I'll try, Mother . . ."

Then, as if to reaffirm her own thoughts, her mother said, "If you don't become pregnant soon we may have to bring the child into the house, especially if it's a boy."

Rie bent over her hands, her mouth open, feeling the pressure of her mother's words. She would have to lie with that disgusting fool every night. "But Father hasn't retired, and when he does my husband will succeed. Why do we need to think of another generation now?" She rested her forehead on one hand, elbow on the table.

"Please, Rie." Her mother looked admonishingly at Rie's unfeminine gesture.

Rie took her elbow off the table.

"It's always well to be prepared in advance in case something should happen to Father. We need to think ahead, for continuity of the house. It's just as important as looking after the family altar and ancestral graves. I know you realize that, Rie. And Father will want to retire before long. He would like to see things more settled. It would set his mind at rest if there were an heir."

Rie sat forward and poured tea for her mother and herself, her hand trembling. Then she excused herself and went out to the garden, her oasis for silence and thought. Still shaken by the news, she leaned against her favorite rock and gazed at the koi swimming lazily in the pond. She knew she would have to try to become pregnant again, as soon as possible. Her honor as daughter of the house depended upon it. She sighed, her lips pursed together tightly. For several minutes she sat in silence, willing away the words she'd heard, wishing she could undo the last twenty minutes. Then coming to a decision, she lifted her chin and returned to her mother's room. She announced her presence, and entered properly on her knees.

"Mother, wouldn't a geisha object to giving up her child?"

"Those women don't. She knows the child will have a better chance in life here in a house of substance than out there in the water world, especially if it's a boy."

Rie sighed and slumped. "Jihei spends so much time out at night, Mother. I don't know what to do." Unbelievable. Now she actually *wanted* Jihei home at night to force himself on her so she could get pregnant. But how could she keep him from going out?

"I've never told you this before, Ri-chan." Hana put down her sewing and looked at

Rie. "But your father had a child by a geisha too."

What? Rie put a hand to her mouth to stifle a cry.

"But since you were already in the *koseki* register, we didn't have to bring the geisha's son in. I was fortunate. It's more difficult for you, having this geisha's child the firstborn. But I know you want to have a child, Rie, as soon as possible. It's so sad that you lost your first." She picked up her sewing again as if to end the conversation.

Rie frowned. "Yes, but what should I do?"

"Try to make yourself more attractive, Rie. Pay attention to your grooming. Cook one of his favorite dishes some evening." She glanced at Rie.

"Oh . . ." Rie put her hands on the table and looked at them critically. The thought of enticing Jihei made her sick to her stomach.

"Put on your best kasuri kimono some night . . . and here." Hana turned to the dressing table behind her, a piece made of polished paulownia wood with carving around the mirror, her favorite antique.

"Here, dear." Her mother held out a small red round lacquer box with a plum blossom design on the cover. "This is a special perfume cream my mother gave me. It's from Kyoto. We can't find it here in Kobe. They say it gives a woman special powers with a man, makes her irresistible." Hana smiled but with an underlying steel that belied the gesture. She opened the lid and held the box under Rie's nose. Not accustomed to using scents, Rie inhaled the aroma, heavier and spicier than anything she had ever smelled.

"Try a bit tonight, dear. It may help."

Lure that vile man to her body. Repulsive! But it was what she had to do.

"Thank you, Mother. I'll try . . ." Her mother gave her a stern look and she quickly amended her words to "I'll do as you say." She cautiously reached for the box and slipped it into her sleeve. She wrinkled her nose at the inevitable prospect.

Late in the afternoon Rie made certain that Jihei was still in the office. She walked over to where he was working and spoke to him softly, out of earshot of her father, Kin and the clerks.

"You know, tonight we'll be having fresh mackerel cooked with miso the way you like it, and sesame tofu. And I thought we could try some of the special sake Toji has been experimenting with." She smiled at Jihei, she hoped enticingly. "Your bath will be ready soon."

Jihei looked at Rie and nodded. "All right." Was he such a dolt he thought nothing of her sudden change of personality?

Rie shook her head as she checked the bath to be sure it was heating and hurried to the kitchen to instruct the cook to prepare the special dishes for the evening. She set aside three bottles of the highest grade of sake. Upstairs she pulled out the tansu drawers holding her kasuri kimonos. She fingered several before selecting a lighter shade of indigo with a larger pattern than she generally wore. She slid her mother's perfume box into her sleeve and took out the kasuri she had selected.

While her father and Jihei were bathing, Rie went again to the kitchen to ask O-Natsu to heat the sake. Jihei and her father returned from the bath, their skin still moist and flushed, their moods relaxed.

When Rie and her mother were seated with their husbands Rie poured, first for her father, then for her husband.

"This is the special sake that Toji has brewed this year. I thought we could enjoy some with our mackerel this evening." She looked at her mother, who urged her to continue, then turned toward Jihei, caught his eye, and smiled as she poured for him.

"Mother, why don't you have a taste too?"

She held the bottle and a cup toward her mother.

"Just a sip, dear." Her mother held up her tiny cup delicately to Rie.

Rie turned back to Jihei. "How do you like it?"

"Here, try some yourself," Jihei said, holding out a warmed flask toward her cup.

She inhaled the yeasty bouquet and savored a sip. "*Mmm.* Wonderful! We should be able to market it at top price."

Her mother sighed and cast a warning glance at Rie not to talk business, but her father, oblivious to the interchange said, "Yes, Rie, I think you're right. It's something new. I haven't tasted anything quite like it before."

Rie smiled inwardly at this sign of approval from her father.

With a nod to Rie, Hana excused herself to prepare her bath and retire early, but Kinzaemon and Jihei continued to enjoy their evening sake. Rie excused herself as well for a quick bath, then hurried up the stairs and lit a lamp in the anteroom. Light from the lamp sputtered and flickered through the wooden carving above the screens, and shadow cranes drifted into the bedroom. She took out the futons and laid them side by side. In the dressing room she took out her mother's Kyoto perfume and applied some behind her ears, neck, and wrists. She smoothed her kimono and obi and surveyed the room quickly. Satisfied, she returned to join her father and Jihei. She paused outside the room and adjusted the collar of her kimono so that a bit more of the nape of her neck showed than was proper. As she entered the room she glanced at Jihei to see how red his face was. It would not do to wait too long. Seated at the table again, she turned her back toward Jihei and lingered over the sake flasks and cups.

She turned back toward Jihei and forced a smile. "I can take a flask upstairs if you like."

"Yes, I'd like to have another sip, a night-cap."

As Rie rose with the sake tray she saw out of the corner of her eye that Jihei was rising to follow her. She could feel his gaze on the nape of her neck as she glided toward the stairway. That the plan worked should have excited her, but it only sent a shiver of apprehension running through her.

In their room upstairs Rie placed the sake tray carefully next to Jihei's futon and water glass. She turned her back toward Jihei and untied her obi. Before she got any further she felt Jihei's arms around her and his face pressed against the nape of her neck.

She stiffened but then forced herself to relax to his touch. She knew Jihei would not leave tonight. She prayed that she would conceive a child, that she would not have to spend many nights this way. For the next half hour she set her mind free and pretended that it was Saburo who touched her, Saburo whose child she would bear.

Over the next few weeks Rie looked for signs that she was pregnant. She examined her body and waited impatiently. When no sign appeared, she despaired. This must be how empresses had felt over the centuries when they failed to produce an heir and instead the son of one of the concubines was brought into the palace in line to the throne. Kinzaemon also was deeply concerned about an heir to provide continuity for the house.

One day when Rie was passing by her father's office, she heard her father and Jihei talking in the inner office, and peered in to see them seated at the low table strewn with ledgers, facing each other.

Kinzaemon ran his hand through his bushy hair. "I heard a rumor the other day," he began.

"Yes?" Jihei moved the abacus nervously.

"I'm told that the geisha O-Toki at the Sawaraya is bearing your child. Is it true?"

Jihei cleared his throat. "Actually, yes. A son has been born, just four weeks ago." He moved his hand across an eyebrow.

Rie stifled a gasp, and absentmindedly rubbed her barren stomach.

Kinzaemon straightened his bulky frame and pulled his kimono more closely around him. "I see." He paused. "A son, is it? And are you sure he is yours?"

"Yes, he is my son."

"And does Rie know about this?"

"I believe she may have heard."

Kinzaemon glanced at Jihei, whose face had reddened noticeably. "Have you seen the child? Is he normal, healthy?"

"Yes, I have, and he seems very healthy . . . eats well . . ." Jihei stopped, uncertainly.

"Of course the house needs a successor," Kinzaemon said. "And Rie has not borne a child yet. Well, then, shall we bring the child into the house? Recognize him as your legitimate heir?" He paused and sighed. "I never did that. My wife insisted that Rie and her husband succeed us. And I didn't wish to bring in an outside child by a geisha." Kinzaemon pulled at his ear and drew the corners of his mouth down. "Of course Rie may not be entirely pleased about it. But she always understands that the interests of the house come first. That was fundamental in our teaching as she grew up."

Rie fought back tears as she rushed off, feeling every bit as disemboweled as a samurai who had committed seppuku.

The following evening when Rie took sake to the dining room she found her father sitting alone.

"Oh, Rie, come in." Her father beckoned toward the seat opposite him.

Rie seated herself and poured for her father. Although she had slept little the night before, she managed a weak smile.

"I want to let you know, Rie, that we plan to bring your husband's son into the house, since there's no sign of your producing an heir." He sipped and glanced at Rie as if to gauge her reaction.

She set the flask down abruptly and looked at her hands, which were shaking. "But Father, what more can I do?" Her voice rose higher than usual.

Her father sighed. "*Uh* . . . do you know the child's name?"

She had heard the rumors whispered by the servants, who had gleaned bits and pieces at the marketplace, each piece of news cutting her more deeply than the last. "I believe it's Yoshitaro. My husband hasn't spoken about the baby, but I think he is four weeks old now."

Kinzaemon cleared his throat. "Then it will be time to bring him in soon. We'll have Jihei go and take care of the formalities at the Sawaraya. We can send O-Natsu with him to carry the baby. I'm glad you understand, Rie." He put down his cup and exhaled loudly.

She bit her lip so hard she tasted blood. Yes, her parents were always sure to mention her understanding. She felt a sense of desperation overcome her. She slumped on the zabuton and when her father left the room she felt tears starting. She rocked back and forth, overcome, desolate, that her father had now deserted her.

CHAPTER 6

Rie's mother supervised preparations for the arrival of the infant, assisted by O-Natsu. They arranged for a wet nurse to come in, a young neighbor named Masa who had a baby of her own. Rie despaired and took no interest in the preparations.

"Rie, you know Kin is really looking forward to having another generation here, for continuity of the house," her mother commented. "We all are. He'll inhale the smell of sake as soon as he's drinking milk here. And once there's a baby in the house, who knows, you may become pregnant," Hana added, as if to console her. "It sometimes happens that way. Did that perfume help, dear?"

She thought of all the nights she had to lure Jihei to her futon.

"Yes, Mother. But I'm not pregnant yet."

Although distressed about the baby, Rie was pleased to see the nursery prepared near the kitchen, away from her room. Wasn't it presumptuous of Jihei to have named the child Yoshitaro, "the good first son"?

On a morning when Yoshitaro was four months old, Jihei and O-Natsu took a ricksha to the Sawaraya, where the transfer was scheduled to occur. O-Haru and O-Toki came to the entrance and ushered them into the formal parlor just beyond the entryway. Jihei and O-Natsu sat opposite O-Haru and O-Toki. A maid brought tea, and after they were served, a second maid carried Yoshitaro in and sat at the end of the table holding the squirming infant. Jihei noticed O-Toki's flawless grooming but avoided eye contact. He was still embarrassed by his errand.

He bowed. "The Omura House is grateful to you," he said stiffly. "Yoshitaro will be recognized as eldest son of the house, my heir. Before long I will succeed. And he will be raised well, trained to become a good brewer."

Jihei bowed again and raised in both hands an envelope which he handed across the table to O-Toki. "You need not be concerned for his welfare," he said. Kinzaemon had told Jihei exactly how much to include in the envelope.

O-Toki held the envelope in both hands

above the level of her head, bowing so low that her face was concealed. But her voice revealed the strain. "I have no words to thank you adequately."

"We are grateful for your continued patronage," O-Haru said as she and O-Toki bowed in unison.

A maid entered carrying a large *furoshiki* of baby clothing and set it on the floor in front of O-Natsu.

Jihei and O-Natsu rose and bowed stiffly. Jihei tried to ignore what he knew was O-Toki's pain. When O-Natsu took the baby in her arms, he began to scream. For just one brief flicker, the mask of the geisha wavered but she quickly held it in check. Jihei picked up the bundle of clothing, carefully avoiding all eye contact.

They left the Sawaraya amid more formal bowing and caught a waiting ricksha. Yoshitaro yelled all the way to the Omura entrance, where he was greeted by Hana, the wet nurse Masa, and Rie, who scowled at the screaming infant as O-Natsu handed him to Masa.

That evening the baby was brought for inspection before Kinzaemon and Hana. Rie and Jihei sat at one side of the table, Rie's parents on the other. Even as Rie's heart was breaking, she made sure that no expression was visible on her face. As she watched her mother undress the baby while the wet nurse held him, she burned with shame. Once again she had let down her family and the house. Then and there she determined that one way or another she would redeem herself, but how?

Yet first things first. It was necessary to confirm that Yoshitaro was a baby boy, normal in all respects. Hana held him toward Kinzaemon, who looked the infant up and down and nodded. She then took each of the baby's hands and feet in turn and shook them gently to test his reflexes. She wrapped him up again.

"Thank you, Masa," Hana said. "You may take him now." She handed over the wiggling infant. Masa stood holding him for another moment to listen to Kinzaemon's verdict.

"He seems a fine, healthy boy, yes. We'll make him into a first-rate brewer." He glanced at Jihei and nodded.

Rie looked around the table at her father, her mother, her husband, these her closest family members, none of whom seemed concerned for her feelings. She did not speak, nor did Jihei. Her mouth tightened. She glanced with distaste at the squirming infant, curdled milk dribbling down his chin onto his wrapper. This puking flesh, creature of her husband's infidelity, would remain here under her nose, an eternal reminder of his geisha's bloodline. A hard knot of rage gripped her stomach at the betrayal of those she loved most. Her fists clenched. She felt her nails press into her palms. She rose abruptly, excused herself, and left the room. As she passed the pillar she stopped and pounded her fists against it.

She walked quickly out the door nearest the garden, opened the gate, and went to her rock. It had grown dark and she could not see the koi in the pond. She leaned heavily against the rock, so often a source of comfort. Tonight there was no comfort anywhere. There was no moon. She could not stop the flood of tears rolling down her face. She bit her lip and reached in her obi for a handkerchief. Not only had she failed to produce an heir, her most important responsibility, but here under her eyes was this geisha's child, this product of Jihei's philandering installed as heir, as the future Kinzaemon XI. She felt as though her life had ended. Her goal of working for the house, her father, proving once and for all that she could be responsible, that she was worthy of her father's love by producing a successor to the Omura line, was beyond her reach. She bowed her head and could not stop sobbing. She sat there ignoring the passage of time. Then she felt black anger overcome her, a wild fury the likes of which she had never felt before.

CHAPTER 7

The morning after the baby's arrival Rie rose even earlier than usual, determined to be the first one up in the family. Hard work seemed the best antidote to the outrage she felt at the illegitimate infant Jihei had brought into the house. She felt energized, determined to somehow redress this betrayal. She walked through the chilly corridors to see to preparations for breakfast. O-Natsu was already there, supervising the kitchen maids. Rie paused. She noticed a small boy with protruding front teeth boiling rice in a huge black cauldron, his thin form completely enveloped in steam. She watched him for several minutes, and then approached O-Natsu.

"Good morning, O-Natsu," she said softly. "Who is the boy boiling the rice?"

O-Natsu bowed. "Oh, good morning. He came with the workers from Tamba this year. His name is Shin'ichi. He's thirteen, almost fourteen." O-Natsu looked at Rie inquisitively and turned back to the stove.

Rie, always alert for good workers, walked over to the boy and watched his fast, efficient work.

"Very good, Shin'ichi. You seem to like to work." She smiled.

The boy bowed rapidly three times. "I have always wanted to work in a brewery, Madam. And this year Toji-san allowed me to come." He bowed again and gave a toothy smile.

"I see." Rie paused. "Well, how would you like to do errands for us in the office?"

Shin'ichi put his hands stiffly at his sides and bowed repeatedly. "Oh, yes, Madam, very much."

"Well then, Shin'ichi, please come to the office tomorrow morning early. We will find someone else to cook the rice." This conscientious boy might prove important in the house's future with Kin facing retirement.

The thin figure continued bowing as Rie nodded, then turned and left the kitchen.

O-Natsu walked over to Shin'ichi. "You have attracted Oku-san's favor." She looked directly at him. "See that you don't disappoint her. She will treat you fairly."

"Oh, I will never disappoint her," he replied. He bowed again.

That evening Rie opened the door of the inner office and found Kin sitting alone, as she hoped.

"Excuse me, may I come in?" she asked softly. She had long been thinking of ways to help the house. A solid idea had formed over the past week.

"Yes, do." Kin beckoned toward the seat opposite him.

"Kin-san," Rie began, seating herself, "I have an idea, two suggestions, for our business." She smiled.

Kin nodded. "Yes?"

"They will help White Tiger, I'm certain."

"Well, what is it? Your suggestion about our Edo shipments was useful." He looked at Rie.

"Can't we expand our moneylending and gold-silver exchange? That way we can counter any risk in increasing production and shipments to Edo." She tapped the table with her fan.

Kin nodded and scratched his cheek. "You may be right. Yes, far less risk in moneylending, gold-silver exchange too. They are traditionally safe, and we always get a faster return on the financial side. More secure too. I'll take it up with your father and husband."

Rie nodded. "You know my husband

seems much more cautious in business than you or Father. Or than I am." She bit her lip. She knew Kin understood.

"That's the survival strategy of smaller houses, O-Josama. They can't afford the risks we can. It's often written in their house rules: 'take no unnecessary risks.' "

"Is that so?" She sipped a cup of tea pensively. "And another thing. A boy is boiling rice in the kitchen. He seems so capable I would like you to consider using him in the office."

"We could try him out. How old is he? Why don't you bring him to the office tomorrow? I'll give him a task, and if he does it well I'll recommend him to your father."

"Thank you, Kin-san. He must be thirteen. Yes, I'll bring him in early." She smiled. Kin was even more receptive than she had hoped. Pragmatism . . . that was the key to approaching him.

Early the next morning Rie met a smiling, bowing Shin'ichi at the kitchen door, before anyone had started work.

"Good morning, Madam," he said in his high piping voice when Rie greeted him.

"Yes, Shin'ichi. Good. Come, we will go to the office and you will meet our *banto*, Kin. I believe he has a job for you this morning." She motioned for him to follow.

Shin'ichi bobbed up and down three times and trailed Rie, who slid open the door to the inner office.

"Good morning, Kin-san. Here we are." She glanced through the door to the outer office where barrels of sake were stacked at one side of the room from floor to ceiling. Near the front entrance was a low table on which stood three small barrels and rows of tasting cups to entice customers.

Kin bowed smartly and, noting her glance toward the door to the outer office, he closed it and turned to Rie and Shin'ichi. Shin'ichi shivered and thrust his hands into his sleeves but stood respectfully back from the hibachi.

"How is your rheumatism this morning, Kin-san?" Rie inquired.

"We have to expect it in winter." He rubbed his hands together briskly.

"Well, I never hear you complain." Rie motioned Shin'ichi to her side.

"Here is Shin'ichi, the boy I mentioned," she said.

Kin looked at the smartly bowing boy. His hawk eyes took in Shin'ichi's erect posture, alert eyes, respectful manner.

"Good. Yes, we can use someone who is not afraid of work, an extra hand. Well,

Shin'ichi, you can begin by picking up an order of yeast this morning at the Hayashi place. Here, this is how to find it." Kin sketched a map on a small piece of rice paper and handed it to Shin'ichi, who looked at it closely, then slipped it into his sleeve.

"It will take you most of the morning to get there and back. You can take the cart outside the number one kura," Kin instructed. He walked back through the corridor and out to the street, Rie and Shin'ichi behind him.

He slid open the front entrance and ducked under the hanging *noren* banner bearing the White Tiger logo.

"Here. You know how to pull one of these, don't you?" Kin indicated the wooden cart.

Rie watched Shin'ichi nod, adjust his straw sandals, then maneuver between the two handlebars. He picked them up and started off down the road at a run, bowing to Rie and Kin as he left.

"I hope you'll be pleased with his work, Kin-san. Be strict with him as you always are. Father won't object, will he?"

"Not if he does his work well," Kin said.

Rie had a hunch that Shin'ichi, young though he was, might prove more capable than any of the clerks working under Kin, and she followed her instinct in matters of business.

Rie walked to her mother's room early one evening several months later. Sounds of the baby playing in the room, mingled with voices, caused Rie to pause outside the shoji. She recognized Jihei's and her mother's voices.

"Excuse me," Rie called.

"Yes," her mother replied. "Come in, Rie."

Rie found her mother and Jihei playing with Yoshitaro, who was crawling back and forth between them, chortling. All three were enjoying themselves. Upon seeing them together, Rie suddenly felt dizzy as if she couldn't breathe.

"Come, Rie. Come and play with Yoshitaro," her mother invited, smiling. "My first grandchild," she said in musical tones. Hana clapped her hands rhythmically and laughed.

No blood relation, Rie wanted to say as she fought down the pain in her chest.

Yoshitaro crawled to Hana, then turned and crawled back to Jihei, fell on his lap, and squealed, never stopping his continual motion. He sat up and clutched Jihei, who helped him to stand. The baby kept one hand on Jihei's shoulder and began to take halting steps around him.

"Oh, look! His first steps!" Hana cried.

Rie looked at Yoshitaro's face next to Jihei's and saw unmistakable hints of the same large nose and long eyebrows.

"He does resemble his father," Rie said finally. She tried to think of something more to say about the baby. "We can start taking him into the office soon," she managed.

Her mother laughed softly. "Not yet, Rie. He's just a baby. But of course he can learn words, gradually." She smiled and nodded at him.

"He is learning now, just look at him. He's bright," Jihei said, taking obvious pleasure in the child.

Hana clapped her hands and began reciting a nursery rhyme: "Momotaro, Momotaro, Momotaro . . ." Yoshitaro stumbled back to Hana and fell. She picked him up and hugged him. "Yes, that's the way," she cooed.

Rie sighed, looked at her mother, and stood. "Good night, Mother." She nodded, not quite a bow, toward Jihei and left the room. She walked slowly up the stairs to her room, dressed for bed, and took out the futon. As she sat in front of her mirror combing her thick hair she choked back a sob and wiped away tears forming in her

eyes. She sighed and lay down. She wondered if she would ever have a child of her
own, if someday she could find a way to
remove the geisha's bloodline from the
house.

The next morning when Rie went down
to breakfast her mother looked at her and
saw how dejected she was. "Ri-chan, why
don't you and cousin Sunao go to the
chrysanthemum festival this morning? I
used to enjoy them so. It would be good for
you to get out of the house a bit, go on a
nice excursion with Sunao."

Rie looked at her teacup, then picked it
up and sipped before answering. Sunao,
daughter of Kinzaemon's younger brother
living nearby, was really Rie's only friend
and roughly her age. Rie put a finger on her
mouth thoughtfully, then glanced at her
mother. "All right, Mother, I'll have one of
the maids go over to Sunao's and tell her
I'll meet her at the exhibition grounds."

"Finish your breakfast, dear."

Rie nodded as she quickly ate some rice
and miso soup. She went upstairs and
picked out one of her finer kimonos.
O-Natsu helped tie the obi, a chore Rie
always found onerous. She asked one of the
clerks in the outer office to find a ricksha
and hummed as she walked out the entrance

near the number one kura to wait for the ricksha.

As soon as she stepped up on the ricksha seat she felt some of the same elation she experienced whenever she had an opportunity to leave the confines of the house. Jihei's oppressive needs, her frustration at his inability in business, and his nightly demands lifted. She looked right and left, enjoying the sight of the rows of large wooden kura that lined the road and the breath of coastal salt air as they jogged along.

At the park she quickly found Sunao and they smiled and bowed in greeting, then walked together beside the rows of chrysanthemums. Anyone who saw them would no doubt take particular notice of two young women in elegant kimonos, Rie knew, but she was so intent on finally having a conversation with an intimate friend she could trust that she was oblivious to all else.

"Sunao, I haven't become pregnant yet. I don't know what more I can do. And now it's too late. You know a geisha's child has been brought in as heir. It's just intolerable!" Rie grabbed Sunao's arm.

"I heard, Ri-chan. It must be dreadful! I can't imagine."

"You are so fortunate, Sunao, having a

child with no difficulty."

"I know this troubles you, Ri-chan, and I'm so sorry. Maybe an herbalist can help. They seem to have powders with magical properties."

Rie looked around at the crowd, individuals and couples, all apparently enjoying themselves, all seeming so carefree. As her glance passed over the crowd, it stopped. Saburo!

"Sunao, aren't they the Kato brothers over there at the end of that row?"

Sunao followed Rie's gaze. "Oh, I guess so. I saw all three at the Akita wedding recently. Shall we speak to them?"

Rie paused, her heart racing, but not wanting to appear overly interested, even with Sunao. After all, as a married woman, that would not do. "If you want to, Sunao," Rie said, affecting nonchalance.

The two walked toward the Kato brothers, admiring chrysanthemums as they went. Rie hesitated, waited until Sunao spoke first. Both bowed at the same time. Rie took in Saburo's fine chiseled features, his above-average height, his elegant bearing, a contrast to his stockier older brother who lacked his fine features and refined manner.

"Kato-sama, how are you?" Sunao asked sweetly.

The elder brother replied, "Omura-san, how nice to see you." Both men bowed slightly.

Rie summoned her voice. "I trust your family is well?" She glanced at the elder brother, then briefly at Saburo, smiling and bowing, her heart fluttering in her chest like a caged sparrow.

The Kato brothers murmured thanks, Saburo briefly catching her eye and then looking away.

"A lovely exhibit, isn't it? Please greet your family for us." Sunao took Rie's arm and they bowed and walked away.

Out of the corner of her eye Rie glanced again at Saburo before turning away and caught him doing the same. Sunao and Rie continued through the exhibit, admiring the variation in colors, sizes, and textures of flowers as they went.

As Rie and her cousin found separate rickshas to return, Sunao remarked, "Aren't those Kato men handsome, Ri-chan?"

Rie smiled and waved as she agreed and climbed into her ricksha to head back to the Omura House. She thought again of Saburo's kindness so long ago, of the surprise warmth of his touch at a time when she needed it most. And here he was again, just as she was being shunted aside for another woman's child. A lump formed in her throat. It occurred to her that she would like to see Saburo Kato again. Yes, she would like very much to see him again. And from the look on his face, the feeling was mutual. But she was a married woman. How in the world could she ever manage such an improper thing?

CHAPTER 8

Rie still relished the memory of the outing with Sunao to the annual chrysanthemum exhibit. Seeing Saburo had supplied welcome relief from the stifling atmosphere of the house, now that the geisha's child had created even greater tension than normal between her and Jihei. How she longed to bring a child of her own into the house. However, with each passing day, the distance between her and Jihei had grown until they spent little time together, inside the bed or out. As her dreams had faded for fulfilling her father's hopes, killing her *self* and enduring her life had become harder. Her one experience of pleasure in the past year had been her recent outing. She smiled again, thinking of the chrysanthemum exhibit and Saburo.

"It was wonderful, Mother. I wish you could have seen it. So many gorgeous varieties on display this year," Rie said as she sat with her mother at breakfast some days later.

"Yes, dear, I know I would have enjoyed it. I just didn't seem to have the energy this time. I guess I'm feeling my age."

Rie glanced at her mother sharply. "Sometimes I think you're working too hard, Mother. You know I can take more of the responsibility for the kurabito now. There are so many things to remember. I ordered some of those new rubber tabi for them."

"Yes, dear, I appreciate it."

"And you should eat more, Mother. You need more than rice and pickles."

Her mother smiled. "You know how much I enjoy these *narazuke,* made with the sake lees." Her mother picked up a pickle and delicately brought her chopsticks to her mouth. "I feel a meal isn't complete without them, even breakfast. And we have always believed rice is what makes the meal. Rice is sacred, you must remember."

Rie sipped her miso soup. "Sunao said she would enjoy going to the special ikebana exhibit that's on now, if we could go together. I think I'll see if she wants to go tomorrow."

"Yes, do, Ri-chan. I think going to the chrysanthemum show did you a lot of good, and this isn't our busiest season."

There was an entirely different reason that Rie wanted to go to the exhibit. A *very* attractive reason. She smiled, holding the secret close to her heart.

The next morning Rie dressed in one of her favorite kimono, even managing the cumbersome obi herself. She caught O-Natsu in the corridor. "O-Natsu, would you tell Mother I have gone to the ikebana exhibit with Sunao?"

O-Natsu nodded. "Shall I call a ricksha for you?"

"There's no need. I know where they wait in the next street."

O-Natsu frowned. "Is it all right, finding one by yourself?"

"Of course." Rie laughed, went to the door to find her geta, and let herself out.

No one need know that Sunao was not accompanying her this time. Rie did not want to worry her mother, but today's was a special outing. She had heard the Kato brothers mention the ikebana exhibit. What Rie would risk for just a long look at Saburo.

Minutes later, as she stepped up into the ricksha she felt a sense of anticipation, almost as if she had grown several years younger, so carefree was her mood. It was always exhilarating to see the large wooden kura lining the main road. She alighted at the exhibition hall, handed coins to the puller, and said she would be looking for him later if he were still there.

Inside the hall the lines were long, and polite chatter about the exquisite arrangements floated on the air. The kimonos of the women were especially elegant, and Rie felt suddenly abashed. She knew Sunao's taste in kimono was superior to hers. Perhaps she should have brought Sunao along after all.

If truth be told, Rie did not appreciate ikebana as much as her mother or Sunao. Somehow she preferred to see plants and flowers in a more natural setting, as in the garden at home. She knew that even there, in her favorite private place, the gardener always pruned in a prescribed way. Nothing grew wild unless one went into some out-of-the-way rural area, something Rie seldom had an opportunity to do.

She turned her attention to an exhibit of her favorite flowers, wisteria, and stopped to admire the arrangements, some in flat obsidian containers, others in white or celadon vases of ingenious shapes, of subtle, impeccable taste. She noted most were in the prescribed three-part placement of flowers and greenery. She tried to remember a few of the most striking designs, thinking perhaps she might try her hand at them. Such fine art was not something that usually occupied her time in the workday of the busy brewery, but she knew it would please her mother. As she paused, a voice at her elbow interrupted her reverie.

"Omura-san, we meet again amid flowers."

Her heart raced. There in front of her was Saburo Kato. More handsome than ever.

"Yes, what a pleasant surprise," Rie managed to say, bowing and smiling. She felt her heartbeat accelerate.

"Shall we look at the prize winners?" Saburo asked.

Rie smiled and nodded, temporarily speechless at her good fortune. She could barely take her eyes off him.

As they walked, Saburo slowed so that they were walking abreast rather than with Rie three paces behind.

"I heard about the inappropriate remarks made by Yamaguchi at your wedding," he said, glancing at Rie. "My father said it was too arrogant, and coming from the president of the Brewers Association. I hope your father was not upset by the insult to your house."

He understood. Here was a man who understood her *and* her family. She paused.

"Thank you, Kato-sama, for your understanding, but I fear my father was annoyed and a bit depressed." She looked directly into Kato's eyes, the man she had always found so attractive. She felt their connection in her inner being, a connection she had never felt with anyone else. And to her surprise she felt no awkwardness in talking with him. Rie felt her spirit soaring, dancing in the air.

His glance rested on Rie's face. "Well, I doubt that he will be reelected. Shall we work together to see that he is not? Of course I am not the heir, but my father and brothers listen to me. I know that you are heir . . . your husband . . ."

She longed to touch him, to feel the protection of his embrace for just a moment.

"Ah, Kato-sama, that would be wonderful. I must be returning home now, but I feel we shall meet again." She knew they would. And that she must not linger today. She bowed.

"Yes, it will be my hope, Omura-san. I look forward to it." He smiled and bowed in return, his eyes lingering longer than what was necessary and sending a warm tingle racing through her. What it took to leave his company, to tear herself away from him.

With one last look at Saburo, Rie hurried out to the ricksha. It was more than she could have hoped, not only meeting him but knowing he cared for her and her house, that they had a common antagonist, and especially that he wanted to see her again. He felt what she did, she was certain. She smiled and hummed all the way to the Omura entrance.

Rie arrived home in a mood of elation. She nearly ran up the slippery stairs to change into her work kimono before joining her mother for lunch. "It was such a special exhibit, Mother," she remarked as she sat at the table where her mother was looking at her food. Rie was hungry and did not notice immediately that her mother was not eating. Rie put down her chopsticks.

"What's the matter, Mother? Don't you feel well?"

"Oh, it's nothing. Just a stomach upset, I imagine. Don't worry."

"Are you sure, Mother?"

Her mother nodded, so Rie excused herself and left for the storeroom, her favorite workplace, and not off-limits to her. She was eager to be alone with her memories of Saburo, of his plan. *Their* plan.

Late in the afternoon she went to her mother's room to see how she was doing. Hana was lying on her futon, her eyes closed. Rie saw that the hibachi coals had gone out. She touched her mother's hands.

"Mother, how are you feeling?" she asked softly.

"Oh, Rie . . ." Hana opened her eyes and struggled to speak. "I am not well." She closed her eyes again.

"Has anyone sent for the herbalist?"

Hana shook her head. Rie relit the hibachi and reached to touch her mother's forehead. A shot of alarm raced through her. Her mother was burning up.

"I see you are in pain, Mother," she said, hiding the panic from her voice. "I'm going to send someone now."

"Oh . . ." Her mother only frowned.

Rie rushed to the kitchen and asked O-Natsu's assistant to go for the herbalist.

"Run! Right now! You know where he lives? Bring him back with you as soon as possible," she ordered.

Rie ran to the inner office and opened the shoji abruptly, without announcing herself.

Her father, Jihei, and a customer looked up, startled. She stood in the doorway.

"It's Mother. She's having abdominal pain. I've sent for the herbalist."

"Oh, I'll come." Her father frowned and rose to follow Rie along the earthen corridor to the step leading to the family rooms.

"I'm afraid it's serious, Father." *Please let me be wrong. Let her be all right.*

Her father gasped. "Good that you called for the herbalist, Rie. Let's see what he has to say."

They entered Hana's room. The light creeping in through the shoji dimly lit Hana's pallid face. O-Natsu had propped up Hana's head and was holding a bowl of rice gruel to her mouth. Hana shook her head, and O-Natsu set the bowl on a tray.

"She won't eat," O-Natsu said, anxiously. She bowed herself out.

Rie and her father sat on either side of Hana's futon and watched her face intently.

The old wizened herbalist arrived with a brown pouch filled with potions and powders tied to his obi. He knelt beside Hana's futon and felt her pulse and pressure points on her arms and legs.

"Hmm," he murmured.

He took from his pouch two powders and measured them into folded papers, which he handed to Rie.

"She must take these with hot water three times each day, beginning now. Send for me tomorrow if she isn't better."

Rie's father followed the herbalist to the door, questioning him as he left.

Rie took the powders and held one packet to her mother's mouth, a cup of tea in the other hand. She raised her mother's head.

"Please open your mouth, Mother. You must take this." *Do not leave me! You must not go. Please.*

Her mother took a small sip.

"One more, Mother. Here." Rie held the second packet of powder to her mother's mouth. *Please work. Please!*

Hana groaned and shook her head. Her eyes moved slowly toward Rie and then to her husband, who had reentered the room and sat near his wife.

"I know," she said feebly, "my time has come." She struggled to continue. "I have had a good life. I am ready."

Kinzaemon dropped his head to his chest, hands clenched in his lap.

"No, Mother, please!" Rie pleaded. She continued to hold the powder to her mother's mouth, but Hana simply closed her eyes.

Rie glanced at her father from time to time as they both sat in consternation at Hana's side. In the evening Rie looked at her father. "Go to bed, Father, and have something to eat. I'll stay here with her."

Her father shook his head. "I want to be with her now."

Hours passed. During the night Rie glanced at her father and saw that he was dozing where he sat, head resting on his chest. Jihei came in and sat for a while, then left. O-Natsu crept in with tea to see if Rie or Kinzaemon wished to be relieved. Rie whispered no.

Alone with her late-night thoughts, tears ran down Rie's cheeks. No one could replace her mother. Rie's father was fond of her, relied on her for the future of the house, she knew. But her mother understood her as only a woman can. She had a tenderhearted way with a woman's problems. Rie sobbed softly as she gazed at her mother's white hands crossed over her chest, hands that had so often held fine needlework with invisible stitches, hands that had nurtured Rie ever since her earliest memories. Now the hands lay so still. Rie watched the futon rise and fall almost imperceptibly with her mother's breathing and felt her own breaths match her mother's, as if to lend her mother her own life force.

At the first faint light of dawn filtering in through the shoji, Rie started at a sound from her mother's futon. She reached toward the futon. Her mother moved as if to sit up but fell back, her eyes and mouth open. Rie touched her hands and felt her pulse. *No. No. No!*

"Father!" Rie reached a hand to her sleeping father's arm. "I think Mother's gone." She sobbed, a hand over her mouth.

The cremation was a most painful experience for Rie, reminding her once again of Toichi, of her failing the house, failing to produce an heir. When would she ever get it right, she wondered, as she sat with her father, shuddering and sobbing as she picked each bone from the ashes with chopsticks? She looked at the cluster of bones, all that remained of her mother. There was the skull that had underlain the delicate features and patrician nose. Rie glanced at her father's devastated face and squirmed as she decided to save him this most painful part of the final devotion. She picked up the skull and separated it from the ashes. When she finished she closed her eyes and imagined her mother's patrician face bent over the needlework she was so fond of. Imagined her sitting in her room in front of her carved paulownia dressing table. For several moments Rie held the vision before opening her eyes to attend to the rest of her difficult task.

The funeral ceremony was a sad, solemn affair, the large room lined with black-clad mourners and priests intoning their droning mantras. Saburo was there too, his heart reaching out to her even across a crowded room. She had heard that he had lost his mother at an early age and had never fully recovered from the loss. She sneaked a glance at him and bowed quickly as his glance locked with hers.

Only once before had Rie experienced such complete and utter grief: the day her brother had fallen into the well. The day she hadn't taken her responsibility seriously. Now, once again, she had failed in her duty. Her mother had not lived to see the grand-child of her blood. It was too late. Watching her father's drawn face, Rie tried to conceal her own desolation. Numbness overtook her, a closing off of all aspects of her normal daily life. For several days she had energy only to sit with her father or in the garden, silent to the world around her.

Though she had never seen her parents demonstrate their affection for each other, she knew it was there, a deep, abiding bond. Her father grew increasingly dispirited in the days and weeks to follow. Added to her own bereavement, Rie felt the heavy weight of an even greater responsibility. Soon it would be up to her and Jihei to maintain the business and tradition of the house. She knew this meant the weight lay squarely on her shoulders, since Jihei had demonstrated so little ability. What kind of support could she count on?

One morning soon after the funeral Rie knelt at the Butsudan altar to light incense and to offer rice before the tablets of her mother and ancestors. Her father entered the room, she could sense without turning. She placed an incense stick in the powdery ash, lit it, bowed and clapped her hands to attract the attention of the gods.

"*Ah,* Rie," her father said behind her when she had finished. "It's so important to keep our communication with the ancestors, the Buddhas, just as we see to the continuity of the house with our heirs. And Rie, your mother was fond of plum wine. Why don't you serve her a cup each morning with the rice? She'll be pleased."

"Yes, Father, I'll do that." She glanced at the new tablet on which her mother's posthumous name was inscribed. A fresh stab of grief overtook her.

"I was gratified that all the major brewers sent family members to attend the funeral. It shows our standing here. You know you need to keep a record of the donation each house made. Then we can return the same amount, with interest, when they have their funerals. Mother always kept strict records."

Rie took a deep breath. "Yes, Father, I have them now. Don't worry." Rie took a rice paper pamphlet from a small wooden cabinet near the Butsudan and pushed it toward her father, seated next to her. "I've entered all the donations."

"Very good, Rie. And the kurabito too. Mother was always so attentive to their needs. This will be your responsibility from now on."

"I know, Father, that's why they have been content here and come back year after year from Tamba. I'll take care of them."

Kinzaemon pushed his bushy hair off his forehead and nodded.

Rie sat at the Butsudan long after her father left the room. Now the enormity of the obligation resting on her shoulders made her catch her breath: the on to her father and nine generations of ancestors, and the burden of the important business of the Omura House, one of the largest in the most ancient and respected industry in all Japan. Soon her father would retire, and the entire responsibility would rest with her. The reality of Yoshitaro, the new heir and the bloodline of the geisha, in the main house sent a wave of agony through her. He was a reminder of everyone she had failed. In the tragedy of her mother's death, she had temporarily forgotten about him. Although her father had been understanding about bringing the child into the house, she could see in his eyes that he had hoped for a child of his own blood. She buried her face in her hands. The time had come to turn her attention now to this intolerable situation.

CHAPTER 9

Rie opened the wooden shutters and looked out at the garden from her upper-story room early one morning. The wintry landscape, in the garden and compound, out on the streets, wherever she looked, was defined by a narrow spectrum of color from brown to gray. In the house she insisted that flowers in red and yellow be displayed to counter the gray monotony that had taken hold since her mother's death. She still hoped for a child, but as the months passed, she had given up on the idea that she would ever have one with Jihei. There must be another way, but how? The glimmer of an idea rose inside her. Something unthinkable. So unthinkable she put it from her mind immediately.

She reluctantly admitted that she was beginning to enjoy the bursts of vibrant energy from Yoshitaro to enliven the somber atmosphere of winter that came with this period of mourning. She regretted that as a married woman she was required to appear in black at weddings and funerals, generally her only occasions beyond the brewery. In the house she wore kimonos of indigo-dyed kasuri fabrics.

When she opened the wooden shutters of her room in the morning and looked at the garden, she watched for the plum blossoms that heralded the beginning of February, and the pink and fuchsia azaleas, harbingers of early spring and the end of the brewing season, precursors of the cherry blossoms. In muggy summertime, the cicadas competed in a buzzing humming chorus that increased in volume with the temperature. In autumn, yellow chrysanthemums reminded her that the brewing season was beginning again. The life of the garden thus marked the seasons of Rie's days following her mother's passing.

Of course, there would be no meeting with Saburo. Perhaps in some future time. In the meantime, just thinking of him consoled her. During the summer months after the brewing was finished, the workload in the brewery abated. The kurabito went home to their farms in Tamba, where they worked in the rice paddies. Apart from selling and shipping sake, the focus shifted to moneylending and gold-and-silver exchange. Because the Tokugawa shoguns had fallen on hard times and their economic condition was reflected in the lives of their daimyo vassals, the samurai were impoverished, forced into the grip of moneylenders. Some of them tried to eke out a living in craft occupations, making umbrellas or fans.

"The samurai are parasites, leeches on us, Father," Rie said, unconsciously echoing her father's sentiments. "It's we merchants who produce the real wealth."

"Quite right, Rie," her father agreed. "They mouth their Confucian maxims and look down on us, but they are completely dependent on us economically."

The House of Omura, like most merchant houses in Kobe and Osaka, benefited from the penury of the samurai class, which depended on the cash and services of the merchants.

Every summer when the days were particularly hot and humid, the Bunraku puppet troupe came from its Osaka headquarters to perform one or two of Chikamatsu's masterpieces for the merchant audiences of Kobe.

Rie turned to Jihei one morning. "Why don't we take Sunao to Bunraku this Saturday? Her husband is away in Edo. I think we can spare the time, and she would enjoy it. Father would too." Rie did not mention that she would also enjoy the outing.

"Not a bad idea," Jihei replied. "Yes, I'd enjoy it too. We can all go."

The Omuras had reserved seats in one of the best sections in the packed theater. Just as Rie, her father, and Sunao were following Jihei inside, he was shouldered aside by a huge figure Rie at first took to be a sumo wrestler.

"Move aside, Omura! Let me pass!"

Rie watched as Jihei struggled to catch his balance. She glanced up in time to see the fat, arrogant face of Kikuji Yamaguchi, and Jihei straightening his collar and brushing off his kimono.

"Incredible effrontery!" he said to Rie, loud enough for anyone nearby to hear. "Who does he think he is?"

"He thinks he's the most important person in Nada," Rie replied. "We'll show him." She gave Yamaguchi a withering glance.

Geishas butterflied in, tittering, long-sleeved hands covering their mouths. They timed their entrance to attract the attention of the entire audience just before the lamps were extinguished.

Rie watched Jihei out of the corner of her eye as he scanned the geisha section and settled on an individual. It must be O-Toki, Rie decided, noticing a geisha with mask-white makeup wearing an apricot kimono that blatantly displayed the nape of her neck. Perhaps that kind of makeup and dress did excite men, as intended. As she watched, the geisha turned toward them, then quickly covered her face with a fluttering fan and turned away. Humiliation bubbled up inside Rie at the thought that she was still barren.

The lamps were snuffed out, and the purple curtain billowed upward on Chikamatsu's perennial favorite, *The Love Suicide at Amijima,* portraying a triangle in which the hero is caught between his duty to his family and his passion for the alluring courtesan. The nasal twanging of the *samisen* accompaniment helped to transport the audience to the magic world of the unfolding drama. As the play advanced toward its climax, the puppets raised their eyebrows, waved their arms, shrieked and wailed in an agony of frustration and despair.

Then came the denouement: the anguished hero committed suicide with his mistress, a lovers' suicide. Rie could hear men clearing their throats and shifting in their seats. When the lamps were relit, she noticed tears glistening on Jihei's cheeks, and several men around them weeping. She smiled ruefully. Chikamatsu was in truth the master playwright. He had so accurately evoked the two separate worlds of Japan, the world of the family and the world of the geisha, the water world where wives never ventured. It was obvious where the sympathies of the men in the audience lay: with the hero and the geisha, not with his wife and children who were left behind.

"What a master Chikamatsu was," Sunao said to Rie as they rode home in a ricksha together.

"And did you notice all the men in the audience weeping?" Rie asked. "We are supposed to sympathize with the hero and the geisha, not the wife and family at home," she added with a wry smile.

"Isn't that the way with most of his plays," Sunao asked rhetorically.

Work at White Tiger continued as if the Bunraku expedition had not occurred. Kobe was home to all the largest breweries in Japan, and competition among them for the Edo market, key to the success of any large brewery, was fierce. Thousands of other brewers scattered throughout the countryside did not enter the Edo market but brewed wherever farmers had a rice surplus and sold locally to loyal clientele.

Rie stood eavesdropping beyond the office one morning, as she often did. "Yamaguchi tried to contract one of the cask ships we've been using, to monopolize the whole ship," Kin said to Kinzaemon and Jihei. "He offered a price higher than the going rate, but the shipper was wary because of his long connection with us. The man just has no scruples."

"Well, it's good that we're in time with this year's shipment to Edo," Jihei said.

"Especially since we contracted the two extra ships to handle expansion this year," Kinzaemon agreed.

Kin scratched his head. "But I'd like to see our gold-and-silver exchange expanded further. Always less risk that way, as Rie says."

Kinzaemon rubbed his chin. "That's what we've always believed. Yes, we could raise it five, maybe ten percent."

"Perhaps as much as fifteen, or twenty," Kin said.

They heard someone running toward the door and looked up. Kinnosuke, as Shin'ichi was now called since he had become Kin's apprentice, entered out of breath and bowed twice.

"There's a messenger from the shipping

contractor in the outer office. He's very agitated," he blurted out. He bowed twice.

Rie backed out of sight, but strained to hear. She moved down the hall toward the outer office. "Have him come in," Kinzaemon said. "No, let's go, Kin and Jihei." Kinzaemon struggled up from the tatami and the three walked quickly to the outer office.

"*Ah*, Hayami-san," Kinzaemon said to the bowing official. "What brings you here?"

Hayami bowed again. "Very sorry to say, Sir. There has been a shipwreck on the way to Edo. One of the ships with part of your shipment has been lost." He bowed again. "It was that dangerous shoal near Nagoya." He wiped perspiration from his face with a towel from his sleeve and sighed.

"Oh! Oh!" Kinzaemon groaned. He pulled at his ear and glanced at Kin.

"It wasn't our whole consignment, was it?" Kin asked, frowning. "We were using five ships."

"Yes, I think one fifth of your total," Hayami agreed.

"How will we repay our loans this year?" Jihei asked, rubbing his eyebrows.

"We'll give you a discount on your next year's shipment," Hayami said. "Fifteen percent. We have no words to apologize

129

adequately." He bowed continuously.

"Yes, we'll need a discount for next year," said Kin. "Let's look at the figures." Kin and Kinnosuke moved to the section of the office where Kin kept the ledgers. Hayami followed them.

Kinzaemon and Jihei walked back to the inner office. Kinzaemon sat heavily and sighed.

"What a disaster," Jihei said, pulling at his eyebrows.

Listening, Rie frowned, pondering what she could do or suggest. She bit her lip, tapped her chin with her fan.

"Brewing is a risky enterprise, as we all know," Kinzaemon sighed. "This is why we need an equal business in moneylending and gold-and-silver exchange. Without that cushion we might be out of business this year, relying on the two-year wait for the return from our brewing investment." He ran his hand through his hair.

Rie's voice came from the hallway, and she hurried into the office. "This is terrible!" She moved a hand up and down her arm. "What do we do now, Father?"

"We haven't lost our whole shipment, Rie. Please ask for some tea for us."

Kin came back into the room with Kinnosuke and stood facing Kinzaemon and Rie.

"It's a loss of one-fifth of the year's shipment," he said in a thin voice. "I'm making arrangements to increase our gold-and-silver exchange ten percent over last year. It will be a struggle to make it till next fall."

Jihei rubbed his hands over his eyebrows. "Other brewers must have lost too," he said.

Rie turned to Hayami. "What about Yamaguchi? Was he using this ship too?"

"I don't believe so, no," Hayami replied.

"Then I wonder," Rie said, "was it really an accident, or another case of Yamaguchi's treachery?"

They sat in fraught silence around the table. Monsoon rains pelted against the roof and added to the gloom inside.

CHAPTER 10

With the death of Hana, the atmosphere and relationships in the house altered. Rie and her father spent more time together, especially in the evenings when Jihei was away. Rie, still protective of her father and wishing to spare him the disappointment of Jihei's lack of commitment, often made excuses for her absent husband as she sat companionably with her father after dinner. They had weathered the storm of the lost shipments, but only through careful planning and tight control of their finances, no thanks to Jihei who once again was out spending her father's money.

"Father, I believe Jihei said he was going to a gathering of other brewers, trying to keep up with the latest news, especially now that you are no longer attending the Brewers Association meetings." Of course Rie doubted Jihei was doing any such thing. More likely, he was spending time at the

Sawaraya with that geisha. "I also need to know what is happening with the business, Father. We don't want Yamaguchi to take advantage of us, now that it's known you may retire soon."

Kinzaemon sighed. "Yes, that's so, Rie. And of course Kin is almost my age, so he may retire soon too. It would be a problem if we both retired at once, a big problem."

Rie sorrowed to see her father looking older, seeming less resilient after his wife's passing.

"Kin told me that he would be able to continue for a while even after you retire. And you know Shin'ichi is doing exceptionally well. Kin says we are fortunate to have him. I believe Kin feels Kinnosuke may be able to succeed him one day." Rie smiled and poured sake as her father held out his cup. "I think Kinnosuke is about fifteen now."

"You did well, Ri-chan, to recognize his ability even as a young boy."

Rie nodded and bowed slightly at her father's compliment. She relished the increased opportunity for her father's companionship, time he had normally spent with Hana while she was alive.

Early one morning several weeks later, as

Rie dressed before going down to breakfast, she sat before the mirror on her mother's paulownia dressing cabinet. Her thoughts turned to Yoshitaro, now walking and making his way into the office. More than once Rie heard Kinnosuke giving him bits of information about the business. Rie did not think this inappropriate. Still, the reality of the geisha's bloodline in the house rankled, never leaving her consciousness for long. What could she do? There was no altering the fact that Yoshitaro was heir, that after Jihei he would become Kinzaemon XI.

This morning as she sat before the mirror she thought of Saburo Kato and their meeting at the ikebana exhibit the morning before her mother died. The tragedy had pushed all thought of their discussion from her mind. Earlier in the week, Rie had received a note of remembrance from Saburo on the anniversary of her mother's death. He had reiterated a desire to work together to prevent Yamaguchi's reelection, and their mutual hope to meet again. Something in the way he'd penned his note had made her think that perhaps he had more in mind.

Was Saburo's talk of working together against Yamaguchi perhaps just his way of forming a bond with her? She hoped so, even though they both wanted to defeat Yamaguchi. She pictured in her imagination meeting Saburo at night, alone. She would make it happen, make it possible to be with him so that she might bear his child, a child growing of love, a child without the blood of a geisha. A child that might someday make it possible to expel the geisha blood-line from the Omura House. She had always felt she belonged with Saburo, not with her dolt of a husband. She would do it.

The idea she hadn't dared let surface so many months ago now blossomed. She pictured his caring brown eyes and pondered for several minutes. Then with a tingle of anticipation and renewed excitement in her step, she went to a tansu and opened a secret drawer where she kept some cash. She took out several coins and placed them in a pouch of finest silk. She inserted the pouch into the sleeve of her kimono and hurried down to breakfast. O-Natsu and others would notice if she delayed too long.

She ate a perfunctory breakfast alone. Her father and Jihei were already in the office, and it was not often they spent time together at this busy hour. She hurried back upstairs, took a brush and inkstone from a tansu drawer, added a bit of water to the inkstone, and quickly rubbed the inkstick back and forth until the ink was of proper consistency. She knew her calligraphy was not highly skilled, but she carefully wrote a few lines on the best rice paper, folded the note, sealed it with wax, and thrust it into her sleeve. She was proud that she could write and use the abacus, skills not common to every woman in brewing families. She went back to the secret drawer, took out a few more coins, and placed them in another small silk pouch. She touched her kimono sleeve to make certain the pouches and note would not slip out, and went downstairs.

In the corridor Rie asked one of the maids to send O-Natsu to her room with tea.

A few minutes later O-Natsu entered on her knees with a tea tray and set it on the tatami in front of Rie. She looked at Rie expectantly.

"Thank you, O-Natsu. I have a very big task for you. It is a great responsibility for the house."

O-Natsu's eyes widened. She bowed. "Whatever O-Josama requires."

She knew she could trust O-Natsu. Discretion was paramount. "Well, O-Natsu, I wonder if you have some relatives in a nice house not too far away who may be having financial difficulties, and who are completely trustworthy?"

136

O-Natsu paused, biting her lip. "Yes, O-Josama, they live not far from here."

"What I want you to do is to go to your relatives tonight. Ask them if they would make their house available two nights from tonight from midnight until dawn. If they agree, give them this money." Rie handed the larger pouch to O-Natsu with both hands. "But tell them they must remain absolutely silent about this, on pain of death. And they must not be there those hours from midnight until dawn." Rie studied O-Natsu closely as she spoke.

O-Natsu gasped. "Are you . . . do you intend to go out at night alone?"

"Yes, O-Natsu, but you must tell no one. This is between us. And do you know the chief servant at the Kato residence?"

"I do, yes."

"And is she completely trustworthy?"

"She is my good friend, and I trust her."

"All right, O-Natsu. Then give your friend this packet of money for her help, and ask that she give this note to the Kato third son, Saburo, to no one else in the house. Tell her she must speak to no one, or there may be consequences. This is a very big responsibility, O-Natsu. Do you understand you must also speak to no one about it?"

O-Natsu nodded and bowed deeply.

"Will you please repeat what I asked you to do?"

Rie sat intently while O-Natsu repeated the instructions.

"Very good. Now when dusk falls this afternoon, please go on your errands, and let me know when you have completed them."

"Certainly, O-Josama. I will do exactly as you say." O-Natsu thrust the bags and note into her sleeve, bowed, and left the room.

Rie smiled and sighed. She looked in the mirror, adjusted her hair, then took out the container of her mother's Kyoto perfume, opened it, and inhaled. She tried to imagine what it would be like to be with Saburo Kato. How would she manage to leave the house at night without being seen, to find a ricksha and make it to the house O-Natsu had indicated? More important, would Saburo really come to the house to meet her?

For the rest of the day and the day following, Rie went about her chores with a distracted air, thoughts of Saburo, his reaction to the note, filling her with anticipation.

CHAPTER 11

Rie awoke early. She sat up abruptly as she realized it was two days since she had sent O-Natsu on her secret errand. To her immense relief and great pleasure, she caught her breath, as the following morning she opened Saburo's note in reply. Her hands trembled as she read his words. Saburo agreed to the rendezvous. She had never felt so elated. She dressed quickly and sat at her mirror combing her hair. How was she to effect her escape from the Omura House and reach her destination by midnight for her rendezvous with Saburo Kato? She would have to go in disguise, cover her face, pretend she was a low-ranking servant.

Although she knew she could never provide the heir for the house, she wanted a child of her father's blood, a child who would carry on the Omura bloodline. Carry the heart and soul of her parents. Besides, loneliness had been a constant companion.

She knew she could never love Jihei, nor he love her, and all her attempts at seduction had ended in failure either because he was too drunk or because he hadn't come home at all. Lately she would lie awake at night, remembering Saburo's eyes, his lips, and the gentleness in his voice. She was in love with Saburo. Deeply in love. And he had given her enough subtle clues that he felt the same. She just hoped that they didn't get caught. She knew the penalty for a woman would be severe, probably even death. Of course there was no penalty for a man, whether married or not. Saburo was not married, and there would be no danger for him, even if he were.

Downstairs, she ate a quick breakfast. When O-Natsu brought in tea and miso soup, Rie saw her opportunity. "O-Natsu, can you find some old clothes that I can use . . . later?" She did not want to be more specific in case one of the maids happened to be listening. Walls and shoji were so thin.

O-Natsu, always quick to guess Rie's meaning, understood. "Yes, I'll find something suitable. You need not be concerned." She nodded and bowed.

Breakfast finished, Rie hurried to the Butsudan to pray to the ancestors, to burn an incense stick, to leave rice and a tiny cup of

140

plum wine for her mother. She sat unmoving for several minutes before the altar, folded hands raised to her chin as she prayed, entrusted her mission to the ancestors. They would surely be listening.

She walked briskly to the storeroom to inventory supplies for the kurabito. She worked to ensure that they were as content with her management of their health and well-being as they had been when her mother was alive.

Next she went to Yoshi's room, where he was playing with an abacus Kinnosuke had given him. At two, her father said it was time he began to learn skills that would be useful later.

"Good morning, Yoshi." She smiled, pleased to see him with the abacus. "Shall we have a lesson in writing today? You did so well starting with *hiragana* the other day." Rie sat next to Yoshi and took a pad of paper from her sleeve.

Yoshi nodded and opened a cabinet where his inkstone and stick were kept.

Rie poured a small amount of water on the inkstone.

"I can do it, Okaa-san." He reached for the inkstick and began to rub it back and forth on the stone.

Each time he called her "Mother" she had

stifled a comment. The first time she had wanted to say "I'm not your mother," but of course she didn't. She needed to treat Yoshi as if she were, and she did her best to behave that way. Yoshi after all had not chosen his parents. He was not responsible for Jihei's action. Besides, he was eager to please, and she had to admit he was an appealing child. In any case, she had learned to adjust her behavior when it had no relationship to her feelings. Was that what her mother had meant when she told Rie women had to "kill the self"?

Yoshi continued busily rubbing the inkstick.

"Very good, Yoshi. I think that's enough." She pushed two sheets of rice paper in front of him. "Now, do you think you can write 'sa, shi, su, se, so' for me?"

Yoshi dipped his brush into the ink and awkwardly wrote the crude syllables, then sat back proudly and looked at Rie.

"That's good, Yoshi, yes. And you remember how I told you to hold your brush so it points straight up and down?"

Yoshi nodded and did his best to hold the brush properly.

Rie spent some minutes this way each morning instructing Yoshi. She found that she began to take satisfaction in watching his improvement and childish enthusiasm. It helped alleviate some of the pain of not having borne an heir herself.

The day seemed to Rie to be passing impossibly slow. She filled the afternoon hours with as many tasks as possible, impatiently hurrying from one to the next. Toward the dinner hour O-Natsu brought a bundle of old clothes to Rie's room.

"I hope these will do," she said as she laid them in front of Rie.

Rie held up the tunic and long scarf and fingered them. "These should be perfect, O-Natsu." Rie wound the scarf over her neck and arranged it so that it covered her face, leaving an opening for her eyes.

"Yes, you look like a poor peon." O-Natsu giggled.

Rie smiled broadly and removed the scarf. "At dinner this evening I'll tell my father and husband that I am tired and will go upstairs early."

"Do you want me to help you leave tonight?" O-Natsu scratched her face.

Rie pondered. "Maybe when it is twenty minutes before midnight you could make certain no one is awake, and that my husband is not here. Let me know. That would be a help. Yes, thank you." It was likely that Jihei would not be around, but she needed to make certain.

When O-Natsu left, Rie sat thinking. She and Saburo Kato had so many things in common. She had never forgotten his sympathy when little Toichi had drowned and he had realized her responsibility. And now they both wanted to prevent Yamaguchi's reelection. They even had similar taste in flowers, so important an indication of a man's sensitivity. And she knew Saburo was as dedicated to the Kato house as she was to hers. He appeared to Rie to have strength of character, something she admired in a man, something so lacking in Jihei. But this was not the time to think of Jihei.

He was nowhere to be seen in the evening, Rie was pleased to see. She dressed in her room for the adventure, making sure her mother's perfume was secure in her sleeve. She sat alone in anticipation.

Late in the evening she heard O-Natsu's voice beyond the shoji. "It's time."

Rie opened the shoji and followed O-Natsu down the stairs, both walking as quietly as possible. O-Natsu led the way to the door closest the storeroom and opened the outer gate. Rie peered out and saw a ricksha standing at the corner. She turned to O-Natsu. "Be sure to meet me here at the gate just before dawn," she whispered.

144

She quickly hailed the ricksha, adjusting the scarf over her face, and instructed the puller where to take her. As the ricksha jogged toward her destination, Rie reached into her sleeve and applied the crème parfum liberally to her neck and wrists. She didn't care if she used it all.

As they neared the house, Rie saw another ricksha standing not far from the gate. She felt a thrill go through her. Saburo was already there as he had said he would be. She alighted and went through the gate to the front shoji. "I'm here," she said, not so loudly that a nearby neighbor might hear.

Saburo was at the door to meet her as she stepped inside. He wore his ordinary kimono, as he had not wanted to attract suspicion either, and his oval face bore an expression of tenderness that she had never seen on Jihei. Rie stood directly before him, unable to hide her excitement or her nervousness, as she fidgeted with the hem of her tunic. Saburo smiled and raised his hands to her face. For a moment they gazed into each other's eyes. Neither knew exactly what to do, what to say. But then Saburo drew her to him and embraced her gently, kissing her face, neck, lips. Trembling, Rie clung to him tightly, then more tightly still.

"I knew when I saw you at the ikebana

exhibit that you had a place in my heart," he murmured. "I knew from the first time I saw you."

She nodded, hearing the truth in his words. "I felt the same," Rie said, breathlessly, remembering the day of her brother's funeral, Saburo's gentleness even then. "Just the same." She felt tears start, but they were tears unlike others.

"As you know, my mother died when I was a child, so I understood your deep loss at the death of your mother. And I remember about your little brother." He ran a finger along her chin. "I was so happy that you responded to my note." He pressed his cheek against hers.

Saburo held her from him so he could look at her. "The heart has its own song," he said, smiling broadly.

Rie felt her whole being smile joyfully. Until now, she hadn't realized how deprived her life had become with Jihei, how lonely she'd been. "*Ah* . . . You would have been a poet in the Old Capital." Her mother had once told her of the poet lovers in the Old Imperial Court, of the beautiful poems they wrote for the women they courted.

"You would have sat behind a screen listening to my poems."

"And I would have chosen your poems

above all others," Rie replied. She had never felt such harmony and peace. She glanced quickly at the tea tray and futon thoughtfully laid out by O-Natsu's relatives. "I'm glad we have no screen now." She had her arms around Saburo's neck.

"We need none." He led Rie toward the futon and pulled off her tunic, kissing her shoulder, caressing her neck with his tongue.

Soon there was not only no screen between them, but nothing else.

Rie felt something in her being released, becoming free. For the first time in her life it seemed there was no separation between her feelings and her behavior. She felt totally new, so new. They lay on the futon, light from the candle revealing the secrets of each other's bodies.

Saburo met Rie with a tender passion that caused her wonder. This was how it was meant to be, she was sure. For the next few minutes, the next few hours, there was nothing for Rie or Saburo but each other.

Some time later, still in the afterglow of love, Rie started. "Have the crickets become silent?"

Saburo pulled away and raised his head. "Perhaps so."

Rie sat up. "Oh! I must get back before

dawn. No one must see me."

"Wait!" he said, drawing her to him. "Why did you come here?"

She knew that he was asking about Jihei, but she only shook her head.

He lifted her chin, forcing her to look him in the eye.

"He has others," she said, lowering her eyes to his lips, unable to look at him directly.

"And the child?"

"Hers," she said, feeling the burn of shame.

"Oh," he said, lifting her chin again. The sympathy she saw in his eyes was too much and a tear trickled down her cheek. "Then maybe we shall have our child of love."

His words were too much to bear. She closed her eyes, knowing she must leave but wanting to savor the gentleness of his touch. Without it, she would shrivel up and die as surely as cherry blossoms on the third day.

"I must go," she finally said.

Saburo touched Rie's back, caressed her shoulders. "I know. Something like this . . ." His voice caught.

Rie sensed he meant to say they might never have this time together again, this timeless time. She longed to tell him they *would* meet again, she would make sure of it, but she did not know if they ever could. They rose and dressed quickly.

"We never spoke of Yamaguchi," Rie said.

They both laughed and held hands.

Rie walked to the door, Saburo behind her. They embraced, then Rie pulled away. She reached for the shoji, and Saburo touched her face.

As Rie moved to leave, Saburo took from a pouch tied to his waist a small tortoiseshell hair ornament and handed it to Rie. "This belonged to my mother. I would like you to have it to remember me."

Rie took it and held it closely. "I need nothing to remember you by. But I shall cherish this always." She kissed him, and reached into her simple obi for a small ivory netsuke which she handed to Saburo. "This was in my grandfather's collection." She had kept it on her always as a cherished memento of her grandfather. "Please keep it with you."

Saburo smiled and put it in an inner pocket. "I will wear it close to my heart so it will never forget its song."

They clung to each other, then Rie broke away.

"Please be careful, Rie. Shall I find you a ricksha?"

"There's no need." She pulled the shawl

over her face. "One should be waiting." She peered out the gate. "I see one at the corner." She turned, embraced Saburo, and stepped out quickly. She glanced back, and saw Saburo watching. Then with immense sorrow, she stepped up into the ricksha to return to her life, to the Omura House.

CHAPTER 12

Rie alighted from the ricksha beyond the house, so as not to awaken the family, and walked as quietly as possible on her wooden geta. She noticed the first hint of dawn above the kura rooftops as she went to the gate.

"O-Natsu," she said softly.

The gate opened and O-Natsu looked at Rie inquisitively.

Rie smiled. That was all O-Natsu was getting out of her. "Is my husband here?"

"No, and I have laid out your futon."

"Thank you, O-Natsu, I'll take a brief rest."

Rie removed her geta and crept upstairs. She discarded the peon's clothes, lay down, and remembered every moment of her rendezvous with Saburo. Then she slept more peacefully than she had in years.

Not long after, she awoke and knew by the birdsong in the garden that the day had already begun. She wished she could remain at leisure to savor her memories, but it was not possible. Yoshi would miss his lessons, and Kin and her father would notice if she did not stop in the inner office to learn the day's plan.

Why was it, she wondered, that society prohibited what she felt in her inner being was right and expected only what her instinct told her was not right? She arose, dressed quickly, and went downstairs to attend to her obligations, her responsibilities, her many duties. During every spare moment, though, she would allow herself to remember. Her private life was hers to keep. She walked into the garden and sat on her favorite rock, stealing a few precious moments to silently thank the gods.

Over the next few days Rie realized something she had never known was possible: her body, her physical being, felt happy, satisfied. She relished the sensation and cherished the memories of a night she knew would remain in her heart as long as she lived. She smiled inwardly every time she thought of Saburo, and she thought of him now each morning when she arose, each night as she retired.

A few weeks later Rie felt the familiar lack of hunger, the slight nausea that had signaled her first pregnancy. O-Natsu agreed that she was indeed pregnant. Rie recalled her failure to produce an heir and prayed that this time she would bear a child, Saburo Kato's child, for it was surely his. Then she realized that this meant she would also once more have to endure the indignity of sleeping with Jihei. This would require some effort and endurance on her part, since Jihei was so seldom home at night. Normally she was relieved at his absence, but this time his presence was required. Rie resented not being able to simply revel in her secret, instead having to plan something so distasteful. She could not discuss so intimate a matter even with O-Natsu, who perhaps might have guessed, and certainly not with Sunao, who would be shocked and also disapproving of her departure from propriety. She puzzled over the problem for several days, knowing that the time to act was limited. The sense of urgency informed her days as she hurried through her normal tasks. Fortunately she was able to eat enough so that her father did not notice anything amiss. Her mother might have taken note.

Two days later, in the afternoon, when Rie was in the kitchen talking to O-Yuki, a maid who worked under O-Natsu, shouting

153

erupted from the area of the storeroom.

"Kaji! Kaji! Fire! Fire!"

Smoke billowed along the corridor toward the inner office and main rooms of the house. Her father, Kin, Jihei, O-Natsu, everyone seemed to be running in all directions. Rie covered her face with her sleeve. Through the smoke she glimpsed O-Natsu and several clerks scurrying through the corridor carrying buckets of water.

"O-Natsu!" she shouted. "Where's the fire?"

"The storeroom and number one kura," O-Natsu gasped.

Rie ran into the courtyard and grabbed a bucket from one of the maids. In the compound a line of clerks pushed hoses along toward the kura. Kin and Kinnosuke were working buckets at the well. Her father, Jihei, and Toji were directing the work, all shouting at once.

Rie looked up in horror as orange tongues licked above the number one kura and storeroom, dangerously close to the inner office. Kin ran back to move ledgers to the outer office, and Rie ran after him to help. Black smoke belching from the brewery billowed over the neighborhood, and neighbors came running to join the sweating, smoke-blackened firefighters. Rie's coughing mixed with sobs as she saw flames leap from the storeroom toward the inner office. She and Kin worked frantically to move all the records to safety.

The smoke and flames drew the city's two competing guilds of firefighters, who converged on the scene simultaneously with their carts and clanging bells. Bannermen from each guild slammed their ladders against the kura wall and clambered to the roof. The man who reached the rooftop first held his banner high with a shout of triumph signaling his men to go into action against the flames.

For the rest of the day the men battled the raging furnace until flames began to subside, to spit and hiss.

Rie ran to the kitchen. "O-Natsu, quickly. We need to prepare food for the men, at least forty of them." O-Natsu, O-Yuki, and two other maids rapidly chopped vegetables, prepared miso and rice, then brought out the best pickles and barrels of White Tiger.

The exhausted, blackened men sat in groups in the still standing number three kura, eating the hastily prepared meal and drinking sake.

Rie watched her father go around the groups of men and thank them for saving the brewery. Would it be his last official act as head of the house, she wondered? She felt a deep sadness overtake her.

All that remained of the number one kura, storeroom, and inner office were charred, hissing coals and ash. Men coughed under the acrid smoke that draped a shroud over the buildings and still rose in the darkened sky.

Spent and speechless, Rie put a hand on her father's arm. She didn't know how she had the strength to fight the tears that threatened.

"We're all exhausted, Ri-chan," he said, returning the pressure of her hand. "We'll talk tomorrow about what we need to do. Now we all need sleep."

Rie caught Yoshitaro in the hall chattering excitedly with the nursery maid, describing the spectacle. This was his future — *their* future — and so much had been destroyed.

Ashes smoldered through the night. Later, as she lay on her futon, unable to sleep, she knew it would be days, weeks, before the smell of smoke left the house. The damage was something they would be paying for for months, more than a year. And how had the fire started?

Fire was a serious hazard. Everyone knew that arson was punishable by death. At night fire watchers walked the streets of the town clacking their wooden sticks together to warn people to be careful, to put out stoves and lamps before they slept. Rie had enjoyed the hollow sound of wood striking wood as she prepared for the night at the hour of the boar. But the sound that meant all was well in the neighborhood would now take on a terrifying meaning for her and everyone in the house.

No one could have started the fire deliberately. The cause would have to be unearthed. Large barrels filled with water were kept atop the kura roofs, a precaution Rie's grandfather had introduced, one generally employed only by temples. Rie tried to put these thoughts from her mind as she tossed on her futon. She touched her abdomen, remembering how precious it had become. Then she saw Jihei enter the room and nestle into his futon, one of the rare times he had stayed home.

This was her chance. She moved closer to Jihei, for once not redolent of sake, but of smoke. She touched his futon, opened it, and murmured, "Anata, wasn't it terrible? How will we ever recover?" She could never address him by his proper name, instead using the word all wives used for their husbands: Anata. Jihei murmured indistinctly, then reached for her, touched her where Saburo had touched her not that long ago. She closed her eyes and imagined herself again in the house of O-Natsu's relatives, with the man who would always remain her lover. When it was over, she felt sick and dirty. She pushed his heavy sleeping form off her, then quickly washed and returned to her own futon, where she willed away all memory of Jihei's repulsive touch. *Saburo,* she thought before finally drifting to sleep, hand on her belly.

The next morning Kinzaemon, Kin, Kinnosuke, Jihei, Rie, Toji, and three junior clerks assembled in the outer office, which reeked so heavily of smoke that it was impossible not to cough. Rie had never seen her father look so despondent, so frail, as he sought to reassure them in a faltering voice.

"The fire has been a catastrophe. We have been fortunate that in nine generations this is the first fire at White Tiger. Thank you all for your efforts in putting it out." He paused to brush the hair back from his forehead. "We are fortunate that the other two kura are still standing. We can produce part of this year's quota in those two." He sighed and glanced around at the faces of the others. "We will begin rebuilding the office, the storeroom, and number one kura starting tomorrow. This is a financial blow, a big one. But if we were a smaller operation we would be totally destroyed. Now we need to ascertain the cause."

Kinzaemon paused and looked around the room again. No one spoke.

"Fortunately Kin and Rie moved our records of nine generations, our ledgers, to the outer office. Otherwise we would have lost it all." He glanced at Rie, and she felt a glow of pleasure at her father's recognition.

Kinzaemon sighed, looked down, then seemed to straighten. "What remains is the tradition and honor of the house, the reputation of White Tiger for excellence. This we have not lost."

Rie felt tears beginning as she heard her father speak of the honor, the reputation, of White Tiger. She looked around the circle of men whose fates were so intimately connected, caught a certain squaring of the shoulders, a firming of the jaw as each responded to her father's words. She felt a surge of energy and hoped she herself would one day be able to inspire the men as her father did.

"Father, I wonder if the water barrels on the roofs were full," she asked sharply.

All eyes turned to Toji, the brewmaster in charge of everything relating to the kuras.

Rie looked at the face that had always reminded her of one of the country entertainers who walked in troupes from village to village during the summer. His eyebrows formed a perfect triangle with his eyes, lending his face an expression that made Rie feel he was about to tell a joke. But there was no mirth in the room this morning.

Toji bowed low, his fists clenched in his lap.

"I learned this morning that one of our kurabito vanished during the night. It was Norio, one of the younger men. We don't know if it had any connection with the fire." Toji bowed after each sentence.

"Very strange," said Kin.

"Yes, most suspicious," Jihei agreed, pulling at his eyebrows.

Kinzaemon nodded. "In any case, we'll have the construction people here tomorrow to make bids on the rebuilding. We need to start with the inner office and storage area, and of course the kurabito quarters above. They can't sleep in the kura many more nights."

Rie rose to go to Yoshi and to give instructions to the maids about removing bedding and clothing from all the cupboards so that things could air. As she opened the shoji to leave, the worker in charge of the koji room bowed and entered the office.

He faced Kinzaemon, bowing again. "They have just found Norio's body at the bottom of a cliff at Mount Rokko. He apparently killed himself in the night, jumped off the cliff. One of the kurabito says Norio was smoking one of those Nagasaki pipes in their room. It must have caught the tatami on fire. That's why the storeroom burned first." He bowed to Kinzaemon and Toji.

Toji knelt and bowed to the floor in front of Kinzaemon. "I have no words to apologize adequately," he said, and bowed again three times, his eyes squeezed tight against his tears.

"It seems he chose his own punishment," said Kinzaemon. "He knew what would have befallen him when he was found."

"He left a wife and three children in Tamba," said Toji.

Kinzaemon turned to Kin. "Send his widow money each year on the anniversary of his death, starting today."

Kin nodded.

Amazed by her father's compassion and sense of tradition, Rie sighed and looked at his ashen, ravaged face.

CHAPTER 13

The construction on the storeroom and number one kura went ahead as scheduled, with the work on the inner office a bit behind. Meanwhile, they used the outer office for all the administrative work of the brewery. One morning, soon after the fire, the office shoji rattled open and Toji entered abruptly, bowing to Kinzaemon, Kin, and Jihei.

"Sorry to interrupt. He paused to catch his breath. Hiroki, one of the kurabito, says that just before the fire broke out he saw someone from the Yamaguchi brewery lurking behind the number one kura. He called out, but the man disappeared. He didn't think much about it at the time, but now he thinks Yamaguchi may have been behind the fire, not Norio." He bowed repeatedly and looked from Kinzaemon to Kin.

Kinzaemon frowned. "Unspeakable! Then Norio's suicide . . . but he thought he was responsible. And Yamaguchi was behind it. Norio's death must be avenged. Yamaguchi must be punished." He put his elbows on the table and held his head with both hands.

Kin bowed. "We won't forget it, Master."

Kinzaemon raised his head and looked at Toji, then at Kin. "I'll talk to Hiroki, and Kin, you talk to Norio's widow when you go to Tamba. Let her know . . . no, perhaps it would be better not to distress her further with the knowledge that his death was unnecessary." He sighed.

Rie could see her father declining as the reconstruction proceeded. The fire, which in earlier years he might have taken in stride, exacted a toll from which he could not readily recover. Rie saw in his face signs of a fatigue that was as much spiritual as physical. She knew the fire had amplified the bereavement he felt over losing Hana not long ago. His resilience eroded, his normally optimistic view of life dimmed. It saddened Rie to see, and it increased her determination to bring down Yamaguchi, the cause of so much destruction.

Not long after the fire, Rie decided it was time to announce that she was pregnant. She told her father that this time she felt the child would be born safely. She hoped this would lighten his mood.

"Rie, that's wonderful," her father said as she sat with him. Jihei was not present, but Rie had already told him. Jihei, of course, thought the child was his and showed as much pleasure as he ever did at anything in the house. "*Ah,* is that so?" Jihei had said when she told him. "That will be good for the house." For once Rie did not see him pulling at his eyebrows. "I'll be glad to have a second child, maybe another son," he added. Rie smiled, but not because of Jihei's pleasure.

"I've chosen the name Fumi, Father, as I feel it will be a girl. And I want a name that portends intelligence, a connection with letters. I would be surprised if she is not an intelligent child."

Kinzaemon beamed, and Rie was pleased to see his depression lift. She brought her hand to her swelling belly and thought of Saburo. How she wished she could share the news with him.

Rie left her father to look through the cupboards in her bedroom for the baby clothing her mother had prepared during her former pregnancy. She also found the clothing she knew her mother had kept for Toichi. These items she wrapped and put away. She did not want the tragic association of Toichi's clothes to affect Fumi. Rie anticipated motherhood in a way she had not thought possible. She took time away from the management of the brewery but did not worry about the lack of attention. The baby she sensed would in some way help the house as much as the work she did in the brewery. She launched into the preparations for Fumi's birth with the same zeal and energy she devoted to other aspects of the family enterprise. She knew Fumi and her future husband would never succeed to the main line, but somehow, some day, Fumi would play a role, of this she was certain. Thinking of her mother, Rie began to sense for the first time her own place in the eternal cycle of death balanced by the birth of new life.

When the day approached, the day she had awaited for nine long months, Rie called for O-Natsu. Rie had been forced to curtail her busy schedule and had to spend more time resting. But she was glad to do so. She did not want to risk losing this baby.

"O-Natsu, please go for the midwife. I know the baby is on her way. Please hurry!"

O-Natsu rushed down the stairs and sent O-Yuki to be with Rie until the midwife arrived.

The midwife was the most experienced in

the neighborhood and arrived with all her birthing materials. She examined Rie carefully.

"Yes, the baby is coming. Take deep breaths. Don't worry. This is a normal birth," she proclaimed. She issued directions to O-Natsu, who was helping.

Rie was glad that Jihei was not there that morning to say to her: "*Yamato damashii.* Don't cry out," as he was likely to do. The midwife had told her this is what some men said as their wives were giving birth. Without him there, she felt free to groan and cry as the baby made her way into the world.

Rie heard the words she wanted to hear. "It's a girl, so the house will prosper," the midwife pronounced. Rie smiled in spite of her discomfort and reached for the baby when the midwife had cleaned her. It was a blessing that the baby was a girl, since there would be little possibility that she would resemble Saburo so closely as to arouse suspicion.

"Fumi," Rie whispered, and put her arms around her baby.

For the next days and months Rie was totally engrossed in her new role, completely happy, more than happy at the secret of Fumi's birth. O-Natsu was the only other person in the house who guessed. Rie did not call Masa, the wet nurse, but fed Fumi herself.

Rie spent less time on the business of the brewery, but after two months she began to take part of each day to attend to matters in the office and new storeroom. When she was away from Fumi, Rie made certain that O-Natsu was in charge of her.

The kurabito quarters above the storeroom had been rebuilt, and Rie had to see to re-supplying clothing and other necessities for the kurabito. This remained her responsibility in addition to caring for Fumi and for attending to Yoshi's lessons. Rie found her days more than full and also satisfying. She was fulfilling her role and responsibility to the house in all respects.

Rie was pleased to see her father showing affection for his new grandchild, as much as he had shown toward Yoshitaro, even though Fumi would have no place in the main house. In the evening after dinner he often held Fumi on his lap. Even Yoshi was curious about the new baby and wanted to hold her. He had tried once to lift her. This Rie forbade as it raised painful memories of her own lapse with Toichi. Rie became a most watchful mother.

Several months later, as Rie held Fumi after dinner and sat with her father,

O-Natsu's voice came from beyond the shoji.

"Excuse me, may I come in?"

"Of course," Kinzaemon replied.

O-Natsu entered slowly, reluctantly, it seemed to Rie. She looked up. "Yes, O-Natsu?"

"Well, I was in the market this morning," she began, then paused, looking first at Rie, then at Kinzaemon.

Rie smiled to hide her uneasiness. "Gossiping again?"

"I was talking to one of the maids who knows people at the Kitaya. She says the geisha O-Yumi has had a child, a girl. They believe she is your husband's child."

Rie gasped. "What! What does he think he's doing, spawning children all over town?" She hugged Fumi closely.

"I believe the problem is that he's not thinking," Kinzaemon replied, pulling at his ear.

"What shall we do, Father? Try to ignore it? Or give my husband a stern talk? Perhaps it should come from you." Rie put a hand over her mouth, aghast at this latest outrage by Jihei.

Rie handed Fumi to her father, touched the column as she passed, and went out to the garden, to her rock, her refuge.

She put her hands on her face and swayed back and forth for several minutes. Just when she was so happy with Fumi, her own special child, whose father was the most important man in her life, Jihei had to destroy her sense of well-being, her chance for happiness. What could she do? How could she recover from yet another assault?

CHAPTER 14

Rie awoke the next morning still angry about this new woman, O-Yumi's child by Jihei, wondering as she had most of the night what action, if any, the house should take about this other child. As she went about her work during the day she kept thinking, pondering. There must be a way to turn this disaster around, to find some way out of this new cloud that had blown into their lives. In the evening she was glad that Jihei was not present because she had an idea.

"Father," Rie began, and paused. She took a deep breath. "You know that Jihei has had another child by a geisha. I've been thinking all day about what we should do."

"Yes, Rie, so have I." Kinzaemon ran a hand through his bushy hair and over his face. "I haven't decided yet what we should do about this disgrace, if anything. Of course the child is not really our responsibility, though if Jihei's philandering becomes public, then it will affect our reputation, inevitably."

"I'm wondering, Father," Rie said as she patted Fumi on her lap, "what if we took in this child as we have Yoshi, though of course she wouldn't inherit or be heir. Couldn't we raise her as our own, then send her out, marry her into another brewing family? That way we'd be expanding our connections, our enterprise."

"*Hmm.*" Kinzaemon took a sip of sake, then closed his eyes for a moment. "That's an interesting idea, Rie, one I haven't really heard of before among brewing houses, though perhaps it happens without becoming.public." He folded his hands on the table in front of him and frowned.

"Well, in fact, Father, if Jihei spawns another child or two we could bring more than one into the house. Just think of the *dozokudan* we could create!" The dynasty her father had always dreamed of began to take shape in her imagination. "It's rather exciting, don't you think?" Rie sat straight, inspired by her own idea. "Of course it would mean more work for me, for the maids, for all of us. But if it expands our enterprise, then we would be able to hire more help. Besides, it would be a better life for the children than in the water world." Rie relished the idea of being able to redeem herself in her father's eyes, to fulfill some of her duty to the house, to enlarge the White Tiger enterprise.

"Let me think about it tonight, Rie." He looked at Rie and reached for Fumi, who went to her grandfather whenever she saw him. She reached for his eyebrows, fascinated. "Sometimes I think you'll be as good a brewer as anyone in the whole district," Kinzaemon said, smiling.

Rie bowed, unable to conceal her pleasure at her father's compliment. She stood and held out her hands. "I'll take Fumi to bed with me, Father. It's her bedtime. Sleep well." She smiled and glanced at her father as he sat motionless, his hands still folded on the table.

The next morning Rie went to the breakfast table early to speak with her father before Jihei arrived from nightly activities.

"Good morning, Father." She handed Fumi to O-Natsu for feeding in the kitchen.

"And what do you think of my suggestion of last evening? I know you have given it some careful consideration." She picked up a bowl of miso soup and sipped.

"Yes, I have, Ri-chan." Her father did not often use this term of affection. "And I like the idea. Yes, let's see if the child is healthy, normal, then we can take her in. I doubt the geisha will object." Kinzaemon continued eating his rice and plum pickle.

"So shall we ask my husband about the baby's health when he arrives?"

"I'll do that, Rie. You won't have to. Then if the infant appears normal, I'll ask him to make arrangements to adopt her, just as he did with Yoshi."

"He may wonder at our motivation. We don't have to explain it to him, do we, Father?" Rie looked at him expectantly.

"There's no need," her father replied.

Rie would enjoy this small pleasure, not explaining to Jihei, keeping him off balance a little.

One afternoon, a few months later, as Rie was caring for Fumi and Yoshi, O-Natsu came into the children's room.

"Look, O-Natsu," Rie said. "Don't they play well together?" Rie was no longer so worried about Yoshi picking up Fumi, but she still warned him always to be careful of his little sister.

"Yes," O-Natsu agreed. "It's good to see." She paused and bowed, her hands crossed formally in front of her.

Rie looked up. "Is something on your mind, O-Natsu?"

O-Natsu bowed again before speaking. "It seems, I was told in the market, that another geisha is pregnant by your husband, O-Toki. She believes it will be another girl." O-Natsu pursed her lips and nearly closed her eyes, so close to tears. She had not heard of Rie's plans for bringing more children into the house and what it might portend. And as much as it angered Rie to know, she would not let his infidelities consume her.

Rie exhaled loudly. *"Huh!"* She paused and turned to Yoshi.

"Yoshi, will you go to Kinnosuke in the office and ask if he has any errands for you?"

Yoshi left the room, eager to go about his favorite activity, helping Kinnosuke.

"I didn't want Yoshi to hear the details. But my husband will give the house a bad reputation in the water world at this rate." She paused. "Don't worry, O-Natsu, my father and I have a plan to deal with this situation, a plan that will help the house in the long run."

Rie stepped into the office and asked her father to join her at the Butsudan, the place where the most intimate details of the family were often discussed, before the ancestors. She followed her father to the main room, noting that he had become more stooped than she had realized. She placed a zabuton in front of the altar for her father and joined him.

Rie bowed slightly toward the Butsudan, then to her father. "Father, O-Natsu has just told me that O-Toki, Yoshi's mother, is also due to have a daughter by my husband. Now there will be two girls that we might bring into the house. I think perhaps we should do so as soon as possible, to avoid news of this scandalous behavior being spread widely around town." She looked at her father inquisitively.

"All right, Rie. I'll speak to Jihei this afternoon and have him go to both places and make arrangements to bring them here as soon as the babies are ready. Yes, his behavior is quite outrageous." He ran his hand over his face.

"And perhaps he will be embarrassed enough to remain at home this evening. I would like to speak to him as well, maybe before you do. Yes, would you wait until tomorrow morning, please?" Rie wanted to embarrass Jihei, if it were in fact possible.

"I have never heard of such behavior in another brewing house. I feel shame," her father said.

She prayed her father wouldn't fall into melancholy as he was apt to since Toichi's death, then his wife's. "We'll turn this disaster into an advantage for the house, Father. I feel certain of it."

That evening Jihei did in fact retire at home for a change. When he entered the bedroom Rie was still up, seated before her mirror, arranging her long luxuriant hair.

Rie spoke as Jihei was lying on his futon, hands behind his head. "I hear that you have fathered two more children with geishas, at the Sawaraya and Kitaya," she said, turning slightly to look at him.

Jihei's face flushed beyond the effects of the sake. He turned so that his back was toward Rie, his face hidden from the glimmer of the lamps. "That is true, yes," he mumbled.

"We want to adopt them," Rie stated firmly. She looked at his reflection in her mirror.

"We . . . we do?" he stammered and turned toward her.

Rie enjoyed Jihei's consternation. She glanced in the mirror again. She wanted to make him wonder. It was a small pleasure she allowed herself in their unsatisfactory relationship.

"Father and I think it would be wise to have three or more children, in case anything should happen to Yoshitaro." Rie continued combing her hair.

"What could happen?" he stuttered. "There's no question about his succession, is there?"

"No question now. It's settled with him. But I've noticed that he isn't the most robust child, haven't you? We never know, no matter how careful we are about a child's health." She stopped, thinking suddenly of Toichi. She had not wanted to bring up her own painful memory just at this point. She only wanted Jihei to worry about Yoshi, though there was no threat to his health. She also wanted to make him wonder about the motive for adopting his two illegitimate daughters.

"So, I believe Father wants you to go to meet the two geishas, to ascertain if the babies are perfectly healthy and normal, then to arrange for their adoption, as you did with Yoshi."

Jihei sat up, frowned, and rested his head in his hands. "I'm not sure that they will want to give up their daughters." He rubbed his face.

"You will persuade them, then. They will realize that their lives will be far better than if they were raised in an okiya. And of course they will be compensated, and their daughters well cared for here."

Jihei groaned and lay back on his futon.

Rie smiled and slept well, thinking of the future expansion of the Omura House. Her father's dream.

CHAPTER 15

The memory of the night Masami became her lover O-Toki would cherish always in some secret recesses of her heart. Only O-Haru of the Sawaraya would know, she who could so well divine anyone's deepest emotion. Masami had asked for O-Toki at the Sawaraya twice before that night, and she had served sake and played the *samisen* for him and his two friends. As she filled the three small cups she took in the features that set Masami apart from his friends: the finely chiseled chin, the skin that seemed almost luminous, the wavy hair, and the compelling black eyes that seemed to penetrate her inner being.

The fabric of her life was woven of men, so many that she thought she was immune to them, until Masami. And the irony was that she should feel this passion for Masami, a man without the worldly position and wealth of the Omuras. Masami was a cooper's son, an honest enough profession, but one that could never aspire to the status of a large brewer. After his first two visits, O-Toki found herself waiting for his next visit as breathlessly as a sixteen-year-old for her first lover. When he appeared alone, and asked for her again, the force of O-Toki's passion surprised even herself.

The next day and the days following, O-Toki found herself anticipating Masami's next visit, regretting that he was not free to come more often. For Jihei she felt only the sense of obligation toward a principal patron. When she became pregnant again, O-Toki knew the child was Masami's, not Jihei's.

It was O-Haru who first noticed the physical changes. She and O-Toki had become friends, something difficult at O-Toki's okiya, where competition so often precluded friendship. O-Toki sat with O-Haru one morning as they manicured their nails. It was a time for confidences.

"Let me see your eyes," O-Haru said.

"Why?" O-Toki asked, looking up at O-Haru.

"Yes," O-Haru began, "I can always tell when a woman is pregnant by looking at her eyes, even before the other signs. You are pregnant, O-Toki. I'm certain."

To O-Toki's dismay, O-Haru was right, as always. As the weeks passed and it became more difficult to conceal her condition, O-Toki had to make a decision . . . two decisions. She spoke with O-Haru again.

"What about Masami? Have you told him you are expecting?" O-Haru asked.

O-Toki stroked her stomach, sadness enveloping her. "He knows I am pregnant and that the child is his. He thinks he is my only patron. But he is in no position to recognize the baby," she said, trying to hide the bitterness she felt. "He is about to be married and won't have much to inherit. He isn't the first son. So he won't be concerned with the child's welfare. He knows I can support her. I say 'her' because I feel the baby will be a girl."

"So you plan to keep the child?"

"I have no plans for an abortion. But no, I won't raise her," she said sadly.

O-Haru raised her eyebrows. "Why not?"

"I let my son go to the Omura House because he'll inherit a powerful house. A boy born here in the water world has such meager prospects." She paused to arrange her hair, and cringed as she glanced at her mirror. What would happen when her beauty faded? Where would she go, she wondered with a sigh? At least her children would be cared for. "Now there's also a reason to give up my daughter, though it pains me more than I can say. Two reasons, or maybe three. I don't want her to grow up here, to do what I do. I want Jihei to adopt her. And as an Omura daughter she'll have a good life and a chance for a respectable marriage. And a third reason: it will give me great satisfaction to tell Jihei she is his child when I know she is really Masami's." O-Toki smiled and pulled her comb through her high coiffure.

O-Haru nodded. "Ah, O-Toki, I've always known you were clever. It's the only kind of power we really have, isn't it, the ability to dissemble? And if I've learned anything working in the water world all my life, it's that nothing is what it seems. There's what we see on the surface but something else beneath it, something quite different, which may possibly be the truth." O-Haru paused and glanced at O-Toki. "But will the Omuras want a geisha's daughter when they already have an heir?"

"What Jihei tells me makes me think his wife and her father are willing. They have recognized a girl from another house, the Kitaya I believe. Jihei has been busy here in the quarter, it seems."

O-Haru pursed her lips and frowned.

"That's strange, isn't it? Not that he frequents more than one house, but that the Omuras want to recognize the daughter of a geisha. A son I can understand, since the house had no children of its own. But the daughter of a geisha stays with her mother. And doesn't Jihei also have a daughter? Daughters are useful to us in old age. The patron gives something toward raising her but does not recognize her. *Hmm.* It's an unusual situation, something I haven't encountered before." O-Haru smoothed her hair slowly.

"In any case, I won't need to discuss the baby's future with Jihei until after she is born."

One evening Jihei went on his errand to the Kitaya to see O-Yumi. She was a woman taller and more mature in years and figure than O-Toki. She also seemed genuinely fond of Jihei. He wondered. *Perhaps the fact that she is getting on in years, starting to lose her youthful bloom, makes her so attentive, almost anxious.* Of course, geishas were all attentive, Jihei knew, but with O-Yumi her devotion seemed to surpass the simple training they all received in serving a man's moods and needs, especially in the case of a patron. Still, it was becoming difficult financially to be the patron of two women, since Rie was keeping such close track of finances now, but Kin gave him a small sum on the side each month, the secret "navel savings" fund that did not enter the ledgers. After all, it was expected that a man of substance would have a woman other than his wife. And Kin was pleased to have Yoshitaro in the house. He knew the importance of maintaining the continuity of house head for White Tiger, and he was after all a man himself.

As soon as Jihei arrived at the Kitaya, O-Yumi hurried to the entrance and greeted him enthusiastically.

"Oh, Master, welcome. I'm so happy to see you."

She led him to the room they regarded as their own. The house was not as lavish as the Sawaraya, but Jihei felt the atmosphere was warmer, less commercial and imposing. And more intimate, as soon became apparent when O-Yumi helped him to undress and put on a house yukata, preparing him for a bath.

"I'll join you in a few minutes," she promised.

The bath was a small private one, not generally intended for guests. Jihei enjoyed the intimacy and inhaled the fragrance of citron left from New Year's that gave the steamy room a lemony aroma. As he waited he mused. *I married according to my parents' wishes and produced an heir for the Omura House. Now I've earned this. A man needs something for himself. But how do I persuade O-Yumi to give up Kazu?*

When O-Yumi joined Jihei she disrobed, washed, rinsed, and stepped into the bath. She embraced him without hesitation. He decided to speak before he lost his nerve.

"How is Ka-chan today?" he asked, releasing O-Yumi's arms from around his neck and looking into her face.

O-Yumi laughed. "She is growing fatter every day, such a joy. I'm so glad I decided against an abortion."

"So am I," Jihei said, pausing. "Actually, the Omura House would like to adopt her." He pursed his lips and frowned, aware that O-Yumi would protest.

"No! I can't give up my daughter! She is mine. She will comfort and support me in my old age. No geisha wants to give up a daughter. I can't." She began to sob.

"But O-Yumi, you won't really be giving her up, you know. You will be able to come to special events . . . her marriage, to watch. And you know she will have a good life and good prospects for marriage being brought

185

up as an Omura daughter. We will care for her well." He refrained from saying "better than you could."

"What will happen to me when I can no longer work, without her to help?" She was biting her nails in distress.

He put his arms around O-Yumi and tried to comfort her as she continued to sob. "You need never worry. I will always make certain you are cared for. Please, O-Yumi. You know we will do our best for her."

O-Yumi put her hands to her face. *"Uh . . . huh . . ."*

"All right, then, I'll come for her tomorrow. Don't worry, please. We will take care of you, *both* of you."

As Jihei left the Kitaya, O-Yumi followed him to the door, her face red from crying. She bowed but said nothing.

CHAPTER 16

The day after Jihei's visit to O-Yumi, he was sent on an errand to the Kitaya with O-Natsu to help as they had done when Yoshitaro was brought home. The difference was of course that Kazu would not become head of the house. Rie knew the sum Kinzaemon instructed Jihei to give O-Yumi was not as large as what was given to O-Toki for Yoshi. At the same time, Kinzaemon told Rie that taking the daughter of a geisha also meant a continuing financial obligation to the geisha. Rie was not happy about the financial arrangements, though she welcomed the daughter for her future value to the house. She knew that when Jihei frequented geishas it was a financial loss to the house, and this she found hard to accept. She felt it was a difficult balance.

Both Yoshi and Fumi were curious about the new baby in the house. They spent time in the children's room talking to her, petting her, kissing her. Rie was pleased to see them playing well together. Yoshi had begun trying to teach words to Fumi, even to teach her to write kana. Rie could see Yoshi becoming an asset even as a young boy. Perhaps he would become a far better house head than Jihei one day. Anyone would.

It was time for the end of brewing season celebration, one of the big events of the year, a grand affair to which well over a hundred guests were invited: heads of major brewing houses, coopers, suppliers, officials, and shogunal commissioners. No expense was spared in the preparations. The maids spent days cleaning, and the kurabito made preparations to serve the highest quality of the year's cellar. A large leaf ball was hung out at the entrance of the brewery, next to the White Tiger *noren* banner to announce to customers that the first sake of the season was ready. It was the one occasion when several geishas were called to serve the guests. Rie sat with her father and Jihei as they planned the event. "Oh, by the way," her father commented, "I hear that the Katos are marrying off their third son. They announced his engagement at the last meeting of the Brewers Association."

Rie froze, stopped looking through the guest list. She felt a knife had slashed through her heart. She could not expect him to remain alone forever, and his family would not allow it, at any rate. Still, her heart seemed to have shriveled at the news, and she hadn't slept well since. She would not want to see his wedding. It would be too painful to watch. Jihei could represent the family and she would make an excuse. For once, she had no desire to see her beloved.

"Which geishas should we call this year?" Kinzaemon asked as he went over the long lists of guests.

"How about calling someone from the okiya that serve the Kitaya and Sawaraya this time?" Rie asked, grateful to think about something other than Saburo.

Jihei looked up, startled and embarrassed. She knew he wanted to ask why they should mention these two establishments, the ones he frequented, but he couldn't without loss of face.

"A good idea, Rie," her father replied. "We can ask the madam in charge of each to furnish two or three names."

Rie smiled and Jihei pulled at his eyebrows.

Unlike weddings and funerals, this was a celebration to which only men were invited, generally heads of houses. Rie was disappointed that Saburo Kato would not be included, as he was third son. Except for Fumi, the light of her life, she often felt lonely and wished she could experience just one more sweet moment like the one she and Saburo had shared when Fumi was conceived. Now, with the impending marriage, she truly knew what it meant to "kill the self," she realized, as she forced her attention to the upcoming celebration.

On the day selected, the shoji were removed to create a huge main room. Several rows of lacquer tables were arrayed in the room, one small table for each guest. On each table were sake cups and small plates containing choice morsels of beans and dried fish to accompany the tasting of the best brew.

The guests arrived in a flurry of festivity as finely groomed geishas flitted through the rows with flasks of sake, kneeling to pour for each guest. Since there were no women invited, it was necessary for geishas to serve the guests. Rie was not able to appear openly, but peered into the room without being seen herself. She thought she could pick out O-Yumi, whom she knew was Kazu's mother, but O-Toki she could not pick out.

Kinzaemon gave the welcoming speech,

urging the guests to enjoy the year's cellar. The event lasted three or four hours, and by the time the last guests had departed, everyone in the house was exhausted. Kin had taken care of financial arrangements for the geishas, and everyone else had performed their proper duties for the occasion.

When it was over, Rie came into the room to hear her father's assessment of the event.

"I think it went well," Kinzaemon said. "Even Yamaguchi behaved." It had been impossible to avoid inviting the president of the Brewers Association, though Rie had hoped they could omit him from the list for this event.

"I heard quite a few favorable comments about the taste of the brew this year," Jihei said. "And I heard a few people wondering about our recipe, which of course we don't share."

Kinzaemon smiled and nodded.

"I wish I could have been in the room," Rie said, hiding the longing from her voice. But as in everything to do with the brewery, she knew this was an all-male custom that would not change.

Six months later O-Toki gave birth to a baby girl she named Teru. During the later months of O-Toki's pregnancy she had not been at the Sawaraya, and it had been some time since Jihei had seen her. He was sent on the same mission that had taken him to O-Yumi and for the same purpose, since this was Rie's plan now. Jihei did not relish this visit, especially after bringing Kazu into the house. For him the visit was a disappointment, without the bath and sensual gratification he expected with O-Toki, a slight, he felt certain. When he mentioned Teru, O-Toki asked, "Would you like to see her?" As O-Toki poured sake for Jihei he noticed an undercurrent of tension. He longed for nothing more than to rise and leave, but how could he refuse to see the baby, his own child?

A maid brought in the infant and handed her to O-Toki. She held her out toward Jihei, who took one of the baby's tiny hands in his but did not offer to hold her. Only a girl, after all.

"I think she has your forehead and eyes, don't you?" O-Toki said pointedly, as she kissed the baby. "I have named her Teru."

"It's hard to tell who they look like when they're so small," Jihei said.

The baby cried, and O-Toki opened her kimono to feed her.

"You probably want to raise her yourself," Jihei began, awkwardly.

"It's usual with a girl, isn't it?" O-Toki

replied, innocently enough. Still, he thought he caught a gleam in her eye that made him uneasy. "She will be a comfort to me in my old age. She will care for me when I'm too old to work."

"You know you need not worry about your old age, O-Toki. That is my responsibility, as I've told you before." Certain that O-Toki wanted to keep the baby, Jihei wondered how to broach the official reason for his visit.

"Actually, the Omura House would like to adopt her, to have a sister for Yoshitaro."

O-Toki rocked the baby before speaking, her jaw tight. She clutched Teru to her. "Why do you need my daughter, our daughter? Don't you have enough children? Won't Yoshi succeed you?"

Jihei gazed at the sake cup in his hand. "It's true that the succession is settled. But you know, for a large house one or two children don't always guarantee security of succession. What if something should happen to Yoshi? My father feels that we need more children. I understand how you feel about Teru." He glanced at the baby. "It may be hard to give her up, but she will have a good life with us, a good marriage. I realize it will be a different life from what she would have with you." He reached over and touched O-Toki on the arm. "So will it be all right then if I come for Teru in a month's time?"

"If you are going to insist, what can I say?" O-Toki kissed the baby, then looked directly into Jihei's eyes, a rare challenge. Then she dropped her chin abruptly, as was fitting. "But you must promise me regular reports, and I would like to be able to see her."

"You will surely be able to see her marriage, and perhaps see her on other occasions as well."

O-Toki smiled at him through tears glistening in her eyes. Then she hugged Teru closely and whispered a farewell.

Jihei felt relieved as he said good-bye and left for home. He still did not understand why it was necessary to bring in another girl.

CHAPTER 17

For the next two years, Rie and Jihei called
an uneasy truce. One evening, when Kinzaemon had retired early and the children
were all in bed, Rie and Jihei sat at the dining table together, something that seldom
happened. Rie was pouring sake for Jihei,
thinking instead of Saburo Kato and his
new wife. Their marriage had sent her into
a spiraling depression that had lasted days,
but Fumi, their love child, had soon pulled
her out of it. The marriage had only tightened her bond with her child, whom she
loved with a fierceness she'd never thought
possible, even more so since it was her one
link to Saburo, a reminder of the love they
had shared. Whenever she looked at her precious Fumi she was reminded of her love
for Saburo. She knew her feeling for Fumi
outweighed what she felt for any of the
other children, but she should take care not
to make her preference too obvious. It

would not be fair to the others, who had not chosen their parents.

Jihei disrupted her musing. "Why don't you drink some of our sake? How can you make decisions about White Tiger when you refuse to enjoy it? Are you unable to drink our own product?"

"No, of course not. Yes, I can drink." Annoyed at his challenge, she held out her cup, and Jihei filled it. She drank the cup down and held it out again.

"Good." Jihei smiled. "That's more like it. You'll soon become a judge of our cellar, the grades of our brew."

Rie held out her cup again. How presumptous of Jihei to assume he was a better judge of White Tiger sake. She lost count after a few cups, unaccustomed as she was to drinking more than a single cup of three sips. It was not really expected of a woman, unless she worked in the water world.

At length Jihei held up a flask and said, "One more? A nightcap?"

Rie felt dizzy. "Oh . . . maybe not," she managed to say. She rose to stand, but stumbled against the table for support.

Jihei smiled. "I'll help you upstairs." He took her arm and assisted her as they wove unsteadily toward the stairs and made their way up, one labored step at a time.

Rie fumbled for a futon and collapsed on it, unable to dress for bed.

Jihei disrobed and moved over Rie without hesitation. "No!" Rie moaned, struggling to prevent him from going further, but Jihei persisted. She had not slept with him since it was necessary after becoming pregnant with Fumi, and she was not at her normal strength. "No!" she grunted again. Feeling angry and violated, she panted and pushed but then collapsed under his weight as he spread her kimono and her legs roughly apart. As she flailed against him, he thrust himself on her, into her, moving vigorously until he abruptly slackened, and lay inert.

Rie was unable to move, not fully aware what had happened, and unable to go downstairs for her ablution ritual. She slept fitfully.

When she awoke in the morning she found herself still in her work kimono, her clothing disarrayed and her body feeling soiled, unclean. She remembered little of the previous night. Then she felt her clothing and realized what had happened. She sat up and rubbed her aching head. Jihei was not in the room. For a few minutes she sat breathing rapidly in anger. Jihei had found a way to exact revenge for her bringing the children into the house. Furious, she got up, dressed, and walked down the stairs toward the bath, not speaking to any of the maids. She went into the bathroom and washed vigorously with the tepid water left from the previous night's baths, trying to remove the disgusting evidence of Jihei's violation.

She went into breakfast alone, wishing there were some way she could erase what had happened from her thoughts, her body.

O-Natsu came in with miso soup and rice. "Are you all right?"

"Yes, O-Natsu." Rie had no desire for conversation. "Please see that the children are doing their lessons."

O-Natsu bowed and left the room, guessing Rie's mood.

Rie drank more than her usual two cups of tea, trying to heal the pain in her head. When she finished, she walked down the corridor to the door to the courtyard, put on geta, and went to the empty barrels. She picked up a bucket, filled it at the well, set it down, and reached for a brush. She scrubbed at a barrel with all her strength, her anger adding to her energy, until she finally put down the brush and sighed, wiping tears from her eyes. How many times in one lifetime must one kill the self?

O-Natsu, concerned about Rie, had gone

along the corridor to the door to the courtyard and stood there watching. O-Yuki came up behind her and looked out.

"You can tell how angry she is when she goes out to scrub the barrels, especially if she's not talking," O-Natsu said.

"I wonder why she's so angry?" O-Yuki asked.

"Who knows? Maybe we'll find out later, maybe we won't. Just watch and wait." They walked back to the kitchen and their day's chores.

By afternoon Rie had recovered enough to go to the nursery, where she found O-Natsu and O-Yuki playing with the three girls. Rie entered and joined them on the tatami. O-Yuki was tossing a red ball to the three children in turn. She was younger than O-Natsu, hardly more than a child herself, and was especially fond of playing with them.

O-Natsu and O-Yuki nodded and bowed as Rie sat down.

"The house has become a lively nursery." O-Natsu laughed, hoping to improve Rie's mood.

Rie caught hold of Fumi, stopping her irrepressible motion, and held her. "Even at this age you can tell how bright Fumi is, can't you?" Rie smiled at Fumi's obsidian eyes, so reminiscent of Saburo's. Fumi helped to erase memories of the painful night. And of Saburo's marriage.

"Well, I have to admit, she does seem more precocious than Kazu or Teru," O-Natsu said. "But I try to treat them all alike."

"I want to give Fumi special training," Rie remarked when she knew Kazu and Teru would not understand.

"Of course all the girls will marry into brewing families, won't they?" O-Natsu asked. "But I guess it's far too early to ask."

"Yes, Kazu and Teru will go as brides to brewing families, but . . ." Rie took out a tortoiseshell comb from her hair, paused, and replaced it.

"How about Fumi?" O-Yuki asked.

"Let's wait and see about her," Rie responded, still arranging her hair with one hand, the other holding Fumi.

O-Natsu leaned forward, both hands on the tatami. "Won't she marry a brewer too?"

"Oh, yes. I have an idea, but we need to wait. It's too early to talk about it." Rie put Fumi down, rose, and left the room.

When she was out of earshot, O-Yuki turned to O-Natsu. "I never know what she's thinking," she said.

"I don't either," O-Natsu admitted. "But

you can be sure she's planning something. Always."

Several evenings later Rie, carrying Fumi on her back, paused outside the shoji to her father's room.

"Father, may I come in?"

"Yes, Rie, please do. I'm sitting here alone."

Was there a slightly different, almost purposeful, note in her father's hoarse voice?

"Have you had your sake yet, Father?" Rie asked and put Fumi down. Rie sat opposite her father. She felt his attitude toward her soften, especially at this hour of the evening.

Her father cleared his throat. "Yes, I still have some here. Will you join me?"

"Just one sip, to keep you company." She held the three-sip cup out, and her father filled it. Rie smiled as Fumi walked toward her grandfather with her arms out, and he reached and took her on his lap.

"Father, I have an idea . . . for the house." She refrained from using the term *business,* though of course they were connected, identical.

"What now, Ri-chan?"

"Well, I know it's way too soon to speak of this, but you've noticed, haven't you, how bright Fumi is? Brighter than Yoshi, really."

"She is your child. Of course she's bright."

He looked at Rie inquisitively.

Rie felt warmed, embraced by her father's affection. "When she's old enough to marry, I want her to have a mukoyoshi, a very good one. I want to set her and her husband up as a *bunke* rather than have her marry out as a bride to another family."

Kinzaemon ran his hands through his hair twice. Rie noticed that though still thick, his hair had gone completely silver since her mother died. *I wish I could talk to you about Mother,* she thought, Hana's sweet face coming to mind.

"Oh? And then?"

"Well," Rie said carefully, "in a bunke, her child could come back to the main house either as heir or his bride, depending on Yoshitaro's eldest child. It would be an ideal combination for the house, Father, don't you think?"

"Thinking so far ahead, Ri-chan. And Yoshi is not a stupid child." He pulled at his ear.

"I know, and I'm glad he enjoys the work, even at his age. But I think with a child of Fumi's . . . a daughter. . . . And of course I'd want to find the best person in Kobe as her husband." Rie took out her comb and turned it over in her hands.

"It would cause a few raised eyebrows,

wouldn't it, if you adopted a husband for her when we already have an heir?"

She reinserted her comb. "Raised eyebrows are not my main concern, Father."

"I'm aware of that, Rie. It's only that we need to consider the opinions and feelings of others in Kobe if we are to do business with them successfully. You know what they always say about the peg that sticks up. It gets pounded down. But it's possible what you suggest may work to our advantage. Let's wait a few years though, quite a few years." He chuckled. "Of course we need to plan in business. And I can see that you are a planner." He smiled, his eyes wrinkling to slits.

Rie reached for her father's hand and gave a gentle squeeze. Sometimes she felt that her father did understand her. Fumi squirmed back to Rie and began to cry.

"She's tired, aren't you?" Rie said, picking her up and kissing her. "I'll take her to bed. Sleep well, Father." *I love you,* she added silently as she carried her daughter to her room.

One morning several weeks later, Rie arose with a sinking feeling. She recognized the signs: the lack of appetite, the slight nausea, and missing a month already. She put her hands to her face, aghast. She knew she was pregnant again, with Jihei's child, the child of the agonizing night when she had drunk so much sake and Jihei had violated her. She would have to bear a child of Jihei's, bring his blood into the family again. This was no happy occasion. She sat alone, tears streaming down her face.

CHAPTER 18

Eighteen thirty-seven was an eventful year in the Omura household. Rie had her second child, a son whom she named Seisaburo. A son to be sure, but he evoked mixed feelings in Rie, feelings she could not share with her father. He was of Jihei's seed, not Saburo's. For her, Jihei's shadow loomed over the child. Rie was relieved to see none of Jihei's features visible on Seisaburo's face. For that she was most grateful. But she felt none of the sense of fulfillment she had felt with Fumi's birth. Her chief regret remained that Fumi had not been firstborn, before O-Toki's son, or that her initial pregnancy had failed. Seisaburo, already a year old, showed early signs of being precocious, Rie had to admit. Yoshi was now nine, Fumi was already six, Kazu five, and Teru four. The girls were having their lessons separately from Yoshitaro.

Yoshitaro's succession, though not imminent, still rankled, a festering sore that would never heal. Her father was of course pleased to have a grandson born of Rie. Even Jihei was pleased. Kinzaemon spent a great deal of time with his grandchildren, and in turn they provided him comfort in his old age. Although he was affectionate with all of them, Rie sometimes thought she saw her father display a special feeling toward her own children.

One afternoon Rie sat with her father after lunch. Jihei and several of the children were present as well.

"He seems a fine, healthy boy, Rie," her father said, holding Seisaburo.

Teru grabbed the baby's blanket and tried to kiss him. "Let me see!" she cried and took the infant's hand.

"Be careful of your baby brother," Rie cautioned.

"Second son," Jihei said. "No question about Yoshi's succession."

Defensive, wasn't he? She had noticed how possessive Jihei was about Yoshi and his position in the house.

"A brewing house can't have too many children," said Kinzaemon. "They will all help the house, help our enterprise."

"They're all capable children," said Rie. "And look at Fumi. She learns so fast."

She smiled at her beautiful daughter.

"So does Yoshi. Always helping Kinno," Jihei rejoined.

"I know Kin is pleased at how well Yoshi is advancing," Kinzaemon said. "And speaking of Kin, I heard him say something about retiring too, soon after me. He'd like to hand over the main responsibility to Kinno. Our operation is growing so fast."

Rie glanced at her father, a sense of sudden loss overcoming her. "Our old customers will surely miss you, Father. You've worked with many of them nearly forty years, and Grandfather worked with their parents."

"Oh, our connections with some of our suppliers and customers go back several generations, many more than two." Kinzaemon nodded and picked up his teacup.

Jihei's face reddened. "I've had ten years to get to know them. I think they're used to dealing with me. And Kinno can do many of the transactions Kin does now."

Rie looked at the baby. "Yes, I've watched Kinno work, not only carrying out orders, but taking charge in an emergency, when something goes wrong. We're lucky to have him to succeed Kin. He's good with customers, and he has a sense of timing too."

"We Nada brewers have always been the

best business people. They say some of those small brewers in the north make the finest sake, but they don't know how to sell beyond their local districts," Kinzaemon said.

"Small brewers always say they're more interested in quality than quantity," Jihei said. "That was my family's philosophy. They don't really want to expand. They think it would affect quality." He pouted.

Rie frowned. "There's nothing wrong with our quality. We produce both quality and quantity. Toji is always experimenting, making improvements." She glared at Jihei.

Kinzaemon nodded slowly. "We have to balance tradition with trying to improve. Sometimes that means doing something new, making some alteration in our production, or trying for an expanded sales route."

"And timing, Father," said Rie. "We have to constantly watch our competition. We can't relax our attention, especially with Yamaguchi. He's so sly."

"Some day White Tiger will be number one, yes Rie?"

Rie nodded, determined to fulfill her father's dream.

"Well, I'm happy you have a son, Rie. We'll leave you. Jihei and I need to get back to the office."

After the men left, Rie pondered. She no longer worried that Jihei spent less time at home in the evening. The problem was the effect of his profligate ways on the reputation of the house. She had noticed that his face was becoming bloated and flushed as its normal state, and that he smelled of sake even during the day. She knew just what to do.

That evening she was alone with her father after dinner. The perfect time for discussion. She turned to him. "I'm afraid Jihei's drinking is becoming a problem, Father. I haven't said anything to him about it. But the smell never leaves him, and his face is becoming so red and bloated." She held her hands over the hibachi.

"Yes, I've noticed, Rie. It's a concern, especially with my retirement coming soon. But so long as he does his work I don't know what we can say. I've seen this happen often in heirs to family businesses. I think it's the family pressures that make them drink. I'll try to speak to him, think of a way to broach the issue."

"It can't be good for his health either." Rie frowned. "Let's hope Yoshi doesn't follow his example. I hope he takes after you instead." She let the words linger in the air for a moment, then glanced at her father.

She knew he understood.

Kinzaemon mumbled as he shuffled toward the office the next morning. He opened the shoji and saw Jihei sitting at one end of the office alone. Kinno's voice could be heard talking to customers in the outer office.

"*Ah, Jihei.*" Kinzaemon settled himself at the table opposite his son-in-law.

"How are you this morning, Father?"

"Well, I have a concern." He placed both hands on the table. "A difficult matter."

Jihei pushed a cup of tea across the table and looked at Kinzaemon, who straightened his collar before speaking.

"I have noticed, Jihei, that of late you have been drinking more than usual." He paused.

Jihei began pulling at his eyebrows and looked down.

"I'm afraid it's being noticed by others, our business associates. When this happens it can endanger our reputation, our business. And our house."

"Oh, I don't drink more than any other brewer. A man needs some relaxation in this work. I'm here in the office all day, ask Kinno. And surely I have provided enough children for the house." He glanced at Kinzaemon, then looked down at his hands.

"It's not lack of heirs that concerns me.

But Yoshi is only nine and it will be several years before he can succeed. In the meantime you will represent the Omura House and White Tiger to the world. And frankly, I've been delaying retirement because I see what's happening to you."

Jihei's eyebrows drew together in a deep frown. He was breathing heavily and struggled to speak.

Kinzaemon paused.

"I was selected for this position, and I have done my best for White Tiger. I have worked hard." His face was a moue.

Kinzaemon's expression was intent. "I know you spend nearly every evening at the Sawaraya. I urge you to curb your drinking. You have let it get out of hand. You owe it to the house." Kinzaemon looked at Jihei, then placed his hands on the table and pushed to his feet. "Don't forget your obligation," he said as he turned and left.

Jihei put his hands to his face, resting his elbows on the table. *Huh!* Obligation, obligation! This was all he'd heard ever since he had married into this family. Being a mukoyoshi was something no one could envy, no matter how wealthy and important his adoptive house. It was suffocating, this network of relationships and obligations that entwined around him, an intricate spider's web. There was no escape, no relief, other than the Sawaraya or Kitaya, a geisha's understanding ways. Of course he needed his sake in the evening. He shook his head and his mouth pulled down at the corners. Kinzaemon was imagining something that was not there. Probably Rie had told him to speak to Jihei. She had never tried to understand him. He would get back at her somehow.

CHAPTER 19

Kinzaemon's retirement in the spring of 1841 was a major event in Kobe brewing circles. For forty years he had shepherded White Tiger through the precarious cycles of the brewing business. He was highly esteemed by all members of the Brewers Association. There was hardly a brewer for whom he had not done some personal favor over the course of the years. That a formal ceremony should mark his retirement and the passing of the mantle to Jihei as Kinzaemon X seemed only fitting. White Tiger was among the largest breweries in all Japan; the status and prestige that accompanied brewing in even the smallest hamlet was many times magnified in a brewery the size of White Tiger.

The ceremony was held in the spring. Kinzaemon insisted that no brewer be slighted, and this meant a long list. Extra help was hired for the occasion. Shoji partitions were removed to make a grand, enormous room. Unfortunately, as the younger son, Saburo would not be among the participants. Rie's heart saddened at the thought. Over the years, she had often thought of contacting him, telling him about Fumi, but the risk was too great, so she had grieved in silence, mourning his loss as she had her mother and Toichi before her.

On the day of the ceremony Rie opened the wooden shutters and looked out at the garden. Early morning dew shimmering on the azaleas reminded her that it was spring and that the brewing was finished. As she gazed out she felt a sense of melancholy, a sadness that it was her father's final day as Kinzaemon IX.

The activity began immediately. Everyone put on a formal kimono, lacquer tables were set in rows, and O-Yuki chased children and attempted to keep them clean and out from underfoot. Food was served with the best brew. Yoshitaro and Jihei sat on either side of Kinzaemon, Rie next to Jihei. Kin, Kinnosuke, Toji, the kurabito and clerks, all were included, with guests from breweries, officials, and customers. Seating in relation to Kinzaemon was according to status.

Lengthy formal speeches were made, as with a wedding or funeral. Kinzaemon spoke first. He bowed and cleared his throat.

"Forty years have passed since I succeeded to headship of the Omura House. During all those years you have granted us the favor of your support and cooperation. For that we are eternally grateful."

Rie detected a hoarseness as her father struggled to keep his emotions under tight control. He asked for the continued patronage of customers and suppliers during the headship of Jihei, now Kinzaemon X. Finally, he prayed for the benison of the gods on the house. As Rie listened, her affection and admiration for her father congealed in a lump in her throat. When he finished he was greeted on all sides by raised cups and shouts of "Banzai!"

Rie felt apprehensive as Jihei rose to speak next. She knew he could never equal her father in business or as a man, even in a speech.

"I am eternally grateful for being chosen to the headship of the Omura House. I will do my best to continue the leadership and long tradition of this house in the production of fine sake." Perspiration glistened on his face as he continued. "I will always strive to ensure that the next generation continues the venerable traditions of White Tiger."

His words were beginning to slur. Rie

wished he would stop. Had he been drinking before this important occasion?

Before finishing he asked for the continued efforts of Toji and the kurabito in maintaining the White Tiger quality, and of Kin and the clerks in selling to Edo and elsewhere. When he stopped, cries of "Banzai" and the raising of cups followed. Rie detected less enthusiasm than for her father's words.

Kin spoke next, of his service of forty years, during which the house had survived fire, shipwreck, and other crises. He mentioned his own retirement, but promised to visit the office when Kinnosuke took over. Rie noticed Kinnosuke looking down modestly.

Toji spoke last, his honest, simple face the picture of loyalty and dedication. Rie felt as moved by Toji's words as by her father's. The skill of Toji and his workers from Tamba was in the last analysis what ensured the quality of White Tiger. He vowed to do his best to maintain its excellence. Rie was thankful she was keeping her eyes downcast, for she could feel tears beginning. Her gratitude for Toji's loyalty was mingled with a sense of poignancy that her father had reached this advanced life passage. She recalled clearly her father's words to her as a child, that one day the future of the house would rest on her shoulders. Now the enormous responsibility did. But with Jihei holding the reins of the house, she knew it would be harder than ever to ensure the house's success.

The next day Jihei poked his head through the kitchen door, where Rie was instructing the cooks on the day's meals. "Rie, Father wants you in the office," he said.

"I'll be right there." The meal plans completed, she hurried to the office, where her father, Kin, Jihei, and Toji were assembled. Each held a tasting cup.

"It's one of the finest sakes I've ever tasted," said Kin. He held the cup to his nose, twirled it twice, took a sip, and spat into the spittoon. "There's something special about this Yamaguchi sake from Nishinomiya. Here, compare it with this from the main brewery in Nada."

Rie held out a cup. "Let me try it."

Toji poured from a small barrel. Rie inhaled the aroma, sipped the Nishinomiya sake, then tried the Nada brew again.

"How could the two be so different?" Rie asked.

"I don't think they changed the recipe," said Toji.

"It has to be one of three things," Kinzaemon said. "The water, the yeast, or the

mold. One of the three is definitely different."

Kinnosuke entered the room, and Kin
gave him samples of the two sakes. Kinno
nodded and looked at Kin and Toji.

"The difference is obvious," Kinzaemon
said. He looked at Kinno. "Go to the Yamaguchi main office. Buy more of each. And
see if you can learn why they're different.
You know some of the clerks there."

Kinnosuke nodded. "Yes, I've been dealing with them these last few years, but you
know they guard their secrets, we all do.
Well, I do know one of the girls working
there. Maybe I can learn something from
her. She may tell me, if she knows."

"Don't delay, Kinno. But do your inquir-
ing discretely," Rie warned.

He bowed as he left. "I'll be back as soon
as possible."

Speculation continued in the office as Rie
excused herself and went to attend to the
children's lessons. In the afternoon her
curiosity about the Nishiomiya sake brought
her back to the office, where Kin and her
father were still pondering the problem. She
was about to leave for the kitchen when
Kinnosuke's voice came from the outer office.

"I bought more sake," he said, "and I got

some information from Nobu. We talked where no one could hear us."

Rie rested her fan under her chin and studied Kinno's face. She thought she detected a special sense of longing when he spoke of Nobu. Well, he was of an age to marry, and it might do well to have access to what was going on at Yamaguchi's.

"Listen!" Kinno could hardly contain his excitement. "She says their toji discovered a new well near their Nishinomiya kura. They used the water from that well for brewing this year. That's why it tastes different from their Nada sake." He straightened, bowed, and grinned.

"Amazing!" said Kinzaemon. "Let's call Toji." One of the clerks ran out of the office.

"We need to get some of that water immediately to try a test batch, even though it's late in the season," Kin said.

Toji entered the office, bowed, and looked at Kinzaemon, then at Kin.

"Taste this, Toji-san." Kinzaemon held out a cup. "Kinno says Yamaguchi found a well near their Nishinomiya kura and used this water for the brew. If we got some of the water could we do a test run this late?"

"We could try a small test and use ice to

keep it cold when the weather turns too warm."

"Are they selling the water?" Rie asked.

Jihei scratched his head. "Selling it?"

"Maybe I can get a sample," Kinnosuke said.

Rie tapped her fan against her shoulder. "I wonder if we need a test when we know it's the water that makes the difference. Maybe we should focus on getting access to the well so we can use it for next year's brewing. Then maybe we could sell some to other brewers."

Jihei looked puzzled. "If it's so good, why would Yamaguchi sell any? And what would other brewers think if we started selling Yamaguchi's water?"

"They'd think we're getting ahead," Rie retorted. Did her husband know *anything*?

Her father smiled, and Kin and Kinnosuke chuckled.

Jihei glowered. "How could we accomplish that? Why would Yamaguchi sell, to us especially?"

"Offer a good price," Rie replied, "and do it right away before any other brewer thinks of it." She paused and straightened. "No! Just a minute. We can't go to Yamaguchi directly, you're right. Send Jihei's cousin Yunoki, or his chief clerk. The family has a heavy obligation to us. They can't refuse. And Yamaguchi won't remember their connection to us. We'll pay for getting access to the well and for purchase. They aren't likely to refuse. They're in financial need. I hear one of their clerks took a lot of cash and vanished." She smiled and hooked both thumbs in her obi. "It's a question of timing."

"This would be a bold move, wouldn't it?" Jihei protested.

Rie sighed and looked at her father, then at Kin.

"We'll be first, I'm certain," Kin said. "That will give us a big advantage. We need to find out who makes decisions there now, with Yamaguchi aging. It may be their chief clerk, Yusuke. I've known him for years."

Rie's voice rose. "Try for a big purchase. If necessary we could mix some of the water with our own well water, do some testing." She took out her comb and fingered it.

"We need to find out the water table of the well too," Toji said.

Rie wished she could go to the Yunoki brewery herself. She sighed. "Kin-san, can you go early tomorrow and talk with Yunoki? Take Jihei with you. Have Yunoki offer Yamaguchi a big loan and then try to negotiate a purchase and access. What do you say, Father?" She ignored Jihei.

Kinzaemon ran his hands through his hair. "Yes, Rie, we should go tomorrow."

"Aren't we moving too fast?" Jihei protested again.

Rie sighed again, louder this time. "Not to move tomorrow would be too slow. We'd lose our advantage."

Kin nodded.

Jihei glared at her. Rie reserved her satisfied smile for herself.

Over the next few months the reputation of the Nishinomiya well, which became known as "Shrine Water," spread among brewers of Kobe and beyond. At a meeting of the Brewers Association, brewer Ikeda said, "This Shrine Water is amazing. Just the right quality of minerals for top grade sake. And you know, Yunoki moved right away and got access to the spring. I hear they're selling the water."

"Damned aggressive!" growled old Yamaguchi. "I don't know why Yusuke allowed it, and I don't know how that small a brewery got the funds. I wish he had consulted with me first."

"Quite a coup," Kin said to Rie later. "It's good you insisted that we move when we did. The demand for Shrine Water is growing; the price has soared."

"I've never done anything that gave me this much satisfaction," Rie said, cradling her elbows and smiling at Kin and her father.

Jihei just glowered at Rie, who had ignored whatever he said, dismissed him. Now Rie worried that he would try to get back at her. But how, that was the question.

CHAPTER 20

"Can you believe it, Father?" Rie asked as she sat with her elderly parent later that evening, her thoughts turning to family. "Yoshi is thirteen, Fumi is ten, Kazu and Teru eight and nine. Even Sei is nearly six. They're growing so fast. I suppose the next time I notice, they'll be old enough to marry." She nodded at her father, and noticed that his silver hair had thinned and the lines had deepened around his eyes.

"It means we're aging just as fast, Ri-chan. It's over ten years since Mother died. Nothing in life ever remains the same. Everything keeps changing." He set the book he'd had in his hand down.

"Yes, it seems so. I'm glad we were able to act as go-betweens for Kinno and Nobu. It's a good connection for us. We can keep better track of Yamaguchi now with Nobu here as Kinno's wife. And I'm glad I was able to find a house for them nearby. So

224

convenient for him."

"You know, Yoshi went to his first Brewers Association the other night with Jihei. Yoshi tells me that the brewers were talking about you and Kinno as an unbeatable combination, almost like watching Kabuki." Her father chuckled. "Selling Shrine Water took them all by surprise when they realized we were behind it." He chuckled again.

"Yes." Rie smiled. She couldn't be more delighted. "It has worked out well."

She put her hand on the calendar. "It's New Year's next Sunday, Father. I think I'll take the children to the temple after breakfast. It can't hurt to have people see the girls looking their best. It will help when it comes time to arrange their marriages if other families have seen them growing up. And they'll enjoy the outing, whether or not my husband goes with us." She just prayed she didn't run into Saburo and his wife for fear of her reaction, seeing them together for the first time. But she knew she would have to face them eventually. Her joy at seeing Saburo's face would outweigh her heartache at seeing him with his wife. She hoped so, anyway.

Fortunately, New Year's was the busiest time of year in any household and kept her in motion so that she didn't have time to

225

think. Not only was it necessary to clear all debts from the year just ending, but gifts had to be prepared for regular customers and suppliers. The house was given a thorough cleaning, decorations of pine and bamboo were placed at the main entrance, and ceremonial lacquerware cups and trays were unpacked and cleaned. Toji brewed a traditional sweet sake to serve callers, but work in the brewery halted for five days so that the kurabito could return home for the holiday.

Three days before the holiday the children gathered around the large stone mortar and pestle near the well as Kin and Jihei pounded the rice into *mochi*. Kin held the hammer-shaped pestle high while Jihei quickly thrust his hand into a water bucket then back into the glutinous rice and water mass before Kin slammed the pestle down on the mortar again. Mochi pounding was a ritual Rie had loved to watch, even as a child. She felt mesmerized by the rhythmic thudding as Kin wielded the pestle. Mochi pounding reminded Rie that it was time to take stock of White Tiger's progress over the preceding year. Her musing was interrupted by Yoshi's voice and she turned to watch the two.

"Let me try," he begged his father.

Jihei stopped and looked at him. "You'll have to be really fast, Yoshi. Move your hands quickly after you turn."

"I will." When Yoshi stepped up to the mortar, Kin slowed his strokes. Yoshi struggled to keep pace until Rie noticed that he was tiring. Jihei soon replaced him. That he was stronger than a thirteen-year-old was the only accomplishment Rie could think of since marrying him.

For several days the kitchen maids worked, preparing the festive foods that would be served New Year's morning and also shared with visitors who came to pay their respects that day and the three days following. Long noodles symbolizing longevity were cooked for the New Year's Eve meal, and even Jihei remained at home with the family that night.

In the morning Rie wished her father felicitations and saw the pride on the faces of the boys as they stood for inspection in their black kimono wraps and brightly colored obis. They sat behind her as she lit incense and poured New Year's sake before her mother's name tablet at the altar already decorated with piles of mochi cakes, tangerines, and bamboo stalks. Then the children were allowed to open their gifts, brightly colored kites for the boys and for the girls a complete set of formal dolls for Girls' Day.

New Year's breakfast was the most elaborate meal of the year: soup with mochi and beautifully arranged morsels of fish cake, pickles, and vegetables in artfully cut shapes and colors, served in small exquisite dishes on individual lacquer tables.

"We're all going to the temple this morning, to pay our respects," Rie said while they were finishing breakfast. "You know this is our family temple, where our family grave is located." She patted Sei's shoulder. "You may come this year, Sei, and bring your paddles."

The children's holiday spirits were contagious, and even Jihei seemed agreeable. "Yes, I'll go with you," he said to Rie, "but I need to be back early to help Father greet the callers."

Rie and the girls walked slightly behind Jihei and the boys as the family strolled like peacocks in their finery through the pine tree–lined temple walkways. She bowed and smiled at neighbors and was careful to speak to brewers as they passed.

Her worries about meeting Saburo and his wife soon faded as she saw brewer after brewer and none was Saburo. She had thought that perhaps she would avoid him after all when suddenly she recognized Saburo Kato and his wife coming toward her. She started, her heart pounding. *Saburo, my own heart!* She should have been the one beside him. They had not been able to arrange a meeting since the night they spent together, the most important of Rie's life. Memories of that precious time crowded in as she attempted to keep her emotions in check and to greet the couple formally.

"Happy New Year," she said, smiling and bowing, her heart breaking. "So wonderful to see your family." She saw three sons, one a striking replica of his father, and a lump formed in her throat. Saburo was still as handsome as he was then, even distinguished now with graying temples, a reminder that they were approaching middle age.

"You're looking well, Mrs. Omura," he said.

How she had missed him. She wanted to embrace him, not walk formally past, but she merely smiled and said, "The boys are helping with brewing already."

"Is that so?" Mrs. Kato bowed. "Already? And your girls are so pretty."

Wasn't it annoying that Mrs. Kato was glancing at Teru, not Fumi? Well, maybe the Katos would consider Teru as a bride for one of their sons. Perhaps even Kazu for another son. Of course for Fumi it was out of the question, something Fumi would never know.

As they walked past, Rie glanced quickly back, and caught Saburo doing the same. Rie felt tantalized, drawn to him as always, but knew a tryst such as the one they had shared was unlikely to happen again, especially now that he was also married. Besides, her family and business responsibilities were now so heavy. She did not have even the smallest chance at the liberty she had taken then.

She let herself steal one last look at him.

At the temple entrance Rie pushed away her thoughts of Saburo, clapped her hands to attract the notice of the gods, then stood silently and offered a prayer for the welfare of the house and brewery. She dropped coins into the offertory box and lit an incense stick. The girls begged for amulets being sold by the priests, and Rie bought three.

When they returned home Rie found her father still greeting callers, visitors below her father in age and status. Each guest was offered a cup or two of ceremonial sake and a package of mochi to take home. Rie thought her father was looking especially tired after the long day, his face haggard and gray. His younger brother had come with his wife, son-in-law, and daughter Sunao, Rie's friend. They chatted and exchanged family news.

Rie glanced at her father. "He looks so exhausted, Sunao. I'm worried about him." She rested her hand on Sunao's arm and frowned at her father's ashen face.

"He does look older than last year," Sunao agreed.

"He stays in his room a lot now, but he especially wanted to come out today and greet people. But uncle is looking well, and you always look so fashionable." Rie scrutinized her cousin's glowing complexion and flawless kimono and obi.

"Yes, Father is what, seven years younger? He still works hard," Sunao said.

"The children could all have played together."

"Yes, maybe next year." Sunao glanced around the room at the children.

"Who does Teru look like?" Sunao asked.

"I'm not sure," Rie answered, her face flushing beneath her cousin's scrutiny. "You know she and Kazu came from distant relatives on Mother's side. They're from the country, both of them." Rie was relieved she could come up with a plausible explanation in a hurry. "I'm sorry we don't have a chance to get together more often," she said as she bade good-bye to Sunao and her parents. "I wish you could come by sometimes. We could go to the flower show next year."

Rie turned back to the room where guests continued to call and mingle in the room around Kinzaemon and Jihei. Maids scurried in still bearing carafes and sweets. Sei began to cry and throw himself on the floor.

"Fumi, would you please take Sei to bed?" Rie said. "And Yoshi, you can go and play cards with the girls now."

Rie saw that the noise and confusion were fatiguing her father. He sat stooped and suddenly silent. Rie and Jihei sat with each set of guests who came to offer greetings until the last visitor departed and darkness was whispering into the room.

Rie hurried over to her father, who was slumped over his tray.

"Father, are you all right?" She put her hand on his shoulder.

"Oh," he murmured feebly and looked up at Rie.

Jihei quickly joined Rie and put his arms around Kinzaemon's shoulders. "Can you get up, Father?"

"Are you in pain?" Rie's voice rose.

Kinzaemon struggled to move his legs as

if to rise. "Rie . . . no," he gasped for breath. "There's . . . something I must . . . tell you." He moved forward slightly, then slumped over on the tatami.

"Father!" Rie gasped and reached for his wrist and pulse. His arm went limp.

"No!" Rie put her hands to her head and rocked back and forth. "No!"

Jihei cradled Kinzaemon's head on his lap and looked at Rie, disbelief on his face.

Rie had spent the day thinking of her children and had neglected her father, the most important person in the world. Now he was dead.

After the initial shock of her father's death Rie felt bereft, totally abandoned. She mourned for days and weeks following the funeral, a ceremony attended by every brewer in the city. The morning after the funeral she sat at the Butsudan weeping, offering sake and rice before the tablet newly inscribed with her father's posthumous name. For nearly eleven years following her mother's death he had been her solace, her support in every major crisis. Now she had just Jihei and the children. She felt utterly alone. There seemed no way to assuage her grief. She alternated between numbness and sorrow. For days she wandered through the garden and rooms of the house that seemed colder now than ever, often ending up in her father's room, as if she half expected to find him there.

One evening, the hour after dinner when she had so often enjoyed her father's companionship, she opened his cupboard and took out his kimonos, piling them on the tatami. She picked up one of the finest formal kimonos, held it to her face and inhaled the camphor aroma mingled with the slightly woodsy scent she associated with her father. Tears ran down her cheeks and she let them fall freely. No, she would give none of the kimonos to Jihei. He did not deserve anything her father had worn. One or two could go to Yoshi, and some to Sei when he was old enough.

O-Natsu became more attentive to Rie than usual and now seemed to Rie the only individual who really understood her. Rie drew closer to Fumi too, a sensitive child nearly eleven, and the bond between them strengthened. As the darkest days of Rie's mourning passed, she again turned to the office for comfort. Working with Kinnosuke began to provide a semblance of normalcy. Kin retired soon after her father died, and she sorely missed his wisdom and experience in the double loss.

Before Kin left he told her what her father wanted to tell her before he died: how proud he was of her, and that he wanted to give her the family seal. Kin handed Rie the seal Kinzaemon had entrusted to him the night before he died, asking that he give it to Rie with his special blessing.

Rie took the seal with both hands, held it to her head, then her heart, and inserted it in her obi. Two tears coursed down her face as she did so.

Rie felt a catch in her throat, an emotion that rendered her nearly speechless. Her father, for whom she had worked so long, had recognized, after all, what she had done. She stuttered. "Thank you for telling me, Kin-san. Thank you." She bowed low.

Jihei showed signs of taking his responsibilities more seriously, but he continued his heavy drinking. While he worked in the office, it was to Kinnosuke and Kin, on his occasional visits, that Rie turned when a serious problem demanded attention. Yoshi as a young teenager became a real presence in the office, now formally ranked as apprentice, although it was understood that he would succeed Jihei. Her father's death made it palpably clear to Rie that the future of the Omura enterprise rested with Kinnosuke and Yoshitaro. And herself.

Chapter 21

After the chance meeting with Saburo and his wife, and the death of her beloved father, Rie poured herself into the business as never before. For the next five years, everything seemed to be going well. Then one day Rie saw Kinnosuke come running past her into the office, his gown flapping and fluttering in the breeze. She quickly followed him.

"Toji is worried about the sake," Kinnosuke said to Yoshitaro and Rie, frowning. "He's been sampling it."

"He's on his way here now," said Yoshitaro in a voice breaking lower.

Toji rushed into the office and knelt on the tatami. He bowed abjectly.

"The sake has gone bad! It's terrible! I've tried three barrels. They're all the same." His head remained bowed.

"No!" Rie cried. "It's not possible!"

"I have no words to apologize adequately," he said, bowing to Rie.

"Let's go and see," said Kinno. He and Yoshi followed Toji briskly out of the room and along the corridor toward the number one kura. Rie followed and stood beyond the door to the kura. She shifted impatiently from one foot to the other as she waited for the men to emerge.

"What a calamity," she said half to herself, half to Yoshi who stood with her. "What will we do? Yoshi, go and ask them to bring samples from all three kura to the office."

He nodded and disappeared through the kura door. Rie walked back to the office and sat at the work table. Minutes later the men reappeared with several flasks. Kinno and Toji were shaking their heads.

"Well?" Rie asked, her heart pounding.

The men put the flasks and cups on the table. Each man poured from the separate flasks, swirled the sake in their mouths briefly and spat into spittoons. All three were frowning.

Jihei stumbled into the room and looked at the three.

"What's wrong?" he asked.

"Taste this," said Kinno.

Jihei picked up a cup. "Awful!" he said with a grimace and spat.

"Let me taste," said Rie. She sipped and spat samples from each flask. "A disaster," she said, frowning.

"This is the first time this has happened in all the years I've been here," Toji said.

"It happened to Kato many years ago, others too. If one or two barrels from one kura are bad, chances are the whole cellar is ruined."

"We have to recognize it's a total loss," Kinno said. He slumped.

"We'll have to discard it all," Toji agreed.

"All of it? All three kura? Nothing to be done?" Jihei picked at his eyebrows.

"How did it happen?" Rie asked, tapping her fan on the table. "We've never had this kind of thing happen before. I've always been so careful to wash the barrels and trained the girls to do likewise. I wonder if I could have missed something? But I keep a close watch."

"Now, don't blame yourself," said Kinno. "You just never know when this is going to hit a brewery. Who knows why? It's happened to many others. Hardly anyone has escaped."

"I wonder if Yamaguchi had something to do with this?" Rie said, frowning.

"It's possible," Kinno said. "Yoshi, bring the ledger books for this year, please."

Yoshi staggered under three heavy ledgers. Rie watched intently as Kinno opened them to the pages of the year's expenses and income. Kinnosuke began working with the abacus.

The room was tense and silent for several minutes except for the rapid clicking of the wooden counters.

"We'll have huge debts with a loss of this magnitude," Kinno said finally. "We'll have to rely on sales of Shrine Water, plus our income from gold-silver exchange and moneylending to survive until next year. I'm not sure if we can make it." He sighed, leaned back, and looked at Rie and Jihei.

No. No! This couldn't be happening. Her father had trusted the house to her. She would not fail him. Rie let out a puff of the cheeks. "We must diversify even more. We have to now in order to survive." She put down her fan and pulled the comb from her hair.

"You're right, no question," said Kinno. "We'll lose customers as it is, we're bound to." He bit his lip.

"What do you suggest?" Jihei wondered.

Did the head of the house have no ideas of his own? Disgraceful.

"How about buying from several small brewers who have little or no brand recognition beyond their local areas?" Kinno asked.

"Excellent idea, Kinno!" Rie cried. "Yes,

we could sell in our barrels under our label, using sake blended from several small brewers. It would be a new product that way." She tapped her fan on the table.

"Could we do that?" Jihei bounced up and down on his heels in a petulant manner.

"Why not?" Rie asked. "Who would object? Shogunal commissioners like White Tiger as well as anyone."

Yoshi looked back and forth from Rie to Kinno with his mouth open.

This was how he'd learn. It was how she had learned — by listening to her father and Kin as a child.

Several streets away, Kikuji Yamaguchi sat, elbows on his table, issuing orders and going through ledgers. He belched.

Yusuke, his aging clerk, sidled up to him with a crablike gait. "Have you heard, Master? White Tiger's brew has turned sour, all of it!" He smiled and looked at Yamaguchi expectantly.

"So!" roared Yamaguchi. "Omura's sake has gone bad! And we didn't have to do anything. Excellent. This is our chance to capture their customers, their whole market. They'll be helpless. Good, Yusuke," he bellowed.

"Master?"

"Start working on Omura's customers.

Get the list at the Brewers Association, can you?"

"I think so, but . . ." Yusuke took three steps backward.

"Don't hesitate." Yamaguchi's jowls trembled as he spoke. "Divert thirty percent from our regular customers to Omura's regular clients. Promise our regular customers more next season, and buy up all you can from smaller brewers."

Yusuke nodded.

"And have three clerks assist you. Get started today. No delay!" he barked.

Several mornings later Kinno approached Rie in the inner office. "Oku-san, I heard some news about Yamaguchi."

Rie looked up quizzically. "What?"

"I hear he's trying to move into our markets, to take over our customers. He has heard about our sake disaster."

"A devil! He's a devil!" Rie frowned darkly.

Kinno scratched his head. "How are we going to stop him?"

No one answered.

Late that morning Rie walked out into the garden as the sun broke faintly through the clouds and caressed the azaleas. She strolled slowly, head down, her hands behind her back in unconscious imitation of her father's walking posture. She halted at the stone and sat. Resting her chin on her hand, she gazed pensively at the pond.

She looked around the garden for a moment, and her eye fixed on the time-haunted fences that enclosed the carefully manicured space. She felt transported to the temple garden, far from the brewery. A sense of timeless peace pervaded her being, and she silently thanked her ancestors for creating this oasis of tranquility. As she looked around, her eyes rested on the clump of bamboo whose leaves rustled in the breeze. Bamboo, a favorite kimono pattern, symbol of adaptability, of bending with shifting circumstances.

As she mused, her father's voice came to her: "A major setback always offers a major challenge, an inevitable part of doing business." She looked back at the bamboo and listened as the leaves whispered softly. Her gaze shifted upward, above the vine-covered fences to the roofs. Her eye traveled along the rooftops over the office and two-story section of the house and beyond, to the towering roofs of the three kuras. The kuras, the kuras! She slapped her knees, rose, and walked back into the office.

Yoshi was working at one end of the room.

"Yoshi, can you find your father and

Kinno?" she asked. "I want to talk to them."

"I can find Kinno, but I don't know about Father."

"Please ask Kinno to come to the office, then."

Yoshi nodded and left.

Minutes later the shoji slid open and Kinno and Yoshi entered. They looked at her expectantly as they sat.

Rie sat perfectly straight. "You know that each time we have had a crisis in the past we have survived because we found a solution other than brewing. That is how we survived. Brewing is the work given us by our ancestors and we must continue it, no question." She paused and looked up as Jihei walked into the room.

She ignored the supposed head of the house.

"Now we need another solution. Selling the sake of small brewers under our own label will not be enough, now that Yamaguchi is moving into our markets. We must look elsewhere. We need something new." She paused and took a deep breath. "I have a question for you, Kinno-san." She tapped her fan on the table. "Do you know of a small brewer in Nada or anywhere in Kobe who is forced to close his brewery this year?"

Kinno scratched his chin. "Let's see. I

think Yanagihara in East Nada . . . I heard something about them. They had a shipwreck and it finished them." He looked at Rie.

Jihei frowned at her. *Frown all you want,* she thought.

She continued. "If it's true that Yanagihara has had to stop, then I propose that we buy his brewery, his kura, and sell it at a higher price. If he had to stop he won't be able to bargain over the price."

Jihei's mouth hung open. "Are you talking about buying and selling kura, dealing in kura? Whoever heard —"

Rie tapped her fan again. "That's just the point. If no one else is doing it, it will be our chance. What do you think, Kinno-san?"

He sucked in his breath in a hiss. "A new idea. Interesting. It might work. *Hmm.*" He scratched his chin. "Let me think a bit." He leaned forward. "As a matter of fact, I hear the Ozawas are having a difficult year; had to cut back on production. I have an idea we might be able to buy one of their kura too."

Rie nodded and smiled at Kinno. "Good."

Jihei frowned. "You're always pushing to be first in everything. I thought a brewer's task is to brew good sake and not worry about anything else, except maybe lending money."

"That doesn't work on our scale here in Nada," Rie said, stating the obvious. Why didn't Jihei understand this by now? "We have to be always on the lookout for something new as well as trying to improve our quality. Otherwise we'd be relegated to second or third class, if we survive at all." She shook her head. "Do you follow what we're discussing, Yoshi?"

"I think so." He nodded.

"All right, Kinno and Yoshi. Our credit is good. See what you can do about the Yanagihara and Ozawa kura. Let's start on it tomorrow."

Jihei frowned and walked out of the office.

Some head.

She had led the house out of this crisis.

Two weeks later Rie sat with Yoshi and Kinno in the office.

"I was right," said Kinno, nodding and placing his hands on the table. "Yanagihara had stopped brewing. He was receptive to selling. I hesitated to make an offer, but Yoshi helped convince me. We had to raise our price a bit. So now we own the Ozawa kura in East Nada and the Yanagihara kura."

"Excellent, Kinno and Yoshi." Rie slapped

her fan on the table.

Just then the shoji opened and Jihei walked in. "I heard what you were saying," he said, his speech slurred. "I think it's too fast. We should proceed one kura at a time."

Yoshi stole a glance at his father, then looked down. "I felt sorry for Yanagihara, having to stop after so many generations," he said.

"It's all right to feel sympathy for someone, Yoshi," Rie said, "and natural. But please remember that such emotions should not intrude when you are doing a business negotiation. Your head must rule, not your heart." She rested a hand on his arm. "But you succeeded. Congratulations." She felt Jihei's glare. He was too drunk to sustain it, though. What an embarrassment he was.

Kinno's eyes crinkled in appreciation, his mouth shaping a toothy grin. "I think we should sell one kura now and keep the other for next winter, when we may be able to increase our production."

"Very well," Rie agreed. "And Kinno and Yoshi, I want you to start giving Sei small jobs in the afternoon. Remember, Yoshi, you were following Kinno everywhere when you were five. That's how you learned so well." She beamed at him. "Teach Sei to do just as you did."

Late one afternoon Rie stopped outside the boys' room. The tutor had left, and she hoped to learn what he was teaching them, especially Yoshi.

"Yoshi," she called as she slid the shoji open and entered the room.

The boys sat at the low table with papers and copy sheets. Sei was painstakingly copying syllables with a brush. Yoshi was reading aloud from a book printed on rice paper. They bowed to Rie.

"Continue, please. What are you reading, Yoshi?"

"Sensei left me these two books." He pushed them across the table.

"*The Way to Wealth,* by Saikaku," Rie read aloud. "Yes, a good lesson, Yoshi. Saikaku says here what a merchant needs is frugality, persistence, a ready mind for figures, mastery of the abacus, a pleasant manner, honesty, and imagination. Just what Grandfather and I have been teaching you. We must keep this so Sei can read it when he's old enough." She read on. "It is not plum, cherry, pine, and maple trees that people desire most around their houses, but gold and silver, rice and hard cash."

Rie burst out laughing, covering her mouth with the book. The boys grinned.

"Of course we value gold and silver, *and*

hard cash. But we also enjoy the plum and cherry blossoms in the garden too. And the other book, Yoshi?"

She picked it up and read, "*The Man Who Spent His Life in Love.*" Then she turned to Yoshi. "Have you read this one?"

"Not yet."

"Well, let me read it first. I'm not sure it's suitable." She slipped the book into her sleeve, rose, and went to the door. "Continue. We'll have dinner soon."

Rie retired early, intending to read Yoshi's lesson book. She set the lamp next to her futon and pulled out the story. She read aloud to herself the words of one of the characters in the story. " 'Many years ago it was observed that a father slaves, his son idles, and the grandson begs.' *Ho!*" she exclaimed aloud. She read the story of the rakish, profligate son who spent his time and money in the entertainment quarter where he squandered the money so painstakingly accumulated by his father. This was a good lesson for Yoshi . . . and for Jihei. She would ask the tutor if he had any more of these stories. She finished the book and decided to leave it on Jihei's seat in the office where he was sure to see it.

Chapter 22

Rie walked to the courtyard one morning and looked at her three daughters standing in front of the barrels in their indigo *mompei* work pants, slapping each other and giggling in their high-pitched voices. Rie tied her sleeves back and walked up to them.

"Talking won't get the barrels clean, girls. Come on, pick up the brushes. I want to see how you're doing. You too, Teru. You're old enough. Watch your sisters. You've washed your hands and feet? And remember, stay away from the kura."

"Yes, Mother," all three replied at once. They bowed quickly and picked up the large brushes next to the hose.

"Get to the back of the barrel first, the bottom. You'll need this small ladder to reach," Rie said. "I know some brewers just run water through the barrels, but that isn't enough. We don't want a repeat of last year's sake."

"But it's so cold, Mother." Fumi shivered and rubbed her hands together. "My hands are freezing."

"I know. Cold weather is what makes good sake. You can stop when you're too cold and warm your hands. Like this." Rie held her hands over her nose and mouth. "And after a while your back gets tired. But there are three of you. I used to do it all alone, so you'll each do only a third of the work."

"But we have more barrels now. We produce more," Kazu said.

"Yes, you're right." Rie laughed. "Use the ladder, Kazu. You'll need it to reach the bottom, there at the side. And Teru, use some force. That's right, Fumi. And it helps to sing. It takes your mind off the cold."

Rie began to hum a rhythmic folk tune and clapped her hands in time to their brush strokes. They all began to sing.

"You'll get to enjoy it after a while, when you realize how important it is for the sake, and for the success of the house."

"You always talk about the house, Mother," sixteen-year-old Fumi said.

"Yes, it's the most important thing in the world, Fumi. In whatever we do we need to think of the house."

Rie mused as she watched the girls. Kazu was already fifteen, taller than average and a capable, responsible model for her younger sister. Teru was obviously attractive and must be watched closely so that she did not behave like a geisha. Rie felt a twinge of guilt that she had given Fumi more attention than her sisters. She turned and walked to the inner office, allowing herself only the briefest of thoughts of Fumi's real father.

Rie opened the wooden shutters one morning and looked out into the garden. The maple leaves were reddening, yellow chrysanthemum buds were ready to burst, and the cicadas had fallen silent. Could summer have come and gone so quickly? Even when the autumn foliage was at its most brilliant, Rie always felt a faint twinge of melancholy at the cold gray winter to come. Of course that was the weather that produced good sake, the colder the better. It also brought on O-Natsu's painful rheumatism and everyone's sniffling noses the whole winter through. And there had not been time to go to Bunraku this summer, regretfully.

The autumn colors in the garden also reminded Rie that it was time to prepare for the start of another brewing season. She prayed that the previous year's disaster would not be repeated. Maids cleaned the kurabitos' room to prepare for their arrival from their farms. Jihei must call the priest for the start of season ritual, a Shinto observance performed in the kura. Rie and the girls were not allowed to witness it. Rie had O-Natsu and O-Yuki ready the fruit and mochi plates to set on the white-draped table at the entrance to the number one kura. Ropes hung with white folded paper amulets were strung above the entrance to each kura. In her father's time Rie knew prayers were said each morning before the Shinto god shelf. Now the ceremony was performed just once annually, though Toji said a prayer himself each morning. Sake brewing required the help of the gods.

The purple-robed priest in his pointed black cap arrived the morning of the ceremony and was greeted by Jihei, Yoshi, Toji, and Kinnosuke. Kin returned for the occasion. The wooden shutters of the main room were open so Rie and the girls could witness the ceremony from a distance as they were not allowed in the kura. Jihei, Yoshitaro, Kinnosuke, Toji, and the kurabito stood in a row in front of the main kura. The priest held his white paper wand in both hands and shook it several times at the entrance to each kura before entering the main kura. He stood at the ceremonial table inside the entrance. The women were silent as they listened to him intone solemn prayers to the god of sake for the success of the season's brew.

Completion of the ritual was the signal for everyone to spring into action. Huge baskets of rice were carried inside the brewery for polishing with the wooden waterwheel. Then the rice was steamed in the huge black cauldron. Next, rice was inoculated with koji mold to produce sweet saccharified rice that would turn all the rice to sugar, while yeast was simultaneously introduced and the process of fermentation begun. The whole operation was the province of Toji and the kurabito.

Rie, forever outside the kura, relied on the sounds and smells as the brewing progressed. She heard the kurabito sing as they worked and knew when the fermentation began by the pungent yeasty smell of something growing that wafted from the kura through the courtyard and permeated the house. When the sake was filtered, Rie was next after Toji and Kinnosuke to judge the brew. Jihei did not always bother to be present.

With the brewing in full swing, White Tiger expanded production in the newly acquired fourth kura. Seisaburo, at age nine, was now an apprentice in the office under his elder brother's and Kinnosuke's supervision. Rie was gratified to see the brothers working together but at the same time distressed that Jihei was becoming increasingly ineffectual as head of the house. He seldom did anything on his own initiative. Planning and decision making were done by Rie and Kinnosuke with Yoshitaro, and, where the kura was concerned, by Toji. Jihei was usually absent during the days *and* evenings, which only relieved Rie. Old Kin came less often, but when he did he never failed to inquire about the sale of Shrine Water. On his latest visit he asked Kinnosuke about the sale of the Ozawa kura.

"We got seventy for it, Kin-san," Kinnosuke told him. "We sold it to Sugiyama. They had a fire in their kura and would have had to stop. They were glad to get it. It enabled them to stay in production this year."

"A good price, yes. Very good," Kin said. "Oku-san must have been happy." Only a few yellowed teeth showed when he grinned.

"Yes, I was pleased," Rie said and leaned toward him. "I can see your rheumatism is troubling you." She glanced at the gnarled, swollen joints on his fingers. "But please come back whenever you feel well enough. It's good for the boys to see you here. Sei was so young when his grandfather died. Your visits are important to us now."

Kin slurped his tea appreciatively and smiled until his eyes vanished in slits. "I'm glad that Toji is still here," he said in his faint, raspy voice. "Yes, I'll come whenever the rheumatism isn't too bad. Brewing is my life." He looked down at his hands.

"As a matter of fact, there is something I wanted to discuss with you," Rie said. "I need your wisdom and experience. You know how lax the authorities have become in enforcing the kabu license regulations." She took out her comb and twirled it in her hands.

"Yes. There's not much the commissioners can do here in Kansai any longer. The shoguns are on shaky ground now, no longer able to control anything, despite their efforts. The whole samurai class is indebted to the merchants. I just wonder what's going to become of these Tokugawa shoguns."

"Well, this is my point, Kin-san. They can't enforce the regulations. They can't dictate the amount we produce. I heard Kinno-san say something about buying or renting additional kabu so we could increase our production. You know he is negotiating to buy two more kura, the old Kuribayashi kura in Nishinomiya. That will put us closer to the Shrine Water. And we'll need more kabu. What do you think? Do you see any risk in buying up more shares, a lot more?"

"I can't foresee any risk. The commissioners can't move against us." He paused to sip his tea. "Yes, I know people have been buying and selling shares. Kinno-san mentioned it. He really is keeping on top of things, isn't he?"

Rie refilled his cup, and he warmed his hands on it.

"We couldn't have done better in our choice of your successor. Not that anyone could ever fill your place." She looked at the old man's lined, sunken face and felt a twinge of nostalgia.

"Well, I've seen you two working together and it's often difficult to say which of you gets an idea first. You two are of the same mind." He grinned toothlessly and chortled deep in his throat. "There's not another pair like you in all Kobe. It's something to watch. Of course you received the best training from your father."

The compliment delighted her.

"Oh, I learned from you too, Kin-san, especially in those years when Father didn't want me near the business."

Kinnosuke walked in and joined them.

"Kinno-san," Rie said, smiling at him.

He looked up and bowed briskly.

"How many more barrels are we using than last season?"

"Ten more, with the new kura."

"And each time we add a kura we'll need that many more barrels?"

"Yes, that's true," he said, and nodded.

"Then shouldn't we think about hiring a cooper and setting him up here instead of buying barrels from outside?" Rie asked as she pulled out her tortoiseshell comb and reinserted it.

"I can make inquiries. I know the Setookas. They might be receptive. They own an old cooperage, and have several sons, so they'll need to send out the younger ones. We've always bought some barrels from them. Setooka comes by at this time of year when he thinks we may need some."

"Good. See what you can do there. We need a cooper and an apprentice or two."

Several months later a coopers' shed was built next to the number three kura, and Masami Setooka's son Goro and his younger brother Kasumi were installed as apprentice barrel makers. All the barrels used in White Tiger were now made on the premises, an economy in production costs.

Rie sat in the parlor one morning renewing a flower arrangement and replacing the rice and plum wine offerings on the family altar. The wooden shutters were open toward the courtyard, affording a view out toward the coopers' shed. At one side of the entrance, wood for making barrels was stacked. At the other side of the door stood Goro, a boy with strikingly fine features. Rie recalled his father's face, the way O-Toki had lingered before him at the end of season celebration years earlier. Not surprising that Goro had inherited a handsome face. But who was the girl talking with him so earnestly, her back toward the house? Rie watched until the girl turned to walk back toward the house. It was Teru, now fourteen and the most beautiful of the Omura daughters. She was smiling to herself as she approached the house, teapot in hand. She walked like a geisha, seductively.

Annoyed, Rie rose and slid open the door to the corridor just as Teru entered from the courtyard.

"Teru, please come in here. I need to talk to you." Rie turned abruptly and walked back into the room. She sat before the Butsudan and indicated a zabuton for Teru.

"Teru, what were you doing over there at the coopers' shed just now?"

"Oh, I was just taking them some tea. It was time for their morning tea."

"And why did you think this was your job and not the kitchen maids'?"

"Oh . . . *uh* . . . they were busy, Mother." Teru looked down and shifted uneasily on the zabuton.

"It wasn't because you wanted to talk to Goro?" Rie persisted.

Teru blushed. "*Uh* . . . well, he does seem nice."

"And what have I taught you about talking with the men, the workers, Teru?"

Teru was silent, her face red, her head still bowed.

"I'm waiting, Teru."

Teru spoke in a voice barely above a whisper. "That we shouldn't."

"Please remember that, Teru. I don't want to have to speak to you again about it. And another thing: who taught you to walk like that?"

"Like what, Mother?" Teru looked up, frowning.

"As if you wanted to attract some man's attention."

"I'm just walking, the same as you and Kazu."

"Not exactly the same. Remember to keep your toes pointed in and your knees slightly bent. You must be more circumspect. Remember who you are." Rie paused. She noted O-Toki pausing several times in front of Masami at a ceremony and guessed that he, not Jihei, was Teru's father.

"As an Omura daughter you will have a good marriage to another brewing house, but you must safeguard your virtue and the honor of the house. Talking carelessly with our workers can endanger our reputation. It is simply not acceptable behavior. I am sorry to have to remind you of this."

Teru's head was still bowed, and Rie saw that she was pouting.

"You may be excused now. Go and finish your abacus lesson."

"Yes, Mother." Teru rose and left the room quickly, without bowing.

Rie sat with her thoughts. She hoped she was being fair with Teru, not venting her old anger about Jihei's mistresses' children. She sighed and had a flash of memory of her own mother and her feelings toward her. She hoped Kazu and Teru felt toward her as Fumi did. Strange, it did not seem like half a lifetime ago that she had sat in this same room with her mother. Teru's beauty was a potential danger as well as an asset to the house. Was there a hint of insolence in her manner? She would bear watching now until her marriage could be arranged. And it must be arranged soon, perhaps as early

as the next year, after Fumi and Kazu were
married.

CHAPTER 23

"Yoshi, you're nineteen now," Jihei said to his son one day as they worked in the inner office. Jihei looked around to make sure they were alone. "There are things you need to learn, things other than brewing. I want you to come with me this evening."

Yoshitaro looked up. "Where are we going?" he asked.

"Somewhere you've never been before. It will be a surprise, a pleasant one. But you're not to tell your mother. Do you understand?"

"Yes, Father."

"We won't have dinner at home this evening. I'll tell your mother that we're going to a Bunraku performance, just you and I. We'll leave after dark."

Jihei had spoken to O-Toki the previous week.

"Yoshi has had his nineteenth birthday. I want him to have his initiation here. Do you

262

have a suitable geisha? Someone with real beauty and experience, a bit older than he but not so old that he'll be put off. What do you think?"

O-Toki smiled. "Yes, it's time. I know he's nineteen. I thought of him on his birthday. A mother does, you know." She raised her eyebrows but continued looking down.

"Do you have someone in mind?"

"I've been thinking about it, actually. Yes, I think O-Sada would be perfect. She's a beauty and much in demand. She has a patron so she's experienced. Her patron needn't know. I'll arrange it with O-Sada."

"I'll bring him a week from tonight. We'll want to have a bath and a meal. He and I can bathe and eat together, but after that. . . ."

"I understand. O-Sada will be very sensitive."

"Will she know you're his mother?" Jihei asked. "You know, Yoshi still doesn't know. He thinks my wife is his mother."

"I'll let her know everything she needs to know, you can be sure." O-Toki did not elaborate.

"Let's go, Yoshi. I had a ricksha called. He's waiting out beyond the number three kura."

Jihei glanced at his son and was pleased

that he had taken special care with his appearance. They looked strikingly alike, Jihei had to concede, only that Yoshitaro was slighter of build. And with his bushy hair and slim figure he might almost be mistaken for an artist or actor, the type that would attract women. Yoshitaro seemed to have caught his father's sense of adventure, Jihei thought as they rode to the Sawaraya. Yoshitaro turned to look at the hawkers, the lights, the scurrying geisha as the ricksha rocked along the bumpy roads.

At the entrance O-Toki and a younger geisha greeted them, a woman whose striking eyes gave her an air of intelligence it was difficult to conceal even with her geisha's makeup and bright kimono. Yoshitaro followed his father and the geisha along the corridors, stumbling as he watched O-Sada and looking curiously at his surroundings. *Good that he especially noticed O-Sada,* Jihei thought.

Seated with his son in the back room always reserved for him, Jihei looked around the room and relished the thought that they were a family — he, O-Toki, and their son, the first time the three had been together since Yoshitaro's infancy.

"So wonderful that you have brought your son this evening," O-Toki said as she and

O-Sada bowed deeply. O-Toki looked at Yoshitaro intently, then glanced down and bowed.

A maid brought in a tea tray, the evening's preliminary. O-Sada poured two small cups and set them before Jihei and Yoshitaro.

"And you will want a bath before you dine. O-Sada will show you to the bath when you have changed." She indicated the house yukata and the women left the room.

Yoshitaro glanced at Jihei, who nodded and rose. They changed into the blue-and-white printed yukata and slid open the shoji. O-Sada motioned for them to follow her. Jihei glanced at Yoshitaro and saw that he was watching O-Sada walk with her small swaying steps. In the bath anteroom O-Sada handed towels to Jihei and Yoshitaro and withdrew as they removed the cotton robes and entered the steaming bathroom. Jihei tried to reassure his son as they soaped and rinsed. "It's the same as at home, Yoshi. We always bathe before dinner here too. Nothing unusual."

They stepped into the vaporous steamy tub. Jihei slapped a hot towel on top of his head and sighed.

"Relax, Yoshi. We're here to forget the pressures of work."

The door slid open and O-Toki and

O-Sada advanced through the mist and knelt behind Jihei and Yoshitaro.

O-Sada smiled at Yoshitaro and asked in a soft voice, "May I massage your back?"

Yoshitaro covered his groin with his hands. Jihei smiled. "Don't worry, Yoshi, she's seen men before."

O-Toki glanced at Yoshitaro, then quickly focused on Jihei's back.

For the next few moments the only sound was water splashing as the women ran their hands around Jihei's and Yoshitaro's backs. Jihei watched O-Sada's hands move up and down Yoshitaro's arms and around to his stomach. Jihei closed his eyes and exhaled loudly.

"A wonderful way to relax, isn't it, Yoshi?" He opened one eye.

Yoshitaro nodded but didn't speak. Jihei saw Yoshitaro's eyes following O-Sada's hands in their exploratory tour of his body.

After a few minutes O-Toki rose and said, "We'll see to your dinner." She motioned O-Sada to follow her.

After the women left, Yoshitaro said, "Do they always come into the bath and massage you?"

"Usually, yes," Jihei answered. "It's part of the whole evening."

"What else?" Yoshitaro asked.

"We'll have dinner and a drink and then . . . we'll see. . . ."

Yoshitaro frowned slightly but said nothing more.

The meal was the Sawaraya's best fare, Jihei could see as tray after tray of small, beautifully arranged dishes was set before them. Most striking was a miniature ship covered with enticing pieces of fresh sliced sashimi.

"Have a drink, Yoshi. It's White Tiger," Jihei said, laughing.

O-Sada held out a flask.

"I think you're old enough to have more than a taste." Jihei winked at O-Toki.

Yoshitaro's face reddened as he sipped his second cup. Jihei drank steadily as the meal progressed. Tastefully cut melon appeared as the final course.

O-Toki and O-Sada sat attentively as maids cleared away the trays.

Jihei half lay on his side, elbow resting on the tatami.

"Let's stay the night, Yoshi. I'm too relaxed to move," Jihei said.

"Will it be all right at home?" Yoshitaro asked with a slight frown.

"Don't worry, Yoshi. Just relax," Jihei said.

O-Toki took Yoshitaro's arm. "Come. I'll show you to your room," she murmured.

"My room?" Yoshitaro asked. "Don't I stay with my father?"

"He'll be nearby. It's all right," O-Toki said gently.

Yoshitaro looked back at Jihei's prone form as he left the room with O-Toki.

Jihei closed his eyes. He heard the shoji slide open again some time later.

"O-Sada is with him in the next room," O-Toki whispered. "I think she'll stay with him most of the night."

"It's a big step for him," Jihei mumbled. "I'm glad he's here with me, and you."

O-Toki yawned. "*Ah,* what happened about your plan to cut back on your wife's production increase?" She glanced at Jihei.

"Oh, it worked better than I thought. Actually I thought only one kura would go sour, but all three did. The whole cellar was spoiled. Couldn't be helped." He closed his eyes and smiled at the thought of his successful revenge against Rie.

"Oh, I'm sorry." O-Toki put an arm across Jihei's chest.

He embraced O-Toki. "Sake brewing isn't the only thing in life."

Some time during the night Jihei was awakened by sounds coming from the next room. He listened closely, aware that Yoshitaro's initiation had begun.

Before dawn Jihei rolled over and sat up. O-Toki was still asleep next to him. He put a hand on her arm. "O-Toki," he said softly. "Wake Yoshi. We need to get back."

O-Toki sat up, pulled her kimono around her and put on her obi. She shuffled out the door. Jihei could hear her calling, "Excuse me," and Yoshitaro's muffled reply mingled with O-Sada's voice.

Jihei dressed quickly and stepped into the corridor. Yoshitaro emerged, hair disheveled, his face a study in confusion.

"Let's wash quickly and leave, Yoshi. We want to get back before breakfast."

Jihei led the way through the corridor to the washbasins. They splashed cold water over their faces and wet down their hair.

"Why didn't you tell me, Father?" Yoshitaro asked.

"Some things a man learns best by experience, Yoshi."

"I mean why didn't you tell me that Mother is not my real mother, that O-Toki is my mother?" He looked at Jihei accusingly.

Jihei paused, his jaw clenched as he hazarded a fierce glance at O-Toki. He gave her one last look, then adjusted his collar and said, "We'll talk about it on the way home, Yoshi."

As they stood at the entrance waiting for the ricksha, O-Toki looked at Jihei, then put a hand on Yoshitaro's arm and said softly, "Yes, Yoshi, I am your mother."

Yoshitaro looked at her, and Jihei once again felt a stab of anger at O-Toki when he realized his son was about to cry.

"It's all right, Yoshi," O-Toki said.

O-Sada took out Yoshitaro's sandals and bowed to him. "Please grace our humble house with your presence again," she said without looking up.

"It's like this, Yoshi," Jihei said after they were seated in the swaying ricksha. "I'm also adopted, you know. Your mother's — my wife's — parents adopted me as her husband. So I was selected especially to continue the Omura House and brewing White Tiger. And she and I, her parents and I, adopted you so that you can continue after me. You are my real son."

He was greeted by angry silence.

"And my wife also regards you as her son and treats you as her son. She and I have raised you, so we really are your parents. We care for you and want you to continue the traditions of the house, as she has always told you. Please don't regard her any differently. The experience you had last night is something completely separate. It has nothing to do with the house, or with marriage. It was about individual human emotions."

"But O-Sada said that is where I was born," Yoshitaro insisted.

"Yes, it is true that you were born there. But you are a member of the Omura House, and after I'm gone you will be the most important member of the house. Don't forget that, Yoshi."

Jihei sat back, exhausted from his predawn exertions. They were silent the rest of the way home. Jihei listened to the creaking of the racketing ricksha on the bumpy road.

He alighted at the rear entrance of White Tiger, between the number one and two kura and left Yoshitaro to fend for himself at the main entrance to the corridor between the storage area and the number one kura.

Just as Yoshitaro entered the corridor the door slid open from the storage room and Rie stood frowning at him.

Yoshitaro bowed, his face suddenly flushed. "*Uh* . . . good morning, Mother."

"I see," Rie said, her mouth an angry line. "So the Bunraku performance lasted all night. Well, I hope you enjoyed the performance."

Yoshitaro bowed again, not looking up. "*Uh*, yes, Mother."

"And your father?"

"I believe he's gone to the kura."

"Most likely, yes," Rie replied. The kura was Jihei's usual escape. "Well, I know Kinnosuke has work for you this morning."

Rie turned and reentered the storage room, sliding the shoji shut with a bang. She stood for a moment resting her trembling hands on the table where she had been working. She scowled, and her angry breath came in rapid gasps. This was the way it had always been with men. Now Jihei was training Yoshitaro to follow in his footsteps, spending on geishas time and valuable money earned by the efforts of herself and the kurabito. Jihei always said geisha entertainment was necessary for business negotiations, but business negotiations never produced babies. When her rage subsided she walked rapidly out through the corridor to the barrels in front of the number one kura. She lifted a small barrel of water from the well to place it beside a huge barrel, tied back her sleeves, knelt, and picked up a brush. She tied a scarf over her hair and attacked the barrel with savage energy.

O-Natsu and O-Yuki came to peer out from the main corridor next to the storeroom.

"You can always tell how angry she is by the way she washes the barrels," O-Natsu said in a low voice. "She's furious because Yoshi didn't return last night. He was out with his father."

"Well, what can she do? It was bound to happen sooner or later. Still, she can't be pleased about it. No woman is," O-Yuki said, "except the geishas." She raised an eyebrow and looked at O-Natsu.

"I'm not even sure about them," O-Natsu said.

Rie scrubbed until her hands were raw and chilled, her fury abated. Then, exhausted by emotion and exertion, she went to her room to change clothes and comb her hair.

Later, she decided to speak to the girls in their room before dinner.

"Kazu, Teru," she called and slid open the shoji to their room. Now sixteen and fifteen, the girls were able to read simple stories and do sums. Fumi was elsewhere. Kazu was a bright, active girl, and Teru had already attracted attention with her sultry beauty. When Rie entered the room the girls were lying on their stomachs on the futon giggling, a book in front of them. They turned and sat up simultaneously as Rie entered the room.

"It's nearly dinnertime," Rie began. She glanced at the book. "What is it you're read-

273

ing? May I see?" She knelt and took the book on her lap.

"Oh, you're reading Saikaku. *Five Women Who Loved Love,*" she read aloud. "Yes, I read it myself just recently. I hope you have understood what Saikaku is telling us? These five women did not know how to behave properly, to control their emotions. They led lives of reckless abandon, and where did it lead them? They ended in tragedy, in disgrace and death by execution or suicide."

She knotted her fist, knowing only too well the consequences if one was not vigilant.

"I've told you often you must be very careful not to meet with any boy alone before you are married. And some of the girls in the stories were no older than you. I hope you'll read all five of these stories carefully and think about them."

If she could not control the nightly exploits of the men in the family, Rie was determined to protect the girls, to give proper guidance until she was able to arrange their marriages.

CHAPTER 24

One morning Rie walked out to the garden for a breath of fresh air, needing relief from the stifling humidity that always hung over the city just before the monsoon rains broke. Only here could she find solitude and respite from the burdens of business, the luxury of time to reflect. She was pleased that Seisaburo showed signs of real ability when it came to the brewing business, but she needed to turn from thoughts of her youngest son to the eldest. Yoshitaro, heir to the house, had just celebrated his twenty-first birthday and had been visiting the geisha O-Sada more than she deemed necessary. The thought that Jihei had orchestrated their meeting still burned. And she had been doubly annoyed to learn that O-Toki had told their son that he was adopted. She fanned herself, her anger boiling over every time she thought of how it had put a wedge in her relationship with

Yoshi these last two years. But be that as it may, the time had come to think of his marriage, and to do more than think of it. She started at the realization that she herself was beyond forty.

For a merchant class family, marriage was a matter of momentous import. The selection of a spouse for the head of the house would inevitably affect the business and welfare of the entire house, beneficially if the selection was made wisely, adversely if adequate care was not taken. Yoshitaro was just one among many things to consider in the plan of arranging the marriage. Choice of a spouse depended on many factors, least among them the emotional preferences of the two individuals. And yet, it had made her parents' relationship much smoother to have some common ground from which to work, unlike with her and Jihei.

Rie fanned herself with her sandalwood fan and watched as her three daughters entered the garden and strolled single file from one end of the garden to the other and back. Their wooden geta struck a rhythm on the stone steps.

It was time to speak to Mrs. Nakano, the ample matron who had negotiated her marriage to Jihei, a woman who delighted in arranging other people's lives.

Rie's thoughts were interrupted by the girls' singing. She glanced at each of them: Fumi, now nearly nineteen and as energetic as herself; Kazu, a tall, willowy eighteen; and Teru, seventeen, with a hint of a geisha's sensuality in her every gesture. Marriage was not so far off for any of them, and Mrs. Nakano's good offices would be required repeatedly over the next few years, for the boys as well as the girls. Rie closed her fan and tapped her knee with it in time to the folk song the girls were singing. Fumi was actually of marriage age already, but Yoshitaro had to be married first.

Rie still smarted at the memory of Jihei taking Yoshi to the Sawaraya. She wished Seisaburo could be spared the experience, but some patterns of male behavior were so deeply ingrained that there was nothing she could do to alter them. She needed to assure that her daughters behaved properly before marriage.

What she must do, no matter what, was to safeguard the interests of the house. This was becoming increasingly difficult to do, what with Jihei's heavy drinking. He was no longer functioning effectively as house head even where formalities were concerned. Rie saw to it that Yoshitaro always accompanied his father whenever a negotiation or meeting was involved. It was simply not safe to leave matters to Jihei alone. Within the house everyone now realized that for all practical purposes Yoshitaro was head of the house.

"What happened at the Brewers Association meeting last evening?" Rie asked Yoshitaro one morning when they were alone. "Did you speak for your father?"

"I did, Mother. It was all right. Father nodded as I spoke. I managed to acquire ten more shares. The Sumidas were willing to sell. They've been having difficulties for some time."

"Good, Yoshi. I'm glad. Now you can see the danger of all that drinking. I know you go to the Sawaraya," she said, fearful that any mention of it would drive a further wedge between them, and yet knowing that he might very well be on the same path as his father if she didn't. "But drinking to excess is ruinous. If it weren't for you we'd be in bad shape now, even with Kinnosuke's management. Appearances are important. People notice. And your father's condition could destroy us, without your efforts. The whole house rests on your shoulders now, Yoshi. This is a heavy responsibility. I'm grateful that you are able to carry on." She smiled at Yoshitaro, who straightened and adjusted the collar of his kimono.

Rie gazed at his face, the face that so vividly reflected his father's, even to the eyebrows. Yoshitaro did not share his father's nervous habit of pulling his eyebrows, a habit that had always given her a vague unease, a sense that Jihei was not quite up to the responsibilities he was being called on to assume. Yoshitaro seemed to take after Kinnosuke's brusque but efficient mannerisms. It was natural enough, since Yoshitaro had been trained not by his father but by Kinnosuke, and by herself.

Rie picked up the teapot and poured for Yoshitaro.

"You know, Yoshi, I don't know how much longer your father can keep up even the appearance of being house head. It's such a worry." She sighed and sipped her tea. "He's really too young to retire, you know. My father was over sixty when he retired, a bit later than usual, to be sure. But your father is only forty-nine. He has a while to go before he can retire respectably. But he may have to retire next year. I know you'll do your best until then, Yoshi. Every public appearance counts where our house's reputation is concerned."

"I know, Mother. I'm aware of it. I'm doing my best to cover for Father at the

Brewers Association."

Rie nodded. "Another thing, Yoshi. I was going to talk to you about this before I became so concerned about your father. Now that you're nearly twenty-two and really acting house head, it's time we thought about your marriage. And we need to do more than think about it. I'll speak to Mrs. Nakano soon. You know she arranged my marriage to your father." Rie removed her comb from her hair and reinserted it. She reached for the teapot and poured again for Yoshitaro.

He frowned. "Already, Mother? Can't we wait a year or two?"

His bond with O-Sada must be greater than she'd feared. She must put a stop to it, soon. "Not really, Yoshi. Fumi is almost nineteen, and we can't wait much longer for her either. Your father and I want to see your marriage settled first. It's most important for the house, far more than the girls' marriages."

Yoshitaro pursed his lips and sighed.

"I'm so glad we had this chance to talk, Yoshi. We're both always too busy or we aren't alone. All right, then. Mrs. Nakano will be very circumspect. She'll help us make the best possible choice for you, so you needn't worry."

Yoshitaro put down his cup, rose, and bowed before leaving the room, yet she couldn't help but notice the slightest bit of curtness in his bow.

Rie put on one of her better kimonos, a formal silk. She must appear properly, if not elegantly attired for her meeting with Mrs. Nakano, who was due to arrive at any minute. Rie hurried down the stairs and instructed O-Yuki to serve tea and the choicest cakes from the Kadatoya as soon as Mrs. Nakano arrived. She glanced into the reception room to make sure that a tasteful vase and ikebana arrangement had been placed in the tokonoma alcove.

Rie trusted that Mrs. Nakano kept in mind all the factors that needed to be considered in the choice of a spouse for a large house like the Omuras, including the presence or absence of contagious or hereditary disease in a family. Only after painstaking investigation by the go-between and due consideration by both families could the go-between arrange the preliminary meeting, the o-miai. After the date was fixed for the meeting, great finesse was needed by the go-between to see that neither party lost face should negotiations not proceed further. To agree to the formal meeting was proof that both sides were serious.

Rie went to the entrance herself to greet Mrs. Nakano. Rie bowed low, crossed hands pressed on her thighs.

"How wonderful to see you again after so long," Rie said. "We are so grateful that you were able to spare time from your busy schedule to visit our humble house."

Both women bowed as Rie ushered her plump visitor into the drawing room and indicated the seat of honor backing against the tokonoma.

"And how is your family, Mrs. Omura?" Mrs. Nakano asked.

"They are all well, thank you, growing faster than I can keep track." Rie laughed, her hand politely over her mouth.

O-Yuki brought in a tray with green tea and small cakes.

"And how old is your eldest son, Yoshitaro, now?" Mrs. Nakano inquired pointedly, her body inclining forward at each utterance.

"He is twenty-two," Rie replied, bowing.

Mrs. Nakano bowed in return. "Then I know you want to consider his marriage."

Rie pushed a lacquer plate with two delicate peach-shaped cakes closer to Mrs. Nakano and bowed even further. "We rely on you." There was no need to be more specific with Mrs. Nakano.

She nodded and put her round white hands to her brocade obi as if to adjust it, though no adjustment was necessary. "Of course your house will want a bride from one of the best families in Kobe. You know the Sawada family, I'm sure. The eldest daughter is fortunately just now of marriage age, and so beautiful. She is nineteen."

"Yes, I have seen her," Rie replied. "But her house does not brew, do they? Aren't they rice wholesalers?" She smiled and dipped her head slightly. It would not do to appear too forceful in rejecting a suggestion from Mrs. Nakano.

"Yes, that is true," Mrs. Nakano replied. "But that would also be useful for your business, to have a marriage connection with a rice dealer, wouldn't it?" Mrs. Nakano picked up her cup and sipped delicately.

"For the eldest son of the main house we really need a bride who knows brewing, who was raised in a brewing house, who can care for the live-in workers during brewing. That is the first requirement for our eldest son's bride." Rie gestured again toward the peach-shaped cakes on Mrs. Nakano's plate.

"*Ah*, I see." Mrs. Nakano paused to cut a minute sliver of cake with a small ivory pick. "Well, I wasn't going to mention it, but you know the Tamiya family, the Nishinomiya brewer. Their daughter Tama is also of the right age. But I'm afraid she is not as beautiful as the Sawada daughter." Mrs. Nakano bowed and looked at the untouched slice of cake.

Rie stiffened. "What about ability? Is she capable?"

"They say both she and her brother are very bright, very well raised. She is older than her brother, so I believe they wish to see her settled first. I feel confident that they would be happy to have a marriage alliance with your house."

"You say her name is Tama? And her age?"

"She is just three years younger than Yoshitaro."

"Tama. Let us hope she turns out to be a real jewel for our house," she added under her breath. "It is possible, yes, that she may be a suitable bride for our house. Please begin the inquiry. I'll inform my husband and Yoshitaro. If your investigation proves positive, and the Tamiyas agree, we can have the o-miai soon. And if she appears suitable, I would like an autumn wedding. But I am being too hasty. We must wait for your report and see if the Tamiyas are willing." She smiled politely.

Mrs. Nakano bowed. "Rest assured that I will do my best." She paused to admire the arrangement in the tokonoma behind her. "And I am gratified to see your house doing so well since your own marriage, now so many years ago."

Rie bowed. "Thanks to you," she said, careful to hide her true feelings about Jihei behind a mask of politeness. She showed Mrs. Nakano to the door. "We are so grateful to you for your help over the years."

After dinner that evening Rie sat with Jihei and Yoshitaro at a small table while the other children sat at a table nearby. Jihei was drinking and Yoshitaro also had a sake cup but drank sparingly, Rie was relieved to see. She cleared her throat and adjusted her comb.

"You know, Yoshi, as I mentioned earlier, we can't postpone your marriage any longer. Mrs. Nakano came this afternoon with a very suitable suggestion. The Tamiya house, you know, the Nishinomiya brewers? Their daughter is the right age. She also mentioned the Sawada daughter, but you know they don't brew."

Yoshitaro brightened. "The Sawada daughter! A real beauty. And I've also seen the Tamiya daughter. Nothing to look at." He wrinkled his nose. "I prefer the Sawada daughter."

Rie took her fan from her obi and turned

to face Yoshitaro. "As you know, Yoshi, where the house and succession are concerned, family and economic considerations are uppermost. The Sawada family are not brewers, the Tamiyas are. Your bride must come from a brewing house." She looked at Jihei, who pulled at his eyebrows and looked at Rie, then back at Yoshitaro.

Jihei cleared his throat. "Yes, Yoshi. As I've told you, individual preferences are a private matter. They aren't concerned with marriage. I believe the Tamiya daughter would be a good match for us. A good house." He glanced at Rie again.

"What's her name?" Yoshitaro asked, frowning.

Rie's tone became more conciliatory. "It's Tama, 'jewel.' She's three years younger than you, just right. So we'll ask Mrs. Nakano to go ahead with arrangements for the o-miai meeting. Then if they agree we can set the wedding date four months from now. That will give us time to make all the arrangements for a fall wedding. It will be quite a big affair."

Yoshitaro sighed and rested his chin on a hand.

"You understand, don't you, Yoshi?" Rie asked.

"I guess so," Yoshitaro mumbled, looking

down, his lips pressed together.

"It's best, Yoshi," Jihei said, downing a cup of sake. "And it's not as if you were going out as a mukoyoshi. You'll be here in your own house."

Yoshitaro looked at his father, a mukoyoshi.

The afternoon chosen for the o-miai arrived. The two families met in a private room in one of Kobe's best establishments. Carved cryptomeria cranes marched along the tops of gilt screens that enclosed the room. The famous two-hundred-year-old garden was revealed beyond the open shutters. Stone steps led along a pathway to a curved bridge over a koi pond and beyond, to banks of green shrubbery so that the eye never encountered a barrier.

Ranged on one side of the lacquer table were Mr. and Mrs. Tamiya and Tama, on the other side, Jihei, Rie, and Yoshitaro, with Mr. and Mrs. Nakano at one end of the table facing the garden. Although the two families were acquainted, the importance of the occasion lent it an ambience of formality and restraint.

Yoshitaro sat stiffly, looking straight ahead and bowing as he replied briefly to Mr. and Mrs. Tamiya's questions.

"And how many years have you been help-ing your father in the business?" Mr. Tamiya asked.

"Nearly sixteen years," Yoshitaro replied.

"*Ah,* is that so? So long, and you are so young," Mrs. Tamiya breathed.

Jihei smoothed his eyebrows. "He has been helping me since he was a small boy of five, even earlier," he said. "He has a natural aptitude for it."

Rie saw Yoshitaro steal a glance at Tama, who was modestly looking down at the table. She did not raise her eyes to look at Yoshitaro, Rie noticed. Remarkable self-control, such a valuable asset, and it re-flected good breeding. She appeared healthy, if not robust. *Good working and child-bearing material,* Rie thought.

"And I understand that Tama knows the abacus and has helped in the office," Rie remarked, smiling and bowing.

Tama bowed but did not look up or speak.

"Yes, she is better at the abacus than I am." Mrs. Tamiya put her hand over her mouth and giggled politely, bowing.

Rie's gaze shifted to Tama's mother, often a portent of a daughter's older age. Mrs. Tamiya appeared in good health and had an appealing calmness of manner, verging on refinement.

The sipping of tea was an incidental but necessary part of the occasion, which ended with more formal bows and glances of mutual appreciation by Rie and Mrs. Tamiya.

Mrs. Nakano tactfully brought the meeting to an end. "We are both so happy that you were able to meet on this occasion." She did not mention any commitment on either side.

Rie wanted to proceed as soon as possible. "It's very apparent that Tama has had good training," she said that evening as she sat with Jihei and Yoshitaro at dinner.

"A good brewing house," Jihei said. "I see no objection."

Yoshitaro frowned. "Such a flat face and large mouth."

Rie impatiently replaced her comb. "Let's agree on the Tamiya daughter. We can't decide on a superficial basis in a matter so vital to the house, Yoshi. Your father and I have explained all this to you. Please try to understand."

"Your personal preferences are a private matter, Yoshi," Jihei said. "Where human feelings are concerned you can do as I do." Jihei spilled sake on the table as he reached to pour for his son.

Rie had the urge to slap her husband's face.

"Even her name is propitious: Tama, 'jewel,' " Rie said, attempting to recover her dignity. "I expect to hear from Mrs. Nakano in a few days."

But she could see the glint of fire in Yoshi's eyes and knew that the matter was far from settled in his mind.

CHAPTER 25

Rie reeled from the news that had just now reached her ears, but which must have been buzzing through the geisha houses for these last two years. How could she have been so blind, she wondered as she went in search of Jihei?

"I must speak with you. Now!" Rie commanded when she caught him in the chilly corridor outside the inner office. "Come to the reception room."

Rie turned abruptly and stalked to the door of the parlor. In a single movement she slid open the door and slipped off her slippers. She hurried into the room and pulled out a zabuton in front of the Butsudan for herself, then slapped a second cushion onto the tatami opposite her. Jihei stumbled into the room after her and slumped onto the zabuton. He glanced uneasily at Rie's frowning face.

She took out her hairpin and began to

twirl it rapidly in both hands on her lap.

"Now I know your true colors at last," she snapped. She leaned forward. "I understand that it was you who ruined our sake. It has become the talk of the geisha houses, I hear." Rie's words split the air in staccato syllables. "What were you thinking, trying to ruin our house? It wasn't enough that you were drinking yourself into idiocy." She breathed rapidly and tried to loosen her obi.

Jihei gasped and reddened, swaying on his zabuton. "But . . . I. . . ."

"You are no longer head of the house. You have brought us dishonor and disgrace, nearly caused our financial ruin. As of now Yoshitaro is head of the house. I do not wish to see you in the house again. Get out!" She spat out the icy words in controlled cadences, then turned to face the Butsudan.

Jihei gasped and blinked, staggered to his feet, and wove back and forth to the door. He slid the shoji open with a bang and stumbled along the corridor, bumping the walls on either side as he headed out the door next to the number one kura.

Rie leaned over and covered her face with her hands. Her breath came in racking sobs, and she reached into her obi for a handkerchief and wiped the tears from her face. She heard Jihei slam the outer door shut. She rose, straightened her obi, and went back into the corridor toward the stairway.

O-Natsu stood at the other end of the hallway wringing her hands. "Can I do anything?" she asked in a hushed voice.

"No, O-Natsu. I am going upstairs. I don't wish to be disturbed. Oh, yes, please see to the children's dinner."

She stomped rapidly up the stairs to her room, went to the window, and sat looking down into the garden. How could she save the house from this unprecedented disaster?

Stunned and desperate, Jihei stumbled along the road in the dark. It was unheard of. How could Rie evict him from his own home? He was still house head. She had no power, no authority. He could not go to the Sawaraya now. O-Toki must have been talking to someone about what he had told her, about the sake souring. Not like her to reveal a confidence. But she must have told someone, maybe O-Haru. O-Haru was a gossip. Where to turn? He paused, swaying in the gloom of the street. His eye caught a red lantern down by the bridge, and he began to stumble toward it. He could get a drink there. They would know him, though it was not a place he frequented. Everyone in this part of Nada knew him. Where was he to go? His mouth felt so dry. He pushed toward the lantern, then bent to duck under the noren and opened the squeaking sliding door.

"Please come in!" came a thin high voice.

Jihei saw a serving girl behind the low counter. She wore a rough kimono and had round red cheeks and was clearly far below the status of geisha.

Jihei didn't hazard her another glance. He slumped down on a stool at the single counter. "Sake!" he grunted.

"Yes." She nodded and turned to get a heated flask and single cup.

"Hurry!" he growled.

"Yes, sir." The girl turned and placed the flask and cup in front of Jihei. She poured quickly before Jihei had a chance to pick up the cup properly. He emptied the cup and poured himself another. Then another. He glanced around furtively and saw that he was the only customer. When the flask was empty he mumbled, "More!"

The girl removed the empty bottle and placed a full one in front of Jihei, pouring the first cup for him. He continued to drink. What could he do? Surely Rie could not have been serious. She had no right, no authority. He was head of the house. He began to nod and sway on the stool. His eyes closed.

"Sorry, sir," came the girl's voice after he had emptied several flasks. "We are closing now. You will have to leave."

Jihei's head had sagged to his chest.

She prodded Jihei on the shoulder. "We are closed now," she said insistently. "Please leave."

"Oh," Jihei groaned. He tried to stand but instead fell off the stool. He reached for the counter to raise himself but slumped back onto the floor. The girl bent to help him up. Jihei leaned against her and reached for her breasts. She brushed his hand off, opened the door, and pushed him out, quickly sliding the door shut behind him.

Jihei lurched into the street and slammed against the rough wooden wall. He gripped his stomach, leaned over, and retched. He wiped his mouth with his kimono sleeve and took a few halting steps away from the wall. He fell and sat immobile, his head down. Then he moved his hands along the ground trying to rise. How could his wife do this to him? And she had never been a real wife, not like O-Toki. But how could he go to O-Toki now? He thrust himself onto all fours and reached for a lamppost to try to stand. He began to shuffle along the road toward the bridge, halting and swaying every few steps, groaning with each breath.

He retched again, and stumbled further. As he arrived at one end of the bridge he reached toward the railing for support. He slipped in the mud, missed the railing, and slid down the steep muddy embankment. His arms flailed frantically as he splashed into the black river below and disappeared.

CHAPTER 26

Rie came to breakfast with her children the next morning. She said little beyond "Good morning, Yoshi."

Before breakfast was finished, Kinnosuke rushed into the dining room out of breath. "Oku-san!" He glanced at Yoshitaro. "Master has been found in the river. He drowned in the night." He gasped in quick sharp breaths and bowed.

Rie glared at Kinnosuke and placed both hands on the table, even as her heart raced. Could he not have told her privately first? She closed her eyes for a moment, her tirade from last night so fresh in her mind. What had she done? "I see." She pushed up from the table. "Come, Yoshi, to the office." She walked purposefully down the corridor followed by Yoshitaro and Kinnosuke. The girls who had been sitting at the table began to weep loudly as Rie made her way to the office.

Rie sat at the table and motioned Yoshitaro and Kinnosuke to join her.

"Just as we've formalized arrangements for your wedding, your father. . . ." She put her hand to her forehead. There was no need to tell the children that she had sent Jihei away or that he was responsible for the sake failure two years earlier. O-Natsu knew, but she would keep quiet.

"What do we do now?" Yoshitaro asked, biting his lip, sorrow written in the lines of his face.

"Of course you succeed now automatically. And you and Kinno need to make the funeral arrangements."

"Why did you push him so hard?" Yoshi looked at Rie accusingly. "That's what drove him to drink as he did. He didn't see any role for himself here, with you making the decisions all along. He felt frustrated. That's why he drank so much, and it only got worse."

Rie glared at Yoshi. "Are you accusing me of being responsible for what he did, Yoshi?"

"I see a connection."

Rie felt her anger rising out of control. "It was your father who caused our sake to sour. He ruined it deliberately! He was destroying our house." She instantly deflated. She hadn't meant to tell him, to hurt him further.

Yoshi stood up, hands on his hips. "I don't believe you. He couldn't have done that." He left the room abruptly.

Rie let out a deep, sobering breath.

That evening Jihei's body lay on the futon in the parlor. The shutters had been closed and the smell of stale sake and death pervaded the room.

Rie paused at the doorway and looked at the lifeless form of the man by whom she had had a child. She arranged zabuton around the futon, and the family seated themselves for the wake. She turned to Yoshitaro next to her.

"It can't be helped, Yoshi," she said softly. "We'll have to postpone the wedding until the year of mourning is over. If only he had not drunk so heavily. All the weddings will be delayed a year." She paused and looked at Yoshitaro.

He nodded, but it was a brusque nod filled with silent anger and accusation.

Silence enveloped the family. Lamplight flickered against the shoji. Kazu, Teru, and Fumi dabbed at tear-filled eyes.

"Sei, go to bed," Rie said, her hand gentle on his shoulder.

Seisaburo stumbled to his feet. He was about to open the shoji when another hand did so from outside.

Kinnosuke knelt at the edge of the tatami and bowed toward Rie and Yoshitaro.

Rie nodded to him and motioned for him to sit opposite her. She looked over at Kinnosuke and bowed slightly to the man she had trained since childhood, a man now so vital to the house and totally dedicated to Yoshitaro. She sighed and looked back at Jihei's corpse. Fumi leaned against Rie, who put an arm around her daughter. Strange that she felt so little for this man she had sent away; mainly relief. No, perhaps not so strange. Hatred had been the real bond between them. And yet she knew that hatred had now created a rift between herself and Yoshi, one she must find a way to overcome.

Early the next morning Rie went down to the kitchen and looked out over the vaulted rooftops. The first light of dawn was just yellowing the sky. Alone in the kitchen, she lit a fire to heat water for tea. O-Natsu and O-Yuki would be in soon. She turned and walked slowly out into the garden. Nothing stirred. No sound was audible. She sat on her favorite rock and rubbed the back of her neck and shoulders. She realized that she had sat at Jihei's deathbed without shedding a single tear. Now her shoulders began to shake and she began sobbing as she released her anguish. Not for the loss of Jihei, for whom she had trouble concealing her distaste. His drinking was just the most obvious of his weaknesses. What she felt was rather a poignant sense that so much of her own life had passed, and relief that he would no longer embarrass or dishonor the house. And finally, sadness for the breach in her relationship with Yoshi. She walked back into the house, paused at the pillar and moved her hands over it thoughtfully.

The children and the business, the house, were still her reason for being. She must find a way to mend her fences with Yoshi. With a last shuddering sigh she walked into the office to ask that a notice be posted over the entrance announcing the funeral.

Rie sat next to Yoshitaro at the head of two long lines of black-kimonoed brewers and their wives. Three Buddhist priests intoned their deep monotonous mantras, rising and falling in sonorous unison. Incense hung heavy in the air and lamps flickered against the shoji and glanced off the elaborate gilt Butsudan. Rie sat absolutely upright looking straight ahead, her face impassive. Out of the corner of her eye she saw that Yoshitaro sat equally immobile at her side and that none of the other four children ranged below him was shedding a tear. Rie felt a sense of family pride as she surreptitiously eyed the five children she had raised so carefully. Her marriage had not been a total loss. It had enabled her to add these five children to the house.

Then a reassuring thought came to her. Now it would never become known that she had banished Jihei from the Omura House, something she really had no authority to do, but Jihei had been too drunk to argue. A huge scandal would have erupted if the news had leaked out. She took a deep breath and pressed her lips together, a twinge of guilt accompanying the relief she felt. If Jihei had not died as he had, that one moment of anger could have very well cost them everything her father had worked his whole lifetime to achieve. She shivered at the thought.

Rie watched with pride as Yoshitaro stood and spoke briefly, thanking all for attending his father's funeral and asking formally for the cooperation of the brewers as he assumed the headship of the Omura House and of White Tiger.

After sake was served, Yoshitaro moved toward the entrance to greet each departing mourner. He overheard Yamaguchi and another speaking as they shuffled toward the door.

"What difference will it make if Yoshitaro is in charge instead of Jihei, anyway?" Yamaguchi said gruffly. "Kinnosuke is far more powerful than Jihei was or his son could ever be."

Yoshitaro did not catch the other guest's reply, but he felt a smoldering anger, nonetheless. As he reached the door Yoshitaro was conscious that his mother was at his side, bowing and joining her words to his as each brewer passed through the door. He knew she was trying to win him over, but he also knew he wasn't ready to make peace. Too much had happened between them.

Later that evening as the family sat together Rie turned to Yoshitaro. She raised a sake flask for him as he held out his cup. Then she picked up a cup, raised it, and toasted him saying, "Now, Yoshi, this is your time." She said no more but rose and went upstairs alone.

Fumi, sobbing, jumped up and ran after her.

Yoshitaro looked around at his glum brother and two weeping sisters. He thought of the comment by the departing Yamaguchi and once again felt the smoldering anger. Of course his mother and Kinnosuke made the decisions. It was natural enough since she had been born in the house. It was moreover necessary, especially since his father had taken to drinking so heavily. What he knew about brewing he had learned from his mother and Kinnosuke. He shifted uneasily in his seat as he remembered his postponed wedding and the bride his parents had selected for him, Tama. Well versed she might be in brewing and even intelligent enough, but Yoshitaro found her flat face plain and unappealing. His affections belonged to O-Sada.

He rose and addressed his siblings, his first act as official house head. "You'd better go to bed. It's been a long, difficult day."

He walked along the corridor, then out through the door next to the number one kura. He hailed a passing ricksha and said abruptly as he climbed in, "The Sawaraya."

At the entrance it was O-Toki herself who greeted Yoshitaro.

"Ah, it is you, my son!" she exclaimed, bowing. "You must be worn out. O-Sada is here. She thought you might come. She will join you in a bit."

O-Toki led the way upstairs to the back room, the one always reserved for his father, Yoshitaro noted.

O-Toki bowed. "Please be seated. I'll be back presently."

Moments later Yoshitaro heard O-Toki's voice again and looked at her more closely as she entered. His natural mother. She knelt, bowed, and poured ceremonial green tea.

Yoshitaro bowed and raised the cup to his lips. "I did not see you at the funeral," he said.

"I was there, in the back room. I could not stay away." She paused and blotted her glistening eyes. "Your father was the most important person in the world to me. He was good to me. He would be so proud of you, to see the way you are taking hold. You will be an illustrious Kinzaemon XI." She bowed again, then moved back to the shoji.

Yoshitaro bowed in acknowledgment of his mother's words — words that contradicted what Yamaguchi had said.

O-Toki rose. "Now I know you will want to spend some time with O-Sada. She will be here shortly." She bowed herself out of the room.

His mother. His *mothers*.

I really have two mothers, my natural mother here in the Sawaraya and Rie, virtual head of one of the most powerful houses in all Kobe. One dedicated to business, the other to pleasure. Many would consider it fortunate, but tonight he felt only pain. Still, he could move with ease between the two worlds, more easily even than his father. A lump formed in his throat. His father had never felt at home in the Omura House. He'd always moved in Mother's shadow. He was far more at ease here at the Sawaraya, but that in the end was his downfall. He lost himself, killed by the very sake they brewed. It was a fate he had no wish to share. Now, he had no choice but to marry Tama, but O-Sada would be his real life partner, just as O-Toki had been his father's. From this day forward, for the rest of his life, he would never take another drink. He would only pretend to drink ceremonial sake.

I will not share my father's fate.

Yoshitaro's musing was interrupted by O-Sada, who entered with a tray of sake and two cups. She bowed and smiled sympathetically before pouring a cup for him.

"You have had a most arduous day. I hope you will be able to relax now. Perhaps a hot bath will help."

Yoshitaro nodded and looked at the beautiful, intelligent face of the woman he had grown to love. He rose and followed O-Sada's swaying figure down to the steaming bath.

Several days later, as Yoshi sat at his desk in

the office, Kinnosuke turned to him.

"Master, we need the seal to affix to this document," he said as he put the finishing touches on the paper.

"I'll get it. I think Mother has it." Yoshi walked to the storeroom where Rie was working.

"Mother, we need the seal in the office for the document Kinno is working on."

"Yes, Yoshi, I'm coming. I will affix it."

Yoshi frowned as they walked to the office. "But I'm house head now. I need the seal for official business."

"I have made final decisions since my father died, and I will continue to do so."

"But. . . ." Yoshi shook his head and clenched his hands.

"This is the way it is, Yoshi."

CHAPTER 27

"Come in, O-Natsu. Join me in a cup of tea?" Rie called when she heard O-Natsu's voice beyond the shoji.

O-Natsu bowed as she entered, smiled, and seated herself opposite Rie. She poured for Rie, then for herself. It had been a year of many changes, least of which was the one Rie'd seen in Yoshi since his father's death. The seal had been a sore point, and he had not failed to let her know it each time a document needed to be signed. She had tolerated his anger, even understood it, but for the sake of the house, she knew she must maintain control. Yoshi didn't have the business acumen necessary to run an operation the size of theirs, and until he did, she could not trust him with it.

"You know, O-Natsu," Rie said, "we two are the only ones who have been in the house this long. Over forty years."

O-Natsu laughed. "Yes, that's so, isn't it?"

"And now that the year of mourning is approaching the end, I want to see Yoshi married as soon as possible. It is unfortunate that it had to be postponed so long, all the marriages." She took her folding fan from her obi and fanned herself slowly.

O-Natsu smiled again. "It will be good to have some activity in the house again. The year has been quiet, hasn't it? Of course we all needed time to mourn the master."

For several minutes the only sound to break the silence between them was the sipping of tea. Conversation was unnecessary to their companionship. Especially false conversation.

At length O-Natsu set her cup down and broke the silence. "Yes, didn't you have some discussion with Mrs. Nakano about the girls as well before the master passed away?"

"Oh, yes, she has them in mind. There will be offers, I am sure, soon after Yoshi's wedding, no doubt." Rie looked at her cup thoughtfully. "Then there will be Fumi, then Kazu and Teru. And of course, finally Sei."

Rie pulled a delicate long-stemmed pipe from her sleeve, filled it from a small pouch in her obi, and lit it, a prerogative of her age and status. Tobacco had entered the country through the Dutch enclave on Deshima

Island, and smoking small pipes had caught on with older women as well as men.

O-Natsu, as though sensing Rie's relaxed mood, also took out her pipe.

Rie nodded. After three short puffs she turned her pipe over on a small raku ware ashtray. "It's important that Yoshi's wife be from a good brewing house." She smiled and nodded.

O-Natsu also tapped her pipe and set it on the ashtray. "I know you have special plans for Fumi and Sei."

"I don't want to overwhelm her with too many marriage arrangements all at once. But I have a plan for Fumi. Sei too. Actually I have something special in mind for Teru as well."

O-Natsu refilled her pipe, then waited for Rie to speak.

"I'll ask Mrs. Nakano to contact the Tamiyas and set the date for the wedding for two weeks after the end of the year of mourning. No need to postpone it longer." She paused to pour tea for O-Natsu and herself. "I'm going to let Yoshi and Tama have the upstairs room. My parents did that for me when I was married, remember? I'll be glad to be back in my old room, close to the garden. It's the first thing I see when I get up in the morning."

"I know," O-Natsu nodded. "Well, I imagine the Tamiyas will be glad to see the wedding over too. The delay can't have been comfortable for them either."

The wedding day was fixed after consulting the calendar, avoiding the unlucky days and selecting one of the most auspicious.

"I've always felt April was the best month for a wedding, especially for a brewing house, at the end of the season. We can turn our whole attention to the occasion," Rie said to her children gathered for an early breakfast on the appointed day. "The cherry blossoms have just come out. Very auspicious for a wedding. Let's all get dressed now. Girls, help each other with your obis."

"I never can get mine right, Mother," said Fumi.

"Kazu will help you. Just be glad you're not the bride, Fumi. It will take two hours to get her dressed," Rie said, patting Fumi on the back.

Fumi wrinkled her nose and walked with an exaggerated swaying after her sisters.

Rickshas were lined up at the main gate waiting to take the family to the Shinto shrine.

Rie stood with O-Natsu as the children emerged for the ride to the shrine. Yoshitaro came first, walking stiffly in his formal black

311

kimono.

"Doesn't he look distinguished!" O-Natsu said loudly enough for the ricksha pullers to hear.

Yoshitaro stepped up into the first ricksha with Rie, who was dressed in the formal black worn by wives and widows alike. To Rie's disappointment, he carefully avoided her eyes. She knew in the long run that this was the right thing and he would thank her later, but she felt an unease recalling his adamant opposition to the thought of marrying Tama, whom he found so unattractive. Rie disliked the idea of imposing an unhappy marriage, perhaps similar to her own. Yet she felt Tama would add strength to the house. That had to take precedence.

Kazu and Teru looked fashionably elegant in their apricot and sea green kimonos. Even Fumi managed to look beautiful in a light blue kimono with a crane pattern at the hem and a beige under kimono and obi. The girls needed to appear at their best to any prospective groom's family. Seisaburo also looked formal as he stepped into the third ricksha.

"Kinno-san and O-Natsu, please take the fourth ricksha," Rie said, and smiled as the runners pulled out into the street.

During the Shinto ceremony Rie scrutinized Tama and found she looked the perfect bride: white silk kimono and brocade obi, face and neck completely whitened, her hair and "devils' horns" covered with the traditional white silk band. No fault could Rie find with Tama's mincing steps, her downcast eyes, her measured bows to each guest present. Even though Tama was not the most beautiful woman, Rie found her more than acceptable. She watched every move as Yoshitaro and Tama exchanged sips from the shallow red lacquer cup. Despite his mixed feelings, Yoshitaro played his role well.

Rie was pleased that every brewer invited appeared for the reception, an assemblage as large as for Jihei's funeral. Yoshitaro's wedding was also a celebration of his status as Kinzaemon XI of the House of Omura. The glittering occasion was proof of the prosperity and reputation of White Tiger and one of the largest affairs of the year 1852. It was now up to Yoshi to adjust to this bride about whom he was less than enthusiastic.

Rie had no firsthand familiarity with the experience of a bride going into a groom's house, no acquaintance with the traditional terrorizing of a bride by a mother-in-law or critical scrutiny by a groom's sisters. Marriage, the abrupt beginning of the most intimate possible relationship, was a harsh test of the mettle of any bride. Rie had been spared what Tama faced: the severity of having to marry into a whole house full of strangers. She did share with Tama what all brides faced: marriage to a total stranger.

What Rie knew above all was that she was responsible for initiating this young bride into the traditions of the Omura House and her role in the White Tiger enterprise. The fact that the house and the business were inextricably linked was why Rie had insisted that Yoshitaro's bride be from a brewing house. Rie did not intend any deviation from the custom that the bride should be the first to rise in the morning and the last to retire at night, the last in the family to enter the bath and the last to eat at the table. For a bride, eating cold rice was an adage that reflected harsh reality.

The morning following the wedding Rie opened the shutters facing the garden and glanced up toward the room she had given Yoshitaro and his bride. The sun had not yet reached the second floor shutters. Just then Rie saw a feminine hand open the wooden shutters and withdraw. Then Rie heard slippers slap quickly down the stairs and head toward the kitchen.

When Rie entered the kitchen, Tama, in a work kimono with sleeves tied back, bowed to the floor three times.

"Oh," said Rie, surprised at Tama's alacrity.

"Please accept my humble efforts to learn and conform to the traditions of the Omura House," Tama said breathlessly.

"Yes, good morning, Tama," Rie replied, nodding.

"I am eager to learn. I shall do my best," Tama repeated.

"Yes, Tama." Rie nodded. "You may help O-Natsu and O-Yuki with breakfast. Please begin by preparing the rice this morning."

Tama bowed again and rose. She took a deep breath and straightened the cotton scarf covering her hair. She turned toward the big rice cauldron.

O-Natsu and O-Yuki exchanged glances without speaking.

It was no small task Rie had given Tama. To be able to cook rice to the exact fluffy palatable consistency was the first test of any woman, a requirement that, if unfulfilled, could send a bride away in disgrace. The proportion of water to rice had to be precise. The word *rice* was synonymous with the word for "meal" or "dinner." All rice served was to be consumed to the last grain.

To waste rice was unconscionable. Moreover, rice was sacred, of the gods. In addition, in the Omura household rice was the critical source of the family's livelihood, the raw material of White Tiger.

Rie joined Yoshitaro and his siblings, who were gathered at the dining table for breakfast. She looked expectantly toward the kitchen. Tama entered bearing a tray with a large wooden Kamakura serving bowl. She knelt at the table and bowed toward Rie, who handed Tama the wooden serving paddle symbolic of the status of wife of the house head. Tama held the paddle with both hands above her head and bowed again. Then, lifting the lid of the serving bowl she took the wooden ladle, filled the first bowl, set it on a tray and, hands trembling, held it out toward Rie. The five brothers and sisters all fixed their eyes on their mother's face. Tension enveloped the room.

With her chopsticks Rie brought a few grains to her mouth, then paused.

"Well, Tama, perhaps just a bit less water."

Rie was instantly sorry at the slight, but it was a necessary one, of course.

Kazu and Teru looked down quickly.

Tama bowed again, biting her lip. "Oh, I have no adequate words of apology," she said.

"You may serve the others now, Tama," Rie replied.

O-Natsu and O-Yuki brought in the pickled plums, miso soup, and tea.

"When you are finished serving breakfast, Tama, you may come to the parlor."

Tama bowed. "Certainly."

Tama filled each rice bowl, placed it on a tray and handed it to a family member, first Yoshitaro, then his brother, then his sisters in order of age. This task finished, she hurried to the kitchen for a hastily eaten bowl of rice with pickles.

Rie finished her breakfast and went to sit before the Butsudan to wait for Tama.

Rie had heard enough stories from O-Natsu about cruel mothers-in-law intimidating frightened, helpless brides, making of them abject slaves. Intelligence was a quality Rie valued, and when she found it in Tama she decided it could be used for the welfare of the house, to foster a daughter-in-law who would work hard and willingly. This same quality Rie had discovered in the small boy who was now her chief clerk, Kinnosuke. Tama would be an ally in her plans for the future of the house, as dedicated to the reputation of White Tiger as she herself. Yoshitaro was O-Toki's son, as Rie had never forgotten and Yoshi had made clearer over the last few years, and while Tama was now his wife, Rie hoped to forge with her a close bond. Tama, on the other hand, had no connection with the Sawaraya. Therefore she was a potential ally. Rie would let Tama know now that while Yoshitaro was formally house head, the representative of White Tiger to the world, in reality it was she, Rie, who had the final word in all important decisions. This was how it was with everything, wasn't it, the *tatemae* appearance and the *honne* reality? A perceptive woman like Tama was certain to recognize the difference.

Rie heard footsteps along the corridor, a pause, then Tama's voice excusing herself as she opened the shoji, bowed properly, and entered the room kneeling.

"Come here, Tama, to the Butsudan."

Tama did as bidden.

Rie turned to face her. "You know that your position as wife of the house head is a most important one," she began, with a nod to acknowledge Tama's bow. "You were selected with utmost care for this role. You are aware, I am sure, that you will be first in the family to rise in the morning and last to retire?"

Tama bowed again, but did not speak, eyes downcast.

"As a person entering the house from outside, you will need to learn the customs of our house as rapidly as possible. I will teach you what you need to know."

"I am unworthy of such an honor, but I will make every effort to justify your faith in me."

"First, please direct your attention to the Butsudan."

Tama bowed toward the altar.

"Here you see the tablets of my mother and father. I offer rice and sake to them each morning, also the plum wine which my mother enjoyed. If I am too busy you will assume this duty, and eventually it will be yours alone. And you will also learn about observing their death anniversaries as the time arises." Rie paused and glanced from the Butsudan to Tama.

"Now, to start with, you need not spend too much time with your husband." Rie knew this might only alienate Yoshi, but duty came first. It was a fact that Yoshi would have to learn.

Tama did not respond, but Rie thought she noticed a slight tightening of Tama's mouth.

"You know the work of the wife of the house head is never finished," Rie continued, "so you must be ever vigilant and alert to any possible problem in the house."

"Most certainly," Tama replied, always ending each statement with a corresponding bow.

"You must take charge, for example, of the scouring of the barrels," Rie said, tapping her folded fan on her lap. "The girls all know how to do this — Fumi, Kazu, Teru. But the responsibility is now yours to see that this critical task is always done thoroughly. The girls will be going out as brides before long, and it is only proper that you see to this matter."

Rie rose. "The workers are your primary responsibility, both the kitchen workers and the kurabito. You need to see that they are well fed and clothed and cared for when they are ill. Without them we could not maintain the reputation of White Tiger. When the kurabito are content, as they are now, they will continue to come back to us year after year."

Tama bowed. "That is what my mother always said also."

Rie looked at Tama and nodded.

"We can go to the kitchen now. You have already met O-Natsu. She is in a special category, like a family member because she has been here so long. You will meet the kitchen helpers."

Rie led the way along the earthen corridor to the kitchen where two maids were scrubbing vegetables. "Here are Michi and Shizu."

Tama bowed slightly to acknowledge the two bowing girls.

"They are the main workers in the kitchen. They prepare the food for the family as well as for the kurabito. You will see that the rice is always properly prepared."

Rie saw a flush rising from Tama's neck to her face. In the corridor they met O-Yuki vigorously flourishing a feather duster.

"And O-Yuki keeps our rooms clean." Rie smiled and turned along the corridor toward the storeroom. "Come, Tama, while the men are gone, I want to show you the kurabito quarters, though of course in the future you cannot go in there, since they are men."

Rie climbed the long steep ladder leading from the storeroom to the large tatami room above, a room lined on two sides by built-in cupboards.

"You will get to know our Toji. He has been here several decades, his father and grandfather before him. He is getting on in years now and is training his son to succeed him. He takes great pride in maintaining the quality of White Tiger."

Tama bowed toward Rie. "Such an honorable tradition, my father always said."

"Yes, let's go down now. Be careful." Rie continued her instruction as they descended the wooden ladder slowly.

"Be sure their clothing is clean at all times and that they are in good health. We have nineteen men here now. You will get to know their names and faces. Here is where they have their meals." Rie pointed to a tatami room off the storeroom. "And I have started to teach some of them to read in the evening, when there is time. You may want to take this over later."

Rie noticed a faint smile on Tama's face.

"Come, we will return to the parlor. You may ask O-Natsu to bring us tea," Rie said.

Rie and Tama sat at the low table in the parlor where the instruction had begun.

"So you see what your main responsibilities are, don't you, Tama?"

Tama bowed.

Rie replaced the comb in her hair.

"I am told you are a good worker. You will need to be. It is no small responsibility, being the wife of the head of the Omura House. I was born here, unlike you, so I was raised with our customs. But you need to learn them all. You can always come to me. I will guide you in the proper course."

"I will do my utmost for the house," Tama

replied, bowing so that her forehead reached the tatami.

Rie smiled with satisfaction as she glanced at her bowing daughter-in-law. Then she paused, because she knew that Tama, as Yoshi's wife, meant trouble. For Rie was quite certain she hadn't heard the last out of Yoshi about Tama and the marriage.

CHAPTER 28

"I have no intention of allowing any of the girls to marry a farmer, which is what the kurabito are most of the year," Rie said to Yoshitaro. "You know I caught Teru talking to Goro twice." Rie tapped her fan on the table.

Yoshi had been surly ever since the wedding. Try as she might to appease him, he had not settled in well with Tama. Rie feared that the two might end up like herself and Jihei. She hoped not, but for now she needed to focus on finding husbands for Fumi and Kazu. Then she would deal with Tama and Yoshi.

"Well, I know you will be careful to watch them, Mother," Yoshitaro replied, employing the barest hint of sarcasm that Rie was determined to overlook.

Because of the house's indebtedness to Mrs. Nakano, both for the arranging of Yoshitaro's marriage and for asking her good offices with Fumi and Kazu, Rie dressed with special care for her meeting with Nada's most sought after go-between.

Rie heard O-Natsu welcome Mrs. Nakano and hurried to the parlor. Rie leaned into a full bow. "Our house is forever grateful for your assistance in Yoshitaro's marriage." She smiled and motioned Mrs. Nakano to the zabuton backing to the tokonoma.

O-Natsu brought in the finest grade of Shizuoka green tea. As Rie looked at Mrs. Nakano's dark green kimono and obi she realized she needed more help from Sunao in the selection of her own kimono.

"And how are your other children?" Mrs. Nakano inquired.

Rie bowed. "Thank you. As you know, since Yoshitaro's wedding had to be postponed due to my husband's passing, Fumi and Kazu have now both reached the age for marriage."

Mrs. Nakano had not inquired about their health as was customary in an arrangement such as this. She bowed abruptly, then quickly adjusted her plump hands on her lap. "Does this mean that you want two husbands for your daughters, two at the same time?" Her voice rose higher than normal.

"Well, they would not be married in the

same ceremony, but I feel they should both be settled this year." Rie smiled, bowed low, and pushed a plate of two delicate plum-shaped cakes closer to Mrs. Nakano.

Mrs. Nakano looked at the exquisite cakes. "It may be difficult to find two brewers' sons of the right age this year, for autumn weddings," she said, no longer smiling.

Rie sat straighter. "In that case we may be satisfied with a wholesaler for one of them, or a shipper. A house related to our business in some way."

"How old are Fumi and Kazu now?" Mrs. Nakano asked.

"Fumi is twenty, and Kazu will soon be nineteen. Just the right ages," Rie replied, smiling and bowing.

"I haven't seen them lately, but I recall at Yoshitaro's wedding they were attractive, especially Teru, if I may say so."

Rie bowed, at the same time pressing her lips tighter together at the praise given O-Toki's daughter. "We need not arrange Teru's marriage for another year or so."

"Let me see," Mrs. Nakano began. She lifted her teacup and paused. "Well, there is a wholesaler here in Nada whose son is the right age, the Nagata family. And, oh yes, the Kawano family has a son of that age as well. They are in yeast production."

"Yes, I know both families." Rie bowed. "You can be sure that Kazu has had strict training. She's accustomed to hard work, and will have the best of trousseaus."

"I am certain," Mrs. Nakano said.

"We would be grateful if you obtain complete information on the Nagatas. Then we can go ahead with the o-miai soon, if they are agreeable. Yes, I would like autumn weddings for Fumi and Kazu, before the brewing begins." She paused and bowed again. "Now for Fumi there is a special requirement. I plan to adopt a mukoyoshi for her, train him here, and send them out in a bunke branch, closely connected to the main house."

Mrs. Nakano hesitated. "A mukoyoshi? But you already have Yoshitaro as house head."

Rie bowed. "I am sorry to trouble you with this special requirement. Of course we hope to find the most excellent clerk in all Kansai. I have heard that the Ikeda family has a second son who is very skilled."

Mrs. Nakano cleared her throat. "I will see what I can learn about the Ikeda son."

"We are eternally obligated," Rie said, bowing lower than usual as she saw Mrs. Nakano to the door. Rie bit her lip, remembering Mrs. Nakano's slight shift in manner at the mukoyoshi matter. It would not do to alienate this woman on whom the house relied so heavily. Perhaps it would help to give an extra generous go-between fee for Fumi's marriage arrangement.

Rie was pleased but not surprised that both the Ikedas and Nagatas agreed to Mrs. Nakano's request for the o-miai meetings, then for the weddings of the two girls. Lucky days were selected for Fumi's wedding in early September and for Kazu's in early November.

Fumi was less than enthusiastic when Rie broached the topic of her marriage. "Not yet, Mother." She puffed out her cheeks.

Bold girl.

"You know you won't really be leaving the house. We'll find a skilled mukoyoshi for you, train him here, then send you out in a branch house. You'll stay close to the main house that way." She smiled.

"But how can you do that when Yoshi is house head?"

"It won't affect his position, you'll see. And when you have a child, he or she might be able to succeed Yoshi."

Fumi's eyes widened. "Really? I'm not sure Yoshi will like the idea. Isn't it unheard of?"

Rie laughed, enjoying Fumi's spirited argument. "I'm going to speak to him, don't worry." Rie was sure she would not enjoy *Yoshi's* spirited argument.

At dinner that evening, Rie had her chance to discuss the matter with Yoshi when the others had left the table.

"Yoshi, you know I think I'd like to keep Fumi here close to the business. I'd hate to see her leave as a bride to another house. I'd rather find a mukoyoshi for her, train him here, then send them out in a branch house, close to us."

Yoshi's face reddened. "A mukoyoshi! What would his position be here? I'm house head, and I have no intention of retiring. I don't see what. . . ."

"Calm down, Yoshi. Of course your position is secure. We'll make it clear Fumi's husband will not remain here. He won't be entered in our koseki." Rie leaned over and poured tea for Yoshi. "You can see that this will help the house, can't you?"

"Well, maybe," he said with an edge of bitterness to his voice. "But why not send Sei out in a branch?"

Rie smiled. "Exactly what I have in mind."

Rie continued her plans for the two weddings of Fumi and Kazu. "This way we can order all the kimono, linens, and chests for both at the same time," Rie said to her daughters. "These kimonos will last the rest of your lives," she added. "And we will give you a sum of cash, Kazu, in the event of divorce by your groom's family, though of course we don't anticipate that. You know a samurai bride can be sent away simply by 'three and a half lines' if they in any way offend the groom's family. And they don't have the protection of their own funds."

Kazu nodded apprehensively.

Although Kazu seemed uncertain about her impending marriage, Rie was gratified that the plan for selecting Fumi's husband was going smoothly.

The summer of 1853 was consumed in frantic activity: visits by lacquerware dealers, silk merchants from Nishijin in Kyoto, long sessions poring over designs and hues, and sittings for fittings by kimono seamstresses.

"I don't have your sense of taste in these matters," Rie told her cousin Sunao, whom she had invited to stay with her for several days during the selections of kimono and patterns.

The house remained in a continual flutter with daily visits by wedding specialists. Early morning calls of *"gomen kudasai"* at the entrance to the office and house did not end until dusk. Fumi and Kazu were continually suspended between excitement over the impending marriages and apprehension about what lay in store for them with strangers for husbands.

"Be strong," Rie said to them one evening when they lingered at the dinner table. "Always remember that you come from the House of Omura. Just as you have been trained to uphold the honor of our house in your behavior, so also when you are married you will uphold the honor of the Nagata house, Kazu. And Fumi will remain in this house until she and her husband leave in a branch house. This will no longer be your home, Kazu. When you marry, your name will be removed from the Omura register and entered in the Nagata register." Rie paused and looked from one intent face to the other, sorry to see the sadness there. "So no matter what your husband or mother does, you know you must endure. Even I have had to endure often, though I was born in this house and had no mother-in-law here."

As Rie looked at the tense expressions on both faces she recalled her mother's words on the eve of her marriage to Jihei. She hesitated, then repeated the words to her daughters: "Sometimes, a woman must 'kill the self' in order to survive. What this means is that we women can never behave selfishly. We must never lose sight of the welfare and interests of the house. These are our reasons for being. When you have children you will understand these things better. But you have understood what I have taught you. These things are the key to your survival and also to contentment in life, the satisfaction of knowing that you have done your duty and done your best for your house." Rie stopped speaking and smiled inwardly at each anxious expression.

Fumi and Kazu had not taken their eyes from Rie's face as she talked. She thought she detected a pout on Teru's face as she listened with her sisters. Rie poured tea for her daughters. She glanced at Kazu's expression of earnest concern. Fumi leaned against her mother, as if for assurance. Rie glanced at Teru. Why was it that Rie always felt a hint of insolence in Teru? Was it because she was O-Toki's daughter, or was it only her imagination? Teru's meetings with Goro were a nagging worry. Rie had done her best to prepare them, even to the point of making certain that O-Yuki handed them all an illustrated booklet of advice to brides, supposedly without Rie's knowledge. Still, Teru's conversations with Goro were a festering concern, and yet she couldn't marry all three daughters at the same time. Jihei's death had already delayed the others.

"Now, get some rest, girls. I have confidence you will do well in your new homes." Rie rose and touched the arm of each daughter. With a touch of melancholy, she watched the girls walk down the corridor whispering, their arms tightly intertwined.

The wedding kimonos for Fumi and Kazu were similar but not identical: the finest white silk with Chinese red lining that could be glimpsed each time the bride took a small pigeon-toed step. The obis were white brocade patterned subtly with plum, pine, and bamboo. Rie made certain that the expenditures for Fumi's wedding was a bit larger, though not so much as to be overtly noticeable.

"I don't want to impose the cost of two wedding gifts in one year for Omura weddings on many brewers or friends, so I'm dividing the guest lists," Rie said to Sunao.

"Then the girls' weddings will be smaller than Yoshi's, won't they?" Sunao asked.

"Oh, yes. His was more important. And Fumi's will be too. Remember, I told you I want to adopt a husband for her."

"How could I forget?" Sunao replied. "I'm looking forward to it. People won't know what to make of it, will they?" She laughed, her plump face dimpled. "It isn't as if you didn't have a son. What an enigma you are sometimes, Rie."

Rie smiled, took out her comb and then reinserted it. She looked at her cousin. "I'm so grateful to you, Sunao, for taking the time to help me. I just don't have your taste in kimonos. And I value your company."

"I enjoy doing it. I always enjoy working with fabrics."

Fumi's wedding was a grand affair, and nearly all brewers in Kobe were invited, including Saburo and his wife, at whom Rie stole surreptitious glances from time to time while he did the same. Rie was able to glance at Saburo just as he looked at her, and they shared the briefest of smiles before both looking at Fumi. Rie realized that Saburo knew Fumi was his daughter; she felt warmed and smiled inwardly.

He would have noticed that the shape of Fumi's face echoed his.

Fumi and Eitaro of the Ikeda family behaved with such propriety. Yoshi gave the speeches on behalf of the house and did a most creditable job. By now the servants were all experienced in serving large numbers of guests and caused Rie no concern.

Despite Yoshi's obvious displeasure that

Fumi and her husband would remain in the house while Eitaro was being trained to assume the burdens of head of a branch family, Rie was pleased by the addition. So far things were going as planned. It was almost too good to be true. Fumi and her husband were given a room just below Yoshi and Tama's. The house was becoming a continual hub of activity, and Tama was assuming some of the household responsibilities so that Rie was able to spend more time in the office on business matters.

Kazu's wedding went as planned, a respectable affair with what everyone said was a well-trained bride. Kazu, Rie was gratified to note, kept her eyes modestly downcast during the entire ceremony and the long laudatory speeches at the reception. Kazu was now a member of the Nagata family and no longer Rie's responsibility.

At the reception Sunao turned to Rie. "Did you hear that, Rie?" Sunao asked, leaning over in a whisper. "Mrs. Akita said she had never seen such a subtle shade of apricot."

Rie squeezed Sunao's hand. "Good. You chose well."

At both weddings Rie's glance lingered on Saburo Kato and she felt the old feeling of longing, of regret that their time together had been so brief, all those years ago. Rie was nevertheless able to exchange special smiles with Saburo as she nodded to three handsome sons who accompanied their parents. Without wishing to appear too obvious Rie asked Mrs. Kato for the names of her three sons.

"They are Hiro'ichi, Jirobei, and Isamu," she replied, smiling. "Jirobei and Hiro'ichi are already married."

"*Ah*, is that so?" Rie said with a proper bow and smile. Mrs. Kato had given her exactly the information she wanted. She looked closely at the youngest son and decided to make careful inquiries of Mrs. Nakano. In all these years Rie had cherished the notion that perhaps Kazu or Teru might marry a son of Saburo.

That night as she combed her hair she smiled at her reflection in the mirror. Only Teru and Sei remained. She hoped to get her married to Isamu, thereby linking her family with the family of Saburo Kato forever.

Over the next few months Rie spoke with Mrs. Nakano again, and began the negotiations that would lead to the fruition of a cherished dream. Rie made certain that Teru realized what a prize she would have as her husband.

■ ■ ■ ■

A cold relentless rain was pelting the roofs of the Omura compound. It was nearly midnight, the hour of the tiger. Teru rolled out of her futon and slipped out of the room and along the corridor to the door to the compound area. She pulled her cloak tightly around her head and ran across to the cooper's shed.

"Goro, are you there?" she said in a loud whisper.

"Over here." He loomed out of the black mist and took hold of Teru's arm. "Come, let's go around to the other side of the shed where it's drier and there's no danger of being seen."

The two slapped through the puddles holding hands, around to the back of the shed.

"Goro, Mother is insisting that I marry that Isamu Kato. The o-miai was three days ago. I can't marry him. I won't!" She clung to Goro and choked out her words.

Goro put his arms around her and held her tightly.

"I know." He rubbed her back.

"I want to be with you. I'd rather die than marry that self-important prig," she moaned.

"What can we do? My parents are already arranging my marriage too."

"There's one way we can be together, Goro. Forever." She gazed into Goro's eyes.

Goro's eyes fixed hungrily on Teru's face. "What do you mean?"

Her voice took on a strangely calm cadence. "You know what they did in the Chikamatsu dramas? I've seen it at Bunraku."

"You mean . . . you mean *shinju,* lovers' suicide?" Goro stuttered out the word.

"Yes! Yes! That way we can be together forever! They can't stop us!"

Goro moved his hand up and down Teru's back. "But . . . could you do that, Teru? Could I?"

"We would do it together, Goro. Give each other the courage. We can go to the beach at night, the way the lovers did in the Chikamatsu play."

Goro looked down at Teru's eager, beautiful face and took it in his hands. He kissed her, for the first time, lingering at the taste of her lips.

Teru pressed her body against Goro's insistently.

He put his hands on Teru's shoulders and moved back to look into her face. "We'd better consider carefully, Teru. Plan in detail and make certain that we have the courage to succeed."

"I'm certain," said Teru, her voice sharp, almost metallic. "The life Mother has chosen for me has no meaning. I can't live that way. A brief time with you, however brief, is better than a whole lifetime with that Kato person. We would be together, Goro, really together." She clung to him fiercely.

"I can see how strong you are, Teru. You have the strength of a tiger, at the hour of the tiger." He smiled briefly. He felt his need for her growing, felt the pressure in his groin.

"The wedding is set for three weeks from now," Teru said. "We can meet here a week from tonight, and be ready to go to the beach." She reached her arms around Goro's neck and kissed him on the mouth. "Be strong, Goro. We'll be together forever." She turned and ran back to the house.

CHAPTER 29

"Only two weeks until Teru's marriage. It will be a relief, won't it, O-Natsu," Rie said, "to have her wedding out of the way? Teru has been such a worry, with her geisha's ways."

O-Natsu nodded.

Rie was glad she had never informed either Kazu or Teru that she was not their birth mother, and that neither O-Yumi nor O-Toki had been invited to the weddings of their daughters. The real parentage of the two girls was not common knowledge among Kobe brewers, though O-Natsu said there were rumors.

"What does it really matter, O-Natsu?" Rie said. "The children of mistresses are often recognized, taken in by reputable houses. What matters is that I have raised them as members of the house. They really are Omura daughters."

O-Natsu refrained from pointing out that

while this was true of geisha sons, it was most unusual to recognize geisha daughters.

Exactly one week had elapsed since Teru's midnight tryst with Goro. The hour of the tiger approached. Several times during the week Teru had gone into the garden or stopped in front of the Butsudan when she found it necessary to be alone with her thoughts, with her fateful decision. She knew it was her resolve more than Goro's willingness that would enable them to act out their plan. She did not want to weaken at the last minute.

Teru pushed out of her futon and reached under it for the white obi sash she had hidden there only hours earlier. She thrust it into her kimono sleeve and moved quietly along the corridor to the door to the compound. She slid the shoji open slowly and looked out into the courtyard. The night was clear and cloudless. She decided against taking her cloak. What difference would the chill of November make? Besides, Goro would warm her. She looked toward the shed and could just make out his silhouette in the moonlight. She glanced back at the house as she emerged from it, this house where she had been taught endurance, discipline, and obedience, those virtues so prized by her mother. Well, Fumi, the perfect daughter and sister, was welcome to them.

She moved quickly to Goro, embraced him without speaking. She looked into his tense, sensitive face and kissed him.

He pressed against her, his arms holding her tightly. "Teru, Teru," he moaned hoarsely.

She looked into his eyes. "Let's not hesitate. We'll be strong, won't we?"

Goro nodded, his eyes locked with hers.

They walked out of the back side of the compound onto the moonlit road, took the road to the ocean and walked in silence, arms entwined, careful to avoid chance meetings with anyone. When they reached the shore they stopped, looked into each other's eyes, and embraced. Teru took Goro's hand and led him toward the narrow sandy strip at the water's edge. They sat on the sand and gazed at each other. Goro moved his hand over the front of Teru's kimono until he found the opening. Teru opened her kimono with both hands and lay back on the sand.

"Now, Goro, and forever," she said. She closed her eyes as Goro moved over her.

They did not count the passing of the time of their passion.

Finally, Goro moved away from her. "Yes,

we were meant to be together," he said, looking down into her face.

"We will always have each other, Goro."

They lay on the sand in each other's arms until Teru noticed the first glimmer of dawn lightening the sky. She sat up and took from her sleeve the long white obi tie. She drew her knees up and tied them loosely together with one end of the white strip, so that she would not be discovered with her legs apart, later.

Goro watched intently.

"Here, Goro, tie the other end around your leg, not so tightly that you can't walk."

He fumbled with the tie. "This way?" he asked as he twined the strip.

"Yes. We can wait until it's nearly light before we enter the water." She took Goro's hand.

"No regrets, Teru?" he asked in a deep, half-muffled voice.

She faced him, her body pressed against his. "No regrets, Goro."

They embraced and stood. For several minutes neither spoke nor moved. Then she took his hand. "Shall we go now?"

They embraced again, then took small, halting steps into the water. Neither knew how to swim. Teru shuddered and gasped at the shock of the cold waves lapping at their feet, their legs, their bodies.

"We can't stop, Goro," Teru said, sobbing.

They walked hand in hand into the sea, waves washing over them. Teru coughed and sputtered, and further on twisted and turned in agony beside her beloved.

Gradually, they began to sink beneath the waves, Teru's hair floating on the surface of the water above her, then nothing, only the muffled sound of water.

"Mother! Mother! Teru's gone! I can't find her anywhere!" Fumi cried as she ran into Rie's room.

"What do you mean, she's gone?" Rie demanded. "She can't be gone. She's getting married in two weeks." Rie frowned, walked purposefully into the corridor and stepped into the girls' room. She looked into the empty room, then walked to the bathroom and looked in. At the kitchen door she stopped.

"O-Yuki, where's Teru? Have you seen her this morning?"

"*Uh* . . . no, I haven't." O-Yuki looked from Rie to Fumi, who was wringing her hands behind her mother.

"Well, search the house, O-Yuki." Rie paused, suddenly apprehensive. "And go to the cooper's shed. See if Goro is there and anyone has seen her."

O-Yuki turned and ran down the corridor and out to the courtyard.

Rie bit her lip and quickly poured herself a cup of tea, then turned to Fumi. "Did Teru say anything to you last night?"

"Nothing special, Mother. Just good night, as usual."

"*Humph!* Something was not usual at all. Go and have your breakfast, Fumi," she said sharply.

When she was gone, Rie stood in the kitchen sipping tea impatiently. She heard the shoji to the courtyard open and O-Yuki's voice call, "Oku-san! Oku-san! The cooper says Goro is gone too!"

Rie gasped and slammed down her cup. "Horrible! I should have known. She was still O-Toki's daughter, not mine, in spite of everything I did."

Rie turned and walked rapidly through the courtyard and to the inner office, where Yoshitaro and Kinnosuke were going over an order.

"Yoshi! Kinno! Teru and Goro have run away together. And the wedding only two weeks away."

"No!" Yoshitaro said. "How could she . . . they?"

"What shall we do?" She walked back and

forth, frowning. "Yoshi, remove her name from the koseki, today!" she ordered.

"I'll go out, Oku-san," Kinnosuke said, "and see what I can learn. They haven't simply vanished into thin air. They can't have gone far. Someone must have seen them." He rose and left the office.

Rie started to speak to Yoshitaro about Teru, but stopped herself. Yoshi was also O-Toki's child. Why complain to him about O-Toki and Teru? She turned and walked along the corridor and out into the garden, past her rock. She paced back and forth on the cold gray stones. What could she do to preserve the name of the house? What could she say to the Katos? And what a disaster to her long-cherished dream. After several minutes she returned to the office, where Tama had joined Yoshitaro.

"I don't know what to say to the Katos, Yoshi," Rie said. She fidgeted with her comb. Her hope of a family bond with Saburo's family was destroyed, adding to her despair.

"Maybe when we know where they have gone we'll know what to say," Tama said, looking up at Rie. "Here, Mother, have some tea. You haven't even had your breakfast."

"I can't eat now, Tama," Rie said. She sat

346

at the table and looked at Tama. "I should have known. I should have guessed," she repeated.

"Don't blame yourself, Mother," Tama said.

"It's not your fault," Yoshitaro said. "She was always strong willed and unpredictable."

The door to the outer office opened and Kinnosuke entered, out of breath. He bowed.

"Their bodies have been found in the water, down by the harbor," he sputtered. "They were tied together." He looked down and bowed again. "I'm very sorry."

Dead. Rie gasped, her face in her hands.

Yoshitaro and Tama both groaned.

Rie forced back tears as she raised her head. "Yoshi and Tama. You must go to the Katos. Tell them Teru has had an accident, has been killed. Don't mention Goro. Apologize abjectly. And Kinno, go to Goro's father and give him whatever is necessary to hush this up. He may not want it known either. And take care of the cremations, will you? We can't have anyone talking about this. Nothing is to be said. Her name will never be mentioned in this house again."

CHAPTER 30

Two or three months had elapsed since Teru's death, and the house had a hushed air about it that felt suffocating. Rie fanned herself as she looked down at the words of sympathy penned by Saburo himself. Tender words that touched her heart and brought tears to her eyes, words that she would cherish forever. She tucked the letter neatly into the folds of her obi, wanting it close to her always. He had also sent a specially arranged ikebana exactly like the one they had so admired at the flower festival all those years ago. She smiled through the tears, feelings of gratitude welling up inside her.

With a sigh, she turned her attention to Tama, who now cooked rice to perfection, always rose first and retired last in the family. Rie could find no fault with her hardworking dedication to Yoshitaro and to the house. But Tama showed no sign of becoming pregnant. Rie hesitated to mention it to

Tama, recalling her own years of frustration at not bearing an heir. Still, it was imperative that Yoshitaro have an heir.

She was also concerned about Yoshi's attitude toward Tama. Yoshi showed no sign of any affection toward his wife, and seemed oblivious to his duty to provide an heir.

One evening as Rie was closing her shutters and preparing for the night she heard O-Natsu's voice beyond the shoji.

"Yes, come in, O-Natsu," Rie said. "Sit down."

Rie turned expectantly toward O-Natsu, whose cheeks were no longer plump or apple-red and whose hair was thinning.

"I know you have been concerned that Tama has not borne an heir," O-Natsu began.

"Yes, O-Natsu. And I have hesitated to mention it to Tama. You understand."

"Yes, I remember well. And I believe this generation is about to repeat. . . ." O-Natsu paused.

Rie caught her breath. "No! You don't mean . . . ?"

"Yes, I'm afraid so," O-Natsu said before Rie could finish her question. "I have learned that a young geisha at the Sawaraya is pregnant, the geisha whom Yoshitaro visits. Her name is O-Sada." O-Natsu bowed. "I thought you would want to know."

"Yes, O-Natsu. I refuse to have another generation of a geisha's child, a geisha's bloodline, in this house!" Rie turned her comb over and over in her hands, took out her fan, and banged it on the table.

O-Natsu looked down at her chapped, work-worn hands. "I believe the child is due in about three months."

Rie sighed deeply. "Thank you, O-Natsu. I don't believe we need to mention it to Tama. I'll speak to Yoshi about this, about his obligation."

O-Natsu wished Rie good night and left.

Rie turned back to her dressing table and combed out her long, thick hair. What a disgusting twist of fate. Maybe it was not just fate. Maybe Yoshi was deliberately staying away from Tama, refusing to sleep with her. Would a geisha's bloodline never cease to flow in the Omura House? What a calamity that Tama had not become pregnant, just as she herself had not until it was too late.

Several evenings later Rie saw her opportunity to speak with Yoshi at the dinner table when the others had left.

She glanced at him and saw that he was about to leave. "Yoshi, we need to talk. I am concerned that Tama has not yet become pregnant."

"She will never become pregnant," he said with a smug air about him.

Rie frowned. "What do you mean, never? In my case it took a while, but how do you know she will *never* become pregnant?"

Yoshi rose. "It will not happen because she will not have the opportunity."

"Sit! You have not been excused. What do you mean by suggesting that she will not have the opportunity? Do you think you can refuse your duty to this house? Impossible! You were adopted as heir, and you must provide a successor."

Yoshi paused in the doorway. "We will have an heir. I have a daughter already."

"I know about your disgraceful philandering at the Sawaraya. And that geisha has had a child. But we will not bring her into this house as we did you."

"Then there will be no heir, no successor," Yoshi said, and walked from the room.

As Yoshitaro went about the business of the day, he recalled with pleasure his visit to O-Sada when she had told him she was pregnant with his child. She had smiled as she watched his face. He had been so enthusiastic, had embraced her.

"My wife has not become pregnant in three years," he told her.

"Perhaps you have given me a better chance than your wife," she had replied, a mysterious glint in her eyes.

He guessed that Rie would eventually relent and want to bring O-Sada's baby into the house, but he dreaded breaking the news to Tama. He knew Rie would do it, if asked, relieving him of the duty. Still, he felt a twinge of guilt, a bit of sadness for Tama, who had worked so faithfully for the house.

Several months had passed and Rie still hadn't relented and let Yoshitaro bring O-Sada's child into the household. Tired of fighting with his mother over the child, he determined to pay O-Sada a visit. He knew it would be an awkward meeting, painful for O-Sada, yet he could not postpone it.

Faced with the prospect of having no heir for the main house, Rie had no choice but to agree to Yoshi's request to bring in Ume, distasteful though the prospect of another geisha's child in the house was.

O-Sada did not attempt to conceal her tears as she nursed her baby. As he watched, Yoshitaro recalled the earlier conversation, the far happier occasion of his previous visit.

He put a hand on O-Sada's arm to calm her. "But Ume will have a good life, O-Sada. She will have every advantage in the Omura House. And a good marriage."

"Yes," she sobbed. "I know, but I don't want to give her up." She stopped and put the baby to her shoulder.

"Be reasonable, O-Sada," Yoshitaro said, leaning into her. "What life can you give her? And you know caring for you will always be my responsibility."

"Yes, it's true," she said softly. "I don't want her to grow up here, like me. O-Toki has told me she had a daughter besides you, and there was another from the Kitaya, all adopted into the Omura House."

Yoshi stiffened.

She put a hand to her mouth. "I thought you knew about Teru and Kazu."

He shook his head brusquely, eyes downcast. Once again his mother, if he could even call her that, had lied to him. He could never forgive her. Three children. He had been told the girls were adopted relatives from the country. No wonder she favored Fumi and Sei, who were no doubt her own.

"It was very hard for her to lose them that way. That's why she is always so happy when you visit. She is proud of you." She sniffed. "But I can't bear the thought that I won't be able to watch Ume grow up and marry."

"I'll tell you about her whenever I come. And I'll do my best to arrange that you can see her sometimes, especially when she marries. But that's twenty years away, so don't worry about it now. I promise she will have the best possible life."

O-Sada sighed and wiped at her tears with her sleeve.

"Come," Yoshitaro urged. "O-Yuki is waiting in the ricksha outside."

O-Sada rose holding the baby, picked up a large furoshiki with the baby's clothes, and shuffled out after Yoshitaro. He took the furoshiki, put an arm around O-Sada, then released her and handed her an envelope. She bowed and handed Ume to O-Yuki, then leaned over to kiss the baby a last time before bowing again to Yoshitaro. He watched from the ricksha as O-Sada turned and stumbled back to the entrance, hands over her face.

Rie looked at Tama. The rest of the family had left the dinner table and they were alone.

"I'm sure you are aware, Tama, that the most important duty of the wife of the house head is to produce an heir. You know, the samurai say a bride is a borrowed womb."

Tama sat opposite Rie, eyes downcast. Rie could see that she was twisting her hands in her lap.

Tama bowed. "I am sorry to have disappointed you."

"Well, it can't be helped." Rie sighed. She had not planned to share her own experience with Tama, but it seemed appropriate now. "You know, Tama, the same thing happened to me when I married. My parents adopted your husband because I had no child for several years after I married."

Tama looked up, her eyes widening. "Oh, I didn't know it happened that way."

"Yes, Yoshitaro is my husband's son by a mistress."

Tama caught her breath. "Oh!" was all she could manage.

Rie felt a measure of sympathy for the girl, knowing how such words stung, how they burrowed beneath the skin to leave pain in its wake. But it was kinder to tell her than to have her find out as Rie had — through gossip on the streets. "Yes, a mistress at the Sawaraya, a geisha. Now Yoshi has insisted on bringing in his daughter from the same establishment, though I have been opposed to it. I cannot prevent it, since we do require an heir, a successor to the main house. Yoshi is house head so I may not be able to prevent this, though I have been trying to stop his plan. I have not succeeded. We will have to bring this child in."

Tama's hands flew to her face. Then she bowed, and ran from the room. Rie could hear her crying as she hurried toward the stairs.

Rie closed her eyes, feeling spent by the encounter and bad for Tama. She was about to take a well-needed rest when she heard a ricksha, and walked toward the entrance, fearing what she would find there.

When Yoshi returned to the house with Ume, Rie and Tama both greeted the baby reluctantly. From the moment Ume came into the house Yoshitaro protected her. He looked in on her in the nursery night and morning, often picking her up, even carrying her into the office to show to Kinnosuke.

"Oh yes," Kinnosuke said, grasping a tiny waving hand. "I can see that she is your daughter." Kinnosuke smiled at the gurgling baby.

"I hope she doesn't grow up to look like me," Yoshitaro said, gazing down at her. "I'd rather she took after her mother," he said softly.

"Well, no matter whom she looks like she'll be very important to the next generation in the house. She'll have an adopted husband, as your mother did. Unless you have a son, of course," Kinnosuke added quickly. "But I'll see that she gets the same training you did," he said, patting the baby.

"Good. And by the way, congratulations! I hear that you have had a second son," Yoshitaro said with a touch of envy in his voice. "I hope Nobu is doing well."

Kinnosuke bowed. "She is thriving, thanks to you. Both of our sons are healthy, and Toru is growing fast. Nearly six. He'll soon be going out as apprentice somewhere, to eat someone else's rice. We can't have him grow up idle or spoiled."

"You'll send him out so young?" Yoshitaro asked.

"Have you forgotten that you were helping me here when you were five?"

"I haven't forgotten, Kinno-san. Yes, I would be grateful if you would have a hand in Ume's training."

As Rie eavesdropped on the conversation she realized she felt nothing for Ume but annoyance that the child was now installed as Yoshi's heir. And now she would be the probable wife of Yoshi's successor, another adopted husband.

"That she has no Omura blood is really regrettable," Rie said to O-Natsu, later that day, the only one in the house to whom she could speak so frankly. Ume was granddaughter of Jihei and daughter of Yoshi.

O-Toki's bloodline was still polluting the house. "But she will be trained to become a true daughter of the Omura House, totally dedicated to our traditions," Rie added, "and she must never be told of her Sawaraya origins. Every hint of it must be expunged from her character." A fleeting memory of Teru flashed through her mind and she flinched.

Seisaburo was now twenty-one and Rie could no longer delay arranging his marriage. She again turned to Mrs. Nakano, this time to find a bride from a brewing family, so that Seisaburo and his bride could establish a new branch family. Yet even as the plans progressed, Yoshi appeared withdrawn like his father had been, and turned more and more to Kinnosuke, avoiding Rie whenever possible. Well, it couldn't be helped. The house came above the individual. She had learned it, and he must learn it too.

The Yamada family were respected brewers and had a daughter of the right age. Rie was satisfied at the prospect of a link with another major brewing house in Nada. She smiled. How proud her father would be. She would inform him when she burned incense at the Butsudan in the morning.

"Must I?" Sei said, when his mother told

him of Mari, the Yamada daughter.

"Yes, Sei, and she is quite pretty as well as being from a highly respected family." Rie took out her comb, paused, then replaced it smartly. How well Mrs. Nakano's daughter-in-law had turned out to be as a go-between after old Mrs. Nakano had retired. She had trained her successor well.

One evening, as Rie was preparing for the night, she sat before her dressing table combing her hair and musing. The face of the family was continually changing. The only child still at home, once Sei was gone, would be Yoshitaro, but already the next generation was beginning with Ume. And Tama. Rie still thought of her as a new member, though a permanent one, although one who had failed a major duty. To be fair, it was Yoshi who had failed.

"I have no intention of sending you back because you have not borne a child," Rie assured Tama one evening. "I know that some samurai families simply hand a bride 'three and a half lines' and dismiss her if she fails to bear an heir. But we are not samurai, and even if we didn't have Ume I would not do that."

Tama held Ume and appeared to be trying to develop affection for the baby, as she bowed and murmured her gratitude.

Rie continued combing her hair, slowly gazing at each graying strand. Now Eitaro was in the house, not actually a house member, but he came to the office each day and worked right alongside Yoshi and Sei. Rie noticed that Eitaro and Seisaburo had formed a close bond from the start, a friendship. Yoshitaro, though, seemed to keep his distance from Eitaro, insofar as possible in the office. Perhaps when Eitaro finished his apprenticeship in the house and was set up in his own branch, Yoshitaro's attitude might change, or would it only become worse?

One morning Rie lit an incense stick in the Butsudan and clapped her hands to attract the attention of the gods, the spirits of her parents. Then she turned toward the tokonoma alcove and began arranging three stalks of yellow chrysanthemums in a shallow black vase.

"Mother, where are you?" Fumi's voice floated in from the corridor.

"In here, Fumi," Rie answered.

Fumi glided into the room and joined Rie in front of the tokonoma.

Rie glanced at her daughter's glowing complexion. "It's good to see you, dear. And you're looking so well, so happy," the last almost a question. "I'm glad we found you a house so close by. It's not really as if you've left, is it?"

"It's very convenient for Eitaro. I know he appreciates being close by. And, you know, I don't think he objected to becoming a mukoyoshi."

Rie smiled. "Why should he? We're a house everyone respects. He'll have his own branch soon. And he seems to be working well with Kinno, and especially with Sei." Rie did not mention Yoshitaro, whose moods had become blacker over the years since his father had died. "It will be good for the future of the house. And speaking of Sei, his marriage will really work out well, don't you think? But you know, it will be hard, being so indebted to the Nakanos after so many weddings."

Fumi reached for a chrysanthemum stalk and pulled it from the vase. "You don't mind, Mother?" Fumi began to rearrange the flowers.

"No, dear. You've always been better at ikebana than I."

Rie sat back on her heels and watched Fumi arrange the flowers, and rearrange them.

Fumi rose abruptly. "I want to see Ume, Mother. I'll bring her," she said as she left the room.

She returned a few minutes later carrying the baby, bouncing her up and down in time to a nursery rhyme she began to hum. The baby gurgled and Fumi hugged her, then put her on the tatami between herself and Rie.

Rie reached over and took her on her lap.

"It seems good to have a baby in the house again, doesn't it, Mother?"

Rie forced a smile.

"Of course you always seem so engrossed in the brewery you probably haven't had time to bond with the baby."

Rie rocked the baby. "The family and the brewery are equally important to me, Fumi. They are really one and the same. And I am the senior member here, have been for some time."

Rie began to sing a folk tune to Ume, who chortled loudly.

Fumi reached for a tea tray on the table and poured a cup for her mother. She pushed the cup toward Rie, and reached for Ume.

"Have some tea, Mother. I really came for a reason this morning."

Rie reached for the teacup, glancing at Fumi. "What is it, dear?"

Fumi paused before answering. "I'm pregnant. I'm going to have a baby." Fumi smiled and leaned back to watch her mother's reaction.

Rie's face lit up. "Wonderful! Are you certain? When is it due?"

"I think in five and half months, Mother."

"And how do you feel? Are you all right? Be careful of your diet, won't you?"

"As you can see, Mother, I'm quite healthy." Fumi laughed.

"That's marvelous, Fumi. Then your baby won't be much younger than Ume. And I hope and pray it's a boy."

"Now, Mother, why would you hope for a boy? You've always told us merchant houses prefer girl babies, so they can find the best mukoyoshi around. But I'm sure you have some reason, some ulterior motive." Fumi laughed and Rie joined in, hand over her mouth. She leaned back and looked at Fumi but did not reply to her question.

CHAPTER 31

Seisaburo's marriage to Mari Yamada of the East Nada brewing family in April 1858, was totally satisfactory to Rie. The wedding also marked the establishment of the southern branch of the Omura House with Seisaburo as head, and of the northern branch under the headship of Eitaro. Rie could barely conceal her pride from the guests gathered in the reception hall. Yoshitaro presided, and Rie had to admit that he needed to be the one to perform this function. She could not make public the fact that she still held the seal without causing Yoshi to lose face among the other brewers who were his peers, but she knew it still rankled.

"It went very well, don't you think, Tama?" Rie asked in the office the day after the wedding.

"Well enough, Mother," Tama said in measured tones. Rie was pleased whenever she caught Tama listening outside the office door, learning what she could of the business, as Rie herself had done growing up.

"And Kinno-san, how are we doing about buying and selling kuras? We have nine brewing now, don't we, counting Eitaro's and Sei's?"

"That's right. We've been able to turn over one every three or four months recently. It may be a seasonal thing, but we're still the only ones doing it. And we're making a good profit at it." He smiled and bowed.

"Good. What are the other brewers saying in the association?" Rie asked, looking at Eitaro and turning her comb over in her hand.

"I think they're amazed, Mother, and perhaps a bit envious too. I heard some of them talking at the last meeting. And Saburo Kato came up to me and remarked about Kinno's ability. They've all noticed."

Rie felt a sudden warmth at the mention of Saburo Kato.

Kinnosuke bowed to Rie. "Thanks to your training, I've learned the importance of timing."

Never one to let Rie enjoy her successes, Yoshi said, "But Mother, Father always cautioned about going too far in advance of the others. You know the old saying about the peg that stands up. Soon you will attract the attention of the wrong person who may not like that we are so successful, more successful than any other house. It might actually turn out to be an embarrassment."

"Yoshi is right," said Kinnosuke. "And you know, Oku-san, I see a lot of political changes now. The loyalists are speaking out against the Bakufu. And the shogunal edicts can't be enforced. The whole samurai class is indebted to the merchants and the structure is collapsing. However, I believe these problems offer new opportunities for us." Kinnosuke leaned forward with his folded hands on the table and looked at Rie.

"Well, what are you suggesting, Kinno? Could we expand our markets somehow?"

He blinked rapidly. "Perhaps with sales in Edo continuing to expand, we could consider opening new routes to markets farther north and south."

Rie took out her fan and held it suspended. "You mean Tohoku and Shikoku, or as far south as Kyushu?"

"I think both directions," Kinnosuke replied.

"But the northerners are so fond of their local sake," Yoshitaro said. "They're loyal to their brands. They're always boasting that their sake is best. It would be hard to break in there."

"That's true, Yoshi," Rie said. "But we don't want to stagnate, or get complacent about our success." Rie paused to give herself time to overcome her irritation. Yoshi was sounding a bit too much like Jihei for her taste. "And since our Edo market is secure, why don't we set up an office there, study the situation? Could you take the time to go to Edo and do that?" Rie asked, tapping her fan on the table and looking at Kinnosuke.

He nodded after each of Rie's sentences. "We have good connections in Nihonbashi. Yes, I'd like to go before other brewers get the idea."

"Especially Yamaguchi. Then leave as soon as you can, Kinno-san." Rie fanned herself rapidly, then replaced her fan in her obi, avoiding the growing resentment she saw in Yoshi's eyes.

Rie called Eitaro over to hear Kinnosuke's report on his trip to Edo. Yoshitaro wanted Seisaburo to be present as well. Rie wondered if Yoshitaro wanted to reduce Eitaro's voice in the discussion. It seemed, no matter the topic, Yoshi was always reluctant to include Eitaro. In any case, Seisaburo's presence in any matter affecting a major decision was welcome. Rie paused before speaking to look around the table at these four grown men, all of whom she had trained: her own son, Fumi's adopted husband, O-Toki's son, and her chief clerk.

She straightened in her seat. "Well, Kinno-san, what did you learn in Edo?"

He bowed to Rie and Yoshitaro. "Everything is changing there. The Bakufu grows weaker by the day. They say the Satsuma and Choshu samurai are on the move, rallying around the Emperor in Kyoto. The loyalists are gaining strength as the Bakufu weakens. The whole structure seems on the verge of collapse."

"*Ho!*" Eitaro and Seisaburo exclaimed almost in unison.

Kinnosuke took a deep breath and continued. "But besides the Bakufu's weakness, some barbarian ships arrived near Yokohama some months ago. The barbarians demanded that the shogun open the country, allow their ships to land and barbarians to live on our shores. They say these were strange ships; they belched forth black smoke."

"Black smoke? And not on fire?" Seisaburo asked.

Yoshitaro frowned. "How could barbarians make such demands of the shogun?"

"Who knows what will happen now?" Kinnosuke said. "But I doubt the Bakufu can survive this crisis: with their own weakness and the loyalist movement in the south, and this added blow by the barbarians. The Bakufu tried to put them off, but I'm told the ships came back with more demands. Now the shogun is forced to open some ports to the barbarians."

"Really, Kinno!" Rie exclaimed. "What will all this mean for brewers?" she asked, rapidly tapping her fan on the table.

"It's hard to say. The situation is changing so fast. But for one thing kabu controls have become a meaningless formality. We can buy as many as we want now from brewers who are going under."

"Then this is the time we should buy more, isn't that so?" Eitaro asked. He rubbed his ink stick on the inkstone, pushed it between himself and Seisaburo, and took a brush from his sleeve.

"Yes," Seisaburo said, "so long as we're certain of our distribution routes and markets."

"That's a big question, isn't it, with this political instability?" Yoshitaro asked, looking at his mother.

Rie turned instead to Kinnosuke. "All right, Kinno-san. Watch the political situation, everyone . . . but Kinno-san and Yoshi, you can coordinate the kabu purchases for the main house with those of Sei and Eitaro. And don't forget to watch Yamaguchi." She fanned herself rapidly.

Eitaro and Seisaburo dipped their brushes into the prepared ink and began making notes.

"And what about finding an agent in Edo?" Rie asked. "Was there too much confusion to do anything?"

Kinnosuke bowed again, blinked and nodded. "No, actually it was a good time to be there. I found a man to be our agent in Nihonbashi. Yoshioka is his name. I checked his references with friends. He knows most of the big wholesalers there, and distributors too along the northern and southern routes out of the city. Keeps his eye on the whole situation. I think we were lucky to get him."

Rie nodded. "Well done, Kinno-san," she said.

Yoshitaro leaned forward. "I think it might be wise to send one of our clerks to work with him, act as our permanent liaison. We'll need to watch the situation closely."

Rie nodded. "Good thinking, Yoshi. Yes, we need to keep close contact there, especially now. Has Yamaguchi set up an Edo office yet?" Rie was relieved to be able to agree with Yoshi, for once.

"Not yet. I should go to Edo again in a few weeks to see how Yoshioka is doing and what is happening in Edo," Kinnosuke said. "I can choose a man to go along and be based there. I discussed the question of northern versus southern routes with Yoshioka. He thinks a southern move would be more strategic now, especially in view of Satsuma and Choshu power along that route."

Rie nodded and looked around the room again at the four men.

At the dinner table one evening Yoshitaro took Ume on his lap. "Ume is three now, Mother. I want Tama to take her out for *shichi-go-san*." A day all children aged seven, five and three looked forward to, when they dressed in their finest for the outing. During the day they enjoyed special treats and played their favorite games.

"I've bought Ume a new red kimono for the occasion," Tama said, smiling at Ume.

"Red kimono, red kimono," Ume cried, waving her hands.

Rie looked at Tama. *Too bad there wouldn't be a chance to get together with Kazu,* she thought, with Kazu's Kimi turning seven this year. She quickly dismissed the thought.

Kazu was no longer part of the Omura House, no longer her responsibility, and the thought of Kazu always elicited painful memories of Teru.

"Hirokichi isn't three yet," Rie said. "His birthday is still four months away, but I don't think he'd like to be left out."

"It wouldn't really be suitable for him to join Ume, Mother," Yoshitaro said. "You know how important the birthday is for this celebration."

He no doubt wanted above all to protect Ume, but did he want to keep Hirokichi away from the house, too? Rie glanced at Yoshitaro and noticed that he was chewing on a chopstick. *Better than pulling at his eyebrows,* she thought.

When the special day arrived, Tama brought Ume dressed in her bright new kimono with matching ribbons in her hair into the office in the morning to greet Rie and Yoshitaro.

"Oh, don't you look pretty!" Rie exclaimed. "And where are you taking her?" She looked at Tama, also wearing a dress kimono.

"We're going to the temple. I know they'll have sweets for the children today."

Ume began to jump and cry, "Sweets! Ume wants sweets!"

Rie took Ume's hand. "You can have sweet bean soup when you come home."

Yoshitaro walked over to Ume and Tama. "Take her through the main office so Kinnosuke can see her," he said. "She's old enough to begin visiting."

Tama bowed and took Ume by the hand. Rie and Yoshitaro both watched as they walked toward the outer office.

"It's good she's such a happy child," Rie said.

"Not only happy, she's also bright and pretty," Yoshitaro said.

Rie smiled. There was no need to tell Yoshi her plans for Ume yet.

CHAPTER 32

"Oku-san," Kinnosuke said to Rie one morning, "Seisaburo has something he wants us to see. He particularly asked that you come too. He says it's going to transform brewing." He blinked rapidly.

Rie looked up quickly. "Transform brewing? What could that be?" She took out her fan from her obi and held it as if to fan herself, but stopped and looked at Kinnosuke.

"I'm not sure. I think his clerk said it has something to do with polishing rice."

"Well, let's go over this afternoon, Kinno-san. Have you told Yoshi?"

"Yes. He's eager to go."

"I want Eitaro to go too. Have someone go and ask him to meet us here after lunch. We'll all go together." She fanned herself. Not surprising that Seisaburo had made a discovery. Already he was well respected in the Brewers Association.

374

Kinnosuke bowed. "I'll have a horse and carriage waiting. It's a long ride to Nishinomiya."

Horse and carriage was a new mode of transport, available to families who could afford it.

Rie enjoyed the ride in the covered black carriage with horse and coachman, a luxury she had recently adopted that now seemed a necessity. With it came the rare chance to visit her son. She leaned forward to look at the looming wooden brewery buildings as they passed, street after street of towering brown structures, apprentices pulling carts piled high with bags of rice or sake barrels, couriers dashing back and forth on their errands. How wonderful to be outside, to feel the pulse of activity that animated her world. And today there was the special excitement about what awaited them at Seisaburo's brewery. She clutched at the side of the carriage.

Seisaburo was waiting at the main entrance to greet them. Rie was pleased at his invitation.

He bowed. "Welcome. I'm glad you could come, Mother. Please come this way."

He led them into his outer office where several clerks in indigo jackets and leggings stood in a row bowing to greet the head of the main house and his mother.

Seisaburo stood as tea was served. "I have exciting news for you. I have discovered something quite astonishing: a new and far faster and more efficient way of polishing rice. I want to show it to you. Mother, you will be able to observe it too, because we cook and polish the rice outside the main kura, next to our storeroom."

Rie took out her fan without opening it. All four visitors leaned forward expectantly.

"First I'll explain it to you, then we can see it in operation. It's a machine that uses steam power rather than a waterwheel to polish rice. I suspect that eventually steam power will completely replace the water-wheel for polishing."

"Steam power!" Yoshitaro exclaimed.

"How does it work?" Eitaro asked.

Rie rested her fan under her chin, eyes riveted on her son, who spoke so confi-dently.

"We use coal to generate the steam power," Seisaburo began. He opened a large drawing on the table and pointed as he spoke. "Here, you can see the process. The heat from burning coal boils water in a tank. This produces steam that expands and cre-ates pressure that forces pistons to move the arm that comes down on the polishing area." He looked around the table at his relatives and Kinnosuke.

"And all this comes from burning coal?" Kinnosuke asked.

"Yes. Coal is the source."

"And how much faster or more efficient is this engine than the waterwheel?" Eitaro asked.

"We can polish forty times as much rice as the waterwheel does in the same amount of time."

The men gasped.

Rie placed both hands on the table. "Forty times! Just imagine!" she exclaimed.

"How did you learn about these steam engines, Sei?" Yoshitaro asked.

"Steam power was being used by those barbarian ships that came to Yokohama a few years ago. I went to Osaka some months ago and saw one of the steam engines in operation. I thought we might apply it to rice polishing, so I studied it carefully and tried to reconstruct it here. It seems to be working well." He smiled proudly.

"Brilliant, Sei! Brilliant!" Rie cried. "And you did this all on your own." She beamed. "Now . . . we'll need a supply of coal, won't we?"

"You're right, Mother." Seisaburo nodded. "We'll need to start a coal plant of our own. I've begun negotiations."

"Kinno-san, Yoshi, study Sei's machine so we can build one of our own. You too, Eitaro," Rie said.

"You can model it after mine, Mother," Seisaburo agreed.

"Make sure you learn how it works," Rie told the others. "Come, let's see it." Rie patted Seisaburo's arm and smiled at him. "This will put us way ahead of Yamaguchi."

Seisaburo led the way through the storage area to the new rice polisher.

Rie could not be more proud of Sei.

Rie had Kinnosuke and her sons carefully study the revolutionary steam-powered rice polisher to adopt it immediately for the main house. Within three months of their visit to Seisaburo it was operating. The Omura enterprise thus became the first brewing house in Japan to use steam power for polishing rice.

"And I'm sure everyone will want to adopt it. But meantime it gives us a big advantage, very big." Kinnosuke worked rapidly with the abacus as he talked. "It looks as if we may jump from fifth to third place this year."

"*Ah,* is that so?" Rie rose and began to pace up and down in the office, hands clasped behind her in imitation of her father. "And I remember my father being so pleased when we climbed from number nine to number eight. But you know, Kinno-san, I have always felt Seisaburo would do something remarkable, even though I shouldn't say it, as his mother."

Just then, Yoshitaro entered the office. The moment Rie saw his face she knew he had heard their conversation. And he wasn't happy.

Rie turned to Yoshitaro one evening after dinner. "Yoshi, please bring me the ledger of donations to the temple. It's in that tansu behind you," she said. "It's time for our annual donation."

"Yes, Mother." Yoshitaro paused. "I was going to mention it to you anyway. We've been approached by the head priest. They're in financial trouble and ask that we double our donation this year." He scratched his chin and looked at Rie.

"Double it?" Rie frowned. "What kind of financial trouble?"

"I believe they had a fire in the old part of the main building. They were lucky to be able to save the rest." He looked at Rie.

"Well, I hope our death records weren't destroyed. But double our donation? That seems too much, don't you think? We should discuss it with Kinno tomorrow."

"We don't have to decide tonight."

Yoshitaro reached for his teacup and took a sip, then picked up the teapot and held it toward Rie.

Rie sipped, then set the cup down on the black lacquer tray. She thought of the evenings she had spent thus with her father. Now she was the parent, not the child, and the relationship was far less peaceful than hers with her father.

"Yoshi," she said abruptly, "this year we will not make a donation to the temple." She took out her comb and fingered it.

"But Mother," Yoshitaro frowned, "we have given to the temple every year, for generations. You know they do the annual memorials for Father and Grandfather, and they care for our graves. How can we refuse?"

"I haven't finished, Yoshi. I'm not suggesting that we give them nothing." She looked at Yoshitaro's perplexed expression and smiled brightly, not revealing the rest of her plan.

"Then what . . . ?" he blurted out.

"What I suggest is that we give it to them, but as a loan at the going rate." She reinserted her comb, a satisfied look on her face.

"A loan, Mother? But we can't give the temple a loan. No one does that. Anyway, what would they use as collateral? What if they couldn't pay the interest, or repay the loan?"

"They have collateral, Yoshi, a great deal of it. They have land, extensive holdings."

"You mean . . . ?"

"Yes, Yoshi, they'll put up collateral, like anyone else who takes a loan. Land can never lose its value."

"I . . . I've never heard of anyone doing this, Mother," he stammered. "I wonder if the temple wouldn't object, refuse the loan?"

"If they need money badly they'll accept it, Yoshi, even as a loan. Where else would they get such a sum? We've been their chief source of funds for many years. They depend on us."

"Well, let's discuss it with Kinnosuke in the morning, shall we?" Yoshitaro said nervously.

"Of course," Rie agreed. "And we should send word to the priest to have him come and meet with you and Kinno."

"You seem confident that Kinnosuke will go along with this idea, Mother."

"Kinno and I almost always agree in a question of business, Yoshi. We think alike," Rie replied without hesitation.

"And he probably wouldn't dare oppose

you when you're determined," Yoshitaro murmured.

Yoshitaro hurried to the office the next morning to discuss his mother's proposal with Kinnosuke before she appeared.

"Your mother's judgment in business matters is usually infallible, Yoshi. I have never known her to be mistaken in a major decision," he said.

And yet Yoshitaro could read the tension in the pallor of the other man's face and the set of his jaw. He couldn't openly oppose Rie, Yoshi knew, but for once it was apparent that he wanted to, something he had never done before. If word got out about what she planned to do, it could ruin them. Why was his mother so headstrong?

As if reading his thoughts, Kinnosuke said, "Loaning to the temple may be unprecedented, but she is correct that the temple is dependent on us financially, has been for many years."

"Then you think we should offer a loan in the amount they want?" Yoshitaro asked, his mouth dropping open.

Kinnosuke paused before answering. "I hesitate to oppose her on this, Yoshi. But I agree with you, it makes one uneasy."

"Won't it affect our reputation if it gets

out among other brewers?" Yoshitaro persisted.

"It might." Kinnosuke sucked in his breath. "First of all there's no guarantee that the priests will accept the loan. But if they do I doubt they'll make it public. We certainly wouldn't. And this is really a family decision, so I won't say anything, unless your mother insists."

Once again, his mother was getting her way on everything. Yoshitaro sighed. "All right, Kinno-san. Let's see what happens when the priest arrives."

Several days later the two chief priests from the family temple in Kyoto arrived at the main entrance to White Tiger, where Yoshitaro and Kinnosuke awaited them. The senior of them was a rotund man with a large shaved head and heavy jowls, his status apparent in his bearing. The second priest was smaller, with a nervous squint and hands that seemed in continual motion. The priests bowed to Kinnosuke and Yoshitaro, though not as low as Yoshitaro and Kinnosuke. The priest's composure reflected his usual role as communicant of the deities and dispenser of their benison rather than his present mission as supplicant. And as both were senior in age as well as being priests, Yoshitaro's and Kinnosuke's respectful posture was only natural.

"We are honored to have your presence in our humble establishment," Yoshitaro said. "Please come this way." He ushered the black-robed figures into the inner office and motioned them to be seated. O-Natsu had been instructed to serve the tea, her advanced age more appropriate to the rank of the priests. Rie had asked her to linger over the tea in the room, hoping to overhear some of the conversation and report back to her.

"We are sorry to trouble you with our request," the elder priest began. "We have had an unusually difficult time this year, particularly after the fire, followed by the drought that hit our region these past two years. We beg your consideration." Both priests bowed. The junior of the two did not speak beyond the usual courtesies during the visit.

Yoshitaro reached to adjust his collar. "We understand your position. We are willing to offer you the total amount —" The two men looked at each other and smiled. "— but as a loan, at the usual terms of interest and collateral." He bowed.

The senior priest's left eye twitched. "A *loan?* I see." He closed his eyes and exhaled, arms folded over his ample stomach. His eyes remained closed, his face as impassive as a Buddha.

For several minutes no one spoke.

Yoshitaro rose. "We will leave you alone." He signaled Kinnosuke to follow him from the room.

Several minutes later Yoshitaro heard the elder priest cough. Yoshitaro and Kinnosuke returned to the room and seated themselves opposite the priests again. All four men bowed.

O-Natsu came in with more tea.

"We will be pleased to accept the terms of your offer," the elder priest said and bowed, eyes nearly closed.

Yoshitaro brought an envelope from his sleeve and pushed it across the table to the priest. The visit was concluded.

O-Natsu shuffled as fast as she could to Rie's room. "Oku-san," she whispered at the door.

"Come in," Rie said impatiently.

"The priests have accepted the loan," O-Natsu announced with a triumphant smile.

Rie blew a sigh of relief and took out her small pipe. "Good." She nodded. Why was it that she had a nagging uneasy feeling about the transaction?

O-Natsu coughed.

"Yes, O-Natsu?"

O-Natsu bowed, in a nervous gesture.

"What is it?"

"I don't believe they were happy about it."

As Rie knelt before the Butsudan altar one morning to pay her customary respects to the ancestors, she wondered if she had done the right thing, giving the temple a loan instead of paying double donation, as requested. A nagging worry made her feel unseasonably warm. She placed the rice bowl and sake cup before her parents' name tablets, then set a stick of incense in the small metal censer and lit the taper. No, it was the right thing to do. She was certain her father would have approved. She bowed, holding her hands together, aware as she did so of another person in the room behind her. She turned.

"Oh, good morning, Yoshi."

"Good morning, Mother." Yoshitaro bowed slightly, and went to one side of the room to slide open a cupboard door. He began riffling through the contents.

"Where is the set of Hina Matsuri dolls, Mother? I thought they were kept here."

Rie turned back to the Butsudan and busied herself. "Oh, I gave them to Fumi,

Yoshi. You know, she wanted the old set the girls had when they were children."

"Well, we need a set for Ume now. We can't let March third go by without a set. We don't want to deprive her on Girls' Day, do we?" He closed the cupboard.

"Yes, Yoshi, you're right," Rie agreed. "The main house needs a set. Tama will see to it, won't she?"

That evening Rie and Yoshitaro lingered at the table while Tama began clearing the dishes away. She glanced at Yoshitaro and nodded.

"Mother, I've asked Tama to order a full set of dolls for Girls' Day next week."

"Fine, Yoshi," Rie agreed. She fingered her comb, and rested her hands in her lap. "And I would like to invite Fumi to bring Mie when we set the dolls out. She's already two, and otherwise Ume will be alone."

Yoshitaro said nothing, but Rie noticed he glanced toward Tama who had reentered the room. Rie marked his silence, typical when Fumi's family was mentioned.

"Let's get the finest set available, Tama," Rie said. "And I'll ask Fumi to bring Mie on the third." Rie glanced at Yoshitaro out of the corner of her eye, but his face was impassive.

The set of dolls that arrived a few days

later at the Omura household was truly impressive: fifteen dolls in their ancient court costume with a five-tiered display stand covered with a red velvet cloth. The emperor and empress stood on the top tier, the emperor to the left of the empress. The court ladies and banquet trays and dishes occupied the second tier. Below them were arrayed the ministers, musicians, and lower officials. Also displayed were a miniature chest of drawers, a hibachi, a dinner table set, bowls, a dressing table, musical instruments and a palanquin in which the Imperial couple rode, all in miniature.

"Wonderful workmanship, isn't it, Tama?" Rie said, examining each piece closely.

"I'll include the peach blossoms tomorrow, Mother," Tama said, "for the feminine traits."

"Oh, by all means," Rie said with a wry smile. "Yes, mildness, peacefulness, and softness."

"Ume is so excited," Tama added.

Rie had been happy at the birth of Fumi's daughter, another child to add to the future of White Tiger. "It will be wonderful to have Ume and Mie celebrate together," Rie said.

Girls' Day, the day Ume and Mie awaited breathlessly, arrived. Both girls danced and waved their arms in front of the display.

Rie took her granddaughters by the hand and sat with them.

"Be careful Ume, Mie. You don't want to touch the dolls. Let's sit quietly and look at them. And O-Natsu has a special treat for you today."

Fumi and Tama sat behind their daughters, whose eyes were riveted on the dolls.

Fumi reached over and touched the back of Ume's pink brocade obi. "What a beautiful obi," she said to Tama. *And so expensive,* she thought, but did not add.

Tama bowed slightly and looked down.

Fumi turned back to the doll display. "It's a really fine set, Mother," she said. "Better than the one we had when we were young, isn't it?"

Rie wondered if Fumi resented anything given to Ume, but she had never favored Ume over Hiro and was trying to balance things in the family. "Yes, well, we are a larger house now, aren't we, with two branch houses," Rie said with a glance at Fumi's face.

O-Natsu slid open the shoji. "The meal is ready, Oku-san," she said, and quickly disappeared toward the kitchen.

The dining table was laden with special foods for the day, also called the Peach Festival. Girls' Day was meant to signify happy marriage as well as to foster the feminine virtues. Sushi, pink and white mochi, and beautifully decorated candies adorned the table. Ume and Mie squealed in delight.

Following the luncheon, Rie drew the two small girls to her side and began to tell them folktales. She looked at her two granddaughters, both happy, bright children, but neither of whom figured prominently in her plans for the future of the main house.

Just then, Rie heard a firecracker go off somewhere in the distance and started. She had an uneasy feeling about the samurai unrest. She drew the children closer, forced a reassuring smile and said, "Now, where were we?"

CHAPTER 33

One evening in 1863 the shoji to the office opened abruptly and Eitaro rushed in, panting.

"Eitaro, what brings you here?" Rie said before he could catch his breath.

"Samurai, Mother! They're roaming the streets tonight!"

Rie jumped up. "Samurai? In the streets?" She gasped. She knew the shoguns, daimyo, and samurai were all indigent, unable to pay their debts, and that many ronin, masterless samurai, were on the loose, but this was the first time they had entered their neighborhood.

"Board up all the doors!" she ordered. "Everyone! Quickly!"

Eitaro, Kinnosuke, and three clerks ran to the doors of the kura, house, and office.

Rie turned to Eitaro. "Where's Yoshi?"

Eitaro frowned. "He left earlier this evening. Shall I go after him?"

"No, stay here. It's too dangerous out there. Let's hope he has the sense to return."

As Kinnosuke slid the latch into place at the door near the number one kura, shouting erupted in the street outside. The sound of footsteps running toward the entrance mingled with cries and sounds of scuffling.

"It's the samurai! They're in our street!" Kinnosuke cried.

A guttural voice roared "Rice! Give me rice!"

"Get out! We're hardworking merchants!"

"That's Yoshi's voice! Open the door! Quickly!" Rie cried.

Kinnosuke and Eitaro fumbled with the latch.

A shout, followed by a chilling scream, pierced the air as the door slid open. Yoshi-taro lurched through the door and sprawled across the threshold, blood soaking through his kimono.

Rie took in the huge figure of a samurai that loomed at the door, disheveled matted hair and beard covering his face except for his wild bloodshot eyes. Torn dirty breeches and jacket half fell off as he raised his sword in both hands.

"Rice! Give me rice and gold!" he growled in a hoarse guttural grunt.

Rie stood in his path, her heart pounding.

"Step back! You'll get nothing until you sheath your sword," she shouted.

He staggered and made two attempts to insert his sword in its scabbard before he succeeded.

"Kinno-san, bring a bag of rice!" she ordered. "Eitaro, help Yoshi and call Tama," she shouted to a clerk.

Glancing down at the pool of blood spreading out from under Yoshitaro's sleeve, Rie knelt quickly, undid her obi and opened Yoshitaro's kimono. Blood oozed from a slash across his upper arm. She hurriedly tied her obi above the wound and yanked it tight until the bleeding stopped.

Tama came running through the corridor. She glanced at her husband, then at the samurai and screamed.

"Bring some cloths," Rie ordered, "and a pan of hot water, Tama."

Kinnosuke dashed in with a bag of rice.

Rie stood. "Give it to him!" she said with a thrusting gesture.

Kinnosuke nodded and heaved the heavy bag at the samurai, who staggered and fell backward to the ground. Kinnosuke and Eitaro quickly bolted the latch again and knelt to examine Yoshitaro. He was groaning, his eyes closed.

They heard the samurai's slurred swearing and grunting as he lumbered off down the road.

"Yoshi has lost a lot of blood," Eitaro said.

Rie leaned over. "We'll send for the herbalist as soon as it's safe for someone to go out," she said.

Tama returned with a pan of hot water and cloths to bathe Yoshitaro's wound.

"Oh, my leg," he cried.

Tama and Eitaro turned him over.

"His leg is bleeding," she cried.

A deep wound gaped in the back of his thigh.

"Bind it quickly above the wound," Rie said sharply. "Eitaro, help her tighten the binding."

Eitaro pulled the cloth tight until Yoshitaro cried out in pain. Rie placed a hand on his chest and looked closely at his face while Tama cradled his head.

"The street is quiet now," Kinnosuke said, blinking rapidly as he leaned over Yoshitaro. "I'll go for the herbalist."

Rie nodded. She turned and walked toward the office, a hand on Eitaro's arm. "I suppose he was at the Sawaraya again. At a time like this! Is it going to kill him as it did his father?" she scolded.

"I don't think his life is in danger, Mother. It is a bad wound, though, the leg wound."

"These samurai parasites are completely lawless," Rie said. "The shoguns can't keep them under control, neither can the daimyo. We'll have to keep a careful watch now. And we need to get together with our neighborhood association. Eitaro, you'd better get home and check on your family."

Yoshitaro lay on his futon for several weeks, despondent and weakened by loss of blood. Tama remained at his side day and night, encouraging him to eat or to drink tea, and the Chinese herbalist came daily with poultices and potions.

"His arm is healing well, but his leg looks bad," he told Tama in the corridor one day. "It is turning purple. I believe we will have to remove it to save his life."

Tama's hands flew to her face and she ran to Rie's room.

"Mother! Come! The herbalist says my husband may lose his leg!" Tears streamed down her face.

Rie rose, took Tama's arm, and propelled her firmly toward the ground-floor room Yoshitaro had taken over. "We'll see," she said.

The herbalist was still standing in the corridor clutching his herb pouch in both hands, looking anxious. "It's true, I'm afraid, Oku-san." He bowed. "It may be necessary, to save his life, and the sooner the better for him. It would be dangerous to leave him as he is."

"Then go ahead, tomorrow if necessary." Rie frowned.

"We'll come for him in the morning, then."

"Eitaro and Kinnosuke will accompany him," Rie said.

That evening Rie sat with Tama, who held five-year-old Ume in her arms.

Rie looked at the two. "Well, Tama, I guess this means there will be no more children from the Sawaraya. Yoshi will not be able to go around at night, or in the daytime either for that matter. The burden of work on Kinnosuke will be much heavier." She sighed.

Tama looked down without speaking.

Yoshitaro continued to languish in his old room on the ground floor. His spirits flagged. O-Sada ghosted through his dreams at night and even his daytime reveries. He despaired of ever seeing her again. Tama came in to sit with him at her needlework when she was not busy elsewhere.

"Try these prawns, your favorite," Tama said one evening, holding the delicacy toward his mouth with chopsticks.

Yoshitaro shook his head and turned away.

"Tama, I know you have tried hard to

rouse Yoshi from his lethargy," Rie said one evening. "It's such a worry. We miss him in the office. I wonder. . . ." Rie paused and looked at the comb she was revolving in her hand. "I think you should come into the office and work with me a bit each day while Yoshi is mending. We don't know when he will be able to resume his work. You can begin to take some of the responsibility in the office. One day you and Yoshi will be responsible for everything." Rie was confident in Tama's ability and her eagerness to learn the business.

"I know." Tama nodded.

"Beyond your usual responsibilities, Tama, I want you to become more familiar with the business side of things. Kinno and I can use some help, especially with Yoshi out of the office these past weeks."

Tama nodded again. "I'll do my best," she said.

Rie detected Tama's interest. Good.

"Please make time to come to the office tomorrow, won't you?" Rie replaced her comb.

Kinnosuke visited Yoshitaro in his room with business questions that required decisions but was unable to rouse him from his torpor. Kinnosuke found Rie in the office and spoke to her about it. "He shows no interest in anything, Oku-san. I know he has suffered a great shock and is not able to get around. But I fear what may happen if he doesn't make some effort. And it's his will he has lost, not his ability."

Rie nodded slowly. "I know, Kinno-san. You're right. I've been considering just what to say."

Moments later she rose and walked slowly to Yoshitaro's room, her head bowed and a hand resting against her face. She slid open the shoji and looked toward the futon where Yoshitaro lay with his eyes closed. Glad that he was alone, she knelt beside the futon and placed her hand on his arm.

"Yoshi," she said softly.

He opened his eyes and looked at her dully.

"Yoshi, you cannot continue this way. You are still head of the house," she said quietly but firmly. "You must get up and perform your duties. The responsibility for the brewery and family rests with you. Tama and Ume are upset that you are lying here, not moving. We all are. Please sit up."

She reached over and placed a backrest behind him.

Yoshitaro struggled to raise himself with his arms and leaned back.

"But how can I manage? How will I get

around?"

Rie looked at his face, grown lean and pallid. "Kinno is having some crutches made for you," she said. "He'll bring them to you this afternoon. You need to practice on them. One of the clerks will help you. It may take time, but you'll get used to them."

Yoshitaro sighed and reached for a glass of water. He mumbled inaudibly.

"Please, Yoshi, remember who you are." Rie flourished her comb and replaced it forcefully. "Show the Omura spirit!" she said, her voice rising.

Yoshitaro looked at her without speaking.

Rie bowed. "We rely on you," she said as she glanced back at the recumbent figure and left the room.

CHAPTER 34

"Yoshi, come on," Rie said as he hobbled slowly toward the office on his new crutches, for the first time without assistance. "Let's go to visit Sei again. Kinno says he has another surprise for us."

"I don't know if I —"

"Yes, of course you can," Rie said before he could finish his sentence. "Kinno is going with us. He's calling a ricksha."

Rie walked past Yoshitaro to the office and signaled Kinnosuke to have a ricksha brought to the entrance. Yoshitaro struggled painfully to the door.

"Very good!" Kinnosuke exclaimed. "You see, you can manage alone. It's just a matter of balance and confidence. Come. The ricksha is here."

Yoshitaro inched along to the main entrance behind Rie and Kinnosuke.

"Here, first sit on this step," Kinnosuke said. "Then use your arms to boost yourself up to the seat. You need to strengthen your arm muscles to bear your body weight. Some exercises will help. Here."

Kinnosuke helped Yoshitaro heave himself up to the seat.

"See, you can do it, Yoshi," Rie said, patting his shoulder. "Now relax and enjoy the ride."

The ricksha rumbled off over the cobblestones. Yoshitaro clung to the ricksha with both hands to balance himself as they bumped along.

"I'm looking forward to seeing Sei's new baby," Rie said.

"Is that the surprise?" Yoshitaro asked.

Rie laughed. "Oh no, we've known that the baby was expected for some time. I have a feeling it's something more to do with brewing. You know how clever he is. Steam power has made such a difference in rice polishing. Other brewers are all beginning to use it."

Rie and Kinnosuke commented on each brewery as they passed the long line of breweries strung in a necklace along the coastal road as far as the eye could see.

"Look at that, Kinno and Yoshi. Hirabayashi has added another kura this year."

"Yes, we need to pay special attention to them now," Kinnosuke replied.

"*Ah,* there's sake in the air today, isn't there, Yoshi? The best of perfumes, I always say. It makes one feel alive, doesn't it?" She smiled at Yoshitaro and was pleased to see him soften.

The ricksha turned a corner and Seisaburo's massive kura loomed before them.

"What is that, Mother, next to Sei's three kura?"

They gazed at the huge red structure made of something other than wood.

"I wonder, Yoshi," Rie replied. "Well, here's Sei."

Seisaburo emerged at the entrance and bowed. "Welcome, Mother. And how are you, Yoshi?"

He put out a hand to help Yoshitaro down from the ricksha.

"Come, Kinnosuke, all of you. I want to show you my new kura."

"A new kura, is it?" Rie asked as they followed Seisaburo into the courtyard. There before them towered a building the size of all kura. But it was unlike any other.

"What have you done here, Sei?" Rie asked.

Kinnosuke was already touching the walls and examining them closely. Yoshitaro leaned against the structure and turned to look at it.

"It's made of brick, you see," Seisaburo explained. "It's the same size, but the bricks make it much easier to control the temperature. And I have a strong feeling it will reduce the danger of spoilage. Everything else is the same. You can taste some of the sake from this kura." He motioned Kinnosuke and Yoshitaro to enter while he stood outside with his mother.

Kinnosuke and Yoshitaro stepped through the kura door and disappeared inside.

"If it's as you say, that it's easier to control the temperature, then we should also be building brick kura, shouldn't we? But what about the cost, Sei? Please go over that in detail with Kinno and Yoshi, won't you?"

"Certainly, Mother. Actually, the cost of building with brick is not all that different from lumber." He smiled.

"Sei, have you made another discovery that will change the way we brew, or at least the buildings we brew in?" Rie put a hand on her son's arm and a smile illumined his face. "Now, you go and give Kinno and Yoshi the details. I'm going to see your baby."

"Yes, have tea with Mari, Mother. She's expecting you. She's eager to show you the baby."

"As I am to see him." Rie paused and

smiled again. "And Sei, you know your grandfather would be very proud of you." Rie turned to enter the house and hummed an old folk tune as she walked. At the front entrance she called out, "Mari, I'm here."

The day after their visit to Seisaburo's house Rie bustled into the office to talk with Kinnosuke and Yoshitaro.

She settled herself at the low table and took out her fan. "What do you think, Kinno, Yoshi? Should we build a brick kura?"

"No question about it, Oku-san. Of course we can discuss it with Toji. But I think we should not only build one or two, but we should consider converting to brick kura exclusively. Seisaburo convinced me that they are more efficient, and also safer than wooden kura. Not as susceptible to fire."

Yoshitaro bit his lip. "But what would we do with our wooden kura, Kinno? It would be expensive to change. We can't abandon them."

"We wouldn't need to convert all at once. We could rent out some of them at first, and demolish others and rebuild on the same spot. I think we can adopt a schedule for gradual conversion, one or two kura each season. That seems to be Sei's plan too."

Rie looked at Kinnosuke and tapped her fan on the table. "Good, Kinno-san. Let's begin this summer and get one brick kura ready for the start of the season. One or maybe two." She paused and looked down at the fan, opening it and turning it over in her hands.

Yoshitaro leaned forward. "Why don't we buy the old Nakanishi property in the next street? Since he died they aren't brewing now, are they? One reason they have failed is that they were never willing to take even the smallest risk."

Rie smiled. "Good, Yoshi. I don't think his widow is going to continue. And their daughter is too young for a mukoyoshi."

Rie turned her fan over and placed it on the table deliberately. "Then see what you can do about purchasing the property, Kinno-san. Those buildings are so old they'd have to be rebuilt anyway. We can build our first two brick kura there, and start with them in the autumn."

Kinnosuke nodded.

"And I want Eitaro to visit Sei too. He should start to convert."

Rie closed her fan smartly and tapped the table.

Some weeks later Rie walked into the garden to try to catch a little afternoon breeze. She reached a handkerchief from her sleeve and wiped the perspiration from her face. The cicadas were in full voice, a summer symphony. She sat on her rock and gazed at the koi in the pond. They were growing so big. The old orange-and-black grandfather koi had been there since her father's time, a venerable fish.

She scratched her chin. What was it Eitaro had said about the Choshu radicals, the loyalist samurai? They had gone so far as to bombard English ships passing through the straits of Shimonoseki. The shoguns had retaliated, joined by Satsuma and Aizu forces in a punitive expedition against Choshu. Choshu samurai had been driven out of the imperial capital in Kyoto. But wait. Eitaro said the Choshu loyalists were at it again, that was it. They were still attacking the barbarian ships, against Bakufu policy. All this political, even military, unrest — these Choshu radicals rampaging around brandishing their swords — this was bound to affect business, especially this close to Kyoto. She fanned herself rapidly, rose, and walked back inside. She would ask Eitaro to join them this evening.

Later, after dinner, Eitaro sat with Rie and Yoshitaro while Tama cleared away the dishes. Rie poured chilled sake of the top grade for Eitaro and tea for Yoshitaro, then held out her cup.

"Just one, Eitaro," she said and sipped slowly. "What's this I hear about Choshu? Tell me what you know." She looked first at Yoshitaro, then at Eitaro.

"Everyone was talking about it at the Brewers Association meeting yesterday," Yoshitaro began. "There's much unrest in Choshu and Satsuma, and it's affecting Kyoto."

Eitaro pushed his hair back from his face. "Choshu is still firing on barbarian ships, the English ships at Shimonoseki. And all this talk of 'Revere the Emperor; expel the barbarians' has support in the south. It's dangerous. The Bakufu has had to sign agreements with the barbarians. They say the barbarians can't be kept out, what with their black ships and guns. And Choshu has been buying up these guns and cannons, using them against the English."

Yoshitaro put both hands on the table and looked down. "But the southern fiefs are so powerful, and I hear Satsuma won't help the Bakufu again. You know, the Satsuma and Choshu forces want to end the shogunate. 'Revere the Emperor, expel the barbarians' is their slogan. That's what they're fighting about. There's a Tosa samurai trying to bring Satsuma and Choshu together, and I hear he's having some success. Satsuma and Choshu, with the support of some samurai from Tosa and Hizen, may change the whole picture."

"No doubt about it, a Sat-Cho alliance could mean the end of the Bakufu," Eitaro said slowly.

Rie handled her cup. "You don't mean it, Eitaro," she said. "What would happen if the Tokugawa shogunate collapses?" she asked looking from her son to her son-in-law.

"We don't know yet, Mother," Yoshitaro said. "Things are so uncertain everywhere, both in Edo and Kyoto."

"Was Sei at the meeting yesterday?" Rie asked.

"Yes, and he spoke up, said he thought Satsuma and Choshu might well be the future center of political power," Yoshitaro said.

"Just imagine!" Rie exclaimed. "What an exciting time to be alive!"

"Exciting, yes, but so unstable, Mother," Yoshitaro said. "And who knows what it bodes for us brewers."

Rie turned to him. "We'll survive, Yoshi. Just remember how many generations have been brewing here through all kinds of crises." She sat back on her heels and inserted her comb. "The key is to keep our wits about us. And try to keep up with everything that's happening in Kyoto and Edo."

Rie sat alone at the dining table one evening after Yoshitaro had left. Tama was in the kitchen working.

"Excuse me," O-Natsu's voice wafted in softly.

"Yes, O-Natsu, come in," Rie replied. She looked at the face of her old servant, now white haired, her step halting. Rie indicated a zabuton at the table.

"What is it, O-Natsu?"

"Well, Oku-san, this is difficult to say." She paused, looked down, and cleared her throat.

Rie looked at her sharply. There was no possibility of another geisha's child.

"I know how loyal Kinnosuke has always been to you and Yoshitaro. He is the most important person to the business."

"Yes, of course, O-Natsu." Rie rested the tip of her fan on her chin. She did not take her eyes off O-Natsu's face.

"Well, it's Nobu, his wife."

Rie frowned. "What about Nobu?"

"She has spoken to someone at the Yama-guchi's, saying you have shown favoritism toward Fumi and Hirokichi, over Yoshitaro and Ume." O-Natsu bowed low and looked at her hands.

Rie placed her fan on the table deliberately. Had she shown favoritism? She must admit, she had. Still, everyone knew that loyalty could never be in question; moreover if Nobu spoke of matters internal to White Tiger at Yamaguchi's, serious damage could result. Yamaguchi had shown that he was continually on the alert to defeat White Tiger.

"Are you certain about this, O-Natsu? This is not some idle rumor?"

"I am afraid it is not a rumor, Oku-san. I have known the person who told me for many years. She is a very close friend, and she would not speak ill of you."

"I see. Thank you, O-Natsu. You have always kept me informed in matters of importance. You are as valuable to me as Kinnosuke." Rie bowed.

"I am so sorry," O-Natsu said as she bowed and left the room.

Rie put both hands to her face and sighed. She would have to ponder what O-Natsu said. It would not do to take any rash action.

The next morning Rie stopped to caress the cypress support, then walked into the

410

garden early, before anyone else was stirring in the house. She wiped the dew off her rock with her handkerchief and sat. She looked over at the koi swimming lazily in the pond. How many decisions affecting the house had she made over the years sitting on this very rock? She rested a hand on her chin and looked down at the gray stepping stones that wound a sinuous pattern through the garden and around the pond.

Kinnosuke was the single most important person to the work of White Tiger, after herself and Toji. She had often thanked the gods for sending him to White Tiger as a young boy, just as she had silently congratulated herself for promoting him in the office. His work was crucial to the success of White Tiger and to its status in the brewing world.

Still, it went without saying that loyalty to the house was absolute. Kinnosuke must have given Nobu the impression that she, Rie, was showing partiality to Fumi and Eitaro and their son, Hirokichi. Hiro was now a precocious child of ten, a few months younger than Ume. But Ume, as Yoshitaro's only child, was Kinnosuke's favorite. He always carried sweets in his sleeve, and Ume ran into the office each morning to greet him, holding out her hand as part of her ritual.

"Good morning, Banto-sama," Yoshitaro had trained her to say. And somehow, during these brief morning visits of Ume's, she began to absorb bits of information about the work of the brewery. And because Rie wanted Hirokichi to learn the work of the main house as well as his branch, she often invited him to the office. But had Kinno noticed some subtle difference in her attitude toward Yoshi and Eitaro, and had he spoken to Nobu about it? But for Nobu to speak to someone at Yamaguchi's was unconscionable disloyalty. Rie stirred uneasily on her rock. She sat there, her heart heavy with what was to come. Was there another option? Another way to proceed? She stared into the distance for the answers, thought of her mother and father. Her promise to her father. *Oh, Kinno,* she thought, the weight of what must be done pressing on her chest. *I am sorry.* She stood and walked slowly back into the house. She would wait until the end of the day, until everyone but Kinnosuke had left. Then she would do what she must.

CHAPTER 35

Rie opened the shoji and walked into the inner office in the early evening. Kinnosuke still sat at his table working with the abacus and ledgers after the others had left. He looked up quizzically and bowed.

She looked at him, dear Kinno-san, and took a deep, fortifying breath. How she hated to hurt him. She wished she could leave him unaware for just a moment longer, but she could not. *Oh Kinno,* she thought. Rie stood holding her fan below her obi with both hands and for a moment said nothing.

"Kinno-san," she began. "Would you come into the parlor please?"

Kinnosuke blinked. "The parlor, Oku-san?"

"Yes, please."

Rie turned, opened the shoji, and walked along the corridor. She heard Kinnosuke's slippers slapping after her. She took two zabuton from a stack at the side of the room and set them in front of the Butsudan, where the spirits of the ancestors attended. She arranged her kimono carefully under her as she sat and indicated a zabuton facing her. She inhaled deeply and paused.

Kinnosuke sat, bowed, and kept his eyes lowered to the tatami.

"Kinno-san, you know how I have valued your work at White Tiger all these many years."

He bowed.

"And your loyalty."

He bowed lower, twice.

"Loyalty can never be called into question. It is absolute." His head was bowed too low to reveal any expression.

"Of course," he murmured.

"Unfortunately it has come to my attention that Nobu has been speaking ill of this house to people at Yamaguchi's. It is disloyal, a dishonor for the house. Speaking to our chief rival about our house cannot be tolerated."

A choked, gasping sound came from Kinnosuke, his head dropping still lower.

"You realize, Kinno-san, that this is a dishonor we cannot abide."

Again Kinnosuke choked and gasped, unable to speak.

414

"You must divorce Nobu," Rie said abruptly. She hated to break his heart, loyal Kinno, yet what else could she do?

"Divorce?" Kinnosuke huffed and looked up, his face white.

"There is no choice," Rie said. She wished such a drastic measure weren't necessary. But it was.

Kinnosuke stammered. "She is . . . she is the mother of my two sons, and my daughter." His eyes blinked and his breath came in rapid gasps.

"Divorce her!" Rie repeated sharply, her heart tightening in her chest. Oh, Kinnosan.

Kinnosuke squeezed his eyes shut to try to contain his tears. His fists clenched on his lap. He began to bow repeatedly.

"I am sorry. I am sorry. I have no words to apologize." He repeated the refrain over and over as he bowed.

Rie stood. "I am sorry too, Kinno-san. So sorry. It is most unfortunate," she said as she rose, walked to the shoji, and left Kinnosuke shaking and bowing in front of the Butsudan. Yet she couldn't help but wonder if she'd done the right thing.

The next morning Yoshi hobbled rapidly into the dining room where Rie was still drinking her tea. "What do you think you have done, Mother, telling Kinno to divorce his wife, and talking about honor? How can you do this, to the person who has helped you achieve what White Tiger has become?" he said, pacing back and forth in front of her. "Questioning his loyalty, indeed! Have *you* no sense of loyalty? Have *you* no concern for anything other than the house? The house is all I hear, nothing about the people in it." Yoshi was gasping for breath.

"Calm down, Yoshi. Kinno knows about loyalty very well. I have not accused him of disloyalty. But his wife, Nobu, has been talking against us at Yamaguchi's. That is something we can't tolerate, and at the very house that has caused us so much grief. It cannot be excused. It is regrettable to cause Kinno unhappiness, but he is well aware of what affects the interests of the house. We can't compromise on this." Rie sighed.

Yoshi stalked from the room and walked to the office. Kinnosuke was seated at his table, head on his hands.

"Oh, Kinno-san . . . I understand that Mother has ordered you to divorce Nobu."

"It is true." He raised his head, tears in his eyes.

"I'm very sorry. You have been happily married so long, and you have your three children. . . ."

Kinnosuke hung his head but said nothing.

"You know, Kinno-san, ever since I was a child I've felt closer to you than to Mother. She can be tyrannical at times. *You* were the one who really raised me, who took pains to teach me. I shall always be grateful to you."

Kinnosuke bowed. "Thank you. As a child you were always so eager to learn. Of course my debt to your mother who gave me this opportunity and trained me is heavy. Her sense of timing in business is without equal. I have learned much from her and can never repay my debt." He bowed again.

"Perhaps you and I can work even more closely together in the future, support each other," Yoshitaro said.

"My loyalty has always been to the Omura House. That is why the charge of my wife's disloyalty is so painful to me. I wonder if I should resign." He looked querulously at Yoshitaro.

"Certainly not! That would serve no purpose, and I'm certain that Mother would not accept it. It would leave us weakened. We have no one to replace you. Your efforts are crucial to our success. I have no question about your loyalty. I cannot work without you."

Kinnosuke bowed low. "Thank you for

your confidence. Then I shall remain with you." He bowed to the floor.

"Thank you, Kinno-san. You have my sympathy in this difficult time. Please let me know if there is anything I can do to help."

Yoshitaro put his hand on Kinnosuke's shoulder and shook his head.

Kikuji Yamaguchi sat at his worktable, leaning backward and forward, backward and forward, belching frequently.

He called his chief clerk Yusuke to his table. "We can do something to stop Omura now. You know, their young Master was wounded in a samurai attack, lost his leg. Kinnosuke is overworked. He can't watch everything."

"That's so," Yusuke said, scratching his bald head. "What do you suggest?"

"We can get control of some of their shipping contracts now that they have less sake to ship. They won't be expecting it."

Yusuke sucked in his breath and closed his eyes. "I see. . . ."

Yamaguchi looked at his aging clerk, face grown lean, shoulders hunched. Was he losing his aggressive push? "Get to the port tomorrow, first thing," Yamaguchi ordered. "Make sure you get the Omura shipping contracts."

Yusuke bowed. "Certainly."

"I'm going over to see Fumi," Rie announced loudly as she took up her parasol and walked out the entrance to the office where Yoshitaro and Kinnosuke were working. Yoshitaro nodded curtly. What little gains she had made with him after the amputation had disappeared after her decree that Kinnosuke divorce his wife. She could only hope that this too would pass. She had done the right thing. The necessary thing. And yes, for the house. The house was the point.

Rie had called Seisaburo to Fumi and Eitaro's. She wanted to talk to her children without having Yoshitaro present, and Fumi offered the best pretext. It would be the first time she had undertaken a family discussion of a problem in the house without involving Yoshitaro.

Rie twirled her parasol and listened to the sound of her wooden geta on the cobblestones and the raucous voice of the tofu man going house to house with his cartload of bean cake.

"I'm here." The bell on the slatted gate tinkled as she slid it open and hurried to the entrance.

"Come in, Mother." Fumi gave a quick bow.

"And here's my precious grandchild," Rie said, patting the head of Hirokichi's sister, Mie, who peered around her mother at her grandmother.

"Sei is already here," Fumi said. "They're in the parlor." She placed slippers on the floor in front of her mother and led the way to the room she had decorated with a special ikebana arrangement for her mother's visit.

Eitaro stood and took Rie's arm. "Please have a seat, Mother." He bowed and indicated a zabuton backing to the tokonoma alcove.

"And how are you, Sei?" Rie asked her son. "What new surprise have you for us today?" She smiled.

"I think it's you who has the surprise today, Mother. Eitaro tells me that you ordered Kinnosuke to divorce his wife."

Rie flushed at the accusation. "I just didn't see any alternative, when I learned that she had been speaking ill of Fumi and Hiro at Yamaguchi's. It was a dishonor, and worse, disloyal."

"What exactly did she say, Mother?" Eitaro asked.

Fumi moved closer to her mother.

"According to O-Natsu's friend, she accused me of favoritism to you and Hiro, over Yoshi and Ume." Rie frowned, at the same time feeling a twinge of guilt.

Eitaro pursed his lips and looked at his hands on the table.

Fumi leaned toward Rie. "And has he divorced Nobu?"

"He did so, of course," Rie replied, feeling a deep regret. "She has left."

"I hope it won't affect Kinno's work," Seisaburo said.

"I doubt it," Rie replied. "You know how close he has always been to Yoshi, and Yoshi is totally dependent on him since his accident. Kinno has been extremely attentive to Yoshi lately, even more than usual. Yoshi has particularly urged him to stay, and they have always been so close."

"Well, I hope it doesn't create a problem for you. Will it be uncomfortable for you to work with him now?" Eitaro asked.

Rie fingered the teacup in front of her. "I'm convinced his support of Yoshi won't waver." She hoped her words didn't reflect a hint of doubt.

"What about his children?" Fumi asked.

"They're still with their father, at least the two sons are," Rie said. "I think Nobu may have taken the daughter with her."

Fumi frowned and hugged Mie.

Rie took out her comb and twirled it in both hands. "It's unfortunate, but it's not a disaster. We mustn't let it paralyze us. This is an exciting time, with so many new opportunities. We need to move in new directions, not be stalled over something that's past." She did not mean to sound cold. She simply had to refocus them away from the personal and onto business. "There's a bigger problem. Now it seems that Yamaguchi has captured our shipping contracts with three of our shippers. We have to do something."

Seisaburo leaned forward. "Well, I've been thinking about shipping anyway. We have to negotiate our charters every winter."

"That's so," Rie agreed.

"Wouldn't it be better if we had more control over shipping?"

"Of course. And now with Yamaguchi's move it's a crisis. Could we buy ships of our own?" Rie asked, taking out her fan.

Sei glanced at his mother. "Buy ships? No brewer has done it yet, which might give us a real advantage, to be independent of the charter agents." He looked at his mother, then Eitaro.

"There's still the question of the loaders, the stevedores," Eitaro said, "but as shippers we'd definitely have more control over costs."

Rie lit up at the news. "Well, what are the risks? What will the long-range effects be? This is something new. We need to think of what would happen if we lost a ship in a storm."

"We're so diversified, Mother, as you have always urged, that I think we would survive the loss of a ship," Eitaro said.

"Then that's decided. Now I have to persuade Yoshi and Kinno," she said, frowning and tapping her chin with her fan. "Of course Kinno has always looked ahead. It may not be a problem. Why borrow trouble, Father always said."

Eitaro cleared his throat. "I was thinking. Could we start wholesaling? We have good sources of Yamada Nishiki rice. This would give us extra funds we could use for buying a ship or two."

"We have no choice about ships. We have to counter Yamaguchi's move," Rie said. "It's true that wholesaling is more traditional, but also the dealers and routes are entrenched. With ships we won't have that kind of opposition, at least from other brewers. None of them has gone into buying ships."

"Ships are the key to our biggest markets,"

Seisaburo urged. "And we have stayed ahead because of our willingness to innovate and take risks."

"I'll go back and talk to Kinno and Yoshi. Give them something to think about besides Nobu."

A few weeks later Yoshitaro hobbled into the number one kura on his new crutches. It was his first venture there since he lost his leg. It was winter, brewing was in full swing, and the kurabito were hurrying from one part of the compound to another. Yoshitaro paused to rest against the wall near the entrance.

"*Ah,* Master. How good to see you again. We were all so concerned."

Yoshitaro looked around. It was Toji, bowing repeatedly, his ruddy face beaming. "Do you wish to, *ah* . . . may I help you?" He glanced at Yoshitaro's one leg, then looked down and bowed.

"Thank you, Toji-san. I'll manage. I just want to look at the filter."

Yoshitaro hopped toward the boat-shaped wooden press where the final stage of brewing took place, the residue of lees filtered out from the brew to leave the liquid clear and nearly colorless. Minutes later two kurabito stopped to bow and ask if he needed help. He shook his head and murmured, "No, thank you." *They're obviously embarrassed,* he thought. He felt an angry flush move from his neck toward his forehead. And the missing leg still pained so that he often bit his lip. The slash of the samurai sword across the back of his thigh was still agony. He leaned against the filter, his crutches resting against it, grateful that the two kurabito had gone elsewhere.

If these men, people he had worked with for years and knew him so well, could not bear to look at him on his crutches, how would he ever face O-Sada? How would she be able to look at the stump, the remnant of his leg? It was so grotesque that he himself could barely stand to look at it. Tama had tried to keep from wincing when she had to change the dressing, but Yoshitaro could sense her distaste. Kinno had been so supportive, a real savior. And his mother treated him as if nothing had happened. He was still Kinzaemon XI of the Omura House, she kept reminding him.

It would be too painful to go again to the Sawaraya. It was possible that O-Toki and O-Sada would welcome him again. They probably would, but it would not be the same. He was still O-Sada's patron and O-Toki's natural son and benefactor. He would not forget their financial needs. They

425

would probably pity him, but pity was not what he craved when he went to the Sawaraya. It was easy to understand why his father had gone there so often over the years. There they accepted a man as he was, made him feel important, even attractive. Attractive. He could never be considered so again. The Sawaraya was the only place a man could totally relax. But nothing could induce him to go back now. How he would survive without those visits, without O-Sada's soft ways, he could not imagine.

As for children, he had no wish to approach Tama. There was no need for further exploration of a possible pregnancy. That meant that Ume, the miracle of O-Sada's love, would be his only child and would represent the next generation. Like Rie, she would one day have an adopted husband. The history of the house would repeat itself. Yoshitaro reached for his crutches to return to the office. He must make sure that Ume became the focus of attention, not only his own and Kinnosuke's, but also his mother's.

CHAPTER 36

As Rie walked toward the kitchen one morning she heard excited voices in the inner office. She hurried along the corridor and opened the shoji.

Kinnosuke glanced toward Rie and said, his thin voice higher than usual, "The loyalists have won, Oku-san. It's happened, just as Seisaburo predicted."

Yoshitaro struggled on his crutches to move closer to his mother. "They say there was fighting in the streets of Kyoto between Sat-Cho samurai and Bakufu forces," he said. "Now they're saying the shogun has relinquished power to the emperor, and the emperor has gone to Edo with his court."

Rie hooked her thumbs in her obi and looked at Yoshitaro, then at Kinnosuke. "Well! The end of the Tokugawa shoguns! I never thought I would see the day. What does this mean for us, I wonder?"

"Too soon to tell, but we've got to be on

guard," Kinnosuke said. "There's going to be an emergency meeting of the Brewers Association this afternoon."

"Make sure Eitaro and Seisaburo know, Yoshi," Rie said, feeling a sense of urgency.

"We'll all go," Yoshitaro said.

Rie tapped her fan on the table. "I want to know everything that's discussed. In detail."

Yoshitaro dipped his head in acknowledgment. "Don't worry, Mother. We'll give you a full report."

Rie spent the rest of the day in agitated activity. She followed O-Natsu and the maids around the house, at one point grabbing the feather duster from O-Yuki and flourishing it furiously in the parlor at each item in the Butsudan and tokonoma. Early in the afternoon she bustled out to the compound, tied back her sleeves, and attacked the barrels with a brush. Then she hurried back into the inner office, took the ledgers onto a worktable, and turned pages, following columns of figures with her fingers. "Don't overlook anything," she muttered to herself. She sat there long after all the clerks had left, unaware of the time until O-Natsu called her to dinner.

"They're still not back, O-Natsu. I don't feel hungry."

O-Natsu set bowls of steaming miso soup and rice in front of Rie. "But you must eat something. They're sure to return soon."

Rie picked up the soup bowl and sipped, then plucked out some tofu with her chopsticks.

She paused. Yes, there was the sound of the outer shoji being opened, the stamping of geta-clad feet on the earthen floor of the entryway, and voices — Yoshitaro's, Kinnosuke's, and Eitaro's too.

Rie rose quickly and hurried to the entrance. "Welcome home! Come and tell me what happened. You must be hungry."

The men gathered around the dinner table and, hoisting up their kimonos to sit cross-legged, cleared their throats.

"I'm glad you've come too, Eitaro," Rie said.

O-Yuki brought in more rice and miso, with small dishes of mountain vegetables, mackerel, pickles, green tea, and sake.

Rie looked at each man then turned to Yoshitaro. "Tell me!" she said.

"Mother, there's a lot to tell and there's nothing to tell. It's really too soon to say what's going to happen in Edo. Until we know the situation there we won't know how it will affect us. All we know for certain is that everything is changing in Edo and elsewhere."

"It took so long just to learn that?" Rie asked sharply.

Kinnosuke blinked several times, his thin face twitching. "What we do know for certain, Oku-san, is that we will continue brewing for the rest of the season, just as if nothing had happened. Of course something has happened, but as Yoshi said, we don't yet know what the effects will be."

"What took so long today, Mother," Eitaro explained, "is that people were discussing various possible outcomes in Edo. But without real knowledge of what's happening it was only speculation. I spoke with Sei and he thinks we should go to Edo, now, at least one of us, to see what we can learn. We need to talk to Yoshioka and the man you sent there, Suganuma. I think that's the best we can do for now." Eitaro turned to the dishes in front of him.

Yoshitaro put down his chopsticks. "What seems certain is that Satsuma and Choshu are in control there now, supporting the emperor. And they've got some samurai from Hizen and Tosa with them. The shogun has retired, without a major battle, just some skirmishes in Aizu and the south. Those samurai were mostly bluster and swagger anyway, attacking unarmed indi-

430

viduals," he added, looking down.

"Yes, Yoshi," Rie said. She reached over and put a hand on his arm. "Well, they haven't stopped you, have they?" She picked up a teapot and poured for him.

Several weeks later Rie stepped into the corridor and caught sight of Yoshitaro hopping rapidly toward the office. She marveled at how adept he had become at getting around on crutches. She was on the verge of complimenting him when she stopped herself. Better not to call attention to his disability, since he himself seemed to be accepting it. At least he no longer complained, and he had stepped back into his role as house head. She followed him into the office, where several clerks were talking excitedly.

"Oku-san, and Master," Kinnosuke spoke up. "It seems there's been a public proclamation by the new government. It's posted outside the old Bakufu commissioners' office. We need to know what it says. I think I'd better go." He blinked several times.

"Yoshi and I will accompany you, Kinno-san. I'm anxious to know too. Send for a ricksha."

Spring had come and gone and with it the kurabito who returned to their farms in Tamba. The end of season celebration had been held, and the kura buildings were quiet. Sales had been brisk following the hanging of the leaf ball at the front entrance. It was the time of year when only the office clerks remained busy.

As the ricksha drew up to the entrance a second ricksha arrived with Eitaro seated in it.

"I see you had the same idea, Mother," he said. "Come, ride with me." He reached a hand out to help Rie up.

"Good. Yoshi will ride with Kinno."

The streets exploded with life, ricksha and carts clogging the narrow lanes, all headed in the same direction. Excitement was in the air as ricksha runners raced for position in the line of traffic. Rie sat back, her arm resting on the side, enjoying the crowds and the sea breeze against her face. She was pleased that her enjoyment had not diminished with age.

The monsoon rains had not begun, and she was grateful for the light wind from across the harbor. She always paused to look at the cask ships anchored there, some on dry dock having their sails or hulls repaired.

As the rickshas neared the main intersection, they jammed every possible space, making it impossible to move.

"We'll walk from here," Eitaro said. He

helped Rie down, made sure that Kinno-suke and Yoshitaro were behind them, and signaled the rickshas to wait.

"Can you make it, Mother?" Yoshitaro asked.

"Yes, Yoshi. How about you? Do you want to wait in the ricksha? There's such a crowd."

"Maybe you'd better wait here, Master," Kinnosuke said.

"No, I want to see the proclamation," Yoshitaro insisted.

As Rie and Eitaro elbowed their way toward the front, Rie could hear men shouting as they read. Yes, they were nearly all men, most of them merchants and townsmen, by their clothing. No samurai were in evidence. Then over at the edge of the crowd Rie spotted a samurai still wearing his swords, his face and head covered by a huge straw hat to avoid recognition.

"He must be embarrassed to appear in this crowd," Eitaro said.

Several inches taller than Rie, Eitaro was able to read the proclamation. He held Rie's elbow as he read. "It proclaims 'the Restoration of the Emperor,' and the emperor and the new era are both named 'Meiji.' Just a minute. There's also a Charter Oath, it says. Let me see if I can read it." He edged closer,

Rie clinging behind him. She looked around, trying to catch sight of Kinnosuke and Yoshitaro.

"I don't see them anywhere," she said, frowning.

"There are five articles in the Oath, Eitaro read: '(1) Deliberative assemblies shall be widely established and all state affairs decided by public discussion. (2) All classes, high and low, shall unite in actively carrying out the administration of affairs of state. (3) The common people, no less than the civil and military officials, shall be allowed to pursue whatever calling they choose. (4) Evil customs of the past shall be abandoned and everything shall be based on the just laws of Heaven and Earth. (5) Knowledge shall be sought throughout the world so as to invigorate the foundations of imperial rule.' That's the end. Well, we still have to know what it all means, don't we?" he said.

"Try to remember those five points, Eitaro. We'll need to talk them over and try to understand what they mean. We need to find Yoshi and Kinno now." She turned.

They squeezed back against the encroaching mob. Rie stumbled, shoved by an insistent plebeian. Eitaro caught her as she was about to fall.

"Oh, there's Yoshi." Just as she spoke an

enormous figure looming ahead pushed against Yoshitaro, causing him to fall to the ground.

"What do you think you're doing here, with your one leg?" roared the man.

"It's Yamaguchi," Rie said. She looked at him as he swaggered away. "Bully!" she shouted. "We'll get him for this," she mumbled. "Yoshi, are you hurt?" she asked, taking his arm. Kinnosuke had already helped him up.

"Well, I nearly fell too, Yoshi," Rie said.

Yoshitaro shook himself. "I'm all right."

"It was hard for anyone to stand," Rie said. "Come, let's go home."

"Edo is no longer Edo, Mother. It's now called Tokyo," Tama said one morning at breakfast.

"Ah, Eastern Capital," Rie said.

"So many things happening there," Yoshitaro said. "All these new notions from America and Europe: banks, railroads, constitutions, political parties, a parliament, a new army and navy, a new solar calendar. It's amazing! One thing I heard Kinno talk about might be useful to us."

"What's that, Yoshi?" Rie asked.

"He said it's a new form of economic organization the government is supporting.

It's called a joint stock company."

"What is that exactly, Yoshi?" Rie asked.

"He said it's a way of spreading the risk among a group of investors," Yoshitaro said.

"We need to learn more about it, then, don't we?" Rie asked.

Later, in the office, Kinnosuke spoke with Rie. "One thing is certain, there are no more kabu shares," he said. "We can produce as much sake as we want with what rice we can procure. No more government controls. The new government has its hands full doing other things." He blinked rapidly and sucked in his breath.

"But doesn't this mean that everyone else can also brew as much as they want, including anyone who has never brewed before?" Yoshitaro asked.

"True," Kinnosuke agreed, "but we have an advantage. We're number three. New brewers just starting out won't be able to compete."

"It seems one key to competing now is to buy as much rice as we can," Rie said, tapping her fan on the table. "So, Kinno-san and Yoshi, shouldn't we send to our suppliers immediately? Offer a slightly higher price, just over the going price, to ensure the largest supply." Rie looked at Eitaro, who had entered the office.

"I think you're right, Mother," he said. "I'm going to move in that direction too."

Eitaro always seemed to grasp the importance of timing faster than Yoshitaro.

Rie broached with Kinnosuke and Yoshitaro the idea of purchasing ships, the suggestion she had already discussed with Eitaro and Seisaburo.

"Since Yamaguchi has taken over most of our shipping contracts we need to buy ships, as soon as possible."

"We don't have a choice, do we?" Kinnosuke said. "It will take negotiation. No brewer has done it, but that doesn't mean it can't be done." He blinked.

"You know the shippers, don't you, Kinno-san?" Rie asked.

"Several." Kinnosuke nodded. "There's a medium-sized shipper in port who's in difficulty, I hear. The head of the house died last month and the succession is in dispute. They may be willing to put one or two ships up for sale."

"Then this is the time to approach them, isn't it?" Rie said.

"It looks as if we should move now," Yoshitaro agreed.

"And there's another possibility," Rie began and took out her fan. "It would mean competition, but I was wondering if we

437

might do some rice wholesaling, as Sei suggested? We have excellent sources now, really more than we need, even with our new kura. It would give us more influence over the price of rice and enable us to expand future production. What do you think, Kinno-san?"

"As you say, there's a lot of competition with the already established routes."

"We could make gradual inquiries. I know it would take some time. I don't expect we could do it all this year, but what about for next year's harvest?"

"We can try, yes," Kinnosuke nodded and blinked.

Rie smiled and poured tea for the two men. Yamaguchi had made it easy to obtain their agreement on buying cask ships. Rie hoped to catch Yamaguchi off guard.

A few months later Rie wanted to visit Seisaburo again, this time alone, without Yoshitaro or even Eitaro. When it came right down to it, Seisaburo was becoming her most trusted business ally, apart from Kinnosuke. His entrepreneurial skill was without peer. Confident though Rie was in her choice of Eitaro, she knew Seisaburo had the edge when it came to innovation. Rie left through the kitchen door, telling only

O-Natsu where she was going. She smiled at the sense of adventure finding her own ricksha gave her, a simple enough act but not part of her daily routine. Seisaburo was not expecting her, but she trusted to luck that she would find him there.

She left the ricksha at the entrance and entered the gate whose tinkling bell announced her presence. Seisaburo's wife, Mari, greeted her with a bow and a smile.

"Welcome! What a pleasant surprise. And you came all this way alone?" She placed slippers at the edge of the hall platform for Rie.

"Oh, yes. Is Sei in the office?" Rie asked without polite preliminaries.

"I am afraid he has gone to our other kura. He should be back by noon, though," Mari said, nodding.

"I wonder if your banto, Hirano-san, would mind if I talked with him?"

"I am certain he would be honored to speak with my husband's mother from the main house. Please wait here a moment." Mari indicated a seat in the parlor near the tokonoma.

Rie sat at the lacquer table. A maid bustled in with tea, but Rie only nodded.

Mari returned, breathlessly solicitous. "Please come this way, Mother," she said.

She led the way along the earthen corridor to the office.

Seisaburo's chief clerk, Hirano, bowed low to Rie. "What an honor to see the mistress of the main house here, Oku-san," he said. Mari excused herself and left Rie alone with the ample, heavy-browed chief clerk.

Rie bowed slightly. "Actually, I had hoped to speak with my son about a rather delicate matter, but as I know you are his loyal banto . . ."

"Is there something I can do to help?" Hirano asked.

Rie looked at him, this sturdy, experienced man in his forties. She herself had advised Seisaburo about hiring him when Sei began his branch house operation, and Hirano was aware of his obligation to her.

"Well, Hirano-san, I have been thinking. Wouldn't it be a good idea to have one of your clerks come to work at the main house for a while? We could send you one of ours in exchange. It would be a good experience for both boys and make our house ties stronger. Having an apprentice eat someone else's rice works both ways, doesn't it?" She did not mention that she hoped to find an apprentice she could keep as Kinnosuke's future successor.

She smiled and looked around the office

at three young clerks working there. Her eye rested on a boy she judged to be the right age, about fourteen, a well-built boy, with a businesslike air about him.

"What about that boy over there? A good worker?" she asked.

"*Ah,* he is my son. Yes, I have been training him, grooming him myself." He bowed. "He has been helping your son."

Rie nodded. "Would you be willing to part with him for a year? Of course you would still be dealing with him on a regular basis, and you would have one of our clerks in exchange." Rie kept her eye on the boy and became more persuasive as she watched him.

Hirano bowed. "I would be honored to have my son work in the main house for a year."

"What is his name?" Rie asked.

"Buntaro. He is thirteen years old, soon fourteen."

"The right age. Good. I'll wait until my son returns. We can formalize the arrangement if it is agreeable to everyone. I'll send you a most able clerk in exchange."

Rie bowed and returned to the house to wait. Mari brought in more tea, then excused herself to take care of her children. "My husband will be back soon, I am sure," she said.

Rie nodded. She hoped Seisaburo would not object to her selection of Buntaro as Kinnosuke's apprentice. Kinnosuke and Yoshitaro might be another matter.

CHAPTER 37

A few days later Rie caught Yoshitaro alone at the dinner table.

"You know, Yoshi," she began slowly, "it might be a good idea to begin thinking about selecting the apprentice who will become Kinno's successor."

"There's no hurry about it, is there? He's still young and we have several clerks about the right age. We could start grooming one of them. No lack of talent or training."

Rie took out her fan, then put it down and poured tea for Yoshitaro.

"That's true, Yoshi. But you know, there's something else to consider. She paused and looked pensively at her fan. "You know what they always say about having a son or apprentice 'eat someone else's rice' so they don't become spoiled or complacent, so they learn other ways of doing things."

"What are you getting at?" Yoshi chewed on a toothpick.

"Well, I wonder if it might not be mutually advantageous for us to take an apprentice from one of our branches, either from Eitaro or from Sei, and send them one of ours in exchange for a year?"

"I suppose it's a possibility. I'd prefer one of Sei's, if you put it that way."

"All right," Rie nodded, pleased that he had so readily acquiesced to her plan. She knew Yoshi would prefer Sei's apprentice to anyone from Fumi's house. "And I wouldn't object to the idea of promoting a clerk from Sei's to be Kinno's successor eventually, if he works out well."

"But what would our clerks think if they were passed over by one of Sei's? And I'm not sure Kinno would agree. Haven't we caused him enough trouble, forcing him to divorce Nobu?"

"You can persuade him, Yoshi. I know you can. And he'll see the wisdom of it. Just think of all the improvements Sei has made in brewing. Having a future banto trained by Sei will enhance our business in the future. It's bound to. It will make our tie with Sei's branch even stronger. You need to be looking toward the future, Yoshi. Kinno may be young now, but he won't last forever. Neither will I." She paused to smooth her hair self-consciously. "We can try him out, see how he works. We don't need to make a decision about Kinno's successor until he has worked here a year or so and proven himself. No need to mention that plan to Kinno yet."

Yoshitaro nodded but frowned, his mouth a study in negativity. "You are very persuasive, Mother."

"You can be too, Yoshi, especially with Kinno. He values your opinion above everyone else's. And after all, you have the final say in any decision."

Yoshitaro raised his eyebrows slightly but said nothing.

The emperor's birthday, a holiday, meant that Fumi was bringing her family for a visit. Emperor Meiji, a child of thirteen at the time of the Restoration in 1868, was now only seventeen. Everyone knew it was the samurai loyalists from Satsuma and Choshu, not the child emperor, who had transformed the country from an isolated feudal regime to something resembling a modern nation-state.

"How good it is to see you all." Rie held out her arms to Hirokichi. Whenever he came to the main house for training, he followed Buntaro around, the new clerk from Seisaburo's branch. Buntaro was now installed as a permanent clerk in the office, and even Kinnosuke had agreed that he be promoted to number one apprentice. Rie smiled whenever she saw Hirokichi and Buntaro together. It repeated the pattern of Yoshitaro and Kinnosuke years earlier, a bond to be fostered.

"And Mie, come here, my dear." Rie put an arm around Mie, who sat down next to her. "Hiro too." Rie handed both children some candies from her sleeve.

"Hiro, you've grown so. How old are you now?"

"I'm eleven, Grandmother. My birthday was three months ago."

"Don't tell me I forgot such an important event! How neglectful of me. So you're the same age as Ume, aren't you, dear?" Rie smiled at Ume and Hirokichi.

"I'm nearly twelve, Grandmother," Ume said, frowning at Hirokichi.

"You're all growing up so fast I can't keep up with you," Rie said laughing. She indicated a plate of cakes to Tama, who passed them and poured tea.

"Hiro is very busy these days, Mother," Eitaro said. "Besides his apprenticeship here he spends time with me the first thing each morning. We go into the kura to check everything."

Rie glanced at Eitaro and thought how good it was for Fumi that her husband was not only capable but also attractive, with his sharply chiseled features and agreeable manner.

"My, is that so?" Rie said. "And how do you like that, Hiro?"

"It smells wonderful in the kura, Grandmother. I like to watch the bubbles grow with the yeast, and the koji room is so warm on cold mornings. It's too bad you can't go into the kura, Grandmother." Hirokichi tossed a ball jauntily as he talked. "Ume can't either," he said, with a superior glance at his cousin.

Ume pouted and stuck her tongue out at Hiro.

"That's right, Hiro. We women can never enter the kura. It's for the safety of the sake. We are taught never to cross the threshold. And our sake has only gone bad once," Rie said.

"Did you enter the kura that time, Grandmother, and make it go sour?" Hirokichi asked.

All the adults laughed, including Rie. Then she thought of Jihei's treachery, and her smile vanished, her mood darkened.

"No, I didn't cause it, Hiro," she said.

Rie leaned over toward Fumi. "I knew

447

Hiro would be a bright child, even before he was born," she said softly, not wanting Hiro to become conceited.

Tama looked at Rie and leaned forward. "And Ume has started scouring the barrels, Mother. She's so thorough. Toji is very pleased with her." Tama, like Yoshi, was always eager to protect Ume. It was a shift since Tama's anguish when Ume was adopted in.

"Yes," Rie said. "That's what I used to do when I was young, Ume." She glanced at Ume. "Your mother did too. It's good to see these traditions carried on by the grandchildren."

"How is Buntaro working out, Mother?" Eitaro asked.

"He's an excellent worker, excellent. And we've promoted him now to Kinno's number one apprentice. Sei is so far away that I'm glad we have this tie. Not like you, close by so that we can talk every day. You know Kinno worked in the kitchen at first. I found him there boiling rice."

"Is that so?" Eitaro said. "I didn't know. So he rose from rice boiler to head clerk?" He nodded appreciatively.

"And Buntaro shows the same promise as Kinno. That's what really pleases me," Rie said. "I'm glad his father and Sei didn't insist that he go back, though I know they miss him." Rie realized that Sei and Buntaro's father were deeply disappointed to lose Buntaro.

"There's a problem with the loan to the temple, Mother," Yoshitaro said in the office one morning.

"Yes," Kinnosuke agreed, worry lines making him appear older than his years. "It was a five-year loan, and they are not able to pay the interest. They haven't paid for the last four months." He looked from Rie to Yoshitaro.

"I see," Rie said. She tapped the table with her fan.

"The priest came from Kyoto yesterday afternoon. He said, correctly, that the principle and interest have reached a total of fifteen thousand yen. They cannot pay the interest on it. He was quite distressed," Yoshitaro said, watching his mother.

"I was afraid that might happen when they asked for such a big loan," Kinnosuke said.

"Yes, it was not totally unexpected," Rie said, although she had hoped it would never come to this. "Now we will have to treat them like any other borrower. Accept some of their collateral." She reached over for the ledger book in front of Kinnosuke.

Yoshitaro frowned. "You mean . . . take the temple's land?" he asked, wide-eyed with shock.

"They have quite a lot of good mountain land that they don't need, and the demand for our wood and coal is increasing. We use a lot ourselves. So many are using steam power now. With the extra money we earn, we can make a larger donation so that they won't be greatly affected, and won't lose face by being unable to repay the loan."

Yoshitaro smoothed the hair back from his face to reveal a gathering storm, and asked, "How can we do this to our family temple? Our ancestral records and graves are there. This would be a huge blot on our reputation. It just isn't done, to take collateral from a temple, any more than it is to loan to them."

"Yoshi, this is a new era. It calls for bold measures if we are to keep up with the times and stay ahead of the competition. We can't cling to old attitudes."

"I didn't like it when we made the loan, but this is even worse," Yoshitaro said, leaning on his crutches. He frowned. "I'm afraid when word of this gets around it will be bad for our business. We'll be criticized. More than that, think of the bad karma that will accrue from taking temple land, taking advantage of the family temple. You can't go against the gods and priests."

Rie sighed. Although she understood his worries, even agreed, it was too late to be timid. It would only make matters worse. Instead, they needed to make the best out of a bad situation. Yoshitaro was at times so obviously Jihei's son, not hers. "Yoshi, don't be fainthearted," she said. "Your father was that way too. Our markets are not only secure, they are expanding. And I doubt others will come to know of this. And as I said earlier, we can make added donations to the temple with our earnings. What do you think, Kinno-san?"

Kinnosuke spoke rapidly. "As the temple is more a family matter, I don't feel I can offer an opinion. The decision is up to you, and the Master. But if you really want my opinion, I think Yoshi may be right."

"We should consult with Sei and Eitaro," Yoshitaro said, taking advantage of Kinnosuke's evasion.

"I am sure they would support me," Rie said.

Yoshitaro stomped around on his crutches. "Well, this is something I refuse to do. And *I* would be the one who would have to inform the priest, not you."

"Business is business, Yoshi!" Rie countered, standing in front of him so he could not escape her. "We often have to do things we do not enjoy. Yes, it's your responsibility as house head. You'll have to go to Kyoto tomorrow. Kinno can go with you and take care of the financial details."

Kinnosuke bowed, but she could see the tension in his face.

Rie knew that if she didn't do something quickly, Yoshi's anger would soon spill over. She touched his arm, but he merely pulled away.

"There's no need to take all their mountain land," Rie said, trying a more conciliatory approach. "This won't change our relationship. I doubt they'll want to publicize these arrangements any more than they did the loan, and in the end, this will help the temple, which is in desperate straits financially and is dependent on the house for support."

"Aren't we all," said Yoshi coldly, staring her boldly in the eye.

Rie ignored the challenge, and instead inserted her fan in her obi, rose, and left the office.

As Rie was preparing for bed that evening, thinking of Yoshi and Kinno's opposition to taking temple land, and even loaning to the temple, her father's words of warning came to her. "You know what they say about the peg that sticks up. It gets pounded down." How many times had she heard this? Competition in business could not be avoided. But had she allowed her zeal for making White Tiger number one to cause her to stray too far from tradition, to get too far ahead of her competitors? Did she detect some resentment in the behavior not only of Yamaguchi but other brewers as well? Moreover, it was known among brewers that she, a woman, was making decisions for White Tiger, not Yoshi. She was venturing into many areas reserved for men. These troubling thoughts coursed through her again and again. How she missed her father and his unerring good judgment.

Rie needed a walk in the garden one morning several weeks later, a chance to take stock of all that had happened in the family and business. She stepped out and felt herself bending, as if under a great weight of worries. She straightened as her geta crunched against the carefully swept gray pebbles. She brushed her hand across her favorite rock and sat. Yoshi had not come around as she had hoped. Instead he had remained sullen, aloof. She sighed. At least her children were married now, all gone. A major part of her responsibility had been discharged. Only with Yoshi and Teru had she failed; Teru still a wound that festered. Now she could focus fully on the business side, though it had never been far from her thoughts, even when the children were present. The temple's mountain land was a valuable addition to the Omura holdings, forested mountain land necessary for coal production and sales. She wished Yoshi and Kinnosuke could understand that.

She gazed at the koi pond and looked for the old fish, the grandfather fish that had inhabited the pond so many years. There he was, still lazing at the far side. As she watched, two red maple leaves circled dizzily down and touched the surface just above him. The koi swished into action and carried the leaves on its back to the center of the pond. She gazed, eyes half closed, and saw a ship, a cask ship carrying barrels of sake to Tokyo, the newly named capital.

The Omura ships now numbered six, and other brewers had followed their lead in purchasing ships of their own. Perhaps it was time to take another step in the shipping venture that had proven so successful. It was a matter of organization, a business issue, a way of deploying resources most efficiently. Kinno would offer some suggestion. His loyalty had really not wavered after divorcing Nobu and now with the tension around the temple, had it? And he had become so protective of Ume, just as he had always been of Yoshi. Surely Kinno would welcome a new move that could propel White Tiger to the forefront in yet another area. Other brewers watched him with great interest and followed his lead in each step he took.

Now with Seisaburo's vision added to her own, Kinno's dedication to the house could only strengthen. How gratifying that Sei was her son, though it was regrettable that his special talents were not shared by Yoshi, who tried so hard to live up to his role as house head. "At least our sake will not kill him as it did his father," Rie mused.

She stirred on the rock, brushed off her kimono, and walked back through the corridor to the office. She lowered herself to the table where Yoshitaro sat.

"Good morning, Yoshi," she said. "Where is Kinno?"

"I believe in the outer office, Mother," he said stiffly. "Shall I get — ?" Yoshitaro stopped, unable to raise himself easily.

"Don't worry, Yoshi. I'll call him," Rie said, wishing that they could bridge the gap that seemed to have divided them since the argument over the loan to the priests.

When Kinnosuke joined them, he and Yoshitaro looked expectantly at Rie.

"Our shipping is going well with our six ships now, isn't it, Kinno-san?"

Kinnosuke nodded. "Quite well, yes. That side of the business has a potential to expand, it seems certain," he said, looking at Yoshitaro as he spoke.

"Just what I was thinking," said Rie, her excitement mounting. "Now what was it you were saying recently about this new form of business organization? Was it called joint stock?"

"That's right. A joint stock company is organized among several stockholders, owners, as a way of spreading the risk. They say it is useful in new ventures," Kinnosuke replied. He looked at Rie quizzically.

"Well, Kinno, do you think our shipping has reached the stage where we could form our own shipping company, perhaps using this new form? Wouldn't it give us still better control over shipping and labor?"

Kinnosuke scratched his head and sucked in his breath. "We were the first to purchase our own ships. I see no reason why we can't be the first to form our own shipping company." He nodded.

Yoshitaro looked back and forth at his

mother and Kinnosuke, then just shook his
head.

CHAPTER 38

Several years had elapsed since White Tiger organized the first brewery-owned shipping company, and in the interim everyone in the Omura household had grown older. Ume was twenty and Hirokichi nearly as old. Yoshitaro was forty-four, and Rie had already passed sixty-five and entered the second cycle of life on the Chinese calendar, still vigorous and intent on keeping ahead of the competition.

Rie, ever watchful of Hirokichi, could not have been more pleased at what she saw. While some might view him as spoiled by Rie and Fumi, for Rie he embodied the innovative spirit of the new Meiji era. A jaunty confidence and optimism radiated from the clean regular planes of his face. He was an attractive young man, liked by everyone and especially popular among the brewers. Now that he was nearly of age, he worked regularly with his father and was a less frequent visitor to the main house. Rie's hopes for the future were materializing in Hirokichi. Her father would be proud to know she would pass the mantle on to his grandson. And if this new joint stock company was successful, the Omura House might finally be number one, just as she had promised him. She smiled, but then with a twinge of guilt her thoughts turned to Ume.

Ume, only child of the main house, was now a beautiful, amiable young woman the age of marriage. While just a hint of Yoshitaro's nose and unruly hair suggested itself, Ume could be considered attractive and of above-average intelligence.

The fortunes of White Tiger were definitely on the rise, yet something nagged at the back of Rie's mind, made her uneasy. She couldn't quite put her finger on it.

Several evenings later the family was at dinner. Tama had brought in the rice and other dishes, and Ume was pouring tea.

"I wanted to speak to you about Ume, Mother," Yoshi said. "Kinnosuke and I are both pleased with the way she has developed. I feel we should be able to select an appropriate mukoyoshi for her soon, someone like Father."

Not like Jihei, Rie thought, but was careful to keep her face a mask. "Yes, Yoshi." She

459

smiled. "I've been giving it some thought too, now that she's nearly twenty. There are several acceptable prospects."

Yoshitaro started to speak again, but began coughing and put a handkerchief to his mouth. He doubled over and could not stop his racking cough. Rie looked at him sharply. Was it her imagination, or had he lost weight?

"He has developed a bad cough lately, Mother," Tama said with a worried glance at Yoshitaro. "Sometimes it keeps him awake at night." She did not mention that it must have also kept her awake, worrying, but Rie could see it in the sallow shadows beneath her eyes.

"Have you called the herbalist, Tama?" Rie asked.

"I'll do that tomorrow early," she replied. "Ume, bring more tea for your father."

Ume rose and left the room.

Rie ate without speaking. That was it, the nagging worry. Yoshitaro had never completely regained his health and spirits since he lost his leg. He had resumed his duties well enough, but lacking the edge of his former enthusiasm. Rie was certain Kinnosuke was aware of it and equally certain that he was protecting Yoshi, helping him out in his work to avoid any unwanted questions.

460

This cough would bear watching.

Glancing at Yoshitaro, his food still untouched, Rie said, "You must eat something, Yoshi."

He took up his chopsticks and picked at his rice. "I'm all right. Don't worry."

Some months later Rie walked into the inner office and found Kinnosuke and Yoshitaro engrossed in conversation at the worktable. Buntaro had joined them.

"Come, Mother," Yoshitaro said. "Buntaro has some interesting information."

"Yes?" Rie smiled at the well-muscled young clerk and seated herself next to Yoshitaro.

"You remember those black ships, the steam-powered ships that appeared at Yokohama with the Americans some years ago?" Kinnosuke asked, blinking rapidly as he spoke.

"Oh, yes," Rie said. "Sei told us about them. Everyone was so frightened by them at first."

"Well," Kinnosuke continued, "Buntaro was at the port yesterday. He says one of these ships has anchored there, and another is expected today."

"What is their cargo? And who owns them?" Rie asked sharply. She turned to Buntaro and took out her fan.

461

He bowed. "They say they are owned by the English and are chartered to a company in Tokyo. Apparently they have brought some of the new foreign goods to sell here in Kobe."

"Foreign goods." Rie paused and looked at Kinnosuke. "Well, we in Kobe have always welcomed Chinese goods, so these foreigners will find a profitable market here. And that means they may be looking for cargo to take back to Tokyo, doesn't it?"

Kinnosuke straightened and sucked in his breath. "That's just what I was thinking, Oku-san. They're much faster than our cask ships, and of course larger and safer. It looks as if they may make our ships obsolete. And it may not take long."

"We should get to the port today, Kinno-san, you and Buntaro-san. Make some of our barrels available immediately, some that we marked for local sales, or some that were scheduled for one of our cask ships."

Kinnosuke bowed twice. "Yes, I believe we'll have to plan how to convert. It will be difficult, costly at first. Our cask crews will need to be trained too."

"See if you can get some of the crew from one of our ships placed on one of the steamships as apprentices, Kinno-san. The important thing is to act now, without losing time." She turned to Buntaro. "Your information was crucial, Buntaro-san. Thank you." She nodded, almost a bow.

He bowed smartly and looked pleased.

She turned to Yoshitaro who was leaning forward intently, trying hard to suppress a cough.

"Yoshi, try to organize this, can you? Kinno and Buntaro can do the legwork . . . but you need to coordinate the operation here." Rie knew she was perfectly capable of organizing, but she hoped to restore Yoshi's energy. She looked at Yoshitaro's pallid face and hoped the challenge would spark some of his old enthusiasm. She toyed with her obi, eyes flashing. "This is wonderfully exciting, isn't it, Yoshi? I feel it's the most important opportunity we've had in years. It may change the way sake is marketed everywhere." She placed a hand on Yoshitaro's shoulder and smiled.

He coughed and bent over, his hands over his mouth.

Kinnosuke and Buntaro both rose and began talking animatedly about their visit to the port. Buntaro darted out to the kura to see about readying some barrels. As Rie left the office every clerk had been alerted and was going into action on Kinnosuke's orders. She tapped her fan on her hand as she walked out, her thoughts on Yoshi rather than business.

One evening Rie sat at her dressing table in the second-floor room she had taken over after Yoshitaro's accident. She fanned out a handful of her long thinning hair and saw that white strands had begun to spread beyond the hair at her temples. She combed and re-combed her hair attempting to conceal this proof of aging. At her last birthday she'd turned sixty-six, and she found it hard to realize that she was older than her father had been when he died. She felt no lessening of energy, no crippling rheumatism or the chilblains most people her age, including O-Natsu, complained of when the damp chill of winter settled in. The most she could say was that the cold energized her, spurred her to an extra burst of activity she always associated with the brewing season. Her health was exceptional; her spirits buoyed each year by the progress of the rice through the fermentation in the kura, so closely was her inner being bound to brewing. She knew it had been the same with her father, but she had never sensed the same intimate connection in either Jihei or Yoshitaro. Watching Hirokichi closely, she thought she could detect in him signs of a sixth sense, an almost physical bond with brewing. Could this somehow be her biological legacy through Fumi? She combed slowly, and paused, her comb in midair as she heard footsteps on the stairs.

"Excuse me, Grandmother," a soft voice wafted through the shoji.

"Oh, come in, dear," answered Rie.

Ume opened the shoji and bowed.

"I've brought you some tea to warm you before you sleep," she said and knelt beside Rie to set the tray down.

Rie looked at her and smiled at the only grandchild of the main house. Ume was always so cheerful, eager to please, and a good worker. Rie looked at the large black eyes, startling against so pale a complexion. She does have a kind of beauty, Rie thought. It was unfortunate that she was not really an Omura daughter.

Ume leaned gracefully to pour tea for her grandmother.

"Ume, now that you are twenty we must think of your marriage, mustn't we?"

Ume looked down at the teapot and bowed.

"Has your mother spoken to you about it?" Rie asked.

"She said something about finding a mukoyishi, Grandmother, but nothing definite."

"Of course there is no hurry, dear. But you are of the age."

Ume looked up quizzically, her dark eyes reflecting an air of mystery in the flickering lamplight.

"We have no lack of prospects, dear. You know we are a major house, and your marriage will be a big event in Kobe."

Rie looked at Ume. This beautiful, conscientious granddaughter tried so hard to please and yet Rie had never been able to accept her as she had Fumi and Sei. She could never know that she was a geisha's daughter and granddaughter. There had been a time when Rie considered bringing Hirokichi in as Ume's adopted husband, since both had been trained in the main house. That was what Yoshitaro expected and Kinnosuke assumed. But for Rie, Ume was ineligible by bloodline to marry the next house head.

Rie had been powerless to keep Yoshitaro, proof of Jihei's philandering, or to prevent Ume, Yoshi's child by another geisha, from entering the house. Now there were grandchildren eminently qualified to succeed, and free of O-Toki's or any other geisha's bloodline, most eligibly Hirokichi. Rie still safeguarded the official seal and refused to give it to Yoshi. Rie's power in the house had grown over the years, and Yoshitaro, weakened by accident and illness, would have to struggle for his goal to have Ume and a husband succeed.

Rie knew in her heart that she had never been able to warm to Yoshitaro as she had to Fumi and Seisaburo. Still, aware of this difference, she had always sought to be fair to Yoshitaro who, though he had not performed brilliantly, had proven an able house head, far more capable than his father. He had shown strength of character, refusing to follow his father's destructive path. Instead, he had been struck by samurai violence, and now by disease.

Rie looked again at Ume's face, the lamplight glowing across her black eyes and striking features. Rie paused and pushed her long hair behind her shoulders.

"We don't need to decide your marriage yet, dear. We can keep it to ourselves for now. This will be our secret, the two of us, all right?"

Rie smiled at Ume and tried to fathom her feelings.

"I guess so," Ume said. She bowed and picked up the tea tray.

"Good night, dear. Sleep well," Rie said, and turned back to her dressing table.

CHAPTER 39

Rie opened the shutters of her upstairs room early one morning, then thrust her hands into her sleeves and shivered. A chill wind was soughing down from Mt. Rokko. Ice crystals glistened and wove a gossamer web on the trees and shrubs of the garden. The faint pink plum blossom buds peering between the leaves and lacy crystals reminded her that it was already February. Why was it that the older one grew, the faster time passed? At sixty-seven she must be nearing the end of her allotted time, a life already longer than most. She was making preparations. Each morning she reported to the ancestors at the Butsudan, whether or not Tama had set out the rice and wine. And each evening before going to sleep she sat quietly for several minutes, reviewing in her mind what she had done for the house during the day. That way there would be no major miscalculations when the time came to join the ancestors. Hadn't her father done something similar when he sat alone in contemplation each evening? This was a comforting thought.

She dressed quickly, put on her padded winter wrap and tapped down the stairs to the kitchen, where she picked up a pair of clippers. At the door to the garden she slipped into wooden geta and foraged out into the icy scene. A chill mist enveloped the garden, and Rie hurried to the plum tree. Rain lashed at her eyes when she reached up and clipped two blossom-laden sprigs. Back in the warmth of the kitchen, she arranged the stalks in a low celadon vase. In the parlor fresh incense burned before the name tablets, proof that Tama had preceded her. She placed the vase carefully before the scroll hanging in the tokonoma alcove, and moved on her knees to the Butsudan.

She lit a second incense stick, then clasped her hands before her face and closed her eyes.

"Father, Hirokichi will do. He will be best for the house," she whispered.

Rie sat in the garden late one afternoon musing about Buntaro's startling information about the black ships, the steamships that had entered Kobe port. All the changes she had witnessed in her lifetime in the brewing and selling of sake flashed through her mind: the discovery of pure Shrine Water that granted divine assistance to brewers near Nishinomiya; the discovery by her own son of steam power to replace the waterwheel rice polishers; the development of kura of brick construction, also by Seisaburo; and now the steamships she and Kinnosuke both knew would replace the cask ships and transform forever the way sake was transported to major markets. And her father had told her of advances before her time, most notably the replacement of the foot treadle by the waterwheel for polishing rice. The dizzying pace of change before her eyes was proof of Japan's progress since the coming of the Western barbarians, just as the Satsuma and Choshu leaders had promised for this new era called Meiji, "Enlightened Rule."

Rie silently thanked the gods that she had been able to grasp the significance of each of these developments almost at the moment of its appearance. Her father and Kin had always praised her sense of timing. Yes, it was true. This did give her an advantage over other brewers, even the sales-oriented Nada brewers. These new steamships were just the latest example. And Kinnosuke had immediately grasped the importance of each step. That White Tiger was at this very moment sending the first barrels of sake by steamship to Tokyo gave Rie a sense of elation, a feeling she knew was central to her life as a brewer.

Brewers as a group were well known for their attachment to tradition, for doing things as they had always done. This conservatism was natural. Brewing sake was the oldest, the primal, business in Japan. In the earliest stories of creation the first mythical hero, Yamato Takeru, had ordered eight barrels of sake for the eight-headed demon, and when the ogre was far gone in his cups, the hero had wielded his sword to slice off the monster's eight heads. All Japanese knew that in every town and village throughout the land the sake brewers were the most honored and respected of inhabitants. Their pride in brewing was legendary. It must be some quirk of fate that granted her this special sense of the importance of timing in this ancient and honored profession.

As these thoughts ran through her mind she inhaled deeply and caught the whiff of salt air pushing inland off the ocean. She smiled. Wouldn't it be wonderful if Hiro-kichi or Buntaro fashioned a miniature model of one of the new steamships? It would be something to put in the parlor, perhaps even in the tokonoma next to the Butsudan. Her father would appreciate it.

The Meiji government issued new regulations delimiting the amount of rice that could be used for brewing sake, and it was therefore imperative that all brewers attend the association meeting. Yoshitaro, Kinnosuke, Eitaro, Seisaburo, and Hirokichi all would attend. During the first two decades of the Meiji era, the government, preoccupied with so many dramatic innovations, had not gotten around to placing controls on brewing. Now every brewer in Nada and Nishinomiya, in fact throughout the country, was concerned to know what the new directives would be. Each association would be assigned an allotment, and limitations on individual brewers would be determined by the Brewers Associations, those close to local conditions. The Nada meeting was doubly important because the president was to be elected as well. Rie felt that Seisaburo had a chance, though at thirty-nine he might be considered young for the position. Still, as head of an Omura branch and with his reputation as one of the region's most successful brewers, Rie felt he could not be ruled out.

"Yoshi, you and Eitaro must support Seisaburo for the presidency," she said, excited by the prospect. She went to the door and saw Yoshitaro and Kinnosuke off for the meeting. "It is so unreasonable that I can't go too," she muttered under her breath as the ricksha pulled off into the street.

Rie invited Seisaburo and Eitaro to return to the main house for dinner after the meeting. She ordered special delicacies for the occasion. The intervening hours passed slowly, interminably. She tried her hand at some needlework to help pass the time in the late afternoon, but soon set it down impatiently. She could still hear her mother's voice after all these years: "Try to be more careful with your stitches, Rie. They're a bit irregular." She looked at them and saw that they still were. A rueful smile played around her lips.

Several hours later Rie heard rickshas and voices of the men returning. She hurried to the door to greet them and quickly surveyed their faces before focusing on Yoshitaro, who stood closest to her.

"It's all right, Mother," he said. "Sei was elected vice president. Kato is president. Yamaguchi was defeated. I could see that he was angry. He had tried to line up votes."

"Good! *Huh!* Yamaguchi's still angry that we got access to Shrine Water, after all these years," she said. "Still, it's good that you're vice president, Sei. I am so proud of you. President next time, yes? Come. Dinner is ready."

Thrilled for her son and for the business and house, Rie led the way into the dining room and motioned the men to be seated. Kinnosuke was included as well, since the dinner was also in the nature of a family business council. O-Yuki brought in tea and three flasks of warmed sake with cups, and the men began pouring for each other, loosening their kimonos.

"Sei had some support, Mother," Eitaro began, "but Kato is senior."

Rie remembered Saburo's elder brother, and was pleased that the Kato family had captured the prestigious position, as Sei's predecessor.

"It's only natural," Seisaburo said. "At my age I didn't really expect to be elected."

"But after Kato's term is up, you'll be next, won't you?" Rie nodded confidently as she spoke.

"Possibly so. By that time I'll be in my forties. But I think Kato will be in for several years. And the new system will be in place by the time I take over."

Rie nodded and turned to Kinnosuke. "What about the new regulations? How will they affect us?"

He rested his chopsticks on his rice bowl. "It's as we thought. The individual allotments will be made by the association, a bit like the old kabu system. It won't be a great hardship. The allotments will be made according to past production, and since ours has been rising steadily we'll be all right, with even an allowance for a bit of expansion."

Rie put down her cup and nodded. Her heart gave a small flutter, something it had begun recently. She ignored it. "Good. Good."

She asked Eitaro to remain behind after the others had left the table. Recently, she had begun to feel her age and knew that it was imperative that she find a successor soon.

She took her fan from her obi and placed it on the table before her. "You know, Eitaro, that the reason I have encouraged Hirokichi all along, had him spend time here with Kinnosuke and Buntaro and, of course, Yoshi, is that I envisioned bringing him into the main house as Yoshi's successor."

Eitaro bowed correctly. "That is what

Fumi has led me to believe. A great honor and opportunity it will be for him, and for us." He bowed again. "It will also be a chance for us to choose Mie's mukoyoshi."

Rie glanced at Eitaro's clean-planed face and turned her fan over several times. "So I'll have Fumi bring him over in a few days. Now that his twenty-first birthday is approaching we can begin preparations."

"I'll mention it to Fumi but of course not to Hiro," he said. He stood, bowed low, and bade Rie good night.

A few days later Rie sent a request for Fumi and Hirokichi to come to the main house. She met them at the entrance and ushered them into the parlor, where a low lacquer table stood in front of the tokonoma. O-Yuki brought in tea.

"How are you, Mother?" Fumi asked.

"As well as can be expected at my age."

Hirokichi smiled. "You seem very healthy, Grandmother."

"Thank you, Hiro. Yes, I can't complain. And speaking of age, now that you are of age, Hiro, we can plan for your future, your marriage in particular."

"That's true, Mother," Fumi nodded, without indicating that she knew what was coming.

"We need to settle your marriage, Hiro.

You know that White Tiger is now number three in all Japan."

"I know, Grandmother," Hirokichi said. "It's impressive."

"We have plans for a great future for you." Rie paused and took out her fan. She toyed with it in her lap. "Yes," she continued. "There is a concern for the succession to the main house. You have been trained carefully, and your parents and I feel it is time to find a bride. You will succeed to the main house, Hiro, at the time of your marriage to a bride of our choice." Rie sat back, satisfied, and glanced at Hirokichi.

He stiffened, his neck and shoulder muscles visibly tensing. He looked down and bowed toward Rie.

"You do me great honor, Grandmother. But I am not ready to marry yet."

"Well, then, in a year, Hiro," Fumi said, frowning.

Hirokichi looked straight ahead. "I cannot marry a bride I do not choose," he said. He bowed again, looking down.

Rie frowned and tapped her fan on the table. "You realize, Hiro, that you have a heavy obligation to the main house. Frankly, you have been trained to succeed. Kinnosuke, and my son too, have taken great care in your training. Now it is only fitting that you marry a bride selected by the main house."

"But I cannot," Hirokichi said, frowning.

Rie stared at her grandson, unaccustomed as she was to such open defiance.

"There is no such thing as *cannot* where obligation to the house is concerned. No question, Hiro." Rie's voice rose sharply.

Hirokichi stood and bowed. "I am very sorry, Grandmother and Mother. But this is something I can never do." He bowed again, turned, and left the room.

Stunned, Rie tapped her fan sharply on the table. "Fumi, it is your responsibility, yours and Eitaro's, to persuade him. It has been our plan, our goal, ever since he was born."

Fumi bowed. "We will do our best, Mother. But you know how stubborn he is. He has been since he was a baby."

Rie knew all about stubborn. "And he has so much talent, apart from his training. Maybe Kinnosuke or Buntaro could talk to him."

Fumi shook her head. "If he won't listen to you and me, I doubt there's anything Kinnosuke or Buntaro could say that would sway him. And he knows Kinnosuke has always favored Ume."

"Perhaps we've spoiled him, Fumi, as your

only son and the eldest boy in his generation. Sei's son is too young still. Yes, I'm afraid I have spoiled him." Rie's mouth turned down at the corners and her whole being seemed to sag. "Well, you and Eitaro will have to persuade him. There is just no alternative."

CHAPTER 40

Two years had elapsed since Rie first broached the subject of marriage with Hirokichi, but he remained stubbornly opposed. He and Ume were nearly twenty-three and still unmarried. The situation could not be allowed to continue. Moreover, Yoshitaro's health was declining dramatically.

Rie hurried to see Fumi and Eitaro one morning to try to end the crisis.

"I'm sorry, Mother, but there's nothing more we can do to persuade Hiro," Fumi moaned. "We've tried everything, but he's adamant." She squirmed uncomfortably.

Rie leaned forward, her voice rising higher than normal. "This is unheard of. It's one thing to be stubborn, but to continue to defy the main house is an outrage. We can't tolerate it. Ume must be married now. She's nearly twenty-three, and we've been approached by several families. We can't postpone her marriage any longer." She looked at Eitaro, then back at Fumi.

"I have no way to apologize adequately, Mother," Eitaro said. "We have done our best for the past two years. We have failed." He bowed abjectly.

"And Mother, this has created so much tension in our house. Hiro doesn't stay at home in the evening. He has taken to staying away more and more."

Rie pursed her lips. "People will think there is something wrong with Ume if she doesn't marry soon. It's such a worry. And with Yoshi's poor health we must settle the succession. I just don't know what to do. And of course Yoshi expects Ume to succeed with a mukoyoshi."

Fumi put a hand on her chin. "The trouble is, Mother, there is someone else he wants to marry."

Rie thought of Saburo, young and handsome, his brown eyes so caring. Then of Jihei. She understood more than anyone would ever guess. But what must be, must be. "Since when do personal wishes enter where marriage is concerned? The house is what matters," Rie tapped her fan on the table.

"Well, you know how Hiro has always been, Mother," Fumi said. "How can we change his character now? He knows he is the eldest and most capable of his generation. You have said so yourself. That's why he is so confident."

"I intended for him to be twelfth house head, but now I don't know. Kinnosuke always called him Botchan, and it's true, he is spoiled. Well, who is this girl he wants to marry?" Rie put down her fan and looked at Fumi.

"I'm not exactly sure, but I'm afraid she may be a geisha," Fumi said, looking down.

"A geisha! Marry a geisha! Preposterous! No Omura man is going to marry a geisha. Patronizing one is bad enough. Marrying one is out of the question. I won't hear of it." She scowled, the corners of her mouth turned down.

"So we've told him, Mother," Eitaro said. "He surely would not have our blessing for such a marriage. We would have to consider disinheriting him. I doubt he would go through with it under those conditions. But the trouble is I'm not sure." He rubbed his nose slowly.

"What a dilemma! And what shall we do about Ume? People are talking," Rie said.

And that night, she lay awake, tossing and turning.

The next morning Rie hurried purposefully into the office after a hasty breakfast. She was glad to find Yoshitaro alone and sat down opposite him.

"Good morning, Yoshi." She smiled at him.

Yoshitaro looked up, his face thinner and paler than ever.

"Where is Kinno?" she asked.

"In the outer office filling orders," he said, his voice rasping. He coughed, a handkerchief to his mouth.

"You know, Yoshi, we can't delay Ume's marriage any longer." Rie twirled her fan on the table.

"I know, Mother." He coughed again, and Rie noticed spots of blood on his handkerchief. He wiped his mouth and struggled to speak. "We've been approached by three families now. Which do you favor?" he asked.

"Of course Hiro was our choice, but he is still being stubborn. Eitaro is threatening to disinherit him if he marries that geisha he told Fumi about." Rie paused and looked down at her fan. "There's only one way out, Yoshi."

He put his handkerchief on his lap. "What's that?" he asked, eyebrows raised.

"Ume will have to marry one of the three, probably the Kuniyoshi son, and establish a branch house. And Hiro will succeed you. We will give him the succession if he agrees not to marry the geisha."

Yoshitaro's hands clenched on his lap. "You mean, force Ume out of the main house? Mother, we can't do that!" His heavy brows drew together in a deep frown. He coughed uncontrollably.

Rie sighed heavily. She cared for Ume, yet what else could be done? She heard a rustling beyond the door to the outer office and guessed that Kinnosuke was listening. "It's not what we hoped for, but it's the only way out of this impasse, Yoshi. Ume will be set up in a branch. We'll be generous with her, and I think Kuniyoshi is the best of the three. He'll do well by us and by her." She squared her shoulders, then poured a cup of tea and pushed it across the table to Yoshitaro. "You must take better care of your health, Yoshi. Have you seen the herbalist lately?"

"Yesterday," he replied abruptly, then bent over and continued coughing.

Rie looked in alarm at the crimson spreading in his handkerchief until it was nearly soaked. She stood abruptly and rushed to the kitchen. Tama looked up, startled.

"Quickly, Tama. Take some damp towels to Yoshi in the office. He's coughing so badly."

Tama reached for towels, dampened two in a basin, and ran to the office, Rie behind her.

Tama knelt quickly and began wiping Yoshitaro's face.

He pushed her hand away. "Don't get so excited, Mother. I've been taking the medicine regularly. But I can't agree to sending Ume out of the main house. It's her birthright." He glared at Rie.

She knelt at the table again.

"Yoshi, dear," she said more gently, "please be reasonable. It's not something I want to do."

"Why not set Hirokichi up as a branch? Or just have him inherit Eitaro's?" Yoshitaro said.

"I've told you, Yoshi, that I think this is the only way to prevent him from a disgraceful marriage that would dishonor the house. And you know how clever he is, Yoshi. He could build White Tiger to the number one position."

"I can't agree." He bent over and coughed again. "I will only allow it if you promise to disinherit Hiro if he refuses a bride the house chooses." He looked down glumly. "And it will make Kinno very unhappy to see Ume sent out. He counts on her to succeed. We both do."

"Yes, you're right, Yoshi." She paused. "But he isn't a member of the house. This is the way it has to be." *The way it has to be.* How many times had she had to say those words over the years? She put both hands to her face, then rose and left the office.

Three weeks later Rie called a full family council at the main house: Yoshitaro, Tama, and Ume; Fumi, Eitaro, Hirokichi, and Mie; and Seisaburo, Mari, and their children, Masako and Nobuo. Rie took greater care than usual in dressing for the morning meeting in the parlor. Zabuton were arranged around two tables placed together. Yoshitaro sat at the head of the table with Rie at his left, Tama on his right.

Rie and Yoshitaro greeted family members as they arrived at the main entrance. Tama set out the best kutani teacups.

Rie had discussed with Yoshitaro what to say. They were finally in agreement. Well, reluctant agreement.

"Welcome to all of you," he began, bowing and glancing around the table. "As you know, we have been discussing the question

486

of succession to the main house and the marriages of Ume and Hirokichi. We have sought your guidance in these matters for these past two years and more."

As he completed each sentence, Rie and Tama both bowed slightly. O-Yuki brought in teapots and poured for everyone.

"Now, as a result of these discussions we have been able to arrive at solutions that will be acceptable to all." He coughed, his handkerchief over his mouth. Beads of sweat formed on his brow.

"First, Ume will marry the Kuniyoshi second son and establish a branch. We have decided to agree to the o-miai meeting and the wedding soon after."

Rie glanced at Ume but could see no sign of emotion on her face. Ume had brought tea to her grandmother several evenings earlier, as had become her habit.

"Sit down, dear," Rie had said. "There is something I would like to discuss with you."

Ume had poured tea and listened attentively.

"I know that two years ago, when I mentioned my hope that you would marry Hirokichi, I could see that you were not enthusiastic, though I knew you would do as we thought best."

Ume had bowed and nodded.

"Now, that marriage does not seem possible," Rie said, picking up her teacup.

Ume's eyes had widened. "Oh?" she said quizzically.

"Yes, dear, we feel the Kuniyoshi son will be the best husband for you. You know, the family has approached us and waited for over a year. So now we have decided to set you up in a nearby branch house, with the Kuniyoshi son as your adopted husband."

Ume had looked down abruptly. "A bunke, a branch house?" she asked in a small voice. "Not here in the main house?"

"No, dear. You will receive a generous sum to begin your own branch. We believe you will do well with the Kuniyoshi son. He is the best of the three, now four, that have approached us. And I believe you will prefer him to Hirokichi. He has become a most stubborn person. He would be difficult to live with."

Ume had looked thoughtful, but said nothing other than good night to her grandmother when she left the room.

Rie had asked Eitaro not to reveal the decision to Hirokichi before the family council met. She did not want to give him another chance to protest. A decision announced at the family council would be final. Now, as she looked out at the familiar faces of the council she made her next proclamation.

"And second," Yoshitaro continued, "Hiro-kichi will succeed me to the main house, but only on condition that he marry a bride of our choice."

Rie glanced at Hirokichi and saw him frown darkly and look down.

"In the event that he refuses to marry the bride we select, he will be disinherited, removed from the koseki register." Yoshitaro covered his mouth and glanced at Hirokichi.

Hirokichi pouted, grunting loudly, his frown deepening.

"We will begin negotiations now for Ume's wedding. Following her wedding, discussions regarding selection of Hirokichi's bride will commence." By this time sweat was pouring down Yoshitaro's face. He wiped his face with his handkerchief and began to cough.

Tama bowed. "Please have some tea and *casutera* cakes." She passed two plates of the new Western-style cakes around the table.

The formal part of the meeting was concluded, and family members began to shift on their zabuton. Some began to sip their tea and make polite conversation.

Hirokichi rose abruptly and left the room.

489

The shoji leading out the front entrance slammed shut, the bell clanging loudly.

Later the same afternoon, as soon as she could free herself from duties in the main house, Rie hurried to Fumi's.

"Oh, Mother," Fumi said as she greeted Rie at the entrance. "I'm not sure Hiro will agree. Eitaro is worried too."

Eitaro joined Rie and Fumi in the parlor. "What Hiro said, Mother, is that if he can't marry O-Fusa he will remain unmarried. He wants to succeed to the main house, but he will remain single."

Rie frowned. Unheard of! What a stubborn young man. "We can't have a bachelor as house head. Being head of such an important house, any house for that matter, is the work of two people, a couple, and an heir is essential as successor," Rie said.

Eitaro bowed. "Hiro says the house has always taken in the children of geishas, so there will be no problem of lack of heirs," Eitaro said. He bowed and excused himself to return to the office.

"Hiro is too clever," Rie said, her mind working. "And he goes too far."

"Well, Mother, he believes he is meeting most of Yoshi's conditions if he does not marry O-Fusa. And actually, our main purpose was to prevent that marriage,"

Fumi said. "So however cunning it appears, don't we have to agree to let him succeed?" she asked.

"He has agreed to only part of the conditions, Fumi," Rie said. "Until he agrees to the rest he will not succeed. Yoshi will back me in this, I am certain."

Mother and daughter sat in an uncomfortable silence.

CHAPTER 41

Ume was married to the Kuniyoshi son as Rie wished, and Yoshitaro had not been able to prevent it. He was very angry about it, Rie knew. The couple was well endowed with facilities and capital to establish their branch house in Nada. Yoshitaro, though he had not seen O-Sada since his accident, managed to arrange for her to be among those who served at the reception, so that she could see her daughter married. Rie was too preoccupied with the guests to take more than a cursory notice of the exceptionally beautiful woman working among the servants at the reception.

Kinnosuke had made it clear he was disconsolate, shocked beyond belief that his protégée, Yoshitaro's only child, should be denied succession, shunted off to a branch family. The assumptions and hopes on which Kinnosuke had based his life work he saw dashed in a single stroke by "Rie and her spoiled daughter and even more spoiled grandson," according to a conversation that Rie had the misfortune to overhear between him and Yoshitaro.

"I must retire now," he announced to Rie and Yoshitaro. His head was bowed and his shoulders tensed.

Rie gasped and leaned toward the spare figure of the chief clerk she had handpicked and trained from childhood. "We know you are unhappy that Ume is no longer in the main house. But Kinno-san, there was no other way to stop Hirokichi from dishonoring the house. This was the only solution. It wasn't what we wanted." She paused and placed both hands on the table. "You know how we value your work. White Tiger would not have reached the number two position without you. Please reconsider, Kinno-san. Please. We cannot do without you." She bowed low. She looked up and saw tears beginning in Yoshitaro's eyes.

Yoshi coughed and sputtered as he tried to speak. "Kinnosuke, you have been my teacher since I was a child, as long as I can remember." He stopped to cough again, and put his handkerchief in his lap. "As you know, my health has not been the best of late. I entreat you, stay on at least until the end of this brewing season. I cannot manage without you." His words trailed off in a hoarse rasping sound.

Rie put her hand to her mouth and bowed, eyes lowered. She did not fail to note that Kinnosuke also bowed as low as possible.

Kinnosuke struggled, a catch in his throat. "*Ah,* Master," he began, and stopped, overcome. "It pains me to see you in such a sad situation, with your ill health, and losing your heir." He paused again and blinked to hold back tears. "I will do as you say. I will stay until the end of this brewing season. Then I must ask you to allow me to retire. I believe Buntaro is capable of taking over."

"Buntaro is capable and well trained, thanks to you, Kinno-san," Yoshitaro said. "But you can never be replaced at White Tiger."

Rie could not speak. She wrung her hands, then bowed, rose quickly, and left Kinnosuke and Yoshitaro looking at each other. As she passed the wooden support she paused and slowly caressed it.

Kinnosuke remained until the end of the season as he had promised, Yoshitaro with him almost constantly. At the same time Buntaro gradually worked more closely with both men, who were grooming him to assume all of Kinnosuke's many duties.

Yoshitaro insisted that Kinnosuke be given a special sayonara dinner. Rie had already planned to give him a handsome pension, and a dinner helped assuage some of her guilt over removing Ume and causing Kinno to retire. Even Yoshitaro was surprised at the size of the pension, an amount so large that when it became known among Nada brewers it caused a minor sensation. Rie wanted it known publicly that the gratitude of the Omura House for his long and loyal service was unbounded. She spared no expense for the dinner, a formal family affair.

Kinnosuke sat at Yoshitaro's left at the occasion, which featured the finest Kobe sashimi and the new foreign import, beef, in a mixture called sukiyaki. Kinnosuke tasted it but turned instead to the sashimi. Beef, a strange unfamiliar flavor, was no doubt as unpalatable to him as it was to Rie.

Yoshitaro attempted a speech after the meal. He spoke from his zabuton, as it was impossible for him to rise or stand easily.

"It is with great regret that White Tiger and the House of Omura bid you farewell," he began with a bow from the waist. "Your outstanding, long, and loyal service to our house is without precedent in all of Nada and has made White Tiger what it is today." Choked with emotion, he bowed several times, tears streaming unchecked down his face.

Watching Kinnosuke and Yoshitaro throughout his halting speech, Rie felt a tightening in her throat. What would the future bring to White Tiger without this extraordinary man? Would she live to regret what she had done the past few months?

Kinnosuke, never garrulous, managed only a few perfunctory words. He bowed and blinked repeatedly. "I owe everything to you, Master, and to Oku-san." He bowed to Yoshitaro and Rie and stopped speaking.

The future of White Tiger was in one sense not greatly different from what it had been. Kinnosuke and Rie had imbued all the clerks in the office and men in the kura with a fierce pride in their sake and a canny business sense. Buntaro proved a talented successor to Kinnosuke, with the same sense of timing and eye to the future. In another sense Rie's concern at Kinnosuke's departure was well founded. She watched Yoshitaro closely and was saddened to see a gradual loss of nerve, a lassitude slowly begin to erode what energy he had regained following his accident. Kinnosuke had been largely responsible for Yoshitaro's resumption of duties after the loss of his leg, Kinnosuke who had been intimately connected with Yoshitaro during his entire working life. The departure of Kinnosuke left Yoshitaro with an emptiness, a dark void that could not be filled. It was obvious that his health was suffering, and as the months passed the physical decline became increasingly apparent. He rarely smiled.

Rie spoke to Tama one morning in the dining room after Yoshitaro had gone to the office.

"I am so worried about Yoshi, Tama. I'm afraid Kinnosuke's retirement was a blow he may not recover from." She sighed and looked at Tama.

"Yes, I know," Tama said. "He seems worse than after the accident. It is his spirit as much as his body that I worry about."

Rie looked at Tama and thought how rare it was to see her smile these days. "And if something should happen to him, with Hiro still refusing to marry, our succession would be a critical problem," Rie said.

"Hasn't Hiro had two or three o-miais?" Tama asked.

"Oh, more than that, Tama. He has refused them all. Fumi is at her wit's end. And now he is twenty-four. What a worry!"

Rie tapped her fan on the table. "I know you have been spending more time in the office, Tama, ever since Yoshi's accident. And now with Ume gone you will be freer to do even more. Isn't it quiet here without Ume?" Rie smiled briefly. She did not really feel like smiling about Ume's departure, but wanted to improve Tama's mood. "Well, we need to try to encourage Yoshi."

"Yes, we must," Tama said. "I'm glad that we have Buntaro."

"But Buntaro is so recent. He was never that close to Yoshi. It was completely different with Kinno." Rie sighed again. "Come, let's see how Yoshi is doing."

Hirokichi's refusal to marry any of the women the younger Mrs. Nakano and other go-betweens brought to o-miai meetings was causing the Omura House great embarrassment and threatened to become a minor scandal. It was not his association with O-Fusa that caused raised eyebrows. Most men who could afford it patronized one or more geisha. But that he was promised succession to the great Omura House and despite that, continued to reject all prospective brides was a violation of all standards of propriety.

Yoshitaro was furious, Rie was irate, and Fumi railed helplessly.

"It's already four years since we sent Ume out, Mother," Yoshitaro complained. "We should have kept her here with her husband as successor, and we would still have Kinnosuke with us. Hirokichi is nothing but trouble for the main house." He coughed, then straightened and pushed his hair back from his face. He scowled. "I never thought Hiro was a good choice. He doesn't deserve to succeed," he said.

"It's too late now, Yoshi," Rie said. "We'll have to make the best of it. I have a feeling he'll come around if we find the right bride."

"There is no right bride for him. How about bringing in Seisaburo's son?" Yoshitaro asked.

"Nobuo is still too young, Yoshi. He's not eighteen yet. It's true that he has had the best training. But we don't want to think of his marriage yet."

Yoshitaro coughed uncontrollably. Rie left the office and went to the garden to try to recover her peace of mind. She sat on her rock to meditate, to try to collect her thoughts. Just then the door to the kitchen corridor opened and Fumi appeared.

"Mother, may I speak with you?" Fumi asked.

"In a minute, Fumi." Rie racked her brain, implored the gods for help in finding a solution to the problem that had plagued the house for so long. Fumi's distress was more than she could deal with at the moment. And Yoshitaro's anger was damaging his health even further. She sighed, rubbed her throbbing temples, and reluctantly rose to go in.

"Oh, Mother, I need to talk to you," Fumi said again as soon as she saw Rie.

"I know. Come, let's go to the parlor. Would you bring us some tea please, O-Yuki," Rie said as she passed the kitchen.

Rie and Fumi sat at the low lacquer table near the tokonoma.

"What shall we do, Mother?" Fumi asked.

"Fumi, I thought you had come with some good news or a new idea," Rie said, frowning.

"No, there's no sign of hope. So many o-miais and Hiro has refused them all. And my husband wants to disinherit Hiro. We can't even do anything about Mie's marriage with this hanging over us." Fumi rested her chin on her hand and leaned toward her mother.

"We can't delay Mie's marriage any longer. Hiro's stubbornness is all over Nada now and it won't help Mie to find a husband, whether or not he succeeds to the main house."

Fumi pouted. "It's just not fair to Mie. I've told Hiro so."

"Complaining will not help us or change his character, Fumi. We need to think of a way out. Hiro is very talented when he puts his mind to his work. I'm still confident about that. I can't support disinheriting him. But five years is too long. We must act now."

CHAPTER 42

Three months after Rie's conversation with Fumi a worse crisis threatened the house. Yoshitaro's health took a sudden drastic turn. One night he hemorrhaged; blood soaked his futon faster than Tama could contain it. Rie sent for the herbalist urgently in the middle of the night, but Yoshitaro was beyond help. Rie put her hand on Yoshitaro's face and neck, and rested her other hand on his. Tama rocked back and forth in distress, covering her face. Before morning Yoshitaro's last rasping breath failed. Rie and Tama sat on either side of his futon, aghast.

When morning finally dawned, alerted family members gathered from the branch houses: Ume and her husband, Eitaro and Fumi with Hirokichi and Mie, and Seisaburo and Mari with their two children.

Rie had no chance to be alone with her emotions before having to greet her children and their families.

"Well," she said deliberately, as they sat around her in the parlor, "we all knew his health was failing, but we didn't expect the end so soon." She glanced at Ume and saw her dabbing at her tears. "And now we are a house without a head." She looked pointedly at Hirokichi. "We are in an untenable position. We will plan to have the memorial service five days from now. Eitaro and Sei, please make the arrangements. Then we will need to take steps about the succession." Rie bowed to her sons and Tama. Rie glanced briefly at Fumi and saw that she was weeping. Hirokichi sat as if made of stone.

In the days before the funeral Rie felt her age and the flutter in her heart had increased with the added stress. She had witnessed the deaths of too many house heads: her father, her adopted husband, and now her adopted son. It was too soon after Kinno's retirement. And it was not the natural order for one's children to predecease one. Lack of a successor was a crisis of major proportions.

The funeral was as large as Jihei's had been. Most of the Kobe and Nishinomiya brewers came. But who should make the formal greetings in the absence of a house head? Rie was tempted to ask Eitaro to make the announcements, but because of Hirokichi's intransigence, she turned instead to Seisaburo.

On the day of the memorial service Rie thought her son looked quite distinguished as he stood at the head of the room filled with black-clad mourners. She scanned the room quickly until her glance rested on a hunched figure in the corner. It was Kinnosuke. Not far away was Saburo, the man who had given her Fumi. The man who had seen her through every crisis, if from a distance. Rie felt a catch in her throat.

"We thank you all for coming today to remember the head of the Omura House." Seisaburo's resonant voice filled the room. "He has joined the ancestors suddenly. In this difficult moment for the house we are especially grateful for your continued cooperation and support," he continued.

When Seisaburo finished his speech, sake was served down the lines of seated mourners. Next to Tama, Rie sat straight-backed, eyes downcast, with neither the need nor ability to speak. She left Tama, Eitaro, and Seisaburo to greet the departing guests. Even to speak to Saburo seemed too great an effort on this painful night.

The next morning Rie found it difficult to

rise at her usual hour. She heard Tama stirring downstairs but could not summon the energy to join her in the kitchen. Well, I am seventy-four, she told herself, and Tama is capable of supervising the household. She turned over on her futon, but a disturbing thought invaded her consciousness. Yoshitaro's sudden demise had left the house without a head. To be sure, business would not stop; she herself had possession of the Omura family seal, the seal that made official any decision or document. Still, she must be up. She threw off the futon, and as she slowly rose heard her knee joints crack. She dressed, slapped down the stairs to the kitchen, and asked O-Yuki for a cup of tea. She sipped slowly, then went to the parlor and peered in. Tama was seated before the Butsudan, incense smoke curling around her bowed head.

Rie turned without speaking and went into the wintry garden. It was March, not a time to linger, but she needed the solitude. She thought about Hirokichi's continued recalcitrance, and tried to dismiss him from her thoughts. He had not shown that he was deserving of the headship yet. She brooded and glanced at the ripples the koi caused on the pond's surface. She paced slowly the length of the garden and back, hands thrust into the sleeves of her padded kimono, her gaze focused on the cold gray stone steps. It was way too late now to recall Ume and her husband to the main house. Soon it would be time to prepare for the end of season celebration, but it would be briefer than usual. Her thoughts rested on Tama, Yoshitaro's steadfast, hardworking widow; Tama, who had worked at her side uncomplaining all these years. Rie nodded and murmured softly, "Yes."

She turned and walked back through the house to the parlor, where Tama still knelt arranging thin reeds and grasses in a black vase.

"*Ah,* Tama," Rie said, joining her before the Butsudan. "How are you this morning, after such a difficult ordeal?"

"Good morning, Mother, and you?"

"Well, I have been thinking, Tama." Rie lit an incense stick and pushed it deeper into the ash mixture.

"You know we cannot exist without a successor to Yoshi."

"I know," Tama nodded, pausing with a stem in her hand to look at Rie.

"I have decided because of Hirokichi's stubborn opposition to have you succeed for the three years allowed."

Tama's eyes widened. "Is it possible for a

woman?"

Rie smiled. "Yes, with the approval of the local officials a woman can succeed for three years. It's in the regulations of the association, though it doesn't often happen."

Tama bowed deeply. "I wonder if I would be capable."

Rie took out her fan. "I have watched you work here for over twenty-five years. You have worked as hard and capably as anyone. I am here to support you. Only remember that it will be necessary for you to speak at some formal occasions. You can practice. And spend more time with Buntaro now."

"I will do my utmost for the house, Mother." Tama bowed deeply, her forehead touching the tatami.

"I know," Rie said softly. "You always have."

Tama's investiture as successor to the headship of the house coincided with the end of season celebration. The celebration was more modest than usual, appropriate to the recent death of the house head and the temporary succession by a woman. Seisaburo made the announcement that his aunt was succeeding to the headship for three years.

Tama's words of acceptance were brief. "We are grateful you have taken the trouble to join us today to celebrate the end of brewing for the season. We humbly request your continued cooperation with the House of Omura." Tama's face reddened with the effort of speaking in front of Nada's important brewers for the first time. "We thank you and ask that you enjoy some of our sake." She then walked among the guests, bowing graciously and greeting them as she had seen Yoshitaro do. It was not common for women of the house to be present at the end of brewing celebration, but this occasion was unusual, a woman becoming house head.

Rie smiled as she watched. Some things a woman could do as well as a man, even better. She looked over at Tama and a shiver of apprehension shook her. Could a woman be house head for longer than the allowed three years? It had never happened before.

Late one evening Buntaro went on an errand to the number one kura. Brewing was finished for the season, and the workers had returned to their farms for the summer. The interior of the kura was completely dark. He tried to focus and moved along the line of barrels, his hand touching each one as he moved. Silence. Only the dull echo of his geta on the earthen floor. He paused. What was that sound? He sensed a presence somewhere in the kura. He listened, did not move. There it was again. Was it the sound of footsteps? Who could it be? The kurabito had all left. The clerks were gone for the night. He crept farther along the line of barrels toward the wall. He paused and looked both ways, peering into the murky darkness. There it was again, the sound. He turned abruptly toward the right and saw something move, a figure.

"Who's there?" he cried.

The person began to run toward the door.

Buntaro raced down another aisle and reached the door just as the intruder came around the corner and nearly collided with Buntaro.

In a series of rapid thrusts Buntaro slammed his knee into the man's groin, banged his knee against his chin, and twisted the man around, pinning his arms behind him. Holding the intruder to the ground with his knees and arms with one hand, with the other hand Buntaro pulled the man's head back by the hair. "What are you doing here? Sent by Yusuke, from Yamaguchi, weren't you?" Buntaro said gruffly. He recognized Yusuke's apprentice, Hachirobei, a slight young man about his own age.

Hachirobei gasped for breath but said nothing.

"Speak!" Buntaro commanded.

Still the culprit made no reply.

Buntaro moved his knees to pin Hachirobei's arms, freeing both hands to encircle his neck.

"Answer now, or you'll never talk again."

Buntaro tightened his grip.

Hachirobei's eyes bulged. He gasped and choked.

"Ready to talk?"

A slight nod of the head.

Buntaro loosened his hold slightly. "Well?"

Hachirobei coughed. "I . . . I was . . . looking for your recipe."

"*Ha!* Another of Yamaguchi's tricks."

Buntaro let go of Hachirobei. He scrambled to his feet, and as he turned toward the door, Buntaro gave him a swift kick.

"Out, rat!" he shouted into the night. "The Brewers Association will hear of this," Buntaro muttered as he walked out of the kura toward the office.

O-Natsu, though older than Rie and long since retired, still came to the house each day to sit a few hours, often in the old nursery, long since empty of children. She

510

had no other family, never having married. Rie found her presence comforting, and since the pace of her own life was slowing, her steps often took her to the nursery of an afternoon. There the two white-haired women would take from their obis their long tiny pipes and reminisce. One would say something, and the other would nod and exhale a thin white wisp. Rie knew that a stranger looking in would not guess that one was mistress, the other servant, so easy was their companionship. The wisdom and plain common sense of O-Natsu Rie found no-where else.

The days and months of Tama's headship passed, and White Tiger prospered.

"Tama," Rie said to her daughter-in-law one morning, "our shipping business is prospering beyond our expectations. I have an idea for something new."

Tama looked at her mother-in-law and marveled at this woman whose face wrinkled around the eyes now and whose voice occasionally cracked, but whose mind was still the most agile she had known. "What is it, Mother?"

"Buntaro says there are rumblings of trouble with China now. He thinks there may be a military confrontation."

"Yes, I heard him say something about it.

He sounded very concerned."

"I want Buntaro to go to the port and buy two of those English steamships, ships that can transport troops. Of course he will negotiate a good price."

"Oh?"

"Then," Rie continued, "we can charter the ships to the government at a good fee. The government will need ships if it transports troops to the continent." Rie tapped the table with her fan. "The English have the best steamships. Then when the fighting has ended we can sell the ships and make a good profit." Rie smiled, sitting straight-backed, her eyes sparkling.

"How clever you are, Mother. Yes, it is a good idea. We should discuss it with Buntaro today."

"He has become even more aggressive than Kinnosuke was, don't you think, Tama?"

"Yes, he does keep up with the pace of the times."

"Come, let's go and speak with him." Rie rose slowly, taking Tama's arm as she did so.

CHAPTER 43

Buntaro hurried to Kobe port soon after Rie and Tama spoke with him about purchasing two English ships and chartering them to the government. As he walked along the wharf he encountered two clerks from another brewery sauntering along, speaking in guttural, gruff voices. They eyed him suspiciously.

"Where to, Buntaro?" one asked.

Buntaro said only hello.

"On a secret mission for the Omura House?" the second said impudently.

"That Omura woman must be possessed by the fox spirit. That's the only explanation for her craftiness," the first clerk said. They both guffawed.

Cheeky fellows, Buntaro thought, and hastened away from them. He was well aware that he was watched wherever he went by curious, even jealous, clerks. It was the price of success. White Tiger's prosperity was legendary, and Buntaro sometimes wondered if being so far ahead of most other brewers didn't have its drawbacks. Was it appropriate to succeed in the competition when one's competitors viewed it as being at their expense? He dismissed these thoughts as he approached the office of the English ship owners. Honest success was the measure of any business negotiation or decision, as his father and Kinnosuke had always taught him. He squared his broad shoulders and walked through the door of the shipping office.

Fumi came through the kitchen corridor door calling for Rie. "Where is she?" Fumi asked O-Yuki, who was working in the kitchen.

"I think she's upstairs in her room," O-Yuki said.

"Not feeling well?" Fumi persisted.

"I'm not sure. Maybe she's just resting."

Fumi padded quickly upstairs to her mother's room and opened the shoji.

"Mother, are you all right?" Fumi asked.

"Oh, come in, Fumi," Rie replied, feeling a little nostalgic after Yoshi's death. It had hit her harder than she'd ever thought possible. Or maybe she was just recognizing her own mortality. She sat at a small table rummaging through a large lacquer box. "I'm fine, Fumi. I was just looking through some of your grandmother's things. I'm sorry you never knew her."

"So am I, Mother," Fumi said. She sat next to her mother and dabbed perspiration from her face.

"What's the matter, dear? You seem upset," Rie asked.

"The same old problem, Mother. It's just that the longer we postpone the marriage, the worse it gets. Mrs. Nakano is at her wit's end. Forty-five o-miais! Can you imagine? And Hiro has had his twenty-seventh birthday. Some people are saying there's something wrong with him." Fumi fanned herself vigorously.

"There's nothing wrong. Nothing that more discipline wouldn't cure," Rie said, holding up a gold-threaded obi tie. "Here, dear, I'd like you to have this. It was your grandmother's favorite. Please don't show it to Tama. I'll give her another one."

Fumi held the gold tie up to examine it. "Lovely, Mother, thank you. I'll cherish it." She thrust it into her sleeve.

"I've been meaning to tell you, Fumi, that I'm going to talk to Hiro soon. I'll make it plain to him: either he accepts a bride or he will be disinherited. Perhaps I'll send for

515

him tomorrow." Rie continued to sort through the items in the box, unwrapping and refolding each carefully.

"Well, I suppose it has come to that." Fumi stopped fanning herself and bit a fingernail. "It's a good thing we didn't wait for Mie to be married. She'd be way over-age for marriage now." Fumi looked at her mother. "Have you been feeling well lately, Mother?"

"Well enough for over eighty, Fumi. But I have to admit, the stairs are becoming harder for me and my heart flutters some-times. I'm thinking of moving back to my old room downstairs. It's closer to the garden too. Come, let's go down and have some tea. Tama will join us. She's working in the office."

Fumi helped her mother up and they descended the stairs to the parlor.

"Would you call Tama, please? And have O-Yuki bring us tea."

Fumi returned with Tama, followed by O-Yuki carrying a tea tray.

Tama knelt, bowed, and smiled. "Buntaro is back from the port, Mother. He managed to purchase one of the two large English steamships."

Rie beamed and nodded. All her plans were falling into place. Why then did she have a touch of melancholy? "And he was so skillful and quick to catch that Yamaguchi thief. Yamaguchi will suffer for it. He won't have thought of buying steamships."

"Yes. I think Buntaro is already planning his Tokyo trip," Tama said. "One of the ships is docked at Yokohama. The other is here in Kobe. He said he wants to go to Tokyo by ship and buy the other there."

"*Ah!*" Rie sighed, feeling her age. "If I were younger I would like to make the trip too. Imagine going to Edo . . . Tokyo, by a steamship! I was going to say maybe you could go, Tama, but we need you here, to settle the matter of Hiro finally. I'm going to talk with him tomorrow. Of course you are more than capable of acting as house head, Tama. But we're over the time limit now, and the officials are asking embarrassing questions, you know."

Tama poured tea for her mother-in-law and sister-in-law.

The following day Hirokichi, whom Rie had summoned to the main house, approached the door to the parlor where Rie waited for him. He bowed stiffly.

"Good afternoon, Grandmother," he said in a deep, resonant voice.

"Hiro, come and sit by the Butsudan with

517

me," Rie said. She patted a zabuton next to her.

"You know, Hiro," she said looking directly at him, "I selected you to succeed your uncle soon after you were born. And when you were younger you justified my choice. But in recent years you have changed. Your commitment to the house is flawed, Hiro. Think about what this means for your life, your future." She paused and leaned forward intently. "Do you understand?"

Hirokichi bowed, his somber expression unwavering. "I will think about it, Grandmother."

"You have had ample time to think about it, Hiro," she said sharply. "I want you to understand the consequences of your continued refusal. We can brook no further delay." She looked at his still bowed head.

He nodded.

"I want to see you again one week from today, Hiro. I expect you to decide to accept your responsibility by then."

One week later Hirokichi appeared at the parlor door at the same hour of the afternoon. He bowed and entered. She prayed that he'd had a change of heart. If not, she would have to play her hidden card.

"Come, Hiro," Rie said. "Sit. Have you

518

decided?" She looked at him intently.

Hirokichi bowed when he was seated. "I will find a bride, Grandmother."

"One the house can accept?" Rie took out her fan and toyed with it.

"I believe so," he said. "In fact, I have found her."

"Really?" Rie's voice rose. "You mean you have found a bride by yourself, without our go-between? What are you talking about? No such thing!" She opened her fan and fanned rapidly.

"Yes, Grandmother. I have found her."

Rie noted a slight smile on her grandson's face and felt a rising anger that her grandson could be so smug.

"But you cannot select your own bride. Remember, the condition was that you marry a bride of our choice. Before I ask who she is, are you certain she will be suitable, acceptable to the main house?"

"Quite certain, yes." He bowed.

"And who might she be, then?"

"Naoko Fujiwara." Hirokichi raised his head and smiled broadly.

Rie put her fan over her mouth to stifle a gasp. "What? A girl from the Kyoto nobility? Where did you get such an idea, Hiro?" She leaned forward. "Have you met her? What makes you think her family would allow her to marry a brewer?" Rie dropped her fan and leaned forward, her hands pressed against the tatami.

"I was introduced to her at a Kabuki performance a few months ago, Grandmother. She is third daughter in her house. I believe she wishes to marry me and that her father will allow it."

"What makes you so certain that she would or could marry you, Hiro?" Rie picked up her fan, her hands resting on the table.

"I am confident about it, Grandmother. I have seen her several times at Bunraku, and we have had some opportunity to talk. She has already spoken with her father. I met him also at a Bunraku performance."

"*Humph!* Too much confidence is as unattractive as too little, Hiro. Well, if her house agrees, it will be the first time a brewer has ever married a bride from the nobility." Rie pursed her lips and looked critically at her grandson.

"Well, isn't that what you have always taught us, Grandmother? That White Tiger should be first in everything?"

Rie quickly picked up her fan, brought it to her face and burst into a peal of laughter. Here, after all, was a grandson fit to succeed to the headship of the house and to honor her father's memory.

"All right, Hiro. If in fact her parents agree, you have my blessing. Yes, I think it will be a master stroke, a good beginning for you as successor." She smiled. "Tama has had the position for five, nearly six years, twice as long as generally permitted. Now we can go ahead with the formal arrangements for the wedding and your succession as well. Of course her family will be responsible for the wedding arrangements." Rie put a hand to her hair. "Won't Mrs. Nakano be surprised, for we should give her the honor of sitting as go-between after all she has done for us. All of Nada will take notice." Rie straightened and smiled at her grandson. "And here, Hiro." She reached into her obi and handed the house seal to Hiro. She thought of Yoshi, the fight they'd had over this very seal, and felt a flash of regret. It was a bittersweet moment. One she would not soon forget.

CHAPTER 44

The wedding reception of Hirokichi and his Fujiwara bride was a glittering event that astounded all of Kansai. The wedding was not only the event of the year; it also marked the investiture of Hirokichi as Kinzaemon XIII. The bride's Kyoto family and friends, exquisitely attired and impeccably mannered, nearly filled the reception hall, with less room for the Omuras and other brewers. Everyone knew the Kyoto nobility had more status than wealth, and that the Omura House was one of Japan's wealthiest brewing families. The marriage was a mutually advantageous union, such as had been happening between families of the samurai and merchant classes. But this was a first, a union between a brewing family and a family of the old nobility. Rie felt awed that her house was now allied in marriage with the ancient Fujiwara house, and yet at the same time, she couldn't help but feel that an era was ending and a new one beginning. She saw in both Naoko, the bride, and the bride's mother, a hint of her own mother's aristocratic features and distinctive nose. If only her parents had lived to see this day.

The entire house and especially the upstairs room was cleaned and readied for the bridal couple. Rie hoped Naoko would learn to feel at home with the customs of the Omura House, but she left to Tama the instructing of the bride. That Naoko's family did not brew was overshadowed for Rie by the anticipation that Naoko's aristocratic Fujiwara blood would benefit the house. Hirokichi by his marriage could gain access to exclusive levels of society about which Rie had only the vaguest knowledge. And although it brought her pride, it also brought home the fact that life would soon be different. Times were changing, customs were changing, and shortly, an era would be ending, the mantle passed to a new generation, one with nobility running through its veins. The geisha's bloodline banished from the house at last. Still, she did not wish her grandson to feel inferior to his noble bride.

"Don't forget, Hiro," Rie told him a few days before the wedding, her head held proudly, "sake brewing is as ancient as the nobility, perhaps even older. In every town and village sake brewers are the most respected people. We have always been the producers, we merchants. The samurai were parasites, and the nobility also lived on what the merchants produced. They still do."

After the wedding, while Hirokichi fell comfortably into the work of the main house with Buntaro, Rie saw that Naoko felt awkward, thrust suddenly into a working family. Rie was certain that Tama would treat Naoko with fairness, even compassion, but the responsibility of instructing Naoko was a daunting one.

"I wonder if she will ever be able to do the work we have done, Tama?" Rie lamented as the two women sat drinking tea one evening in Rie's room.

Tama raised her eyebrows. "I don't know, Mother. Her background is so different, and she is not accustomed to hard work. She has been trained in the polite arts. She does very well with ikebana, and I have seen some of her fine needlework. And you know she has brought her koto with her."

"That won't go very far in the brewery, will it?" Rie said sharply, then softened her tone. "Well, it's a good thing that all the women in the house know what to do without being told by Naoko. I doubt that the house will suffer, at least while we are

alive. I wonder in what new direction Hiro
and his bride may take White Tiger?" She
paused and took out her small pipe, once
again feeling the winds of change stirring.

Rie hated to admit that she was feeling
her age, her legs and knees less agile, her vision losing clarity. She worked consciously
to keep her back straight, not bent from
years of bending and bowing as with other
women her age. She went to the office less
often now, but expected Tama and Hirokichi
to come to her to report on problems and
decisions, whether important or minor matters. She felt comfortable with having given
the seal to Hiro, but a sense of loss, too. It
meant her own road would soon be coming
to an end.

One morning Tama came to Rie's room
before noon and called at the door,
"Mother, may I come in?"

"Of course, Tama." She looked at her
daughter-in-law, now graying at the temples,
her plain face somehow a reminder of her
faithfulness.

"There's good news, Mother," Tama said
brightly.

"Is that so?"

"Buntaro is back from Tokyo. He says the
war with China is over. He and Hiro think
the time has come to sell the two ships we

chartered to the government."

"Good, Tama. Yes, I'm glad both Buntaro and Hiro know about timing, and you too. Yes," Rie said, and reached for Tama's hand to help her rise. "I'll go to the office with you. I want to see about the price."

Tama stepped aside so that Rie could precede her slowly down the corridor to the office. When Rie entered, clerks working in the room stopped to bow low and leave the office.

"Good morning, Grandmother," Hirokichi said with a bow.

"How good to see you in the office," Buntaro said.

"What's this I hear about the war being over, Buntaro-san? Is it really true?" Rie asked.

"Yes, I arrived in Tokyo just a few days after the fighting stopped. It's given our shipping a boost, but I'm glad it's over," Buntaro replied.

"I know it's time to sell now; the sooner the better," Hirokichi said.

"Just so, Hiro," Rie nodded.

"So Buntaro and I are going to Tokyo tomorrow. I'm fairly certain the government will want to buy back the two ships they used for transporting troops."

Rie nodded. "We've owned them just a bit

over two years, and they were indispensable to the government during the war." Rie paused. "Ask at least sixty percent more than we paid for them. Then if they want to bargain, don't go below thirty percent more," she said.

"Yes." Hirokichi nodded. "That's about what Buntaro and I were thinking."

"Yes, do go tomorrow, Hiro-chan," Rie said. She nodded to Buntaro and her grandson and left the office. She shuffled slowly along the corridor, thankful that the fortunes of White Tiger rested in the hands of the two aggressive, forward-looking young men in the main office. That Naoko was not familiar with the requirements of a brewer's wife was perhaps less important in the long run. Naoko was gradually becoming accustomed to what was surely a more frugal, less luxurious lifestyle, wasn't she? She paused at the pillar and rested her head against it.

The same afternoon Rie went down the corridor to the nursery. She wanted O-Natsu's company. There were times when it was so satisfying.

Rie slid open the shoji.

Old O-Natsu looked up. "*Ah,* is it you, Oku-san? Good. Good." She nodded, tried unsuccessfully to rise, and moved a zabuton over toward Rie.

Rie sat and moved toward the teapot on the table. She reached for two cups and poured.

"Heh, heh," O-Natsu chuckled. "Good for the house, this new bride, isn't she?"

"There are some advantages to having a Fujiwara bride." Rie nodded and sipped her tea. "What makes you say so?"

"Pregnant already, I think," O-Natsu said.

"What? Has someone said something?" Rie glanced up quickly.

"No need," O-Natsu said, nodding. "Just look at the eyes. I had a glimpse at them this morning in the kitchen." Her smile revealed several toothless gaps.

"Well, O-Natsu, I'll make certain. And it isn't that I doubt you. You have always been the first in the house to learn of a pregnancy, haven't you?" Rie laughed, her hand over her mouth, a reflex even in O-Natsu's company.

That night as she sat before her dressing table combing her long white hair Rie mused. Having Hirokichi and his Fujiwara bride as successors was far better than if Ume had married Hirokichi. Now the bloodline of O-Toki and Jihei and the influence of the Sawaraya were finally gone from the house. Rie's revenge against Jihei was complete. Naoko's baby would have none of O-Toki's blood. The bloodline of the main house would be pure, even enhanced by the Fujiwara infusion. Rie nodded and smiled at herself in the mirror. "Yes, Hiro, you are good for the house," she muttered. How proud her father would be when she reported at the Butsudan.

Hirokichi and Buntaro returned from Tokyo elated by their success in selling the two ships at a handsome profit. It was not White Tiger's only success since Hirokichi had become house head.

Hirokichi came to Rie's room one morning looking unusually jaunty and elated.

"What is it, Hiro-chan?" she asked as soon as he entered the room.

"We've made it, Grandmother! White Tiger is now number one! It was announced at the Brewers Association last night." He grinned, his well-muscled arms akimbo.

She gasped. This was the day she had striven for ever since that day at the well, when she had lost the heir, had shirked her duty. Rie looked at Hirokichi, and bowed several times. She quickly took a handkerchief from her sleeve and dabbed at tears that threatened to overflow.

"*Ah,* Hiro-chan. What I have worked for all my life. . . ." She paused and held up a bony hand. "Come, give me a hand. I must go to the Butsudan."

"Yes, Grandmother, I'll accompany you."

Rie hobbled slowly to the parlor on the arm of her grandson pausing briefly to touch the aged column. She removed her slippers and shuffled to the Butsudan in her tabi. Hirokichi placed a zabuton in front of the altar. Rie knelt slowly, clapped her hands and closed her eyes.

Hirokichi pulled up a cushion and sat quietly next to his grandmother. When she opened her eyes and turned to him he said, "I have more news for you, Grandmother. Naoko is going to have a baby in a few months."

Rie nodded and smiled. "Good."

"We would like your permission to build a house at the side of the compound here." He pointed toward the vacant area beyond the old well.

"A new house, Hiro? You don't want to live here with me?" Rie queried, frowning. A vague disappointment settled in her bones. She had worked so hard, only to see the children scatter to the four winds.

"Oh, it isn't that, Grandmother. But Naoko has seen some of the new Western-style houses in the city. She thinks it would reflect the spirit of the new era and enhance the reputation of our house."

"I see." Rie was silent for several minutes. Hirokichi waited. "Well, Hiro, you have done well. And it may be that Naoko will help you advance our status even more. I have never opposed doing something new. Yes, you may build it. I wonder what it will look like."

"You will see, Grandmother, you will see."

Two months later the purple-robed priest came to bless the site for building Hirokichi's house. Rie watched him shake his white paper wand just as he did for the opening of the brewing season.

The house Hirokichi built was unlike anything Rie had seen. She watched from the parlor when the shutters were opened in the morning as the structure took shape, each of two stories fronted by a railed veranda behind which were arched doors. Built along Western lines and inspired by pictures Naoko had seen, its two-story frame dwarfed the old main house in style if not in height.

"I wonder why they are covering the wood with white," Tama said to Rie one day as they sat together and watched the builders put the final touches on the house.

"It must be what Naoko saw in those foreign picture books," Rie said. "Well, Hiro wanted something new, and that is what they have. The baby will be born in the new house." She nodded slowly. "Everything changes," she said, and took out her tiny pipe.

Hirokichi moved into the grand new home in time for the birth of the baby, a girl born auspiciously on New Year's Day. Rie and Tama celebrated the doubly felicitous occasion with Hirokichi beside them. All the branch families came to pay their respects to Rie and Hirokichi at the old main house. Even Ume and her husband appeared. Rie felt a great contentment descend on her as she looked around the room at Fumi and Seisaburo and their children, and a great sadness as well, knowing that life has a cycle: spring, summer, autumn, winter. She turned to Hirokichi and reached for him to pour her a cup of congratulatory New Year's wine.

"You know, Hiro, I'm happy it's a girl. It will be good for the house," she said, smiling at the old adage until her eyes disappeared.

"I hope she will grow up to be like you, Grandmother."

Rie smiled and bowed. He had deeply pleased her. "I'm anxious to see her," she said.

Two weeks later Naoko came to the door carrying the baby. Rie and Tama exclaimed over the tiny struggling infant and ushered Naoko into the parlor.

"Please, sit here in front of the Butsudan," Rie said. "Tama, bring a zabuton."

When Naoko was seated she held the baby out to Rie, who reached for her gingerly.

"We have named her Hana, Grandmother, after your mother."

"Ah," Rie said, and bowed over the baby, tears starting in her eyes.

"I want to invite you and Aunt Tama and Mother Fumi to our house, Grandmother," Naoko said. "The day after tomorrow please come in the afternoon. I will play my koto for you."

When Naoko left with the baby, Rie turned to Tama. "Well, I guess now I need a special invitation to visit my grandson in his new house," she said, pride mingled with a poignant sense of herself as a person passed by with the changing times. Then she shuffled off to her room.

CHAPTER 45

Rie and Tama could still see workmen coming and going, making last minute changes to the elegant new home in the compound and house servants bustling in to help Naoko. Rie enjoyed the activity vicariously from the vantage point of the parlor shutters that were opened to the courtyard.

Fumi arrived in the afternoon to join Rie and Tama for the much anticipated visit.

"I haven't seen the inside of the house yet, Fumi, only what you see from here," Rie said.

"Nor have I, Mother. Come, let's go over."

Fumi and Tama took Rie's arms and helped her across the courtyard.

A servant greeted them at the large arched doorway and ushered them into the parlor, a room unlike any the three had seen before.

"Mistress will be with you presently. Please be seated," she said, and left the room.

The women looked around for zabuton.

"I thought it was finished," Fumi whispered.

"Where are the tatami?" Tama asked. "Just bare wood. And I don't see any zabuton."

"What are those things with the long legs?" Rie asked, looking at square wooden pieces with backs and padded cushions.

The women were still standing, looking around in puzzled bewilderment when Naoko entered exquisitely attired in a pale blue kimono, smiling and bowing.

"Oh, I'm sorry to keep you waiting, Grandmother," she bowed. She hurried to Rie's side. "Please be seated," she said, holding Rie's arm. "This is a Western-style chair, Grandmother. Can you sit in it?" She helped Rie into the chair, where Rie sat uncomfortably, her feet dangling above the floor.

"And Mother, Aunt Tama, please take a seat. I am so honored that you were able to visit today," she said in her politely soaring voice.

The maidservant entered and placed tea and cakes on small, high wooden tables next to the chairs. Rie noted that the cakes were from the Kadatoya in Kyoto.

"How is the baby today?" Fumi asked.

"She is fine and healthy, thanks to you,"

Naoko said. "I'll bring her here after I have played. She is napping just now. Please help yourselves." She indicated the cakes on the tables.

The long koto sat on a mat on the wooden floor, a zabuton facing it.

Naoko seated herself gracefully and leaned forward. She placed bone picks on her fingers and paused, her hands resting lightly on the thirteen strings.

The visitors fixed their eyes on Naoko, a vision of elegant aristocratic beauty as her fingers began to dance over the strings. The liquid tones of the koto filled the room with a mellifluous familiar melody. Naoko's fingers raced faster and faster until the three older women were mesmerized.

Well, Rie mused as she listened, her family never had the leisure for these refinements. They had only heard the koto or samisen when they went to a concert, so infrequently. If they had a chance to squeeze in anything but brewery work they tried to teach the kurabito to read and write a bit. *I guess the Omura House is going to become something very different now.* She sighed, feeling yet again that life was changing, and with it would come an end of an era.

Naoko played another selection before turning to Rie. "I don't want to tire you,

Grandmother," she said.

"Oh, I am enjoying your music, Naoko. We have never had the opportunity to hear the koto in the house before. Thank you." Rie nodded. "And Naoko, please tell us what that large black box with the black-and-white teeth is." Rie pointed to a piece of furniture standing against the far wall.

"Oh, that is called a piano, Grandmother. Come, I'll show it to you."

The women approached the piano cautiously. Naoko played a scale and a few chords. "When Hana is old enough she will have lessons on the piano," Naoko said in her lilting voice. She rose from the stool. "I'll bring Hana now. Excuse me," she said, and disappeared through a doorway.

Naoko returned carrying the infant wrapped in a white lace-trimmed garment, a white bonnet on her head. The three older women surrounded Naoko, exclaiming and reaching for the baby's waving fists.

"*Ah,*" Rie said, her gaze on the lovely baby girl. "My first great-grandchild. I am so pleased that you have named her Hana."

"Yes, my husband thought you would be. He was particular about choosing her name." Naoko bowed.

When the visit was over the women walked back toward the old main house. Before they reached the entrance, Hirokichi walked rapidly toward them. "Grandmother, Mother, have you heard?"

"*Eh* . . . what is it, Hiro?" Rie asked.

Hirokichi took Rie's arm. "We reported Buntaro's discovery of Yamaguchi's treachery at the last Brewers Association meeting, you know."

"Oh?"

"They say Yamaguchi committed suicide yesterday."

Rie stopped and looked at her grandson, her heart fluttering suddenly, and yet she was surprised at how little satisfaction the news gave her. "*Ah* . . . so that is how he ended?" She paused. "Then I must tell my father. He would want to know." She bowed slightly to Hirokichi and continued into the parlor, where she knelt in front of the Butsudan, Tama and Fumi behind her. Rie bowed and was silent for a few moments. Then she turned and asked Tama to bring tea.

The three women sipped slowly.

Tama leaned forward. "I could never get used to that kind of furniture and that hard floor. Don't they have tatami? I didn't know if I should ask."

"I wonder," Rie said. "Well, Fumi did you ever think the day would come when you had to wait for a special invitation to visit your son's house?"

Fumi shook her head and smiled with a hint of pride. "It's a new age, Mother. Who knows what new things Hiro will introduce?"

"I am thankful he is house head now and that my time will soon end. He has raised White Tiger to number one," Rie said. "That is enough."

"We were already well on the way, Mother, weren't we?" Tama said firmly.

Rie laughed softly, her fan over her face. "Yes, Tama, well on the way."

That night as Rie sat in her room alone the thought came to her that she herself wished to select the characters for her tombstone. She took out inkstone, brush, and rice paper from her black lacquer writing box inlaid with mother of pearl. She poured a few drops of water onto the inkstone from a miniature iron pot, and rubbed the inkstick back and forth until the ink was of proper consistency. She dipped the tip of the brush into the ink, held the brush over the rice paper, and paused. She wrote "spring blossom" a few times. Then she dipped the brush again and wrote "autumn reverie" twice. Next she wrote "tranquil water." She sighed and dipped the brush again, the pain that Toichi's death had caused her all those years ago receding with the last word written. She wrote the characters for "first sake," then smiled and set the brush down on the inkstone.

She went back to her dressing table and picked up her comb. "First sake," she said to herself and smiled until her eyes were nearly slits.

Rie heard Fumi's voice in the corridor one morning.

"Fumi? Come in, dear."

Fumi opened the shoji to her mother's room. She sat and faced Rie.

"How nice to see you." Rie smiled. "Have a cup of tea, dear."

Fumi inclined her head, as though noticing for the first time how her mother had aged and become mellowed, without the hard edge she'd once had. "Mother, Eitaro and Sei want to have a family gathering to celebrate your eighty-eighth birthday."

"Oh, dear, let's not talk about my birthday." Rie shook her head, her lips pressed firmly together.

"But Mother, your eighty-eighth is so important. You know you always told us how important it is because the numbers resemble the character for rice. We must celebrate."

Rie broke into a wrinkled smile. "Oh yes, that is true, dear. All right."

"Wonderful! It will be doubly special because Hiro has a surprise for the occasion."

"*Ah,* Hiro often has surprises for us, doesn't he? I wonder what it is this time."

"You will see, Mother." Fumi sipped tea with Rie for a few minutes, then excused herself, saying the celebration would be in time for her birthday, two weeks hence.

The entire family assembled for Rie's important birthday. All the children and grandchildren: Sei and Mari and their children, Fumi and Eitaro with Mie and her husband, even Ume and her family and Kazu and her family had been called for the event. Rie touched her special hair ornament — the one Saburo had given her — and smiled.

The maids had removed the shoji in the main room and set out many lacquer tables in rows, as for a wedding reception or end of year celebration.

Hiro brought in a man carrying several large pieces of equipment. "This is Mr. Akita, Grandmother. He is going to take a picture of you, your likeness. This is a new

541

invention that has come into the country recently. Your picture will then remain for all future generations of the family to see and enjoy."

"My picture? What an idea. I don't really want people to see what I look like now, Hiro-chan." She tried to adjust her hair, to arrange herself in a more presentable way. She sat absolutely straight as Mr. Akita set up his equipment with the tripod and black cover.

"You look beautiful, Grandmother. And I want us to toast you on your birthday." He raised a cup and all the family followed suit, with cries of "Happy Birthday, Grandmother."

Rie looked around at her assembled family and bowed, trying her best to conceal her tears. All the family was present, though Kin, Kinnosuke, and Buntaro were also part of what she had worked all her life to achieve. White Tiger was now the largest sake empire in all the land.

Rie's days and months passed quietly, often in her room or in the nursery with O-Natsu, sometimes in the parlor in front of the Butsudan, occasionally making her way slowly down the hall to the office to speak with Hirokichi and Buntaro.

One day Rie hobbled out into the courtyard and paused at the huge barrels where she had spent so many vigorous hours. She glanced toward the dark door of the kura and inhaled her favorite scent, the yeasty aroma of brewing sake. Then her gaze rested on the old well, and for a moment she could almost imagine Toichi there. She had done what she had set out to do and taken a small step toward redemption in the process. But now, looking back, she knew that redemption wasn't enough. What her father had given her was so much more than what she could have ever given him in return. He had given her a rich sense of tradition, and now she was passing that tradition on to Hiro-kichi.

With that, Rie walked deliberately into the main house and into the front room where she carefully placed a zabuton directly before the altar, then sat so that she faced it. The morning light was glancing in through the open shutters. She reached for an incense stick, lit it, and placed the small vase in front of her father's name tablet. Smoke swirled up around her head and curled toward her mother's name tablet. The image of her mother's face came to her, the delicate outlines of Hana's chin and patrician Kyoto nose. She sat motionless for several minutes, and heard her mother's voice call ever so faintly, "Rie."

Rie jumped, startled. She strained to listen but could not hear the voice call again. She looked again at the Butsudan. There they all were, the name tablets of the generations of Omuras: her father, Kinzaemon IX; Jihei, Kinzaemon X; Yoshitaro, Kinzaemon XI; Tama, still alive, who intervened in the chain but whose name as a woman would not figure in the formal succession, though she had been intermediary as number XII. And finally there would someday be Hirokichi, who had married a Fujiwara bride from the nobility and succeeded as Kinzaemon XIII.

Rie's eyes filled as she was overcome with memories of so many generations, so many deaths. She glanced out the open shutters into the courtyard where the sunlight was filtering past the old well. A pang of grief shook her. Her eyes moved on toward the barrels. There beside a barrel heaved on its side was a bent, white-haired figure in a worn, indigo-dyed kimono. Who was it? She leaned closer to the open shutter and peered out. It was O-Natsu, surely it was O-Natsu. Wasn't she holding someone by the hand? Rie caught her breath. Yes, it was Hirokichi's two-year-old daughter, Hana, Rie's mother's namesake.

What was it the country women in the south said? Rie remembered hearing the ancient folktale from O-Natsu. A woman should not live to see her great-grandchild. Food was too scarce in those poor farming districts. So a son took his old mother on his back when her great-grandchild was born, took her up to a mountaintop and left her there to die.

Rie smiled and allowed a tear to run down her cheek at the painful thought. There was no one to see. How fortunate that she was Rie, daughter of Kinzaemon IX, widow of Kinzaemon X, mother, yes mother, of Kinzaemon XI, and grandmother of Kinzaemon XIII of the House of Omura, and now White Tiger was number one in all Japan. She sat perfectly straight before the Butsudan, inhaled the yeasty aroma and smiled.

ACKNOWLEDGMENTS

I am indebted to many individuals who offered suggestions, encouragement, inspiration, and technical assistance during the writing of this novel. My agent, Natasha Kern, said, "I'm the perfect agent for your book," and, in fact, was. Editors Carol Craig and Carrie Feron believed in the book from its inception and guided it with unerring vision through to completion.

A host of friends offered continual support, among them Paul Wood, Sue Riford, and Pat Palmer on Maui; in Boulder, members of my writing group — Thora Chinnery, Diana Vari, Carol Dow, and Sherri Jennings — as well as other friends: Hualing Hu, Takeko and Art Sakakura, Keiko Beer, Billie Corrigan, Sherry Oaks, Jody Berman, Faye Kleeman, Polly Christensen, Mariko Sumida (Honolulu), and Kitty Felion (Erie, Pennsylvania). I am immensely grateful to them, as well as to Masami

547

Yabune in Japan and also to those who helped me through the idiosyncracies of computers: Sherry Oaks, Nancy Fritch, and Polly Christensen.

I was fortunate to have guidance and information on the history of the sake industry, Japan's most ancient industry, from two leading authorities, Professor Manabu Yunoki of Kwansei Gakuin University and Professor Sakurai of Chiba University.

The book would never have been written without the many brewers who shared stories of their families, their brewing traditions, and the technology of the brewing process. As I traveled from Akita, Niigata, and Fukushima in the north to Kyushu in the south, brewers were more generous of their time and hospitality than I could have hoped. In some cases I was a guest for a week at a time and had an opportunity to observe brewing at each stage and to explore the inner recesses of the architecture of house and kura. I was given lectures on brewing by brewmasters, I tasted enticing grades and varieties, and was wined and dined along with brewers at ceremonies celebrating both the start and end of the brewing season. Out of respect for traditions of brewing houses I do not here identify individual brewers who have been so kind and helpful. It is my hope they will realize the depth of my gratitude.

This is a work of fiction. While certain incidents are based on historical events and eras, the characters depicted are products of the author's imagination.

Joyce Chapman Lebra
Boulder, Colorado
2008

■ ■ ■ ■

A$^+$
AUTHOR INSIGHTS,
EXTRAS, &
MORE . . .
FROM JOYCE LEBRA AND AVON A

■ ■ ■ ■

NOTE TO READERS

Imagine yourself near Kobe, Japan, in the year 1830, a time when the feudal Tokugawa shoguns are on the verge of collapse. The real economic strength of Japan is in the hands of the prosperous merchant class, the chonin, and among them sake brewers are the most powerful. As you bounce along the coastal road in your ricksha you see rows of towering brown wooden structures, the kura, where sake is being brewed. You pull your cloak tighter around your throat against the icy wind blasting down from Mt. Rokko, for it is winter, the height of the brewing season.

Pull up to the entrance of one of the breweries where the noren hanging over the door announces the name of the brand. As you stoop under the noren and enter the main office you are assailed by a pungent yeasty aroma, the scent of sake, that pervades the room and beyond into the house itself. This enterprise is also the house; the two are one and the same. Beyond the outer office and the inner one are the rooms where the family lives. Clerks are scurrying back and forth waiting on customers and dealing with suppliers of the koji mold and yeast used in brewing. If you listen carefully you can hear the singing of the kurabito, the brewery workers, a rhythmic tune matching their tasks as they work.

This is a man's world in a male-dominated society. Brewing is a masculine occupation. Women, even senior members of the house, are not allowed to enter the kura for fear of pollution. Even to step near the entrance is to court danger. The entire process of brewing is surrounded with purification rituals. Sake is the most ancient and honored industry in the land; none can be married or buried without sake being imbibed.

The one exception, a niche in this all-male structure, comes with the birth of a baby girl in a large merchant family. You will hear the midwife announce loudly, "It's a girl, so the house will prosper!" And you know this to be true, since with only a girl child, the house can, when the time comes, adopt a husband for the daughter, a husband who has proven himself the ablest clerk around. As house head he will then propel the house and enterprise to success. This is what usually happens. In those rare cases where, due to a miscalculation and despite careful investigation by the marriage go-between, the husband proves to be a disappointment, the door to this androcentric structure can be pushed open a crack, and the house daughter can, if she is capable, step into the role and power of a house head, acting behind the scenes.

A century and a half later when I was visiting during one of my many trips to Japan, I became fascinated by the intertwining of enterprise and family in traditional businesses. I briefly explored five businesses until I realized that the sake industry was Japan's most ancient, and was also extremely familial and traditional. These features made it irresistible to me as a historian. I then spent many months visiting breweries ranging from Akita and Niigata in the north to Kyushu in the south. I benefited from the gracious hospitality and willingness of brewers to share family traditions and information about brewing technology. More than once I enjoyed a brewer's hospitality for days at a time.

I then considered the prospect of house daughters in brewing families. While exploring this possibility I encountered one example of a woman who had been so successful that it seemed she was an embarrassment to her descendants, who were extremely reluctant to speak about her. A sociologist pointed out to me that I was "storming the family castle," that the details of a family's history are often too intimate, too private, to share with outsiders. This only whetted my interest further. The only alternative, then, was to write fiction, to imagine the life of such a woman. This woman became Rie.

Joyce Chapman Lebra
Boulder, Colorado
2008

DISCUSSION QUESTIONS FOR READERS' CLUBS

1. Were you surprised by how powerful sake brewers were in the eighteenth and nineteenth centuries?

2. Why was this house happy to have a daughter as an only child?

3. Was Jihei a typical mukoyoshi, adopted husband/househead?

4. What challenges did Rie face as a woman? What advantages did she have as house daughter?

5. Why was Rie so unhappy to have Yoshitaro adopted as househead and heir? Would you be?

6. Do you think arranged marriages worked at the time?

7. Why were people so surprised Rie wanted to adopt a mukoyoshi for Fumi?

8. Some Americans have asked, why didn't Rie have the nerve to sneak into the kura when no one was looking? What do you think?

9. What would have happened had Rie been discovered during her assignation with Saburo? What would have happened to Saburo?

10. What was your reaction when Rie demanded that Kinno divorce Nobu?

ABOUT THE AUTHOR

Joyce Lebra, a recognized authority on the cultures of Japan, India, and Asia/Pacific women, is professor emerita of Colorado University. She lived in Japan many years and authored twelve nonfiction books.

The employees of Thorndike Press hope you have enjoyed this Large Print book. All our Thorndike, Wheeler, and Kennebec Large Print titles are designed for easy reading, and all our books are made to last. Other Thorndike Press Large Print books are available at your library, through selected bookstores, or directly from us.

For information about titles, please call:
(800) 223-1244

or visit our Web site at:
http://gale.cengage.com/thorndike

To share your comments, please write:
Publisher
Thorndike Press
295 Kennedy Memorial Drive
Waterville, ME 04901